Valentin et Orson:
An Edition and Translation of the Fifteenth-Century Romance Epic

MEDIEVAL AND RENAISSANCE
TEXTS AND STUDIES
VOLUME 372

VALENTIN ET ORSON: AN EDITION AND TRANSLATION OF THE FIFTEENTH-CENTURY ROMANCE EPIC

Edited and translated by

Shira Schwam-Baird

ACMRS
(Arizona Center for Medieval and Renaissance Studies)
Tempe, Arizona
2011

Published by ACMRS (Arizona Center for Medieval and Renaissance Studies)
Tempe, Arizona
© 2011 Arizona Board of Regents for Arizona State University.
All Rights Reserved.

Library of Congress Cataloging-in-Publication Data

Valentin et Orson (French romance). English & French (Middle French)
　Valentin et Orson : an edition and translation of the fifteenth- century romance epic / edited and translated by Shira Schwam-Baird.
　　　p. cm. -- (Medieval and Renaissance texts and studies ; v. 372)
　"The present volume contains the first modern scholarly edition of the text of the Maillet book of 1489. Moreover, its facing-page translation constitutes the second translation into English ever made of the French prose Valentin et Orson, and probably the first based directly on the 1489 edition"--Introd.
　Includes bibliographical references.
　ISBN 978-0-86698-420-1 (alk. paper)
　1. Charlemagne, Emperor, 742-814--Romances. I. Schwam-Baird, Shira I. II. Title.
　PQ1581.V35E5 2011
　843'.2--dc22

　　　　　　　　　　　　　　　　　　　　　　　　　　　　2011002928

∞
This book is made to last. It is set in Adobe Caslon Pro,
smyth-sewn and printed on acid-free paper to library specifications.
Printed in the United States of America

TABLE OF CONTENTS

Acknowledgements — *vii*
Introduction — *ix*

Valentin et Orson — 15

Appendix A: Editions — 531

Appendix B: Woodcuts — 535

Bibliography and Works Cited — 539

Acknowledgments

No scholar works in a vacuum, and it is a pleasure to be able to thank the various individuals and institutions whose support and help make our work possible and fruitful.

My first thanks go to Leslie Zarker Morgan, who initially made me aware of the existence of this text, and who continued to encourage me as the time needed to complete the project seemed to grow rather than shorten over the passing years. I am also grateful to Lorraine Stock, whose interest in the wild man inspired my own.

I am deeply appreciative for the excellent services of the University of North Florida's library staff, in particular those responsible for Interlibrary Loan, whose hands passed on to me all sorts of rare and unusual volumes. Thanks are also due to the many libraries and institutions that allowed me to consult some of their most precious materials: the Morgan Library in New York, the Bibliothèque Nationale de France in Paris, the Bibliothèque de l'Arsenal in Paris, the Musée Condé library in Chantilly, the Bodleian Library in Oxford, and the British Library in London.

Thanks are due to Elizabeth Poe, once dissertation advisor and now friend; and to William Kibler, who generously answered many email queries on language conundrums.

Thanks are also due to the editors and staff at the Arizona Center for Medieval and Renaissance Studies: Robert Bjork, who, early on, expressed faith in this project by granting me a pre-completion contract and then had patience when life (in the form of union contract negotiations and hurricanes) interfered with completion of the project; and Roy Rukkila and Leslie MacCoull, who guided me through the process of making a book out of a book project.

And finally, my deepest gratitude is due to David, husband and life partner, whose love and moral support keep me sane.

INTRODUCTION

Valentin et Orson is a fifteenth-century romance epic of anonymous authorship recounting the adventures of twin brothers separated at birth who discover each other, their family origins, love, and many enemies to fight in the course of their story. Georges Doutrepont includes *Valentin et Orson* on his list of late medieval *mises en prose* with the longest continuing popularity (*Mises en prose*, 677–78),[1] and, indeed, from the time of its first edition by Jacques Maillet in Lyon in 1489 until the mid-nineteenth century, *Valentin et Orson* was continually adapted, re-edited, and republished (with progressively modernized language) in Lyon, Paris, Rouen, Troyes, Lille, and Epinal. The list of editions included in Appendix A is an indication of its publishing longevity. Although there are no extant manuscripts of this text, and the 1489 Maillet edition is the first surviving version of the tale in French, it is believed, for reasons explained below, to have been the expansion of an earlier French metric narrative, now lost.[2]

The tale is known in English by way of a *c*.1510 Middle English translation and subsequent renditions such as reprints, more or less adapted from that translation (one version made up part of Scrooge's childhood reading, rediscovered during his return journey with the Ghost of Christmas Past); plays; Arthur Dickson's 1937 edition of the Middle English translation; and, most recently, Nancy Ekholm Burkert's 1989 illustrated children's album, *Valentine & Orson* (which, ironically enough, came out in a French translation in 1990).[3] Despite this continuous popularity, the extant French incunabulum has never been seen in a modern critical edition, a lacuna that the present work aspires to fill.

Late medieval prose works have often been considered excessively long and disjointed, and indeed, in contrast to the rhymed works on which many of them are

---

[1] The other popular titles cited by G. Doutrepont (*Les Mises en prose des épopées et des romans chevaleresques du XIVe au XVe siècles* [Brussels: Académie royale, 1939]) are *Fierabras*, *Galien*, *Girart de Roussillon*, *Ogier le Danois*, *Les Quatre Fils Aymon*, *Le Chevalier au Cygne*, *Gérard de Nevers*, *Gui de Warewic*, and *Huon de Bordeaux*. In its publishing history, *Valentin et Orson* was occasionally published in multiple text volumes that sometimes included *Galien*, *Les Quatre Fils Aymon*, or *Huon de Bordeaux*.

[2] See discussion of the text below.

[3] See Arthur Dickson, *Valentine and Orson: A Study in Late Medieval Romance* (New York: Columbia University Press, 1929; repr. New York: AMS Press, 1975), 284–98, and Bibliography.

based, they can seem difficult to read. Doutrepont felt the need to justify his 1939 study of the *mises en prose* by pointing out that these works contribute to the understanding of the evolution of the national literature from its early days of rhymed narrative in the twelfth, thirteenth, and fourteenth centuries to the fifteenth- and sixteenth-century prose works. He added that the adaptation of poetic works to prose allowed later audiences to know, and apparently love, stories that might otherwise have been lost due to their "antiquated" language and outdated style. (The fact that they *were* loved is attested to in the number of manuscript copies, incunabula, and later redactions that have survived.) He also used the philological argument that studying such works gives us insight into the development of the language itself in transition from Old French through Middle French to the language of the Renaissance. And finally, he states, one can begin to understand the evolution of tastes of an entire society by studying what stories they enjoyed and in what format they enjoyed them (*Mises en prose*, 14–15). Most often for this period that format was wordy and elaborated—not a style readily appealing to most modern readers.

However, by now we are past the point at which an apology must be made for focusing on a late medieval text of prolix style. Since the latter part of the twentieth century, texts of the fourteenth and fifteenth centuries, both new compositions and prose *remaniements*, have garnered interest in various quarters, resulting in the establishment of the respected journals *Le Moyen français* and *Fifteenth Century Studies* (commenced in 1977 and 1978 respectively), the preparation of many modern scholarly editions, and the writing of numerous articles and books addressing the questions and concerns such texts have raised.[4] The present edition of *Valentin et Orson* hopes to expand the discussion of late epic and join the ranks of modern editions like *Lion de Bourges* (edited by Kibler), *Fierabras* (edited by Keller and Miquet), and *Tristan de Nanteuil* (edited by Sinclair).

The Text

Valentin et Orson is the *mise en prose* of a rhymed narrative in French that has not survived. The existence of this original was first posited in 1846 by Gustaf Edvard Klemming, the Swedish scholar and editor of a surviving verse redaction in Middle Low German called *Valentin und Namelos*.[5] Klemming pointed out that

---

[4] See the collection of articles in *Echoes of the Epic: Studies in Honor of Gerard J. Brault*, ed. David P. Schenck and Mary Jane Schenk (Birmingham, AL: Summa Publications, 1998), of which the articles by Catherine M. Jones, "'Modernizing' the Epic: Philippe de Vigneulles," (115–32), and Hans Erich-Keller, "Une *Chanson de Roland* en prose," (133–40) are two good examples.

[5] Gustaf Edvard Klemming, *Namnlös och Valentin: en Medeltids-roman* (Stockholm: Norstedt, 1846), vii. In the same volume is found Klemming's edition of an Old Swedish translation of *Valentin und Namelos*.

Valentin und Namelos predates the Maillet edition, incorporates the same narrative connection to the Charlemagne cycle, and, most importantly, contains multiple references to a French source.[6] Nevertheless, no more than roughly half the Maillet edition is based on this earlier version. The other half spins out the tale with an abundance of battles, searches, encounters, and events of all sorts—an inventive expansion that allowed the story to wander, not quite aimlessly, but certainly with a good deal of latitude. Moreover, the entire text, including the first half that follows its source in basic outline, is considerably lengthened by a longiloquent style brimming with narrative detail and protracted speeches. In this, it is a typical *mise en prose*, as per Doutrepont's description:

> [P]rose rendering is, in most cases, more than a simple translation or reworking of a twelfth-century rhymed poem into a fifteenth- or sixteenth-century prose text. The 'translator' alters his original, either by lengthening it or shortening it.[7]

There is no question here that the alterations came in the form of prolongation, not abbreviation.

Very useful for understanding the relationship between the lost original and the Maillet edition is Dickson's side-by-side comparison of parallel episodes in the French *Valentin et Orson* (VO) and the Middle Low German *Valentin und Namelos* (VN). This text from the first half of the fifteenth century is not only the most complete of the translations, but also the closest to the presumed French original.[8] This exercise demonstrates that the first thirty-four chapters of VO (out of a total of seventy-four) correspond more or less to the sequence of events in VN, with an additional two parallel events occurring in later portions of VO.[9]

---

[6] According to Dickson, Klemming's theory of a lost French original has been "universally accepted" (Dickson, *Study*, 5). He gave it the title *Valentin et Sansnom* (*VS*). Surviving fragments of verse redactions in Dutch also predate the Maillet edition. See Dickson, *Study*, 3–10.

[7] "... le dérimage est, dans bien des cas, plus que la simple traduction, ou le simple remaniement, d'un poème rimé au XIIᵉ siècle en une prose du XVᵉ ou du XVIᵉ. Le translateur, alors, retouche son original, en l'allongeant ou en l'abrégeant" (*Mises en prose*, 15). (All translations are my own.)

[8] See Dickson, *Study*, 159–64. I am following Dickson in referring to the versions by their initials VO and VN.

The Middle Low German version in "romance couplets" is the most complete of the rhymed translations. The Swedish version is primarily but not entirely in verse, and the other metric versions are found only in fragments in Middle High German and Middle Dutch (the latter manuscripts from the fourteenth century being the oldest of all). There is also a complete prose version of VN in Middle High German from 1465. See Dickson, *Study*, 8–10.

[9] These are the Second Rescue of Rosamond and Namelos in VN corresponding to Valentin's rescue of Esclarmonde in VO's Chapter 61, and the Second Woman episode in

The full translation in this volume of the Middle French text into English precludes the need for a lengthy plot summary (the "analyse" conventional in French editions of medieval texts); nevertheless, a brief summary is in order. The eponymous heroes of *Valentin et Orson* are twins, born to King Pepin's sister, Bellissant, and Alexander, the emperor of Greece. Having been banished owing to a false accusation of adultery, their exiled mother gives birth in a forest. Accident separates the three of them so that Orson grows up wild in the forest after having been suckled by a she-bear, while Valentin is raised as a foundling by his own uncle Pepin at the French court yet with no knowledge of his origins. In the meantime, their mother finds refuge in the household of a Saracen giant. Hairy and mute, Orson must be vanquished by his brother Valentin before the slow process of his civilizing may begin, but completion is possible only after the supernatural intervention of a bronze head that reveals the secret of the brothers' noble birth and the way to restore speech to Orson. As knights, the brothers fight Saracens, giants, and even a dragon, as well as various lackeys of their evil cousins, Henry and Hauffroy (Pepin's illegitimate sons). About halfway through the narrative they are reunited with their parents, but that is in no way an end to their adventures or, even, to their family troubles. At times captured by their enemies, they find themselves liberated not infrequently by the magical intervention of the necromancer Pacolet, owner of a marvelous flying wooden horse. Both brothers fall in love and marry (Orson more than once), and both end their lives somberly. After mistakenly killing his disguised father on the battlefield, Valentin embarks on a life of penance, whereas Orson, after years of both knighthood and rule, chooses a hermit's existence.

Genre

Such a summary raises the question of genre, and *Valentin et Orson* is nothing if not a polymorphic text. Indeed, there are moments when certain antics of Pacolet approach the level of fabliaux.[10] But it is primarily the coexistence of elements usually considered typical of either epic or romance—the warring against Saracens, high treason, a falsely-accused queen,[11] the wild man motif, love, magic,

---

VN corresponding to Orson's love affair with Galasie in VO Chapter 62 (whom he marries after the death of his wife Fezonne in Chapter 70).

[10] One thinks in particular of Pacolet's trickery, as when, for example, he disguises himself as a woman to "seduce," trick, and kill a rival sorcerer, Adramain, who had been instrumental in the kidnapping of Esclarmonde (Chapter 31), or when he convinces the King of India, a Saracen, that he is Mohammed, come both to free him from his Saracen enemy Brandiffer and to deliver the latter into his hands (Chapter 47).

[11] For a study of this motif see Nancy B. Black, *Medieval Narratives of Accused Queens* (Gainesville: University Press of Florida, 2003).

and the quest for identity—that marks it as belonging to the later evolution of vernacular literature in medieval France in which the heroic *chanson de geste* and the chivalric romance of knight-errantry and love blend in prose format to please the tastes of a fifteenth-century audience. Should it be considered a romance? Dickson certainly thought so when he named it a "late medieval romance" in the title to his source study, and Valentin's knight errantry and conduct (most of the time) demonstrate the strict awareness of the tenets of chivalric duty common to a knight of romance narrative.[12] On the other hand, as a part of the genealogical expansion of the Carolingian story, it can certainly lay claim to the label "epic," and, as befits the epic tradition, Saracen hordes are repeatedly fought and defeated by Christian armies as they attack Rome, Constantinople, or other Christian strongholds, and no fewer than three Saracen princesses fall in love with one or the other of the two brother heroes. Nevertheless, Dickson believed that the link to the Carolingian story was tenuous and superficial at best, especially in the source romance *Valentin und Namelos* (which is indicative of the material of *Valentin et Sansnom*), but also in *Valentin et Orson*, for although Pepin is a central figure, Charlemagne appears only intermittently as the child Charlot who never seems to grow to maturity, and indeed, it is barely mentioned that he will eventually succeed his father on the throne of France after Pepin is killed treacherously by his illegitimate sons Hauffroy and Henry.[13] Even within single episodes, generic aspects may be mixed. For example, the Green Knight, a giant, demands the hand of a certain maiden in marriage, agreeing to leave off his suit only if a champion can be found to defeat him in single combat. Moreover, he hangs all those whom he defeats by the neck on a tree next to his pavilion—a common Arthurian motif. But unlike such villains in Arthurian lore, this Green Knight is a Saracen, and when he is finally defeated by Orson, he converts to Christianity and henceforth never deserts the Christian side, thus resembling the eponymous hero of *Fierabras* more than Mabonagrain of *Erec et Enide*.[14]

Doutrepont explains this coming together of genres in terms of the three traditional "matières" or "Matters" in the introduction to his book on the late "mises en prose":

---

[12] His most glaring act of disloyalty, that of accepting the task of leading a Saracen force against his uncle King Pepin's army while in mercenary service to a Saracen king (undertaken while in search of his kidnapped beloved Esclarmonde), is an exception, and may be a reflection of the particular historical phenomenon of Christian mercenaries in medieval Muslim armies. This question has been considered in Shira Schwam-Baird, "The Romance Epic Hero, the Mercenary, and the Ottoman Turk Seen through the Lens of *Valentin et Orson* (1489)," *Medievalia et Humanistica* 34 (2008): 105-27.

[13] See Chapter 67.

[14] Chapters 15, 16, 19, and 20.

In any case, one cannot deny that in the long run, these French, Breton, and classical stories from antiquity appear to form a single mass, so undefined are the boundaries between them, so purposefully mixed together are their themes. The distance that separates them is less and less marked as medieval literature develops and creates for itself a wide compass. In other words, many of the basic elements of the so-called Matters of France, Brittany, and Rome came to fuse in an undifferentiated whole, and one must employ the powerful litmus paper of modern philology to break apart such strongly combined substances (*Mises en prose*, 4).[15]

It is just such an approach that inspires Dickson's study, a classic work of "modern philology" attempting to trace and identify the sources of all the disparate elements making up this textual artefact of late medieval literature.

But what causes this phenomenon, and is it a question of blending or influence? Is there a true nature separate and essential each to epic and romance to distinguish one from the other, which, when borrowed or incorporated, creates the new model of late vernacular literature? Or is Doutrepont right in suggesting that generic distinctions simply do not make sense for late medieval vernacular literature?

The conventional view holds that the *chanson de geste* depicts conflict between Christian and pagan, while romance is the genre of individual quest and adventure. But as William Kibler points out, the so-called second generation of *chansons de geste* quickly evolved to plots other than that of the Christian–Saracen struggle (such as that of the rebellious barons), such that the early *chansons de geste* should be seen as the exception to the genre rather than the rule. Indeed, he states, ninety percent of the extant *chansons de geste* could be said to be "impregnated with narrative motifs and affective themes of the courtly romances."[16] Can one speak of essentially different genres in that case? Kibler differentiates between the so-

---

[15] "En tout cas, l'on ne saurait nier qu'à la longue, les récits français, bretons et antiques paraissent devenir ou former une seule et même chose, tant leurs limites respectives sont indécises, tant ils confondent volontiers leurs thèmes. La distance qui les sépare est de moins en moins accusée à mesure que la littérature médiévale se développe et se crée un plus large domaine d'action. En d'autres mots, beaucoup d'éléments premiers des dites matières de France, de Bretagne et de Rome la grant arrivent à se fusionner en un Tout indistinct, et il faut les puissants réactifs de la philologie moderne pour désagréger des substances aussi fortement combinées."

[16] "On sait aujourd'hui que 90% et davantage des chansons de geste sont imprégnées des motifs narratifs et thèmes affectifs des romans courtois. Il n'y que les rares *Chanson de Roland, Gormont et Isembart*, ou *Chanson de Guillaume*, où l'on peut reconnaître la chanson de geste de la définition. Au lieu de vanter la perfection de tels poèmes, ne vaut-il pas mieux voir en eux des exceptions, plutôt que la règle?": William Kibler, "La 'chanson d'aventures'," in *Essor et fortune de la Chanson de geste dans l'Europe et l'Orient latin* (Modena: Mucchi, 1984), 509–15, here 510. As examples of the "second generation" texts Kibler names the *Prise d'Orange* and the *Charroi de Nîmes*.

called "second generation" texts, which at least were admired by scholars, and "late epics" or "late *chansons de geste*," which usually were not.[17] So different are the later texts that Kibler suggests they deserve a generic classification all their own, that of *chanson d'aventures*, to suggest their romance format and yet differentiate them from romance *per se* ("La 'chanson d'aventures'," 510).[18]

Some of this drive for a new generic classification is clearly inspired by a desire to counter the general scorn in which earlier scholars, enraptured by the violent purity of the prototypical *Chanson de Roland* and its fellow texts (predating 1150), held the later examples.[19] Robert Francis Cook, in the name of a "philologie profonde," took up the defense of the late French epic against Bédier's charge of its constituting "que de méchants romans d'aventure."[20] For Cook, these texts are simply late examples of *chanson de geste*, which, despite their differences from the earlier *chansons*, nevertheless provide the matter for important philological study, particularly for questions of genre. He points out, moreover, that limiting ourselves to studying only the texts we easily like prevents us from arriving at a clear understanding of an extensive body of works. The "new philology" he proposes would allow us to establish a deeper and truer literary history of the genre ("'Méchants romans'," 72). Elsewhere, Cook begins the building of that "new philology" with his 1986 article on the "Unity and Esthetics of the Late *Chansons de geste*," a study in which he notes a structural similarity among late epic cycles that lent itself to what he posits as an episodic mode of public reading.[21]

Sarah Kay similarly attacks the well-entrenched notion that the *chanson de geste* knew its pure existence only in its earliest examples (i.e., the prototypical *Chanson de Roland* and its fellow texts dating from before 1150), and that it was then "influenced" by the rising popularity of romance ("influenced" meaning "adulterated" according to those modern critics enamored of "the rugged

---

[17] François Suard, for example, refers to them collectively as "the late French epic" in "L'épopée française tardive (XIVᵉ–XVᵉ s.)," in *Etudes de philologie romane et d'histoire littéraire offertes à Jules Horrent*, ed. Jean-Marie d'Heur et Nicoletta Cherubini (Liège: [s.n.], 1980), 449–60.

[18] By the time of the late works, the short assonanced *laisse* that had distinguished the epic is replaced by the rhymed couplet of romance.

[19] Kibler cites respectfully the noted French scholar Jean-Charles Payen who deplores "la décadence de l'épopée bourrée d'éléments romanesques, et écrit: «le XIVe siècle sera désastreux pour la pauvre chanson de geste abâtardie en roman de chevalerie»": Kibler, "La 'chanson d'aventures'," 510; quoting from J.-C. Payen, *Le Moyen Age*, I: *Des Origines à 1300* (Paris: Arthaud, 1970), 135.

[20] From Joseph Bédier, *Les Légendes épiques*, 3ʳᵈ ed., vol. 1 (Paris: Champion, 1926), quoted in R.F. Cook, "'Méchants romans' et Epopée française: pour une philologie profonde," *L'Esprit Créateur* 23 (1983): 64–74, here 67.

[21] R.F. Cook, "Unity and Esthetics of the Late *Chansons de geste*," *Olifant* 11 (1986): 103–14.

splendours and uncompromising bellicosity" of the early texts).²² In her reading, it is not a question of influence by the motifs of a later genre or of a shift from one genre to another. Rather one must understand the simultaneity, the contemporaneity, of the two genres. Basing her distinctions as much on form as content, she does clearly classify texts as one or the other in her 1995 study *The Chansons de geste in the Age of Romance: Political Fictions*, but she sees them as fellow travelers sharing traits, and attempts to correct the standard 'horizon of expectation' for the *chansons de geste* by demonstrating what the two genres share, and, in particular, the political nature of each.²³

Danielle Quéruel makes a similar point in her work on fifteenth-century *mises en prose* of chivalric romance. The prose renditions represent much more than an effort to translate earlier rhymed text into prose; rather they are an attempt to create something new, modern, and fitting for the fifteenth century. (One could draw an analogy between the *mises en prose* and current film adaptations of nineteenth-century novels: the story and characters may be recognizable, but the medium and language are clearly different and appeal to the contemporary audience in a way that the supposedly "antiquated" language of the novel cannot, at least not to the general audience.)

Though her work concerns chivalric romance, Quéruel's point is relevant to the present subject: "prose writing in the fifteenth century tends to abolish the formal distinctions between the literary genres."²⁴ She is echoed by Michel Zink, who has noted a blurring of borders between genres and a fusion into "a common model of prose narration" occurring in the late medieval period.²⁵ Taken with Doutrepont's earlier contention, quoted above, that "the Matters of France, Brittany, and Rome came to fuse into an undifferentiated whole," it would seem that, rather than speak of a "mixing" of genres in late epic, we should consider that the

---

²² See Sarah Kay, "Contesting 'Romance Influence': The Poetics of the Gift," *Comparative Literature Studies* 32 (1995): 320–41, here 320.

²³ See introduction to Sarah Kay, *The Chansons de geste in the Age of Romance: Political Fictions* (Oxford: Clarendon Press, 1995), 1–21, esp. 6–8.

²⁴ "... l'écriture en prose du XVᵉ siècle tend à abolir les distinctions formelles entre les genres littéraires": Danielle Quéruel, "Des mises en prose aux romans de chevalerie dans les collections bourguignonnes," in *Actes du VIᵉ Colloque international sur le moyen français*, vol. 2, *Rhétorique et mises en prose au XVᵉ siècle*, ed. Sergio Cigada and Anna Slerca (Milan: Vita e Pensiero, 1991), 173–93, here 189.

²⁵ Zink, quoted in W. Kibler, "From Epic to Romance: The Case of Lion de Bourges," in *The Medieval Opus: Imitation, Rewriting and Transmission in the French Tradition*, ed. Douglas Kelly (Amsterdam: Rodopi, 1996), 327–55, here 332, n. 10: "In the introduction to *Apollonius de Tyr*, Zink writes 'à la fin du moyen âge l'abolition des frontières entre les genres traditionnels, chanson de geste, roman, chronique, vie de saint, définis primitivement dans une large mesure par leur forme, et leur fusion dans un modèle commun de narration en prose préparent le public à recevoir des récits plus variés et moins cohérents dans leur contenu, dans leur vision du monde et dans leur leçon.'"

very survival of epic may be tied up in the notion that prose adventure of all sorts is what late medieval audiences craved, and thus that is what unifies these various texts and defines the genre.

Generic labels raise expectations in readers as to the content and form of the text; thus the question of genre is important, and this present edition of *Valentin et Orson* will make available a text the study of which will contribute to that discussion. In practice, the term 'romance epic' or "épopée romanesque" (meaning medieval epic literature in the various Romance languages) is used by the Société Internationale Rencesvals, which of course emphasizes epic as the base. In an academic world that classifies by discipline, genre, and language, epic will continue to be distinguished in some measure from romance, but an understanding at least of the partial artificiality of the distinction should be noted and taken into account in all studies of relevant texts.

The Incunabulum

In the history of the French book the incunabulum of *Valentin et Orson* constitutes a visual and textual artefact of its period. Printing began in Paris in 1470 when the rector of the Sorbonne, Jean Heynlin, brought in German printers to set up an operation and produce books of rhetoric and classical letters for use by students at the university.[26] Two years later printing commenced in Lyon (Martin, *Livre illustré*, 53). Not being a university town, Lyon had no powerful guilds of copyists, miniaturists, and illuminators to oppose the new art of printing books.[27] Moreover, not needing to meet the needs of a learned public, Lyon catered to more popular tastes and a less refined clientele, producing books that appealed to a popular audience. That often meant books in French, rather than Latin (Claudin, *Imprimerie*, 1: xiii-xiv), of which *Valentin et Orson* was typical. It was the first book produced under the name of Jacques Maillet, an "imprimeur" and "libraire" (printer and bookseller) active in Lyon from 1489 until his death in 1514.[28] Like many in his profession, he may have engaged in renting or buying and selling equipment such as font sets and woodcuts (Rondot, *Graveurs*, 109), an activity which will be relevant in the discussion of the woodcuts below.

Three copies of Maillet's edition of *Valentin et Orson* are known to have survived, found today in New York, the Pierpont Morgan Library; London, the British Library; and Paris, the Bibliothèque Nationale (Dickson, *Study*, 156). Each copy contains 136 non-paginated folios of prose text printed in a gothic

---

[26] André Martin, *Le Livre illustré en France au XIVe siècle* (Paris: Alcan, 1931), 5–6.

[27] Anatole Claudin, *Histoire de l'imprimerie en France au XVe et au XVIe siècle*, 4 vols. (Paris: Imprimerie Nationale, 1900–1914), 1: xi-xii.

[28] Natalis Rondot, *Les Graveurs sur bois et les imprimeurs à Lyon au XVe siècle* (Lyon: Mougin-Rusand, 1896), 181–82.

font and arranged in a two-column format.[29] The text itself is continuous with no organization by paragraph and little punctuation, but it is divided into seventy-four chapters, each of which begins with a lengthy title announcing the primary matter of the chapter.[30] Although a line space separates the end of one chapter from the title of the next, no space separates the title from the chapter it announces. Only a large hand-drawn initial marks the first word of each chapter. Both the Morgan Library and Bibliothèque Nationale copies have a complete set of initials, but in the British Library copy only guide letters appear where the initials were to be added.[31]

Seventy-three of the seventy-four chapter titles begin with "Comment" and continue with a full sentence. A few contain a second "et comment" to signal a second major event in the chapter. A single title (Chapter 70) begins with "Pour raconter comment." A table of contents begins on the second folio recto (folio 2r according to my numeration) and continues for six pages, or until 4v. Chapter numbers are given in roman numerals.

Signature numeration for each signature ($a - r^8$) appears fairly regularly on the bottom left corner of the first four leaves of each signature (thus *ai, aii, aiii,* and *aiiii* for the first signature, *bi, bii, biii,* and *biiii* for the second signature, and so on), and is noted parenthetically in the edition.

After *Valentin et Orson*, Maillet is known to have printed other French texts: *Fierabras* (1489), *Jason et la belle Medée* (1491), *Baudoin comte de Flandres* (1491), and *Le Songe du Vergier* (1491). Though Latin texts, including a Latin Bible, mix with French in his later production, the substantial number of works he printed in the vernacular is in keeping with Lyon's place in early French book production.

In his edition of *Valentin und Namelos*, Wilhelm Seelmann listed both the French and English language editions of *Valentin et Orson*.[32] He identified twenty-eight French editions from the 1489 incunabulum to an undated nineteenth-century edition from Epinal (*Valentin und Namelos*, xxx-xxxi). The editor of this volume has identified and examined twenty-one editions and adaptations in French for the same period, not all of which appear on Seelmann's list. A

---

[29] This edition belongs to what Guidot calls the "gothic" period of printed editions of *mises en prose* (1480 to 1530). See Bernard Guidot, "Formes tardives de l'épopée médiévale: mises en prose, imprimés, livres populaires," in *L'épopée romane au Moyen Âge et aux temps modernes: Actes du XIVe Congrès International de la Société Rencesvals 1997*, ed. Salvatore Luongo (Naples: Fridericiana, 2001), 579–610, here 587.

[30] Guidot points out that one of the merits of the *prosateurs* (those who reworked verse texts into prose) was to organize the material with chapters and rubrics: "Formes tardives," 595.

[31] The guide letters in the copies containing the hand-drawn initials sometimes peek out from behind the initials; in others they are completely covered (or nearly so) by the added initial.

[32] W. Seelmann, *Valentin und Namelos* (Norden and Leipzig: Soltau, 1884).

somewhat different list appears in Brunet.[33] Helwi Blom, whose particular interests lie in the *Bibliothèque Bleue*, states that there are about fifty editions, but identifies only forty-one.[34] However, combining all lists and barring any errors of identification, there were indeed at least fifty printed versions of the story of Valentin and Orson in French over nearly five centuries.[35]

The Woodcuts

The city of Lyon is notable for having produced the first illustrated printed book in France in 1478 (Martin, *Livre illustré*, 53). Some of the early Lyonnais printers were Germans who had crossed the Rhine to set up presses first in Paris and two years later in Lyon, and, for this book and others, they used woodcuts brought in from Germany and Switzerland. In time a distinctively Lyonnais style of woodcut illustration developed, influenced by the cuts of Germanic origin that continued to cross the border with regularity (Martin, *Livre illustré*, 54–55).

The drawing in early Lyonnais woodcuts is simple, primarily linear with almost no shadow and little development of landscape or architecture. Instead, effort went into rendering basic physical and facial expression (Claudin, *Imprimerie*, 1: xiv). The woodcuts in Maillet's *Valentin et Orson*, except for the frontispiece (clearly by a different and superior hand to that of the other images), conform to this popular and relatively inexpensive style.

Most woodcuts from this early period, called "factotum" cuts, were made to be non-text-specific in subject matter so as to serve more than one text. Thus one sees relatively generic scenes such as a kneeling messenger delivering his missive to a king, jousting knights, mass battle scenes, and marriage tableaux, and these may appear in completely different works produced by the same printer. A case in point is Maillet's 1491 *Jason et Medée* in which nearly all the woodcuts are identical to ones used in his *Valentin et Orson*.[36]

---

[33] J.-C. Brunet, *Manuel du libraire et de l'amateur des livres*, vol. 5 (Paris: Firmin-Didot, 1864), 1035–37.

[34] Helwi Blom, "Valentin et Orson et la *Bibliothèque bleue*," in *L'épopée romane au Moyen Âge et aux temps modernes: Actes du XIVe Congrès International de la Société Rencesvals 1997*, ed. Luongo, 611–25.

[35] See list of editions in Appendix A.

[36] The copy of *Jason et Medée* in the Bibliothèque de l'Arsenal in Paris is neither paginated nor foliated, thus I refer to folios according to the signatures. The cut in *Jason* on b.^{2}.v is identical to that on 15v in VO; b.^{6}.v = 126r; e.^{1}.v = 115v; f.^{5}.r = 14v; g.^{1}.r = 103r; g.^{4}.v = 51v; i.^{5}.v = 115v (repeat of e.^{1}.v); m.^{6}.r = 23v. However, the woodcut on l.^{6}.r of a wedding scene, though similar to one in Maillet's 1489 *Valentin et Orson*, contains nevertheless some small changes and is produced by a different hand. That cut is identical to a cut on a.^{3}.v in Arnoullet's 1495 *Valentin et Orson*, a book in which nearly all the cuts are

Moreover, woodcuts were often used more than once in the same text. Maillet's *Valentin et Orson* is endowed with a total of forty illustrations, several of which are repeats, so that only thirty-two individual woodcuts in all were used.[37] Indeed, two cuts appear three times each—a scene with a kneeling messenger delivering his missive to a king, and one of a king conferring with multiple attendants—both obviously useful cuts the subject matter of which was likely to occur more than once in many different texts, and, in fact, the kneeling messenger cut is one that also appears in Maillet's *Baudoin comte de Flandres*.[38]

Throughout the 1480s there developed in Lyon a fund of woodcuts that printers borrowed, rented, or bought from one another (Martin, *Livre illustré*, 59). By studying various incunabula one can trace some of these borrowings. For example, most of the woodcuts in Jacques Arnoullet's 1495 edition of *Valentin et Orson*, also produced in Lyon, are identical to cuts in the Maillet edition. Moreover, such borrowings, rentals, and sales occurred as well between cities, as demonstrated, for example, by the fact that four woodcuts from the printer Pierre Schenck's edition of *L'Abuzé en court*, published in Vienne in 1484, are identical to cuts in Maillet's 1489 *Valentin et Orson*. Whether Maillet himself bought them from Schenck or they came first by way of some other printer is probably impossible to know, but the fact *that* they traveled is clear.[39] Woodcut engravers

---

identical to those of Maillet's edition. Clearly a cut must have been lost or damaged and a second hand redid the scene.

[37] See description of all woodcuts in the incunabulum in Appendix B.

[38] Reproduced in Claudin, *Imprimerie*, 4: 104. Claudin claimed that this copy of Baudoin was owned by a M. J. Baudrier, author of the *Bibliographie lyonnaise du XVI*[e] *siècle*. Seeing that Claudin published his study before World War I, the book may have changed hands since then, but I have been unable to discover anything about this volume or locate another copy of this rare early edition. The volume Claudin was fortunate enough to consult may have remained in private hands. The kneeling messenger can be interpreted as either delivering a message, that is, handing it over to the king, or receiving a message to be delivered, and indeed, is used for both purposes in the text.

[39] The copy of *L'Abuzé en court* in the Bibliothèque Nationale in Paris is neither paginated nor foliated, but does have clearly marked signatures, thus I refer to folios according to the signatures. The cut in *L'Abuzé* on b.[2].r is identical to that on 64r in VO; b.[4].r is identical to 27r; b.[8].v is identical to 9v; and c.[8].r is identical to 128v. The woodcut on b.[8].v is reproduced in Martin.

Claudin traces relationships among printers by way of the printing type. Schenck, the named printer of *L'Abuzé en court*, was associated with a Lyon printer named Gaspard Ortuin. Later Schenck disassociated himself from Ortuin and must have taken the font characters used in two jointly produced works with him to Vienne in 1484, for they were used to produce *L'Abuzé* (Claudin, *Imprimerie*, 3: 382–83). Claudin also believes it likely that Ortuin did the typesetting for Jacques Maillet on several works bearing Maillet's name as printer, as the character set used in all of Maillet's first published books appears to be the same as that used in Ortuin's c.1486 *Ponthus et la belle Sidoyne*. Since

themselves, mostly anonymous, were often independent itinerant artists, moving from one printer to another, contracting themselves out for a time (Rondot, *Graveurs*, 113–14). Their movements may help explain the movement of cuts from printer to printer and city to city.

The placement of the factotum woodcuts in the text of the 1489 edition conforms to the plot of the narrative, but the images often have only a tenuous relationship to the action they supposedly represent. The employment of the image of the kneeling messenger mentioned above is just one example. It first occurs in Chapter 8 when Alexander, the emperor of Greece, sends for Pepin to come see the judicial combat between the archbishop and the merchant who is defending the queen's reputation. Thus the image is supposed to represent the sending of a message, that is, the sender handing over the message to the messenger, and the cut does indeed show the exchange of a paper or parchment. In the second instance, in Chapter 24, Pacolet is bringing news to the Saracen giant Ferragu concerning Valentin and Orson, the guests of his sister Esclarmonde, and their discovery of their true identity as the sons of Alexander and Bellissant. Here, of course, there is no question of a written message, for Pacolet arrives in person to tell Ferragu the news, and the generic scene lacks all individualization of representation of the colorful necromancer. The third instance occurs in Chapter 40. In the previous chapter, Valentin had been charged by King Lucar to carry a message of defiance and challenge to the King of India, and in Chapter 40 he delivers his message. Thus here the scene represents the purely oral delivery of a message (no written message mentioned), and of course, once again, there is no individualization of the cut to represent Valentin, the noble knight. The cut shows us an ordinary generic messenger.

Editions and Translations

The present volume contains the first modern scholarly edition of the text of the Maillet book of 1489. Moreover, its facing-page translation constitutes the second translation into English ever made of the French prose *Valentin et Orson*, and probably the first based directly on the 1489 edition.

Maillet was both a bookseller and a printer, it would not have been unusual, according to Claudin, to have someone else do the printing and yet have his own name in the book as printer. However, Claudin also admits that it is possible Maillet may only have borrowed or bought the font from Ortuin (Claudin, *Imprimerie*, 4: 97–99). Nevertheless, this connection between Schenck and Maillet by way of Ortuin may explain the use of some of the same woodcuts in Schenck's and Maillet's works. See also Rondot, *Graveurs*, 145–46 for his discussion of Ortuin (spelled Hortuin in Rondot), 162 for Schenck, and 181–82 for Maillet.

The first translation of the prose *Valentin et Orson* was done by Henry Watson *c*.1505.[40] Little is known of him beyond what he himself states in the prefaces to his translations indicating that he was in the employ, probably as an apprentice, of the printer Wynkyn de Worde, his "worshipful master."[41] He stresses his youth, excusing mistakes in his translation on that basis, and tells us that he has undertaken the task at his master's bidding (Dickson, *Valentine and Orson*, xiv-xv). Of the first edition of his translation only a fragment has survived—four leaves pasted in another book and discovered in 1816 (Dickson, *Valentine and Orson*, xi). To prepare a modern edition of Watson's translation, Dickson had to use the second edition of 1548–1558, published not by Wynkyn de Worde but by William Copland.

Dickson believes that Watson was working not from the 1489 Maillet edition, but rather from a subsequent French edition, which would account for occasional abbreviations of passages and variances from the French text in the English translation.[42] This "process of progressive abbreviation and corruption" as the texts were re-edited and adapted for subsequent publication affected both the French and the English texts (Dickson, *Valentine and Orson*, xvii).

Nevertheless, Watson's work was the starting point for the long history of this story in the English language, for virtually all such versions descend from his early sixteenth-century translation. Dickson provides an "incomplete" list of seventy-four English editions of the text in an appendix to his source study (Dickson, *Study*, 284–98). A footnote in Helen Cooper's article on *Valentine and*

---

[40] In 1929 in *Study*, Dickson gives "1510?" as the approximate date of the Watson translation, pending further study (3, 285). By the time of his 1937 edition of the Watson text (Arthur Dickson, ed., *Valentine and Orson: Translated from the French by Henry Watson*, EETS o.s. 204 [London: Humphrey Milford/ Oxford University Press, 1937; repr. 2000]), he has pushed the possible date up to "1503–05?" (xiv) based on the examination of the surviving fragment by "Mr. Frank Isaac" who informed Dickson that "the type and the character of the impression indicate that it was printed by de Worde about 1503–05" (xi).

[41] Watson is the known translator of at least three other texts for Wynkyn de Worde, and may have done two others (Dickson, *Valentine and Orson*, xiv-xv).

[42] He posits the edition as one mentioned in Brunet's *Manuel du libraire*, a volume printed in Lyon by Martin Havart in 1505, known only by an entry in a sales catalog from 1863 (Brunet, *Manuel du libraire*, col 1035–36). It is apparently still in private hands. However, that would preclude the 1503 end of the "1503–1505?" date suggested in his 1937 edition of *Valentine and Orson*. To be sure, Dickson reasonably hypothesizes that the Watson translation could be based on an edition now lost, but that it must be one that predates what he calls the fourth edition (fifth on the list in Appendix A), printed in Paris under the name Veuve Jehan Trepperel and Jehan Jehannot, 1511–1525, a copy in the Staatsbibliothek, Munich, not examined by the present editor (Dickson, *Valentine and Orson*, xvii).

Orson[43] mentions that George Keiser "who is working on a bibliographical history of both the texts and illustrations of *Valentine*, has noted some two hundred editions from both sides of the Atlantic" (154, n. 3). As of the present moment, no such bibliography has been published, but such numbers testify to the longstanding popularity of the story in English.

Editing and Translating Principles

All normal abbreviations marked in the incunabulum with a bar have been expanded without comment. However, sometimes the bar is missing on a letter where an abbreviation was clearly intended. In such instances, I have expanded the presumed contraction, but placed the added letters between square brackets. Where agreements normative in the fifteenth century are lacking (apparently due to typesetting error), these have similarly been added in brackets. However, agreement of the past participle is irregular in this text and I have not emended cases where it would be considered lacking only according to the rules of modern French.

Punctuation around roman numerals has been left intact, but in instances where numbers are spelled out in normal sentences modern punctuation has been employed.

Not infrequently when the pronoun *il* follows *que*, one sees the form *qui* (either written out in full or in abbreviated form). I have chosen to transcribe this as *qu'i*.[44] Elsewhere *i* occurs in lieu of *il* which I have left similarly unemended.

Where letters are simply missing or a word obviously misspelled, apparently owing to typesetting error, I have made the change and explained in a footnote what the original printed text contained. However, many inconsistencies in spelling typical of the period have been allowed to stand. Where the typesetter repeated a word (usually at the beginning of a line after including it at the end of the previous line), I have eliminated the repeat and indicated such in a footnote.

Although the font used clearly differentiates *n* from *u*, they are occasionally substituted one for the other in the text, probably in keeping with their near interchangeability in handwritten manuscripts. In fact, the bar over a letter usually indicating an *n* (or *m*) to follow the letter carrying the bar is used not infrequently for a following *u* (such as in the word *moult* spelled with the abbreviation of a

---

[43] H. Cooper, "The Strange History of Valentine and Orson," in *Tradition and Transformation in Medieval Romance*, ed. Rosalind Field (Cambridge: Brewer, 1999), 153–68.

[44] "Peut-être cette confusion formelle avec le relatif qui nous indique-t-elle que l'on prononçait alors [i], le l final s'étant amui devant consonne; en effet, une farce de la fin du XVe siècle offre plusieurs fois la forme y": Christiane Marchello-Nizia, *La langue française aux XIVe et XVe siècles* (Paris: Nathan, 1997), 223.

bar over the *o*; i.e., *mōlt*). Wherever the letters have been interchanged, I have changed to the appropriate letter without comment.

The letter *i* is regularly used for *j*, which apparently was not included in the font set used to typeset the incunabulum. Therefore I have substituted *j* for *i* wherever appropriate without comment.

The letter *z* is frequently used in place of *s* to mark the plural of nouns (i.e., *les navirez, vivrez* [68r], *quelz coupz, frerez* [52r]) and pronouns (i.e., *ilz, lesquelz*), or in words such as *forez*. To avoid confusion between the second person plural or formal of verbs and plural past participles, I have added an acute accent to the plural past participles; i.e., *ils sont entréz*. In cases where *z* marks the second person singular of verbs, the presence of the subject pronoun usually dispels any confusion with the second person plural or formal; i.e., *oyez tu* [49v].

The *le* for a feminine antecedent (usually a Picardism in Old French) is rare in this text, but since it recurs several times (see Chapters 8, 19, 28, 29, and 61) I have let it stand and commented upon it in a note.

Although I believe in translating as literally as possible, excessively awkward language has a negative impact on clarity, and clarity in English was the overarching principle to be balanced with fidelity to the original text.

Occasionally the narrator begins to report conversation in indirect discourse and switches mid-sentence to direct discourse. Without removing the relative construction, I have simply placed quotation marks around the speech when it becomes direct. For example, when first person speech occurs after *que*, which would normally be expected to introduce indirect discourse, I have left the *que* but surrounded the first person speech that follows with quotation marks. According to Christiane Marchello-Nizia, this kind of sudden switch from indirect to direct discourse is not uncommon in Middle French.[45]

To relieve what in English would be the stultifying monotony of long series of declarative sentences and clauses linked by simple conjunctions like *et* and *puis*, I have sometimes introduced in the translation a variety of adverbs and conjunctions.

I have regularly changed word order where too literal a translation would be awkward.

Where two words, usually closely synonymous adjectives, are used, I have translated with one close equivalent, if using synonyms in English was too awkward or no second adjective appropriate in meaning was available. For example, in a single sentence in Chapter 3 one finds both instances in three doublings. The sentence in the original reads: "Si me veullez oÿr *reciter et declairer* ung cas qui grandement *touche et ataint* vostre *profit et honneur* plus que nulles riens." I have translated this sentence into English in the following manner: "Please let me *tell* you of a case that *most definitely touches* your *honor and welfare* more than anything

---

[45] See Marchello-Nizia, *La langue française aux XIVe et XVe siècles*, 441.

else." With *reciter et declairer*, the doubling is simply stylistic with no particular emphasis, and is translated with the one verb "tell." The double synonyms *touche et ataint* serve to emphasize a point (reinforced with "grandement"), thus I used "most definitely touches" to give the sense of urgency the evil archbishop is expressing. However, "honor and welfare" sounded balanced as a translation in English of "profit et honneur." Such are the choices translators must make at all times.

Sources of the Story

Arthur Dickson's source study of 1929 contains a thorough account of the various folk-tales, fairy-tales (or "märchen", as Dickson prefers to call them), romance motifs, and epic themes that can be identified as supplying narrative material for both *Valentin und Namelos* (and thus also presumably **Valentin et Sansnom*) and subsequently *Valentin et Orson*. We owe Mr. Dickson a great debt of gratitude for carrying out the kind of work rarely done today. That the author of *Valentin et Orson* drew on and was inspired by a wealth of source material is beyond question. This in and of itself is no fault, since most medieval narrative draws on oral and written traditions, and indeed was expected to do so. Excellence was judged by how skillfully the author fashions known material into a well-told tale. For modern readers, the heaping up of narrative motifs, themes, and incidents in this text results in a rather uneven hodgepodge of a story that achieves excellence of narrative tension only within certain distinctive episodes, such as the conquest and taming of Orson the wild man, and Valentin's encounter with the Saracen queen Rozemonde. But, as stated above, the late medieval, Renaissance, and even early modern audiences enjoyed the story sufficiently to keep reediting and adapting it in subsequent editions over the course of the next three to four centuries.

Few of Dickson's findings of source material have been challenged, owing in part perhaps to the lack of critical attention paid to this tale, but, in fact, scholarly disagreement has resulted from only one of his contentions, namely, that the märchen of the Jealous Sisters (a specific type of twin-tale) constitutes the core source of *Valentin und Namelos* (which later was expanded into VO).[46] Alexander H. Krappe states clearly that he does not disagree with Dickson's basic thesis, that *Valentin et Orson* "represents an accumulation of motives and incidents of different character and origin, but mostly taken from older romances and fairy tales" ("Valentine and Orson," 493). However, he sides with the conclusions of an earlier article by Rendel Harris,[47] namely, that the story of Valentin and Orson

---

[46] See Alexander Haggerty Krappe, "Valentine and Orson," *Modern Language Notes* 47 (1932): 493–98.

[47] J. Rendel Harris, "Valentine and Orson: A Study in Twin-Cult," *Contemporary Review* 126 (1924): 323–31.

"has for its nucleus a tale of twins in a primitive form, comparable with the legends of Romulus and Remus" ("Twin-Cult," 323).

Harris takes pains to show the parallels between the basic Valentin and Orson story and ancient twin-tales: the exiled mother, exposed twins (although here it is for reasons other than the desire to rid oneself of the products of a multiple birth deemed either uncanny or sacred in ancient times), the fight between the twins, and the contrast between the twins with one rough and/or hairy, the other smooth (Harris, "Twin-Cult," 323–24, 328). Krappe argues compellingly that it is more likely that both *Valentin et Orson* and the märchen of the Jealous Sisters (in which it is just as often a jealous mother-in-law or a mother-in-law working in conjunction with jealous sisters who brings misfortune onto an innocent wife/queen) draw, each of them, on the essential elements of the twin-tale, rather than the former being derived from the latter. Nevertheless, to be fair to Dickson, certain details of *Valentin und Namelos* that did not make it into *Valentin et Orson* link VN more closely to the märchen than VO.[48] For example, in VN, it is the queen's jealous mother-in-law who is the source of her troubles, whereas it is the lust of an evil archbishop that brings on the false accusation against the queen in VO.

In any case, the primary conclusion to be drawn from these discussions is the debt that the author/compiler of *Valentin et Orson* owes to the myriad folk-tales, romances, and epics from which he drew his basic material. For *Valentin et Orson* is much more than the expansion of a single märchen or a twin-tale. Dickson names some forty or so folklore sources, romances, hagiographic sources, and epics from which the author of VO drew to fashion his narrative (Dickson, *Study*, 266–68). And one of the oldest motifs and probably the most delightful in this story is that of the wild man.

Orson, the Wild Man

Both Dickson and Krappe acknowledge the centrality of the wild man motif, and Dickson devotes a fair amount of space in his source study to the history of this multifaceted figure of medieval romance (Dickson, *Study*, 113–27). Orson fits into a long tradition of representation of *l'homme sauvage* in Western literature and art, a motif explored by many scholars.[49] Unfortunately none of the

---

[48] See Dickson, *Study*, 23–24, and the discussion of *Valentin und Namelos*, 28–153.

[49] Roger Bartra, *Wild Men in the Looking Glass: The Mythic Origins of European Otherness*, trans. Carl T. Berrisford (Ann Arbor: University of Michigan Press, 1994); Richard Bernheimer, *Wild Men in the Middle Ages: A Study in Art, Sentiment, and Demonology* (Cambridge, MA: Harvard University Press, 1952; repr. New York: Octagon Books, 1970); Timothy Husband, *The Wild Man: Medieval Myth and Symbolism* (New York: Metropolitan Museum of Art, 1980); Bruno Roy, "En marge du monde connu: les races de

woodcuts in the 1489 edition, which, as mentioned above, are all factotum prints and thus not specific to the text, depicts Orson as a wild man. It is not until the 1539 edition produced by Olivier Arnoullet in Lyon (although possibly in his 1526 edition) that an image of Orson graces the volume.[50]

Orson appears twice in wild man mode, each time paired with his brother. The first is the frontispiece to the book and shows the brothers as two mounted figures. Orson is furry (except for his hands and bare feet), bearded, shaggy-haired, and crowned with a leafy circlet. Valentin is clothed as a knight in armor except for a cap with three long trailing feathers that replaces the conventional helmet. Each rides a properly saddled and bridled horse, and they are nicely framed by a scalloped arch. The style of drawing is relatively rough with simple parallel-line hatching for shading. On a wide banderole beneath them is the title: "Lystoire du noble valentin et orson."

The second image comes at the beginning of the chapter entitled "Comment valentin conquist orson en la forest & lamena au roy pepin a orleans." It shows the two brothers mounted once again, but this time their horses stand in parallel, both facing right, looking toward a robed, crowned figure holding a scepter, presumably King Pepin, welcoming Valentin back after his victory over his brother. The drawing style resembles that of the frontispiece, but is executed in a rapid, even sketchier fashion. Orson's horse is bridled but not saddled; Orson has no crown of leaves; and Valentin's cap is down to one feather.

The figure of the wild man is employed, to be sure, for its entertainment value, but the taming of Orson, as he undergoes a transformation from wild man of

---

monstres," in *Aspects de la marginalité au Moyen Age*, ed. Guy H. Allard (Montreal: Aurore, 1975), 70–81; Shira Schwam-Baird, "Terror and Laughter in the Images of the Wild Man: The Case of the 1489 *Valentin et Orson*," *Fifteenth-Century Studies* 27 (2002): 238–256; Lorraine Kochanske Stock, *The Medieval Wild Man* (forthcoming with Palgrave Macmillan); Franck Tinland, *L'Homme sauvage: Homo ferus et homo sylvestris: de l'animal à l'homme* (Paris: Payot, 1968); Hayden White, "The Forms of Wildness: Archaeology of an Idea," in *The Wild Man Within: An Image in Western Thought from the Renaissance to Romanticism*, ed. Edward Dudley and Maximillian E. Novak (Pittsburgh: University of Pittsburgh Press, 1972), 3–38.

[50] One copy of Olivier Arnoullet's edition of 1526 resides in the Herzog-August-Bibliothek in Wolfenbüttel, Germany. Both the online library catalog and Seelmann attest to this edition containing ninety woodcuts. Seelmann says that the first depicts two riders, which suggests its being identical to the frontispiece described below; however, not having examined the cuts myself and having no other source of information, I cannot say with certainty whether the woodcuts are all factotum cuts or whether at least some, if not all, were made specifically for the edition and thus include an image of the wild man Orson. I have however examined two copies of the 1539 edition, one at the Musée de Condé in Chantilly, the other at the British Library. This edition contains only thirty-five woodcuts, many of which are repeats, so that, in fact, there are only nineteen separate images.

the woods to full-fledged knight, reveals the model of chivalry promoted by his fifteenth-century creator. In his wild state Orson is an animal, using his remarkable strength to wound and kill indiscriminately. Captured by his twin brother, Valentin, and brought to Pepin's court, he is at first an uncontrollable *vilain* who wreaks havoc on the civilized life of the court, inviting laughter at his boorish manners and providing much of the comic relief in the tale. But in time he is completely transformed and takes his rightful place as a king's son and ruler of men, a role that seems innate to Valentin at his earliest maturity.

The narrator highlights the contrast between the two brothers early in the tale. Chapter 10 recounts that despite his status as a foundling of unknown parentage, Valentin's beauty and natural inclination for all things chivalrous cause Pepin to both love him and equip him for knighthood (an expensive gesture), and Valentin justifies Pepin's love by excelling in jousts and tournaments. But the very next paragraph reminds us that at the same time "his brother Orson is in the forest, hairy and covered with fur just like a bear, leading the life of a wild beast."[51]

Valentin represents a classic ideal of knighthood; his noble birth draws him instinctively toward horses and arms for which he demonstrates native talents, and his sense of religion and honor is evident. Moreover, by the time he faces Orson in the forest, he is a proven warrior, having already battled Saracens; fighting the wild man who had nearly killed Pepin is his next adventure. When battle is joined between them, they fight according to their present state, Valentin the knight employing steel weapons and his wits, Orson the wild man depending on nails, brute strength, and an uprooted tree.

The battle between the brothers rages on for some time (no text of this sort would be worth its salt without lengthy descriptions of marvelous blows, wounds, and blood), but a moment comes when Orson manages to wrest Valentin's shield from him, stopping to examine it "for the beauty of the colors he had not been accustomed to see."[52] Like the fascination with the horse, this moment demonstrates a savage's marveling at the unknown and unrecognized, but perhaps as well a preliminary inkling of Orson's own natural inclination to things chivalrous owing to his royal blood. If so, it is nevertheless momentary, and Orson tosses the object aside to resume his attack.

The battle terminates only after both combatants are thoroughly exhausted and Valentin makes a verbal appeal to Orson to give himself up and come with him to be baptized and civilized. According to the narrator, Orson understands by signs that Valentin wishes only his own good, and the "natural inclination that does not lie," as the narrator puts it, persuades Orson to surrender to his

---

[51] "... son frere Orson est dedens la forest velu et couvert de poil tout ainsi come ung ours, menant vie de beste sauvage (p. 72)."

[52] "... pour la beaulté des couleurs qu'i n'avoit point acoustume de voir (p. 94)."

brother.⁵³ Thus does Orson make the first step away from wildness and toward civilized life.

The next scenes involving Orson, recounting the brothers' journey back to Orléans, exploits the humor inherent in the wild Orson's *vilain* behavior (Chapter 13). When the frightened villagers hide behind locked doors rather than respond to the hungry and weary Valentin's request for lodging, he threatens to turn the wild man loose on them, and carries through when his menacing fails to convince them. Orson breaks down doors, the brothers seize what they need, and Orson's rapacious eating and drunkenness, when he is plied for the first time with wine, are treated as a huge joke. Similar incidents take place as they arrive at Pepin's court. All are frightened at Orson's appearance, and, once allowed in, he exhibits bestial eating and drinking manners, in the fashion of the *vilain* Reynoart from *Aliscans*, that amuse Pepin.⁵⁴

Pepin immediately recognizes Orson's potential; noting how well-formed he is despite his hairiness, he declares that, once properly dressed, Orson would make a handsome knight.⁵⁵ At once Valentin requests and arranges for the baptism he had promised Orson in the forest. Nevertheless, the wild man's education has hardly begun, for at the meal after the baptism, Orson seizes food from Pepin's plate, gets staggering drunk, and earns Valentin's reprimand. Moreover, though provided a room, the newly Christianized wild man ignores the civilized bed and sleeps on the floor as he was wont to do in the forest. Clearly, though Orson possesses a native beauty appropriate to his noble birth which his wildness cannot disguise, baptism alone cannot sweep away the habits of fifteen years in the forest or reverse the consequences of having been suckled with a she-bear's milk.

True to the wild man type, Orson demonstrates a decidedly unchivalrous sexual aggressiveness and lewdness. When the king's daughter Esglentine, curious to see the wild man, has Valentin bring him to her chamber, Orson throws himself on the bed and invites the attendant ladies by signs to come join him. This makes them all laugh, and so it goes no further. But his lasciviousness gives way to a more proper devotion only when he falls in love with "la belle Fezonne" further on in the tale. He also gets into a scrape with one of the cooks in the kitchens in a scene lifted out of *Aliscans* (Dickson, *Study*, 180).

---

⁵³ ". . . selon le cours de nature qui ne peult mentir, Orson se getta a deux genoulx et tendit les mains devers son frere (p. 96)."

⁵⁴ Dickson was the first to note that these scenes of inebriation and a scrape with the kitchen staff may have been inspired by the exploits of the vilain Reynoart from the late twelfth-century *Aliscans*. See Dickson, *Study*, 180.

⁵⁵ "Seigneurs, par le Dieu tout puissant, moult est merveilleuse chose de cest homme sauvaige voir et regarder. Moult est bien formé et belle estature de corps et de tous membres. Et combien qu'il soit velu s'il estoit vestu comme l'ung de nous, fort seroit plaisant a veoir et beau chevalier sembleroit" (p. 102).

Pepin's illegitimate sons, Hauffroy and Henry, detest Valentin, whom they see as a rival for their father's affection, and do all they can to harm him. While Orson is being displayed in Esglentine's chamber, the evil brothers enter, accuse Valentin of trying to compromise their sister's virtue, and move to attack him (Chapter 14). By this time, Orson is devoted to his conqueror, and like the loyal lion of Yvain, attacks his attackers, and, without the intervention of Valentin and the ladies, would surely have killed them. Pepin is ready to imprison the wild man until the true nature of his action is explained. Though his motivation is less the loyalty of chivalry and more that of a devoted beast, it is no less his first noble act.

In one of the illegitimate brothers' plots against Valentin, they arrange for a cousin, Grigar, to attack and seize Valentin on the road, and throw him in a prison with a plan later to kill him (Chapter 17). But Grigar fails to capture Orson, who finds his way back to court and attacks Grigar at the king's table. Some call for Orson's death after this supposedly unprovoked assault, but the king notes that Orson had assailed no one but Grigar and thus probably had a reason. Orson then manages through signs to accuse Grigar of the attack against Valentin and challenges him by throwing down his cap ("chapperon") in defiance. Thus he passes from his wild man behavior—the brute attack—to chivalrous procedure—the challenge to combat by gage, though his transformation is nowhere near complete yet. Orson has continually to be restrained from assaulting Grigar whenever he sees him,[56] and once the combat starts, he fights like a wild man, starting with a growl, a baring of his teeth, and a showing of his nails. Grigar is armed and mounted while Orson fights from the ground, using no weapons besides his brute strength. There is none of the savage elegance of skill with sword and lance, only messy viciousness, with Orson seizing Grigar's weapons one after another and beating Grigar to a pulp until his utter defeat and confession (Chapter 18).

Valentin and Orson leave court to rescue "la belle Fezonne," daughter of the Duke of Aquitaine, from the importunate suit of the Green Knight (Verd Chevalier) (Chapter 20). Valentin fights him bravely throughout a day and into the evening, but cannot defeat him, for, as it turns out, only the son of a king who has never suckled a woman's milk can win victory over this Saracen giant. Valentin has the happy thought to send in Orson as his replacement the next day, for he surmises that at the very least he has suckled no woman's milk. True to type, Orson, who is happy to fight the Green Knight, takes up an enormous cudgel to use in combat, and must be persuaded to wear Valentin's own armor and bear his weapons so that the substitution may work. Once armed Orson looks the knight "preux" and "hardy," but in the course of combat, he depends on sheer brute force

---

[56] "Tousjours estoit Orson pres de frapper Grigar le faulx et mauldit trahytre. Mais le roy le fist prendre et retenir devers luy en luy faisant signes que plus nul il ne frappera tant qu'il soit ou champ" (p. 128).

to put his enemy at his mercy. Once the Green Knight is overpowered, Orson performs the task that only the one destined to defeat him can do, namely, lifting a certain shield off a tree, the task Valentin had failed to do the previous day, and the Green Knight agrees to baptism.

Orson's triumph gains him the promise of Fezonne's hand, but the twins' priority is to discover the truth of their birth (they still have no idea they are related); thus they set off to Esclarmonde, the Green Knight's sister, whose marvelous Brass Head tells all—their family relationship and the means to restore speech to Orson. By Chapter 26, when Orson returns to Aquitaine disguised as an errant knight to test Fezonne's faithfulness, his behavior is completely transformed. So accomplished is he that Fezonne's father, who has weakened in his commitment to Orson in the latter's prolonged absence, presses his daughter to marry this valiant newcomer who has just saved him from a new threat. Despite the lovely impression this "new" knight has made on everyone,[57] Fezonne remains loyal to the one who had won her heart, and all turns out happily in the end. Valentin and Orson make a grand entrance, and with Orson now clothed as in his previous visit, everyone recognizes him. The narrator winks at us perhaps when Fezonne expresses her joy to her beloved at his return which saves her from being forced to marry another knight, "who," she says, "greatly resembled you in the nose and the mouth."[58] "My dear," Orson answers her, "I know the truth. And know that since I last saw you I have learned to speak, and I am the one who in your chamber today requested your love."[59] Pleased with her fidelity, Orson seems undisturbed by her failure to recognize him, and we are left with the lesson that a radical change of behavior affects recognition more than does physical appearance.

A certain model of chivalry emerges from the course of this transformation. First of all, noble birth is determinate in the acquisition of chivalry and transcends all other influences. Ever since the rustic Perceval was overcome by his first sight of knights in Chrétien's tale, the understanding that the truth of knighthood "will out" despite a decidedly unchivalrous upbringing is the standard stuff of romance. Both Perceval and Orson have a natural talent for the combat skills of a knight, and learn quickly that which in reality took many years of strenuous training to acquire; but both also take longer to gain the social graces that must accompany the knight into the courtly setting, and earn the court's and the reader's laughter for their initial gaffes. Nevertheless, there is an

---

[57] "Tant fut Orson saige et bien aprins en maniere et contenance que pour la prudence et saigesse de luy en son palais a disner le retint avec ses chevaliers. Et quant il fust a table assis tant fust sa maniere fort plaisante et sa [61verso] contenance a tous aggreable que des barons et chevaliers fust moult regardé (p. 232)."

[58] ". . . moult fort bien vous resembloit de nez et de bouche (p. 246)."

[59] "[J]'en sçay la verité. Sachez que depuis que ne vous veis j'ay aprins a parler, et suis celuy qui au jour d'uy en vostre chambre d'amours je vous ay prié (p. 246)."

inevitability that the transformation will take place due to the reader's knowledge of their noble birth. Moreover, beauty is an integral element of nobility. No amount of hairiness can hide the pleasing form that marks Orson inevitably as a gentleman.

Secondly, the acquisition of speech is primary in Orson's case. Although hairiness is an essential mark of wildness, the narrator makes no remark as to when he literally sheds this characteristic, especially curious in light of the fact that *Valentin und Namelos* states that upon bringing Orson to court, Valentin sees to it that he is bathed and shorn of his long body hair before being properly clothed and taught to walk and behave. In the prose version it is simply assumed that at some point Orson's appearance becomes less wild, and it is rather the changes in his behavior that are prominent in the final transformation, especially the acquisition of speech. Without it, Orson's disguise as an errant knight seeking his fortune in service to the Duke of Aquitaine would not have worked, but having it completes what is already a full metamorphosis into a properly dressed, properly armed, properly behaved, and now properly spoken specimen of chivalry.

Overall Orson conforms to an essentially conventional paradigm of chivalry that includes courage, skill at arms, and ferocity against foes, especially Saracens. Courtliness of address towards kings and ladies is no less requisite, and physical beauty graces all knights worthy of the label. In Orson's case, in his status as conqueror of the Green Knight, he enhances the model with chosenness, a not infrequent characteristic of romance heroes, and the one particular characteristic in which he exceeds his brother Valentin in chivalric worth. In fact, few characteristics that have ever been cited as comprising the epitome of chivalry were overlooked in this late example of the romance epic genre to paint for us Orson, the fascinating *sauvage* turned *chevalier*.

If I have spent these several pages only on the delightful Orson, it is not because other enchanting characters are lacking: Bellissant, the falsely accused queen; Esclarmonde, the kidnapped Saracen princess who is the object of Valentin's affection and long quest;[60] Rozemonde, the Saracen queen determined to have a husband to her liking;[61] Pacolet, the Saracen magician in service to the Christians, and his wonderful flying wooden horse.[62] They all deserve scholarly attention and will attract it with the availability of this text.

---

[60] Jacqueline de Weever, *Sheba's Daughters: Whitening and Demonizing the Saracen Woman in Medieval French Epic* (New York: Garland, 1998).

[61] Rozemonde is particularly interesting and is the subject of an article: Shira Schwam-Baird, "A Husband to Her Liking: The Wily Saracen Queen Rozemonde in the 1489 *Valentin et Orson*," *Olifant* 26.1 (2007): 45-66.

[62] Michelle Szkilnik, "Pacolet ou les infortunes de la magie," *Le Moyen français* 35–36 (1994–1995): 91–109.

Contents

[TABLE DES CHAPITRES]

[2recto]¹Vous² princes et aultres seigneurs qui prenés plaisir a lire tous livres, je vous veul racompter la vie des nobles seigneurs Valentin et Orson, nepveux du vaillant et redoubté roy Pepin, jadis roy de France. Pour voir la declaraition dudit livre plus amplement, lisez³ premierement ceste presente table en laquelle on trouvera que ce present livre contient lxxiiii. chapitres, lesquels parlent de plusieurs belles et diverses matieres, lesquels pourront voir ceulx qui liront ce premier chapitre long a long.

Comment le roy Pepin espusa Berte, dame de grande renommee. i. cha[pitre]

Comment l'empereur fut trahy par l'archevesque de Constantinoble dont mauvais mal luy en vint comme vous orés apres. ii. chapitre.

Comment l'archevesque apres ce qu'il fut escondit de la dame Bellissant pour son honneur sauver, contre la noble dame pensa et machina une grant trahison. iii. chapitre.

Comment l'archevesque se mist en habit de chevalier et monta a cheval pour suyvir Bellissant qui estoit bannye. iiii. chapitre.

Comment Bellissant enfanta deux beaulx enfans dedans la forez d'Orleans, dont l'un fut appellé Orson et l'autre Valentin, et comment elle les perdit. v. chapitre

De l'ourse qui emporta ung des enfans de Bellissant parmy le bois. vi. c[h]a[pitre]

Par le conseil mauvais de l'archevesque furent elevé plusieurs nouvelles coustumes en la cité de Constantinoble;⁴ et comment sa trahison fut congneue. vii. chapitre.

Comment l'empereur Alexandre, par le conseil des plus saiges, envoya querir le roy Pepin pour voir la verité de la querelle du marchant et de l'archevesque. viii. chapitre.

---

¹ On 1v, full-page woodcut showing king on horseback, with crown and scepter, wearing sword; both horse and man turned to look back behind them; small dog running alongside; rocks in diagonal across lower left; castle perched on rocks on upper left; another castle perched on a hill behind the king far off in distance on right side of image.

² *a ii* appears at bottom right corner of 2r.

³ Text has *lise*.

⁴ Text has *Par le conseil mauvais de l'archevesque qui fust eslevé plusieurs nouvelles coustumes en la cité de Constantinoble*. I have taken the wording as it appears at the head of the actual chapter 7 which makes better sense.

[CONTENTS]

My lords and princes, you who take pleasure in reading all kinds of books, I wish to tell you the story of the noble lords Valentin and Orson, nephews of the valiant and respected King Pepin, long ago king of France. For a fuller understanding of this book, first read this table of contents where you will discover that this book contains seventy-four chapters, which speak of many beautiful and diverse subjects, and which those who read this first chapter completely will be able to see.

Chapter 1 How King Pepin married Bertha, a lady of great renown.

Chapter 2 How the emperor was betrayed by the archbishop of Constantinople, from which much harm came to him as you will hear later.

Chapter 3 How the archbishop concocted and put into effect a treacherous plot against the lady Bellissant after she rejected him in order to preserve her honor.

Chapter 4 How the archbishop dressed himself as a knight and rode off to follow the banished Bellissant.

Chapter 5 How Bellissant gave birth in the forest of Orleans to two beautiful children, one named Orson and the other Valentin, and how she lost them.

Chapter 6 Concerning the she-bear who carried off through the woods one of Bellissant's children.

Chapter 7 By the evil order of the archbishop, several new rules were put into place in the city of Constantinople; and how his treachery became known.

Chapter 8 How the emperor Alexander, according to the advice of his wisest men, sent for King Pepin to come see the outcome of the fight between the merchant and the archbishop.

Comment le marchant et l'archevesque se combatirent en champ pour sçavoir la verité de l'occasion de Bellissant; et comment l'archevesque fut desconfit. ix. chapitre.

Comment le roy Pepin prist congié de l'empereur et se partist de Constantinoble pour retourner en France; et comment apres il ala a Rome contre les Sarrasins[1] qui la cité avoient prinse. x. chapitre.

Comment Hauffroy et Henry eurent envye sur Valentin pour la grant amour de quoy l'empereur roy de France l'aymoit, comme il luy estoit tenu. xi. chapitre.

Comment Valentin partit d'Orleans pour aler combatre Orson son frere de[2verso] dans la forez, comme vous pourés oÿr cy apres. xii. chapitre.

Comment Valentin, apres ce qu'il eust conquis Orson, se partit de la forez pour retourner a Orleans. xiii. chapitre.

Comment Hauffroy[2] et Henry voulurent tuer Valentin en la chambre de la belle Esglentine. xiiii. chapitre.

Comment le duc Savary envoya devers le roy Pepin pour avoir secours contre le Verd Chevalier qui a force vouloit avoyr sa fille Fesonne. xv. chapitre.

Comment plusieurs chevalier[s] vindrent en Acquitaine pour cuider avoir la belle Fesonne. xvi. chapitre.

Comment Hauffroy et Henry firent gaitter Valentin sur le chemin pour luy et Orson faire mourir. xvii. cha[pitre].

Comment le roy Pepin commanda que devant son palays le champ fust apparellé pour Orson et Grigar ensemble veoir combatre, lequel fut fait. xviii. chapitre.

Comment Grigar, apres ce qu'il fut conquis par Orson, confessa au roy la trahison de Hauffroy et de Henry contre Valentin faitte. xix. chapitre.

Comment Valentin par la grace de Dieu s'avisa d'envoyer le lendemain au matin Orson pour combatre[3] contre le Verd Chevalier; et comment Orson le vainquist et conquesta, comme vous orés apres. xx. chapitre.

Comment la nuyt que Orson eut juré la belle Fesonne, l'ange s'aparut a Valentin; et du commandement qu'il luy fist. xxi. chapitre.

Comment le roy Pepin partit de France pour aler vers l'empereur de Grece porter nouvelles de sa seur Bellissant; et comment devant son retour fist guerre au souldant qui avoit assiegé Constantinoble. xxii. chapitre.

---

[1] Text has *sar/ sarrasins*, a mistake that apparently was due to carelessness setting the type when breaking a word from the end of one line to the next.

[2] Text has *Hauffsoy*.

[3] Text has *combate*.

Chapter 9	How the merchant and the archbishop fought a duel in order to establish the truth concerning Bellissant; and how the archbishop was defeated.
Chapter 10	How King Pepin took leave of the emperor and left Constantinople to return to France; and how afterwards he went to Rome to fight the Saracens who had taken the city.
Chapter 11	How Hauffroy and Henry were jealous of Valentin because of the great love the emperor king of France bore him.
Chapter 12	How Valentin left Orleans to fight Orson his brother in the forest, as you will be able to hear below.
Chapter 13	How Valentin, after having defeated Orson, left the forest to return to Orleans.
Chapter 14	How Hauffroy and Henry tried to kill Valentin in the chamber of the fair Esglentine.
Chapter 15	How Duke Savary sent to King Pepin for help against the Green Knight who wanted to claim his daughter Fezonne through force.
Chapter 16	How many knights came to Aquitaine to try to win the fair Fezonne.
Chapter 17	How Hauffroy and Henry sent men to lie in wait on the road for Valentin in order to kill both Orson and him.
Chapter 18	How King Pepin ordered the field to be set up in front of his palace for him to watch the duel between Orson and Grigar, which was done.
Chapter 19	How, after being defeated by Orson, Grigar confessed to the king the treachery carried out against Valentin by Hauffroy and Henry.
Chapter 20	How Valentin, by the grace of God, thought to send Orson to fight the Green Knight the following morning; and how Orson defeated him, as you will hear below.
Chapter 21	How the angel appeared to Valentin on the night Orson had pledged himself to the fair Fezonne; and concerning the order he gave him.
Chapter 22	How King Pepin left France to bring news to the emperor of Greece concerning his sister Bellissant; and how before his return he made war against the sultan who had besieged Constantinople.

Comment Valentin et Orson arriverent au chasteau ou estoit la belle Esclarmonde; et comment pour la teste d'araing ilz eurent cognossance de leur generation. xxiii. chapitre.

Comment par ung enchanteur qui avoit nom Pacolet le geant Ferragu sceut les nouvelles de sa seur et de Valentin; et de la trahyson d'iceluy Ferragu. xxiiii. chapitre.

Comment Pacolet par son sort delivra Valentin et Orson des prisons du roy Ferragu; et comment il les mist hors de sa terre avec leur mere Bellissant et la belle Esclarmonde. xxv. cha[pitre].

Comment le roy Ferragu pour a[3recto]voir[1] vengance de Valentin et de sa seur Esclarmonde fist assembler tous ceulx de sa terre; et comment descendit en Acquitaine. xxvi. chapitre.

Comment Orson voulut essaier la voulenté et loyauté de la belle Fesonne devant qu'il l'espousast. xxvii. cha[pitre].

Comment Ferragu[2] pour avoir secours manda le roy Trompar et l'enchanteur Adramain; et comment Valentin partit d'Acquitaine pour aler a Constantinoble. xxviii. chapitre.

Comment Pacolet delivra Valentin et le Verd Chevalier de la prison au souldant Meradin; et comment il deceut ledit souldan. xxix. chapitre.

Comment le roy Trompar ariva devant Acquitaine pour secourir Ferragu, et amena avec luy Adramain l'enchanteur par qui Pacolet fut trahy et deceu. xxx. chapitre.

Comment Pacolet prist vengance de l'enchanteur Adramain, lequel l'avoit trahye, desrobé la belle Esclarmonde. xxxi. chapitre.

Comment les chrestiens pour avoir des vivres saillirent de Constantinoble;[3] et comment Valentin et le Verd Chevalier furent prins par les Sarrasins. xxxii. chapitre.

Comment le roy Pepin print congié de l'empereur pour retourner en France; et de la trahyson de Henry et de Hauffroy a l'encontre de Orson. xxxiii. chapitre.

Comment Orson, quant on le vouloit juger, mist opposition et demanda champ de bataille contre ses accusateurs, laquelle chose par les xii pers luy fut acordé. xxxiiii. cha[pitre].

---

[1] *a iii* appears at bottom right corner of 3r.
[2] Text has *Ferragur*.
[3] Text has *constā/noble*, probably due to a typographical error made at the line break.

Chapter 23	How Valentin and Orson arrived at the castle where dwelt the fair Esclarmonde; and how they learned the truth of their birth from the bronze head.
Chapter 24	How Ferragu learned about his sister and Valentin from a magician named Pacolet; and concerning the treachery of this Ferragu.
Chapter 25	How Pacolet used a spell to deliver Valentin and Orson from King Ferragu's prison; and how he helped them get away, along with their mother Bellissant, and the fair Esclarmonde.
Chapter 26	How King Ferragu assembled all those of his land in order to avenge himself against Valentin and his sister Esclarmonde; and how he traveled down to Aquitaine.
Chapter 27	How Orson wanted to test the will and loyalty of the fair Fezonne before marrying her.
Chapter 28	How Ferragu sent for King Trompart and the magician Adramain for help; and how Valentin left Aquitaine to go to Constantinople.
Chapter 29	How Pacolet delivered Valentin and the Green Knight from the prison of Sultan Meradin; and how he deceived the sultan.
Chapter 30	How King Trompart came to Aquitaine to help Ferragu, bringing with him Adramain the magician by whom Pacolet was betrayed and deceived.
Chapter 31	How Pacolet took vengeance upon the magician Adramain, who had betrayed him and kidnapped the fair Esclarmonde.
Chapter 32	How the Christians rode forth from Constantinople to find provisions; and how Valentin and the Green Knight were taken by the Saracens.
Chapter 33	How King Pepin took leave of the emperor to return to France; and concerning Henry and Hauffroy's treachery towards Orson.
Chapter 34	How Orson opposed a trial, asking instead for judicial battle against his accusers, which was granted him by the Twelve Peers.

Comment Valentin en querant Esclarmonde arriva en Anthioche; et comment il combatit et vainquit le serpent. xxxv. chapitre.

Comment Valentin, apres ce qu'il eut conquit le serpent, il fist baptiser le roy d'Anthioche et tous ceulx de sa terre; et de la royne Rozemonde qui de luy fut amoureuse. xxxvi. cha[pitre].

Comment le roy d'Anthioche, pour tant qu'il avoit renoncé la loy de Mahon, fut par Brandifer, le pere de sa femme, mis a mort; et comment l'empereur de Grece et le Verd Chevalier furent par Brandiffer prins devant Crethophe. xxxvii. chapitre.

Comment la belle Esclarmonde, apres que l'an fut acomply, contrefist le malade affin que le roy d'Inde la Major ne l'espousast; et du roy Lucar qui [3verso]voulut venger la mort du roy Trompar son pere a l'encontre du roy d'Inde la Major. xxxviii. chapitre.

Comment le roy Lucar en la cité d'Esclardie espousa la belle Rozemonde. xxxix. chapitre.

Comment Valentin partit d'Esclardie pour aler en Inde la Major porter la deffiance du roy Lucar. xl. cha[pitre].

Comment Valentin fist son messaige au roy d'Inde de par le roy Lucar, et de la responce qui donnee luy fut. xli. chapitre.

Comment Valentin retourna en Esclardie, et de la responce du roy d'Inde la Major. xlii. chapitre.

Comment Rozemonde trouva maniere de soy faire prendre et emmener au roy d'Inde la Major. xliii. cha[pitre].

Comment le roy Lucar fit tant que Brandiffer demoura avec luy devant Inde et envoya en Angorie Valentin, acompaigné de cent mil hommes contre Pepin, roy de France.[1] xliiii. chapitre.

Comment par le sort et subtil engin de Pacolet fit mettre a mort les payens qui par Brandiffer celle part contre le roy Pepin tenoient et avoyent esté envoyéz. xlv. chapitre.

Comment Valentin apres la bataille retourna[2] devant Inde vers le roy Brandiffer et en fist porter mort le roy Murgalant. xlvi. chapitre.

Comment Valentin oÿt nouvelles de son pere; et comment Pacolet delivra le roy d'Inde par son sort et luy livra Brandiffer a sa voulenté. xlvii. chapitre.

---

[1] Text has *Fance*.
[2] Text has *retoruna*.

Chapter 35 How Valentin, in search of Esclarmonde, arrived in Antioch; and how he fought and vanquished the serpent.

Chapter 36 How Valentin, after defeating the serpent, had the king of Antioch and everyone in the land baptized; and concerning Queen Rozemonde who fell in love with him.

Chapter 37 How the king of Antioch was put to death by Brandiffer, his wife's father, for having renounced the faith of Mohammed; and how the emperor of Greece and the Green Knight were captured by Brandiffer before the walls of Christopolis.

Chapter 38 How, once the year was up, the fair Esclarmonde pretended to be ill so that the king of India Major would not marry her; and concerning King Lucar, who wanted to take vengeance on the king of India Major for the death of King Trompart his father.

Chapter 39 How King Lucar married the fair Rozemonde in the city of Esclardy.

Chapter 40 How Valentin left Esclardy for India Major to bring King Lucar's challenge.

Chapter 41 How Valentin delivered the message from King Lucar to the king of India, and concerning the answer given him.

Chapter 42 How Valentin returned to Esclardy, and concerning the reply of the king of India Major.

Chapter 43 How Rozemonde found a way to have herself taken and brought to the king of India Major.

Chapter 44 How King Lucar convinced Brandiffer to remain with him outside of India and send Valentin to Angory, accompanied by a hundred thousand men, against Pepin, king of France.

Chapter 45 How the pagans sent by Brandiffer to fight King Pepin were put to death by means of Pacolet's spell and crafty plot.

Chapter 46 How Valentin returned after the battle to King Brandiffer's encampment before the walls of India, bringing King Murgalant's corpse with him.

Chapter 47 How Valentin heard news of his father; and how Pacolet freed the king of India with his magic, and delivered Brandiffer up to him to do with as he wished.

Comment Hauffroi et Henry trahyrent leur pere le roy Pepin et les douze pers de France. xlviii. chapitre.

Comment Haufroy pour sa trahison parfaire arriva devant Brandiffer et Lucar; et comment par sa trahyson luy propre fut deceu. xlix. chapitre.

[4recto]Comment[1] la belle Galasie, apres qu'elle congneust la grant trahyson de Hauffroy, le fist mettre en ses prisons moult estroitement. l. chapitre.

Comment le roy Brandifer et Lucar prindrent dedens Hierusalem le roy Pepin avec les douze pers de France. li. chapitre.

Comment le roy d'Inde la Major pour sa part des prisonniers emmena Pepin, mais pas ne sçavoit qu'il fust roy de France. lii. chapitre.

Comment le roy Pepin estant avec le roy d'Inde eut congnoissance de la noble et belle dame Esclarmonde et de son fait. liii. chapitre.

Comment le roy Brandiffer emmena a Chastel Fort les douze pers de France, et puis les fist emprisonner en moult diverses horribles et dures prisons. liiii. chapitre.

Comment le roy Brandifer, apres ce qu'il eust assemblé ses gens a Faleizie, il monta dessus la mer pour aler en la cité d'Angorie pour combatre contre les chrestiens. lv. chapitre.

Comment Brandiffer sceut que Lucar estoit en la cité d'Angorie detenu prisonnier; sy manda a Valentin ung message pour l'appointement faire de le racheter et getter hors de prison. lvi. chapitre.

Comment le duc Millon d'Angler, qui estoit nommé roy de France pour saulver Pepin, fut delivré des prisons de Brandiffer en change de Lucar. lvii. chapitre.

Comment Valentin et le duc d'Angler saillirent de la cité d'Angorie sur l'ost des payens et mescreans; et comment les payens perdirent la bataille.[2] lviii. chapitre.

Comment le roy Pepin fut rendu par le roy d'Inde la Major en eschange de son mareschal qui avoit nom Lucar.[3] lix. chapitre.

Comment le roy Pepin se partit de la cité Angorie et s'en retourna en France pour Artus de Bretaigne qui sa femme Berthe vouloit espouser et le royaulme tenir. lx. chapitre.

---

[1] *a iiii* appears at bottom right corner of 4r.

[2] Text has *batail*.

[3] He is not named in the text, nor does the wording as it appears at the head of the actual chapter include the name of the King of India's marshal, thus this appears to be an error.

Chapter 48	How Hauffroy and Henry betrayed their father King Pepin and the Twelve Peers of France.
Chapter 49	How Hauffroy came to Brandiffer and Lucar to carry out his treason; and how by his treachery he was himself deceived.
Chapter 50	How, after learning of Hauffroy's great betrayal, the fair Galasie had him thrown into her dungeon under strict guard.
Chapter 51	How King Brandiffer and Lucar captured King Pepin and the Twelve Peers of France in Jerusalem.
Chapter 52	How the King of India Major took Pepin away as his share of the prisoners, without knowing he was king of France.
Chapter 53	How King Pepin, while in the custody of the King of India, recognized the noble and fair lady Esclarmonde and learned her story.
Chapter 54	How King Brandiffer brought the Twelve Peers of France to Château Fort, and locked them up in harsh and horrible dungeons.
Chapter 55	How, after having assembled his men in Falezie, King Brandiffer took sail for the city of Angory to fight against the Christians.
Chapter 56	How Brandiffer found out that Lucar was being held prisoner in the city of Angory, and so sent a message to Valentin to arrange ransom and get him out of prison.
Chapter 57	How Duke Millon d'Angler, who had pretended to be the king of France in order to save Pepin, was delivered from Brandiffer's prison in exchange for Lucar.
Chapter 58	How Valentin and the Duke d'Angler rode forth from the city of Angory against the army of pagans and miscreants; and how the pagans lost the battle.
Chapter 59	How King Pepin was returned by the King of India in exchange for his marshal whose name was Lucar.
Chapter 60	How King Pepin left the city of Angory and returned to France because of Arthur of Brittany who wished to marry his wife Bertha and take over his kingdom.

Comment Valentin alla en Inde la Major et contrefit le medecin pour voir Esclarmonde. lxi. chapitre.

[4verso]Comment Valentin prist Chastel Fort et delivra son pere, l'empereur de Grece, et tous les aultres prisonniers. lxii. chapitre.

Comment l'empereur de Grece, Orson, et le Verd Chevalier demourerent en garnison a Chastel Fort; et comment Hauffroy et Henry firent mourir le roy Pepin. lxiii. chapitre.

Comment apres la mort du noble roy Pepin, le duc Millon d'Angler voulut faire couronner Charlot son filz. lxiiii. chapitre.

Comment l'empereur de Grece partit de Chastel Fort pour venir devant la cité d'Angorie les chrestiens secourir. lxv. chapitre.

Comment les chrestiens saillirent d'Angorie; et de l'ordonnance de leurs merveilleuses batailles. lxvi. chapitre.

Comment Valentin tua son pere l'empereur de Grece en la bataille. lxvii. chapitre.

Comment le duc Millon d'Angler retourna en France, et Valentin et Orson son frere alerent en Grece. lxviii. chapitre.

Comment Valentin prist congié de la belle Esclarmonde pour aler a Romme par devers le pape pour son peché confesser. lxix. chapitre.

Pour raconter comment Valentin, en grant douleur de son corps, acheva et parfist sa penitance pour son pere lequel il avoit occis. lxx. chapitre.

Comment le roy Hugon fist demander la belle Esclarmonde pour femme; et comment il trahyt Orson et le Verd Chevalier.[1] lxxi. chapitre.

Comment Bellissant et la belle Esclarmonde sceurent la trahyson et la faulce entreprinse du roy Hugon. lxxii. chapitre.

Comment Orson et le Verd Chevalier furent des prisons delivrés par appointement de la guerre qui fut puis au roy Hugon. lxxiii. chapitre.

Comment au bout de sept ans Valentin dedans le palays de Constantinoble fina ses jours. lxxiiii. chapitre.

---

[1] Text has *Comment le roy hugon et la belle esclarmonde qu'il fist demander pour femme, et comment il trahy orson et le verd chevalier*. I have taken the wording as it appears at the head of the actual chapter 71 as it makes better sense.

Chapter 61   How Valentin went to India, pretending to be a doctor, in order to see Esclarmonde.

Chapter 62   How Valentin conquered Château Fort and delivered his father, the emperor of Greece, and all the other prisoners.

Chapter 63   How the emperor of Greece, Orson, and the Green Knight remained to defend Château Fort; and how Hauffroy and Henry had King Pepin murdered.

Chapter 64   How, after the death of the noble King Pepin, Duke Millon d'Angler wanted to crown his son Charles.

Chapter 65   How the emperor of Greece left Château Fort to come before the walls of the city of Angory to help the Christians.

Chapter 66   How the Christians sallied forth out of the city of Angory; and concerning the conduct of their amazing battles.

Chapter 67   How Valentin killed his father the emperor of Greece in the battle.

Chapter 68   How Duke Millon d'Angler returned to France, while Valentin and Orson his brother went to Greece.

Chapter 69   How Valentin took leave of the fair Esclarmonde to go to Rome to confess his sin to the pope.

Chapter 70   Recounting how Valentin, with great pain of body, carried out and completed his penance for having killed his father.

Chapter 71   How King Hugo asked the fair Esclarmonde to marry him; and how he betrayed Orson and the Green Knight.

Chapter 72   How Bellissant and the fair Esclarmonde discovered King Hugo's treachery and wicked plot.

Chapter 73   How Orson and the Green Knight were delivered from prison by an agreement to wage war afterwards against King Hugo.

Chapter 74   How Valentin at the end of seven years ended his days in the palace of Constantinople.

Valentin et Orson

[CHAPITRE 1]

[5recto] Comment[1] le roy Pepin espousa Berte dame de grant renommee. i. chapitre.

Veritablement nous trouvons aux croniques anciennes que noble et vaillant roy Pepin[2] si espousa et prist a femme Berte, dame de grant renommee, saige et prudente qui en son temps eust et souffrit, par envye grande, habondance de pestilla[n]ce et tribulation. Car elle fut chassee et expellee de la compagnie et habitation dudit roy son mary par une faulce et mauldite femme vielle et envenimee en malice. Laquelle vielle pour la premiere nuytee trouva façon et maniere de bailler et delivrer une sienne fille au lieu de la bonne royne Berte, et elle mena et conduisist ceste trahison pour maintenir sa fille avec le roy au lieu de Berthe son espouse.

Lequel roy d'icelle fille eut deux filz, Hauffroy et Henry, qui ou temps de leur regne moult fort greverent et gasterent le pays de France, et furent de fier courage plain[s] et de male voulenté. Ces deux furent cause de mettre la royne Berthe en exil, dont luy convint mainte douleur et angoisse souffrir. Et en exil fut ladite dame moult longuement, usant et passant ses jours en larmes et gemissemens. Mais puis apres de son amere et douleureuse fortune, Dieu le createur des peines et tourmens, vray protecteur, deffendeur, et trespiteulx, voulut la bonne dame en son aversité misericordieusement secourir, et en tant que Dieu, createur du monde, au moyen et a l'intercession de plusieurs barons de France, desirant le bien et utilité dudit royaulme, la royne Berthe fust acordee au roy, lequel en grant pitié et honneur la receust. Et apres peu de temps en elle engendra ung filz. Ce fut le trespuissant et redoubté roy Charlemaigne, lequel puis apres fut debouté et dechassé hors du royaulme par les dessudis, Hauffroy et Henry, ainsi que plus a plain appert en ce present livre. Mais atant je vous veul parler de la matiere subjecte ja devant proposee, et par especial du fait et du gouvernement du vaillant Valentin et de son frere Orson.

Or est vray que le roy Pepin avoit une seur nommee Bellissant, belle, plaisant et tresgracieuse en toutes choses, bien aprinse et endoctrinee, et l'aima le roy Pepin son frere de bonne amour cordiale. Et tant qu'il avint que pour le bruit et renommee d'icelle, laquelle de grans et de petis estoit prisee et amee, pour la beaulté et tresgracieulx parler, maniere et contenance qui en elle [5verso]resplendissoient plus que en nulle aultre dame.

Le roy Alexandre, empereur de Constantinoble, fut espris de son amour et embrasé tresardamment, si ne demoura pas longuement que pour celle cause; il

---

[1] Woodcut showing wedding scene. Ecclesiastical figure flanked by couple, attendant at left of scene, all four placed under arch.

[2] Text has *peepin*.

CHAPTER 1

How King Pepin married Bertha, a lady of great renown.

Truthfully we find in the ancient chronicles that the noble and valiant King Pepin married and took to wife Bertha, a lady of great renown, wise and prudent, who, in her time, because of the great malevolence of others, suffered an abundance of trial and tribulation. For she was driven away and dismissed from the company and home of the king, her husband, by a false and cursed old woman, poisoned with malice. On the wedding night, this old woman found the means to substitute her own daughter for the good queen Bertha, and she carried out this treason in order to install the girl with the king in the place of Bertha, his wife.

The king had two sons with this girl, Hauffroy and Henry, who, at the time of their reign, wrecked and ravaged the land of France, and they were full of malice and ill will. These two caused Queen Bertha to be exiled, a state in which she suffered much pain and anguish. The lady spent a long time in exile, passing her days in tears and moans. But then, after her bitter and painful misfortune, God, the creator of pain and torment, the true and compassionate protector and defender, determined in his mercy to aid the good lady in her adversity, such that God, the creator of the world, through the intercession of several barons of France, whose interest was the welfare of the kingdom, brought about a reconciliation between Queen Bertha and the king, who received her with great mercy and honor. Shortly after he fathered a son through her. He became the powerful and feared King Charlemagne, who later on was driven away and exiled by those mentioned above, Hauffroy and Henry, which will appear more clearly in this book. But for the moment I wish to speak to you about the subject matter already proposed, and especially about the deeds and actions of the valiant Valentin and his brother Orson.

Now it is true that King Pepin had a sister named Bellissant. She was beautiful, agreeable, and gracious in every way, well-taught and educated, and she loved King Pepin, her brother, with a true and heartfelt love. And such was her reputation and renown that it so happened that she was prized and loved by all people great and small for her beauty and her gracious speech, manner and composure, which shone in her more than in any other lady.

King Alexander, emperor of Constantinople,[1] was smitten with burning love for her, so he did not wait very long before he came to France in the highest

---

[1] The historical emperor Alexander reigned 912–913.

vint en France a tout moult hault et grant estat, acompaigné de plusieur[s] contes et barons qui tous estoient en grant pompes et ricesses. Sy ne demeura pas longuement apres sa venue qu'il manda tous les plus grans princes et seigneurs de sa court et de son tinel, et leur commanda mettre en hault et honnourable estat, et leur commanda qu'ilz alassent vers le roy Pepin demander en mariage pour avoir a femme et espouse sa seur Bellissant, laquelle luy fut accordee par ledit Pepin a moult grant joye. Sy fut par toute la court tant d'ung costé come d'aultre feste demenee pour les joyeuses nouvelles de l'assemblance et alliance de l'empereur Alexandre et du franc roy Pepin qui sa seur luy donna.

Les nopces furent faites en grant habondance[1] a honneur et triumphe, et ne fault pas demander se alors fut largesse de toutes choses. La feste dura longuement. Puis l'empereur et ses gens prindrent congié de son beau frere le roy Pepin pour soy en aler a Constantinoble avec sa seur, la tresgracieuse Bellissa[n]t. Le roy fist abiller ses gens pour acompaigner l'empereur. Chascun monta a cheval, et y avoit grant quantité de damoiselles et de grans dames qui compagnoient Bellissant. Ceulx qui demourerent si plourerent pour le departement de Bellissant.

Le roy le convoya plusieurs jours tant qu'ilz arriverent a ung port ou ledit empereur voulut monter sur mer. Si prist la endroit congié du roy Pepin en lui rendant graces plus que ne le vous sçaroye dire de l'honeste chiere et la bonne reception qu'il luy avoit fait. Et entre les aultres choses de sa seur Bellissant, laquelle de pure et reale voulenté il luy avoit donné pour femme.

A ces motz le roy Pepin de France commença a embrasser Alexandre en luy disant, "Beau sire et trescordial seigneur et amy, au respect et regard de ma puissance, je ne vous ay pas receu en triumphe ne sy hault excellent magnifice comme je deusse, mais de tant je congnois la gracieuseté de vous que de mon petit pouoir vous estes content. Et a moy ne sont pas les graces ne mercys, mais sont a vous, quant tant vous m'avés voulu decorer, et de vostre personne honnourer que ma seur avés prinse a femme. Et sachez que d'icy en avant j'ay bonne voulenté et ferme propos que nous soions bons amys ensemble, et quant au regard de moy je suis celluy qui de ma puissance vouldroye le corps et les biens mettre et habandonner pour vous servir et secourir en tous lieux et en toutes places selon mon pouoir."

Puis s'en vint Pepin vers sa seur Bellissant et luy dist, "Belle seur, souviengnez[2] vous du lieu dont vous estes yssue, et faites en maniere que moy et voz amis et tout le sang royal puissons avoir de vous joye, prouffit et honneur. [6recto] Vous alés en pays estrange, loing de vostre nation. Gouvernez vous par saiges dames, et vous gardés de mauvais conseil croire. Vous estes la creature du monde que j'ay plus chier aymee. Sy me seroit la mort prochaine se par vous je n'avoye toutes bonnes nouvelles."

Moult donna le roy Pepin de beaulx et de bons enseignemens a sa seur. Incontinent l'embrassa et la baisa moult doulcement, en pleurant tendrement pour

---

[1] Text has *habonbance*.
[2] Text has *souviengne*.

and grandest manner, accompanied by several counts and barons, all exhibiting great pomp and wealth. Nor did he wait long after his arrival to call for all the greatest princes and lords of his court and his entourage. He commanded them to accouter themselves in a high and honorable state, and ordered them to go to King Pepin to ask for the hand of his sister, Bellissant, in marriage, which was accorded him by Pepin with great joy. Then the entire court rejoiced in the delightful news of the union and alliance between the emperor Alexander and the noble King Pepin who was giving him his sister.

The marriage was celebrated with great opulence, honor, and triumph, and no need to ask if there was largesse in every aspect of it. The feast lasted a long time. Then the emperor and his people took leave of his brother-in-law King Pepin in order to depart for Constantinople with his sister, the most gracious Bellissant. The king outfitted his men to accompany the emperor. Each one mounted his horse, and there was a great number of maidens and high-born ladies who accompanied Bellissant. Those who remained behind wept for the departure of Bellissant.

The king escorted him for several days until they arrived at a port where the emperor planned to set sail. There he took leave of King Pepin, thanking him more profusely than I could tell you for the proper welcome and excellent reception he had given him. And among other things, he thanked him for his sister Bellissant, whom with regal goodwill he had given him as wife.

At these words, King Pepin of France began to embrace Alexander, saying to him, "Fair sir, kindly lord and friend, as to my power, I did not receive you with the triumph nor the high and excellent magnificence that I should have, but I recognize all the more your own goodness in that you are content with my limited means. And thanks are due not to me but to you, for so much did you wish to honor me, and honor me personally, that you have taken my sister to wife. And know that henceforth I heartily wish and intend that we be close friends, and that as to myself, I am one who would, to the fullest extent possible, place himself and his possessions at your disposal, in order to serve you and aid you in any situation whatsoever according to my abilities."

Then Pepin came to his sister Bellissant and said to her, "Fair sister, remember whence you came, and act in a manner by which I, your friends, and all those of royal blood can have joy, profit, and honor from you. You are going to a foreign land, far from your own country. Be guided by wise ladies, and be careful not to believe ill counsel. You are the one creature in this world that I have loved most dearly. Death would come quickly to me if I did not have excellent news of you."

King Pepin gave many fine and good instructions to his sister. Thereupon he embraced her and kissed her very gently, weeping bitterly for his sister's departure.

le departement de sa seur. Et la france dame, qui le cueur eult piteux et dolent, peu de chose respondit, car de ses plaisans yeulx et du cueur souspiroit si grandement que le parler luy estoit chose tresforte. Adonc prindrent congié dames et damoiselles, barons et chevaliers, tant de France que dudit empereur. La y eut maintes larmes plourees et maint souspirs gettéz pour Bellissant. Le roy Pepin s'en retourna en France et l'empereur monta sur la mer, et eut bon vent et le temps a son plaisir, tant que en peu d'espasse luy et les gens arriverent a Constantinoble. Sy fut receu a grant honneur et triumphe, dont le reciter seroit long. Mais ne demoura pas longuement que le grant honneur qui fut fait a Bellissant et la joye que chascun mena fut muee en pleurs et lamentations pour la france dame Bellissant qui par trahison et accusation deceptive fut en exil gettee ainsi que vous orés reciter.

[CHAPITRE 2]

Comment l'empereur fut trahy par l'archevesque de Constantinoble dont mauvais mal luy en vint, comme vous orés. ii. [chapitre]

En la cité de Constantinoble avoit ung archevesque lequel sur tous les aultres l'empereur aymoit et tenoit chier plus que nul homme. Et luy faisoit des biens a grande habundance et largesse, tant avoit de confidence. L'empereur audit archevesque le fist de son hostel gouverneur et sy le fist son confesseur principal et sur tout secret dont eut depuis le cueur dolent. Car le faulx archevesque, ingrat et non cognoissant des grans biens et haulx honneurs qu'i luy avoit fait et par chascun jour faisait le bon empereur, par amour desordonné, deshonneste, vituperable, villaine, embrasé fut et esprins de puante luxure et de plaisir charnel pour la clere et beauté souveraine de Bellissant, la royne gracieuse, doulce et courtoise tant, et si ardamment que ung jour qu'il avisa la royne toute seule en la sale paree, vint aupres d'elle soy assoir. Et la commenca a regarder en sourriant, de quoy la dame ne fit maniere ne semblant, car tant estoit desloyal l'archevesque privé et familier de la maison que jamais n'eust cuidé personne nee, que faire ne penser il vousist chose contre l'empereur fors que tout honneur. Or n'est il point de pire ennemy que celui qui est familier de la maison quant a mal se veult appliquer, comme bien le monstera le faulx et mauldit archevesque.

Lequel estant assis empres elle, de la tant aymee et renomee[1] dame, il ouvrit sa bouche venimeuse, puante, et sale et parla en telle maniere:

---

[1] Text has *renome*.

And the noble lady, whose heart was full of sorrow, answered little, for from her pleasing eyes and her heart she was sighing so forcefully that speaking was quite difficult for her. Then they all took leave of one another, the ladies and maidens, the barons and knights, those of France as well as those of the emperor. There many tears were shed and many sighs heaved for Bellissant. King Pepin returned to France while the emperor set sail, enjoying a good wind and making good time so that he and his entourage soon arrived in Constantinople. He was received with great honor and pomp which would take too long to recite. But not long after, the great honor that was shown to Bellissant and the joy that each one felt were turned to tears and lamentation, for the noble lady Bellissant was sent into exile by means of betrayal and false accusation, as you will hear told.

CHAPTER 2

How the emperor was betrayed by the archbishop of Constantinople from which much harm came to him, as you will hear.

In the city of Constantinople there was an archbishop whom the emperor loved above all others, holding him dearer than any other man. Generously he gave him goods in great abundance, so much did he trust him. The emperor gave this archbishop charge of his house, making him his principal confessor and privy to all secrets, for which his heart was pained later on. For the false and thankless archbishop, not grateful for the great possessions and high honors that the good emperor had given him and continued to give him every day, was kindled by reckless, dishonorable passion and shameful villainy, so ardently smitten by stinking lust and carnal desire for the bright and sovereign beauty of Bellissant, the gentle, courteous, and gracious queen, that one day when he saw the queen all alone in the great hall, he came to sit next to her. And he began to look at her and smile, which the lady took no notice of, for so much was the disloyal archbishop an intimate friend and frequenter of the royal household that never would anyone have imagined that he was willing to do or think anything harmful to the emperor, but only all things honorable. But there is nothing worse than one who is an intimate friend of the household when he wants to do evil, as the false and cursed archbishop will soon demonstrate.

While he was seated near the well-loved and highly reputed lady, he opened his dirty, stinking, venomous mouth and spoke in the following manner:

"Ma treschiere et souveraine dame, je suis vostre petit [6verso]serviter et chappellain. S'il vous plaist oÿr et entendre une chose que je vous veul dire, laquelle en douleur et en melancolie j'ay porté, enduré, et soffert en mon courage moult longuement. Sachez, ma dame redoubtee, que la beaulté de vostre corps et plaisant figure, formee et compassee oultre tout, vostre humain corps de naturelle operation a ravy, espris, et embrasé mon cueur qui nuyt et jour ne peult penser sinon a vous tant seulement. Et qui plus est, je pers repos, boire, et menger, maniere et contenance quant il me souvient de voz beaulx yeux et clere face. Sy requiers a Dieu qu'il vous doinst voulenté et courage de moy pour amy recepvoir, et que je vous puisse servir et complaire a vostre gré, plaisir, et voulenté. Car s'il est ainsi que vous me refusés pour amy, je n'ay espoir ne confort plus prochain que la mort invoquer.

"Helas! dame, vous qui estes en toutes choses renommee, doulce, benigne, courtoise, et debonaire, ne soyez cause de ma mort abreger. Mais me veullez vostre[1] amour ottroyer par tel convenant que je feray loyal et secret en amours, plus que ne fut jamais homme. Et qui plus est, n'aiez paour ou crainte de Dieu pour ce fait offenser ou peché faire, car je suis vicaire de Dieu en terre. Si vous pouroie donner absolution et penitance facile et legiere."

A ces motz deceptis diaboliques, plains de traïson et decevance, la dame prudente, saige, et eloquente bassement respondit, "Ha, faulx et desloyal et irregulier archevesque! tempté et plain de diabolique voulenté! Comment oses proferer de ta bouche, qui sacree doit estre, parolles tant villaines, deshonnestes,[2] et abhominables, contre le profit et majesté imperiale de celuy qui tant doulcement t'a nourry et monté en honneur plus que a toy n'apartient? Dont te peult venir ne mouvoir celle male diction d'estre cause de ma damnation, qui me dois en la saincte foy, en meurs et condicions enseigner, ainsi que l'empereur pense et du tout se confie? Ja Dieu ne plaise que le sang de France dont je suis extraite, ne la majesté du puissant empereur soit honnye ne en riens deshonnouree. O faulx et mauldit homme! regarde que tu veulx faire, qui me veulx despouller et desvetir de tout honneur, et metre mon corps a honte et vergongne vituperable et mon ame en la voye de damnation eternelle. Delaise ta folle oppinion, car a telle fin comme de mon amour n'y peuz parvenir ny attaindre. Et se plus oultre tu en parles, soyes certain que je le ferai sçavoir a l'empereur, et lors pouras bien dire que de ta vie sera fait. Va t'en d'ici et n'en parle plus."

De telle responce fut l'archevesque trop courucé. Si n'osa plus avant proceder sur ce fait puis que de la dame il n'auroit ja l'amour. Et ainsi confus s'en retourna, car oncques ne vit semblant ne maniere ne signe ou il peust prendre reconfort ne esperance de pouoir parvenir en son entente. Grandement se repentit de sa folie quant rebouté et refusé se vit de la dame, mais remede n'y trouva de sauver son honneur fors que par trahison, car il pensa bien en lui mesmes que l'empereur

---

[1] Text has *voostre*.
[2] Text has *deshonnstes*.

"My dear and sovereign lady, I am your humble servant and chaplain. Please hear something that I wish to tell you, which I have carried in pain and melancholy, indeed endured and suffered in my heart for a very long time. Know, worthy lady, that the beauty of your body and your pleasing figure, formed and proportioned better than any other, your goodly self by its very nature has ravished, smitten, and kindled my heart which cannot think of anything day and night but you alone. And what is more, I lose sleep, all appetite and composure when I think about your beautiful eyes and bright face. Thus I pray God that He give you the desire to accept me as your lover, and that I may serve you and please you according to your will and pleasure. For if you refuse me as your lover, I have no hope for any quicker comfort than to call for death.

"Alas, lady, you who are honored in all things, gentle, good, courteous, and noble, do not be the cause of hurrying my death. But please grant me your love with the understanding that I will be loyal and discreet in love, more than any other man ever was. And what is more, fear not that you will offend God or commit a sin by this, for I am the vicar of God on earth. Thus I can give you absolution and an easy and light penance to do."

At these false and diabolical words, full of treason and deception, the prudent, wise, and eloquent lady answered in a low voice, "Oh, false, disloyal, and inconstant archbishop! tempted to, indeed filled with diabolical desire! How dare you proffer such evil, dishonest, and abominable words from your mouth (that should be sacred) that run counter to the well-being and imperial majesty of the one who has brought you up so kindly and raised you in honor more than you deserve? From where can this evil speech possibly come, inciting you to be the cause of my damnation, you who are supposed to teach me about holy faith and proper moral behavior, as the emperor believes and trusts you do above all? May it never please God that the blood of France, from which I descend, nor the majesty of the powerful emperor be shamed or dishonored in any way. Oh, false and cursed man! Look at what you wish to do, you who wish to strip me of all honor, and put my body to abject shame and my soul on the way to eternal damnation. Abandon your mad idea, for you can never achieve such an end nor win my love. And if you speak any more of this, be certain that I will make it known to the emperor, and then you will certainly be able to say that your life is done. Go away from here and speak no more of it."

The archbishop was quite upset at such a response. He didn't dare proceed any further in the matter since he would never have the love of the lady. And thus unsure what to do, he left, for he never saw any sign whatsoever in which he could take comfort or hope of being able to fulfill his intention. He greatly repented of his folly when he saw himself refused and rejected by the lady, but he saw no way to save his own reputation except through perfidy, for he worried that

ne sceust par la roy[7recto]ne Bellissant la male voulenté de son courage. Trop a temps commença la folie et tart s'en repentit. Ainsi avient souvent que ce que fol pense il demeure estre parfait.

[CHAPITRE 3]

Comment l'archevesque apres ce qu'il fut escondit de la dame[1] Bellissant pour son honneur saulver contre la noble dame pensa et machina une grant trahison. iii. [chapitre][2]

En pensee et sousy trop parfait et ennuyeulx fut l'archevesque, doubtant que l'empereur ne le fist mourir pour sa faulte criminelle, laquelle contre sa haulte seigneurie et magnificence il avoit commise. Si se pensa de saulver son honneur tout au mieulx que il pourroit, et tant fit que pour la male diction couvrit et pour monstrer apparance de leauté et preudommie, en faignant et dissimulant que de tout son pouoir il vouloit et desiroit le bien et honneur et valeur et utilité de l'empereur.

Le jour de l'Ascention Nostre Seigneur, il vint par devers l'empereur et le tyra a part et luy dist en telle maniere, "Treshault empereur, il est vray que je cognois les grans graces et benefices que vous m'avés donnéz et ottroyéz, et sçay bien que par vous je suis en honneur monté et elevé plus que a moy n'apartient. Et sy m'avez fait comme indigne et insuffisant maistre et gouverneur de toute vostre maison, du tout a moy vous confiant plus qu'en nul aultre de vostre court. Sy ne doy pas estre en lieu ne en place ou je seuffre ne endure vostre estat estre diffamé et vostre renommee mys au bas. Car ainsy me soit Dieu propice que j'aimeroye plus chier devant tous de moy soubmettre a subite mort finer mes jours que voir ou escouter devant ma presence langaiges ou parolles qui a vostre honneur et domination et seigneurie fussent mal convenables ne licites.

"Si me veullez oÿr reciter et declairer ung cas qui grandement touche et ataint vostre profit et honneur plus[3] que nulles riens. Sire, il est vray et certain que Bellissant, vostre femme, seur du roy Pepin de France, laquelle vous avez voulu tan priser et honnourer que pour femme et espouse l'avez prise, ne vous tient pas foy ne loyaulté comme doit. Car pour tout vray elle aime autre que vous, et qu'elle vous est[4] desloyalle. Mais tant y a que je ne veulx pas mener ne nommer celuy qui de vostre femme fait sa voulenté, car vous sçavez que je suis prestre sacré. Il

---

[1] Text has *dnme*.
[2] Woodcut of seated king and ecclesiastical figure, each with open book.
[3] Text has *plu*.
[4] Text has *ē (en)*.

the emperor might find out from the queen Bellissant about the evil intention of his heart. He began the folly too soon and repented of it too late. Thus it often happens that what a fool thinks to do remains unaccomplished.

CHAPTER 3

How the archbishop, in order to preserve his honor, concocted and put into effect a treacherous plot against the lady Bellissant after she rejected him.

The archbishop was pensive and terribly worried, fearful that the emperor might execute him for the crime he had committed against his exalted lordship. He thought how he might save his reputation the best he could, and came up with a way to cover up his wicked speech and appear loyal, feigning to have nothing in mind but serving the honor and dignity of the emperor.

On Ascension Day, he came to the emperor and took him aside, saying to him the following: "O most exalted emperor, truly do I recognize the great favors and benefits you have granted me, and I know well that I have been honored by you more than I deserve. And, as unworthy as I am, you have made me the governor of your entire household, putting your confidence in me more than in anyone else in your court. Thus it is incumbent on me, wherever I am, not to put up with anything that would defame you or tarnish your reputation. For, God help me, I would rather submit myself to public execution than personally to see or hear anything inappropriate or illicit connected to your honor or lordship.

"Please let me tell you of a case that most definitely touches your honor and welfare more than anything else. Sire, it is absolutely certain that Bellissant, your wife, the sister of King Pepin of France, whom you have wished so to praise and to honor that you have taken her to wife, is not keeping faith with you as she ought. For it is certain that she loves someone other than you, and that she is disloyal. However, the case is such that I do not wish to name the one that is having his way with your wife, for you know that I am a consecrated priest. It is true that

est vray que la verité de ceste chose m'est venue en confession; si ne la doy ne ne veul pas reciter en ma[n]iere que je vous [7verso]nomme celluy qui tel deshonneur vous pourchasse. Mais que de tant vous me veullez croire que en toute la court n'y a plus dissolue ne deshonneste femme que la vostre que tant chier vous tenés dont vostre corps est en danger et peril—ja elle pourchasse nuyt et jour maniere de vous faire mourir affin de mieulx faire sa voulenté.

"Et pour tant je suis tenu de vouloir vostre profit et honneur garder. Je vous avertis et fais assavoir que vous la veullez aviser et corriger tout au mielx et plus secretement que faire pourés, ou aultrement je tiens vostre honneur perdue et vostre personne deshonnouree. Car trop est grande infameté entre les princes que vous cuidés avoir espousé la seur du roy de France pour la fleur de beaulté, de prudence et de noblesse, et vous avez une putain que de vostre vie est ennemye, et vostre mort desire et appelle de jour en jour, dont j'en suis desplaisant. En laquelle chose veullez remedier tout au mieulx que vous pourés pour vostre honneur garder."

Quant l'empereur entendit le parler du traitre archevesque, ne demandés pas s'il en fut au cueur tresamerement dolant et couroucé, car de tant est il plus dolant quant on luy en raporte mauvaises nouvelles. L'empereur crut de legier les parolles du faulx archevesque, car en lui avoit sa confidence plus qu'en homme vivant. Il creut trop de legier, par quoy grant inconvenient puis apres il en sourdit. Il n'est plus grant danger a prince que croire de legier.

L'empereur ne respondit riens car tant fut espris de couroux, et navré au cueur parfondement qu'il perdit maniere et contenance. Et s'en ala parmy le palays imperial gemissant et gettant souspirs tresangoisseux. Puis ne se tint atant mais ne peult son ire refraindre ny atremper. Mais s'en entra sans parler ne faire semblant dedens la belle chambre de Bellissant qui garde ne s'en donnoit. Et sans dire mot a dame ny a damoiselle, cruellement et de fier courage vint prendre la belle dame enchief[1] vis, et par les cheveulx de son chief la getta a terre sy rudement que de la face vermeille il luy fist le sang saillir. Adonc se prist la dame trespiteusement a plourer et crier.

"Helas, helas, monseigneur! Quelle chose vous meult de moy si oultrageusement frapper et batre? Car oncques jour de ma vie je ne vous fis que tout honneur et leal service de mon corps."

"A! putain!" ce luy dist l'empereur, "je suis trop bien informé de vostre vie. Que mauldite soit l'eure et le jour que de vous premier me vint cognoissance." Si la fiert de rechief sy fort et sy grant coup que la noble dame perdit[2] le parler, et cuiderent les dames et damoyselles qu'elle fust morte. Sy firent ung cry sy grant que les barons et chevaliers de la court l'oïrent et vindrent en la chambre dont les ungz leverent Bellissant la royne et les aultres prindrent l'empereur en parlant a luy par telle maniere:

---

[1] Text has *enchier*.
[2] Text has *pedit*.

the truth came to me by way of confession; I must not nor wish to name the one who is perpetrating such a dishonorable thing against you. But if you will believe me, there is no more dissolute or dishonest woman than your wife, whom you have held so dear that you yourself are now in danger—for already she seeks a way, day and night, to bring about your death, the better to have her way.

"Therefore I am determined to work for your welfare and guard your honor. I must advise you to take heed and correct her as well but also as quietly as you can; otherwise I hold your honor to be lost and your reputation tarnished. For it is too great an infamy among princes to think that you married the sister of the king of France, believing her to be the flower of beauty, prudence, and nobility, and instead you have a whore, an enemy who desires daily your death, all of which upsets me terribly. You must attempt to remedy this situation as best you can to save your honor."

When the emperor heard the words of the treacherous archbishop, no need to ask if his heart was both grieved and furious, for it is all the more upsetting when someone brings you bad news. The emperor believed right away the words of the false archbishop, for he trusted him more than any other being alive. He believed much too easily, by which great disaster later came about. There is no greater danger for a prince than to believe what he hears too quickly.

The emperor said nothing in response, so overwhelmed was he with anger, and so deeply struck in his heart that he lost all composure. He made his way through the palace moaning and letting out sighs of anguish. Then, at that moment, he could no longer hold himself back nor contain or temper his anger. Rather, without speaking or giving any kind of sign, he entered the beautiful chamber of Bellissant, who suspected nothing. Without saying a word to lady or maid, cruelly and with a fierce heart, he seized the fair lady by the face, and by the hair of her head he threw her to the floor so violently that he made the blood spurt from her rosy face. At this the lady began to weep most piteously.

"Alas, alas, my lord! What is it that moves you to hit and beat me so outrageously? For never in my life have I ever done anything but honor you and offer you my loyal service."

"Ah, harlot!" said the emperor, "I am all too well informed concerning your life. Cursed be the hour and day that I first heard of you." Then he struck her again so hard and with such a great blow that the noble lady lost her ability to speak, and the attending ladies and maidens thought she was dead. They cried out so loudly that the barons and knights of the court heard them and came running to the chamber where some of them lifted up Queen Bellissant and the others took the emperor aside, speaking to him in the following manner:

"Helas, sire, comment avés vous si cruel courage de vouloir deffaire sy vaillant et noble [8recto]dame qui de tant est de tous chiere ame, en laquelle ne fut oncques veu ne apperceu blasme ne deshonneur? Pour Dieu,[1] sire, soyés ung petit plus atrempé et moderé, car a tort et sans cause entreprenés ceste querelle contre la bonne dame."

"Ne parlés plus," dit l'empereur, "je congnois, je fais et sy sçay comme la chose va. Et qui plus est par le Dieu tout puissant, je suis deliberé totalement de la mettre a mort. Et se nul d'entre vous m'en dist du contraire, je luy feray perdre la vie et possessions et heritages."

A ces motz parla un tressage baron et dit, "Redoubté sire, advisés et considerés que vous voulés faire. Vous sçavés que la dame que vous avés espousee est seur du roy de France, nommé Pepin, lequel est puissant, fier et de grant courage. Et devez fermement croire que se vous faites a sa seur Bellissant oultrage ou villennye, il est homme pour soy venger par telle façon que trop de dommage pourra porter en ce pays et en pourront mourir maintz bons et vaillans seigneurs et vous mesmes en exil, en honte et confusion, dont ce seroit pitié. Et d'aultre part la bonne dame est grosse d'enfant, et ainsi que vous voyés, si est peril a vous de la ferir ne toucher si rudement."

Apres ces parolles la dame se getta a deux genoulx a terre devant l'empereur; en parlant et en plourant dit moult piteusement, "Helas, monseigneur, ayés pitié de moy, car oncques mal ne villennye ne voulus penser. Et sy vous n'avés pitié de moy, veullés au moins avoir pitié de l'enfant que je porte en mon ventre. Car je suis grosse et ensainte de vostre[2] fait dont Dieu par sa grace me doint joye de le delivrer. Helas, sire, je vous supplie et requiers que dedens une tour me facés mettre et enfermer tant que le temps[3] sera venu que je delivre et enfante, et apres mon enfantement faites de mon corps ce qu'il vous plaira."

Tant et si piteusement parloit la douce dame en larmoiant des yeulx et du cueur souspirant, et que trop avoit le cueur dur qui se sçavoit tenir de plourer. Mais l'empereur, qui par le faulx et mauldit[4] archevesque fut deceu et courocé au cueur, n'eust oncques de sa femme compassion ne pitié. Mais cruellement et fierement luy respondit, "Faulce putain desordonnee, de tant que tu es grosse d'enfant je me dois petit resjouir, car je suis tant de ton gouvernement informé que je n'y ai riens, et que desloyalment tu t'es abandonnee a aultres que a moy."

Quant ilz virent que l'empereur ne vouloit pour nulle riens son ire appaiser ne refraindre, tout par ung commun acord l'ont prins et mené hors de la chambre, et le plus doulcement qu'ilz ont peu, l'ont tenu en paroles en luy remonstrant sa faulte. Et la dame est demouree en la chambre qui du sang avoit sa face tainte et salle. Les dames du plus pres d'elle luy ont apporté de l'eaue clere pour soy laver.

---

[1] Text has *aieu*.
[2] Text has *voostre*.
[3] Text has *le te temps*.
[4] Text has *mualdit*.

"Alas, sire, how can your heart be so cruel as to want to harm such a valiant and noble lady who is so loved by everybody, in whom no one has ever seen or perceived blame or dishonor? By God, sire, calm yourself, for wrongly and without cause you commence this quarrel with the good lady."

"Speak no more," said the emperor, "I know exactly how things are. And what is more, by God Almighty, I am determined to put her to death. And if any of you contradicts me, he will lose his life, his possessions, and his patrimony."

At these words a wise baron spoke up and said, "Worthy sire, think and consider what you wish to do. You know that the lady you have married is the sister of the king of France, one Pepin, who is powerful, proud, and of great courage. And you should realize that if you commit any outrage or villainy against his sister Bellissant, he is a man to avenge himself in such a fashion that would bring much harm to this country, and many good and valiant lords could die over it, and you yourself end up in exile, shame, and confusion, which would be a pity. And besides, the good lady is pregnant, and as you can see, it is perilous for you to strike her or touch her so violently."

After this speech the lady threw herself down on her knees before the emperor; speaking through her tears she said woefully, "Alas, my lord, have mercy on me, for never have I intended any evil or villainy. And if you have no pity on me, at least have pity on the child that I carry in my womb, for I am pregnant by you with a child for which I pray God in His mercy to grant me the joy of delivering safely. Alas, sire, I beg you to shut me up in a tower until the time comes when I will be delivered of this child, and then you can do with me as you like."

So very piteously spoke the lady, while copious tears streamed from her eyes and sighs poured forth from her heart, that only the most hard-hearted could have kept himself from weeping. But the emperor, whose heart had been deceived and enraged by the false and cursed archbishop, had not an ounce of pity or compassion for his wife. Rather he answered her cruelly and fiercely, "False-hearted, brazen strumpet, I can take little joy in the fact of your pregnancy, for I am so well informed of your behavior that I know I had nothing to do with it, and that you faithlessly abandoned yourself to others than myself."

When the barons saw that the emperor would by no means restrain his anger, they all by common accord took him and led him out of the room, and, as gently as they could, they remonstrated with him. And the lady, her face bloodied, remained in her chamber. The ladies who served her brought clear water to wash her.

Et a celle heure entra dedens sa chambre son escuier nommé Blandimain, et quant il la vit il commença a plourer en luy disant, "Ha, madame, [8verso] madame, je voy bien que faulcement vous estes trahye. Sy requiers a Dieu que mauldite soit la personne qui ce mal vous a pourchasé. Pour Dieu, ma tresdoulce dame, prenez en vous ung peu de resconfort, et se vous me voulez croire, je vous remenray en France devers le roy Pepin, vostre frere, qui a vous me donna et bailla pour vous servir en voz necessitéz, laquelle chose je vouldroye faire de ma puissance.[1] Croiez mon conseil et nous en retournons en vostre pays. Car vous estes seure que l'empereur vous fera mourir briefment a honte et deshonneur."

Lors respondit la dame, "Helas, Blandimain, mon amy, trop me seroit chose vituperable et a moy deshonneste de m'en aler en telle maniere sans aultre deliberation. Et pourroit on dire et croire de legier que l'empereur auroit droit et rayson et que je seroy coupable du fait. Sy aime mieulx et plus chier mourir de mort que blasme recepvoir du fait dont je suis innocente et sans cause acusee."

Apres les choses ainsi ditez, l'empereur, qui fut avec les barons ung petit moderé et refrigeré de son ire, envoya querir Bellissant sa femme, et fut amenee par devant luy. Quant il la vit le cueur de dueil luy trambla de ce qu'il ne l'osa pas faire mourir pour doubte du roy Pepin son frere. Par rudes parolles lui dist, "Faulce et mauvaise femme, par vous est mon honneur vituperee.[2] Sy jure a Dieu que se ne fust pour l'amour de vostre frere et vaillant roy Pepin je vous feisse ardoir et brusler en feu. Mais pour l'amour de luy sera vostre vie prolongee pour le present. Si vous fais assavoir que de ceste heure je vous bannys et expelle de mon pays et empire, vous commandant espressement que demain vous partés de la cité. Car se plus vous y voy, jamais n'aurez respit que mourir ne vous face. Et sy fais commandement a tous ceulx de mon pays que nul ne soit tant hardy de vous compaigner ne convoyer, fors seulement vostre escuier Blandimain, que de France amenastes avec vous. Alés ou vous vouldrés et a vostre aventure, car jamais a mon costé ne a mon lit ne coucherez."

Tantost apres le commandement de l'empereur qui fut court et soudain, sans sejour ne dilation, la royne Bellissant et son escuier Blandimain monterent a cheval et vuiderent la ville. Si fut par la cité des seigneurs et des dames et de tout le menu peuple, tant des grans comme des petis, fais pleurs, cris, et lamentations en sy grant nombre que telle pitié ne fust veue oncques ne oÿe. Chascun couroit a la porte pour commander a Dieu a la belle dame qui par le faulx archevesque est piteusemen dechassee. Et au saillir de la cité fut le cry sy grant et si piteulx que c'estoit pitié de l'oÿr.

Or s'en va Blandimain qui conduisoit et menoit Bellissant la dame, et ont prins le chemin pour tirer vers le pays de France. Et quant la dame fut hors des murs de la cité et qu'elle se vit aux champs povrement adornee et comme povre

---

[1] Text has *pussance*.
[2] Text has *vitupeeree*.

At that moment her squire, Blandimain, entered her chamber, and when he saw her he began to weep saying, "Ah, my lady, my lady, I see that you have been falsely betrayed. I pray God that the person who perpetrated this evil against you be cursed. For God's sake, my most gentle lady, try to comfort yourself a bit, and if you want, I will take you back to France to King Pepin, your brother, who gave me to you to serve you in all your needs, which I would like to do to the best of my ability. Accept my counsel and we will return to your country, for you are certain that the emperor will soon put you to a shameful and dishonorable death."

Then the lady answered him, "Alas, Blandimain, my friend, it would be too shameful and dishonest a thing for me to leave like that without any other deliberation. And then people could say and believe that the emperor was right and that I was guilty of the act. Thus I prefer to die than to be blamed for an act of which I am innocent and accused without just cause."

After these things were said, the emperor, whose barons had calmed him down a bit and whose anger had cooled somewhat, sent for his wife Bellissant, and she was brought before him. When he saw her, his heart trembled with bitterness over the fact that he didn't dare kill her for fear of King Pepin her brother. He spoke to her rudely: "False, depraved woman, by you is my honor shamed. I swear to God that if it were not for love of your brother, the valiant King Pepin, I would have you burned alive. But out of respect for him your life will be prolonged for the present. I hereby inform you that from this hour I banish you and expel you from my country and my empire, commanding you expressly to leave this city tomorrow. For if I ever see you here, never will you escape execution. Moreover, my command is that none of my subjects shall dare be so bold as to accompany you except your squire, Blandimain, whom you brought from France with you. Go where you will and where chance takes you, for never by my side nor in my bed will you ever sleep again."

Right after the emperor's declaration, which was sudden and short, without any delay, the queen Bellissant and her squire Blandimain mounted their horses and left the city. All through the city there were lords, ladies, and common people, great and small, who wept and cried in such great numbers that never had such unhappiness ever been seen or heard. Each one ran to his door to commend to God the beautiful lady who had been driven out by the false archbishop in this dreadful way. And at their going forth from the city the cry was so great and so grievous that it was terrible to hear it.

So it was that Blandimain led forth the lady Bellissant, and they took the road that led towards France. And when the lady was beyond the walls of the city, and she found herself in the fields, poorly dressed, looking like a disreputable

personne infame [9recto]villainement[1] dechassee, alors elle considere le lignage et sang royal dont elle estoit partie et yssue, la treshaulte magnificence imperiale ou elle avoit esté mise. Puis pensa la miserable et dolante fortune que sur elle estoit si soudainement tournee.

"Helas, helas, pourquoy tarde la mort, qu'elle ne vient a moy pour ma vie abreger et mes angoisses et douleurs a fin mettre? Las! de malleure fus je nee pour telle peine souffrir, et de sy hault estat cheoir en telle povreté, car de toutes les malheureuses je suis la nonpareille. Or sont toutes mes joyes en tristesse muees, mes ris en pleurs changéz, mes chans en souspirs convertis. En lieu de robe de drap d'or dont souloie estre paree, je suis comme femme publique, de injures et vituperez commise et adornee. Et pour pierres precieuses grosses de valeurs inestimables de toutes pars, me convient le demourant de ma povre vie dolante semer et couvrir mes habis de grosses larmes et dueil qui mes jours et ma vie me feront finer. O vous, pastourelles et bergieres des champs! considerés ma grant douleur et plourés mon dolant exil. Or pleust a Dieu que je fusse de aussi basse condicion et estat descendue que la plus povre du monde, au moins je n'auroye nul regret de moy veoir en telle povreté. Helas, pourquoy me allume le soleil et pourquoy me soustient la terre?[2] Car je n'ay besoing que de la fontaine dangereuse de tristresse et mortelle misere pour donner a mes yeulx force et habondance de larmes, car il n'est pas en ma puissance humaine et corporelle de ma destresse langoureuse souffisamment plourer. O faulce envye et trahyson! je te doy bien du cueur mauldire, car par toy je suis au jour d'uy la plus dolente creature qui soit vivant sur la terre. Helas, mon frere roy Pepin, que ferez vous de ceste dolente? Or vous vausist il mieulx que oncques sur terre je n'eusse esté enfantée, ou que du ventre de ma mere je n'eusse esté en terre boutee."

En faisant ceste dure complainte, la dame demoura pasmee sur le cheval et a terre fust tombee, quant Blandimain s'aprocha pour la[3] soustenir. "Helas!" dist il, "madame, prenez en vous confort et ne veuillez entrer en tel desespoir. Ayez ferme fiance en Dieu, et ainsy comme vous estes innocente, sachez qu'il vous confortera et vostre bon droit gardera." Adonc il avisa une moult belle fontaine vers laquelle il mena sa dame, et au plus pres la fist assoir pour un peu reposer et reprendre courage. Sy vous laisseray a parler d'eulx et parleray de l'archevesque qui fut perseverant en sa malice damnable et diabolique.

---

[1] *b i* appears at bottom right corner of 9r.
[2] Text has *trrre*.
[3] Text has *le*.

pauper, and shamefully banished, she thought about the lineage and the royal blood of which she was descended, and the imperial magnificence in which she had been placed. Then she realized the miserable and grievous fortune that had suddenly come upon her.

"Alas, alas, why does death delay, why doesn't it come shorten my life and my anguish and put an end to my sorrows? Alas! I must have been born in misfortune to end up suffering such pain and falling from such a high estate to such poverty, for of all the unhappy women in the world there is none such as I. Now are all my joys turned to sorrow, my laughter changed to tears, my song converted into sighs. Instead of the cloth of gold I was wont to wear, I am like a common strumpet, given over to and adorned with insults and blame. And instead of being covered with great precious stones of inestimable value, it is now my lot for the rest of my sorrowful pauper's life to sprinkle and adorn my clothes with great tears and mourning that will bring an end to my days and my life. Oh you, shepherdesses of the fields, consider my great sorrow and weep for my painful exile. Now even if it pleased God that I be of as low a condition and estate as the poorest pauper in the world, at least I should have no regret to see myself in such poverty. Alas, why does the sun shine on me and why does the earth support me? All I need now is the harsh fountain of grief and mortal misery to give my eyes strength and effusion of tears, for it is not within my human bodily power sufficiently to weep my unhappy distress. Oh, false desire and betrayal! I must curse you from the bottom of my heart, for it is because of you that today I am the most sorrowful creature alive on this earth. Alas, my brother King Pepin, what will you do with this sorrowful creature? It would have been better for you had I never been born into this world, had I never left my mother's womb."

Bitterly bemoaning her fate, the lady fainted in the saddle and would have fallen to the ground, but Blandimain came forward to support her. "Alas!" he said, "my lady, comfort yourself and do not give yourself over to such despair. Have a firm faith in God, and since you are innocent, know that He will comfort you and keep you." Then he spied a beautiful spring towards which he led the lady, and there he had her descend to rest a little and regain strength. Now I will leave off speaking of them and will speak of the archbishop who persevered in his damnable and diabolical malice.

[CHAPITRE 4]

Comment l'archevesque se mist en habit de chevalier et monta a cheval pour suivyr Bellissant qui estoit bannye. iiii. chapitre.

[9verso]Quant[1] l'archevesque vit que la dame estoit partie, il se pensa qu'il yroit apres et que d'elle il feroit sa voulenté. Il laisa rochet et aumusce et comme irregulier et apostat a sainté son espee et monte, et frappe des esperons, car il estoit monté a l'avantage, et tant que en peu de temps il fit grant foison de chemin. Il demandoit a ceulx qu'i rencontroit nouvelle de la dame, et on luy disoit le chemin qu'elle tenoit. Tant chevaucha le traytre qu'il entra en une forez moult longue et large. Le grant chemin prist et s'efforça d'aler. Si n'eut gaires chevaulché que il aperceut la dame avec Blandimain, qui estoit aupres de la fontaine ou la dame sy estoit descendue pour soy rafreschir et ung petit reposer. Car lassee et pesante estoit, plaine de plours et gemissemens de la destresse et couroux tresamere qu'elle soustenoit[2] sur son cueur.

"Dame," dist Blandimain, "resconfortez vous."

L'archevesque tira vers eulx et avisa la belle Bellissant, mais elle ne le recogneut point de loing pour ce qu'il portoit habit dissimulé. Mais quant il approcha bien le cogneust.

"Helas," dit elle, "Blandimain, or voy je venir vers nous le faulx home archevesque qui de mon exil est cause. Las! j'ay trop grant paour qu'il ne me veulle faire villennie."

"Dame," dit Blandimain, "n'ayez de luy ne paour ne doubte, car s'il vient pour vous faire ne mal ne desplaisir, je metteray mon corps pour le vostre deffendre jusques a la mort."

A ces motz fut venu l'archevesque. Il mist le pié a terre et salua la dame le mieulx qu'il peult et dit, "Treschiere et honnouree dame, se tant est que voulez ma voulenté acomplir et croire mon conseil, je feray tant que en peu de temps l'empereur qui vous a dechassee sera de vous veoir bien joyeulx et content. Et serés en vostre premier estat restituee et mise en plus grande triumphe que jamais ne fustes. Et pour tant pensés y, car je le fais pour vostre grant honneur et proffit."

"Ha!" dit la dame, "desloial et cruel aversaire de tout honneur imperialle, je doy bien avoir cause de toy aimer et chier tenir, quant par ton faulx mal as donné a entendre que je suis miserablement adornee et plus que ne fut oncques povre bergiere, privee de honneur royal et imperiale seigneurie. Tu m'as mis a chemin

---

[1] Woodcut depicts a nobleman armed with a sword on horseback. He wears a hat with a feather, and bears a falcon on his right hand. A man with a plain cap follows on foot.

[2] Text has *suostenoit*.

[CHAPTER 4]

How the archbishop dressed himself as a knight and rode off to follow the banished Bellissant.

When the archbishop saw that the lady had left, he thought to go after her and have his way with her. He left behind his surplice and bishop's cap, and, like a renegade and apostate priest, he belted on his sword and mounted his horse. He was well-mounted and spurred on his horse so much that in little time he covered a lot of ground. He asked for news of the lady from those he met, and they told him what road she had taken. The traitor rode on until he entered a vast forest that stretched on and on. He took the main road and hurried onward. He had ridden only a little way when he saw the lady with Blandimain, who was near the spring where the lady had descended in order to refresh herself and rest a little, for she was tired and heavy, and shaken by tears and groans from the distress and bitter anguish she carried in her heart.

"Lady," said Blandimain, "take heart."

The archbishop rode towards them and spied the fair Bellissant, but she didn't recognize him at all from afar because of his disguise. However when he came closer she knew him well.

"Alas," she said, "Blandimain, now I see coming towards us the false archbishop who is the cause of my exile. Alas! I greatly fear that he plans to molest me."

"Lady," said Blandimain, "have no fear of him, for if he comes to hurt or offend you, I will risk my body to defend you to the death."

As he spoke the archbishop arrived. Getting off his horse, he greeted the lady as best he could and said, "Most dear and honored lady, if you are willing to follow my wishes and accept my advice, I will arrange things so that before you know it the emperor who has driven you out will be filled with joy to see you. You will be restored to your previous estate and to greater triumph than ever. So think about it, since I am doing it for your greater honor and well-being."

"Ha!" said the lady, "you most faithless and cruel adversary of all imperial honor, well should I have cause to love you and hold you dear, when it is by the wicked lies you told that I am brought down to this miserable state, lower than the poorest shepherdess, deprived of royal honor and imperial majesty. You put

de danger de user et finer mes jours en douloureuse destresse, car plus n'y a au monde dolente femme que je suis."

"Dame," ce dit l'archevesque, "delaissés telles parolles. Par moy il ne vous peult que [10recto]bien[1] venir, car assés suis puissant pour vostre douleur et vostre desconfort muer en joye et en liesse plus que jamais vous n'eustes."

En disant ces paroles il s'enclina vers la dame, si la cuida baiser, et Blandimain sault avant qui prist l'archevesque et luy donna si grant coup qui le getta a terre. Si luy rompit deux dens de la bouche. L'archevesque se leva, fut dolant et despiteulx et tira son espee, et Blandimain prist ung glave qu'i portoit avec luy, et ont assailly l'ung l'autre que tous deux furent fort navréz.

En ce point combatant vint sur eulx ung marchant arriver, moult notable, et de tant loing, qui les vit. Il escrie, "Seigneurs, seigneurs, delaissez en pais vostre debat et me veullez conter et dire dont la chose procede. Si sçaray de vous deux lequel a tort ou droit."

"Sire," dit Blandimain, "laissez nous faire nostre entreprise, car je ne feray pais avec luy."

"Alasse," dist la dame, "veuillez nous secourir, car vecy le faulx prestre mauldit qui mon honneur veult tollir a force et oultre mon courage. C'est l'archevesque damné qui d'avec l'empereur a tort m'a fait partir et par son faulx langaige de sa compaignie expulser."

Quant le marchant entendit le parler de la dame, il en eut grant pitié, et dit a l'archevesque, "Sire, laissez vostre entreprise et ne touchez la dame, car vous poués bien sçavoir que se l'empereur estoit de vostre fait informé, honteusement et en publique lieu devant tous vous feroit mourir."

Tantost que l'archevesque entendit le marchant parler il delaissa la bataille et se prist a fouir parmy le bois. Car il fut trop dolent et courroucé de ce qu'il fut congneu. Il pensoit bien faire sa voulenté de la dame, mais il entreprinst chose par quoy en la fin sa trahyson fut sceue et descouverte comme dit vous sera.

Apres le depart de l'archevesque, la dame demoura au bois sur la fontaine, tristre et douloureuse, et Blandimain qui estoit avec elle bien navré. Le marchant qui estoit demouré dit, "Helas, dame, je voy bien que par le trahytre et faulx archevesque vous avez esté degettee et dechassee d'avec le puissant empereur. Or me doinst Dieu tant vivre que une fois je le puisse accuser de la faulte villaine et sa mort pourchasser. Dame, a Dieu je vous dy qu'i reconfort et pacience vous doinst."

Le marchant prent congé et Blandimain le mercia doulcement. Blandimain monta la dame a cheval, puis monta sur le sien et alerent en ung hostel qui pres de la estoit ou il[s] se tindrent sept ou huit jours pour garir Blandimain. Et quant Blandimain fut reposé et afermy et qu'il peult chevaulcher, ilz se mirent a chemin vers le païs de France.

---

[1] *b ii* at bottom right corner of 10r.

me on the road where I risk finishing my days in grievous distress, for there is no woman in the world more sorrowful than I."

"Lady," said the archbishop, "leave off such speech. Nothing but good will come to you through me, for I am powerful enough to turn your sorrow to joy and delight greater than you ever had."

As he pronounced these words he bent towards the lady, thinking to kiss her, but Blandimain jumped forward, seized the archbishop, and gave him such a great blow that he knocked him to the ground. He even broke two teeth in his mouth. The archbishop, hurt and enraged, got up and drew his sword, so Blandimain took a blade that he carried with him, and they assailed each other until each was seriously wounded.

As they were fighting, a well-known merchant, who was coming from afar, happened upon them and saw them. He cried out, "My lords, my lords, cease this fight and tell me what this is all about. I will be able to judge who is in the right and who in the wrong."

"Sir," said Blandimain, "let us continue, for I will not make peace with him."

"Alas," said the lady, "please help us, for you see here a cursed false priest who wants to ravish my virtue by force and against my will. This is the damnable archbishop who had me wrongly banished by the emperor, whose lies caused me to be expelled from his company."

When the merchant heard the lady speak, he was filled with compassion for her, and said to the archbishop, "Sir, stop this and don't touch the lady, for you should be quite aware that if the emperor knew what you had done, he would have you shamefully and publicly put to death."

As soon as the archbishop heard the merchant speak, he left off fighting and fled through the woods. He was very upset and angry that he had been recognized. He was thinking to have his way with the lady, but what he did caused his treason finally to be discovered and known, as you will find out.

After the archbishop's departure, the lady remained in the wood near the spring, sad and grieved, with Blandimain who was seriously wounded. The merchant who had remained behind said, "Alas, my lady, I can clearly see that because of this traitor, the false archbishop, you were banished and driven away by the powerful emperor. I pray God that I will live so long as to be able to accuse him of his villainous act and pursue his death. Lady, may God give you comfort and patience."

The merchant took his leave and Blandimain thanked him gently. Blandimain helped the lady onto her horse, then mounted his own, and they went to a lodging nearby where they stayed seven or eight days to cure Blandimain. And when Blandimain was rested and recovered and could ride again, they set out on the road to France.

Et commencha la dame tresfort a getter grans souspirs et complaintes disant, "Helas, Blandimain, mon amy, que pourra mon frere le roy Pepin et tous les seigneurs dire de mon piteux cas quant ilz sçauront que pour fait si dissolu et deshonneste et par si villain blame je suis de l'empereur et de sa contree piteusement separee et honteusement mise aux champs come femme publique et desordonnee et a tout le monde haban[10verso]donnee.¹ Et helas, or suis je certaine que mon frere tost croira que du fait soie coupable, si me fera mourir a honte, car fort a le courage hault."

"Dame," ce dit Blandimain, "n'aiez aucune doubte, car ce n'est chose a croire sy de legier. Vostre frere est saige et discret et si est furni de bon conseil pour prendre garde sur ceste matiere. Ayés fiance en Dieu et il vous donnera confort et vostre bon droit gardera."

En parlant de ceste matiere, Blandimain, qui la dame consoloit, tant chevauça avec elle que apres qu'ilz eurent passés maintz païs sauvages et plusieurs divers royaulmes, ducéz et contés, et tant firent qu'ilz arriverent au païs de France. Et passerent par Orleans pour aler a Paris ou le roy avoit acoustume de soy tenir. Lors entrerent en une forez fort grant qui est a trois lieues d'Orleans, en laquelle piteuse chose a raconter avint a la dame Bellissant comme je vous feray mention.

[CHAPITRE 5]

Comment Bellissant enfanta de deux beaulx filz dedens la forez dont l'ung fut appellé Orson et l'autre Valentin, et comment elle les perdit. v. chapitre

Bellissant fut dedens la forez chevauchant; laquelle dame estoit grosse et enfanta dedens comme ja devant vous a esté mention faite. Or advint que son corps eut terminé et parfait contraignit la dame mal d'enfant sentir. Si commença a soy descendre et debriser sur son cheval, en soy plaignant tendrement. Et Blandimain luy demanda, "Madame, que avez vous que tant vous plaingnez fort?"

"Helas, Blandimain," dit la dame, "mettés le pié a terre, si me descendés bas et me couchés sur l'erbe. Et pensés d'aler dillagamment aulcune femme querir car le te[m]ps est venu que je doy enfanter et ne puis plus attendre."

Blandimain descendit et mist la dame au pié d'ung hault arbre lequel il avisa et choisit pour mieulx recognoistre la place ou il la laissoit. Puis monta a cheval et chevauça tant fort qu'il peult pour avoir une femme que la dame peult secourir.² Et Bellissant demoura seule et sans compaignie, fors que de Dieu et de la Vierge Marie qui luy ayda et fist tant de secours que dedens la forez elle enfanta deux

---

¹ Text has *habandonne*.
² Text has *srcourir*.

The lady began to sigh deeply and lament saying, "Alas, Blandimain, my friend, what will my brother King Pepin and all his lords say regarding my miserable situation when they find out that I have been pitifully banished from my husband and his country for a supposedly depraved and shameful act, absolutely blameworthy, and sent into the fields like a common incorrigible harlot, abandoned by everyone? Alas, I am certain that my brother will believe me guilty right away and will put me to shameful death, for he is very proud."

"Lady," said Blandimain, "fear not, for this is not something to be believed so easily. Your brother is wise and discreet and is furnished with too good a set of advisers not to be careful concerning this matter. Have faith in God and He will comfort you and keep you."

They continued to speak of this subject, and Blandimain continued to console the lady while they rode and rode until, after having passed through many wild countries and several different kingdoms, duchies, and counties, they arrived in the territory of France. They passed through Orleans on their way to Paris where the king was accustomed to hold court. Then they entered a huge forest that was three leagues from Orleans, where a thing terrible to recount befell the lady Bellissant, as I will explain to you.

CHAPTER 5

How Bellissant gave birth in the forest to two beautiful children, one named Orson and the other Valentin, and how she lost them.

Bellissant rode through the forest; the lady was pregnant and gave birth there, as was mentioned earlier. Now it happened that her pregnancy came to term, and the lady felt her labor begin. She started slipping and falling off her horse, while complaining quietly. Blandimain asked her, "My lady, what is the matter that you complain so?"

"Alas, Blandimain," said the lady, "get off your horse and help me get down and lay me on the grass. Then go see if you can quickly find some woman, for the time has come that I must give birth and cannot wait any longer."

Blandimain dismounted and brought the lady to the foot of a tall tree that he had spotted and chosen in order better to recognize the place where he was leaving her. Then he remounted and rode off as quickly as he could to find a woman to help the lady. Bellissant remained all alone and without company, except for God and the Virgin Mary who helped her and aided her so much that there in

beaulx filz. Mais ne furent pas si tost venus sur terre que la dame souffrit dolente peine comme vous orés.

Tout ausitost que la dame eut les deux enfans de son ventre mis et produis au monde, et ainsi qu'elle estoit dessoubz l'arbre seule couchee, vers elle vint une grande ourse et velue a grant merveilles, qui en faisant chiere trop horrible et effroyee de Bellissant s'aprocha, et ung de ses deux enfans prist entre ses dens et parmy le bois s'en fouit. Si fut adonc la dame dolente et non sans cause. De voyx feble et lasse commença moult piteusement a crier, et a ses deux piéz et a deux mains s'en va parmy le bois apres la cruelle beste qui son enfant emportoit. Las! mais trop petit luy valut sa poursuyte, car jamais son enfant ne verra tant que par divin miracle son enfant luy fera rendu. Tant chemina la dame parmy la forez en plourant [11recto]pour[1] son filz et tant fort se traveilla d'aler apres que une tresforte maladie la print, et demoura pausmee et contre la terra se coucha ainsi comme femme morte.

Je vous laisseray a parler d'elle et vous parleray de l'autre enfant qui tout seul demoura. Il avint que iceluy jour que le roy Pepin partit de Paris acompaigné de plusieurs grans barons, ducz, contes et chevaliers pour aler a Constantinoble veoir sa seur Bellissant. Si tira vers Orleans et tant chemina qu'il entra dedens la forez ou estoit sa seur acouchee, mais nulle riens n'en sçeut pour celle fois. Or est il vray comme de Dieu fut le plaisir que le roy Pepin par la forez passant avisa desoubz le hault arbre l'autre filz de Bellissant qui tout seul et desus la terre gisoit. Si chevauche celle part et dist a ses barons:

"Seigneurs, par le Dieu qui tout crea, j'ay fait icy moult belle trouve et bonne encontre. Regardés comment vecy ung beau enfant!"

"Par ma foy," dirent les barons, "vous dites verité."

Or dit le roy, "Je veul qu'il soit nourry a mes despens tant que Dieu luy donnera vie. Et qu'il soit gardé bien songneusement, car s'il vient a eage, je lui feray du bien largement."

Adonc le roy appella ung sien escuier et luy bailla la charge de l'enfant en luy disant, "Prenez cestuy enfant et le portez a Orleans et le faites baptiser et luy querés une nourrice. Et faites que on pense de luy tout au mieulx qu'il sera possible."

Bon droit avoit Pepin se de l'enfant estoit amoureulx, car il estoit son nepveu, mais pas ne le sçavoit. L'escuier print l'enfant et le porta en la ville d'Orleans, le fit baptiser et lui donna son nom car nommer le fit Valentin, car tel estoit le nom de l'escuier. Puis demanda une nourryce et fist penser de l'enfant ainsi que on luy avoit baillé la charge.

Le roy lequel par la forez tousjours chevaucha et tira son chemin, car il avoit grant desir d'estre en la cité de Constantinoble pour voir sa seur Bellissant que tant aymoit. Et ainsi que par le bois passoit il rencontra Blandimain qui menoit une femme; si le cogneust le roy. Blandimain mist le pié a terre et salua le roy.

---

[1] *b iii* appears at bottom right corner of 11r.

the forest she gave birth to two beautiful sons. But hardly had they arrived on earth before the lady suffered grievous sorrow, as you will hear.

Almost as soon as the two children came forth into the world, and as the lady was lying all alone under the tree, a huge she-bear, marvelously hairy, came towards her, and, making horrible frightening faces, approached Bellissant and grabbed one of the children with her teeth and took off into the forest. The lady was at once anguished and not without cause. She began to cry out most piteously with a weak and feeble voice, and crawled off on all fours through the forest after the beast who was carrying away her child. Alas! her pursuit was hardly worth it, for never will she see her child again until by divine miracle her child will be restored to her. So far did she make her way through the forest, weeping for her son, and so much effort did she make that a sudden malaise overcame her, and she lay there on the ground in a faint like a dead woman.

I will leave off speaking of her and will speak to you of the other child who remained all alone. It so happened that very day that King Pepin left Paris, accompanied by several great barons, dukes, counts, and knights, to go to Constantinople to see his sister Bellissant. He was riding towards Orleans and had made such progress that he entered the forest where his sister was lying, although he knew nothing about it at that time. It happened to be God's pleasure that King Pepin, passing through the forest, spied Bellissant's other son under the tall tree, lying there on the ground all alone. He rode over there and said to his barons:

"My lords, by the Lord God who created all, I have made a lovely discovery here. Look at this beautiful child!"

"By my faith," said the barons, "you speak truly."

Now the king said, "I want him to be raised at my expense for as long as God gives him life. Let him be carefully kept, for when he comes of age, I will do much for him."

Then the king called one of his squires and gave him charge of the child saying, "Take this child and bring him to Orleans; have him baptized and find him a wet-nurse. And make sure that he is taken care of in the best way possible."

Pepin was right to love the child so, for he was his own nephew, though he didn't know it. The squire took the child and brought him to the city of Orleans, had him baptized and gave him his own name, Valentin, for such was the squire's name. Then he asked for a wet-nurse and took care of the child as he had been commanded.

The king continued his journey through the forest, for he had a great wish to be in the city of Constantinople to see his sister Bellissant whom he loved so. But just as he was passing through the wood, he ran into Blandimain who was bringing a woman [for Bellissant]; he recognized the king right away. Blandimain got off his horse and greeted the king. After his salutation the king said to

Apres le salut fait le roy luy dit, "Blandimain, beau sire, contez nous des nouvelles et entre les aultres choses, dittes nous comment se porte ma seur Bellissant."

"Chier sire," dit Blandimain, "quant au respect et regard des nouvelles, a peine vous en sçauroye dire de bonnes. Car trop a de mal vostre seur Bellissant par la trahyson du faulx langaige d'ung mauldit archevesque; elle a esté de l'empereur bannye et hors de son pays chassee. Car tant luy a donné l'archevesque de parolles fausses a entendre que se ne fussent les seigneurs de sa court qui a vostre fureur ont doutee et crainte, l'empereur l'eut fait ardoir et mourir devant tous."

"Blandimain," dit le roy Pepin qui fut triste et dolent, "de tant tien je l'empereur a fol qui n'a fait ma seur mourir, car par le Dieu tout puissant, se presentement je la tenoye, jamais de mort elle [11verso]ne seroit respitee que de mort mauvaise ne la feisse mourir. Or avant, seigneurs," dit Pepin, "nostre voyage est fait. Retournons a Paris, car plus oultre je ne veul aler. Je sçay trop des nouvelles de ma seur sans plus en demander ne enquerir."

A ces parolles tourna son cheval pour retourner en faisant et menant grant dueil en son courage. A luy mesmes se print a dire, "Ha, vray Dieu," dit Pepin, "tant souvent est homme deceu par femme. Or suis je bien venu au rebours et contraire de mon intention. Moy qui de ma seur pensoye et cuidoye une foys en ma vie avoir toute joye et plaisir et d'Alexandre l'empereur estre a moy secourir et tenir chier. Et par elle je suis grandement diffamé et mis a trop grant deshonneur."

En ceste melencolye si tresgrande chevaucha le roy Pepin longuement tant qu'il arriva a Orleans. Adonc Blandimain qui bien veit et cogneut le courage du roy Pepin et qui pour doubte de la dame plus ne luy en declaira. Sy s'en retourne vers l'arbre ou il l'avoit laissee, mais point ne la trouva dont il fut marry et de grant couroux plain. Si descendit et loya son cheval, et commença sarcer par le bois. Et tant ala et fit qu'i trouva la dame sur la terre qui de cueur plourer estoit sy lassee pour son enfant qu'elle ne pouoit parler que a trop grant peine.

Et Blandimain l'embrassa et la mist sur les piéz, puis luy demanda, "Helas! que vous peult icy avoir amenee?"

"Ha, Blandimain, tousjours croit ma douleur fortune et double ma destresse langoureuse. Vray est que quant vous me laissastes si vint a moy une ourse qui ung de mes enfans emporta. Et je me mis apres dedens le bois pour luy cuider oster. Mais je n'ay sceu retourner a l'arbre ou j'ay laissé mon aultre enfant."

"Dame, je viens du pié de l'arbre, mais je n'ay point trouvé d'enfant. Si ay je regardé de toutes pars."

Quant la dame oÿt Blandimain plus que devant mena douleur amere, et de rechief s'est pasmee. Et Blandimain la lieve, qui de grant pitié a plourer s'est prins. Vers l'arbre la mena ou l'enfant avoit laissé, mais quant ne le trouva getta si grans souspirs et sy piteux qu'il sembloit que le cueur de son ventre luy partist.

"Ha lasse," dist elle, "or n'est il au monde plus dolente ne plus desconforté femme que je suis, car de tout en tout suis vuide de joye et de plaisir et de liesse. Et suis plaine de douleur, comblee de misere et de destresse intollerable,

him, "Blandimain, fair sir, tell us the news, and among other things, tell us how is my sister Bellissant."

"Dear sire," said Blandimain "as to news, I can hardly give you any that is good. Your sister Bellissant has been harmed by the betrayal of false language on the part of a cursed archbishop; she has been banished by the emperor and driven out of his country. The archbishop so convinced him with his false words that had it not been for the lords of his court who feared your anger the emperor would have put her to death by fire in front of everyone."

"Blandimain," said King Pepin, who was sad and grieved, "I consider the emperor a fool not to have put my sister to death, for, by almighty God, if I had her right now in my power, never would she have respite from the shameful death to which I would put her. Let us go, my lords," said Pepin, "our voyage is done. Let us return to Paris, for I wish to go no further. I have more than enough news about my sister and wish to know no more."

With these words he turned his horse around to return, all the while grieving in his heart. He began saying to himself, "Ah, true God," said Pepin, "man is so often deceived by woman. Now I am come to the very reverse of what I intended. I once believed that I would have great joy and pleasure from my sister, and that Alexander, the emperor, would be my friend and succor. Instead she has brought me great shame and dishonor."

In this overwhelming melancholy Pepin rode for a long time until he arrived in Orleans. Blandimain, who clearly perceived and understood Pepin's state of mind, dared say no more to him for the good of the lady. Instead he returned to the tree where he had left her, but he didn't find her there, which worried and upset him. So he got off his horse, tied him to a tree, and began to search the woods. He searched so much that soon he found the lady on the ground, weeping so desperately for her child that she was exhausted and could barely speak.

Blandimain gathered her in his arms and put her on her feet, then asked her, "Good heavens! what could have brought you here?"

"Oh, Blandimain, my misfortune only increases and my distress doubles. What happened is that when you left me, a bear came and took away one of my children. I followed her into the woods, hoping to get him back. And then I couldn't get back to the tree where I left my other child."

"Lady, I have just come from the foot of the tree, but I saw no child there. And yet I looked everywhere around there."

When the lady heard what Blandimain said, she grieved more bitterly than ever, and once again fainted. Blandimain lifted her up, and began himself to cry, so filled was he with grief. He led her to the tree where she had left the child, but when she didn't see it, she heaved such piteous deep sighs that it seemed her heart would burst.

"Alas," said she, "now there is truly no woman in the world more sorrowful and desperate than I, for in every way possible am I empty of joy, pleasure, and happiness. I am filled with pain, laden with misery and intolerable anguish,

de toutes tribulations aggravee, et entre toutes les desolees la plus desolee. Helas, empereur, vous estes cause de ma mort avancer. A tort et sans cause, par mauvais conseil, de vostre compaignie m'avez privee, car sur mon ame oncques jour de ma vie de mon corps ne fis faulte. Or ay je perdu, par vous, voz propres enfans legitimes, du sang royal yssus, par lesquelz j'espoire une fois de mon tort estre vengee. La mort a moy, pour ma langueur mettre a fin car trop plus m'est la mort agreable que [12recto]languir[1] et vivre en telle martire."

Quant Blandimain vit la dame si tresamerement desconfortee, le plus doulcement qu'il peult la prist a conforter et la fit porter en ung petit village. Si en fit bien penser, baigner et garder tant qu'elle fut bien guarie, saine et enbonpoint, et que de ces grans souspirs, gemissemens et pleurs elle fut ung peu apaisee, car il n'est si grant dueil que en temps on ne mette en oubly.

Adonc Blandimain commencha a dire et compter a la dame comment il avoit trouvé le roy son frere, lequel luy avoit demandé des nouvelles, et qu'il estoit iré et couroucé encontre elle.

Si luy dit, "Dame, par Dieu, j'ay grant doubte que devers le roy vostre frere vous ne soyez mal venue. Car tout ausitost qu'il a sceu que l'empereur vous a degettee d'avec luy, il a monstré semblant d'estre contre vous fort couroucé, ainsi que celuy qui trop de legier veult croire que sa faulte soit de vous."

"Ha, Dieu," ce dit la dame, "or m'est il avenu la chose que plus je doubtoie. Bien puis a ceste heure dire que de toutes pars me suivent et envyronnent douleurs et angoisses, quant d'avec l'empereur mon espoux sans cause suis dechassee. Jamais a Paris je ne retourneray, mais je m'en iray en estrange contree si loing que jamais n'aura nul de mon fait cognoissance ne ne sçaura que je suis. Se mon frere me tenoit, il me feroit mourir. Or vault il mieulx son ire et sa fureur eviter que de la mort attendre."

Et Blandimain lui a dit, "Dame, ne plourés plus. Car vous estes seure que jamais je ne vous laisseray jusques a la mort. Mais suis deliberé de vivre et mourir avec vous et de vous tenir compaignie ou sera vostre plaisir d'aler."

"Blandimain," dit la dame, "alons a nostre aventure. Je vous mercie de vostre bon vouloir, car du tout en vous je me fie."

Ainsy se sont mis a chemin la dame et Blandimain qui du tout ne sont pas joyeulx mais chargéz d'angoisses.

Je vous laisseray a parler d'eulx, et vous diray de l'ourse qui emporta l'enfant parmy le bois.

---

[1] *b iiii* appears at the bottom right corner of 12r.

overcome with every tribulation possible, and of all unhappy women the most unhappy. Alas, emperor, because of you I shall be brought to an early death. Wrongfully and without cause, through evil counsel, you have deprived me of your company, for, by my soul, never a day of my life did I commit a sin of the body. Now, because of you, I have lost your own legitimate children, the issue of royal blood, by whom I hope one day to be avenged of the wrong done to me. Death, come to me, come put an end to my sorrow, for death is more agreeable to me than languishing in this martyrdom."

When Blandimain saw the lady's bitter desperation, he picked her up as gently as he could to comfort her and brought her to a little village. There he had her well taken care of, bathed, and watched over until she was fully healed, healthy, and plump, and her heavy sighs, moans, and tears were somewhat calmed, for there is no sorrow so great that in time one does not begin to forget it.

Only then did Blandimain begin to recount to the lady how he had encountered the king her brother, who had asked him news, and who was now angry with her.

He said to her, "Lady, in God's name, I am afraid that you will not be welcomed by the king your brother. As soon as he knew that the emperor had cast you off, he seemed very angry with you, obviously believing too easily that the fault is yours."

"My God," said the lady, "now the very thing I most feared has occurred. Now I can truly say that sorrow and anguish follow and surround me on every side for having been driven off by the emperor my husband. Never will I return to Paris; rather, I will go to some foreign land so far away that no one will know anything about me or who I am. If my brother had me in his power, he would have me put to death. It is better for me to avoid his wrath than to wait for death."

Blandimain said to her, "Lady, weep no more. For you can be sure that I will never leave you till the day I die. Rather I am pledged to live and die with you and keep you company wherever it will be your pleasure to go."

"Blandimain," said the lady, "let us go where chance leads us. I thank you for your kind willingness, for I trust you in all things."

Thus the lady and Blandimain took to the road, not joyfully, of course, but rather filled with anguish.

I will leave off speaking to you of them, and will tell you about the she-bear who carried the child off through the woods.

[CHAPITRE 6]

De l'ourse qui emporta ung des enfans de Bellissant parmi le bois. vi. cha[pitre]

L'ourse qui avoit pris ung des enfans de Bellissant pas ne le devora, mais le porta en sa terrierre en une fosse profonde et obscure qui estoit sans clarté. En laquelle fosse avoit iiii. oursons fors et puissans. L'ourse getta l'enfant parmy les oursons ainsi comme celle qui leur baille a mengier, mais Dieu qui jamais ses amis n'oublye monstra evident miracle, car les oursons nul mal ne lui firent, mais de leurs pates velues commencerent a le plaigner moult doulcement. Quant l'ourse vit que ses petis oursons ne le vouloient devorer, elle fut fort amoureuse de l'enfant et tant que parmy les oursons le garda et alaitta ung an entier. Si fut l'enfant pour cause de la nutrition de l'ourse tant velu ainsi comme une beste sauvage.

Si se prist a cheminer parmy le bois et devint grant en peu de temps et commença a fraper les aultres de la forez tant que toutes le doubtoient et fuioient devant luy. Car si terrible estoit qu'il ne craingnoit de riens paour, en tel estat me[12verso]nant vie de beste. Fut l'enfant l'espace de xv. ans tant qu'il devint fort, grant, et puissant que nul par la forez n'osoit passer. Bestes et hommes il les abatoit et mettoit a mort. La chair mengoit crue ainsi comme les aultres bestes et vivoit de vie bestialle et non pas humaine. Il fut appelé Orson pour cause de l'ourse qui le nourrist et allaita, et pelage avoit comme ung ours. Tant fit de mal parmy le bois et tant fut redoubté que nul tant fut hardy ou de grant vaillance ne passoit parmi la[1] forez que tres grandement ne doubtast l'omme sauvage. Si fort acreut le bruit de luy que ceulx du païs environ a force et puissance le chasserent pour le prendre, mais riens n'y vault chose qui contre luy fust faite, car il ne doubtoit filés ne glaives, mais tout rompoit et mettoit par piesses devant luy. Or est il devant la forez menant vie de beste sauvage, sans nul drap vestir et sans parole dire.

Et sa mere Bellissant, qui bien le cuidoit avoir perdu, s'en va comme femme desconfortee par le pays a l'aventure. Et Blandimain la conduit et conforte tant et si bien qu'il peult. La dame tousjours avoit regret a ses deux enfans, car perdu les a, et prie souvente fois et de bon cueur a Dieu et a la Vierge Marie que ses deulx filz luy peust sauver.

Par plusieurs lieux passerent Blandimain et Bellissant, et tant alerent et par mer et par terre qu'ilz arriverent au port de Portingal sur lequel y avoit ung chasteau fort. En en celui chasteau demouroit ung geant si grant et si puissant que nul cheval tant fust fort ne le pouoit soustenir. Il avoit a non Ferragu. Or avint qu'il saillit hors du chasteau et vint dessus le port pour son tribu demander aux passans

---

[1] Text has *la la*, one before and one after the line break.

[CHAPTER 6]

Concerning the she-bear who carried off one of Bellissant's children through the woods.

The she-bear who had taken one of Bellissant's children did not eat him; rather she carried him to her den in a deep, dark gully where little light shone. In this gully were four strong and powerful bear cubs. The she-bear threw the baby to the cubs for them to eat, but God, who never forgets those He loves, produced a miracle, for the cubs did not harm him: rather they began to play with him quite gently with their furry paws. When the she-bear saw that her little cubs didn't want to devour him, she fell completely in love with the child, so much so that she kept him with her cubs and nursed him an entire year. The child then became as hairy as a wild beast because of the she-bear's milk.

He began to wander the woods, and grew quickly, and began to attack the other beasts of the forest so that all feared him and fled before him. He was so terrible that he feared nothing, and led the life of an animal. By the time he was fifteen years old he had grown so big and powerful that no one dared pass through the forest. Both beasts and men he attacked and killed. He ate raw flesh like other animals and lived a bestial life, not a human one. He was called Orson because of the she-bear who nursed and nourished him, and he had the fur of a bear. He caused so much harm in the woods and was so feared that no one, no matter how brave or valiant, passed through the forest without greatly dreading the wild man. His reputation grew so that the local people hunted him, trying to capture him, but nothing worked, for he feared neither nets nor swords and only tore and broke everything he confronted. And so he lived like a wild beast in the forest, wearing not a stitch of clothing nor speaking a word.

His distraught mother, who was sure she had lost him forever, took to the road again with no fixed destination. Blandimain led her and comforted her as best he could. The lady continued to miss her two children, for she had lost them, and she prayed often and with a fervent heart that God and the Virgin Mary might preserve her two sons.

Blandimain and Bellissant passed through many places, traveling by sea and by land until they came to the port of Portugal where there was a castle fortress. In this castle lived a giant so large and so strong that no horse, no matter how brawny, could hold him. His name was Ferragu. It so happened that he sallied forth from the castle and came to the port to levy his tribute from the passengers,

ainsi que de coustume avoit de prendre sur chascune navire. Il entra dedens le bateau ou estoit Bellissant qui estoit fort garny de plusieurs marchandises. Et tantost qu'il avisa Bellissant qui tant fut belle, il la prist par la main et la mena en son chasteau devers sa femme, car il estoit marié a une dame tresplaisante et belle. Et Blandimain ala apres la dame que le geant Ferragu maine en grant honneur et sans luy vouloir faire villennie.

Il la presenta a sa femme. Voulentiers la receut et eut grant joye de sa venue pour la gracieuse contenance qu'elle veoit en Bellissant. Le geant commanda a sa femme que Bellissant fust chierement gardee comme son corps et Blandimain son escuier pareillement. Elle fut a grant joie au chasteau receue, car bien estoit aprinse en meurs et en science, et bien savoit parler et soy honestement gouverner entre grans et petis. Et quant de ses enfans avoit souvenance, tendrement plouroit en son cueur. Mais tousjours la resconfortoit la femme du geant et dessus toutes personnes au plus pres d'elle la tenoit, car elle l'aimoit de si grant amour que sans elle ne pouoit ne boire ne menger. Longtemps fut au chasteau de Ferragu.

Si vous en laisse a parler et vous diray de l'empereur et du faulx archevesque.

[CHAPITRE 7]

Par le conseil mauvais de l'arche[13recto]vesque furent elevé plusieurs nouvelles coustumes en la cité de Constantinoble, et comment la trahison fut cogneue. vii. cha[pitre].[1]

L'empereur Alexandre apres qu'il eut dechassee et deboutee vituperablement sa femme Bellissant hors de sa compagnie, fit plusieurs durs et piteux regretz pour elle et se repentit en son courage. Mais l'archevesque mauldit de Dieu tousjours l'entretenoit en sa folle oppinion, et l'empereur le creoit. Et tant luy donna de puissance et d'auctorité sur tous les aultres que ce qu'il commandoit estoit fait, tant eust de gouvernement et de seigneurie, qu'il mist sus et esleva en la cité de Constantinoble coustumes et usages contre droit et contre rayson.

Or avint que en la cité avoit une foire laquelle on tenoit le xv. jour de septembre et de plusieurs païs venoient les marchans a celle foire. Et quant le jour fut venu que on la devoit tenir, la ville fut toute plaine de marchans de divers pays et de plusieurs contrees. La fit l'empereur garder la foire comme de coustume estoit, et bailla la garde a l'archevesque qui, pour luy acompaigner, fit armer deux cens compaignons. Lesquelz partirent de la ville pour la foire aler garder.

---

[1] Woodcut depicting a crowned king backed by several councillors facing a man in a robe and cap and his companion. Hands are raised in gestures indicating speech.

as was customary for him to do with each ship. He entered the boat Bellissant was traveling on, which was filled with all kinds of merchandise. As soon as he saw Bellissant, who was so beautiful, he took her by the hand and led her to his castle, to his wife, for he was married to a most pleasant and lovely lady. And Blandimain followed the lady [Bellissant] whom the giant Ferragu led with great respect, without wanting to cause her any harm.

He presented her to his wife, who received her most willingly, joyful for her coming, for she saw such graciousness in Bellissant. The giant ordered his wife to watch over Bellissant as she would her own self, and Blandimain her squire as well. She was joyfully received at the castle, for she was well-educated, in terms of both her manners and her knowledge, being both well-spoken and well-bred in her bearing towards everyone. However, when she remembered her children, she wept bitterly in her heart of hearts. Yet the giant's wife always comforted her and was close to her more than anyone else, for she had such great affection for her that she never wanted to eat or drink except in her presence. And so, for a long time she lived in Ferragu's castle.

And now I will leave off speaking of this matter and will tell you about the emperor and the false archbishop.

CHAPTER 7

By the evil order of the archbishop, several new customs were put into place in the city of Constantinople; and how his treachery became known.

After having ignominiously exiled his wife Bellissant and banished her from his company, the emperor Alexander suffered many heartfelt regrets for her and repented in his heart of hearts. But the archbishop cursed by God kept encouraging him to maintain his foolhardy attitude, and the emperor believed him. So much power and authority over others did he give him that whatever he commanded was done, be it concerning government or lordship, so that he was able to put into place certain customs and practices in the city of Constantinople that ran contrary to right and reason.

It so happened that in the city there was a fair that fell always on the fifteenth day of September. Merchants came from many countries to attend this fair. When the day came on which it was to take place, the city was full of merchants from diverse countries. It was customary for the emperor to have the fair guarded, and he gave responsibility for maintaining the guard to the archbishop, who had two hundred men armed in order to accompany him. These men left the city to go guard the fair.

En ycelle foire fut present le marchant dont j'ay mention faite devant, c'est assavoir celuy qui trouva Blandimain et l'archevesque qui se combattoient. Bien le recogneust l'archevesque mais nul semblant n'en fit, car trop il doubtoit que sa faulceté ne fust congeue. Moult voulentiers l'eust fait mourir, mais il n'avoit pas la puissance sans trop grant esclandre.

A ce jour ledit marchant, qui fut bien garny de drap d'or et de soye, vendit et delivra plus que nul des aultres, pourquoy en la fin de la foire l'archevesque sy envoya devers luy ung sergent pour luy demander tribu en quoy il estoit tenu pour cause de la vendition de sa marchandise.

Le sergent vint a luy disant, "Sire marchant, il vous fault payer dix deniers pour livre de ce que vous avez vendu, car ainsy est il ordonné."

"Or va!" dit le marchant. "Que mal puisse avenir a celuy qui telle coustume a mise sus. C'est le faulx et desloyal archevesque, que Dieu mauldie, car long temps y a que mourir doit honteusement et a deshonneur."

Lors quant le marchant eust ainsi diffamé l'achevesque le sergent leva son baston et frappa le marchant en la [13verso]teste si grant coup que le sang en saillit. Et quant le marchant se sentit frappé, il tira son espee et frappa le sergent par telle fasson qu'il l'abatit mort. Lors se leva grant bruit et grant commotion de peuple par toute la foire, en telle maniere que les aultres sergens prindrent le marchant et le menerent devers l'archevesque, qui le vouloit faire mourir sans sejour ne dilation. Mais le marchant, qui fut saige et bien avisé, demanda la loy; c'est a dire qu'il vouloit estre ouÿ en ses raisons et deffences, et la justice fut sage et moderee, si lui fut ottroié. Adonc l'archevesque le fit mener devant l'empereur car grant voulenté avoit de le faire jugier a mort. Mais en desirant la mort aultrui il pourchassa la sienne comme vous orés.

L'archevesque fit presenter le marchant au palais. La fut present l'empereur qui le juge comanda a mettre soy en chaiere. Et l'archevesque fit par ung avocat rigoreusement proposer contre le marchant en l'accusant du murtre qu'il avoit fait et de la grant injure qu'il avoit dicte contre la reverence de l'archevesque.

Quant le propos fut fait contre le marchant, a deux genoulx se getta devant la majesté de l'empereur, et luy comenca a dire,[1] "Treshault et excellent seigneur, s'i vous plaisoit de vostre benigne grace de moy donner audience par devant tous voz barons, je vous diray chose qui est de grande importance et dont vostre honneur imperialle est chargee."

"Marchant," dit l'empereur, "or parlés seurement car licence je vous donne."

"Sire," dit le marchant, "commandez que les portes de vostre palais soient de toutes pars closes, afin que nulluy ne puisse de ce lieu partir."

L'empereur creut le marchant et dit devant tous hautement, "Seigneurs, barons et chevaliers qui desirés et devés aimer l'onneur et le proffit du triumphant empire, entendés a mon parler. Le temps est venu que la trahison du mauldit

---

[1] Text has *die*.

At this fair was present the merchant I mentioned earlier, that is to say, the one who found Blandimain and the archbishop fighting one another. The archbishop certainly recognized him, but gave no sign of it, for he greatly feared his falseness becoming known. Most willingly would he have had him killed, but there was no way to carry it out without a great scandal.

On that day the merchant, who was well-furnished with gold and silk cloth, sold and delivered more than all the others, which is why at the end of the fair the archbishop sent an officer to him to demand the tribute due him on the merchandise sold.

The officer came to him and said, "Sir merchant, you must pay ten deniers for every pound you have sold—those are orders."

"What are you talking about?" said the merchant. "May evil befall the one who instituted such a custom. It's the false and disloyal archbishop, may God damn him, who has long deserved to die shamefully and ignobly."

When the merchant had thus defamed the archbishop, the officer raised his club and dealt the merchant such a heavy blow on the head that blood spilled out. When the merchant felt himself hit, he drew his sword and struck the officer in such a way that he killed him on the spot. Then such noise and commotion were raised throughout the fair that the other officers seized the merchant and led him to the archbishop, who wanted to execute him without delay. But the merchant, who was smart and well-informed, invoked the law; that is to say that he wanted a chance to explain his reasons and defenses. The judge was wise and moderate, and thus it was granted him. Therefore the archbishop had him brought before the emperor, greatly desiring that he be sentenced to death. But in desiring another's death he brought about his own, as you will hear.

The archbishop presented the merchant in the palace. There present was the emperor who commanded the judge to take the bench, and the archbishop had an attorney present a vigorous accusation of murder against the merchant as well as of libel concerning what he had declared against His Reverence the archbishop.

When this accusation was made against the merchant, he threw himself on his knees before His Majesty the emperor and began to say to him, "Most exalted and excellent lord, if it please you in your benevolent mercy to grant me a hearing in the presence of all your barons, I will tell you something of great importance which involves your own imperial glory."

"Merchant," said the emperor, "go ahead and speak in surety, for I give you permission."

"Sire," said the merchant, "order all the doors of your palace to be closed so that no one may leave this place."

The emperor believed the merchant [and carried out his suggestion]. The merchant declared loudly before everyone, "My lords, barons and knights, you who desire and must love the honor and well-being of this glorious empire, listen to what I have to say. The time has come that the betrayal of this cursed

archevesque que vous voyez icy doit estre cogneue et declairee publiquement et devant tous voz reverences. Helas, sire empereur, c'est le mauldit home par qui vostre bonne femme a esté a tort de vous deboutee a honte. En luy avez fait povre nourriture que luy, qui vous devoit vostre honneur garder, ung jour requist la belle dame Bellissant, laquelle comme saige et prudente le refusa. Et quant ce pervers traitre prestre entendit et aperceut que la dame jamais ne feroit sa plaisance, pour doubte que son peché ne fust descouvert, il a tant fait et pourchassé que les faulces paroles qu'il vous a donné a entendre que vostre dame Bellissant est faulce et desloyalle envers vous et qu'elle a son corps habandonné a d'aultres que a vous. Laquelle chose sauf l'onneur de vostre haulte excellence reverence et de tous les seigneurs de vostre haulte magnificence il a menty comme faulx infidele a vous. Et se pour ce plus grande approbation de cestuy cas voir, vous me demandés comment je la sçay et qui la verité m'a declairee, je vous dy, sire, que ung jour passé, bien tost que vostre femme fut de vostre païs bannye, en chevaulchant parmy ung bois, je trouvay cestuy prestre irregulier et apostat qui estoit en [14recto]armes et en habit dissimulé, oultre Dieu et l'ordonnance de sa vocation. Et en iceluy bois avoit assailli tresfierement Blandimain qui gardoit et conduisoit en sa dolente fortune et la tresnoble et franche dame Bellissant vostre femme.

"Et ainsi que je veis leur debat, je commençay a dire, 'Messeigneurs, laissez en paix vostre debat!' Et la dame qui fort piteusement plouroit me commença a dire, 'Marchant, mon amy, veuillez moy secourir contre celuy faulx archevesque, qui a force et contre mon courage veult mon honneur tollir. Helas,' ce dit la dame, 'c'est celuy par qui je suis en exil mise et chasee d'avec l'empereur et de sa contree.'

"Si frapay mon cheval pour les separer, mais cestuy archevesque prist tost et soudainement sa fuite par le bois, car trop luy vint a desplaisance quant il veit qu'il fut cogneu. Helas, hault empereur et puissant roy, j'ai plusieurs fois pensé en mon courage de vous declairer ceste matiere mais parler je ne vous en osoie. Informés vous du cas et se vous trovés du contraire, si me faites mourir."

Quant l'empereur oÿt les parolles du marchant, du cueur comença a souspirer et plourer des yeux grosses larmes. Et puis dit a l'archevesque, "Ha, faulx et desloyal servant, je te dois petit tenir chier et honnourer. Je me suis perforcé toute ma vie de toy bien faire et mettre en honneur, et tu m'en rens deshonneur et trahison pour loyalle preudommie. Or ainsi me soit Dieu amy que mon courage me disoit tousjours que je seroye par toy deceu et trahy une fois en ma vie. Helas! la chose que plus doubtoye m'est avenue. Tu m'as fait de tous les grans le plus petit, et tous les princes le plus diffamé et malheureux. Las! je doy bien haïr ma vie, quant il fault que par ta faulce trahyson soye privé de la chose qui plus j'aymoye. De mal eure j'ay creu ton conseil si de legier."

"Ha!" ce dit l'archevesque, "ne soyez ja pour moy courrucé pour chose que le marchant vous dye. Car oncques de tout ce fait je n'en sceus rien, et n'en suis coupable mais innocent je suis et tel je me veul tenir."

"Tu mens," dit le marchant, "car de la trahyson tu ne te peuls excuser et se tu dis du contraire, je veul combatre en ung champ pour ceste querelle soustenir.

archbishop (whom you see here) be known and declared publicly and in the presence of all Your Reverences. Alas, lord emperor, it is because of this damnable man that your good wife was wrongfully and shamefully cast off by you. In him you have wasted the goodness you invested, for he, who was supposed to guard your honor, instead one day tried to seduce the fair lady Bellissant, who, wise and prudent lady, refused him. And when this perverse traitor priest heard and realized that the lady would never succumb to his pleasure, fearful that his crime would be discovered, he libeled her with false words, telling you that your lady Bellissant was false and unfaithful towards you and that she had given herself to men other than you. With all due respect, most exalted and excellent emperor and lords, he has lied to you like a faithless infidel. And if, in order to see some substantial proof of this case, you ask me how I know this and who explained to me what really happened, I tell you, sire, that some time ago, soon after your wife was banished from your land, while riding through the woods, I found this irregular and apostate priest out of his proper ecclesiastical robes and fully armed as a knight, contrary to God and the requirements of his vocation. In this wood he had fiercely attacked Blandimain, the squire who was guarding and guiding the most noble and virtuous lady Bellissant, your wife, in her unfortunate state.

"When I first saw their fight, I began to say, 'My lords, cease this strife!' And the lady, who was crying piteously, began to tell me, 'Merchant, my friend, please help me against this false archbishop who wishes to ravish my virtue by force and against my will. Alas,' said the lady, 'it is he who is responsible for my being exiled and cast away from the emperor and his land.'

"I spurred my horse forward to separate them, but the archbishop suddenly took off and fled through the woods, for he was upset at being recognized. Alas, exalted emperor and powerful monarch, I have thought many times in my heart to tell you all of this but I didn't dare speak to you. Investigate the matter, and if you find that I am wrong, then put me to death."

When the emperor heard the words of the merchant, he began to sigh deeply and weep abundantly. Then he said to the archbishop, "Oh, false and faithless servant, I owe you little love or honor. All my life I have done my utmost to do good by you and honor you, while you repay me with dishonor and treason in return for loyal honesty. Now, as God is my friend, I always thought in my heart of hearts that one day in my life you would deceive and betray me. Alas! the thing I most feared has occurred. You have debased me and rendered me the most unfortunate and dishonored of all princes. Alas! I have every reason to hate myself since by your wicked betrayal I am deprived of the one I loved the most. Woe unto me that I so easily believed your counsel."

"What!" cried the archbishop, "don't be already angry at me because of what the merchant tells you. I know nothing of what he is talking about. I am not guilty of this thing, and I insist on my innocence."

"You are lying," said the merchant, "for you can't worm your way out of this treason, and if you continue to lie, then I want to fight a judicial duel to support

Et sy offre mon corps a mort estre livré se devant la nuyt fermee je ne vous rens par devant tous faulx trahytre tout mort ou vaincu ou tu confesseras ton cas. Et afin que nul ne pense que mon courage s'acorde aux ditz, je te livre mon gaige et pense de toy deffendre."

Et quant l'empereur Alexandre vit que le gaige fut getté, il dit a l'archevesque, "Or est il temps que selon justice et droit vous pensés et avisés de vous combatre au marchant ou de loyaulté dire et verité recongnoistre."

"Ha, sire, vous devez sçavoir que de faire bataille et champ d'armes je doy estre[1] tenu pour excusé, car je suis prelat et prestre sacré, dont il n'apartient nullement de moy combatre. Car en ce faisant [14verso]je fausseroye et reprouveroye la dignité de sainte esglise."

"Par ma foy," dit l'empereur, "en ceste querelle n'a point d'escusation. Mais convient que vous combatés au marchant lequel de trahison vous accuse, et se faire vous ne le voulés, je vous tiens pour coupable du fait."

De telles parolles oÿr fut l'archevesque moult effroyé car il voit et cognoit que combatre luy fault. Sy a dit a l'empereur, "Sire tresredoubté, quant il vous plaist que de mon corps je monstre et preuve que je suis innocent de cestuy cas est bien raison que je le face, combien que ce soit contre mon estat."

Or pensa bien et se cuida excuser l'archevesque de la bataille entreprendre. Mais petit luy valut son parler et ses excusations, car l'empereur commanda que l'archevesque fut gardé tellement qu'il le peult avoir a sa voulenté toutes les fois qu'il luy plairoit. Et aussi fit prendre le marchant et commanda que on pensast de luy bien et honnestement. Puis assembla l'empereur son conseil et fut le jour terminé, le champ prins, et lices faites pour le marchant et l'archevesque faire combatre. En laquelle bataille Dieu, qui est vray juge, monstrera evidamment par devant tous que trahison et barat doivent tousjours retourner a son maistre, comme vous orés.

[CHAPITRE 8]

Comment l'empereur Alexandre par le conseil des plus sages envoya querir le roy Pepin pour voir la verité et querelle du marchant et du faulx et mauldit archevesque. viii. chapitre[2]

Apres que la journee fut terminee et le champ fut commandé a preparer et les lices faire, il vint nouvelles a l'empereur que le roy Pepin estoit a Romme venu pour aider et conforter le pape a l'encontre des infideles et ennemis de la sainte

---

[1] Text has *esstre*.

[2] Woodcut depicting messenger down on one knee, holding spear, handing a message to a standing robed and crowned figure, with one attendant partially seen behind him.

my accusation. Thus I offer myself to a sentence of death if by tonight I cannot render you dead or vanquished or confessed as a false traitor in the presence of all. And so that no one will think my heart not in accord with my words, I challenge you—get ready to defend yourself."

When the emperor Alexander saw the challenge launched, he said to the archbishop, "The time has come according to the laws of justice that you prepare yourself to fight the merchant or that you speak loyally and tell the truth."

"Oh, sire, you must know that I must be excused from doing battle or entering a field of arms, for I am a prelate and holy priest, thus it is not seemly for me to do battle. In doing that I would defraud and betray the dignity of the holy church."

"By my faith," said the emperor, "in this quarrel there is no exemption. Rather you must fight the merchant who accuses you of treason, and if you do not want to do it, I will hold you guilty as charged."

The archbishop was frightened to hear such words, for he understood and realized that he must fight. So he said to the emperor, "Most respected sire, when it pleases you that I myself demonstrate and prove that I am innocent in this case, then it is reason enough for me to do it, however it runs counter to my estate."

The archbishop really thought that he could recuse himself from undertaking this combat. But his speeches and excuses were of little value, for the emperor ordered that the archbishop be guarded so closely that he could command his presence whenever it pleased him. He also had the merchant taken into custody and ordered that he be taken care of properly. Then the emperor assembled his council, and the day was determined, the field chosen, and the lists prepared for the merchant and the archbishop to fight. In that battle, God, who is the true judge, will render evident before everyone that treason and deceit will always come back to haunt their master, as you will hear.

[CHAPTER 8]

How the emperor Alexander, according to the advice of his wisest men, sent for King Pepin to come see the outcome of the fight between the merchant and the false and cursed archbishop.

After the day was fixed and preparation of the field and the lists ordered, news came to the emperor that King Pepin had come to Rome to aid and support the pope against the infidels and enemies of the holy Christian faith.[1]

---

[1] This reflects an actual historical event, the Arab attack on Rome in 846.

foy crestienne. Et adonc il fut avisé par les plus saiges de son palais que devoit aler querir ledit roy Pepin afin d'estre present audit jour de la bataille pour plus honneste excusation de l'empereur, et qu'i veit et congneust clerement que par mauvaise trahyson avoit fait sa femme separer hors de sa compaignie, ou que a bon droit et juste querelle il l'avoit degettee. A cestuy conseil s'acorda l'empereur et tranmist et envoia a toute diligence a Romme certains messagiers ausquelz il bailla lettres pour porter au roy Pepin qui lors a Romme estoit en la saincte foy deffendant contre les infidelles comme dessus vous ay dit.

Les messagiers se sont partis [15recto]de Constantinoble et ont tant fait que par mer et par terre ilz sont venus a Romme devers le roy Pepin lequel ilz saluerent et luy en fait reverence telle qu'il apartient a faire a roy en telle maniere que de coustume estoit.

Puis ont dit, "Tres redoubté crestien et excellent roy, je vous presente ceste lettre de par le puissant empereur, mon maistre. Si veullez regarder le contenu d'icelles, et sur ce plaise a vostre majesté royale de nous donner responce."

Le roy Pepin prist tantost la lettre et l'a ouverte et regardee. Et apres qu'il l'eut leue il parla devant tous haultement en disant, "Seigneurs, par le Dieu tout puissant, veci nouvelles de grant admiration. L'empereur me mande que ma seur Bellissant, que donné luy avoie, a esté de par lui a tort et sans cause mise en exil par ung faulx archevesque qui lui a donné a ente[n]dre une me[n]songe. Lequel de son cas fort detestable est accusé par ung marchant qui sus ceste querelle veult vivre et mourir en combatant l'archevesque devant tous en champ de bataille. Et que soit certain, ledit marchant, comme hardi de son cas poursuivir a l'aide de Dieu et bonne et loialle equité, soy confiant, il a getté et livré son gaige contre l'archevesque. Or est ainsi que le jour qu'i se doivent combatre et que ma seur que tant j'aimoie, je pourroie cognoistre s'elle a commis la faulte dont elle est accusee. Et s'il est ainsi que l'empereur injustement luy ait fait ce deshonneur, je vous jure par mon serment royal que de luy je prenderay vengance, car la grant faulte qu'il a faite ne pourroit jamais estre reparee."

Adonc commanda le roy Pepin que chascun de sa court fut pres et apparellé pour l'acompaigner en Constantinoble car il vouloit aler au jour de l'entreprise qui estoit fait entre le marchant et l'archevesque. Si furent tous pres pour le commandement du roy faire.

Pepin partit de Romme en moult belle compaignie; et tant a chevaulché qu'il est venu sur la mer et monterent sur les gallees et tant qu'ilz sont venus arriver a Constantinoble. Et quant l'empereur sceut la venue du roy Pepin, il commanda que on sonnast les cloches, et que par toute la cité on demenast joye. Si grandement comme faire sera possible chascun fut joyeux de la venue de Pepin, et l'empereur monta a cheval moult sumptueusement acompaigné, saillit hors de la cité pour aler a l'encontre. Mais tantost qu'il vit le roy Pepin et qu'i luy souvint de Bellissant, il commença a plourer et souspirer si piteusement que parler il ne peult sinon en gettant grosses larmes et faisant grandes lamentations de cueur et de bouche trop angoiseusement.

Thereupon his wisest advisors suggested that he go invite King Pepin to be present the day of the judicial duel, as the best way for the emperor to justify himself, so that he [Pepin] could see and clearly understand either that it was by evil treachery that he had driven his wife out of his presence, or that he had been correct and just in exiling her. Accepting this advice, the emperor sent messengers right away to Rome to carry letters to King Pepin who was there defending the holy faith against the infidels, as I told you above.

The messengers left Constantinople, traveling quickly by sea and by land until they reached Rome and King Pepin, whom they greeted with proper reverence, as custom and obligation demand one do before a king.

Then they said, "Most respected Christian and excellent king, I present you this letter from the mighty emperor, my master. Please read what it says and may it please your royal majesty to give us your response."

King Pepin took the letter immediately, opened it, and looked at it. After having read it he declared in a loud clear voice before all, "My lords, by almighty God, here is news to amaze one. The emperor informs me that Bellissant, my sister, whom I had given him, was wrongly and without justification exiled by him because of the lying testimony of a false archbishop. This archbishop has been accused of his hateful crime by a merchant who is willing to stake his life in the matter by means of a judicial duel in the presence of all. And to make it certain, this merchant, like a bold man, confident of pursuing his case with both God's help and fair and proper justice, has launched a challenge to the archbishop. Thus the day they are supposed to fight, I should be able to know whether my sister, whom I loved so, committed the sin of which she is accused. But if it turns out that the emperor shamed her unjustly, I swear to you by my royal oath that I will take vengeance, for the immense wrong he committed could never be repaired."

Thereupon King Pepin ordered everyone in his court to ready himself to accompany him to Constantinople, for he wanted to be there the day of the duel between the merchant and the archbishop. Everyone was ready to carry out the king's command.

Pepin left Rome with a full entourage, and they rode until they came to the sea and boarded the ships, and soon arrived in Constantinople. When the emperor knew that King Pepin had arrived, he commanded that all the bells be rung and that everyone celebrate throughout the city. Everyone celebrated Pepin's arrival as grandly as they could, while the emperor mounted his horse and sallied forth from the city with a sumptuous entourage to meet him. However, as soon as he saw King Pepin and remembered Bellissant, he began to weep and sigh so piteously that he could not communicate except with abundant tears and anguished lamentations of the heart and the mouth.

Et le roy Pepin qui avoit le courage fier et orgueilleux pour le plourer riens ne luy chault. Il ne fit semblant ne signe que pour son plourer eut pitié ne compassion, mais lui dit en ceste maniere, "Empereur, laissés le plourer et ne vous desconfortez pour tant se ma seur avez perdue, car qui pert une putain il n'en doit faire esmay. Et puis que ma seur est telle n'ayés pour elle ne sousi ne desplaisance."

"Ha!" dit l'empereur, "pour Dieu ne veullez dire de vostre seur telles parolles, car je croy seurement que en elle est toute [15verso]loyauté et preudommie et que a tort et sans cause je l'ay de moy dechassee."

"Par ma foi," ce dit Pepin, "de tant vous doit on plus blasmer et peut chascun cognoistre la grande sapience qui en vous deust estre quant par ung seul mal donner a entendre vous avez si diligamment creu que par vous ma seur est comme putain publique vituperablement d'avec vous dechassee. Et sachez que je suis bien petit tenu d'amer celuy qui tel blasme et deshonneur fait a ma personne et a tout le sang royal de France."

Quant l'empereur Alexandre oÿt et entendit les parolles et le courage du roy, il fut moult dolent et courocé en son cueur. Il a respondu simplement, "Helas, sire roy Pepin, ne vous veullez mouvoir en ire, mais moderer vostre courage, car s'il plaist Dieu le tout puissant la verité sera congneue."

"Empereur," dit Pepin, "trop avez atendu. Car on dit communement que trop tard est de fermer l'estable quant le cheval est perdu. Or s'en est alee ma seur en exil (povre esgaree!) je ne sçay quelle part, dont bien me doit le cueur douloir quant il fault que pour vous je la perde, car je suis bien certain que jamais ne le[1] verray. Helas! on se doit bien garder de faire si hastif jugement car on a tost fait une male besongne de quoy on se repent apres tout a loisir. Et vous sçavez que renommee est chose chiere car quant on la pert, ou soit a tort ou soit a droit, on l'a tard recouvree. Peu avez prisee l'onneur de ma personne quant sans nulle deliberation ne avoir consideration que plusieurs telles choses souvent se font par envie..."[2]

En disant ces paroles l'empereur et le roy Pepin entrerent dedens Constantinoble en moult grant honneur. Et quant ilz furent dedens la cité, l'empereur voulut loger le roy Pepin et ses gens en son palays moult honestement. Mais le roy Pepin n'y voulut entrer, mais fit loger et tenir ses gens tous ensemble aupres de luy et ne voulut recepvoir de l'empereur ne dons ne presens quelconques, combien que de choses assés luy fit presenter, tant de vivres que de joyaulx riches paremens. Moult fut le roy Pepin en grant pensee de sa seur Bellisant car tous ceulx de la cité luy assermoient que c'estoit la meilleure dame que jamais fut trouvee et que par trahyson et injuste querelle elle avoit esté accusee et bannye.

---

[1] The *le* for a feminine antecedent (usually a Picardism in Old French) is rare in this text, but since it recurs several times (see Chapters 19, 28, and 29) I have let it stand.

[2] Sentence appears to be unfinished. See translation.

But King Pepin, who had a fiercely proud heart, cared nothing for his tears. He made no sign of feeling pity or compassion for the other's weeping, but instead spoke to him in the following manner, "Emperor, leave off crying and don't distress yourself for having lost my sister, for he who loses a whore shouldn't be upset. And since that is what my sister is, have no care or heartache for her sake."

"Oh!" said the emperor, "for heaven's sake, do not speak so of your sister, for I truly believe she was nothing but fidelity and honesty and was wrongly and without just cause cast off by me."

"By my faith," said Pepin, "then one should blame you all the more, and that way everyone will realize what great wisdom you should have had, for you were so quick to believe a single accusation that you cast off my sister shamefully like a public harlot. And I'll have you know that I am little inclined to love someone who brings such blame and dishonor to me and to the royal blood of France."

When the emperor Alexander heard the words and the thoughts of the king, he was quite upset and cut to the quick. However, he answered simply, "Please, my lord King Pepin, do not give in to wrath, rather moderate your feelings, for if it pleases God, the all-powerful, the truth will be known."

"Emperor," said Pepin, "it's too late. Everyone says that it is too late to close the stable door once the horse has escaped. Now, my sister (poor wandering soul!) has gone into exile I know not where, which I cannot help but be upset about since the fault is yours that I have lost her, for I am sure I will never see her again. Alas! one should be very careful about jumping to conclusions, for one rushes into trouble that one later regrets at one's leisure. And you know that reputation is a dear thing, for when one loses it, whether rightly or wrongly, it takes a long time to recover it. You cared little for my personal honor when without any deliberation or consideration of the fact that such things often occur through jealousy [you banished my sister]."

While speaking these words the emperor and King Pepin entered Constantinople with great pomp. Once they were in the city, the emperor wanted to lodge King Pepin and his people in the palace as befitted them. But King Pepin refused to enter, rather lodging and putting his people all together near him, and refused to receive any presents or offerings whatsoever from the emperor, however many things were presented to him, both provisions and sumptuous jewels. King Pepin was deep in thought about his sister Bellissant, for everyone in the city assured him that she was the best lady that every lived, and that only by treason and unjust allegation had she been accused and banished.

[CHAPITRE 9]

Comment le marchant et l'archevesque se combatirent pour sçavoir la verité de l'occasion de Bellissant; et comment l'archevesque si fut desconfit. ix. cha[pitre][1]

Tout ainsi que le jour fut venu que l'archevesque et le marchant se devoient ensemble combatre, [16recto]l'empereur les fist devant luy amener et commanda a eulx armer et incontinent pour parfaire l'entreprise de la chose encommencee. Adonc lx. chevaliers de la nation de l'archevesque l'alerent armer et fut richement et en pompes habillé. Et l'empereur si commanda que devant luy et en sa presence on amenast le marchant et qu'il fust armé aussi bien et en la maniere comme son propre corps. Et devant qu'il fust armé, l'empereur le fit chevalier et lui donna la colle en lui promettant donner villes, chasteaulx, et grandes richesses se par luy l'archevesque pouoit estre vaincu et desconfit. Et quant les deux si furent arméz et leurs blasons en leurs colz pendus, on amena leurs chevaulx et monterent dessus. Pour aler au coup, lors commanda l'empereur aux chevaliers et aux sergens qu'ilz acompaignassent l'archevesque jusques au lieu et que de luy ilz se donnassent garde afin que il ne peust fouir, car subtil estoit et homme cauteleux.

Le marchant fut monté sur son cheval, bien armé en tous lieux et forte espee sainte, sy chevauche vers le champ, et premier entra dedens. Apres luy alerent de la cité de Constantinoble sy grant nombre de peuple que fort seroit a le nombrer. Et ne demoura pas longuement que l'archevesque entra ou champ moult fort et haultement acompagné car il estoit moult riche et de noble nation.

La fut le roy Pepin qui moult voulentiers regarda le marchant.

"Mon amy, Dieu te doinst grace d'avoir victoire contre le faulx homme car par la foy de mon corps, se au jour d'ui par toy est vaincu l'archevesque et que la verité de ma seur je puisse au vray cognoistre, je te guerdonneray si haultement que de ma court te ferai premier et le plus grant."

"Sire," dit le marchant, "je vous mercie du bon vouloir que vers moy avez. Sachez de certain que j'ay fiance en Dieu et a la Vierge Marie qui me garderont le bon droit que j'ay en ceste querelle. En telle maniere que je demonstreray devant tous la trahyson de ce mauldit archevesque."

Ainsi dit le roy, "Dieu le veulle ottroyer a qui je te recommande."

A ces motz le marchant se departit devant le roy Pepin pour aler l'archevesque assaillir. Sy vint ung herault que tous deux les fit jurer et faire sermens acoustumés. Et apres le serment pris on fit le champ vuider et tout le peuple qui estoit dedens saillir hors, fors que les deux combatans.

---

[1] Woodcut of two armed and mounted knights jousting with rocks in background.

CHAPTER 9

How the merchant and the archbishop fought a duel in order to establish the truth concerning Bellissant; and how the archbishop was defeated.

When the day came that the archbishop and the merchant were to fight each other, the emperor had them brought before him, commanding them to arm themselves forthwith so as to conclude the matter between them. Thereupon sixty knights from the archbishop's country went to arm him, and he was richly and sumptuously arrayed. Then the emperor ordered that the merchant be armed in his presence and arrayed as well and in like manner to himself. But before arming him, the emperor knighted him, dubbing him and promising him cities, castles, and great wealth if he could defeat the archbishop. When both were fully armed, with their shields hung at their necks, their horses were brought and mounted. Finally, the emperor commanded the knights and officers to accompany the archbishop to the field and watch that he not escape, for he was a sly and crafty man.

The merchant, now mounted on his horse, well armed all around and girded with a stout sword, rode first into the field. Behind him entered so many people from the city of Constantinople that it would be impossible to count them. Not long after the archbishop entered the field with a lavish entourage, for he was quite rich and from a noble country.

King Pepin was also there, looking at the merchant with much interest.

"My friend, may God grant you victory over this false man, for, upon my soul, if you vanquish the archbishop today so that I can know the truth about my sister, I will reward you so lavishly that you will be first in my court."

"Sire," said the merchant, "I thank you for your goodwill towards me. You should know that I have absolute confidence in God and in the Virgin Mary to defend the right that I fight for in this quarrel. In this manner I will make manifest to all the treason of this cursed archbishop."

The king answered him, "May God, to whom I commend you, make it so."

After this speech the merchant left King Pepin to go attack the archbishop. A herald came up who made both combatants swear the usual oaths. Once that was done, the field was emptied; everyone left, except the two combatants.

Or sont il[s] sur les rens; si vindrent d'une part et d'aultre ceulx qui la charge en avoient leur presenter leurs lances et frapperent des esperons et vont l'ung a l'autre. Lors se rencontrerent si tresmerveilleusement que des copz qu'i[lz] donnerent les lances rompirent. Et tant fut le coup grant que tous deux sur leurs chevaulx passerent oultre. Et quant ilz furent au bout du champ ilz retournerent l'un sur l'autre leurs espees en mains et se joingnirent ensemble. Sy grant coup se donnent que les escus qu'i[lz] portoient font les pieces voler et cheoir a terre.

Quant l'archevesque vit que le marchant si rudement le assault, il pensa a luy que tant bien se tendroit que la nuyt seroit venue, et que telle estoit la loy que quant ung home appelloit l'autre de champ de bataille [16verso]il convenoit qu'il l'eust vaincu devant soleil couché ou il seroit pendu. Et pour ce se pensa l'archevesque de soy fermement tenir. Et le marchant, qui la coustume sçavoit, de tant plus s'efforçoit de faire fortes armes contre l'archevesque qui le suivit de pres et tant pressa les coups que du coup qu'il luy bailla luy abatit une oreille et une grande partie de son haubergon qui estoit de fin achier. Tant fut le coup grant et merveilleux que le marchant ne peult son espee retenir, mais luy cheust bas. Et quant le faulx archevesque vit que le marchant fut sans baton, il frappa son cheval d'estoc en telle maniere qu'il lui creva ung euil. Lors s'effroïa le cheval qui se sentit fort navré, et tant courut et saillit parmy le champ que le marchant getta bas. Tant luy fut fortune contraire qu'il demoura pendu par le pié a l'estrier de la celle. Et le cheval qui point n'aresta le traisna tant et si piteusement que tous ceulx de l'assemblee dolans et desplaisans en estoient et par eulx ilz disoient que du marchant il n'y avoit plus espoir ne resconfort.

Et quant le roy le vit, au martyre danger et inconvenie[n]t ausquelz le marchant estoit, il se prist a plourer moult piteusement en disant bassement, "Helas! helas! marchant, or voy je bien clerement que de tes jours il n'en y a plus en ce monde. Helas! or puis je bien cognoistre magnifestement et de certain que ma seur est coupable de l'occasion dont elle a esté chargee, et que Dieu veult monstrer evidamment a tous que a bon droit l'empereur de sa compaignie la degettee. Et s'elle eust esté de dessus les sains fons en terre portee et ensevelie bien eust esté heureuse et de bonne heure nee, car par elle est le noble sang de France a deshonneur livré. Et ainsi me soit Dieu amy que se je la tenoie je la feroie mourir de mort villaine et angoisseuse." Moult de divers souspirs fist le bon roy Pepin.

Et l'archevesque[1] en toute sa puissance faire son cheval vers le marchant aller ne peult ne de luy approcher qui bien sembloit estre chose miraculeuse. Or fut le marchant tant traisné par le champ de son cheval en telle maniere que le cheval cheut a terre. Et quant le cheval fut bas, le marchant se leva qui preux, vaillant et hardy fut, et quant l'archevesque aperceut le marchant qui estoit relevé, il vint courant a lui et lui donna deux ou trois coups si merveilleux que moult fut le marchant estonné et esturdy. Si se tira arriere pour reprendre son alaine,[2] puis

---

[1] Text has *archevesqui*.
[2] Text has *alaime*.

They lined up; those in charge brought them their lances; they spurred their horses and came at each other. Their first clash was so extraordinary that their blows shattered their lances. So great was the blow that each rode past the other. When they each reached the end of the field, they turned and came back to attack each other with sword in hand. They gave such blows that hacked-off pieces of their shields flew and fell to the ground.

When the archbishop saw the merchant assaulting him with such vigor, he began to think that he had better be able to hold on until nightfall, for the law said that when a man challenged another to a judicial duel, he had to conquer him before sunset or he would be hanged. And so the archbishop thought mainly about holding on. But the merchant, who also knew the custom, pushed himself all the more to do feats of arms against the archbishop, who pressed him closely and gave him such a blow that he whacked off an ear and a significant portion of his fine steel hauberk. It was such a mighty and terrible blow that the merchant could not hold on to his sword, but let it fall. When the false archbishop saw that the merchant was weaponless, he struck his horse with his sword in such a way that he gouged out one of his eyes so that the horse, feeling itself badly wounded, took fright, and set off running and bucking all over the field until he knocked the merchant off his back. His luck was so contrary that he remained hanging by his foot in the saddle stirrups, and the horse, who never stopped running, dragged him around in so pitiable a manner that everyone watching was worried and upset, saying to one another that there was no hope for the merchant.

When the king saw that the merchant was in such danger and distress, he began to weep most piteously, saying softly to himself, "Alas, alas, merchant, now I see quite clearly that your days are numbered. Alas! now I can't help seeing that my sister is indeed guilty of the offense for which she has been charged, and God is clearly demonstrating that the emperor was justified in casting her off. And if she had been carried from the holy font of baptism directly to the earth to be buried, then she would have been happy and fortunate, for by her the noble blood of France has been dishonored. I swear by almighty God, if I had her in my power, I would put her to a shameful and painful death." Good King Pepin sighed repeatedly.

Meanwhile the archbishop, despite all his strength, could not get his horse to approach the merchant, which seemed a miraculous occurrence. All this time the merchant was being dragged so much around the field by his own horse that finally the horse collapsed. Once he was down, the merchant stood up—brave, valiant, and hardy man!—and when the archbishop realized that the merchant had gotten up, he came galloping towards him and gave him two or three forceful blows that left the merchant stunned and dizzy. Drawing back to catch his breath, then advancing adroitly, he gathered his courage to strike the archbishop

s'avança subtillement et de grant courage frappa l'archevesque en telle maniere que a terre luy fist son espee cheoir, et oultre son harnoys le navra tellement que le sang luy fist en bas courir.

L'archevesque mist son cueur et sa force de soy venger et broche son cheval pour courir au marchant. Mais il fut subtil et tira ung grant couteau pointu et le getta contre le cheval de l'archevesque. Si le frappa au corps sy rudement que le cheval commença a regiber et saillir dont l'archevesque fut en trop grant[1] danger de cheoir bas. Et [17recto]au[2] saillir du cheval il perdit son escu et la le marchant le getta hors des licices[3] afin qu'il ne s'en peust plus ayder. Et quant il eut ce fait, il frappa son cheval de son espee par le ventre, tant qu'il l'abatit par terre et le cheval et l'archevesque. Lequel incontinent se releva, mais le marchant fut diligent qui si grant coup luy donna que tout plat l'abatit a terre. Et puis saillit sur luy et luy osta le heaume pour luy coupper la gorge. Et quant l'archevesque se vit en ce danger, plain fut de trahyson, et a dit au marchant, "Las! amy, je te prie que de moy veullez avoir pitié, et me donne temps et espace que je me puisse confesser, afin que mon ame ne puist estre en danger, car a toy je me rens comme vaincu et coupable."

Quant le marchant oÿt parler l'archevesque il fut courtois et debonnaire et se fia au beau parler de l'archevesque et le laissa lever. Et quant le faulx prestre fut sur les piéz levé il n'eut desir ne voulenté de soy confesser. Si a tantost prins et saisy le marchant et l'a tombé par terre, et a sailly dessus disant par moult grant ire, "Marchant, jamais ne m'eschaperas que mourir ne te face devant tout le monde oultrageusement et honteusement, ou tu feras a ma voulenté et du tout ce que je te commanderay."

"Ha!" dit le marchant, qui trahy se vit, "archevesque, je vois et cognois bien que je suis en vostre mercy et que de moy pouez du tout faire a vostre plaisir. Si vous prie que me dites quelle chose vous voulez que par vous je face et je l'acompliray, s'il vous plaist de moy sauver la vie."

"Marchant," dit l'archevesque, "voycy que tu feras. Je veul que devant l'empereur et le roy Pepin tu tesmoingneras en publique que a tort et sans cause tu m'as de ce fait occupé et accusé faulcement et par envye, et de ce fait tu me descharges et prenderas la charge par tel convenant que, se faire tu le veulx, je te jure et prometz toy de mort garder et faire ta paix devers l'empereur et le roy Pepin. Et en oultre plus je te jure en foy de gentillesse et de l'ordre de prestrise toy donner en mariage une mienne niepce que j'ay, moult riche, belle et plaisant et tresgracieuse. Si pourras bien dire que jamais en ton lignage plus eureulx ne plus riche ne fut trouvé. Et pour tant avise et considere se tu le veulx faire en telle maniere, et choisi ou de vivre ou de mourir, car par nulle aultre voye eschaper tu ne me pourras sans perdre la vie."

---

[1] Text has *trorp gant*.

[2] *c i* appears at bottom right corner of 17r.

[3] Not clear if this is a typographical error and should be amended to *lices* or if it is some variation on *liceïs*, attested to in Godefroy, meaning "collect. de *lice*, barrière."

in such a manner that not only did he make him drop his sword, but he wounded him so badly through his armor that the blood ran down.

The archbishop now gathered his courage and strength to avenge himself, spurring his horse to chase after the merchant. But he was clever and pulled out a large, sharp knife to throw at the archbishop's horse. He struck him so forcefully that the horse began to buck and jump, which put the archbishop in great danger of falling. Indeed as the horse jumped about he dropped his shield, whereupon the merchant threw it outside the lists so that it could no longer help him. Once this was done, he struck the archbishop's horse through the belly so that he sent both horse and rider to the ground. The archbishop rose immediately, but the merchant was quick to deal him a mighty blow that sent him sprawling to the ground. He pounced on his adversary, wrenching off his helmet to slash his throat. However, when the archbishop, who was full of treachery, saw himself in danger, he said to the merchant, "Please, friend, I beg you to have pity on me and give me time and space to confess so that my soul will not be in danger, for I give myself up to you as one both vanquished and guilty."

When the merchant heard the archbishop, he reacted courteously and humanely, and, believing the archbishop's words, let him get up. But once the false-hearted priest was on his feet, he had no desire at all to confess. Rather he grabbed hold of the merchant, brought him to the ground and jumped on him, saying furiously, "Merchant, you will never escape me—either you will do exactly what I tell you to do, or I will kill you horribly and shamefully in front of everyone."

"Oh," said the merchant, who saw himself betrayed, "archbishop, I realize that I am at your mercy and that you can do with me as you like. I beg you to tell me what you want me to do and I will do it, if you will only spare my life."

"Merchant," said the archbishop, "here is what you must do. I want you to testify publicly before the emperor and King Pepin that you accused me of this deed wrongly and without cause, that you did it falsely and through jealousy, and that you take back your accusation and rescind your charge so that, if you wish it, I promise to keep you from death and make peace between you and the emperor and King Pepin. Moreover, I swear to you by noble faith and my priestly order to give you in marriage to a niece of mine who is rich, beautiful, graceful and agreeable. You will be able to say that no one of your lineage has ever been as rich or happy as you will be. And so think carefully if you want to do as I say, and choose either to live or to die, for there is no way you will be able to escape me without losing your life."

Incontinent que le marchant entendit l'archevesque ainsi parler il fut moult pensif et dolent et non sans cause. Sy reclama en soy Dieu et la Vierge Marie que son bon droit luy voulsissent garder et preserver de mort. Puis respondit en telle maniere, "Sire archevesque, vostre rayson est belle et bonne et suis prest du tout vous complaire et obeÿr, en moy fiant que foy et loyaulté vous me ferés et tiendrés."

"Oy," dit l'archevesque, "je ne vous feray faulte."

"Or de par Dieu," dist le marchant," allons vers l'empereur et les barons; si vous descouperay de la tres[17verso]grant injure que contre vous j'ay proposee."

"C'est bien dit. Or vous relevés sus et vous viendrés avec moy."

A ces motz le marchant se leva sus. Et quant il fut levé il se recorda de l'archevesque qui trahy l'avoit, soy faingnant de soy vouloir confesser et comme devant est mention faicte, dont il prist en luy courage et se pensa de luy jouer de pareil tour, car on dit voulentiers que trahyson est telle que tousjours retourne a son maistre. Lors prist l'archevesque de sy grant courage que tost dessoubz luy l'abatit. Puis luy dit, "Archevesque, bons m'avez aprins a jouer de ce jeu. Et pensés de vous confesser a moy car aultre confesseur n'aurez que moyen."

Or pensa[1] l'archevesque par plusieurs fictions et parolles faire tant que du marchant il se peust deffaire, mais le marchant jamais plus en luy ne se confia, ne il ne luy donne plus temps ne espace de soy relever. Mais tantost et a grant diligence lui creva les deux yeulx, et tant de coups luy donna que de soy revencher n'eut force ne pouoir. Et quant le marchant vit qu'il estoit a son pouoir et liberal arbitre subget et submis, et que de luy plus ne doubtoit, a terre le laissa et se leva et appella les gardes du champ, puis leur dit, "Seigneurs, ycy pouez cognoistre se j'ay fait mon devoir de l'archevesque, s'il est vaincu. Vous voyez que je l'ay mys en tel point que quant bon me semblera, je le puis tuer et occyre a mon apetit. Et pour tant je vous prie que il vous plaise faire venir par deça l'empereur Alexandre et le roy Pepin, afin que [puissent escouter] toutes leurs haultes magnificences et triumphantes seigneuries l'archevesque confesse[r][2] par devant tous a droite querelle estre par moy accusé, et injustement et sans cause avoir prins la deffence contre moy."

Lors allerent les gardes du camp querir l'empereur Alexandre et le roy Pepin, lesquelz vindrent et de plusieurs barons acompaignéz au lieu ou estoit l'archevesque dolent et confondu. Sy luy prist l'empereur a demander la verité de tout le fait, et le faulx archevesque devant tous recogneust le fait et la maniere, et comment a tort avoit contre la noble dame Bellissant parlé, et sans nulle cause son exil par fallace et mauvaise trahyson pourchassé. Helas, pensés quantes piteuses larmes de dueil angoisseux alors getta l'empereur, car tant furent ses crys piteux et sez lamentations dolentes, que l'abondance des larmes de ses yeulx descendoient de toutes pars, et sa face arrousoient en telle façon et maniere que tous ceulx

---

[1] Text has *psa*.

[2] There seem to be some words missing. I have attempted an emendation (in brackets) to help the sentence make sense.

As soon as the merchant heard what the archbishop said, he was very pensive and sorrowful and not without reason. He silently prayed to God and to the Virgin Mary to watch over him and keep him from death. Then he answered in the following manner, "My lord archbishop, your reasoning is good and right, and I am ready to obey and do as you ask, trusting you to keep your word to me."

"Yes," said the archbishop, "I will not let you down."

"Well then, by God," said the merchant, "let us go to the emperor and his barons; I will retract the grave accusation I made against you."

"Well said. Now get up and you will come with me."

At those words, the merchant rose. When he was up he remembered how the archbishop had betrayed him, pretending to want to confess, as was told you before. From that he took courage and thought to play him a similar trick, for, as people say all the time, treachery always returns to its master. So he took hold of the archbishop with such determination that he soon had him pinned under him. Then he said to him, "Archbishop, you taught me well to play this game. Now think about making your confession to me, for no other confessor or means will you have."

The archbishop racked his brains for a subterfuge or words by which he could overcome the merchant, but the merchant knew better than ever to trust him again, nor would he give him time or space to get up. Instead, with impressive speed and force he gouged out both of his eyes, giving him so many blows that there was no possibility of his having the strength or ability to defend himself. Then when the merchant saw that he was in his power, completely subject to his will, so that there was no further reason to fear him, he left him on the ground, rose up, and called the guards on the field, telling them, "My lords, you can see here whether I have fulfilled my charge concerning the archbishop, whether he be vanquished. You see that I have overcome him to such a point that I could kill him if and when I liked. For that reason I beg you please to call Emperor Alexander and King Pepin, so that their majesties and their lords may hear the archbishop confess in front of everyone rightly to have been accused by me, and unjustly and without cause to have taken up his defense against me."

Thereupon the field guards went to get Emperor Alexander and King Pepin, who came accompanied by many barons to the place where the archbishop lay powerless and in great pain. The emperor demanded to know the truth about everything, and the false archbishop finally revealed publicly what he had done, how he had wrongly accused the noble lady Bellissant, seeking her banishment without just cause but through lies and evil treachery. Alas, think how many piteous tears of anguished grief were shed by the emperor! So pitiful were his cries, so sorrowful his lamentations, that the abundance of his tears flowed everywhere,

qui les veoient sy grant dueil demener, estoient contrains a plourer et souspirer pour la pitié de luy.

Et se l'empereur demena grant dueil, ne demandez pas se le roy Pepin estoit alors en tristesse et desconfort. Helas! ce n'estoit[1] pas sans cause que si grant dueil demenoient quant ilz veirent et cogneurent que trop legier croire et par faulce trahyson perdu avoient la belle et plaisante Bellissant, [18recto]seur[2] du roy Pepin, le roy de France, de l'empereur espouse. Et fut entre l'empereur et le roy joie en tristesse en deux pars assemblee—joye pour le roy qui de sa seur congneust la loyauté preudommie, douleur et desplaisance pour l'empereur qui du fait se trouva coulpable pour tant que alors sceut et congneust que a tort et sans cause l'avoit dechassee d'avec luy.

Et apres toutes lamentations, la confession de l'archevesque oÿr et de sa trahyson, l'empereur assembla son conseil pour aviser et juger de quelle mort l'archevesque mouroit. Si fut deliberé qu'il seroit boully en huylle tout vif, et ainsi fut fait.

Apres lequel jugement chascun se retire en son repaire. Et quant le roy Pepin fut retrait en son logis, l'empereur dolent et souspirant vint par devers luy et mist les genoulx a terre, puis luy dist en plourant, "Helas! sire, trop ay vers vous commis crisme detestable et deshonneste. Or voy je clerement ma faulte miserable et honteuse, et cognois que par ma folie et legiere credence je suis et ay esté cause de vostre seur mettre en exil et perdition. De laquelle chose je vous requiers pardon, et devant vous je me presente comme coulpable vostre grace expectant. Et en recognoissant ma faulte villennie et pour satisfacion et amende je rens et remay du tout en voz mains le royaulme de Grece qui justement et de bon droit est a moy et apartient, car jamais je ne quiers avoir nom d'empereur ne de roy tant que sur terre serez en vye. Mais veul comme servant du tout a vous obeïr car bien l'ay deservy."

Quant le roy Pepin entendit le bon vouloir et la grant humilité de l'empereur, de luy print pitié et luy pardonna par devant tous les barons. Et apres leur paix faicte par ung commun acord, deliberent entre eulx d'envoier par tous païs messaigiers pour la noble dame Bellissant querir et serchier. Apres lesquelles choses Pepin print congié de l'empereur pour retourner en France.

---

[1] Text has *ce ne n'estoit*.

[2] *c ii* appears at bottom right corner of 18r.

drenching his face so thoroughly that everyone who saw his bereavement could not help weeping and sighing out of pity for him.

And if the emperor mourned, no need to ask if King Pepin was also sad and upset. Alas! It was not without reason that they grieved so when they realized that by gullibility and by false treachery they had lost the fair and lovely Bellissant, sister of King Pepin, the king of France, and wife of the emperor. Both the emperor and the king felt joy and sadness at the same time—joy for the king who could now see his sister's noble fidelity, grief and displeasure for the emperor who knew he was guilty in this matter, realizing that wrongly and without just cause he had cast her off from him.

After all the expressions of grief and hearing the archbishop's confession of his treason, the emperor assembled his council to take advice on what sentence to pass on the archbishop. It was decided that he be boiled alive in oil, and so it was done.

After the judgment was carried out everyone retired to his dwelling. But when King Pepin was in his lodging, the emperor, sad and full of sighs, came to see him, dropping to his knees to say to him through his tears, "Alas, my lord, I have committed a hateful and dishonorable offense against you. Now you see clearly my miserable and shameful error, and realize that through my foolish gullibility I was the cause of placing your sister on the road to exile and perdition. I beg your pardon for this, and present myself as a guilty petitioner for your mercy. In recognition of my false villainy and to make amends to you, I remit to your hands the kingdom of Greece which by right belongs to me, for never will I seek to have the name of emperor or king as long as you are alive. Rather I wish to obey you like a servant, for that is what I deserve."

When King Pepin heard the good will and the great humility of the emperor, he took pity on him and forgave him in the presence of all the barons. After they made their peace by common accord, they decided between themselves to send messengers everywhere to seek the noble lady Bellissant. After these events Pepin took leave of the emperor to return to France.

[CHAPITRE 10]

Comment le roy Pepin print congié de l'empereur et partist de Constantinoble pour retourner en France; et comment apres il ala a Romme contre les Sarrasins que la cité avoient prinse. x. cha[pitre][1]

Le roy Pepin se partit de Constantinoble apres les choses dessudites, et tant chevaucha qu'il arriva en France et s'en ala a Orleans pour soy refreschir, car voulentiers estoit oudit lieu pour le deduit des forez qui sont a l'environ. Si commanda que pour sa bienvenue on feist table ronde, et ainsi [18verso]fut fait.

Et quant vint a l'eure de plain disner, le chevalier que Valentin avoit nourry et a qui le roy l'avoit donné, le print par la main et le presenta devant le roy en luy disant, "Sire, vecy le povre orphenin que vous trouvastes en la forest d'Orleans, et lequel vous me baillastes pour nourrir et garder. Or l'ay je nourry jusques a ceste heure presente tel que vous le voyez, non pas a mes despens mais aux vostres. Si vous supplie, chier sire, que de l'enfant veullez avoir memoire, car tost deviendra[2] grant, si est temps de penser."

Et quant il eut oÿ le chevalier parler, il appella l'enfant Valentin, et le print par la main. Si le vit tant saige et bien aprins en meurs et condicions, que de celle heure luy donna toutes les couppes, tasses, pos, gobelés et aultres riches vaisselles qui pour lors estoit aprestee a la court servir. Puis a dit le roy devant tous les princes de sa court qu'i veult que Valentin soit chierement gardé et doulcement nourry. Et pour la grande beaulté et honneur de sa personne le roy voulut et ordonna que le jeune enfant Valentin, qui n'avoit lors que xii. ans, fut mis et nourri avec sa fille Esglentine qui tant estoit belle et saige et bonne et bien aprise, que tout le monde en disoit honneur et bien. Les deux enfans furent nourris[3] ensemble, et aimerent bien l'ung l'autre d'amour juste et loyale en telle maniere qu'ilz ne sçavoient avoir liesse l'ung sans l'autre, et principalement Esglentine, fille du roy, voyant et considerant la prudence de Valentin fut tant d'amour esprise en honneur et bien que sans luy ne peult avoir soulas ne recreation.

Valentin devint grant et de belle estature, en toutes choses bien aprins. Il aima fort chevalx et armes et voulentiers il se trouva en joustes et tournois. Et la ou il se trouvoit il emportoit le pris et l'onneur. Alors le roy, voyant sa vaillance et la bonne voulenté et courage de luy, il luy donna chevaulx et harnoys, terres, tenemens, rentes et grandes possessions, si que ne demeura pas longtemps que de luy fut bruit par toute la court, dont plusieurs eurent sur luy maintes fois envye. Et souvent luy

---

[1] Woodcut of mounted figures, led by a crowned horseman, riding toward a distant city on a hill.

[2] Text has *devinndra*.

[3] Text has *tourris*.

CHAPTER 10

How King Pepin took leave of the emperor and left Constantinople to return to France; and how afterwards he went to Rome to fight the Saracens who had taken the city.

King Pepin left Constantinople after the events described above. He rode until he arrived in France and went straight to Orleans to refresh himself, for he was glad to be in that place because of the sport in the forests around there. He commanded that a round table be set up for his welcome, and so it was done.

When it was time for dinner, the knight to whom the king had given Valentin and who had brought him up took him by the hand and presented him to the king, saying, "Sire, here is the poor orphan whom you found in the forest of Orleans, whom you gave to me to raise and take care of. I have done so up to the present time, as you can see, not at my expense but at yours. Therefore I beg you, most gracious sire, to remember the boy, for soon he will be grown and it is time to think about such things."

Once the king had heard what the knight had to say, he called the lad Valentin and took him by the hand. Seeing how wise and well-bred he was in comportment and temperament, he gave him right then and there all sorts of chalices, cups, pots, goblets, and other costly vessels that were used at the time to serve at court. Then the king said in the presence of all the princes of his court that he wanted Valentin to be taken care of lovingly and brought up gently. And for the great beauty and honor of his person, the king desired and ordered that the young child Valentin, who was no older than twelve at the time, be brought up and raised with his daughter Esglentine, who was so beautiful, wise, good, and well-bred that everyone spoke well of her. The two children were raised together and loved each other with a proper and devoted love in such a way that they couldn't be happy without one another, especially Esglentine, daughter of the king, who, seeing and noting Valentin's abilities, was so smitten with an honorable love that without him she could have no comfort or rest.

Valentin grew tall and of handsome stature, and was well-educated in all things. He adored horses and arms, gladly participating in jousts and tourneys. Whenever he took part he took away the prize and the honor. Therefore the king, seeing his valor, good will, and courage, gave him horses and armor, lands, fields, endowments, and valuable possessions, so that it wasn't very long before everyone at court was talking about him, which caused some people to be quite jealous of

disoient en reproche que ce n'estoit que ung trouvé et ung povre sans cognoissance de nul parens, pour Dieu nourry et eslevé, desquelles parolles Valentin plouroit souvent. Et quant la belle Esglentine le veoit couroucer, elle plouroit tendrement et de toute sa puissance elle le resconfortoit. Et Valentin en la court du roy Pepin entre les barons, chevaliers, dames et demoiselles si bien et gracieusement se gouvernoit que nul ne sçavoit dire de luy fors que tout bien et honneur.

Et son frere Orson est dedens la forest velu et couvert de poil tout ainsi come ung ours, menant vie de beste sauvage ainsi que devant est mencion faite, et comment en cestuy chapitre vous sera declairé. Car sachez que bien tost apres la venue du roy Pepin luy estant a Orleans, vint ung messagier envoié de par le pape, lequel secours, aide, et confort luy demandoit contre les paiens et ennemis de la foy chrestienne qui avoient prinse Romme. Et quant le roy Pepin entendit que les Sarra[19recto]sins[1] estoient dedens Romme il fit en toute diligence son armee aprester, laquelle Valentin fut fait chief et principal gouverneur.

Et quant Esglentine sceut que Valentin s'en va, moult fut dolente et courroucee, comme celle qui l'amoit et tenoit chier entre tous les aultres. Adonc le manda la belle tout secretement pour parler a luy.

Et quant il fut venu elle luy dit en souspirant moult tendrement, "Helas! Valentin, mon amy, or voy je bien que vous n'aurez plus ne joie ne consolation quant departir vous fault pour aler en bataille. Helas! vous estes ma seule amour, mon seul confort et refuge de ma plaisance. Or pleust a Dieu que je[2] n'eusse parent ny amy en ce monde qui me gardast de faire ma voulenté. Car ainsi me veulle Dieu aider que jamais aultre que vous n'auroye en mariage, si seriez roy de France et je seroie rayne."

"Ah, madame," dit Valentin, "laissez vostre ymagination et n'ayez le cueur dessus moy si ardant, car vous sçavez que je suis ung povre donné, pour Dieu nourry a la court de vostre pere, et que je ne suis en nulle maniere homme qui vaille de vous ne de la plus povre demoiselle qui soit avec vous. Pensez aultre part et faites en maniere que vous monstrez de quel lien vous estes extraite. Et a Dieu, je vous dy, qui vous veulle avoir en sa garde."

A ces motz se partit Valentin et laissa Esglentine dolente et esplouree pour son departement.

Le roy et tout son ost est prest pour monter a cheval et partent d'Orleans pour aler devers Romme. Lors le roy Pepin appella les seigneurs de sa court et leur dit ainsi, "Vous sçavez que tout le monde fait bruit d'ung homme sauvaige lequel est dedens ceste forest, pour quoy j'ay grant vouloir et affection de le veoir prendre devant que je voise et passe plus oultre."

A ces parolles se consentirent et acorderent tous les seigneurs de la court. La chasse fut ordonnee et entrerent ou bois. Ilz prindrent plusieurs bestes sauvages, mais de trouver Orson le sauvage chascun en avoit grant paour fors que Valentin

---

[1] *c iii* appears at bottom right of 19r.
[2] Text has *le*.

him. As a result they reproached him often with the fact that he was no more than a poor foundling with no knowledge of who his parents were, that he was a charity case, words that often made Valentin weep. When the fair Esglentine saw him get upset, she wept bitterly and comforted him as best she could. But Valentin conducted himself so well and with such grace in the court of King Pepin among all the barons, knights, ladies, and maidens that no one could report anything about him that wasn't good and honorable.

In the meantime his brother Orson lived in the forest, hairy and covered with fur just like a bear, leading the life of a wild beast, as was mentioned before and will be further explained to you in this chapter. For know that soon after King Pepin returned to Orleans, a messenger sent by the pope came to request help, aid, and support against the pagans and enemies of the Christian faith who had taken over Rome. When King Pepin heard that the Saracens were in Rome, he hastened to prepare his army of which Valentin was made the leader.

When Esglentine found out that Valentin was leaving, she was very sad and upset, as one who loved him and held him dearer than anyone else. Therefore the fair maiden sent for him secretly to speak to him.

When he arrived she said to him, sighing deeply, "Alas! Valentin, my dear, now I see that you will have no more joy or consolation, for you must leave to go off to battle. Alas! you are my only love, my only comfort and refuge of my delight. May it please God that no parent or friend in this world keep me from following my inclination. God help me if ever I marry anyone other than you, for you would be king of France and I would be queen."

"Ah, my lady," said Valentin, "don't let your imagination run wild and don't set your heart on me so ardently, for you know I am a poor foundling, a charity case at your father's court, and in no way a man to deserve you or even the poorest of the young ladies in your service. Place your thoughts elsewhere and act in a manner commensurate with the lineage from which you are descended. I must say goodbye, and may God keep you."

With these words Valentin withdrew, leaving Esglentine sad and tearful because of his departure.

The king and his host were ready to mount their horses and leave Orleans for Rome. At that point King Pepin called together the nobles of his court and said to them, "You know that everyone talks about the wild man in this forest, for which reason I have a great desire to see if we can capture him before going any further."

All the nobles of the court consented and agreed with the king's spoken wish. The hunt was organized and they entered the woods. They captured many wild beasts, but everyone was afraid of finding Orson the wild man, except for

qui estoit son frere, lequel desiroit sur tous avoir a luy bataille. Tant alerent et coururent parmy le bois que le roy Pepin vint arriver devant la fosse obscure ou se tenoit Orson le sauvage. Et quant il vit le roy il saillit hors subitement et courut contre luy. Si le print et saisit des ongles qu'il avoit grans et le getta a terre moult durement. Et le roy qui cuida mourir cria hault demandant secours. Si vint vers luy ung vaillant chevalier, et quant il vit le sauvage qui vouloit estrangler le roy, il tira son espee pour luy courir sus. Et quant Orson vit l'espee nue flamboier et reluyre, il laissa le roy et courut au chevalier, et le print et le serra par si grant courage que homme et cheval il getta par terre. Lors le cheval se releva sus qui eut paour et s'en fuit parmy le bois, et Orson tint le chevalier, lequel a ses ongles agus l'estrangla et piteusement mist par pieces. Et quant le roy vint a ses gens qui par le bois estoient, ausquelz il raconta le danger ou il avoit esté [19verso]et la mort piteuse du chevalier, desquelles nouvelles oÿr moult furent esbahis tous ceulx qui la furent presens. Adonc se sont mis ensemble et sont aléz vers la fosse de Orson pour le cuider prendre et tuer. Ilz ont bien trouvé le chevalier, mais Orson n'ont point veu car a Dieu ne plaisoit pas qu'il fust conquis fors que de son frere Valentin, lequel prendra Orson ainsi que vous oréz. Et quant le roy vit que le sauvaige ne peult avoir ne prendre, il se laissa a tant pour ceste fois et se mist en chemin pour son voyage parfaire a Romme.

Les batailles furent arengees et l'oriflamble de France baillee a ung moult vaillant chevalier qui avoit nom Millon d'Angler, saige et de tresbonne conduite. La furent presens Gervais et Sanson, son frere, qui vailla[n]s chevaliers estoient, et plusieurs aultres ducz, contes et barons. Or on tant chevauche que ilz ont passé le pays de Savoye et Lombardie et toutes les Ytalyes. Puis sont venuz a Romme et ont demandé la bataille et la maniere et le fait des Sarrasi[n]s. Et on leur a conté comment ung admiral riche et puissant et de fier courage avoit la cité de Romme prinse, et plusieurs crestiens mis a mort et destruis, et avoit deffaites les esglises et fait les temples des ydoles, et la contraingnoit pape, cardinaulx, archevesques et evesques a servir et officier en la mode et maniere de leur loy mauldicte et tresdampnable. Et quant le roy Pepin oÿt et entendit ces nouvelles il fut moult dolent, piteulx et desplaisant de la grande misere, griefve et douloureuse destresse en quoy les povrez crestiens estoient detenus. Il aprocha la cité de Romme et fist son ost assembler ses gens d'armes et mettre en point, et ses batailles constituer et ordonner, car du tout eut courage et voulenté de la foy crestienne venger et deffendre. Laquelle chose il fit comme apres il est declairé plus au long.

Apres que le roy Pepin eut assiegé la cité de Romme il appella ses barons et chevaliers et leur dit en ceste maniere, "Seigneurs, vous sçavez et cognoissez que ce chien admiral infidele et ennemy de nostre foy a mis plusieurs vaillans crestiens a mort, et a vituperé l'esglise de Romme ou Nostre Seigneur Jesucrist estoit tant devotement servi et honnouré. Lesquelles choses nous doivent commouvoir a pitié et a larmez. Et pour tant je suis deliberé, a l'ayde de Jesus nostre createur, moy confiant, de combatre et expeller les paiens et Sarrasins hors de la cité de Romme et de tous les pays. Si avisez par entre vous lequel vouldra entreprendre la

Valentin who was his brother and who desired more than anyone to fight him. They covered such a distance galloping through the forest that finally King Pepin came to the dark gully where the wild Orson lurked. When he saw the king he burst forth suddenly and ran at him. He took hold of him, seizing him with his long nails and hurling him forcefully to the ground. The king, who thought he was about to die, cried out for help. A valiant knight came running to him, and when he saw the wild man who was trying to strangle the king, he drew his sword to attack him. But when Orson saw the naked blade glimmer and sparkle, he dropped the king and darted over to the knight, seizing him and gripping him with such great strength that he flung both man and horse to the ground. At that point the terrified horse leapt up and went tearing off through the woods, while Orson held onto the knight, strangling him with his sharp nails and tearing him to pieces in a most ghastly way. When the king located his men who were scattered in the woods, he recounted the danger he had been in and the pitiful death of the knight, which horrified everyone present. As a consequence, they gathered together and went to Orson's gully, thinking to capture and kill him. They did indeed find the knight, but Orson was not to be found, for it did not please God that he be conquered by anyone save his brother Valentin, who will capture Orson as you will hear. But when the king saw that there was no way to lay hold of the wild man, he gave up for the present and began his journey to Rome.

The battalions were organized and the oriflamme of France entrusted to a most valiant knight called Millon d'Angler, a wise and highly competent man. Also present were Gervais and Samson, his brother, both stalwart knights, and many other dukes, counts, and barons. They rode steadily until they passed the lands of Savoy and Lombardy and all of the Italies. Then they came to Rome where they sought war and asked for information on the Saracens' situation. They were told how an emir, wealthy, powerful, and fiercely brave, had taken the city of Rome. He had put to death many Christians and destroyed churches to set up temples with idols, and now was forcing the pope, the cardinals, archbishops, and bishops to officiate and serve there in the cursed and damnable fashion of their religion. When King Pepin heard this report he was extremely sad and upset, and filled with pity for the terrible misery, grief, and painful distress in which the poor Christians were caught. He approached the city of Rome, commanding his host to have the soldiers assemble and arm, and to set up the battalions, as he was eager to avenge and defend the Christian faith. This was all done as will be told to you presently.

After King Pepin laid siege to the city of Rome, he called together his barons and knights and spoke to them in the following manner: "My lords, you are fully aware that this infidel dog of an emir, enemy of our faith, has put numerous valiant Christians to death, and has insulted the church of Rome where our Lord Jesus Christ had always been so devotedly served and honored. These things cannot but move us to pity and tears. For that reason I am determined to fight and expel the pagans and Saracens from the city of Rome and all the country around with the help of Jesus, our creator, in whom I place my trust. Decide among

charge d'aler porter a celuy admiral de par moy une lettre de deffiance. Car je luy veul livrer et bailler journee et combatre pour nostre saincte foy exaulcer, soustenir et deffendre jusques a la mort."

Quant le roy eut ainsi parlé [20recto]nul[1] ne se traist avant pour la responce donner. De ce fait nul ne s'en ose entreprendre fors l'enfant Valentin, qui devant le roy se presenta et parla devant tous en disant, "Sire, s'il vous plaist, a vostre licence, je veul entreprendre le message et parleray devant tous, paiens et leur fier admiral, en telle maniere que a l'aide de Dieu et de sa doulce mere vous cognoisterés que j'aray fait vostre messaige a vostre prouffit et a mon honneur."

Du grant vouloir et du vaillant courage de Valentin fut le roy moult joyeulx, et tous ceulx de la court esmerveilléz. Adonc appella le roy ung secretaire auquel il fit escripre lettres de deffiance, puis les bailla a Valentin pour porter a l'admiral payen. Et Valentin monta a cheval et la prit congié du roy et de tous ceulx de la court, puis s'est mis en chemin en la garde de Dieu soy recommandant, et s'en est venu a Romme. Si ne fault pas demander si fut voulentiers regardé, car tant beau se contenoit a cheval et en armes que nul ne le voit qui grant plaisir n'y prengne.

Or ala vers le palais ou estoit l'admiral qui en ses salles estoit triumphantement et en grant pompes. Valentin entra dedens et vint devant l'admiral et le salua en telle maniere, "Jhesus, qui nasquit de la Vierge Marie et qui pour nous tous souffrit mort et passion, veulle garder de mal et deffendre le hault et puissant roy Pepin. Et Mahommet de telle puissance qu'i te veulle aider et secourir, redoubté admiral, ainsi que je vouldroye."

Quant Valentin eult ainsi parlé l'admiral se[2] leva et comme fier et orgueilleux a dit, "Messagier Valentin, retourne toy afin que plus je ne te voye. Si dy au roy Pepin qui de Jhesus tient la loy, qu'il croie en Mahommet et que sa creance renonce et du tout en tout delaisse et mette bas. Ou sachez de certain que je suis deliberé de le faire mourir et tout son païs destruire. Or t'en va, messaiger, et plus ne fay devant moy de demouree car de oÿr tes parolles mon cuer ne le peult souffrir.[3] Grant folie as entrepris que si fierement es entré[4] dans mon palais pour telle chose devant ma haulte seigneurie et dire. Or saches bien que se je sçavoye que par ton orgueil ou presumption tu eusses ceste chose entreprise, jamais vers le roy Pepin tu ne retournerois."

Quant Valentin oÿt le fier parler de l'admiral, il fut fort doubteux, craintif, et esmerveillé, et non pas sans cause, car la mort luy estoit prochaine se de Dieu

---

[1] *c iiii* appears at bottom right of 20r.
[2] Text has *le*.
[3] Text has *fouffrir*.
[4] Text has *as entré*. According to R. Gardner and M. Greene, "*Estre* was required as the auxiliary verb in the compound tenses of certain intransitive verbs, such as *naistre, mourir, aler, venir* (and its derivatives), *partir, entrer*, etc., the same as in Modern French:" Rosalyn Gardner and Marion A. Greene, *A Brief Description of Middle French Syntax* (Chapel Hill: University of North Carolina Press, 1958), 42.

yourselves who is willing to take on the job of carrying a challenge from me to this emir, for I wish to engage him in battle in order to glorify, sustain, and defend unto the death our holy faith."

When the king had thus spoken, no one stepped forward to answer him. No one dared undertake this deed except for the lad Valentin, who presented himself before the king and spoke in front of everyone saying, "Sire, if it please you to give me permission, I would like to carry the message and speak before them all, the pagans and their doughty emir, so that, with the help of God and His gentle mother, you will see that I have delivered your message to your benefit and my honor."

The king was thrilled with Valentin's firm resolution and bold heart, while everyone from the court marveled. Then the king called a secretary to write the challenge, then gave it to Valentin to bring to the pagan emir. Valentin mounted his horse, took leave of the king and all those of his court, and set off, commending himself to God's keeping, and so came to Rome. No need to ask if he was looked at eagerly, for he was so handsome riding his horse fully armed that there was no one who saw him who didn't take great pleasure in the sight.

He rode to the palace to find the emir who sat triumphantly in his hall, surrounded by great splendor. Valentin entered, coming up to the emir and greeting him in the following manner: "May Jesus, who was born of the Virgin Mary and who suffered death and passion for us all, keep from harm and defend the exalted and powerful King Pepin. And may Mohammed aid and succor you with such power as I would wish him to have, worthy emir."

Once Valentin had finished, the emir rose up, declaring proudly, "Messenger Valentin, go back where you came from and get out of my sight. Tell King Pepin, who clings to the religion of Jesus, to put his faith in Mohammed, renouncing and suppressing his present belief. Otherwise I am determined to kill him and destroy his country. Now go away, messenger—don't remain in my presence, for I will not abide your words. It was great folly for you to undertake so arrogantly to come into my palace and make such a speech in my exalted presence. And realize that if I knew you to have come here on account of your own arrogance or presumption, never would you return to King Pepin."[1]

When Valentin heard the emir's haughty speech, he was both amazed and quite afraid, and not without cause, for his death would have been quick in coming had God not consoled him. But so inspired by God was he that he gave a

---

[1] The emir has obviously picked up on the mockery in Valentin's greeting which can be read with a double meaning. He lets him go on the assumption that the mockery is from Pepin.

n'eut esté consolé. Mais tant fut de Dieu inspiré qu'il donna responce solitaire, tant pour la vie du corps que pour la vie de l'ame. Et comme saige, bien avisé et aprins de responce donner parla en telle maniere, "Helas! treshault et puissant admiral, ne veullez penser ne premediter que par orgueil je soye venu devant vostre magnificence, car, sire, quant vous sçaurez la maniere et le fait comme je suis venu vous seriez tous esmerveilléz."

"Dy nous comment tu es venu et tout ton cas, car ainsi me soit Mahommet en aide que je prendray plaisir, confort [20verso]et consolation a oÿr vostre entreprise reciter et vostre courage multiplier en tout honneur et bien."

Lors parla Valentin et dit, "Sire admiral, il est vray et certain que par faulce et desloyalle envye j'ay esté accusé devers le roy Pepin, et luy a on dit que de grant peur et de grant crainte que j'avoye de me trouver aux armes je vouloye retourner en France. Pour laquelle chose le roy est contre moy couroucé et plain d'ire. Hier matin me fit prendre pour moy faire la teste couper. Et quant je me veis en ce danger, pour alonger ma vie, je me vantay devant tous d'une tres grant folie, car je juray devant tous ceulx de la court que je viendroye devers vous pour vous et tous voz barons deffier de par le roy Pepin. Et oultre plus je me vantay que au departir de vous je demanderoye trois coups de lance sur vostre corps qui tant en vaillant et renommé pour loz et bruit acquerir. Pour tant je vous supplie que ceste chose m'acordez, car aultrement devant le roy Pepin no[n] seroye retourner que mourir ne me feist."

"Beau filz," dit l'admiral, "par Mahommet le tout puissant, vous n'en serez point escondit, mais vous ottroye de ceste heure la jouste. Et afin que les François qui ceste cité ont assiegé puissent veoir vostre vaillance, je feray hors de la ville les joustes appareiller et ordonner."

"Grant mercis," dit Valentin qui a terre se getta pour baiser les piéz de l'admiral en signe de humilité et obeïssance. Mais on dit en commun proverbe que on deschausse souvent le soulier dont on vouldroit avoir coupé le pié.

Valentin estoit renommé ou palais de l'admiral en fort grande pensee, tousjours priant et requerant Dieu qu'i luy donnast puissance de tant faire, qu'il peust sçavoir et cognoistre de quel lieu il estoit venu et qui estoit son pere et sa mere. Et ainsi qu'il estoit en grant pensee l'admiral luy print a dire, "Beau sire, vous me semblez moult pensif et pesant."

"Il est vray," dit Valentin, "et non pas sans cause, car j'ay trop grant doubte d'estre par vous en la jouste occys et mis a mort. Si vous prie qu'il vous plaise de moy faire venir ung prestre qui de mes pechéz me puisse donner absolution."

Adonc commanda l'admiral que on fist venir ung prestre. Quant il fut venu il le bailla a Valentin en luy disant, "Or tenez et vous confessez, car de toutes voz confessions je ne vous donneroye vaillant ung bouton."

singular response, as much for the life of his body as for that of his soul. A wise, clever, and quick thinker, he spoke in the following manner: "Alas, most exalted and mighty emir, please don't think or assume that it is through arrogance that I come into your magnificent presence, for, sire, when you will understand the manner and reason for my coming you will be all amazed."

"Tell us then how it is that you have come and what your situation is, for, Mohammed help me, I will take pleasure, joy, and delight in hearing you explain your undertaking, if it sheds the light of honor and goodness on your attitude."

Then Valentin spoke, saying, "My lord emir, it is true and certain that through false and faithless jealousy someone denounced me to King Pepin, saying that I was so terribly afraid of going to war that I wanted to return to France. For that reason the king is furious with me. Yesterday morning he had me arrested in order to cut off my head. When I saw myself in such danger, I made a foolish boast in front of everyone in order to prolong my life, for I swore before the entire court that I would come in your presence to challenge you and all your barons on King Pepin's behalf. Moreover, I boasted that before leaving I would demand three jousts by lance with you, who are so bold and renowned, in order to acquire praise and admiration. Therefore I beg you to grant me this boon, for otherwise I couldn't return to King Pepin without his putting me to death."

"My handsome lad," said the emir, "by Mohammed almighty, you will not be refused—no, I will grant you this joust right away. And so that the Franks who have laid siege to this city may see your valor, I will have the jousts set up and arranged outside of the city."

"Thank you very much," said Valentin, throwing himself down on the ground to kiss the feet of the emir as a sign of humility and obedience. But as everyone says in the well-known proverb, one often takes the shoe off the foot [to kiss it] that one would like to have cut off.[1]

Though admired in the palace of the emir, Valentin was quite pensive, constantly praying and beseeching God to give him the strength to do what he needed to do, and that he might one day know his origins and who his mother and father were. While he was lost in thought, the emir took him aside and said to him, "Fair sir, you seem to me rather pensive and troubled."

"True," said Valentin, "and not without cause, for I am greatly afraid of being killed by you in the joust. Therefore I beseech you to please have a priest come see me who can give me absolution of my sins."

Thereupon the emir ordered that a priest be brought. When he had come, the emir sent him to Valentin saying, "Now, go ahead and confess, but I wouldn't give a button for all your confessions."

---

[1] Cf. Joseph Morawski, ed., *Proverbes français antérieurs au XVe siècle* (Paris: Champion, 1925), 84 (no. 2322); James Woodrow Hassell, *Middle French Proverbs, Sentences, and Proverbial Phrases*, Subsidia Mediaevalia 12 (Toronto: Pontifical Institute of Mediaeval Studies, 1982), 199 (no. P160).

Valentin prit le prestre par la main et le tira a part. Et quant ilz furent assembléz Valentin luy a dit, "Helas, sire, vous estes prestre et devez entre les aultres avoir voulenté et courage de nostre saincte foy garder. Si veullez oÿr et entendre ce que je vous diray. Il est vray et vous le sçavez que je me doy au jour d'uy combatre contre le faulx admiral qui tant est ennemy de nostre foy. Or sçay je bien que payens et Sarrasins sauldront hors de la cité pour voir la jouste qui hors les murs est terminee. Si vous diray que vous ferez—vous direz secretement aux crestiens qui par la cité sont, qui ne saillent nulz dehors. Mais [21recto]se tiengnent en armes sans bruit ne commocion. Et adonc que payens seront hors ilz prenderont les gardes des portes en telle maniere que quant les Sarrasins vouldront entrer dedens la cité que vous leur cloez les portes. Et dites aux crestiens qu'i mandent au roy Pepin ces nouvelles, et qu'i face tenir ses gens en armes afin que quant il verra le point et l'eure, qu'i viennent courir sur les payens; de la ville qu'i sauldront d'aultre part et par telle maniere seront au jour d'uy vaincus et desconfis."

Et quant Valentin eut dit au prestre il se confessa, et apres sa confession le prestre se partit et s'en ala qui a Dieu le commanda. Lors l'admiral fit mener Valentin en sa chambre pour disner et prendre refection, et commanda qu'i fust servy honestement tout ainsi que sa personne.

Valentin fut a table assis avec plusieurs barons. Moult bien se sçeut contenir honnestement par devant tous les aultres. Et quant le disner fut fait et les tables leveez, l'admiral appella ung sien nepveu et avoit nom Salatas. Il luy commanda qu'il fist armer Valentin si bien et d'aussi bon harnoys que pour sa personne. Et si commanda et donna[1] en charge a son dit nepveu que on delivrast a Valentin tout le meilleur cheval qu'en sa court pourroit estre trouvé ne choisi. Et quant l'admiral eut ainsi parlé a son nepveu, il entra en la sale paree et la fut armé par plusieurs paiens vaillans et cognossans des armes. Et Salatas prit Valentin et le mena en une belle sale paree, puis fit aporter de plusieurs harnois, et des meilleurs qu'i peult trouver fit armer Valentin ainsi que par l'admiral son oncle luy estoit commandé. Et quant il fut armé il saillit sur ung destrier et l'admiral saillit en la place monté et en armes moult triumphant.

Lors chevaucherent tous deux vers la maistresse porte de Romme, car vers celle part le roy Pepin si avoit mis le siege. Et quant ilz furent au champ Valentin print son escu et le pendit a son col ou il avoit ung champ d'argent alié d'asur. Et sur celluy champ il y avoit ung cerf d'or unglé et denté de sable, et aupres de celluy cerf ung arbre. Lesquelles armes estoient signifiance qu'il avoit esté trouvé en la forest. Et lesquelles armes luy avoit donné le noble et puissant roy Pepin.

Or vindrent les François sur les rens dont moult furent joyeux. Sy fut le cry si grant par la cité de Romme que tous les paiens saillirent hors pour aler veoir les

---

[1] Text has *doona*.

Valentin took the priest by the hand and pulled him over to one side. Once they were together Valentin said to him, "Alas, sire, you are a priest and should more than anyone else have the will and the desire to keep our holy faith. Please listen closely to what I will tell you. It is true and you are aware that today I am to fight the treacherous emir who is so much the enemy of our faith. Now I know that the pagans and Saracens will issue out of the city to see the joust which is set up outside the walls of the city. I will tell you what you shall do—secretly you will tell the Christians within the city that they not sally forth outside. Rather they must arm themselves without any noise or commotion. Then, when the pagans are outside, they will overpower the guards at the gates so that when the Saracens try to enter the city you will close the gates against them. In addition, tell the Christians to send this information to King Pepin, that he should have his men armed and ready so that, when he sees the right moment, he has them descend upon the pagans; then those from the city should assail them from the other side, and that way they will be vanquished and undone today."

Once Valentin had explained all this to the priest, he made his confession, after which the priest departed, commending him to God. Then the emir had Valentin brought to his room to dine and take refreshment, commanding that he be properly served just like himself.

Valentin was seated at the table with several barons. He knew how to conduct himself properly in company. When the dinner was done and the tables removed, the emir called over a nephew of his named Salatas. He directed him to arm Valentin as well and with as good equipment as would be appropriate for himself. He also told his nephew and charged him to have the best horse given to Valentin that his court could find or choose. After having said all this to his nephew, he entered his main hall and there was armed by several valiant pagans well versed in weaponry. In the meantime Salatas took Valentin and led him to another handsome hall, then had several suits of armor brought in, choosing the best he could find with which to arm Valentin, just as his uncle the emir had commanded him. Once he was ready, he rode out on a charger, and the emir issued forth mounted and splendidly outfitted.

Then both of them rode toward the principal gate of Rome, for that was where King Pepin had laid his siege. When they were in the field, Valentin took his shield, decorated with a field of silver and azure, and hung it on his neck. On the field was a golden stag, with claws and teeth of sable black, and next to the stag was a tree. This coat of arms signified that he had been found in the forest, and had been granted him by the noble and powerful King Pepin.

Now the Franks came out to the jousting range for which they were very happy.[1] The cry was so great throughout the city of Rome that all the pagans

---

[1] The verb is indeed plural (*furent*) and I have not altered it. However it seems that it would make more sense for it to be singular, implying that Valentin was happy to see the Franks after his harrowing time among the Saracens.

joustes. Et les crestiens qui estoient dedens se myrent tous en armes le plus secretement qu'ilz peurent, et prindrent toutes les gardes des portes en telle maniere que nul ne peult retourner dedens. Et le roy Pepin de ce cas averty tenoit ses gens tous en armes pour le vaillent et preux Valentin secourir a son besoing.

Si fut l'eure venue que la jouste deult commencer. Sy s'eslongnerent l'ung de l'autre et coucherent leurs lances et poignirent leurs destriers, en si grans [21verso]coups donnans que lances et heaulmes l'ung a l'autre rompirent. Si retournerent arriere pour la seconde lance et est venu contre l'admiral; si l'a encontré et feru par telle maniere que tout oultre le corps luy a la lance passee. Lors cheut mort l'admiral dedens le champ en gettant grant cry. Et quant les payens veirent l'admiral mort et desconfit, ilz couroient sus a Valentin pour le mettre a mort, mais Valentin en grant hardiesse frappa son cheval et de l'espee d'armes fit si grant vaillance que tous les payens passa et plusieurs en passa et occist.

Et lors fut le roy Pepin en son ost qui en la bataille entra. Lequel fut si durement assailly des paiens que enmy le pré fut a terre mis et abatu. Mais Valentin vint la qui luy fit tel secours que sur son cheval le monta. Et quant il fut remonté il dit a Valentin, "Enfant, vous avez ma vie sauvee. Mais s'il plaist a Dieu il vous sera rendu."

Lors commença grant cry tant d'une part comme d'aultre, et fut la bataille forte et fiere, tant que les payens furent contrains a eulx retraire. Mais quant ilz voulurent dedens Romme entrer, les crestiens qui dedens estoient leur saillirent dessus. Et veirent les estandars et bannieres du roy Pepin plantés et mis sur les murs dont payens et Sarrasins furent fort esmerveilléz. Ilz furent assaillis tant de l'ost du roy que de ceulx de la cité que honteusement et a deshonneur finerent miserablement leurs jours. En icelle bataille sur le champ demoura CC.M. payens et tout par l'entreprinse, vaillance, et courage de Valentin qui tant vigoureusement se porta que trois fois en icelluy jour preserva et garda de mourir le roy. Et en icelle vaillance faisant eust quatre chevaulx mors contre luy et dessoubz luy. Ainsi pour la sienne prouesse et hardiesse de conqueste et prise, dont grant joye et liesse fut par toute crestienté, et principalement en la cité de Romme et aux parties prochaines, chascun crya "Montjoye!" au roy Pepin de France. En telle maniere aquist pris que par la voys du peuple par le pape Clement fut empereur couronné. Moult bien gouverna et augmenta l'esglise en son temps. Il fit a tous justice et rayson et tant que chascun disoit de luy bien. En ce temps estoit pape de Romme Clement quatriesme de ce nom que empereur consacra le roy Pepin.

issued forth to go watch the jousts. Meanwhile the Christians within armed themselves as quietly as they could, overcoming all the guards at the gates so that no one would be able to come back in. Moreover, King Pepin, advised of the plot, kept his men armed and ready so as to help the brave and valiant Valentin in his need.

Then it was time for the joust to begin. The combatants rode to the ends of the field, couched their lances, and spurred on their horses, inflicting such violent blows on each other that they shattered each other's lances and helmets. They pulled back for the second lance and Valentin rode towards the emir, meeting him and striking him so that his lance passed straight through the emir's body. And so the emir fell slain onto the field with a death cry. When the pagans saw the emir defeated and dead, they charged Valentin to kill him, but Valentin with great boldness spurred his horse and performed such feats of arms with his sword that he passed through all the pagans, killing several of them as he passed.

Then King Pepin and his host entered the battle. He was so heavily assailed by pagans that they knocked him down to the ground in the middle of the field. But Valentin rushed to his rescue with such support that he got him back on his horse. Once remounted he said to Valentin, "My child, you have saved my life. May it please God that you be likewise rewarded."

Then a great cry went up, as much from one side as from the other, and the fighting was heavy and fierce, so much so that the pagans were forced to retreat. But when they wanted to reenter Rome, the Christians inside fell upon them. Moreover, they saw the standards and banners of King Pepin planted and set up on the walls, which amazed and confused these pagan Saracens. They were assailed as much by the king's army as by those of the city, so that shamefully and to their dishonor they finished their days miserably. Two hundred thousand pagans remained on the field after this battle, and all because of the initiative, valor, and courage of Valentin, who conducted himself so vigorously that three times that day did he preserve and save the king from death. Moreover, in accomplishing such deeds, four horses were killed under him. And so, thanks to Valentin's prowess and boldness in conquest, for which there was great joy and gladness throughout the Christian world, and especially in the city of Rome and nearby areas, everyone cried out "Montjoye!" to King Pepin of France. In this way Pepin won such praise that by the consent of the people he was crowned emperor by Pope Clement. Well did he govern and fortify the church in his time. He dispensed such fair justice to all that everyone spoke well of him. At this time Clement was pope of Rome, the fourth of that name,[1] who consecrated Pepin as emperor.

---

[1] The actual Clement IV reigned 1265–1268, not at the time of the historical Pepin the Short.

[CHAPITRE 11]

Comment Hauffroy et Henry eurent envie sur Valentin pour la grant amour de quoy l'empereur roy de France l'aimoit comme il luy estoit tenu. xi. cha[pitre].

Apres que le roy Pepin par la grace de Dieu et par la puissance des armes eut chassé les infideles de la foy hors des parties rommaines, il vint a Orleans. Et la trouva royne Berte sa femme qui en grant joye le receust avec son jeune filz Charlot et sa fille Esglentine, laquelle fut moult joyeuse que Valentin estoit en santé revenu. Si ne sejourna pas longuement que vers elle le manda et il vint moult volentiers.

Lors quant la belle [22recto]le vit, elle doulcement le salue en disant, "Valentin, mon amy, bien soyez venu. Bien estes digne d'estre chier tenu et honnouré, car on dit que par dessus tous aultres vous avez acquis triumphe et victoire dessus les payens qui Romme tenoient en leur subjection."

"A, madame," dit Valentin, "a Dieu en sont les louenges. Chascun dit ce qu'il veult, mais quant a moi, je n'ay fait chose que on ne doie pour promesse tenir, et oultre plus le roy vostre pere m'a fait tant de bien et de honneur que jamais en ma vie rendre ne luy pourroie pour service que je lui face."

Et en disant ces parolles, Hauffroy et Henry, ardans et esprins d'envye, sont entréz en la chambre de la belle Esglentine. Et quant Hauffroy et Henry furent entréz ilz luy dirent en ceste maniere, "Valentin, que venez vous icy faire en la chambre de nostre seur, qui riens ne vous apartient? Trop vous monstrez fol et hardy d'entrer en la chambre royale, car vous n'estes sinon que ung trompeur et ne sçet nulz qui vous estes, ne de quel lieu vous estes venu. Sy vous gardez et je le vous conseille de plus vous trouver avec elle que mal ne vous en vienne."

Valentin dit a Ha[u]ffroy, "De vostre seur n'ayez nulle doubte. Car en nul jour de ma vie vers elle ne pensay fors que tout bien et tout honneur. Pour tant se je suis povre et on ne sçait qui je suis, si ne vouldroie faire ne penser[1] chose qui fust contre la majesté royale. Et afin que doubte vous n'en ayez et que vostre seur Esglentine par moy n'ait aulcun blasme de ceste heure je vous prometz de n'y jamais entrer en sa chambre." A ces parolles partist Valentin de la chambre et la belle dame Esglentine demoura toute seule plourant et souspirant moult tendrement.

Valentin monta au palays pour le roy servir qui a la table estoit ja assis. La furent Hauffroy, Henry et Millon d'Angler qui tous avec Valentin servoyent le roy a la table. Et quant il fut levé de table il appella Valentin, lequel dit devant tous:

"Seigneurs, vecy Valentin lequel m'a bien et loyallement servy et secouru en mes necessitéz. Afin que chascun de vous le puisse sçavoir, et pour les bons

---

[1] Text has *pensez*.

CHAPTER 11

How Hauffroy and Henry were jealous of Valentin because of the great love the emperor king of France bore him.

After King Pepin had chased the infidels out of Rome and its environs by the grace of God and with force of arms, he came to Orleans. There he found Queen Bertha his wife who, along with his young son Charlot, received him with great joy, and his daughter Esglentine who was joyful that Valentin had returned safe. Not long after she sent for him, and he came willingly.

When the girl saw him, she greeted him sweetly saying, "Valentin, my dear, welcome. You deserve to be cherished and honored, for they say that you more than anyone triumphed and brought victory over the pagans who were holding Rome in subjection."

"Oh, my lady," said Valentin, "all praise is due to God. Everyone says what he likes, but as I see it, I did no more than one must in order to keep a promise. Moreover, the king, your father, has been so good to me and honored me so much that never in my life could I repay him, whatever service I render him."

As he spoke these words, Hauffroy and Henry, gripped with burning jealousy, entered the fair Esglentine's room. Once there, they said, in the following manner, "Valentin, what are you doing here in our sister's chamber, where you don't belong? You show yourself to be foolish and overly bold by coming into the royal chamber, for you are no more than a beguiler, having no idea who you are or where you come from. You'd better watch yourself, and I advise you not to be found anymore with her lest some evil come your way."

Valentin addressed Hauffroy: "Have no fear for your sister, for never in my life have I thought of her with any intention other than goodness and honor. Though I may be poor and no one knows who I am, I would never do or think anything contrary to the majesty of the royal family. So that you may have no doubts on the subject nor your sister Esglentine be blamed on my account, from this time on I promise you never again to enter her chamber." With these words Valentin left the room, and the fair lady Esglentine remained all alone, weeping and sighing most heartily.

Valentin went to the main part of the palace to serve the king who was already seated at table. There also present were Hauffroy, Henry, and Millon d'Angler, who, with Valentin, were serving the king at table. When he rose from the table he called Valentin and spoke before all the company:

"My lords, this is Valentin, who has served me faithfully and well, and aided me in my need. So that each one of you may know this, and also because of the

services qu'il m'a fait, en attendant de mieulx avoir, je luy donne la conté de Clarmont en Auvergne."

"Sire," dit Valentin, "Dieu le vous veulle rendre, car plus me faites de biens que jamais je ne vous[1] desservy."

De tellez parolles oÿr furent Hauffroy et Henry fort dolans. Si dirent l'ung a l'autre, "Cestuy trouvé (que Dieu mauldie!) est en grace du roy en telle maniere que se nous n'y mettons remede, il fera une fois cause de nostre grant dommaige. Car le roy n'a d'enfans que nous et le petit Charlot duquel nous pourrons faire a nostre voulenté apres la mort de nostre pere. Mais il est chose vraye que Valentin le supportera et aydera a l'encontre de nous. Si nous fault aviser maniere de le mettre en indignation du roy et pourchasser sa mort. Car aultrement [22verso] venger ne nous en pourrons du tout a nostre plaisir le royaulme gouverner sans nul contredit."

Adonc parla Hauffroy et dit a Henry, "Frere, j'ay trouvé la maniere par quoy le faulx garson sera trahy et deceu. Je vous diray comment. Nous dirons et ferons entendant au roy nostre pere qu'il a violé nostre seur et que nous l'avons trouvé couché avec elle tout nu, et quant le roy sara ces nouvelles, je suis tout certain que mourir le fera honteusement."

"C'est bien dit," respondit Henry. "Or soit la chose menee a fin; si en serons vengéz."

En ce point demourerent en pensant et ymaginant tousjours contre Valentin mauvaistié et trahyson, car de sa mort ont plus d'envye que de nulle rien. Et Valentin sert le roy si bien a gré que le roy sur tous aultres desire de le veoir et avoir en sa compaignie, car tous les jours de bien en mieulx se maintenoit en priant Dieu qu'i luy voulsist donner cognoissance du lieu dont il estoit venu.

Et Orson son frere est dedens la forest qui tant est craint et doubté que nul n'ose pour luy le bois approcher ne passer. Les complaintes en viennent au roy de jour en jour grandes et merveilleuses de toutes pars. Si avint ung jour que ung povre vint au roy tout navré et sengle[n]t et luy dit, "Sire, je me plains a vous du sauvaige, car ainsi comme le bois je passoye, moy et ma femme, en portant pour la provision de nostre vie pain, frommaige et chair et autres vivres, le sauvaige est venu qui tout nous a osté et mengé. Et qui plus est, il a prins ma femme et en a fait deux fois a sa voulenté!"

"Or me dy," ce dit le roy, "de quoy te desplait il plus, ou d'avoir perdu tes vivres ou de ta femme."

"Par ma foy, sire," ce dit le bon homme, "de ma femme suis trop plus desplaisant."

"Tu as droit,"[2] dit le roy. "Or t'en va en ma court et may a pris la perte car rendue te sera." Apres appella le roy ses barons pour prendre avis sur le fait du sauvaige. Si fut deliberé par eulx que le roy feroit crier par tout a l'environ qui luy

---

[1] Text has *vour*.
[2] Text has *Tu a droit*.

good services he has rendered me, I have given him the county of Clairmont in Auvergne, until I have something better to offer him."

"Sire," said Valentin, "may God repay you, for you do me more honor than I deserve."

Hauffroy and Henry were very unhappy to hear this announcement. They said to one another, "This foundling (may God curse him!) is in the king's good graces to such a degree that if we don't do something, one day he will cause us harm. For the king has no children but us and little Charlot, with whom we can do as we like after the death of our father. But it is true that Valentin will support him and help him against us. Thus we must find a way to make the king angry with him [V.] and get him killed. Otherwise we will not be able to take revenge or rule the realm as we please without opposition."

Thereupon Hauffroy said to Henry, "Brother, I have found a way by which we can betray and deceive that false boy. I will tell you how. We will say, making the king our father understand, that he has violated our sister and that we have found him lying in bed with her completely nude, and when the king hears this news, I am certain that he will put him to shameful death."

"Well said," replied Henry. "Now let the thing be carried out; thus we will be avenged."

In this vein they remained, always thinking up and imagining wickedness and betrayal against Valentin, for they desired his death more than anything. In the meantime Valentin served the king so willingly that the king wanted to see him and have him in his company more than anyone else, for every day he comported himself from good to better, all the time praying God that He would give him knowledge of his origins.

And in the meantime, Orson his brother was in the forest, so dreaded and feared that no one dared approach the wood or pass through it because of him. Day by day strange and incredible complaints came to the king from all sides. It so happened that one day a poor man came to the king and said to him, "Sire, I bring a complaint to you about the wild man, for just as we were passing through the wood, my wife and I, carrying provisions—bread, cheese, meat, and other necessities—the wild man came upon us, taking everything and eating it. And what is more, he took my wife and had his way with her twice!"

"Now tell me what upsets you more," said the king, "losing all your food or what happened to your wife."

"By my faith, sire," said the good man, "I am much more upset about my wife."

"You have spoken well," said the king. "Now go to my court and put a price on your loss, for it will be paid to you." After this the king called his barons to ask for advice about the situation with the wild man. It was determined by them that the king would have it announced all around that whoever could bring him the

pourroit ou mort ou vif rendre l'omme sauvaige il auroit mil mars vaillant. Si fut le conseil tenu et le cry publié. Si vindrent de plusieurs pais chevaliers nobles de tous estas pour prendre Orson et le pris conquerir.

Lors le roy Pepin estant en son palays avec plusieurs grans seigneurs et nobles barons qui de ceste matiere parloyent et faisoient grans amirations entre eulx. Entre lesquelz seigneurs et barons Hauffroy, ennemy mortel dudit Valentin, commença a dire en telle maniere:

"Syre, vecy Valentin que vous avez nourry et mis en grant honneur. Lequel a requis nostre seur Esglentine d'amour desordonnee et de deshonneur et moult grant villennie. Et pour ce que je suis bien informé de cestuy cas je luy conseille que pour veoir ce qu'il scet faire et pour monstrer sa vaillance qu'i voise conquerir le sauvage qui tant est craint et redoubté, et vous luy donnerez Esglentine, vostre fille; sy sera de tous poins sa voulenté acomplie."

"Hauffroy," dit le roy, "ton parler est mal [23recto]gracieulx et plain d'envie. Car jassoit ce que Valentine soit povre et de bas lieu venu et que je l'aye trouvé parmy la forest, je le trouve si doulx, humble et debonaire que mieulx semble gentil et de noble courage que tu ne fais. Lesse le parler de luy, car les bonnes meurs et condicions qui en luy sont, apreuvent et monstrent qu'il est venu et extrait de bon lieu et de noble lignaige. Et pour le bien que j'ay trouvé en luy, je veul et me plaist qu'il aille avec ma fille la veoir a son plaisir, car de noble cueur il ne peult venir que tout honneur. Et tant en luy je me confie qu'il ne vouldroit penser contre mon honneur chose qu'il ne soit honneste et licite."

Et quant Hauffroy oÿt le roy qui si fort le reprent en sousportant Valentin, il fut au cueur desplaisant et dolent, mais semblant il n'en monstra.

Lors parla Valentin qui bien entendit les parolles de Hauffroy. "Hauffroy, a tort et sans cause avez de moy parlé, sans que en riens je vous aye meffait. Et pour maniere de refusion vous voulez que je voise combatre le sauvage afin que je y puiste mourir et que de moy vous soyez vengé. Mais je fais a Dieu serment que jamais n'arresteray en place tant que j'aye trouvé le sauvage, et quant je l'aray trouvé, a luy me combateray en telle maniere que mort ou vif devant tous l'amenray ou je y fineray mes jours. Et s'il avient que Dieu me donne puissance de celluy conquerir, jamais ne me verra nul en ceste contree tant que j'aray trouvé le pere qui m'engendra afin que je puisse sçavoir et cognoistre se je suis bastart ou legitime et pour quoy je fus laissé au bois."

Quant le roy entendit l'entreprise de Valentin, si fut au cueur desplaisant, car de le perdre il avoit plus grant paour que de nul de tous les aultres de sa court. Il mauldit Hauffroy et Henry qui luy font telle chose entreprendre. Puis il appella Valentin et luy a dit doulcement, "Helas, Valentin, mon enfant, avisez que vous voulez faire. Car de combatre l'omme sauvage ce me semble par vous une chose impossible. Vous sçavez et cognoissez assez que par luy sont mors plusieurs vaillans hommes, et ont delaissé ceste entreprinse aulcuns nobles champions. Et pour ce ne soyez si hault que pour le parler d'eulx vous perdez la vie, car trop est

wild man dead or alive would be rewarded with a thousand golden marks. The advice was accepted and the announcement made public. As a result there came from many countries noble knights of different station to try to capture Orson and conquer the prize.

One day Pepin was in his palace with several important lords and noble barons who were speaking and wondering about this matter among themselves. Among the lords and barons was Hauffroy, the mortal enemy of Valentin, who began to speak in the following manner:

"Sire, look at Valentin here, whom you have raised and placed in a most honorable position. He has made to our sister advances of unlawful love, dishonor, and the worst knavery. And since I am well informed concerning this matter, I suggest that he go conquer this wild man who is so dreaded and feared, in order to see what he can do and to prove his valor—then you will give him your daughter Esglentine, and his desire will be completely satisfied."

"Hauffroy," said the king, "your speech is ungracious and full of jealousy. For even though Valentin may be poor and from low station, and even though I discovered him in the forest, I find him so gentle, humble, and of natural nobility that he seems nobler and of more excellent character than you. Cease speaking of him, for his proper behavior and demeanor prove and demonstrate that he must descend from a good place and a noble lineage. And because of the goodness I have found in him, I would be happy for him to see my daughter whenever he wishes, for from a noble heart can come nothing but honor. I trust him so much that I am sure he wouldn't even desire to think of anything dishonest or illicit contrary to my honor."

When Hauffroy heard the king defend and support Valentin so vigorously, he was displeased and distressed internally, but he made no show of it.

Then Valentin spoke up, having clearly heard Hauffroy's speech. "Hauffroy, you have spoken wrongly about me and for no good reason, without my having done anything to you. Moreover, in order to refute it, you want me to go fight the wild man, so that I may die and you be avenged of me. Nevertheless I swear to God that I will not stop in one place until I have found the wild man, and when I find him, I will fight him, so that dead or alive I bring him to you or die in the attempt. And if it so happen that God give me strength to conquer him, never will anyone see me in this country until I have found the father who sired me so that I may know and be fully aware of whether I am a bastard or legitimate and why I was left in the woods."

When the king heard Valentin's plan, he was heartsick, for he feared losing him more than anyone else in his court. He cursed Hauffroy and Henry who made him undertake such a mission. Then he called Valentin over to him and said to him gently, "Alas, Valentin, my lad, consider carefully what you wish to do. For fighting the wild man seems to me an impossible task for you. You know and are aware that he has killed several valiant men, and many noble champions have given up this mission. So don't be so overproud that because of their nasty

cruelle chose a atendre de telle beste qui est sans rayson et sans naturel entendement. Pour Dieu, mon enfant, souffrés et endurez les parolles des envyeulx, car belle vertu est de pouoir endurer et souffrir faulces langues parler."

"Haa, sire," dit Valentin, "pour Dieu pardonnez moy, car jamais ce propos ne changeray. On m'apelle en repreuche trouvé, dont je suis moult doulent quant je ne puis sçavoir qui je suis ne de quel lieu. Je prens congié de vous et adieu je vous dis, car demain au plus matin je pense de prendre le chemin et la voye pour mon entente et entreprinse mettre a fin."

A ces motz se partist le vaillant et preux Valentin et print congié du roy Pepin. Et lendemain au matin il ala oÿr la messe, puis apres monta [23verso]a cheval pour querir le sauvaige.

Or ne fault il point demander se la belle Esglentine mena grant dueil et geta souspirs grans et gemissemens tresangoisseux toute la nuyt. Et quant le matin fut venu, elle appela une damoiselle qui estoit d'elle prochaine, puis luy a dit, "M'amie, alez vers Valentin et luy dites que je luy mande que devant qu'i departe qu'i vienne parler a moy, et que pour nul qui vive il n'ait doubte d'entrer dedens ma chambre, car sur toutes choses je desire et si est ma voulenté singuliere qu'il prenne de moy congié devant qu'il departe."

Lors ala la damoiselle vers Valentin et luy fist le messaige ainsi que par Esglentine luy estoit enchargé. Et quant Valentin entendit les nouvelles il respondit en ceste maniere, "Madamoiselle, je sçay et cognois que toute l'amour qui est entre moy et madame Esglentine est loyalle, juste, et de bonne equite. Et si sçay bien tant d'elle qu'elle ne vouldroit penser chose qui l'onneur d'elle peult en aulcune maniere amendrir. Ainsi me soit Dieu en tesmoignaige que de ma part jamais envers elle je ne poursuivis ne pensai que bien et honneur. Mais envie est de telle nature que jamais n'a repos, et plus tost sont les envieulx de leur nature enclins et habandonnéz a mal dire, et leur malice prouver et exercer contre loyaulté et preudommie et contre ceulx qui selon Dieu veullent et pretendent a vivre quant ilz veullent acquerir honneur. Or me prent il en ceste maniere, car je sçay de certain que Hauffroy et Henry, les freres de madame Esglentine, ont voulenté et courage de ma mort pourchasser, pour quoy, madamoiselle, vous irez par devers elle et luy direz que ne luy desplaise se d'elle je ne prens congié, et qu'elle ait fiance en Dieu, car c'est celuy seul qui fait justice et garde le droit a ceulx qui a tort seuffrent injure et sans cause sont blasmés."

Apres ceste responce s'en retourna la damoiselle moult dolente et couroucee de ce que Valentin monta a cheval pour son voyage faire.

speech you lose your life—such a cruel thing to die at the hands of such a beast without reason or natural understanding. For God's sake, my boy, pay no attention to the envious, for it is a fair virtue to be able to bear with and ignore the speech of false tongues."

"Oh, sire," said Valentin, "for God's sake, pardon me, for never will I change my mind. They call me a foundling in reproach, which I am very unhappy about, not knowing who I am or whence I come. I take leave of you and bid you adieu, for tomorrow at dawn I plan to take to the road to carry out my plan."

With these words the valiant and brave Valentin departed, taking leave of King Pepin. The next morning he went to hear mass, then mounted his horse to go seek the wild man.

No need to ask whether the fair Esglentine mourned, sighing deeply and moaning in anguish all night long. When the morning dawned she called a damsel who was close to her and said, "My friend, go to Valentin and tell him that I order him to come talk to me before he leaves, and that he fear no one about coming into my chamber, for more than anything it is my particular desire that he take leave of me before he departs."

So the damsel went to Valentin and gave him the message just as Esglentine had charged her. When Valentin heard the message, he answered in the following manner: "Damsel, I know that the love between myself and my lady Esglentine is loyal, just, and proper. Moreover, I know well that she would not think anything that could in any way lessen her honor. Thus may God bear me witness that never in my life have I sought anything from her or thought about her in any way other than to her well-being and honor. But envy is predisposed to take no rest, and the jealous are inclined by their nature, indeed completely given over, to speaking ill of others, manifesting their malice, and taking action against loyalty and honesty, especially against those who try to live according to God so as to win honor. I am caught in this bind, for I know for certain that Hauffroy and Henry, my lady Esglentine's brothers, wish to bring about my death, for which reason, damsel, you will go to her and tell her that she please not be angry if I do not take leave of her, and that she may place her hope in God, for He alone renders justice and keeps watch over those who suffer insult and blame without cause."

After this answer the damsel turned around, very sad and upset that Valentin then mounted his horse to leave on his journey.

[CHAPITRE 12]

Comment Valentin partit d'Orleans pour aler combatre a Orson son frere dedans la forest comme vous purrez ouyr. xii. chapitre[1]

Or s'en va Valentin et monté sur son cheval seul et sans compaignie fors que ung sien escuier que avec luy mena. Et se partit d'Orleans et tant chevaucha qu'il vint et arriva en la foretz en laquelle estoit Orson le sauvaige. Et quant [24recto]il fut aupres du bois il dit a son escuier qu'il luy baillast son heaulme et print congié de luy disant, "Vous demourrés icy et ne vendrés plus oultre avec moy. Car telle est mon entreprinse et ainsi je l'ay juré et promis que tout seul entreray au bois pour le sauvaige combatre. Prie Dieu pour moy que secourir me veulle. Et se le corps y demeure, je vous recommande mon ame." Et a ces motz entra Valentin dedens le bois et l'escuier demoura plourant et souspirant tendrement.

Valentin serche et chevauche parmy le bois pour le sauvaige trouver, mais par ung jour entier n'en peult avoir nouvelles. Et quant le jour fut passé et la nuyt commença a raprocher il descendit de dessus son cheval et l'atacha au pié d'ung arbre. Puis print du pain et du vin que avec luy portoit et ung peu se repeut. Et quant il eut mengé et que la nuit fut venue et le jour fut du tout failly, lors Valentin pour doubte de la nuyt monta dessus ung arbre et la demoura.

Et quant le jour fut venu il regarda entour de luy et il veit son frere Orson qui par le bois couroit comme beste sauvaige. Lequel avisa le cheval de Valentin, et tyra par devers luy. Et quant il le veit si beau et sy plaisant, de ses mains velues fort l'aplania en luy faisant feste, car jamais n'avoit acoustume de telle beste veoir. Et quant le cheval sentit et aperceut le sauvaige qui de toute pars le gratoit et touchoit, il commença a ruer et regiber des piéz moult durement. Et Valentin, qui sur l'arbre estoit, regardoit les manieres du sauvage qui moult fut terrible de regard et fort a doubter et craindre. Et lors reclama a Dieu et la benoite Vierge Marie moult devotement, en luy priant et requerant de tout son cueur que du sauvaige le voulsist preserver et du tout deffendre et encontre luy donner victoire de le conquerir.

Or tournoye tant Orson autour du cheval de Valentin que le cheval qui fut fier le commença a frapper et le cuida mordre. Et quant Orson l'aperceut il aherdit le cheval pour le boutter a bas et a luy se combatre. Et quant Valentin vit que le sauvaige vouloit son cheval tuer et destruire il s'escria et dit haultement, "Sauvaige! laisse mon cheval et atens, car a moy aras bataille!"

---

[1] Woodcut of mounted hunter in profile with falcon on wrist, riding toward trees on left.

CHAPTER 12

How Valentin left Orleans to go fight Orson his brother in the forest, as you will be able to hear.

Now Valentin left, riding alone and without company save for his squire whom he had brought with him. He left Orleans and rode so far that he came to the forest where Orson the wild man lived. When he approached the woods he told his squire to hand him his helmet, and took leave of him saying, "You will remain here and not come any further with me. For this is my undertaking, just as I swore and promised to do, to go into the woods to fight the wild man. Pray to God for me, that He grant me His help. And if it turns out that I leave my body here, I commend to you my soul." With these words Valentin entered the woods while his squire remained behind, weeping and sighing deeply.

Valentin rode and searched throughout the woods to find the wild man, but for an entire day he could find no trace of him. Once the day ended and night began to approach, he got off his horse and tied him up at the foot of a tree. Then he took some bread and wine he had brought with him and refreshed himself a bit. Once he had eaten and the night had fallen and daylight was completely gone, then Valentin, fearful in the dark, climbed a tree and remained there.

When day dawned he looked around him and saw his brother Orson who was running through the woods like a wild beast. He saw Valentin's horse and headed towards him. When he saw how handsome and pleasing he was, he caressed him enthusiastically with much delight, for he was not accustomed ever to see such an animal. When the horse felt and perceived the wild man touching and scratching him on all sides, he began to kick and buck dangerously with his feet. Valentin, up in the tree, watched the behavior of the wild man who was terrible to behold and much to be feared. He called on God and the Virgin Mary most devoutly, praying and beseeching them with all his heart to preserve him from the wild man, and defend him, and grant him victory over him.

Orson turned so much around Valentin's horse that the horse, who was fierce, began to strike out and tried to bite him. When Orson realized this, he seized the horse to knock it down and fight it. When Valentin saw that the wild man wanted to kill his horse, he cried out loudly, "Savage! Leave my horse alone and wait, for I am the one you will have to fight!"

Lors le sauvaige laissa le cheval et leva ses yeulx contremont l'arbre. Et quant il a veu Valentin il lui a fait signe des mains et de la teste que par pieces le mettera, et Valentin fait le signe de la croix et se recommande a Dieu. Puis tira son espee et saillit en bas vers Orson. Et quant Orson vit l'espee dont Valentin le cuida ferir, il se tira arriere et du coup se garda. Puis vint [a] Valentin et a force de bras a terre il le getta et dessoubz luy il le mist, de quoy Valentin fut fort esbahy et desconforté, car il cuida bien en icelle place mourir et finer ses jours, car tant sentoit Orson puissant que eschaper de ses mains n'avoit esperance. "Hé, vrai Dieu," [24verso]dit il, "ayez pitié de moy et ne souffrés ma vie par cestuy sauvage estre si piteusement finee."

Par plusieurs fois cuida Valentin tourner Orson dessoubz luy mais il n'en eut point la puissance. Et quant il vit que par puissance de corps il ne le pouoit gaigner, il tira ung couteau fort pointu de quoy il frappa Orson ou cousté destre tellement que le sang en saillit a grant randon. Adonc se leva Orson qui navré se sentit, et de la douleur qu'il eut comme tout en rage getta ung cry sy grant que le bois il fit tout retentir. Puis revint a Valentin et si fierement a tout les ongles agus et trenchans a luy se prist que de rechief a terre le getta. Si se combatirent tant et si merveilleusement les deux freres que forte chose seroit de vous raconter leurs batailles et la maniere. Et quant Orson le sauvage si rudement et de telle facon prist le chevalier Valentin que de son col luy arracha l'escu et le blason, et quant il l'eut osté, moult fort le regarda pour la beaulté des couleurs qu'i n'avoit point acoustume de voir, puis le getta contre terre et retourne a Valentin et aux grifz et aux dens si fermement serre que harnois et haubergon debrisa et rompit. De ses ongles le frappa jusques a la chair nue de Valentin tellement que le sang en fit courir a grant randon. Et quant Valentin se sentit navré moult fut triste et dolent, si commença de cueur et de courage Hiesucrist a reclamer, "Helas!" dit il, "vrai Dieu, en toy est ma seule esperance, mon seul refuge et mon resconfort. Si te prie humblement que de moy veulles avoir pitié. Et ainsi[1] que par ta digne puissance tu gardas et sauvas Daniel entre les lyons veulles moy garder de cest homme sauvaige."

Et quant Valentin eut fait sa priere a Dieu, il va devers Orson a tout son espee pour le cuider frapper. Mais Orson saillit arriere et va vers ung petit arbre lequel il ploya et rompit et en fit ung baston moult merveilleux et vint a Valentin et ung tel coup luy en donna que sur ung genoul le fit tomber a terre. Valentin se releva comme preux et hardy. Si commencerent entre eulx treffiere bataille et dure. Moult avyoent les deux freres grant voulenté et courage de l'ung l'autre destruire, mais ilz ne cognoissoient pas qu'ilz estoient freres ne le cas de leur fortune. Orson fut sy cruel et fort qu'il eut plusieurs fois tué Valentin si n'eust esté son espee qui sur toutes aultres choses doubtoit et craingnoit pour cause du couteau dont Valentin l'avoit frappé. Tant et si longuement ensemble se combatirent que en plusieurs manieres et tant que tous deux si demourerent lassés et fort travailléz.

---

[1] Text has *aisni*.

Thereupon the wild man let go of the horse and raised his eyes up to the tree. When he saw Valentin, he made signs with his hands and head that he would tear him to pieces, while Valentin made the sign of the cross and commended himself to God. Then he drew his sword and jumped down towards Orson. When Orson saw the sword with which Valentin sought to strike him, he pulled back and avoided the stroke. Then he ran at Valentin, throwing him on the ground with his powerful arms and pinning him down, for which Valentin was fearful and overcome, for he believed that he was about to die and end his days in that place; so powerful could he feel Orson to be that he had no hope of escape from his hands. "Oh, true God," said he, "have pity on me and do not allow my life to end so pitifully in the hands of this wild man."

Several times Valentin tried to turn Orson under him but he wasn't powerful enough. When he saw that by body strength alone he couldn't win, he drew a sharp knife and struck Orson so hard on the right side that the blood gushed forth. Orson, feeling himself wounded, got up and, because of the pain, let out such a cry of rage that it made the woods echo. Then he lunged back at Valentin, attacking him so fiercely with all his sharp nails that once more he dashed him to the ground. And so the two brothers fought so long and to such an extreme that it would be difficult to recount it all. Once Orson the wild man took hold of the knight Valentin so roughly and in such a way as to wrest from him his shield, but once he had it in his hands, he gazed at it amazed for the beauty of the colors that he wasn't used to seeing at all. But then he cast it to the ground and returned to Valentin, whom he gripped so firmly with his claws and his teeth that armor and mail he pierced and broke. He smote Valentin so severely on his naked flesh with his nails that the blood gushed forth. And when Valentin felt himself wounded he was so distressed that he began to pray in his heart to Jesus Christ: "Alas!" said he, "true God, in you is my only hope, my only refuge, and my only comfort. I beg you humbly to have pity on me. Just as you kept and saved Daniel in the lions' den by your worthy strength, please keep me from this wild man."

Once Valentin had made his prayer to God, he approached Orson with his raised sword, thinking to strike him. But Orson leapt backwards, going to a little tree that he bent back and broke to make himself a marvelous club, and then, returning to Valentin, he gave him such a blow that he sent him down on one knee. However, Valentin raised himself like a brave and hardy man. Once again they began a fierce and tough battle, both brothers desiring nothing more than to destroy the other, but not recognizing that they were brothers nor the cause of their fate. Orson was so cruel and strong that he would have killed Valentin several times had it not been for his sword, which above all other things he feared because of the knife with which Valentin had struck him earlier. So much and for so long did they battle each other every possible way that both were worn out and exhausted.

Adonc parla Valentin a Orson et lui commença a dire, "Helas, homme sauvage, pour quoy ne vous rendés vous a moy? Vous vivez en ce bois tout ainsi comme une povre beste et n'avez cognoissance de Dieu ne de sa mere ne de sa sainte foy parquoy vostre ame est en grant danger. Venés vous en avec moy et vous ferés que saige. Baptiser vous feray et la saincte foy [25recto]apprendre.[1] Et si vous donneray assez de chair, de poisson et de pain et de vin boire et menger, vesture et chaussure vous donneray richement et userez voz jours honnestement ainsi que tout homme naturel doit faire."

Quant Orson oÿt parler Valentin il entendit et aperceut bien par ses signes que Valentin vouloit et desiroit son bien. Et alors parla Valentin de Dieu, et selon le cours de nature qui ne peult mentir, Orson se getta a deux genoulx et tendit les mains devers son frere Valentin, luy faisant signe que pardon luy veulle faire[2] et du tout a luy veult obeïr et complaire pour le temps a venir. Et luy monstre par signes que jamais jour de sa vie ne luy fauldra de son corps ne de ses biens. Sy ne fault pas demander se Valentin fut joyeulx quant il veit[3] le sauvaige par lui conquis et mis en subjection. Et en demena grant liesse et non pas sans cause, car plus en avoit conquis d'onneur et de proesse que nul chevalier de son temps n'eust osé entreprendre, tant fust il preulx, courageulx et hardy.

Il a prins Orson[4] par la main, puis luy a monstré signe qu'il chemine devant luy jusques dehors le bois. Et Orson a prins la course devant Valentin et tantost ont esté hors de la forest. Lors Valentin a prins une des sangles de son cheval, et pour doubte du danger a parmy le corps estroitement lyé Orson afin que ne luy ne aultre ne peust dommager. Et quant il l'eut lyé, il monta a cheval et print Orson et l'emmaine avec luy comme une beste lyé, le tenant sans ce que jamais ledit Orson luy fit quelque mal semblant qui estoit chose miraculeuse.

[CHAPITRE 13]

Comment Valentin apres ce que il eust conquis Orson se partit de la forest pour retourner a Orleans devers le roy Pepin qui la estoit. xii[i]. [chapitre]

Valentin tant a fait avec l'ayde de Dieu qu'il a vaincu et conquis Orson le sauvaige. Il est monté a cheval pour aler a Orleans et est tant alé qu'i est entré en ung grant villaige. Mais tout ainsi que les gens d'icelluy lieu ont veu le sauvaige

---

[1] *d i* appears at bottom right corner of 25r.
[2] Text has *faire*, that is, a bar over the *i* to indicate a following *n*, which is not needed.
[3] Text has *veic*.
[4] Text has *Valentin*, but only the name Orson makes sense in light of the next sentence.

Finally Valentin spoke to Orson saying, "Alas, wild man, why not give yourself up to me? You live in these woods like a poor beast, possessing no knowledge of God or his mother or the holy faith, which puts your soul in great danger. Come with me—you'll be acting wisely. I will have you baptized and teach you the holy faith. Then I will give you sufficient meat, fish, bread, and wine to eat and drink, rich clothes and shoes to wear, and you will spend your days honestly like every natural-born man should."

When Orson heard Valentin speak, he understood and perceived well by his signs that Valentin desired only his well-being. Then Valentin spoke of God, and, following the natural inclination that cannot lie, Orson threw himself to his knees and held out his hands to his brother Valentin, begging by signs that he pardon him and expressing that he wished to obey him and please him in the future. He also showed him by signs that never in his life would he fail him in person or possessions. No need to ask whether Valentin was glad when he saw the wild man conquered and subdued by him. He was extremely happy, and not without cause, for he had won more through honor and prowess than any knight of his time had dared to undertake, so daring, brave, and bold was he.

He took Orson by the hand, signaling him to walk in front of him until they were outside the woods. So Orson took his place in front of Valentin and soon they were out of the forest. Then Valentin took one of the girths from his horse, and tied Orson up tightly to make sure that he couldn't harm himself or anyone else. Once he was tied up, he mounted his horse, taking Orson and leading him like a captured beast, without Orson ever seeming to want to harm him, which was a miraculous thing.

CHAPTER 13

How Valentin, after having defeated Orson, left the forest to return to King Pepin who was in Orleans.

With God's help, Valentin was able to do so much that he defeated and conquered Orson the wild man. He mounted his horse to return to Orleans and rode until he entered a large village. But as soon as the people of that place saw the wild man that Valentin was leading, they began running away, escaping into

que Valentin menoit il[1] ont commencé a fuir et entrer es maisons. Et de la grant paour qu'ilz eurent ilz fermerent leurs portes en telle maniere que nul n'y peut entrer. Valentin les escrye que de luy ilz n'aient doubte et qu'ilz euvrent leurs portes, car ilz veullent logier, mais pour nulle riens qu'il peust dire nul ne luy voulut de sa maison faire overture.

Lors leur cria, "Par le Dieu tout puissant, se vous ne me donnez logis pour la nuyt passer et prendre repos, sachez que je desliray le sauvage et laisseray aler. Si suis bien certain que il me aura tantost trouvé logis a mon plaisir."

Moult de foys requist Valentin que logis peut avoir, mais chascun avoit telle doubte du sauvaige que nul n'ose sa porte ouvrir. Et quant Valentin vit que nul ne le vouloit loger, il deslya Orson puis luy a fait signe qu'i [25verso]frappe contre la porte d'une grant maison qui la estoit en laquelle on tenoit hostelerie. Et Orson print une grosse piesse de bois pour frapper contre la porte et par si grant force a frappé encontre que au troisiesme coup il la rua par terre, puis sont entréz dedens.

Et quant ceulx de la maison virent que le sauvaige avoit rompu la porte, ilz saillirent hors par la porte de devant, si que nul ne demoura dedens. Et Valentin ala devers l'estable et loga son cheval, puis a prins Orson et sont aléz vers la cuisine ou il ont trouvé chapons et plusieurs viandes qui en une broche estoient aupres du feu. Lors Valentin a fait signe a Orson qu'il tournast la broche, car la viande n'estoit pas cuitte, mais Orson aussitost comme il vit la viande il mist la main a la broche et en tira de viande grant partie, puis ne demanda pas s'elle estoit bien ou mal cuitte, mais la menga tout ainsi comme ung loup fait sa proye. Puis avisa une chaudiere plaine d'eaue, si boutta la teste dedens, si en but tout ainsi que le cheval fait en la riviere.

Et Valentin luy fait signe qu'i laisse a boire de l'eau et qu'il luy donnera du vin. Puis a prins ung grant pot et amené Orson en la cave ou estoit le vin. Et quant il eust tyré du vin plain pot il le bailla a Orson, et Orson lieve le pot et commence a gouster du vin et moult bon le trouva et friant. Si beut si largement que sans reprendre son alaine tout le pot vuida, puis getta le pot a terre et fait signe a Valentin qu'il tyre d'aultre vin. Et Valentin leva le pot et print grant plaisir a voir et regarder les contenances de Orson le sauvaige.

Et quant Valentin eut emply le pot du bon vin, Orson avisa ung grant chaudiere. Sy a prins le pot et a boutté le vin dedens, puis la porte au cheval de Valentin pour luy faire boire. Et quant Valentin le vit, il luy fist signe que le cheval ne buvoit que de l'eaue, et Orson luy monstre que le vin vault mieulx que l'eaue. Plusieurs aultres choses faisoit Orson parmy la maison qui trop long seroit a raconter.

La nuyt fut venue que temps il fut d'aler coucher. Valentin se repeust et fist repaistre Orson qui le vin n'espargna pas. Mais tant en beut qu'il fut ivre, puis se coucha pres du feu et commença a ronfler et a dormir tresmerveilleusement. Et

---

[1] *Ilz* had not completely replaced *il* as the plural form of the third person masculine plural subject pronoun in Middle French. See Gardner and Greene, *Middle French Syntax*, 46.

their houses. And because of their great fear, they fastened their doors in such a way that no one could get in. Valentin called out to them not to be afraid and to open their doors, for he wanted lodging, but nothing he said could induce anyone to open his door.

Then he shouted, "By almighty God, if you won't offer me lodging and a place to rest tonight, I will unbind the wild man and let him loose. Then I warrant he will soon find me lodging to my taste."

Many times did Valentin request lodging, but everyone was so afraid of the wild man that no one dared open his door. When Valentin realized that none was willing to lodge him, he untied Orson, gesturing to him to knock at the door of a large hostelry that was there. So Orson picked up a huge piece of wood to knock at the door, and struck with such force that at the third blow he dashed it to the ground, whereupon they both entered.

When the people in the house saw that the wild man had broken through the door, they scampered out through the other door—not a single one stayed behind. So Valentin stabled his horse, and took Orson into the kitchen where they found capons and other meats on a spit roasting over a fire. Then Valentin gestured to Orson that he turn the spit, for the meat was not yet cooked, but as soon as he saw the meat Orson laid hands on the spit and tore off a huge chunk of it, not caring whether it was well cooked, but eating it just like a wolf devours his prey. Next, seeing a cauldron filled with water, he thrust his head inside, drinking just as a horse does from the river.

Then Valentin gestured to him to stop drinking water, that he would give him some wine. Taking hold of a large pitcher, he led Orson to the cellar where the wine was kept. After filling the pitcher, he offered it to Orson who lifted it and began tasting the wine, finding it quite delectable. He drank so deeply that, without catching his breath, he emptied the whole pitcher, then threw it down, gesturing to Valentin that he refill it. Valentin picked up the pitcher, taking great pleasure in watching the wild Orson's antics.

Once Valentin had refilled the pitcher with good wine, Orson spotted a large pot. Grabbing it, he poured the wine into it, then took it to Valentin's horse to drink. When Valentin realized what he was doing, he gestured to him that the horse drank only water, but Orson signed to him that wine was better than water. There were lots of other things Orson did in the hostelry but they would take too long to recount.

With night arriving, it was time to go to sleep. Valentin ate and fed Orson, who spared not the wine. So much had he drunk that he was intoxicated, so he lay down near the fire and began to snore and sleep most marvelously. Valentin,

Valentin le regarde en disant en soy mesmes, "Vray Dieu tout puissant, tant que c'est peu de chose de ung homme endormy et de l'omme qui par boire pert sens et memoire. Or voy je cestuy homme sauvaige en qui il n'a maintenant ne force ne puissance et pourroit estre tué devant qu'il fust esveillé."

Et quant il eut ce dit pour plus esprouver la hardiesse de Orson, il le boutta d'ung pié si fort qu'il l'esveilla, puis luy fist signe qu'il y avoit gens entour la maison. Dont se leva Orson comme tout effroyé et print ung gros tison qui ou feu estoit et courut vers la porte et donna si grant coup enco[n]tre la porte [26recto]que[1] toute la porte en retentist. Et Valentin se print de sousrire[2] pour quoy Orson cogneut bien que Valentin faisoit ce pour l'essaier. Si a fait signe Valentin qu'i voise reposer et que de riens il n'eust paour ne sousy car bien le gardera. Puis Orson se recouche devant le feu, son baston entre ses bras. Et Valentin fut toute la nuyt aupres de luy qui toute la nuyt veilla et riens il ne dormit pour doubte qu'il ne fust assailly, car tant fut le bruit grant que chascun laissa sa maison et se retrahirent en l'esglise. Et toute la nuyt sans repos sonnerent les cloches pour le peuple assembler qui a grant nombre et puissance d'armes toute la nuyt pour Orson firent le gait.

Ainsi passa la nuit tant que le jour fut venu. Et quant Valentin vit que le jour estoit grant il monta a cheval et a lyé Orson et s'est mis a chemin vers la ville d'Orleans, et tant que a ung joeudy il est arrivé dedens la ville. Et quant il fut aperceu menant Orson le sauvaige, ilz ont fait si grant cry que parmy la cité ne fut oncques si grant bruit. Chascun court en sa maison et ferment leurs portes, puis montent aux fenestres et regardent Orson le sauvaige. Les nouvelles vindrent au roy Pepin que Valentin estoit arrivé et qu'il avoit conquis Orson le sauvaige et avec luy le menoit. Desquelles nouvelles le roy Pepin en fut moult grandement esmervellé. Et en faisant le signe de la croix dit en telle maniere:

"Ha, Valentin, mon enfant, de bonne heure fus tu né. Benoit soit le pere qui t'engendra et la mere qui au bois t'enfanta, car je voys et cognois que de Dieu tu es aymé, et que par toy nous monstre miracle evident."

Et le peuple d'aultre part est aux fenestres qui crie a haulte voix en disant, "Vive entre les aultres le vaillant Valentin! Car au monde n'a plus preulx ne plus vaillant, et bien est digne d'onneur et de louenge avoir, quant par sa prouesse et vaillance il a celuy conquis qui jamais n'osa de nus estre assailly. De luy porter honneur et reverence chascun y est tenu, car par luy sommes delivréz et a seureté mis de la chose que plus nous redoubtions."

Valentin chevaulcha parmy la ville d'Orleans tant que il vint devant les portes du palais. Et quant les portiers le veirent venir ilz coururent fermer les portes pour l'amour et doubte du sauvaige. Lors leur dit Valentin, "Ne vous doubtez de riens. Mais alez vers le roy disant que sur ma vie du sauvaige je le fay seur, luy et tous les seigneurs et barons, car de tant le cognoy que a nul homme vivant soit petit ou grant ne portera dommaige."

---

[1] *d ii* at bottom right corner of 26r.
[2] Text has *ssousrire*.

watching him, said to himself, "True and almighty God, what a small, weak thing is a man asleep, and moreover a man who loses his sense and memory from drinking. Now I see this wild man without force or strength, who could be killed before he woke up."

Having said this, Valentin decided to test Orson's boldness, kicking him with his foot so hard that he woke him up, gesturing to him that there were people surrounding the house. Orson, alarmed, rose up, seizing a thick log from the fire, running to the gate and giving it such a blow that the entire gate shook. When Valentin began to laugh, Orson understood that Valentin had only done it to test him. Then Valentin gestured to him that he should rest and fear nothing, for he would guard him. So Orson lay down again in front of the fire, his club in his arms. In the meantime Valentin kept guard near him all night long, not sleeping at all for fear that he be assaulted, for the commotion had been so great that everyone left his house to gather in the church. There all night long without respite the bells rang to assemble the people, great numbers of whom armed themselves well and kept watch for Orson.

So the night passed until dawn. When Valentin saw that it was full morning, he mounted his horse, tethered Orson, and set out for the city of Orleans, making such good time that he arrived in the city on Thursday. When people perceived that he was leading Orson the wild man, they raised a huge cry, greater than any noise ever heard in the town. Everyone rushed home to shut their doors, then mounted to the windows to watch Orson the wild man. News came to Pepin that Valentin had arrived, having conquered Orson the wild man, and was bringing him with him. Pepin was absolutely amazed at the news. Making the sign of the cross, he spoke in the following manner:

"Ah, Valentin, my lad, you were born in a lucky hour. May God bless the father who engendered you and the mother who gave birth to you in the wood, for I see that you are beloved of God, who through you has performed a true miracle."

The people on the other side at their windows cried out loudly saying, "Long live the dauntless Valentin above all others! For there is no one in the world braver or more valiant. Worthy is he of all honor and praise, when by his courage and valor he conquered the one whom no one else dared to attack. All of us owe him honor and esteem, for by him are we delivered and made safe from the thing we most feared."

Valentin rode through the city of Orleans until he came before the gates of the palace. When the gatekeepers saw him coming they ran to close the gates because they feared the wild man. Then Valentin said to them, "Don't be afraid. Go to the king and tell him that I warrant for his safety from the wild man on my life — his safety and that of all his lords and barons — for I know him so well that he will not harm anyone at all."

Les messagiers sont montéz contremont le palais et ont dit au roy Pepin les nouvelles et commandement et que Valentin prenoit la charge et garde du sauvaige Orson. Dont commanda le roy Pepin que on le feist entrer et qu'on ouvrit les portes. Valentin entra dedens [26verso]et print Orson par la main. Et quant la royne Berthe et la belle Esglentine sceurent qu'ilz estoient au palays avec toutes les dames elles fouirent en leurs chambres de la grant paour qu'elles en eurent. Et Valentin monta en hault et est entré en la sale ou le roy Pepin estoit acompaigné de tous les nobles barons de sa court. Et Hauffroy et Henry qui de leurs semblance monstroient grant signe d'amour a Valentin. Et bien luy sembloit qu'il fust moult joyeulx de la grande entreprinse et de la prouesse que Valentin avoit fait, mais ilz ne furent oncques plus dolens en leurs cueurs, car jamais n'esperoient que Valentin puisse vif retourner. Ilz mauldisoient le sauvaige quant il ne l'avoit tué et destruit.

Le roy Pepin et tous ceulx de sa court regardoyent Orson moult voulentiers. Lors dist le roy Pepin, "Seigneurs, par le Dieu tout puissant, moult est merveilleuse chose de cest homme sauvaige voir et regarder. Moult est bien formé et belle estature de corps et de tous membres. Et combien qu'il soit velu s'il estoit vestu comme l'ung de nous, fort seroit plaisant a veoir et beau chevalier sembleroit."

Lors parla Valentin au roy Pepin en ceste maniere, "Sire, je vous requiers que baptiser vous le facez. Si aprendra la foy et la creance de la loy crestienne, car tel est mon desir et ainsi luy ay promis."

"Bien me plaist," ce dist le roy. "Je veul que ainsi soit fait." Lors il commanda a ung prestre que il le baptisast, et furent ses parrins le roy Pepin et le duc Millon d'Angler, Sanson et Gervais, moult vaillans chevaliers, et Valentin aussy. D'aultre part y fut la royne Berthe et plusieurs aultres dames de grant renon. Et aultre non ne luy baillerent que celuy qu'il avoit prins en la forest.

Quant Orson fust baptisé le roy se asist a la table pour disner et Valentin le sert de sa couppe car c'estoit son office. Et quant il fut assis il commanda que on fist entrer Orson dedens la sale pour voir ses manieres et contenance. Orson fut devant le roy qui moult fort le regarde. Il avisa la viande qui devant luy estoit. Il print dedens le plat ce qu'il en peust emporter et commence a menger vitement et a gros morseaulx. Et quant il eult mengé il regarde d'aultre part ung serviteur lequel aportoit dedens ung plat ung paon pour le roy servir. Lors y courut Orson et au serviteur l'osta, puis s'asist a terre emmy la place de la sale et commence a menger. Et quant Valentin l'aperceust il luy monstre signe que mal se gouvernoit dont Orson fust honteulx, car sur toutes choses il craingnoit et redoubtoit naturelement Valentin. Et le roy Pepin commanda que on le laissast faire, car il prenoit plaisir a ses contenances regarder. Quant Orson eut bien mengé il avisa ung pot qui estoit plain de vin, si la tantost saisy et tout d'ung tret le beut puis va get[27recto]ter[1] le pot a terre et a commencé a secourre la teste, dont le roy et tous

---

[1] *d iii* appears at bottom right corner of 27r.

The messengers went up to the palace and told King Pepin the news and Valentin's instructions and how he vouchsafed for the wild man Orson. So King Pepin commanded that they open the gates and let him in. Valentin came in, leading Orson by the hand. When Queen Bertha and the fair Esglentine knew that they were in the palace they fled to their rooms with all their ladies out of their great fear. But Valentin climbed upstairs and entered the hall where King Pepin sat accompanied by all the noble barons of his court. Hauffroy and Henry made much display of affection over Valentin, and it seemed to him that they[1] were most happy about the great deed and exploit he had accomplished, but, in their hearts, never had they been so unhappy, for never had they wanted Valentin to return alive. They cursed the wild man for not having killed and destroyed him.

King Pepin and his entire court looked at Orson with great interest. Then King Pepin spoke: "My lords, by almighty God, it is truly a marvelous thing to see and contemplate this wild man. He is well formed, of handsome limb and stature. However hairy he is, if he were clothed like the rest of us, he would be most pleasant to behold, and would appear a most comely knight."

Then Valentin spoke to Pepin in this manner: "Sire, I beg you to have him baptized. That way he will learn the faith and belief of the Christian religion, for such is my desire and so did I promise him."

"It pleases me well," said the king. "Let it be done." So he ordered a priest to baptize him, and his godfathers were King Pepin and Duke Millon d'Angler, Samson and Gervais, and many other valiant knights, including Valentin. On the other side were Queen Bertha and many other ladies of high renown, but they gave him no other name than the one he had taken in the forest.

Once Orson was baptized the king sat down at table to dinner, Valentin serving him from his cup, for such was his duty. When he was seated he ordered that Orson be brought into the hall to observe his manners and behavior. Orson stood before the king, who looked at him closely. When he noticed the meat that was placed in front of the king, he grabbed from the platter what he could carry away and began eating quickly with huge bites. When he had eaten, he saw a servant on the other side carrying a peacock on a platter to serve to the king. So he ran over and snatched it away from the servant, then sat down on the floor in the middle of the hall and began to eat. When Valentin saw him, he gestured to him that he was behaving badly, which made Orson ashamed, for, more than anything else, he naturally feared and respected Valentin. But King Pepin directed that they should leave him alone, for he enjoyed watching his antics. Once Orson had eaten his fill, he noticed a jar full of wine, so he seized it right away, drank it in one gulp, then threw the jar to the ground and began to shake his head, which

---

[1] Although the subject pronoun and verb are clearly singular, all other signs in the text point to Valentin's belief that both Hauffroy and Henry seem happy to see him.

ceulx de la court ont moult commencé a rire. Et quant la nuit fut venue, a Valentin fut baillee une chambre pour coucher, en laquelle fut ordonné et paré ung lyt pour Orson. Mais pour neant ont le lit appareillé, car si tost qu'il entra en la chambre, il se coucha a terre et tantost s'en dormit, car aultrement n'avoit aprins de dormir en la forest.

[CHAPTER 14]

Comment Hauffroy et Henry pour leur enuye prindrent conseil pour tuer Valentin en la chambre de la belle Esglentine. xiiii. chapitre.[1]

Moult fut joyeuse et plaisante la belle Esglentine de ce que Valentin avoit le sauvaige conquis. Si luy manda par une damoiselle qu'il luy amenast Orson le sauvaige. Lors Valentin appella Orson, si le print par la main, si le mena en la chambre de Esglentine en laquelle avoit plusieurs dames et damoiselles qui voulentiers regarderent Orson. Et Orson en riant se getta sur ung lit et regarda les dames en faisant plusieurs signes et manieres qui aux dames estoient moult plaisantes. Mais tout ce qu'il faisoit point ne l'entendoient, de quoy elles estoyent moult desplaisantes. Si appellerent Valentin et luy demanderent que c'estoit que le sauvaige leur monstroit par ces signes, et Valentin leur dist, "Mes dames, sachez de vray que le sauvaige monstre par ces signes que moult voulentiers vouldroit baiser et acoler les dames et damoiselles qui icy sont," dont elles commencerent a rire et regarder l'une l'autre.

Et ainsi que ensemble se devisoient et qu'i s'esbatoyent en la chambre de Esglentine pour la venue du sauvaige, Hauffroy vint devers Henry et luy a dit, "Beau frere, trop mal va nostre fait, car vous voyez que ce garson meschant et malleureux trouvé Valentin de jour en jour monte et acroist en honneur entre les princes, seigneurs et dames. Et entre les aultres choses le roy est plus de luy amoureulx qu'il n'est de l'ung de nous, laquelle chose est et peult estre en grant avilissement[2] et bassement de nostre honneur."

"Hauffroy," ce dist Henry, "vous dictes verité et parlez comme saige. Et quant a moy je ne fay point de doubte que par luy une foys nous [27verso]ne soyons desprisez se longuement il dure et regne."

"Frere," dist Hauffroy, "oyez que je vous diray. Valentin est maintenant en la chambre de nostre seur Esglentine, laquelle chose nous luy avons longtemps a deffendue. Si aurons bone excusation de le prendre et mouvoir guerre et debat

---

[1] Woodcut of two standing figures conferring; one tree and river as background.
[2] Text has *avisement*, which makes no sense in this context. I have emended to "avilissement," more likely the intended synonym to "bassement."

made the king and everyone in the court begin to laugh uproariously. When night fell, Valentin was given a room to sleep in, where a bed was also ordered and set up for Orson. But the bed was set up for nothing, for as soon as he entered the chamber, he lay down on the floor and fell directly asleep, for in the forest he had learned no other way to sleep.

CHAPTER 14

How Hauffroy and Henry conspired to kill Valentin out of jealousy in the chamber of the fair Esglentine.

The fair Esglentine was pleased and happy that Valentin had conquered the wild man. She sent a damsel to ask him to bring Orson the wild man to her. So Valentin called Orson, and, taking him by the hand, led him to Esglentine's chamber where there were many ladies and damsels who looked at Orson with much interest. And Orson, laughing, threw himself on a bed and looked at the ladies, making all kinds of signs and gestures that the ladies found very funny. But they didn't understand at all what he meant, which displeased them. So they called over Valentin and asked him what the wild man wanted to show them by these gestures, and Valentin explained to them, "My ladies, understand that the wild man is gesturing to indicate that he would very much like to kiss and hug the ladies and damsels here," for which reason they all started to laugh and glance at one another.

While they were talking and enjoying together the presence of the wild man in Esglentine's room, Hauffroy came to Henry and said to him, "Fair brother, our plan goes badly, for you see that this wretched foundling Valentin rises and gains more honor from day to day among princes, lords, and ladies. And what is worse, the king loves him more than either of us, which is likely greatly to decrease our standing."

"Hauffroy," said Henry, "what you say is true and wisely said. As for me, I have no doubt that one day because of him we could end up repudiated if he lives long."

"Brother," said Hauffroy, "listen to me. Right now Valentin is in our sister Esglentine's room, something that we have long forbidden him. Thus we have a good excuse to seize him, accuse him, and incite him to fight. So if you want to

contre luy. Et pour tant se croire me voulez, nous irons en la chambre et par nous sera mis a mort; puis nous jurerons au roy que avec nostre seur l'aurons trouvé faisant d'elle sa voulenté."

Ainsi parlerent les deux trahytres et desloyaulx, et ainsi comme les juifz par leur envye ilz crucifierent et machinerent la mort de Nostre Seigneur a tort et sans cause, tout ainsi firent Hauffroy et Henry Valentin qui tant estoit debonnaire et a tous obeÿssant, que oncques de sa bouche ung villain mot ne saillit. Et apres qu'ilz eurent fait et achevé leur faulce et mauldite entreprinse ilz alerent en la chambre de la belle plaisante Esglentine. Et tout aussitost que Hauffroy fut entré il a dist a Valentin, "Mauvais et desloyal homme, or congnoissons nous que de ta folie et oultrageuse voulenté ne te veulx point restraindre ne retirer. Mais en perseverant en ta malice et folle oppinion, en pourchassant de jour en jour le deshonneur de nostre pere le roy Pepin, par le moyen et acord de nostre faulce et desloyale seur Esglentine de laquelle vous faictes a vostre plaisir et voulenté tout ainsi que de une femme malleureuse et dissolue, pour quoy c'est bien droit et rayson que mal vous en viengne, et puis que le roy de ce fait ne tient compte, c'est force que vengance de vous nous prengnons."

En disant ces parolles Hauffroy a levé la main, si a frappé Valentin tellement que par la bouche luy a fait le sang cler saillir. Puis Henry s'est approché qui d'ung glaisve trenchant et agu a cuidé Valentin frapper moult oultrageusement. Et quant Orson a veu que on vouloit oultrager Valentin, il est sally avant et a baillé si grant coup a Hauffroy que de sa main velue a terre l'abatit. Puis est couru vers Henry et tellement entre ses bras l'a estraint derrier[1] que se n'eussent esté les dames qui Orson appaiserent et pacifierent, jamais de sa vie n'y eust heu respit.

Lors se leva le cry en la chambre sy grant que grant partie des seigneurs et barons de la court vindrent en la chambre. Et quant ilz ont aperceu que Orson sy malmenoit les deux filz du roy ilz l'ont voulu frapper de glaisves et de espees et tous contre luy se sont mis en deffence pour le vouloir tuer et mettre a mort. Adonc Valentin pour Orson secourir tyra son espee. Si a juré que s'il y a plus homme qui Orson frappe ne touche quoy qu'il en doive avenir la vie luy ostera. Puis fait signe a Orson que plus il ne frappe, et Orson atant se retrayt sans nul oultraige faire.

Et Hauffroy et Henry sont aléz vers le roy Pe[28recto]pin[2] dolens et courroucéz. Puis luy a dit Hauffroy, "Ha, sire, mal fut oncques né Valentin que si chier vous tenez, car seans a amené le sauvaige par qui moy et mon frere avons esté en danger et peril de mort. Sire, trop mal ferez se plus vous le laissez vivre car dommaige et deshonneur vous portera de brief. Pour Dieu, faictes qu'i soit noyé ou pendu, car riens ne vault la garde de sa compaignie."

Quant le roy Pepin oÿt les nouvelles moult tristre et delent en fust. Et a dit qu'i fera le sauvaige en une tour mener et fermer en telle maniere que jamais

---

[1] Text has *derrie*.

[2] *d iiii* appears at bottom right corner of 28r.

follow my advice, we'll go into that room and we'll kill him; then we will swear to the king that we found him having his way with our sister."

So spoke the two faithless traitors, and just as the envious Jews crucified and wrongly plotted the death of Our Lord without just cause, so schemed Hauffroy and Henry against Valentin, who was so kind, so happy to serve everyone, from whose mouth never sprang a base word. After they had finalized their wicked, villainous plans, they marched off to the chamber of the fair and pleasant Esglentine. As soon as Hauffroy entered, he said to Valentin, "Evil, faithless man, now we know that you have no desire to restrain your madness and outrageous lust. Since you persist in your malice and perverse notions, attempting day by day to dishonor our father King Pepin by means of and in agreement with our false and disloyal sister Esglentine, with whom you take your pleasure and have your way as if she were any unfortunate dissolute woman, for which reason you should rightly come to harm, and since the king does nothing about this, we must perforce take vengeance on you."

Thereupon Hauffroy lifted his arm and struck Valentin with such force that bright red blood gushed from his mouth. Next Henry approached, thinking to smite Valentin most outrageously with a sharp pointed sword. However, when Orson saw that they wanted to attack Valentin, he sallied forth and landed such a blow on Henry with his hairy hand that he dashed him to the ground. Then he ran up to Henry, squeezing him so tightly in his arms from behind that if it had not been for the ladies who calmed Orson down, never would he have let him go.

The noise was so loud then in the chamber that most of the lords and barons of the court came running to the room. When they realized that Orson was mistreating the king's two sons, they wanted to attack him with swords and blades, all of them on the defense against him, intending to put him to death. So Valentin drew his sword to come to Orson's rescue. He swore that if any man struck or touched him he would kill him on the spot no matter what. Then he gestured to Orson to stop fighting, and Orson retreated right away without causing any harm.

So Hauffroy and Henry, angry and upset, went straight to King Pepin. Hauffroy addressed him: "Ah, sire, alas that Valentin, whom you hold so dear, was ever born, for he brought the wild man here who very nearly killed my brother and me. Sire, it would be wrong for you to let him live, for he will soon bring you harm and dishonor. For God's sake, have him drowned or hanged, for keeping his company is worthless."

When King Pepin heard the news he was truly saddened. He said that he would have the wild man shut up in a tower in such a way that he would never

saillir n'en pourra fors que par congié. Le roy fist venir Valentin pour demander de ce fait, et Valentin luy compte l'entreprinse telle qu'elle avoit esté faicte par Hauffroy et Henry. "Sire," dist Valentin, "je estoie en la chambre de madame vostre fille en la compaignie de plusieurs dames et damoiselles qui fort desiroient a veoir Orson et principalement madame Esglentine. Je luy avoye mené; si ne sçay pourquoy ne a quel tiltre messeigneurs voz deux filz Hauffroy et Henry sont en la chambre entréz en moy disant que de vostre fille vouloye faire a mon plaisir et que de pieça le sçavoient bien. Et en disant fieres et orgueilleuses parolles Hauffroy par oultageuse voulenté m'a frappé, et Henry de son espee ma vie m'a cuidé oster. Orson voyant que mon corps estoit en danger est alé devers eulx et les a tous deux rué par terre en telle maniere que pour celle cause le bruit et le cry en est tel que vous le voyez."

"Est il vray," dist Pepin, "ainsi que vous dictes?"

"Oy, sire," ce dist Valentin, "sur la peine de ma vie. Aultre chose ne aultre cause je n'y sçay."

"Et par Dieu," dist le roy Pepin, "Orson a fait son devoir et ce qu'i devoit faire. Et vous, Hauffroy et Henry, gens estes envieux et de male voulenté plains. Je voys et cognois clerement que de toute vostre puissance vous querez de jour en jour nuyre a Valentin. Bien estez de mauvaise nature de pourchasser son mal quant vous voyez que je l'ayme et que loyaument me sert. Je vous deffens de luy mal vouloir; et le laissez atant, car de luy ne me veul pour aultre deffaire. Et se suis bien certain que mon deshonneur jamais il ne le vouldroit querir ne serchier."

Ainsi se departent Hauffroy et Henry qui moult furent dolens et desplaisans. Valentin demoura en la sale avec les aultres seigneurs et barons de la court. Et Orson s'en va parmy le palais. Il entre en la cuisine et voit la viande que le cuisiner habilloit pour le soupper. Sy est approché de luy et a prins deux chapons tout cruz et les mengue et mort ainsi comme ung chien. Et le cuisiner print ung peteil et en frappa Orson si grant coup que tout ployer le fist; dont se baisse Orson et print le cuisinier et le getta dessus terre. Et tant de coupz luy donna que a peu qu'i ne fut mort.

Les nouvelles vindrent au roy que Orson tuoit le cuisinier [28verso]du palais et que nul n'osoit de lui approcher, dont le roy fut fort courroucé et fist venir Orson et luy a fait signe que il le fera pendre. Mais Orson ala tantost querir le pesteil et monstra au roy comment le cuisinier l'avoit rudement frappé. Et quant le roy cogneust le cas il pardonna tout a Orson et commanda que nul ne le touchast plus. Et Valentin[1] luy monstra mode et maniere de soy gouverner parmy le palais pour le temps a venir. Valentin print la chairge et si bien l'enseigna que depuis il ne fit a nul mal ne desplaisir qui premier en luy n'en faisoit. Et en ce point demourerent longuement avec le roy Pepin qui estoit leur oncle, mais il n'en sçavoit riens.

---

[1] The text inserts *qui* here unnecessarily.

be able to get out except with permission. But the king also had Valentin come tell him what had happened, and Valentin recounted the incident and how it had been instigated by Hauffroy and Henry. "Sire," said Valentin, "I was in the room with my lady your daughter in the company of several ladies and damsels who had expressed a strong desire to see Orson, especially my lady Esglentine. I brought him to her; I have no idea why or for what reason my lords your two sons, Hauffroy and Henry, burst into the chamber saying that I wanted to take my pleasure with your daughter and that they knew it long ago. While pronouncing this arrogant and aggressive speech, Hauffroy struck me without provocation, and Henry prepared to kill me with his sword. Orson, seeing my life in danger, came towards them and knocked them both to the ground in such a way that a great ruckus ensued, which brought all this to your attention."

"Is this true," asked Pepin, "just as you say?"

"Yes, sire," replied Valentin, "on pain of death. I know of nothing else or any other cause."

"Well then, by God," declared King Pepin, "Orson did his duty and what he was supposed to do. And you, Hauffroy and Henry, you are jealous and filled with ill will. I can clearly see that you seek day and night with all your might to injure Valentin. You are truly wicked to attempt to harm him when you see that I love him and that he serves me faithfully. I forbid you to try to hurt him; leave him alone, for I want no one else. I am absolutely certain that he would never attempt to dishonor me."

Hauffroy and Henry thus left, thoroughly disheartened and discouraged, whereas Valentin remained in the hall with the other lords and barons of the court. Orson, however, wandered around the palace. He entered the kitchen and saw the meat that the cook was preparing for that night's supper. He approached and grabbed two completely raw capons, eating and chewing them like a dog. So the cook took hold of a pestle with which he struck Orson so hard that he doubled over; then Orson stooped down, seized the cook, and threw him to the ground. So many blows did he give him that he nearly killed him.

Word came to the king that Orson was killing the palace cook and that no one dared approach him, which greatly angered the king. He had Orson brought to him and gestured to him that he would have him hanged. But Orson went right away to get the pestle, showing the king how the cook had viciously hit him. When the king understood how things stood, he forgave Orson everything and ordered that no one ever touch him. Then Valentin taught him how to comport himself in the palace from that time forth. Valentin took charge of him and taught him well, so that thenceforward he caused no harm or unpleasantness unless someone provoked him first. In this manner they remained a long time with King Pepin who was their uncle, though he was completely unaware of it.

[CHAPITRE 15]

Comment le duc Savary envoya devers le roy Pepin pour avoir secours contre le Verd Chevalier qui a force vouloit avoir sa fille Fezonne. xv. chapitre.[1]

En celuy temps que Orson et Valentin estoient ensemble a la court du roy, de par le duc Savary vint ung chevalier devers le roy lequel apres qu'il eust fait toute reverence au roy parla en ceste maniere:

"Franc roy puissant et sur tous redoubté, le bon duc Savary, a qui servant je suis, par devers vous m'envoye requerant que par vous puisse estre secouru contre ung faulx payen qui l'a assiegé, et se nomme le Verd Chevalier, qui par force d'armes et malgré son courage sa fille veult avoir qui est la plus belle qui puisse estre. Et si a trois freres moult hardis et puissans, c'est assavoir Garin, Anseaulme, et Gerin le plus jeune."

"Messeigneurs, sachez que voulentiers secourrons le bon duc et si luy aiderons en son besoing de toute nostre puissance."

"Sire," dist le messaiger, "Dieu vous en sache gré, car vous ferez aulmoisne, et vous remercye de par mon maistre cincq cens fois."

En disant ces paroles vint dedens le palays ung aultre messagier, lequel apres la reverence de humilité au roy faicte luy a dit, "Excellent et sur tous redoubté prince, veullez en toute diligence vostre ost et voz gens d'armes envoyer vers la cité de Lyon, car des Alemaignes sont yssus et saillis plus de cent mil combatans qui vostre royaulme veullent du tout destruire et mettre en subjection."[2]

Quant le roy eut les nouvelles oyés et entendues il fust moult esbahy, et fist venir l'archevesque de Rains, le duc Mil[29recto]lon[3] d'Angler, Gervaiz et Sanson. Puis leur a dit le cas du messagier et conseil leur demanda sur ce point pour sçavoir quelle part il devoit aler, ou devers Acquitaine le bon duc secourir ou devers Lyon pour son païs garder.

A laquelle chose respondit Millon d'Angler, "Sire, sur ceste matiere vous devez estre tout conseillé. Car plus pres vous est vostre chemise que vostre robe. Vous ne devez pas deffendre le païs d'aultruy pour le vostre laisser, pour quoy sans aultre conseil avoir vous yrez vers Lyon pour vostre pays garder et deffendre. Et quant vous aurez voz ennemis chasséz et expellés dehors de vostre terre et royaulme, adonc pourrez vous seurement aler secourir le bon duc Savary qui vous demande secours."

---

[1] Woodcut of standing messenger delivering a message to a figure in a feathered cap and robe with sword at side.

[2] Text has *subietion*.

[3] Text has *Millost*.

CHAPTER 15

How Duke Savary sent to King Pepin for help against the Green Knight, who wanted to claim his daughter Fezonne by force.

During this period when Orson and Valentin were together at Pepin's court, a knight came to the king from Duke Savary. After bowing to Pepin, he delivered the following message:

"Noble and mighty king, respected above all others, the good Duke Savary, whom I serve, has sent me to you to request help against a false pagan, named the Green Knight, who has besieged him. He wishes to take possession of the duke's daughter against her will by means of force, and she is the most beautiful girl that ever was. Three brothers she has, strong and bold, namely Garin, Anseaulme, and Gerin, the youngest."

"My lords, willingly will we come to the aid of the good duke and help him in his need with all the strength at our disposal."

"Sire," said the messenger, "may God reward you, for you will be performing a true act of charity. I thank you five hundred times in my master's name."

As he spoke, another messenger came into the palace, who bowed humbly before the king and addressed him: "Most excellent and respected prince, I beg you to assemble your army with all your men at arms as quickly as you can to send them to the city of Lyon, for the Germans have attacked, sallying forth with more than a hundred thousand soldiers to destroy your realm and subject it to their rule."

When the king had heard this news, he was astonished, and called for the archbishop of Reims, Duke Millon d'Angler, Gervaiz, and Sanson, explaining to them the messenger's information and requesting their advice, namely, which direction he should take—to Aquitaine to help the good duke, or to Lyon to defend his own land.

Millon d'Angler answered him, "Sire, you must accept counsel on this matter. Just as your shirt is closer to you than your gown, you must not defend another's land while your own is neglected, for which reason you should go directly to Lyon to keep and defend your country without taking any other advice. Once you have chased off your enemies and expelled them from your lands and kingdom, then you will surely be able to go help the good Duke Savary who requests your aid."

Le conseil creust et accepta le roy, et au messagier du duc Savary dist que, "Pour le present de moy ne peult avoir secours, car mener me fault mon ost sans sejour ne dilation vers le pays de Lyon. Je suis desplaisant que je ne le puis secourir a son besoing et nonpourtant vous luy direz qu'i se tienne tousjours ferme contre le Verd Chevalier, et que moy ayant fait mon entreprinse, grant secours je luy emmerray, et de gens si grant nombre qu'il sera bien content."

"Sire," dist le messagier, "trop mal luy vient a point que venir vous n'y pouez car il en a grant afaire pour le present. Mais puis qu'il ne peult estre aultrement fait, je vous remercye de vostre bon vouloir, et au congé de vostre haulte majesté je me depars de vous." Et a ces motz le chevalier et messaiger du duc Savary s'en ala vers le pays d'Acquitaine et compta les nouvelles et l'empeschement du roy Pepin. Et quant le duc sceust que venir ne luy pouoit du roy Pepin de France secours, moult en fust desplaisant et dolent, car le Verd Chevalier grant guerre luy faisoit, et de trop pres l'avoit assiegé.

Et devez sçavoir que iceluy Chevalier Verd estoit frere de Ferragu le geant qui Bellissant la dame faisoit garder en sa maison, laquelle estoit mere de Valentin et du sauvaige Orson, ainsi que vous avez devant oÿ dire et declairer.

Or fut le duc Savary dedens Acquitaine moult pensif et dolent pour le Verd Chevalier qui telle guerre luy faisoit pour sa fille. Il a fait crier et commander que tous ceulx de son ost soient en point et en armes et le lendemain au matin il veult saillir hors contre le Verd Chevalier pour les paiens combatre. Chascun se mist en point et firent devoir d'eulx armer. Et quant le jour fut cler, les clarons et trompettes sonnerent, et gens d'armes de toutes pars, tant de pié comme de cheval, se sont mis a chemin pour saillir hors de la ville. Grant haste avoit le duc Savary du Verd Chevalier assaillir, mais tel se cuide avancer qui aulcune fois fait son dommaige, et ainsi en print au duc come il sera dit.

Le duc Savary saillit hors d'Aquitaine a grant compaignie. Et quant il fut aux champs il sonna tromppettes [29verso]et clarons, et comme vaillant champion ses ennemis assaillit et vint ferir sur eulx. Et Sarrasins et payens qui grant nombre furent ont couru aux armes et commença merveilleuse bataille. Et le Verd Chevalier frappa a tout sa hache d'armes que premier qu'il arrestast tua deux chevaliers. Lors le duc Savary est devers luy tiré, et ont l'ung l'autre moult fierement assailly. Vaillant estoit le bon duc, mais nonpourtant du Verd Chevalier combatre entreprenoit moult grant folie. Car telle estoit la predestination d'iceluy Verd Chevalier et par sort estoit predestiné que jamais ne seroit ne conquis ne vaincu sinon par homme qui fust filz de roy, et qui n'eust jamais de femme esté nourry ne alaitté. Si ne se pensoit pas que jamais tel homme peust estre trouvé, mais tel enfant est sur terre vivant qui le combatera et vainquira—c'est Orson le sauvaige comme vous orrez.

Ensemble se combatirent moult longuement le duc Savary et le Verd Chevalier mais trop entra avant le bon duc, car quant il se cuida retirer pour aler vers son ost, tant fut des payens poursuivy et de toutes pars sy ensarré que fortune le contraindit d'estre rué par terre, parquoy il fust prins prisonnier de ses ennemis.

The king believed and accepted this advice, and to Duke Savary's messenger he said, "For the present, I cannot help you, for I am obliged to lead my army without delay to the land of Lyon. I am truly sorry that I cannot help him in his need; nevertheless you will tell him to hold firm against the Green Knight, and, once I have accomplished my goal, I will bring him such aid and such a number of men that he will be content."

"Sire," said the messenger, "it will be hard for him that you cannot come, for he has much to deal with at the present time. But since there is no help for it, I thank you for your good will, and if your majesty is agreeable, I will take my leave." With these words the knight messenger of Duke Savary left for the land of Aquitaine to recount the news and the reason why King Pepin could not come. When the duke found out that King Pepin of France could not come help him he was very unhappy and upset, for the Green Knight was waging terrible war against him and had besieged him very closely.

You ought to know that this very Green Knight was the brother of Ferragu the giant who kept the lady Bellissant in his house, she who was mother to Valentin and the wild man Orson, as you have heard explained previously.

So Duke Savary was in Aquitaine, worried and upset because of the Green Knight who was waging such war against him in order to possess his daughter. He sent out word that all the men of his host should arm and prepare themselves to sally out the next morning to fight against the Green Knight and his pagans. Everyone took great care to arm himself and get ready. Once the day dawned they blew the trumpets and sounded the clarions to issue forth from the city. Duke Savary was in great haste to attack the Green Knight, but often he who hopes to advance does so only to his own disadvantage, and so it happened to the duke, as I will explain.

Duke Savary sallied forth from Aquitaine with a great company. When he reached the fields he blew his trumpets and clarions, and, like a valiant champion, attacked his enemies, striking hard against them. The pagan Saracens, who comprised a great host, ran to arm themselves, and thus began an amazing battle. The Green Knight swung hard with his great battle-axe so that at first blow he killed two knights. Then Duke Savary rode over to him, and they assaulted one another fiercely. The good duke was valiant; however, in fighting the Green Knight, he had done a foolish thing, for it had been predicted that it was the fate of the Green Knight never to be conquered or vanquished in battle except by a king's son who had never suckled woman's milk. Of course he did not believe ever to find such a man, but such a one did exist who would one day fight and vanquish him—that was Orson the wild man, as you will hear later on.

Together they fought for a long time, Duke Savary and the Green Knight, but the good duke had advanced too far into the enemy host, for when he thought to withdraw to his own men, he found himself pursued and surrounded on all sides by so many pagans that he was knocked down and taken prisoner by his

Et le prindrent paiens et le menerent au Verd Chevalier que telle joye enmena que pour nul tresor ne l'eust voulu laisser aler. Et le duc en son cueur reclama Dieu et la Vierge Marie.

Quant les crestiens sceurent que le duc estoit prins, dolens et esbahis sont en Acquitaine retournéz. Lors commença le peuple a grant dueil demener, et a faire grans regretz et lamentations pour leur bon duc qui tant aimoient. La furent ses trois filz, Garin, Anseaulme, et Gerin le jeune qui pour leur pere font grant dueil.

Mais sur tous passoit la plainte et lamentation de Fezonne, laquelle en ses cheveulx desrompant qui plus luisant que l'or estoient en gettant de ses yeulx grosses larmes et disoit, "Helas! de malle heure fus je nee, quant il fault que pour moy tant de vaillans vaisseaulx et nobles chevaliers pour moy ont tel douleur et si piteusement finent leurs jours. Et qui plus est mon cueur a chose fort amere a souffrir et a porter se le bon duc mon pere, qui est pour l'amour de moy entre les mains de ses ennemis mortelz, est piteusement prins, dont mourir luy conviendra par douleur angoisseuse et piteuse destresse. Helas! mon treschier pere, trop chierement m'avez aimee, quant mon amour vous est vendue si chiere, qu'i convient que par moy la mort vous soit livree."

Si fort se complaint en plourant la belle Fezonne que elle a courage et voulenté de soy tuer. Ainsi pleure et suspire la belle.

Et le Verd Chevalier est en son pavillon qui a fait venir devant luy le duc et luy a dist moult fierement, "Or vois tu mantenant que tu es en ma subjection, et que j'ay puissance de toy faire mourir ou de sauver ta vie. Sy te diray et deviseray que tu feras—donne [30recto]moy ta fille Fezonne a femme et la vie te sauveras et la meneray en la verde montaigne ou moult richement couronner le feray."

"Sarrasin," dit le duc, "je te diray ma voulenté. Saches que ma fille jamais tu n'auras se baptiser tu ne te fais, et que de Jhesus prengne la loy et creance."

"Savary," ce dit le chevalier, "de telle chose ne me parle jamais, car ja jour de ma vie en ton Dieu je ne croyray. Et si te dy puis que mon conseil tu ne veulx croire je te feray mourir et de finer ta vie villainement. Et si feray Acquitaine ardoir, brusler et mettre a execution et tous les hommes et femmes et petis enfans feray tous mettre a mort."

"Payen," dist Savary, "Dieu me veulle par sa grace contre toy ne ta malle et cruelle voulenté deffendre et garder. Car en luy je me fie et en luy est toute ma seule esperance."

Longuement furent en parlant de ceste matiere le Verd Chevalier et le duc Savary qui en Dieu reclamant du cueur souspire tendrement, et le Verd Chevalier le regarde. Et quant il a veu les grans lamentations qu'i faisoit et piteulx pleurs qu'i gettoit, il luy a dist, "Franc duc, delaissez le plourer, car tant suis esprins et ardamment embrasé de l'amour de vostre fille que pour l'amour d'elle je n'ay vouloir ne courage de vous oster la vie. Mais suis du tout deliberé de donner congé par tel convenant que se dedens six mois vous m'amenrez chevalier qui pour puissance d'armes me puisse conquerir vostre fille je quitteray et en mon pays je m'en retourneray avec toute mon armee sans de riens vostre terre degaster ne destruire.

enemies. The pagans took hold of him and led him to the Green Knight, who was so overjoyed that no treasure could have induced him to let him go. The poor duke, however, prayed to God and the Virgin Mary in his heart.

When the Christians realized that the duke had been taken, they returned, sad and disheartened, into Aquitaine. Then the people began to mourn, sorrowfully lamenting their good duke whom they loved so much. His three sons were there, Garin, Anseaulme, and Gerin the youngest, who greatly mourned their father.

But the plaint and lamentation of Fezonne surpassed all the others, for she tore at her hair (that shone brighter than gold) and wept copious tears, saying, "Alas! Woe is me, when for my sake so many brave vassals and noble knights suffer and end their days so terribly. And what is worse, my heart must suffer and bear a bitter burden if, because of his love for me, the good duke my father has fallen into the hands of his mortal enemies and been taken prisoner, for which he will surely die out of pain, anguish, and distress. Alas! my cherished father, you loved me too dearly, for my love is sold to you at too high a price, when as a result death comes to you on my account."

So violently did the fair Fezonne grieve and weep that she was ready to kill herself. Thus did the lovely girl cry and sigh.

Meanwhile the Green Knight, who was in his tent, had the duke brought before him, and spoke to him most fiercely: "Now you see yourself subjected to me, and it is in my power to kill you or save your life. I will tell you what you must do—give me your daughter Fezonne as wife and I will spare your life. Then I will bring her to the Green Mountain where I will have her richly crowned."

"Saracen," said the duke, "I will tell you my will. Know that you will never have my daughter unless you have yourself baptized and take up the faith and belief of Jesus."

"Savary," said the knight, "don't ever speak to me of such a thing, for never in my life will I believe in your God. And I declare to you that since you don't wish to accept my counsel, I will have you put to a shameful death. Moreover, I will have Aquitaine put to the torch, and execute men, women, and children—all of them will die."

"Pagan," said Savary, "may God in His grace protect and defend me against you and your cruel and evil will. For in Him do I place my trust and in Him is my only hope."

For a long time the Green Knight and Duke Savary spoke of this matter, and the duke beseeched God from the depths of his heart and sighed profoundly, while the Green Knight watched him. When he saw his great lamentations and piteous tears, he said to him, "Noble duke, leave off this weeping, for I am so smitten and burning with love for your daughter that for her sake I have not the heart or will to take your life. Instead, I have decided to let you go under the condition that, if within six months you will bring me a knight who can defeat me in battle, I will leave your daughter and return to my country with my entire army without hurting or destroying anything of your land. But if it turns out

Et s'il avient que dedens ledit terme je ne soye conquis et vaincu, je auray vostre fille pour femme et espouse et en mon pays sans aultre guerre faire l'ameneray."
Pour tant firent entre eulx la paix et les triesves cryer l'espace de six mois. Et apres le cry fait, le Chevalier Verd donna congé au duc Savary. Sur la foy de Jhesucrist luy jura les dessusdictes triesves tenir et loyaument garder l'appointement par eulx dessus devisé, et ou cas du deffault luy donne sa fille sans nulle excusation ou contradicion. Puis vint a Acquitaine et fit par tout sçavoir et publier la forme de l'appointement. Et quant il eust fait les triesves par six mois crier, il manda son conseil et leur declaira la maniere comment il avoit fait avec le Verd Chevalier. Si ont avisé et deliberé par entre eulx que le duc envoiast messagiers par tout le pays d'environ pour serchier et querir chevalier que par sa prouesse et puissance puisse le Verd Chevalier combatre. Et apres le conseil ainsi prins le duc fist venir plusieurs messagiers de toutes nacions crestiens, puis leur a baillé lettres esquelles estoit contenu la grande beaulté de sa fille et l'entreprinse du Verd Chevalier. Et si mandoit le duc ces lettres que celluy qui pourroit le Verd Chevalier conquerir il luy donnera sa fille. Les lettres furent baillees a douze [30verso]messaigiers qui eurent la charge de les porter par tout le pays jusques a douze royaulmes crestiens et en furent les nouvelles publiees et magnifestees.

[CHAPITRE 16]

Comment plusieurs chevaliers sy vindrent en Acquitaine pour cuider avoir la belle Fezonne. xvi. cha[pitre].[1]

En celuy temps durant les triesves, le roy Pepin de France sy estoit alé contre les ennemys devers Lyon acompagné de soixante mil hommes. Et tant fist qu'il chassa et mist a desconfiture ung roy nommé Lempatris, lequel encontre Pepin les payens et Sarrasins conduisoit en moult grande puissance. Celuy Lempatris estoit roy de Saines et de Hollande et de Frise. Et avec ce il tenoit le pays de Monemarche qui estoit une ville forte et puisante en laquelle se retrahirent les paiens pour la doubte du roy Pepin. Et quant il sceut qu'ilz furent tous encloz en ladicte ville et forteresse, le roy les assiega en telle maniere que il les affama, et tant qu'ilz se rendirent et se mirent du tout a sa voulenté. Et quant il eut la ville prinse il fist les payens baptiser et croire en Jesucrist, et donna la ville au mareschal de France qui estoit appellé Guy.

Apres ces choses le roy Pepin a tout son ost retourna en France et arriva a Paris. Si eust tantost les nouvelles par ung messagier du duc Savary comment il

---

[1] Woodcut of party of knights riding through castle portcullis, seen from rear.

that within the said term I am neither defeated nor vanquished, I will take your daughter to wife and will bring her to my country without waging further war."

On that basis they ceased hostilities and had a truce proclaimed for six months. And after the announcement, the Green Knight set Duke Savary free. In the name of Jesus Christ the duke swore to observe the above-mentioned truce and faithfully to keep the appointment settled between them, and that, if he defaulted on the agreement, he would give up his daughter without excuse or resistance. Then he went to Aquitaine, and published and made known everywhere the terms of the agreement. Once the six-month truce was announced, he called together his council and explained to them how he had reached an agreement with the Green Knight. Then, having deliberated among themselves, they advised the duke to send messengers to all the surrounding countries to seek a knight who would have the prowess and ability to fight the Green Knight. Once he had accepted this counsel, the duke convoked several messengers from all the Christian lands, entrusting to them letters in which was described the great beauty of his daughter and the endeavor of the Green Knight. And the duke wrote in these letters that he would grant his daughter to the one who could defeat the Green Knight. The letters were given to twelve messengers charged with bearing them far and wide to twelve Christian realms where the tidings were disseminated and circulated.

CHAPTER 16

How many knights came to Aquitaine to try to win the fair Fezonne.

At this time, while the truce was in force, King Pepin of France rode off to Lyon to attack his enemies, accompanied by sixty thousand men. He fought so well that he drove out and defeated a king named Lempatris, who had brought a great army of pagans and Saracens to fight against Pepin. This Lempatris was king of Saxony, Holland, and Friesland. Moreover, he controlled the land around Monemarche, a strong, powerful city to which the pagans retreated out of fear of King Pepin. When he realized that they had withdrawn into that fortress city, the king besieged them so closely that he starved them into submission to his will. Once the city was taken, he had all the pagans baptized and converted to belief in Jesus Christ, giving the city to Guy, the Marshal of France.

Subsequent to these events, King Pepin and all his host returned to France and arrived in Paris. Right away he received tidings from a messenger sent by

avoit prins triesves au Verd Chevalier. Et quant il sceut la maniere comment et la condicion de leur appointement il dist devant tous ses barons en riant, "Seigneurs, qui vouldra avoir belle amye, il est temps qu'i se monstre vaillant, car celuy qui pourra le Verd Chevalier combatre par fait d'armes il aura en mariage la tresplaisante Fezonne, fille du duc Savary, et si aura avec elle de sa terre et seigneurie la moitié. Et qu'il soit vray, vecy les lettres. Tenés et regardez entre vous le contenu d'icelles."

Chascun regarda ces lettres moult voulentiers. Mais il n'y eust si hardy ne si vaillant qui l'entreprinse voulust faire fors que Valentin qui devant tous dit au roy Pepin, "Treschier et redoubté sire, sy plaist a vostre majesté de moy donner congé et licence que en Acquitaine esprouve mon corps contre le Verd Chevalier. Sire, donnez moy congé que departe [31recto]de la contree de France, car j'ay moult fort grant desir de laisser le païs. Et tant chevalcheray que jamais n'auray repos tant que je aye nouvelle de la mere qui me porta, car tresfort il me desplaist que sy longuement j'ay demouré sans sçavoir qui je suis."

"Valentin," dist le roy, "ne vous chaille qui vous soyez, car assez suis puissant pour vous donner des biens largement et vous monter en honneur et vous faire puissant et tous ceulx de ma court. Et aussi chier vous tieng comme se vous estiez de mon propre sang."

"Sire," dist Valentin, "pour Dieu soit et me pardonnez, car de long temps je l'ay voulu."

Quant le roy vit que Valentin estoit du tout deliberé d'aler en Acquitaine, il luy donna congé par tel convenant qu'il luy fist promettre de retourner vers luy apres que au Verd Chevalier se seroit combatu et se Dieu luy donne sancté et vie. Valentin luy promist.

En partant il print congié pour aler en Acquitaine. Adonc fust Esglentine dolente plus que jamais, plaine de pleurs et de gemissemens angoisseulx. Elle manda Valentin lequel vint devers elle. Puis luy a dit la belle en plourant tendrement, "Je voy bien que de vous jamais je n'auray joye ne consolation, et que du tout vous estes deliberé de laisser le pays de France. Helas! Or pleust a Dieu que ce fust mon honneur de moy en aler avec vous, car ainsi Dieu me veulle secourir se jamais j'ay aultre homme a espoux fors que vous. Mais puis qu'il est ainsi que de ma voulenté je ne puis user, et que mon liberal arbitre est par aultre puissance gardé et qu'il est force que le corps demeure par deça, mon cueur, mon courage, et voulenté a vous seront jamais sans nulle aultre intention fors que d'amour juste, loyalle et sollitaire je vous aymeray. Et afin que a voz affaires et necessitéz vous puissez secourir et subvenir a vostre indigence quant vous aurez necessité, vecy la clef de mon escrin que je vous presente. Prenés or et argent a vostre voulenté, car assés y a de quoy."

"Madame," dist Valentin, "d'or ne d'argent je n'ay envye. Fors seulement que trop me tarde que je ne sçay qui je suis. Et sachez que d'une chose je suis fort esmerveillé—c'est que je porte une croix sur l'espaule tout ainsi tanné que le fin or. Je ne sçay dont tel signe me peult venir, pour tant suis deliberé de n'arrester jamais

Duke Savary of the truce agreed upon with the Green Knight. Once he heard how things had been settled, he laughed and said to his barons, "My lords, he who would like to win a beautiful friend must speak up now and show himself valiant, for the one who will defeat the Green Knight in battle will have in marriage the most lovely Fezonne, daughter of Duke Savary, and gain moreover half of the duke's land and holdings. It's true, just look at this message. Take it, all of you, and see what is written there."

Everyone looked at the letter with interest. But no one who wanted to undertake the challenge was bolder or more stalwart than Valentin, who said to King Pepin in the presence of all, "Most dear and respected sire, may it please your majesty to grant me leave to go to Aquitaine to test myself against the Green Knight. Sire, please allow me to leave the country of France, for I have a great desire to quit this land. I will ride without respite until I learn at last who my mother is who carried me in her womb, for it makes me unhappy to have gone so long without knowing who I am."

"Valentin," replied the king, "you mustn't let it bother you, not knowing of your origins, for I am powerful enough to give you ample riches and raise you in honor, making you and my entire court powerful. I hold you as dear as if you were of my own blood."

"Sire," said Valentin, "for God's sake, please forgive me, for I have wished to do this for a long time."

When the king saw that Valentin was determined to go to Aquitaine, he granted him leave on the condition that he promise to return once the Green Knight was defeated, if God granted him health and life. Valentin promised to do so.

Upon his departure for Aquitaine, he took proper leave. Esglentine was more upset than ever, full of tears and anguished moans. She sent for Valentin, who came to see her. Then the lovely girl said to him, through her abundant weeping, "Now I see that I will never have joy or consolation from you, and that you are absolutely determined to leave the country of France. Alas! If only it pleased God that I had the honor to accompany you, for God help me if I ever have a man other than you as husband. But since I have no choice in this matter, and my free will is fettered by another authority, though my body is forced to remain here, my heart and desire will ever be with you without any intention other than that I will love you justly, loyally, and exclusively. And so that you will have everything you need, here is the key to my coffer. Take as much gold and silver as you like, for there is more than enough."

"My lady," said Valentin, "I have no desire for gold or silver. I only desire to know who I am. You should know about something that amazes me—I bear on my shoulder a mark, a cross the color of fine gold. I cannot tell from whence such a sign comes to me; however, I am determined never to rest until I have knowledge

tant que de ma nativité je puisse avoir cognoissance. Adieu vous dy, madame, et pour moy plus ne plourez, par la foy de mon corps. Se Dieu veult que je soye du lieu venu que je puisse nullement estre digne en valeur ou lignage de vostre extraction, jamais je n'auray a femme ne espouse aultre que vous. Et ainsi se je treuve que je ne soie digne de vous avoir a femme par faulce de haulteur de lignaige, de vous ne vouldroye estre vostre mary, car au temps a venir les envyeux demanderoient 'qui sont les [31verso]parens, freres ou cousins de celluy malleureux abollé qui a tant le roy abusé qu'i luy a donné sa fille pour femme et espouse?' Et pour tant je veul et desire sçavoir sur toutes choses de quel estat je suis."

Et a ces motz se departit Valentin et laissa Esglentine en sa chambre plourant bien piteusement, et lors commença a considerer que amour de femme est forte chose et merveilleuse, car bien voit que s'i luy plaisoit, Esglentine la fille du roy s'en yroit avec luy a sa voulenté. Mais le sens et la rayson qui estoit en luy dominerent et preserverent en tous temps de faire chose villaine, ne de quoy peust jamais avoir deshonneur ou reproche. A tant lesse Esglentine[1] et se mist a chemin.

Et quant vint au partir il fut conduit et convoyé de plusieurs nobles et grans barons de la court, dont Hauffroy et Henry furent moult joyeulx a rebours et pour leurs faulces envyes de quoy de long temps ilz estoient plains. Ilz machinerent et aviserent que sur le chemin ilz seroient pour prendre Valentin et Orson qui avec luy menoit, et les ferons mourir et leurs vies definer honteusement pour et afin que a jamais ilz fussent vengéz de la chose dequoy ilz desiroient plus d'estre.

[CHAPITRE 17]

Comment Huffroy et Henry firent gaitter Valentin sur le chemin pour luy et Orson faire mourir. xvii. cha[pitre].

Quant[2] Valentin et Orson furent departis de la court du roy Pepin pour aler en Acquitaine douleur et melencolie avec envye decepvable et mauldite entra plus que devant et aggrava les cueurs et courages de deux desloyaulx et mauldis trahitres Hauffroy et Henry en telle maniere que pour parvenir a leur faulce, mauldite et decepvable entreprinse, ilz parlerent a ung cousin germain qu'ilz avoient et tant firent que par entre eulx fut avisé et deliberé que trente hommes puissans et vaillans gaitteroient et si metteroient garde sur l'enfant Valentin et le sauvaige Orson en telle maniere que ou ilz seroyent trouvéz sans nulle remission ilz fussent destruis et mis a mort. Apres son conseil il fist assembler xxx. hommes des plus redoubtéz qu'il peut finer, puis les envoya et fit aler en armes et en point dedens une forest bien large par laquelle Valentin et Orson devoyent passer.

---

[1] Text has *Esglztine*.
[2] Text has *Qquant*.

of my birth. I bid you farewell, my lady, and please do not weep for me any longer. If it is God's will that I be of such extraction that I can in any way be worthy of your lineage through my own, then never will I have a wife other than you. But if I find that I am not worthy to marry you from lack of high lineage, I would not want to be your husband, for afterwards jealous naysayers would ask 'who are the parents, brothers or cousins of this miserable wretch[1] who has so abused the king that he has given him his daughter as wife and spouse?' For that reason I desire to know more than anything of what estate I am."

And with these words Valentin departed, leaving Esglentine in her chamber dissolved in tears, which made him consider how powerful and marvelous a thing is the love of a woman, for he could clearly see that, if he wished it, Esglentine the daughter of the king would go off with him wherever he went. But sense and reason ruled in him and preserved him at all times from committing a villainous act, or anything that could bring him dishonor or reproach. Thus he left Esglentine behind and started on his way.

When he left, he was accompanied by many nobles and barons of the court. Hauffroy and Henry were overjoyed at his departure, for they had long been filled with false envy. They plotted and planned how they might capture Valentin and Orson, who was traveling with him, on the road, in order to kill them and put a shameful end to their lives, so that they might be avenged on the one being they most hated.

CHAPTER 17

How Hauffroy and Henry sent men to lie in wait on the road for Valentin in order to kill both Orson and him.

When Valentin and Orson left the court of King Pepin to go to Aquitaine, distress and gloom mixed with deceitful and cursed jealousy dug even deeper into the hearts and spirits of the two disloyal and wicked traitors, Hauffroy and Henry. In order to succeed in their evil enterprise, they spoke to a cousin of theirs, determining with him to take thirty strong men to lie in wait for the noble young Valentin and the wild man Orson. Once they found them, they were to slay them at once and without delay. After this council, he assembled thirty of the toughest men he could find, and sent them fully armed into the deep forest through which Valentin and Orson were to pass.

---

[1] The closest reference I could find for this word is in F. Godefroy, *Dictionnaire de l'ancien français*, 10 vols. (Paris: Vieweg, 1880–1902; repr. Geneva: Slatkine, 1982), "**aboler**, v.a., effrayer." However, context seems to lead one to the translation I have chosen.

Si ne demoura pas longuement que Valentin et Orson, qui couroit a pié devant luy plus que ung cheval, entrerent en la forest. Adonc les aperceust Grigar et ses gens que estoient en embuche. Et quant Grigar vit Valentin il saillit contre luy, son espee tiree pour[1] le tuer. Et tel coup a donné au noble chevalier Valentin que parmy le harnoys il luy a entammé la chair tant que le sang en sallit. Puis luy dit, "Valentin, icy mourir vous conviendra car trop avez vescu."

Et quant [32recto]Valentin vit qu'il estoit navré et que de toutes pars assailly de ses ennemys, a Dieu se recommanda et a la Vierge Marie, puis leur a dit, "Messeigneurs, ma mort avez juree, et voy bien maintenant que par vous a tort et sans cause me convient mourir. Mais se Dieu plaist en cestuy jour je vous venderay ma mort tant et si chierement que jamais tous ensemble vous ne retournerez."

Et adonc tyra son espee et de telle maniere frappa le premier que devant luy trouva que il luy fendit la teste jusques aux espaules et puis mourut. Puis ala aux aultres par si tresgrant courage que devant que il arrestat ne que de luy osassent aprocher il en abatit cincq ou six tous mors parmy le bois. Et Orson sault avant, tout effroyé; a tout ses grandes mains velues frappe et deschire tous ceulx qui treuve parmy sa voye en telle maniere que de ses ongles les deschire et de ses dens les mort et estrangle. Il les gette par terre l'ung sur l'autre puis passe pardessus en les frappant et murtrissant moult laydement. Valentin est d'aultre part qui tient l'espee toute nue dont si vaillamment se combat que nul n'ose des deux freres aprocher.

Grigar crya tout hault, "Valentin, rendez vous, car mourir icy vous fault." Lors l'enfant Valentin a Dieu se recommanda, qu'il le veuille garder de mal et a son besoing secourir. Puis tira vers Grigar contre luy; si commença bataille de Grigar et de ses gens piteuse a compter encontre Valentin et Orson son frere, qui vaillamment et en grant resistance et a force de leurs corps contre leurs ennemis se deffendirent tant que des plus hardis et puissans par eulx furent mors en la place. Mais combien que en Valentin et en Orson eussent de grant proesses et hardiesses de corps monstrees, nonpourtant par le grant nombre des aultres qui xxx. estoient, fors et puissans, le bon Valentin fut de si pres estraint que fortune le contraignit a estre par ses ennemis prins. Et quant ilz l'eurent prins ilz l'ont lyé estroitement et rudement l'ont mené dont Orson commença a courir apres en cryant et ulant comme une beste mue et treshorriblement que tout le bois faisoit resonner et retentir. Mais riens n'y valut sa poursuite, car Valentin fut mené hastivement parmy le bois si que de Orson il ne peust plus estre veu. Lors commanda Grigar que on suivist Orson tant que mort ou vif on le prengne. Mais pour neant vont apres, car de si grande puissance court et saulte parmy le bois que nul tant soit hardi de luy n'ose aprocher. Ainsi eschapa Orson des trahystres.

Et menerent Valentin jusques a ung chasteau qui estoit en celle forest, lequel estoit moult fort et puissant. De celuy chasteau en estoit gouverneur ung baron

---

[1] Text has *pout*.

Before long Valentin and Orson entered the forest. Orson preceded him on foot, running faster than a horse. Soon Grigar and his men, waiting in ambush, saw them. When Grigar caught sight of Valentin, he rushed out toward him, sword drawn, to slay him, and indeed gave the noble knight Valentin such a blow that he cut through the harness to his flesh so that blood flowed. Then he declared to him, "Valentin, here must you die, for you have lived too long."

When Valentin saw that he had been hurt and was assailed on all sides by his enemies, he commended himself to God and to the Virgin Mary, and then addressed his attackers: "My lords, you have sworn to kill me, and I can see now that wrongly and without just cause I must die today at your hands. But if it please God, I will make you pay so dearly for my death that never will all of you return alive together."

At that moment he drew his sword and struck the first one he saw before him with such force that he severed his head from his shoulders—and the man fell down dead. He turned to face the others with such courage that before stopping, and before they ceased daring to approach him, he had slain five or six in the woods. Then Orson leapt up, alarmed, and with his huge hairy hands he beat and tore all those he found in his path, ripping them apart with his nails and strangling them to death with his teeth. He cast them to the ground one on top of the other, then stomped over the pile most viciously. Across from him was Valentin, brandishing his naked sword with which he fought so fiercely that no one dared approach the two brothers.

Finally Grigar called out, "Valentin, give yourself up, for you have no choice but to die here." At that point the noble young Valentin commended himself to God, asking Him to keep him from harm and help him in his need. Then he headed towards Grigar, and there began a battle, pitiful to recount, of Grigar and his men against Valentin and his brother Orson, for they fought and resisted so valiantly and defended themselves with such force against their enemies that many of the hardiest and boldest among them died then and there. But however much Valentin and Orson excelled in prowess and demonstrated great valor, the brave Valentin was surrounded and captured by his enemies who, as a force which had started out as thirty strong men, still outnumbered them. Once they had taken him, they tied him up tightly and roughly bore him away, while Orson began to run after them, howling and bellowing horribly like a mute beast till he made the woods echo with the sound. But his pursuit was for nought, for they rode away so quickly with Valentin that Orson lost sight of him. Then Grigar ordered his men to follow Orson and take him dead or alive. But they followed him in vain, for he skipped and leapt so fast through the woods that no one was bold enough to dare approach him. Thus did Orson escape the traitors.

They brought Valentin to a strong, solid castle in the forest governed by a robber knight, a relative of Grigar, to which the wicked, greedy renegades usually

desrobeur de gens qui estoit le parent de Grigar. Et portoyent tous ensemble leur butin les faulx trahytres envyeulx. Mais riens n'en sçavoit le roy Pepin qui fermement [32verso]ne cuidoit que nul ne fust au pays de plus grant preudommie.

Quant Valentin fut ou chasteau entré ilz l'ont pris rudement et mené dedens une tour obscure et tenebreuse et au plus parfont d'une grant fosse en prison l'ont bouté. Et quant Valentin fut en la tour encloz se print piteuseme[n]t a plourer, en priant et reclamant Dieu et la Vierge Marie qu'i luy donnassent grace de ce lieu eschapper.

"Helas," dit Valentin, "or suis je venu a la chose que plus je doubtoye, c'est assavoir es mains de mes ennemys et de ceulx qui ma mort desirent, de jour en jour demandent, et pourchassent. Si requiers a Dieu devotement que de cestuy danger me velle secourir. Helas, bon roy Pepin, jamais jour de ma vie ne vous verray et de ma mort riens ne saurez, car en ceste fosse obscure et orde me conviendra mourir. Adieu, Orson, a Dieu soyez tu, car pour l'amour de moy tu as la mort sofferte. Et se tu m'aymoyez d'amour parfaite, aussi faisoye je toy outant et plus que se tu eusses esté mon propre frere. Helas, ma doulce mere que j'ay tant desiree de vous veoir, jamais de vous n'auray cognoissance dont trop amerement mon povre cueur souspire et mes yeulx fondent en larmes sur tous les plus dolens, quant il me fault mourir sans sçavoir qui je suis. Mais quant il plaist a Dieu que tellement mourir je doye, je luy recommande mon ame."

En telle maniere se complaint Valentin dedens la chartre obscure, et ses faulx ennemis sont parmy le chasteau qui entre eulx de son fait tiennent leur conseil. Lors aulcuns ont[1] dit, "Seigneurs, le plus expedient remede qui soit c'est de faire mourir Valentin sans aultre deliberation."

"Seigneurs," dit Grigar, "de telle chose je ne suis pas consentant, mais d'oppinion que nous gardons Valentin en la prison lequel ne nous peut eschapper, et que nous alons devers Hauffroy et Henry leur dire et racompter le fait de ceste entreprinse. Si nous sçaurons donner conseil sur ceste matiere." A celuy conseil s'acorderent tous et furent deliberéz d'aler a Paris ou estoit pour lors le roy Pepin. Grigar apres ce conseil pris chemin pour aler[2] a Paris.

Et Orson estoit dedens le bois piteulx et plourant qui toute celle nuyt avoit repose au pié d'ung arbre. Et quant le jour fut venu il se mist en chemin et par luy s'est pensé que jamais n'arestera qu'il n'ait fait savoir au roy la maniere de la trahyson et comment Valentin a esté prins et emmené. Il a prins son chemin et plus tost que ung cheval a Paris est couru. Mais premier y arriva Grigar le trahytre et ainsi qu'i fut au palais entré. Il ala vers Hauffroy et luy compta le cas, comment Valentin estoit prins et emprisonné dont il fut moult joieulx. Mais moult il luy despleut quant on luy dist que Orson est eschappé. Nonobstant il se confortoit de ce que Orson ne sçauroit retourner a Paris, et oultre plus de ce que point ne

---

[1] Text has *on*.
[2] Text has *alet*.

brought all their booty. Yet King Pepin knew nothing of this, for he firmly believed that there were no more honest men than these in his land.

When Valentin entered the castle, they placed rough hands on him and led him into a dark gloomy tower, where they threw him into the deepest dungeon in the prison. Once Valentin was shut up in the tower, he began to weep most piteously, praying and beseeching God and the Virgin Mary to grant him the boon of escape from this place.

"Alas," said Valentin, "now have I come to that which I most feared, that is to say, into the hands of my enemies, those who desire my death, indeed who seek it every day and pursue it. Therefore I beseech God most devoutly to succor me in this danger.[1] Alas, good King Pepin, never will I see you again, nor will you know anything about my death, for I must die in this gloomy, filthy dungeon. Adieu, Orson, may God be with you, for you have suffered death for my sake. And if you loved me with perfect love, I too loved you as much as and even more than if you had been my own brother. Alas, my dear mother, whom I have wished so much to see, never will I know who you are, which makes my poor heart sigh and my eyes well with the most bitter tears, for I have to die before discovering who I am. But since it pleases God that I must die in such a manner, I commend my soul into His keeping."

And so Valentin lamented in his gloomy prison while his wicked enemies throughout the castle gathered together to deliberate his fate. Some of them said, "My lords, the most expedient solution is to put Valentin to death without delay."

"My lords," said Grigar, "I cannot consent to that; rather I believe we must keep Valentin in prison, for he cannot escape, and we must go to Hauffroy and Henry to recount the outcome of our undertaking.[2] They will know what advice to give us about this matter." All agreed with his advice, and decided to go to Paris where King Pepin was in residence. After the meeting Grigar set out for Paris.

In the meantime, Orson was in the forest, distressed and weeping, passing that entire night at the foot of a tree. Once the day dawned, he took to the road, determined never to rest until he made it known to the king the way in which Valentin had been betrayed and taken away a prisoner. He set out and, faster than a horse, raced off to Paris. However, Grigar the traitor arrived there before him and entered the palace. He went directly to Hauffroy and explained the situation to him, how Valentin had been taken and imprisoned, which filled Hauffroy with joy. But he was quite displeased when told that Orson had escaped. Nevertheless, he comforted himself with the thought that Orson would never know the road

---

[1] The language is conventional, probably an allusion to the language of the Psalms, such as Psalm 30: 9, 16.

[2] A surprising comment, given the explicit instructions to kill Valentin that Grigar had been given. The author is apparently more concerned about providing the opportunity for Orson to challenge and fight Grigar, so that Valentin can be rescued, than he is about verisimilitude.

parloit et qui ne sçauroit pas ra[33recto]compter¹ la maniere de ceste entreprinse. Mais leur intention fut bien tournee au revers, car Orson ne sejourna pas longuement que tantost a Paris arriva. Et a celuy jour qu'il fut venu les deux trahitres avoient prins conseil entre eulx que Grigar devoit lendemain retourner au chasteau pour faire mourir Valentin sans nulle remission.

De bonne heure arriva Orson a ce jour, lequel tout aussitost qu'i fust au palais entré, il monta contremont et sans sejour ne dilation entra dedens la sale paree en laquelle estoit Pepin le bon roy qui pour celle heure estoit a table assis pour disner, acompaigné de plusieurs nobles chevaliers. Quant Pepin vit Orson bien cuida que Valentin fut retourné. Orson aloit par la sale piteusement criant et batant sa forcelle pour laquelle chose le roy et tous les aultres l'ont fort regardé. Et quant Orson vit les chevaliers a la table assis il les regarda moult horriblement en faisant hydeulx signes. Lors avisa et congneust Grigar entre les aultres qui tenoit la teste enclinee contre la table pour doubte d'estre congneu. Quant Orson le vit il courut celle part et sy grant coup luy donne que ung orelle luy avala a bas. Puis frappe derechief pardessus le visaige ung si fort et puissant coup² que les de[n]s luy rompit et ung oueil luy creva, dont Grigar se print a crier moult hault tant que tous ceulx de la sale ont la noise et le debat aperceu.

Et Orson retourna arriere qui sy grant coup luy donna que a terre l'abatit et si getta a bas la table et tout ce qui estoit dessus, de quoy toute la compagnie fut toute esmervellee et fort troublee. Et la fust mort Grigar par Orson le sauvaige se ne fust ung vaillant prince qui la estoit qui des mains Orson le gette. Puis a dit tout hault, "Helas, sire roy, voyez et considerez le piteulx point en quoy le sauvaige Orson a mis cestuy bon chevalier. Pour Dieu, sire, faitez que la vie luy soit ostee, car top est chose perilleuse de tel homme garder."

"Seigneurs," ce dit le roy, "sur ceste matiere convient aviser par bon conseil. Car je vous prometz et ainsy je le croy que Orson le sauvaige sans aulcune grant cause n'a pas frappé Grigar. Faites le venir devant moy, sy sçauray son intention et la cause de son debat."

Orson fut amené devant le roy. Lors luy demanda le roy pour quoy il avoit fait devant sa majesté royalle si grant oultrage. Et Orson luy a fait signe que Grigar avoit tué et murtry faulcement Valentin en la forest. Puis va monstrant signez merveilleux que de ceste chose il se vouloit combatre contre Grigar, pour loy de champion, pour luy faire devant tous confesser sa mauldite entreprinse et dampnable trahyson. Puis a tiré son chapperon et par moult grant oultrage l'a getté a Grigar par maniere de gaige et de deffiance.

Et quant le roy vit cela il appella les seigneurs et aultres barons [33verso] et leur a dit tout hault, "Seigneurs, or avez vous veu comme cestuy homme sauvaige par devant tous a getté et livré gaige de bataille a Grigar et comment il se veult a luy combatre. Pour quoy veullez moy tous dessus cest afaire dire voz

---

¹ *e i* appears at bottom right corner of 33r.
² Text has *cout*.

back to Paris, and that moreover, without the ability to speak, he would never be able to recount what had occurred. However, their plans were completely upset, for it didn't take Orson long to reach Paris. And the very day that he came, the two renegades had decided between them that the next day Grigar would return to the castle to put Valentin to death without delay.

Fortunately Orson arrived that day, and, as soon as he entered the palace, he mounted without delay to the great hall, going directly to Pepin, the good king, who was at that hour seated at table for dinner, accompanied by many noble knights. When Pepin saw Orson, he thought at first that Valentin had returned. But Orson entered the hall crying piteously and beating his chest, which made the king and everyone in the hall stare at him. Then, when Orson saw the knights seated at the table, he glared at them with a horrible look and made frightening gestures. Then he caught sight of Grigar among the others, though he was keeping his head bent towards the table for fear of being recognized. When Orson saw him, he ran over to him and gave him such a blow that he took off one of his ears. Then he hit him again on his face with such force that he broke his teeth and gouged out an eye, for which reason Grigar began screaming so loudly that everyone in the hall heard the noise and tumult.

Orson came back with another great blow that knocked Grigar to the ground, overturning the table as well with everything on it, which amazed and upset the company. Grigar would have died right then and there at the hands of Orson the wild man if it hadn't been for one valiant prince who seized him from Orson's hands. Then he declared out loud, "Alas, royal sire, cast your eyes on the piteous state that this good knight is in because of the savage Orson. For God's sake, sire, have him put to death, for it is too dangerous to keep such a man."

"My lords," said the king, "such a matter deserves to be considered in council. For I assure you that I cannot believe that Orson the wild man would smite Grigar without good cause. Bring him before me; I will know his meaning and the cause of this conflict."

Orson was brought before the king, who demanded to know why he had committed such an outrage before his royal majesty. And Orson gestured that Grigar had killed Valentin wickedly in the forest. Then he communicated by gestures that he wished to challenge Grigar to combat over this matter, according to the laws of the judicial duel, in order to make him confess publicly his cursed plot and damnable treason. Then he pulled off his hood and cast it forcefully at Grigar's feet to signal his challenge and defiance.

When the king saw this he called together his lords and barons and declared to them, "My lords, now you have seen how this wild man has publicly cast his challenge to battle Grigar, and how greatly he desires to fight him, for which reason I require you to tell me your thoughts on his matter, for I wonder very

voulentéz, car trop suis esmerveillé en mon cueur de ce que Orson entre les aultres chevaliers de ma court a frappé Grigar par sy grant fureur sans nul aultre toucher. Seigneurs, dictes en vostre oppinion, car trop me doubte de faulceté de quelque part qu'elle doyve venir. Et quant est a ma part sans le vostre conseil et deliberation je seroye d'oppinion que la bataille fust entre les deux jugee."

Quant le roy eust parlé en telle maniere les barons furent d'acord et d'oppinion que Grigar et Orson pour ceste querelle se combatissent. Lors fut la bataille adornee et fit le roy amener Grigar devant luy et luy dist que Orson combatre luy convenoit. Quant Grigar sceust et entendit que contre Orson combatre luy convenoit trop fut dolent et non pas sans cause, car venu est le temps que la trahyson que tant a esté couverte et celee sera devant tous publié et magnifestement declairee. Grigar regarda Hauffroy de semblance mal asseuree et de cueur effroyé. Lors Henry l'appella et luy dist, "Grigar, ne vous doubtez en riens, car je vous prometz et fay assavoir que nous ferons vostre paix vers le roy nostre pere en telle maniere que de vostre personne n'aurez dommaige ne villennie en maniere du monde, par ainsy que vous jurerez[1] de non jamais dire ne confesser le cas pour chose qu'il vous puisse avenir."

"Helas," dist Grigar, "trop mal va de mon cas; je voy bien que par vous la mort me fault souffrir."

Et quant il eut ce dit il ala devers le roy disant, "Sire, je vous requiers ung don; c'est que de vostre grace vous plaise que a l'omme sauvaige je ne me combate point. Car, sire, vous sçavez que ce n'est pas homme contre homme qui chevalier puisse avoir ne acquerir honneur; et aussy ce n'est pas ung homme naturel, mais est beste irraysonnable et sans nul espoir de mercy."

"Grigar," dist le roy, "d'escusation n'y a il point. La bataille est jugee par le conseil de toute la court. Rayson vous y condempne et droit veult que ainsi soit."

De celle responce fut Grigar moult fort pensif, dolent et desconforté. Lors luy a dit Hauffroy, "N'ayez doubte, car sy bon droit vous avez, Dieu vous fera aydence et vous fera escu et deffence en ceste querelle. Et quant est de ma part je vous feray armer bien et souffisamment comme ou cas apartient."

Quant Orson entendit que combatre se devoit, il demena grant joye. Moult grans signes faisoit au roy que Valentin estoit mort et destruit, desquelz signes le roy Pepin tresfort s'esmerveilloit. Tousjours estoit Orson pres de frapper Grigar, le faulx et mauldit trahytre, mais le [34recto]roy[2] le fist prendre et retenir devers luy en luy faisant signes que plus nul il ne frappera tant qu'il soit ou champ. Puis a dit a Grigar, "Or vous alez armer et pensez de bien faire vostre fait."

"Ha, sire, je vous ay longuement servy et de toute ma poussance me suis perforce de vous en toutes choses obeÿr, tant en bataille comme dehors. Mais mauvais salaire m'en rendez, quant contre ung homme sauvaige ou n'y a sens ne rayson me voulez faire combatre."

---

[1] Text has *iurerz*.
[2] *e ii* appears at bottom right corner of 34r.

much why it is that, of all the knights in my court, Orson struck Grigar with such fury without touching anybody else. My lords, give me your opinion, for I am wary of falseness from whatever direction it may come. As for my part, even without your counsel and deliberation, I am of the opinion that a judicial battle is due between them."

Once the king had spoken thus, the barons were all agreed in their opinion that Grigar and Orson should fight to settle this quarrel. So the battle was ordered, and the king, who had Grigar brought to him, explained that he was to meet Orson in combat. When Grigar realized and understood that he had to fight Orson, he was very upset, and not without cause, for the time had come when the treason that had been kept hidden up to this point would become public and known to all. Grigar, with fear in his heart, glanced uncertainly at Hauffroy. Then Henry beckoned him over and told him, "Grigar, don't worry about anything, for I promise you that we will make peace between you and the king our father so that no harm will come to you of any sort, as long as you swear to say or confess nothing, whatever happens."

"Alas," said Grigar, "my case goes badly; it's clear I must suffer death for your sakes."

Having said that, he went to talk to the king. "Sire, I beg of you a favor: namely, that it please you in your goodness to release me from fighting the wild man. For, sire, you know that this is not a case of man against man, by which a knight can acquire honor; moreover, he is not a natural man, but rather an irrational beast without any hope of mercy."

"Grigar," said the king, "there will be no release from this battle. It has been agreed upon by the counsel of the entire court. Reason obligates you to it and right rules that it shall be so."

Grigar was worried and unhappy with this response. Then Hauffroy said to him, "Fear not, for you are so much in the right that God will come to your aid, serving as shield and defense[1] in this quarrel. And as for my part, I will arm you well as befits the situation."

When Orson heard that he was to fight, he was overjoyed. He gestured wildly to the king, trying to communicate that Valentin was dead and murdered, which filled the king with wonder. Orson kept threatening to strike Grigar, the wicked and cursed traitor, but the king had him seized and held back, gesturing to him to explain that he mustn't strike until he was in the field. Then he said to Grigar, "Now go arm yourself, and be sure to do it well."

"Ah, sire, I have served you for a long time, and in all things I have striven to obey you with all my strength, both in war and in peace. However, you repay me ill, forcing me to duel with a wild man who has neither sense nor reason."

---

[1] Cf. Psalms 28:7; 115:9, 10, 11; 144: 2.

"Grigar," ce dit le roy, "se bon droit vous avez, de riens ne vous devez esmouvoir car je vous prometz que bien armé ferez et Orson sera mis au champ tout nud et sans armeure. Vous serez a cheval et il sera a pid sans nul glaive porter, parquoy vous n'avez cause de reculer a vostre droit deffendre. Ne sçay comment il vous en prendra mais bien monstre semblant qu'en vous il y a a dire. Faictez vostre devoir et gardez vostre droit car aultre chose vous n'aurez de moy. La cause est consummee et la conclusion faicte et prinse de mon conseil."

[CHAPITRE 18]

Comment le roy Pepin commanda que devant son palays fust appareillé le champ pour Orson et Grigar ensemble veoir combatre, lequel fut fait. xviii. chapitre.

Apres ce que Grigar eust mis plusieurs excusations et oppositions de soy combatre contre Orson et que par le conseil fut deliberé de la bataille faire, le roy Pepin commanda le champ estre ordonné et fait devant son palays. Et quant le champ fut pres Orson qui estoit attendant entra dedens pour attendre Grigar qui fut armé par Hauffroy et Henry qui tout au mieulx qui sceurent l'armerent. Et quant il fut armé il print congé d'eulx en leur disant, "Seigneurs, je voy mourir pour vous. Malle fut pour moy la journee quant je entreprins celle chose."

"Taisez vous," dit Henry, "et ne vous donnez nul esmay, car ja le vous ay promis et tenir le vous veul que se vous estes par Orson vaincu nous ferons vostre paix au roy nostre pere tellement que de vostre personne ne mal ne dommaige n'aurez. Et se mal vous vouloit pour ce fait poursuyvir plus tost en mourroit cent mil que faulceté vous fust faicte de nostre part. Soyez tousjours secret et ne congnoissez riens de toute l'entreprinse qui a esté faicte."

Or fut armé Grigar et monté a cheval. Il tyra vers le champ qui devers le palais fut ordonné. Et quant l'eure de combatre fut venue, le roy Pepin vint aux fenestres pour la bataille veoir et regarder. Et quant toute la court fust assemblee et les juges ordonnéz et disposéz pour juger de la bataille, on commanda aux parties de faire leur devoir. Lors entra Grigar ou champ moult fier et orgueilleux et monté a l'avantage dont en la fin mal [34verso]luy en print. Il touche le cheval et tire vers Orson en luy disant, "Paillart! vous m'avez trop oultragé de m'avoir osté ung oeuil par ton cruel oultrage. Mais je te monsterray que a tort tu m'as assailly."

Et quant Orson l'a veu venir, il l'a bien entendu. Et a estendu ses bras et monstré ses ongles et ses dens en rechinant moult laidement. Lors Grigar baissa sa lance et touche le cheval devers Orson, et quant Orson vit la lance approcher il fist ung sault arriere, et Grigar, qui a son coup faillit, sa lance coucha et ficha contre terre.

"Grigar," said the king, "if right is on your side, you have nothing to worry about, for I assure you that you will be well-armed, whereas Orson will take to the field bare and without armor. You will be on horseback while he goes on foot without a sword to carry. Thus you have no cause to withdraw from defending your right. I don't know how it will all turn out, but it certainly seems that something is amiss. Do your duty and defend your right, for you will gain nothing else from me. This trial has been agreed upon and the decision made by my council."

CHAPTER 18

How King Pepin ordered the field to be set up in front of his palace for him to watch the duel between Orson and Grigar, which was done.

After Grigar tried multiple reasons to excuse himself from the battle against Orson, all of which failed to move the council, King Pepin ordered the field to be set up in front of his palace. Once it was ready, Orson, who had been biding, entered to wait for Grigar, who was being armed by Hauffroy and Henry as best they could. Once armed, he took leave of them, saying, "My lords, I am going to my death for your sakes. It was an evil day for me when I undertook this affair."

"Hold your tongue," said Henry, "and don't worry, for I promised you, and I mean to keep my promise, that if you are beaten by Orson, we will make your peace with the king our father, so that you suffer no harm. And if he tried to harm you in any way because of this matter, rather a hundred thousand men should die before we would fail you. Guard our secret and say nothing of this deed we have undertaken."

Grigar finished arming and mounted his horse, riding towards the field set up before the palace. When it was time for the combat to begin, King Pepin went to the windows to watch the battle. Once the court was assembled and the judges charged and prepared to adjudicate the duel, the combatants were ordered to do their duty. Then Grigar entered the field, proud, bold, and mounted to advantage, although it turned to his disadvantage later on. He spurred his horse and rode up to Orson saying, "Villain! you have committed an outrage against me by cruelly gouging out my eye. But I will prove that your attack was unwarranted."

When Orson saw him coming, he understood everything. Spreading wide his arms, he displayed his nails and teeth, and grimaced menacingly. Then Grigar lowered his lance and spurred his horse towards Orson, but when Orson saw the lance approaching he jumped backward, and Grigar, having failed to hit him, got his lance stuck in the ground. Seeing this, Orson ran towards him and took

Et quant Orson le vit il retourna[1] contre luy et ampongna sa lance et tant fort il a tiré que des poingz il la luy osta. Et quant il tint la lance tellement l'en frappa que il luy fist perdre l'ouÿr et l'entendement. Quant Grigar fut frappé il touche le cheval des esperons en fuyant parmy le champ. Et Orson court apres en rechignant des dens moult despiteusement et en faisant signe au roy que Grigar luy rendra. Et quant Grigar aperceust le danger grant en quoy il estoit en souspirant a dist a part luy, "Ha, Hauffroy et Henry, or est ma fin venue.[2] Icy mourray pour vous. Je l'avoie bien dict—mal est la chose commencee et mal finera."

En ce point fut Grigar, et Orson en nulle maniere navrer il ne peult. Et quant Orson vit ce il getta la lance en bas, puis vint contre Grigar et si pres le serre que son cheval a prins par le coul et tant l'a detours demené que a terre l'a fait trebucher. Mais quant il sentit son cheval a la terre tomber il vouloit saillir hors de la selle et au saillir il perdit son escu, car il voul a bas. Et Orson courust oultre luy et tantost l'a saisy puis dessus luy l'a mis et est alé au cheval et a monté dessus en faisant signes merveilleux, chevaulchant apres Grigar qui parmy le champ fuyoit. De veoir la contenance[3] de Orson furent plusieurs tous esbahys et le roy Pepin entre les aultres de ce cas moult pensif et doubteulx. Sy a dist par devant tous, "Par le Dieu tout puissant, seigneurs, je m'esmerveille moult de ce fait, et ne sçay que penser ne a quelle fin ceste chose veult venir. Mais quoy qu'il en soit ne qu'il en aviengne, c'est mon oppinion que trahyson [y a][4] de quelque part." Il a ainsi parlé le roy, doubteux et pensif dessus ceste entreprinse.

Et Orson a cheval estoit monté. Pour Grigar poursuivir est descendu du cheval et est venu par bas a Grigar. Il luy a donné tel coup qu'i l'a abatu par terre. Et puis est sailly dessus et luy a osté l'espee et la dague. Puis luy a donné ung coup si grant que le bras et l'espaule luy avala tout bas. Alors il luy donna ung aultre moult merveilleux et horrible coup parmy le corps tant que l'eschine luy couppa et rompit. Et Grigar s'escrie haultement que tout le monde l'entendit en demandant ung prestre pour ses pechéz confesser et avoir l'asolution. [35recto] Et[5] quant les gardes du champ l'ont entendu ung moult noble chevalier qui de ce faire avoit la charge vint tantost devers Grigar et luy demanda quelle chose il demandoit. Lors luy dist Grigar, "Sire, faictes descendre le roy Pepin, car je veul devant tous dire et confesser la faulceté de mon cas." Adonc la chose fust signifiee au roy, lequel descendit du palays et entra du champ pour Grigar oÿr et entendre plus clerement.

---

[1] Text has *retoura*.
[2] Text has *venuee*.
[3] Text has *contenānce*, indicating an unnecessary *n*.
[4] The phrase makes no sense without the addition of a verb at this point.
[5] *e iii* at bottom right corner of 35r.

hold of the lance, jerking it with such force that he got it away from him. Once he had hold of it, he delivered such a blow that he knocked out Grigar's hearing and wits, at which point Grigar spurred his horse to escape across the field. But Orson pursued him, gnashing his teeth horribly and gesturing to the king that Grigar would yield to him. When Grigar realized the great danger he was in, he said to himself with a bitter sigh, "Well, Hauffroy and Henry, now my end is come. Here will I die for you. I was right—this began badly and will end badly."

So it was that Grigar could not find a way to wound Orson. And when Orson realized that, he threw down the lance, came up to Grigar, and took such tight hold of his horse by the neck that he was able to turn him round and round until he made him stumble. When Grigar felt his horse tumble down, he tried to leap from the saddle, but in doing so lost his shield which flew out of his hands. Then Orson ran past him, snatching and donning the shield, then seizing and mounting the horse, all the while making extravagant gestures, and finally chasing on horseback after Grigar who, for his part, was trying to flee across the field. Everyone was amazed at Orson's exhibition, including King Pepin who was very thoughtful. He said to his entourage, "By almighty God, my lords, I marvel much at this situation and don't know what to think, nor how this will all end. But whatever happens, I believe there is treachery here somewhere." So spoke the king, anxious and pensive about this matter.

Orson had been riding Grigar's horse, but he got off the horse to pursue him the better, smiting him with a blow that knocked him to the ground. Then he leapt upon him and wrested away his sword and dagger. The next blow cost him his arm and shoulder. Then he smote him with another terrible but marvelous strike through his body that broke his spine. Grigar cried out loudly (everyone could hear him) for a priest so that he might confess his sins and receive absolution. Once the guards on the field heard his cries, a noble knight in charge of these matters came to Grigar and asked what he required. Grigar replied, "Sire, bring King Pepin, for I wish to recount everything and confess my falseness in this case in the presence of all." The matter was announced immediately to the king, who came down from his palace and entered the field to hear all Grigar had to say.

[CHAPITRE 19]

Comment Grigar apres ce que il fut conquis et vaincu
par Orson confessa au roy la trahyson de Hauffroy et de
Henry contre Valentin ainsi faicte. xix. chapitre[1]

Quant Grigar a veu le roy il luy a cryé mercy en luy disant, "Helas! sire, trop ay failly vers vostre haulte magnificence, mais a ce m'a contraint Hauffroy et Henry son frere, car pour complaire a leurs voulentéz je me suis perforce de Valentin prendre et mettre a mort cruelle. Et si ay tant fait de diligence que en une forest je l'ay pris et tenu de si pres qu'il est contraint a tenir prison tant que par entre eux[2] soit deliberé et regardé de quelle mort il devra mourir et estre jugé."

Quant le roy entendit les nouvelles et la verité de ceste chose il commanda que Grigar fust prins et pendu, puis monta a cheval pour aler vers la prison en laquelle estoit Valentin. Et quant Orson aperceut que le roy fust a chemin mis avec quatre ducz et quatre contes dont il estoit richement acompaigné, il va devant en monstrant le lieu ou Valentin fust prins. Moult droit le mena et aloit plus que ung cheval ne pouoit aler, et tant fait de manieres sauvaiges que toute la compaignie souvent faisoit rire. Et dist bien souvent le roy Pepin, "Seigneurs, moult est grant chose que de cest homme sauvaige qu'i tant aime Valentin. Et bien sachez que ses manieres me esmouvoient fort a luy vouloir du bien faire et pourchasser."

Moult l'aymoit le roy et bien le devoit faire et raison estoit, car il estoit son nepveu dont riens il ne sçavoit. Et ancores pas ne le saura tant que par Esclarmonde, la seur du geant Ferragu, qui la belle Bellissant gardoit, la chose fut cogneue, car icelle Esclarmonde avoit ung chasteau et dedens avoit une teste d'arain qui par art d'ingroma[n]ce luy di[35verso]soit tout ce que avenir luy devoit. Et si estoit icelle teste de tel art composee que jamais ne devoit definer tant que le plus preux et vaillant du monde enterra dedens le chasteau, car adonc devoit elle perdre son parler et toute sa puissance. Or viendra celuy qui a fin le mettra, et sera Valentin qui la belle Esclarmonde prendra, de quoy trop de dangiers perilleux passer et endurer luy conviendra, ainsi comme puis apres vous sera dist.

Si laisseray a parler de ceste matiere et retourneray vers Pepin qui va vers la forest pour Valentin sauver et preserver de mort. Il a tant fait qu'il est entré en la forest et va suivant Orson qui au chasteau le maine. Mais quant ilz furent au chasteau ceulx qui le roy congneurent les portes vont fermer et aux portiers fut commandé sur peine de la vie que nul du chasteau ne luy fist ouverture. Adonc quant le roy vit que ou chasteau entrer ne pouoit mais que par force, il commanda

---

[1] Woodcut of seated king at left on canopied throne, speaking to two standing robed figures at right.

[2] Text has *vous*; however, since Grigar is addressing King Pepin at this point, the *vous* is inappropriate for explaining what Hauffroy and Henry were plotting.

CHAPTER 19

How, after being defeated by Orson, Grigar confessed to the king the treachery carried out against Valentin by Hauffroy and Henry.

When Grigar saw the king, he begged him for mercy saying, "Alas! sire, I have miserably failed your exalted magnificence, but I was coerced by Hauffroy and Henry his brother. In order to satisfy their desires, I was obliged to capture Valentin and put him to a cruel death. I carried out their orders so well that I did capture him in the forest; then I put him in prison to await their decision as to how he would be put to death."

As soon as the king heard the truth about what had happened to Valentin, he ordered Grigar to be taken away and hanged, then mounted his horse to ride to the prison where Valentin was being held. When Orson realized that the king was leaving, amply accompanied by four dukes and four counts, he ran ahead of them to show them the way to Valentin. He led them straight there, galloping faster than any horse, and moving the entire company to frequent laughter with his wild antics. King Pepin remarked, "My lords, it is truly incredible that this wild man loves Valentin so. His admirable behavior makes me want to help him, to do him some good."

The king truly loved him, and he had good reason to do so, for Orson was his nephew, though he didn't realize it. Nor would he know it until it became known through Esclarmonde, sister to the giant Ferragu who was keeping Bellissant, for Esclarmonde had a castle, and in the castle was a brass head which, through its magic arts, could tell her the future.[1] Moreover, magic had constituted the head in such a way that it would cease functioning the day the bravest and most valiant knight entered the castle, for on that day it would lose its ability to speak and all its power. Now the one who will put an end to the brass head will come, and it will be Valentin, and he will marry Esclarmonde, but she will have to endure many perils and dangers for him, as will be told to you in time.

But I will leave off speaking of these matters and will return to Pepin, riding towards the forest to rescue Valentin and preserve him from death. He rode so quickly that soon he was in the forest, following Orson's lead to the castle. But when they arrived at the castle, those who recognized the king rushed to shut the gates and ordered the gatekeepers, on pain of death, not to open to him. As soon as the king saw that he couldn't enter the castle unless by force, he ordered his

---

[1] A. Dickson treats the long history of the topos of the Oracular Head at great length (see *Study*, 187–216).

a ses gens la place estre assaillie. Si ne demoura pas longuement que le bois qu'ilz taillerent et couperent emplirent les fossez et puis aprocherent les murs et a force d'armes entrerent dedens le chasteau. Ilz prindrent les trahystres et estroitment les lierent. Puis alerent aux basses prisons ou Valentin estoit en moult grant povreté et miserablement detenu. Ilz l'ont getté hors et au roy l'ont mené. Et quant il vit le roy il se mist a deux genoulx en luy rendant graces du grant danger et peril dont il l'avoit mis hors.

 Lors le prindrent les barons et grans seigneurs en luy faisant honneur et grant feste, et luy conterent du cas comme il aloit et comment Orson estoit pour luy contre Grigar combatu en champ de bataille. Et quant Valentin oÿt ces nouvelles il embrassa Orson moult doulcement et aussi Orson luy. Si ne fault pas demander se la joye de entre eulx fust grande. Et apres cela fait, le roy commanda que les trahytres fussent menéz au bois et la fussent tous a ung arbre pendus et estranglés sans nulle remission.

 Puis parla le roy Pepin a Valentin et luy a dist, "Valentin, mon amy, puisque Dieu vous a fait celle grace d'estre de la main de voz ennemis joyeulx et en sancté delivré, je vous donne conseil que avec moy retournez. Si ferés comme saige et bien avisé."

 "Sire," dist Valentin, "pour Dieu pardonnez moy, car jamais ne retourneray tant que je saiche au vray qui je suis et de quelz gens extrait. Je m'en voy en Acquitaine vers le Chevalier Verd, car ainsi je l'ay juré et promis. Je prens congé de vous comme povre servant qui tousjours vouldroye obeÿr et vostre majesté servir de ma povre petite puissance." A ces motz se departirent le roy et Valentin.

 Si laisseray a parler du roy et parleray de Valentin et de Orson qui s'en vont en Acquitaine pour combatre contre le Verd Chevalier que nul [36recto]homme[1] ne doubte, car ainsi que devant vous ay dit, jamais il ne sera vaincu fors que par ung filz de roy qui jamais de femme n'ait esté nourry ne alaité.

 Ainsi s'en vont ensemble Valentin et Orson vers le pays d'Acquitaine. Tout le monde couroit pour voir Orson le sauvaige qui nud et velu estoit comme ung ours. Chascun de luy se rit mais il n'en tient compte. Lors luy fist faire Valentin ung jaceran de fin acier de telle façon que chapperon et tout tenoit ensemble. Et quant Orson l'eust vestu moult luy sembla sauvaige et moult voulentiers l'eust despoullé, mais trop fort craingnoit Valentin et tout ce qu'i luy commandoit sans nul contredit il le faisoit. Quant Orson fust vestu du jaceran d'acier moult fort se regarda et tenoit fort orgueilleuse contenance.

 Or il avint ainsi qu'ilz passoient leur chemin Valentin avisa ung tresbeau escuier qui par la chevaulchoit, lequel moult tendrement plouroit et souspiroit. Quant Valentin le vit, "Amy," dist il, "qui vous meult de plourer? Avez-vous mauvaises gens trouvé, ou se de bestes sauvaiges avez paour ou crainte? Car de ma puissance je vous donneray confort."

---

[1] *e iii* appears at bottom right corner of 36r.

men to attack the stronghold. Before long the moat was filled with the wood his men had cut down, which enabled them to approach the walls and enter the castle by force of arms. Apprehending the traitors, they tied them up tightly. Then, descending to the lowest dungeons where Valentin was being held in the greatest misery, they brought him out and led him to the king. When he saw the king he knelt down in gratitude for his liberation from great peril and danger.

At that point the barons and great lords came round him, celebrating and delighting in his release. Moreover, they told him how it had come to pass that Orson had fought against Grigar for his sake on the dueling field. When Valentin heard this, he embraced Orson gently, and Orson returned his embrace. No need to ask if they were joyous to find one another again. After this, the king commanded that the traitors be led into the woods, there to be hanged from a tree without delay.

Then King Pepin spoke to Valentin: "Valentin, my friend, since God has graced you with delivery safe and sound from the hand of your enemies, I advise you to return with me. It is the wise thing to do."

"Sire," said Valentin, "I beg you in God's name to pardon me, for I will never return until I know for certain who I am and from what people descended, although first I will go to Aquitaine to the Green Knight, for so have I sworn and promised. I take my leave from you as a poor servant who wishes always to obey and serve your majesty to the best of my humble abilities." With these words the king and Valentin took leave of one another.

Now I will leave off speaking of the king and will tell you about Valentin and Orson who are going to Aquitaine to fight the Green Knight who feared no one, for, as I told you before, he will never be defeated except by a king's son who has never suckled woman's milk.

So Valentin and Orson set off together for the country of Aquitaine. Everyone came running to see the wild man Orson, who was naked and hairy as a bear. Everyone laughed at him, though he paid no heed. However, Valentin had a coat of mail made for him of fine steel, fashioned with a hood so that it was all of one piece. When Orson first put it on, it drove him mad and gladly would he have torn it off, but he feared Valentin and did everything he commanded him to do without protest. Once clothed in the coat of mail, he considered himself quite strong and held himself proudly.

Now it happened, as they wended their way, that Valentin espied a handsome squire on horseback who was weeping and sighing in a heart-wrenching manner. When Valentin saw him, he said, "Friend, why are you crying? Have you come into contact with evil people, or are you afraid of wild beasts? I will gladly comfort you in any way I can."

"Helas," ce dist l'escuier, "de tout ce je n'ay nulle doubte. Mais sachez que la chose qui me meult a moy plaindre c'est mon maistre que j'ay perdu, le plus piteulx, courtois et vaillant chevalier qui jamais fust sur la terre."

Valentin dist, "Comment l'avez vous perdu?"

"Sire," dist l'escuier, "il estoit alé en Acquitaine pour le Verd Chevalier combatre pour avoir la plus belle qui fust au monde vivant. C'est la plaisante et tresgracieuse Fezonne qui tant a le cueur gracieux. Mais jamais nul ne l'aura se le Verd Chevalier ne rent confus et vaincu par champ de bataille. Or sont plusieurs chevaliers mors et vaillans champions, et quant il les a conquis, il les fait pendre a ung arbre qui est emmy la place. Auquel arbre a plusieurs pendus, jusques au nombre de xxxii. De nul ne prent mercy, tant est cruel felon et de mauvais courage."

"Saincte Vierge Marie!" dist Valentin, "je croy que c'est ung dyable quant telles choses fait. Mais s'il plaist a Jhesus, je yray en Acquitaine; a combatre son corps je esprouveray le mien, car j'ay tant oÿ faire de mencion de la belle Fezonne que se de brief je ne meurs par armes j'en sçauray la verité."

"Ha, sire," dit l'escuier, "pour Dieu n'y alez point, car de combatre a luy vostre peine perdrés, et vous estes tant beau chevalier que jamais ne vis tel. Ne perdez pas la vie pour ce diable combatre, car tant de fors et vaillans chevaliers luy ay veu mettre a mort que de vous j'ay grant doubte se en bataille contre luy entrez."

"Escuier, mon amy, en Acquitaine je yray et sçauray du Verd Chevalier la verité, et s'il a mauvaise cause, contre luy me combatray. Mais premier se je puis a la belle Fezonne parleray et par son conseil useray sur le fait de ceste matiere."

Et Orson l'entendit. Il mon[36verso]stre signe a Valentin qu'il est amoureux de la belle Fezonne pour luy monstrer[1] qu'il est amoureux du Verd Chevalier combatre et aimera Fezonne. Et quant Valentin le vit de joye s'est prins a rire. Ainsi vont les deux freres cheminant par le pays pour venir vers Acquitaine.

Si ont tant chevaulché que ilz ont aproché la cité. Valentin la vit de moult loing car elle estoit fort haulte. Il appella ung homme qui passoit le chemin et luy demanda, "Mon amy, dites moy quelle cité c'est la devant moy."

"Sire," dist l'autre, "c'est Acquitaine."

"Or me dites," dist Valentin, "ou se tient le Verd Chevalier."

"Sire," dist le bon homme, "il se tient vers la cité ou vous alez combatre a luy?"

"Oy," dist Valentin.

"Ha, sire," dist il, "vous entreprenez grant folie, car jamais de luy vous n'aurez victoire. Montez sur ceste petite motte et regardez[2] ung hault arbre auquel y a tant de pendus, plus de xl. qui ont esté tous mis a mort. Il n'y a plus que xv. jours d'attente que le duc d'Acquitaine sera contraint de luy donner sa fille, la plus belle du monde dont ce sera grant dommaige."

---

[1] Text has *monstre*.
[2] Text has *rtgardez*.

"Alas," said the squire, "I have no fear of any of those. What moves me to tears is that I have lost my master, the most courtly and valiant knight, and the most to be pitied, that ever lived on earth."

Valentin asked, "How have you lost him?"

"Sire," said the squire, "he had gone into Aquitaine to fight the Green Knight in order to win the most beautiful girl in the world, the lovely and most gracious Fezonne, who has a such a sweet heart. But no one will ever have her without defeating the Green Knight on the field of battle. Already many knights and valiant champions are dead, and when he defeated them, he hanged them from a tree in the middle of the field. He has hanged at least thirty-two from that tree. He grants mercy to no one, so cruel and evil-hearted is he."[1]

"Holy Virgin Mary!" said Valentin, "I believe he must be a devil to do such awful things. But if it please Jesus, I will go to Aquitaine; in fighting him, I will prove myself, for I have heard such wonderful things about the fair Fezonne that as long as I do not first die fighting, I will know the truth about them."

"Oh, sire," said the squire, "for God's sake, do not go there, for it will be useless for you to fight him, and you are such a handsome knight—I have never seen one handsomer. Do not lose your life fighting that devil, for I have seen him kill so many strong and valiant knights that I greatly fear what will happen if you go into battle against him."

"My dear squire, I will go to Aquitaine and find out the truth about the Green Knight, and if his cause is evil, I will fight him. But first, if I can, I will speak to the fair Fezonne and follow her advice in this matter."

Orson heard it all. He made a sign to Valentin that he was in love with the beautiful Fezonne, and that he longed to fight the Green Knight and win Fezonne. When Valentin saw and understood, he was so tickled that he started laughing. And so the two brothers continued on their way to Aquitaine.

They rode with such speed that soon they approached the city. Valentin saw it from afar, for it stood on high. He called over a man who was passing them in the road and asked, "My friend, tell me what city that is up ahead."

"Sire," the other answered, "that is Aquitaine."

"Now tell me," said Valentin, "where the Green Knight is to be found."

"Sire," said the good man, "he is just outside the city. Are you going there to fight him?"

"Yes," said Valentin.

"Oh, sire," he said, "that is a great folly, for you will never have victory. Climb up this little hill and look at the tall tree where so many men hang, more than forty killed. In just fifteen days the Duke of Aquitaine will be forced to give him his daughter, the most beautiful girl in the world, which will be a terrible shame."

---

[1] The hanging of the corpes of conquered knights in a tree is the first of several motifs in this chapter that evoke the Arthurian world. See Dickson, *Study*, 186–87.

"Amy," dist Valentin, "Jesus luy aidera." Ainsi que Valentin a iceluy homme parloit, il vit ung ancien homme en habit de pelerin qui vers eulx arriva, mal vestu, et avoit une grande barbe toute chenue et blanche, qui bien avoit quatre vingz ans de age. C'estoit Blandimain, l'escuier de Bellissant, qui au chasteau l'emena ou estoit le geant Ferregu, comme mencion vous en a esté faicte par devant.

Valentin salua le pelerin, puis luy demanda dont il venoit et il luy respondit, "Sire, je viens de Constantinoble. Mais je n'ay peu entrer dedens la cité pour ung payen souldan qui tient la ville assiegee. Je n'ay peu mon messaige faire et m'en retourne."

"Pelerin," dist Valentin, "dy moy du Verd Chevalier, s'il a point prins finement."

"Nenny," dist le pelerin, "de ce je vous fay bien certain et si vous donne conseil que de celuy combatre vous ne vous entremettez, car se cent vous estiez il vous feroit tous mourir. A Dieu je vous commande, car il m'en fault aler."

Ce dit Valentin, "Dites ou vous alez."

"Sire," dist Blandimain, "je voys droit a Paris, car au roy Pepin de France me convient aler faire ung messaige de par une seur qu'il a, laquelle de longtemps fust bannye de Constantinoble a tort et mauvaise cause sans l'avoir deservy. Or est la franche dame en la maison d'ung geant qui moult doulcement le[1] garde. Lequel veut aler en France pour ceste querelle sçavoir se Pepin se consent. Car tant cognoist la dame de bonnes meurs et condicions plaine que pour elle se veult en ung champ de bataille contre l'empereur de Grece combatre qui desloyallement et faulcement l'a dechassee et deboutteé."

"Amy," sy a dist Valentin, "je te prie que en nom du Dieu tout puissant que tu retournes en Acquitaine avec nous. Et quant je me seray combatu au Verd Chevalier, se Dieu mon createur me donne victoire [37recto]contre luy, je retourneray avec vous en France et pour l'onneur du roy Pepin je entreprendray le champ, car a luy je suis plus tenu que a nul homme qui vive. C'est celuy qui m'a esté pere et m'a nourry, tant que pour faire son vouloir et commandement je doy bien avoir couraige et voulenté."

"Sire," dist Blandimain, "jamais de ce ne consentiroye. Je voys faire mon messaige pour la tressaige et treshonnouree dame Bellissant, car baillé m'en a la chairge et loyallement je le veul servir. A Dieu soyez vous tous qui de mal et de peril vous veulle deffendre."

Blandimain se partist et a Paris son chemin print, et Valentin le regarde moult fort. Helas, ce n'est pas sans cause; il avoit bon droit se son cueur luy atiroit, car c'est celuy qui longuement et loyallement a sauvé et gardé sa mere, mais de tout ce riens ne sçavoit.

Ilz reprindrent leur chemin et tant sont aléz que aupres de la cité d'Acquitaine sont arrivés. Valentin fort regarda la ville qui moulte estoit plaisante. Puis avisa Valentin une fontaine et tira celle part, puis descendit de son cheval en bas, puis

---

[1] Another occurrence of *le* for *la*; see Chapter 8, p. 58, n. 1.

"My friend," said Valentin, "Jesus will come to his aid." Just as Valentin was speaking to the man, an elderly man clothed in pilgrim's garb came towards them. He was poorly dressed, had a great white beard, and was at least eighty years old. It was Blandimain, Bellissant's squire, who had brought her to the castle of the giant Ferragu, as I recounted to you earlier.

Valentin greeted the pilgrim, asking him whence he came, and he answered, "Sire, I come from Constantinople. However, I was not able to enter the city because of a pagan sultan who is besieging the city. I was not able to deliver my message, and so I am returning."

"Pilgrim," said Valentin, "tell me about the Green Knight, if he has yet met his end."

"Not at all," said the pilgrim, "I am absolutely certain of this, and I advise you not to undertake combat against him, for were you a hundred, he would kill you all. I commend you to God, for I must be on my way."

Then Valentin said, "Tell me where you are going."

"Sire," said Blandimain, "I am going straight to Paris, for I must go to King Pepin of France to deliver a message concerning his sister, who was long ago wrongly and undeservedly banished from Constantinople. Now the noble lady lives in the house of a giant who keeps her in a respectful manner. If Pepin consents, he wants to go to France to find out about this affair. So well does he respect her, as a lady of noble manners and rank, that for her sake he wishes to meet the emperor of Greece, who so falsely and disloyally banished and exiled her, on the field of battle."

"Friend," said Valentin, "I beg you in the name of almighty God to turn back to Aquitaine with us. And when I have fought with the Green Knight, if God my creator has given me victory against him, I will return with you to France, and for the honor of King Pepin, I will undertake this battle, for there is no man alive to whom I am more beholden. I am willing to do anything for him, for he raised me as if he were my father."

"Sire," said Blandimain, "I could never consent to this. I will go deliver my message for the most wise and honorable lady Bellissant, for that is my charge, and loyally will I serve her. May God watch over you all and keep you from evil and peril."

Blandimain left to make his way to Paris, while Valentin gazed after him intently. Indeed, it was not without cause; he had good reason to feel his heart pulled in that direction, for this was the man who had faithfully guarded and long watched over his mother, even though he knew nothing about it.

They took to the road again, riding so quickly that they soon arrived in Aquitaine. Valentin looked with interest at the lovely city. Then he noticed a fountain and rode in that direction, getting off his horse and lying under a tree

se coucha dessoubz ung arbre qui estoit aupres pour soy rafreschir, car grant chault avoit. Ung peu se reposa et dormit et Orson le regardoit. Et quant il fut reposé il se leva sur les piedz pour monter a cheval, mais il vint la arriver ung chevalier fier et orgueilleux que pour le grant orgueil de luy estoit appellé l'Orgueileux Chevalier, car fier estoit tant que jamais jour de sa vie n'avoit nul salué et si estoit d'une condicion telle que celuy qui ne le saluoit a luy avoit bataille dont plusieurs avoit fait mourir.

Il vint vers la fontaine et mist le pied a terre et Valentin le regarde que nul mot ne luy dit, puis avisa Orson qui asseurement le regardoit. L'Orgueilleux Chevalier en son cueur eust despit. Il s'aprocha d'Orson et a le bras levé, puis luy donna tel coup qu'i luy fist saillir le sang de la bouche. Et quant Orson se sentit frappé il a le chevalier sarré entre ses bras si rudement que soubz luy l'a abatu a terre. Puis print ung cousteau qui pendoit a la sainture du chevalier et de celuy le frappa au corps tant que le sang en saillit. Et le chevalier qui frappé se sentit moult haultement s'escria.

Lors s'aprocha Valentin et osta le chevalier d'entre les mains d'Orson et luy dist, "Beau sire, tort avez de frapper cestuy povre homme qui nul mot ne peut parler."

Lors dist l'Orgueilleux Chevalier a Valentin, "Orgueilleux ribault, pourquoy ne me salues tu?"

Il a tiré ung glaisve pour le ferir, et Valentin tira son espee et si grant coup il luy donna que a terre l'abatit tout mort. Puis luy a dit, "Je vous aprendray a gens saluer."

Quant le Chevalier Orgueilleux fut mort ses gens dolens et espoventéz se prindrent tous a fuyr vers la cité d'Acquitaine, et sont entrés dedens et ont compté les nouvelles de leur maistre l'Orgueilleux qui est mort. Desquelles nouvelles fut moult fort [37verso]courroucé et desplaisant le duc d'Acquitaine, car son cousin estoit.

Valentin oÿt le bruit que les gens demenoyent pour la mort du Chevalier Orgueilleux qui sur la fontaine avoit esté a mort mis, si monta a cheval et entra dedens la ville. Et quant il fust dedens il se loga en la maison d'ung moult riche bourgoys, mais quant ilz furent logéz ne demoura guairez que les nouvelles vindrent au duc d'Acquitaine que ceulx qui son cousin avoyent occuys estoyent dedens la ville logéz. Il commanda que on les luy amenast, et quant il eut commandé les messagiers sont partis pour Valentin et Orson aler querir, lesquelz devers luy sont venuz. Lors parla le duc en ceste maniere:

"Amis, ditez moy qui vous estes et se vous estes chevaliers ou non, de quel pays estes vous et a quel prince vous servez."

"Sire," dist Valentin, "chevalier suis servant au roy Pepin qui France tient."

"Chevalier," dist le duc, "mon cousin avez occys et mis a mort."

"Il est vray," dist Valentin, "je ne dy pas du contraire, et quant il eust esté de mon propre lignaige, autant en eusse je fait, car orgueilleux estoit et de fier courage. Il ne daignoit parler au grans ny au petis. Et par son orgueil a mon

next to the fountain to refresh himself, for he was very hot. He reposed there a little and slept while Orson watched over him. Once he was fully rested, he got to his feet and was about to mount his horse when a fiercely proud knight appeared. So arrogant was he that they called him the Haughty Knight, and so full of pride in his elevated rank that he never greeted anyone himself, yet anyone else who failed to greet him properly was immediately challenged to battle, and thus in that way several had met their deaths.[1]

He came to the fountain and got off his horse while Valentin looked at him without saying a word. Then he noticed Orson, who watched him boldly. The Haughty Knight's heart filled with anger. He approached Orson with his arm raised and gave him such a blow that blood flowed from Orson's mouth. In reaction to the blow, Orson clutched the knight roughly in his arms and threw him to the ground under him. Then he seized a knife that was hanging on the knight's belt and smote him with it until the blood ran. The knight, feeling his wounds, cried out loudly.

Then Valentin came up and wrested the knight from Orson's grip, telling him, "Good sir, you are wrong to hit this poor man who cannot speak a word."

Then the Haughty Knight said to Valentin, "You arrogant scoundrel, why haven't you greeted me properly?"

He drew his sword to attack him, so Valentin drew his own, and dealt him such a mighty blow that he fell down dead. Then he addressed the corpse: "That will teach you to greet people."

When the Haughty Knight was dead, his men, horrified and upset, fled to the city of Aquitaine to recount the news that their master, the Haughty One, was dead. The Duke of Aquitaine was quite angry and upset at the news, for this was his cousin.

Valentin could hear the uproar of the people about the death of the Haughty Knight, who had been killed by the fountain, but he mounted his horse anyway and rode into the city. Once there he found lodgings in the house of a rich burgher of the town, but soon after they settled in, the news came to the Duke of Aquitaine that his cousin's murderers were lodged in the town. He ordered that they be brought to him, and once he had commanded it, the messengers went out to find Valentin and Orson, who came to appear before him. Then the duke spoke in the following manner:

"Friends, tell me who you are, whether or not you are knights, from what country you come, and what prince you serve."

"Sire," said Valentin, "I am a knight in the service of King Pepin, ruler of France."

"Knight," said the duke, "you have killed my cousin."

"This is true," said Valentin, "I do not deny it, and had he been of my own blood, I would not have acted differently, for he was haughty, and had a fierce heart. He refused to speak both to the great and the humble. Because of his

---

[1] Another common Arthurian motif, the Haughty Knight. See Dickson, *Study*, 186–87.

compaignon feru tant que a terre il l'a fait trebucher. Dont quant j'ay ce veu, tyré ay mon espee et tel coup en ay donné que a terre je l'ay mis mort. Je suis ung estranger qui en ceste ville suis venu pour le Verd Chevalier combatre en champ et pour la belle Fezonne qui est tant renommee. Vous en avez fait faire les voys que tous chevaliers viengnent. Si me semble de droit et juste equité que par tout vostre pays on doit aler a seurté parmi le chemin."

Quant le duc d'Acquitaine oÿt Valentin qui bien parla il dit, "Chevalier, bien respondu avez. Se mon cousin est mort, c'est par son orgueil et fier courage. De sa mort suis dolent mais remede n'y a. Le cas je vous pardonne et veult estre pardonné. Mais au sourplus de vostre entreprinse sur le Verd Chevalier, vous viendrés en mon palais et verrez la belle pour laquelle vous estes venu en ceste part. Avec elle trouverrez quatorze chevaliers d'estrange terre venus tout de nouveau qui pour l'amour de elle au Verd Chevalier se veullent combatre. Alez y et saluez ma fille comme il [est] de coustume, car ainsi est ordonné que tous chevaliers qui pour l'amour de elle viennent par deça devant que faire bataille au Verd Chevalier a elle se presente. Et en signe d'amours ilz prengnent ung aneau d'or d'elle."

"Sire," dist Valentin, "je suis pres de ainsi faire que l'ordonnance dit et d'aultre part je suis vostre petit serviteur comme celluy du tout a voz bons commandemens vouldroye obeïr de ma puissance." Lors monte le duc au chasteau et Valentin et Orson l'acompaignerent moult honnourablement.

Ilz entrerent en la sale ou les chevaliers sont qui la belle Fezonne acompaignent. [38recto]Et quant Valentin la veit il ala devers elle en grant reverence. Le salut luy donna disant devant tous haultement, "Dame, de qui le bruit et le renon de beaulté corporelle sur tous les dons de nature fait les cueurs des humains contens et repeust par ung oÿr racompter, et de qui le regard et belle contenance toute fleur de noble chevalerie resplendissant, celuy Dieu qui tout peult vous veulle garder et deffendre de villain reproche, et vous veulle du Verd Chevalier preserver et deffendre; pas n'est digne de vostre corps toucher. Ma chiere et treshonnouree dame, plaise vous sçavoir que Pepin, le trespuissant roy de France, par devers vous nous envoye et si vous fay present du plus hardy et vaillant homme qui soit vivant sur terre. Dame, regardez le, car il ne doubte homme et si n'a paour de glaisve tant soit agu ou bien trenchant. Se il sçavoit bien parler, en tout le monde on ne sçauroit son pareil trouver. Sy pouez estre seure et croire fermement que le Verd Chevalier contre luy ne pourra mais le rendra confus et vaincu tout aussitost que a luy se combatra."

"Sire," dist la pucelle, "au puissant roy de France je rens cent mille mercys, et a vous qui avez tant de peine prins pour moy. Mais dictes moy, je vous prie, pourquoy aultrement vous ne vestez et habillez honnestement iceluy vaillant homme que vers moy amenez, car il est a merveilles bien fait et de ses membres bien formé, droit et hardy semblant, et croy que se il estoit baigné et estuvé la chair de luy seroit blanche et tendre."

"Dame," dist Valentin, "jamais ne porta robe tant que l'autre jour pour veoir sa contenance je luy feis faire ce jaseran lequel il a vestu, car c'est la premiere robe

arrogance, he attacked my companion so violently that he knocked him down. So, when I saw that, I drew my sword and gave him such a blow that I slew him. I am a stranger, come to this city to meet the Green Knight in field of battle for the sake of the fair Fezonne who is so renowned. You have opened your roads for all knights to come. It seems only right and just to me that one be able to ride in safety on the road in your land."

After the Duke of Aquitaine listened to Valentin, who had spoken well, he said, "Knight, you have answered well. If my cousin is dead, it is through his haughtiness and fierce heart. I am sorry for his death, but there is no help for it. I pardon you concerning this matter and wish also to be pardoned. Moreover, concerning your enterprise with the Green Knight, you will come to my palace to see the fair one for whose sake you have come to this place. You will find fourteen knights from foreign lands with her already, all new arrivals who wish to fight the Green Knight for her sake. Go and greet my daughter as is the custom, for it has been arranged that every knight who comes here to do battle with the Green Knight for her sake must present himself to her. And as a sign of love each receives from her a gold ring."

"Sire," said Valentin, "I am ready to do as ordered, and declare myself your humble servant, willing to obey your good commandments to the best of my ability." Then the duke went up to the castle with Valentin and Orson accompanying him in an honorable fashion.

They entered the hall where the knights waited upon the fair Fezonne. When Valentin saw her he approached her respectfully. He proffered his greeting, declaring in a ringing voice before the company, "My lady, whose renowned beauty gladdens and nourishes the heart of men more than any other gift of nature just from hearing it spoken of, and who attracts the entirety of the splendid, noble flower of chivalry, may all-powerful God guard and keep you from evil reproach, and may He preserve and keep you from the Green Knight, who is not worthy to touch you. My dear and most honored lady, may it please you to know that Pepin, the most powerful king of France, sends us to you, and moreover presents you with the boldest and most valiant man alive on earth. Lady, look at him, for he fears neither man nor sword, however sharp or trenchant. If he only knew how to speak properly, in all the world there would be none to equal him. You may be sure and believe firmly that the Green Knight would not be able to withstand him; he would soon confound and vanquish him as soon as he fought him."

"Sire," said the girl, "I render a hundred thousand thanks to the mighty king of France and to you who have taken such pains on my behalf. But tell me, I beg you, why do you not properly attire this valiant man whom you bring to me, for he is marvelously well-made and well-formed in all his limbs, appearing straight and bold, and I believe that, if he were bathed and washed, his flesh would be white and delicate."

"Lady," said Valentin, "he had never worn clothes until the other day when, to see how he would react, I had made for him this coat of mail that he has put

que jamais il porta. Et sachez que tout nud et sans nulle vesture vint a Paris dont il est natif; la chair si est dure et forte, si ne craint ne vent ne froidure tousjours."

En disant ces parolles la belle Fezonne regarda[1] fort Orson et ainsi que Dieu voulut que amour et nature s'i adonnast, elle fust esprinse de Orson et pointé au cueur tresardamment et entre les aultres que jamais avoit veu de luy fust esprinse[2] d'amours plus que nul aultre, et combien qu'i ne fust pas polly ne sy mignonnement vestu ne habillé comme plusieurs aultres. Touteffoys on dist communement que il n'est nulles laides amours quant les cueurs s'i adonnent.

Lors quant Valentin eust ainsi parlé il dist a la pucelle, "Belle, quant est de moy, je vous diray mon cas. Car sachez que pour l'amour de vous a force d'armes vaillamment conquerre je suis venu en ceste partie, et si ay fait serment que jamais en France ne retourneray tant que au Verd Chevalier je me soie combatu et esprouvé mon corps. Car sachez que pour l'amour de vous la mort je veul endurer ou le Verd Chevalier, vaincu et desconfit, je vous amenray."

"Helas, sire," dit la belle Fezonne, "pour moy [38verso]n'ayez courage de vostre vie mettre a l'aventure. Car mieulx ayme aultre que soy mesmes en choses en quoy la vie pent, telle amour ne me semble pas juste mais desordonnee. Las! trop de vaillans gens et de nobles chevaliers sont mors pour moy dont dommaige trop grant est de ma longue demouree."

"Dame," ce dit Valentin, "de ce me pardonez, car ainsi je l'ay entreprins."

"Chevalier," dist la belle, "bien vous en puisse prendre." Lors tira deux aneaulx d'or dont l'ung donna a Valentin et l'autre a Orson, puis sont aléz a la table avec les aultres quatorze chevaliers ou moult fort notablement le duc Savary les fist servir. Mais entre tous les aultres qui en la table furent, la belle Fezonne dessus tous gettoit son regart sur Orson et Orson la regardoit par ung desir d'amour embrasé et esprins d'ung ardant et gracieulx appetit.

Or avint ainsi que les chevaliers en la table se seoyent, le Verd Chevalier s'y vint frapper a la porte pour veoir la belle Fezonne dont tant esprins estoit, car ilz avoient fait ensemble que le duc d'Acquitaine et luy que par ung chascun jour une foys il pouoit venir et entrer ou chasteau sans nul contredit pour la belle Fezonne veoir a son gré. Et adonc quant il fut entré il s'escry a tout en hault, "Vaillant duc d'Acquitaine, avez vous champion qui pour la belle dame a mon corps se veuille employer?"

"Oy," ce a dist le duc, "ancores ay je xvi. dedens ma sale qui pour prouesse monstrer a l'encontre d'ung chascun[3] et de vous sont venus de plusieurs[4] païs en ceste terre."

Or dist le Verd Chevalier, "Faictes que je voye et que je entre dedens la sale pour la belle regarder."

"Entrez," ce dit le duc, "car licence en avez."

---

[1] Text has *regadar*.
[2] Text has *espeinse*.
[3] Text has *chas*, probably owing to line break.
[4] Text has *plusieus*.

on, and that is the first garment he has ever worn. You must understand that he came to Paris, the city in his native region, completely nude and without any clothing whatsoever; his flesh is so tough that he fears neither wind nor cold."

While they spoke, the fair Fezonne gazed at Orson, and as it was God's wish that love and nature should be joined, she was smitten by Orson, her heart struck with more ardent love than it had ever been for any other she had ever seen, despite the fact that he did not have refined manners, nor was he elegantly dressed or attired like most others. Just as people say, there are no ugly lovers when hearts are sincerely devoted.[1]

After speaking thus to the girl, Valentin addressed her again: "Fair one, as for myself, I will explain my situation to you. I have come here to win your love through valiant conquest, having taken an oath not to return to France until I have fought and proved myself against the Green Knight. For your sake I will endure death or will bring you the Green Knight, vanquished and overcome."

"Alas, sire," said the fair Fezonne, don't put your life in such danger for my sake. For when one loves another better than himself in matters where his life hangs in the balance, such love seems to me not proper but reckless. Alas! so many bold men and noble knights have died because of me that it is a shame I have lived this long."

"My lady," said Valentin, "you must pardon me, for I am determined to undertake this thing."

"Sir knight," said the lady, "may you find success." Then she drew forth two gold rings, giving one to Valentin and the other to Orson, after which they joined the other fourteen knights at the table, where Duke Savary made sure they were honorably served. But Fezonne fixed her gaze on Orson more than on any of the others sitting at table, and Orson, for his part, smitten with a gracious yet ardent hunger, returned her gaze with the desire of burning love.

Now it happened, while the knights were thus seated at table, that the Green Knight came knocking at the gate to see the fair Fezonne with whom he was so smitten, for it had been agreed between the Duke of Aquitaine and himself that he could come once a day to see her at his pleasure in the castle without hindrance. Upon entering, he spoke up loudly, "Valiant Duke of Aquitaine, have you a champion who wishes to challenge me for the fair lady?"

"Yes," said the duke, "I still have sixteen in my hall who, in order to demonstrate their prowess against you and the others, have come to this land from many other countries."

Then the Green Knight said, "Let me see them, and let me enter the hall so that I may see the fair lady."

"Enter," said the duke, "for you have permission."

---

[1] Cf. Hassell, *Proverbs*, 35 (no. A85).

Le Verd Chevalier entre en la sale et regarde les chevaliers qui la estoient. Et quant il les eut regardéz il leur dit en ceste maniere, "Seigneurs, buvez et mengez et faictes bonne chiere car demain sera vostre jour venu. Et sachez que tous pendre je vous feray au plus haulte de mon arbre."

Lors l'oït Valentin qui trop fut malcontent, si lui respond, "Chevalier, de celle chose dire vous pouez garder, car au jour d'uy est venu qui contre vous se combatra plus roidement que nul aultre. Vous en avez plusieurs a mort livréz, mais celuy est venu qui vous vainquira par champ de bataille."

Or entendit Orson que de luy on parloit et si cogneust que le Verd Chevalier estoit celuy par qui la jouste fust commencee et que c'estoit celuy par qui tant de chevaliers avoient la mort prinse. Si le regarda moult fort et puis saillit hors de la table et en estraingnant les dens print le chevalier par les rains et le charga sur son col ainsi comme il eust fait ung enfant. Et quant il l'eust chargé il regarda ung mur et getta le Verd Chevalier encontre si rudement que tous ceulx de la place cuidoient qu'il eust le col rompu. Et quant il l'eust ainsi rué il s'en retourna soy aseoir a la table parmi ses compaignons et en riant leur monstra [39recto]signes qui portreoit sur son col tieulx troys hommes comme le Verd Chevalier.

Adonc se prindrent tous les chevaliers de la sale a rire moult fort et dire l'ung a l'aultre, "Or est venu celluy par qui le Verd Chevalier sera mys a desconfiture. Et Fezonne perdra trop quant il ne sçet parler, car bien est digne d'avoir honneur entre tous les preulx et vaillans."

Or regarda Fezonne les manieres et les contenances de Orson; elle fust au cueur frappee du dart d'amours par le plaisir de Dieu qui les cueurs des deux de grace enlumina en telle façon que du tout a luy son courage donna. Et tousjours avoit dessus Orson son regard et l'ayma si tresardamment que tous les aultres elle oublia pour celuy avoir pour amy. Et non pas sans cause se elle estoit de son amour esprinse, car sy vaillamment avoit sarré le Verd Chevalier que a celle heure il l'eust tué et occys devant tous s'il eust voulu. Mais combien que sur luy assez puissance, nul mal pour l'eure presente ne luy voulut faire, car on dit voulentiers que noble courage jamais ne peult mentir.

Non pourtant le Verd Chevalier reputa ce fait pour trop grant oultrage, et dist tout en hault devant toute la compaignie, "Seigneurs, cestuy homme sauvaige m'a tiré et deceu, car a moy est[1] venu sans parler aulcunement ne dire mot. Je vous prometz et fay assavoir que demain au plus matin je suis homme pour luy. Afin que tous les aultres y prengnent exemple en despit et pour son oultrage, je feray ung gibet lever et au plus hault de tous les aultres qui par moy ont esté vaincus, je le feray pendre et estrangler."

Orson aperceut bien que le Verd Chevalier estoit de luy mal content et qu'i le menassoit. Si se leva sus et commence a bourbeter tresfort, faisant signe que le

---

[1] Text has *en*.

The Green Knight came into the hall and looked at the knights gathered there. And when he had finished gazing at them, he spoke to them thus: "My lords, drink and eat and be merry, for tomorrow your day of reckoning will come. You know that I will hang all of you from the very top of my tree."

Valentin was not pleased hearing this, and answered him thus: "Sir knight, you should watch what you say, for today one has arrived who will fight you more vigorously than any other before. You have delivered many men to death, but the one who will vanquish you on the field of battle has come."

Now Orson understood that they were speaking of him, and also realized that it was the Green Knight who had initiated the jousts and put so many knights to death. He stared at him for a moment, then leapt up from the table, and, gnashing his teeth, seized the knight around his waist and threw him on his shoulders as if he were no more than a child. Once he had him on his back, he spotted a wall and threw the Green Knight against it so hard that everyone there thought he had broken his neck. Then, after having roughed him up like that, he returned to his seat at table among his companions and laughingly showed them through gestures that he could carry on his back three men like the Green Knight.

At this point all the knights in the hall began to laugh uproariously and say to one another, "The one has come who will be able to beat the Green Knight. But what a shame for Fezonne that he cannot speak, because otherwise he is worthy of honor among all brave and bold men."

Fezonne observed Orson's manners and ways and was struck in the heart by the arrow of love, for such was God's pleasure. He lit up both their hearts in such a way that she gave him all her love. Her gaze never left Orson, and she loved him so ardently that she forgot all others and wanted only him for her lover. And it was not without reason that she was so taken with love for him, for he had locked the Green Knight in such a hold that he could have killed him on the spot in front of everyone had he wished it. But however much power he had over him, he didn't wish to do him further harm at that moment, for everyone says that a noble heart can never betray its word.[1]

Nevertheless, the Green Knight considered this to be a great outrage, and declared aloud before the entire company, "My lords, this wild man has attacked and deceived me, for he came at me without any word of warning. I promise you and make known that tomorrow at dawn I am the man for him. So that he will serve as an example to all the others in spite of and because of his outrage, I will have a gibbet raised, and I will have him hanged by the neck higher than any of the others I have vanquished."

Orson could clearly see that the Green Knight was angry with him and threatening him. So he got up and began to babble loudly, gesturing that the next

---

[1] Cf. Morawski, *Proverbes*, 16 (no. 437); Hassell, *Proverbs*, 78 (no. C233).

lendemain a luy vouloit avoir bataille. Et en signifiance il print son chapperon et en signe de gaige le getta au Verd Chevalier. Dont parla Valentin au Verd Chevalier en disant, "Sire, veez gaige que le sauvaige vous gette; se contre luy vous pouez, pensés de le lever."

Lors fust le Verd Chevalier d'orgueil et de despit si fort esprins que nul mot ne respondit, et le duc d'Acquitaine qui estoit present luy dist, "Franc chevalier, icy aura dure bataille entre vous et cestuy sauvage. Si me doubte fort que a luy vous n'ayez moult fort afaire et se tant vous pouez faire que sur luy vous acquerés victoire bien vous pourrez vanter que de tous chevaliers vous estes le plus preulx et hardy et que de nul ne devez avoir crainte ne doubte. Et qu'il soit vray bien le vous a monstré devant tous qu'il est hardy de cueur et de courage."

"Par mon dieu," dist le Chevalier Verd, "demain pourrez tous veoir et cognoistre quelle sera sa puissance, car jamais en sa vie du champ ne retournera que pendre ne le face tout au plus hault des aultres."

A ces motz [39verso]saillit hors du chasteau et ala responce devers son pavillon, et les aultres seigneurs et chevaliers demourerent en la sale avec la belle Fezonne qui grant chiere demenerent a grant joie et disoient l'ung a l'autre que venu estoit le jour que le Verd Chevalier trouveroit son maistre.

Grant bruit fust parmy la cité de Orson le sauvaige. Chascun desira de le veoir en telle maniere que si tresgrant multitude de gens vindrent au palays que pour la presse qui y estoit le duc d'Acquitaine commanda a fermer les portes. Quant Orson oÿt le bruit il monta aux crestiaulx et saillit aux fenestres pour le peuple regarder. Lors l'apercerent les gens et le monstrerent[1] l'ung a l'autre en parlant, en devisant de luy en plusieurs façons et manieres. Or fut la nuyt venue qui fut temps de soupper. Chascun fut assis, et quant le duc fut levé de table ung peu vindrent d'esbatement, puis alerent dormir chascun en sa chambre ainsi qu'il avoit esté ordonné. Et quant Valentin fut couché il fist signe a Orson que aupres de luy se couchast, mais Orson n'en fist conte. Il se coucha a terre tout plat et estendu ainsi que de tous temps avoit en la forest aprins. Ainsi passa la nuyt.

Et quant le jour fut venu, Valentin et Orson furent dedens la sale devant Fezonne la belle; avec luy quatorze chevaliers qui en Acquitaine estoient venus pour l'amour de la tresgracieuse et tresplaisante dame conquerir et son amour avoir. La ont tenu conseil tous ensemble du Verd Chevalier combatre, car a celuy jour luy avoit promis le duc d'Acquitaine que champion luy liverroit.

Sy parla entre les aultres ung chevalier moult noble et de moult noble sang et dist en ceste maniere, "Seigneurs, s'il vous plaist a tous je suis deliberé de faire contre le Verd Chevalier le premier champ de bataille." Ceste requeste luy fut acordee de par l'assistence de toute la chevalerie, et s'en ala armer le chevalier lequel avoit nom Galeran, et estoit venu du pays de France. Et quant il fut armé il vint devant la tresplaisante[2] et tresgracieuse dame Fezonne et d'elle print congé

---

[1] Text has *monstrrrent*.
[2] Text has *tresplalsante*.

day he wished to do battle with him. To prove this, he took his hood and threw it at the Green Knight as a challenge. Then Valentin addressed the Green Knight, saying, "Sire, see here the challenge that the wild man has cast down before you; if you think to have any power against him, take it up."

At that moment the Green Knight was so overcome with arrogance and scorn that he didn't answer a word, so the Duke of Aquitaine, who was present there, spoke up: "Noble knight, it will be a hard battle between you and the wild man. I greatly fear that you will have your hands full with him, and if you can manage to best him, then you will be able to boast that of all knights you are the strongest and boldest and need fear no other. He has certainly demonstrated in front of everyone here that he possesses a bold heart."

"By my god," said the Green Knight, "tomorrow everyone will be able to see and recognize what his strength is, for never will he return alive from the field without my hanging him higher than all the others from my tree."

With these words he left the castle and went directly to his tent, while the other lords and knights remained in the hall with the fair Fezonne, joyously eating and drinking, and telling each other that the day had come that the Green Knight would find his master.

Throughout the city people were talking about Orson the wild man. So many people wanted to see him that a great multitude came to the palace, creating such a crowd that the Duke of Aquitaine ordered the gates to be shut. When Orson heard the noise, he climbed up to the battlements and went out to the windows to observe the people. Then the people below saw him and pointed him out to each other, talking and making different comments about him. Night fell, it was time to dine, and everyone was seated. When the duke got up from table, there was some entertainment, then everyone went to his room to sleep as had been arranged. When Valentin was in bed he signaled to Orson that he lie down next to him, but Orson paid no attention to him. He lay down flat on the floor, resting as he had learned always to do in the forest. And so passed the night.

When the daylight came, Valentin and Orson presented themselves in the hall to the fair Fezonne; with her were fourteen knights who had come to Aquitaine to win the love of this most gracious and pleasant lady. There they all held council together on fighting the Green Knight, for on that day the Duke of Aquitaine had promised to deliver him a champion.

A most noble knight of highly noble blood spoke up and said, "My lords, if it please you all, I am determined to be the first to face the Green Knight on field of battle." This request was granted him by the entire group of knights, and the knight, named Galeran, from the country of France, went to arm himself. Once ready, he came before the lovely and gracious lady Fezonne, and took leave of her

moult joyeusement et en grande reverence. Et celle qui de toute honneur fut garnie et tout bien aprinse congé ottroya en luy disant, "Franc chevalier, je prie Dieu de paradis et la glorieuse Vierge Marie qu'i vous veullent conduire et de dommaige preserver en telle facon et maniere que a joye et a honneur puissés devers moy retourner."

Quant le chevalier eust prins congé de la belle Fezonne, il monta a cheval et tira vers la tente du Verd Chevalier. De si loing qu'i le vit frappa des esperons et de cruel courage courust au chevalier Galeran et si grant coup luy donna que de son cheval a terre l'abatit. Puis descendit et son heaulme lui osta de la teste pour quoy Galeran, qui la mort doubta, se rendit en la mercy du Verd Chevalier, mais peu [40recto]prouffita, car sans nulle pitié le harnoys luy osta et le pendit au hault de l'arbre tout ainsi que des aultres avoit fait par devant. Pour la mort d'icelluy Galeran fut grant le cry par toute la cité d'Acquitaine, car beau chevalier estoit et moult loué et prisé de ses compaignons.

Or cogneust bien Orson que le Verd Chevalier avoit mis a mort Galeran. Il fait signe des mains qu'il le veult aler combatre a celle heure presente sans sejour faire. Mais Valentin luy fait signe qu'il se retire, car premier il y vouloit aler. Atant se teust Orson, car il craignoit tousjours Valentin. Lors Valentin se arma et ala vers la belle Fezonne pour prendre congé d'elle. Si ne fault point demander se elle faisoit grans regretz et se elle gettoit souspirs couvers dedens son cueur.

"Helas," dit la belle et plaisant dame, "veullez deffendre et preserver celuy tant noble, beau, et tant gracieux chevalier qui pour l'amour de moy sa vie veult mettre en dangier." Fort regreta Fezonne le plaisant et gracieulx Valentin, mais sur tous en son couraige Orson. Et elle avoit bien cause, car pour elle espouser l'avoit Dieu mis sur terre.

Apres le congé prins de la dame et de toute la chevalerie, Valentin monta a cheval pour aler combatre le Verd Chevalier, mais ainsi qu'i se mist au chemin a luy vint ung chevalier qui de l'amour de Fezonne estoit fort esprins et embrasé.

"Sire," dist il a Valentin, "ayez ung peu de pacience; laissez moy aler le premier."

"Amis,"[1] dist Valentin, "je t'en donne congé. Va a Jesus qui puissance et victoire te veulle donner d'icelluy conquerir."

Celuy chevalier avoit nom Tyris et estoit natif du pays de Savoye. Mais tant avoit en son cas que pour soy mettre a l'aventure avoit tout le sien despendu si que plus riens n'avoit. Il print congé des seigneurs puis monta a cheval et sans nul sejour faire il chevaulcha jusques au pavillon du Verd Chevalier. Et quant vit Tyris de Savoye de luy aproché, il saillit hors de sa tente moult fier et orgueilleux.

Et Tyris luy a escryé hault, "Sire Verd Chevalier, or montez a cheval et pensés de vous deffendre, car de Dieu je vous deffie qui tout le monde a fait et pour nous souffrit mort."

---

[1] A late but infrequent example of the *s* of the Old French nominative in Middle French. See other examples on pp. 268 and 272.

most joyously and with great respect. And she, adorned with every virtue and very well brought up, granted him leave, saying to him, "Noble knight, I pray that the God of paradise and the glorious Virgin Mary guide you and preserve you from harm, so that you may return to me in joy and honor."

Once the knight had taken leave of the fair Fezonne, he mounted his horse and rode off to the tent of the Green Knight. As soon as he saw him, he spurred his horse, and with a ferocious courage rode toward the knight Galeran, striking him such a heavy blow that he knocked him from his horse to the ground. Then he got off his own horse and removed Galeran's helmet, for which reason Galeran, who feared death, yielded himself to Green Knight's mercy, but it did him no good, for without any pity he removed his armor and hanged him high from his tree, just as he had done to all the others before. A great cry went up throughout the city of Aquitaine for the death of Galeran, for he was a handsome knight, much praised and prized by his companions.

Now Orson realized that the Green Knight had killed Galeran. He gestured with his hands that he wanted to go fight him right away without delay. But Valentin signaled to him to step back, for he wanted to go fight him first. Orson quieted down at once, for he still feared Valentin. Then Valentin armed himself and went to the fair Fezonne to take leave of her. No need to ask whether she lamented and sighed repeatedly in her heart.

"Alas," said the fair and pleasant lady, "may God protect and preserve this so very noble, handsome, and gracious knight, who, for my sake, is willing to put his life in danger." Fezonne bewailed the pleasant and gracious Valentin, but the one most in her heart was Orson. And she had good reason to feel that way, for God had put him on earth in order to marry her.

After taking leave of the lady and all the knights, Valentin mounted his horse to go fight the Green Knight, but just as he started out, a knight desperately in love with Fezonne came to him.

"Sire," he said to Valentin, "have a little patience; let me go first."

"Friend," said Valentin, "I give you leave. Go with Jesus and may He grant you the power and the victory to conquer the Green Knight."

This knight, named Tyris, was a native of Savoy. So infatuated was he that he had spent all his fortune in order to participate in this adventure, and thus had nothing left. He took leave of the lords, then mounted his horse and without delay rode to the Green Knight's pavilion. When he saw Tyris of Savoy approaching him, he issued forth from his tent full of pride and arrogance.

Tyris cried out loudly, "Sir Green Knight, mount your horse and defend yourself, for I challenge you in the name of God who created the whole world and who suffered death for us."

Le Verd Chevalier qui Tyris entendit appella pour son cheval avoir ung de ses serviteurs. Puis mist le pié a l'estrier et est sailly de dessus son cheval. Il a mis l'escu verd et a prins sa lance. Puis sont alongnéz l'ung de l'autre et ont tellement encontré l'ung l'autre que le Verd Chevalier oultre le corps de Tiris sa lance luy passa et a terre l'abatit. Et le Verd Chevalier descendit et a prins une corde, puis tira hors le chevalier Tiris et ou col la corde luy mist et l'a pendu avec les aultres dont Sarrasins menerent grant joye.

Et quant Valentin vit que Tiris fut mort et a l'arbre pendu dolent fut de sa mort et au cueur desplaisant. Il fit le signe de la croix devant luy et a Dieu se recommanda [40verso]et[1] desirant sur toutes choses tant faire que de son pere et de sa mere peust avoir cognossance. Et quant il eut a Dieu sa priere faicte il frappa des esperons et ala en la tente du Verd Chevalier qui pour la semblance de Orson bien le recogneut et de luy plus se doubta que de nul aultre jamais n'avoit fait.

Il appella Valentin et luy dit, "Chevalier, entendez que je vous diray. Voyez vous la devant en cest arbre ung verd blason? Alez le moy querir et le m'aportez et je le vous deserviray."

"Sire," dit Valentin, "assez avez de varlés aultre que moy. Faites qu'i vous servent, car par moy n'aurez vous le blason."

"Par ma loy," dit le Verd Chevalier, "le blason m'aporterez, ou je vous fais assavoir que jamais a mon corps n'aurez bataille."

Quant Valentin vit que le Verd Chevalier pour le blason apporter vouloit prendre excusation de combatre comme vaillant et hardy chevalier, chevaulcha devers l'arbre ou le blason pendoit. Mais il perdit sa peine, car il ne le peult oncques oster dont il fut desplaisant. Lors vint au Verd Chevalier et luy dit fierement, "Va querir ton blason car avoir je ne le puis. Mauldit soit il de Dieu qui si fort luy atacha et pendu soit celuy qui envoyé m'y a."

"Amy," dit le Vert[2] Chevalier, "je te diray pourquoy je t'y ai envoyé. Sachés de vray et pour certain que celuy escu que tu voys la jadis vint de faerie et par une faee il me fut donné. Or il a telle vertu que jamais nul tant soit vaillant ou fort du lieu ou il est ataché oster ne le pourra fors celuy seulement par qui je doys estre conquis et vaincu. Pour tant je t'ay envoyé a celle part car de toy avoye doubte. Mais maintenant en suis seur quant le blason tu n'as peu avoir ne a moy aporter. Pour tant retourne toy du lieu dont tu es venu et tu sauveras ta vie. Car tant me semblez beau chevalier que de ta mort je n'ay nulle envye; de laquelle eschapper tu ne pourras se tu prens a moy bataille. Et afin que tu ne penses pas que je veulle dire ces parolles par faintise ou folle abusion, saches que de nul tant soit victorieulx je ne seray vaincu sinon d'ung homme qui sera filz de roy et qui aura esté nourry sans femme allaiter, par quoy tu peulx cognoistre se tu es tel ou non."

---

[1] Text has *er*.
[2] Rare instance of spelling with a *t*.

The Green Knight, hearing Tyris, called for one of his servants to bring his horse. Then he placed his foot in the stirrup, leapt up on his horse, girded on his green shield, and took up his lance. They withdrew to opposite ends of the field, then rode towards each other, clashing with such force that the Green Knight thrust his lance through Tyris's body, killing him at once. Getting off his horse, the Green Knight took hold of a rope. Then he pulled the knight Tyris [to the tree], tied the rope around his neck, and hanged him with the others, for which the Saracens cheered.

But when Valentin saw that Tyris was dead and hanging from the tree, he was aggrieved for his death. He crossed himself and commended himself to God, reiterating his foremost desire to gain knowledge of his father and mother. His prayer done, he spurred his horse and rode up to the tent of the Green Knight, who recognized him for his resemblance to Orson and feared him more than he ever had any other.

He called Valentin, saying, "Sir knight, listen to what I tell you. Do you see that green shield hanging in the tree there before you? Go fetch it and bring it to me and I will repay you."

"Sire," said Valentin, "you have servants enough. Have them fetch it, for you will not get the shield from my hands."

"By my faith," declared the Green Knight, "you will bring me the shield, or I swear you will never get to fight me."

When it seemed to Valentin that the Green Knight wanted to use this matter of fetching the shield to avoid fighting him like a proper stalwart knight, he rode over to the tree where the shield was hanging. But it was no use, for he was irritated to discover that he could not remove it. Then he came back to the Green Knight and said to him fiercely, "Go get your own shield, for I cannot remove it. May God curse both him who affixed it and him who sent me there."

"Friend," said the Green Knight, "I will tell you why I sent you there. You should know that the shield you see hanging there was charmed long ago and given me by a fairy. Its special power is such that no one, however valiant or strong, can remove it from where it is attached except the person by whom I am destined to be conquered and vanquished. For that reason I sent you over there, for I feared you. But now I am safe, since you were not able to dislodge the shield or bring it to me. Thus I say to you, return to whence you came and you will save your life. You seem to me such a handsome knight that I have no desire to kill you, and you will not be able to escape that fate if you do battle with me. And to prove to you that I am not saying these words out of weakness or mad trickery, understand that I will never be vanquished by anyone, however victorious he might otherwise be, except by a man who both is the son of a king and has never suckled a woman's milk. You will know whether this description fits you or not."[1]

---

[1] The object that may be handled only by the chosen hero, an example of "geis" (a tabooed object), is not only an Arthurian motif but common in Celtic folklore. See John Revell Reinhard, *The Survival of Geis in Medieval Romance* (Halle: Max Niemeyer, 1933).

De ces nouvelles oÿr fut Valentin fort dolent et au cueur moult desplaisant et pensif. "Helas," dit il, "sire Dieu tout puissant, trop mal va de mon cas se de vostre benigne grace je n'ay secours et confort car bien sçay que je ne suis pas tel que iceluy payen dit. Mais puis que tant j'ay fait que jusques icy je suis venu pour ceste entreprise faire, jamais je ne retourneray que je n'asçay mon corps contre celluy que tant de vaillans champions a fait mourir."

Lors appelle Valentin le Verd Chevalier et luy dit en ceste maniere, "Chevalier, je voys et cognois bien que pas ne suis celuy par qui devez estre conquis, mais nonpourtant quel que je soie, jamais d'icy ne partiray tant que [41recto]contre[1] vostre corps je ne me soye combatu."

"Par Mahon," dist le payen, "folie trop grande te maine, et semble que par trahyson tu me veullez vaincre et conquerir, mais tost te monsterray que ton oultrecuidance te tournera a dommaige villain et honteulx."

Lors a prins son cheval et subtillement est sailly dessus, et appella ung sien varlet qui avoit nom Gobart, et luy commanda qu'il luy aportast une boiste en laquelle il avoit dedens du baulme de Nostre Seigneur Jesucrist. Lequel ongnement ainsi que nous trouvons par escript est de si grande vertu et merite que il n'est plaie mortelle ne si dangereuse quant elle en est oincte que tantost ne soit guerie. Iceluy ongnement avoit le payen de longtemps avec luy gardé, et en plusieurs grans dangiers l'avoit souvent deffendu. Apres qu'il eust ce fait il frappa des esperons, la lance sur la cuisse. Puis sont venus l'ung contre l'autre et si fermement ont l'ung l'autre rencontré de leurs deux lances que les pieces de toutes pars sont volees. Les chevaulx passerent oultre et quant vint au retour ilz tirerent leurs espees luisantes pour l'ung l'autre assaillir.

Valentin fut trespreux, hardy et dilligent des armes tant que de son espee au Chevalier Verd bailla ung coup si grant que le harnoys tailla et rompit tant que du corps luy fist le sang aval courir a grant randon. Et quant le Verd Chevalier se sentit feru et navré il leva hault son bras et de son espee qui portoit frappa Valentin sur la cuisse si grant coup que de la chair luy getta bas ung grant morceau. Puis luy dist, "Vous pouez cognoistre se de l'espee je sçay jouer. Assés je vous avoye dit devant que de mes mains vous conviendroit finer voz jours se contre moy le champ entreprendre vous vouliez. Trop a temps venistes devers moy et tard vous en retournerez, car j'ay esperance que tantost je vous penderay et atacheray a la plus haulte branche qui soit en celuy arbre pour le lieu reparer et tenir compaignie aux aultres malleureux qui par leur orgueil et folie ont la mort soufferte."

"Payen," dist Valentin, "de ce ne se fault ja trop fort vanter car ancores ne m'as tu pas. Pense de toy deffendre car a moy auras a faire." En disant ces parolles ont les deux chevaliers de rechief leur bataille commencee, et Valentin frappa adonc le payen sy grant coup que de son escu luy abatit ung grant quartier. Et le Verd Chevalier frappa sur Valentin par si grant force et puissance que dessus son

---

[1] *fi* at bottom right corner of 41r.

Valentin was troubled and unhappy to learn this information. "Alas," said he to himself, "almighty Lord God, my case will go badly if I do not have your beneficent grace and support, for I know that I am not the one the pagan speaks of. But since I came here with the purpose of undertaking this matter, never will I return without taking my measure against him who has killed so many valiant champions."

Then Valentin called the Green Knight and spoke to him thus: "Knight, I know perfectly well that I am not the one destined to conquer you, but nevertheless, whoever I may be, never will I leave here without facing you in battle."

"By Mohammed," said the pagan, "great folly leads you. You seem to think you can conquer me through treachery, but I will soon show you that your overweening confidence will turn into shameful defeat."

He took hold of his horse and quickly leapt on its back, calling a servant of his named Gobard, and ordering him to bring him a coffer that contained the balm of Our Savior Jesus Christ. It is written that this ointment is of such power and merit that no wound, however mortal or dangerous, would not be healed right away by its touch.[1] The pagan had possessed this ointment for a long time, and in several very dangerous situations it had helped him. After doing this, he spurred his horse with his lance couched on his thigh. Then they rode towards each other, clashing with such force that both their lances shattered in pieces that went flying off in all directions. The horses passed each other, and, when the knights turned to come back, each drew forth his shining sword to assault the other.

Valentin was brave, bold, and so skillful in arms that with his sword he gave the Green Knight a mighty stroke, breaking and slashing through his armor, and causing the blood to flow freely from his body. But as soon as the Green Knight felt himself to be cut and wounded, he raised his arm high and brought down his sword with so formidable a blow on Valentin's thigh that he gashed out a piece of his flesh. Then he declared, "You can see whether I know how to use a sword. I told you before we started that you would end your days by my hand if you chose to fight me. You came to me too promptly and will leave late, for I plan to hang you soon from the highest branch of that tree, where you will dress it up nicely and keep the other wretches company who through their pride and folly have suffered death."

"Pagan," said Valentin, "I wouldn't boast too much if I were you—you don't have me yet. Watch out for yourself—you won't find me so easy to deal with." Saying these words, the two knights recommenced their battle, and Valentin delivered such a mighty blow to the pagan that he whacked off a whole quarter of his shield. Then the Green Knight struck Valentin with such force and

---

[1] The wound-healing balm connected to Christ is another of the several motifs in this chapter that evoke an Arthurian setting. See Dickson, *Study*, 186–87.

heaulme son espee rompit. Et du grant coup qu'i donna a Valentin il fust estourdy en telle maniere que de son cheval il cheut a bas contre terre, mais tant fut de courage vaillant que tantost se releva. Et quant le payen vit que il se relevoit il tyra hors ung tresgrant cousteau qu'il avoit qui estoit pointu et le getta contre luy. Mais Valentin vit le cousteau venir et du coup se garda. Lors le Verd Cheva[41verso]lier qui se trouva sans glaisve, il tourna le cheval pour baston recouvrer, et Valentin fust pres que de son espee couppa ung des piedz du cheval tellement que payen et cheval a terre cheurent. Et quant il fut a bas a terre a coup se leva sus et vint vers Valentin et a force de bras ont l'ung l'autre serré. Si ne fault pas demander se chascun d'eulx monstra et employa sa puissance et sa force, et pour briefve parole faire tant fust la guerre des deux chevaliers fiere et merveilleuse que l'ung et l'autre furent moult fort navréz. Mais tant il avoit que combien que Valentin par sa puissance d'armes donnast plusieurs coupz au payen, riens ne luy prouffita, car du baulme qu'i portoit tantost estoit sain et guary comme devant.

 En ce point furent combatant si longuement que le jour sy leur faillit, et si travaillé se sentirent et non pas sans cause. Dolent et tresdesplaisant fust le chevalier paien que Valentin n'avoit peu desconfire, et jassoit ce qu'i fust moult las, si[1] n'en monstroit il pas le semblant, mais il dist a Valentin, "Chevalier, d'ores en avant il convient la bataille cesser, car je voy que vous estes travaillé et moult fort las. Et d'aultre part la nuyt s'aproche et descline le jour. Si me seroit petit d'onneur quant en ce point je vous conquerroye. Retournez en Acquitaine ceste nuyt vous reposer, car bien vanter vous pouez devant toutes gens que jamais plus vaillant que vous a mon corps ne jousta. Mais demain au matin retournez en ce champ et vous pourrez bien dire adieu tous voz amis car jamais eschapper de mort vous ne pourrez."

 Valentin fust joyeux de lesser le payen car lasse estoit et fort navré. Si ala vers son cheval, lequel en ung verd pré estoit entré. Il le print par le frain et monta dessus pour retourner en Acquitaine. Et quant ceulx de la cité veirent qu'il estoit retourné ilz menerent grant feste. Le duc et les barons saillirent a la porte qui Valentin receurent moult honnourablement entre lesquelz fut Orson qui en faisoit grant chiere. Entre ses bras le print, et quant il fut au palais le duc d'Acquitaine luy demanda des nouvelles du Verd Chevalier.

 "Sire," dist Valentin, "il est en son repaire dedens son verd pavillon la ou il se repose. Tant est puissant et fort que je ne cuide pas que nul, tant soit fort ne vaillant, le puisse conquerir se Dieu par sa grace n'y monstre evident miracle."

 "Valentin," dist le duc, "bien avez ouvré, car onques nul n'en retourna qui ne mourust a honte par les mains du Verd Chevalier. Bien avez monstré que sur tous les aultres vous estes chevalier et plain de grant proesse."

---

[1] Text has *sil*, which cannot be *s'il* since the subject of the verb *monstroit* follows.

might that he broke his sword on his helmet. Though the blow dizzied Valentin to the point of pitching him from his horse to the ground, he immediately raised himself up in heroic determination. The pagan, seeing him rise, drew and hurled at him the long pointed knife he carried. But Valentin saw the knife coming and sidestepped the blow. The Green Knight, finding himself without a sword, turned his horse to go seek a club, but Valentin was close enough to cut off one of his horse's feet, so that both horse and pagan fell to the ground. Quickly he rose from this prone position, coming towards Valentin till they were locked in a hostile embrace. No need to ask whether each one strove with maximum force, and, in brief, so fierce and marvelous was the struggle between these two knights that each one was seriously wounded. But however much Valentin managed to wound his pagan opponent through his warrior skills, it did no good, for he was immediately cured as soon as he applied the balm he carried.

By now they had been fighting so long that daylight began to fail. Moreover, they were exhausted, and not without cause. The pagan knight was sorrowful and angry that he had not been able to overcome Valentin, and, however weary he was, he would not admit it, instead saying to Valentin, "Knight, we should cease the battle for the present, for I see that you are tired and exhausted. Moreover, night is falling and the daylight is fading. I would gain little honor if I conquered you under such conditions. Return to Aquitaine to rest yourself this night, and you can surely boast that no one more doughty than you has ever jousted with me. But tomorrow morning come back to this field, having made your farewell to all your friends, for you will never be able to escape death."

Valentin was happy to leave the pagan, for he was weary and seriously wounded. He made his way towards his horse in a nearby green field. He took him by the reins, mounted, and headed towards Aquitaine. When the city's inhabitants saw him return, they were overjoyed. The duke and his barons came out of the gate to greet Valentin with great honor. Among them was Orson, who took him in his arms and made great cheer over him. When they reached the palace, the Duke of Aquitaine asked him for news of the Green Knight.

"Sire," said Valentin, "he has repaired to his green tent to take his rest. He is so powerful that I don't believe anyone, however strong and valiant, can conquer him if God in his grace does not perform some miracle."

"Valentin," said the duke, "you have done well, for no one has ever returned from battle with the Green Knight; rather all have died shamefully at his hands. You have demonstrated most forcefully that you are a worthy knight and full of great prowess."

"Franc duc," dist Valentin, "de ma proesse contre luy je ne me puis ancores vanter car demain au matin doit estre entre luy et moy nouvelle bataille. Or me soit Dieu en ayde et resconfort, car sans luy nul ne peut contre le Verd Chevalier par force cor[42recto]porelle[1] avoir victoire."

Apres celle victoire Valentin fust desarmé, puis ala en la chambre de la belle Fezonne. Sy ne fault point demander s'elle fust de sa venue moult joyeuse quant Valentin sain estoit retourné. Chascun en tenoit grant compte pour sa proesse et vaillance; des grans et des petis fust prisé. Et quant vint au soupper le duc d'Acquitaine tant d'onneur luy voulut faire que a sa propre table au plus pres de luy le voulut faire seoir comme sa personne.

Le soupper se passa en devisant de plusieurs choses. Apres Valentin se retrahit en prenant congé du duc et des aultres barons. Puis entra en une chambre secrete pour ses plaies mediciner, car trop fort navré estoit. Et quant il fut mediciné, il entra ou lit pour prendre repos. Et le Verd Chevalier est en son pavillon qui de son baulme fait oindre ses plaies, car il n'y a plaie si grande que tantost de cest ongnement ne soit guarie comme devant. Si vous laisseray a parler de luy et parleray de Valentin lequel est en sa chambre faisant grandes complaintes et piteuses lamentations.

[CHAPITRE 20]

Comment Valentin par la grace de Dieu s'avisa d'envoyer le lendemain au matin Orson pour combatre au Verd Chevalier; et comment ledit Orson le vainquist et conquesta comme vous orés. xx. [chapitre][2]

Toute celle nuyt fust l'enfant Valentin en son lit qui sans prendre repos de cueur tendrement souspiroit en disant paroles piteuses bassement a part luy.

"Helas! vray Dieu puissant, or voy je bien maintenant que mon entreprinse jamais n'en viendray a fin se par vostre grace et sainte bonté de moy n'avez pitié en moy donnant secours et resconfort contre ce faulx payen qui a ma mort juree. Helas! or avoy je entreprins et estoit mon intention fermee de propos arresté et deliberé que jamais a nul jour mon corps n'auroit repos jusques a ce que je puisse sçavoir de quel pere je fus engendré et de quelle mere je fus porté et enfanté sur terre. Mais je cognoy bien que ce que l'omme propose n'est pas chose parfaicte ne de legier achevee. Pour moy je le puis bien dire, car quant je entreprins le champ de bataille contre le Verd Chevalier trop me fust Fortune contraire puis qu'il est tel que jamais ne peult estre vaincu si non d'ung chevalier qui soit filz de roy et qui en

---

[1] *f ii* appears at bottom right corner of 42r.
[2] Woodcut of two knights jousting (repeat of woodcut on 15v).

"Noble duke," said Valentin, "I cannot yet boast of my prowess against him, for tomorrow morning there will be another battle between him and me. May God help me, for without that no one can gain victory over him by physical force alone."

After this victory, Valentin was disarmed; then he went to the fair Fezonne's chamber. No need to ask whether she was overjoyed to see that he had come back safe. Everyone made much of his prowess and valor; both great and small honored him. When he came in to supper, the Duke of Aquitaine wanted to do him honor by having him sit at his own table right next to him.

The supper was filled with much conversation. Afterwards Valentin retired, taking his leave from the duke and the other barons to go to his private chamber to have his wounds dressed, for he was seriously hurt. Once he had been treated, he went to bed to get some rest. At the same time, the Green Knight was in his tent, having his special balm massaged into his own injuries, for there is no wound so serious that this ointment cannot heal it right away. And now I will leave off speaking of him and will speak of Valentin who was in his chamber, groaning and moaning most piteously.

CHAPTER 20

How Valentin, by the grace of God, thought to send Orson to fight the Green Knight the following morning; and how Orson defeated him, as you will hear below.

All that night long the lad Valentin tossed and turned restlessly in his bed, sighing deeply and speaking softly to himself.

"Alas! true and almighty God, I can see that I will never be able to accomplish my goal if you do not take pity on me through your grace and holy goodness, granting me aid and succor against this false pagan who has sworn to kill me. Alas! I had fully intended never to rest a single day until I discovered what father engendered me and what mother bore me and put me on this earth. But I have learned that what man proposes is not necessarily easily achieved. I can say that with certainty, for Fortune was against me when I undertook battle against the Green Knight, since he can never be vanquished by any knight if he is not a king's son who has never suckled a woman's milk. Not only can I not claim

telle maniere [42verso]ait esté nourry ou temps de sa jeunesse que de nulle femme n'ait esté alaité. Lors or ne suis je pas celuy qui si digne puisse estre que d'estre filz de roy, et qui en telle maniere aye esté nourry ou temps de ma jeunesse. Cy ne voy confort en mon fait qui de mort me peust preserver fors seulement invoquer et requerir la grace de mon createur Jesus et sa doulce vierge mere que de ce danger me veulle preserver et mettre hors sans deffiner mes jours sy trespiteusement."

En ceste contemplation moult grande fust Valentin toute la nuyt sans prendre repos fors que sa fortune plourer et doubter[1] son aventure. Et quant il eust par tout pensé et par divine inspiration il s'avisa de Orson le sauvaige lequel il avoit en la forest conquis; sy se pensa que par celuy il pourroit estre secouru, "car je croy bien que de femme il n'avoit jamais esté alaité, et que par aventure pouoit estre avenu que une royne en la forest l'auroit enfanté."

En ces choses considerant la nuyt print fin et le jour esclarcist. Ainsi se leva Valentin chargé de pensee ennuyeuse et de mellencolie plain, et vint devers Orson et par evidens signes luy demonstra que il vestit ses armeures et print son cheval pour aler en son lieu combatre le Verd Chevalier. De ces nouvelles fut Orson moult fort joyeulx, en saillant et en menant grant joye parmy la sale. Si fist signe que le Verd Chevalier jamais de ses mains eschapper il ne pourra. Et en ces signes faisant il avisa une massue de bois grosse et pesante. Si la mist sur son col et en branlant la teste il faisoit signe des bras et des mains que nul aultre harnois contre le faulx payen il ne veult porter, et de cheval ne de lance ne d'aultre harnoys quelconques pour combatre le geant il n'a cure.

"Amy," ce dist Valentin, "cela ne ferez vous pas. Mais je veul que de mes armeures vous soyez armé et portant le blason qui par le roy Pepin me fust donné, et sy chevaulcherez le destrier que je amenay de France." Au vouloir de Valentin se consentit et acorda Orson, car sur toutes choses vouloit obeïr a Valentin et a ses commandemens comme son subject et serviteur.

Lors commanda Valentin que on luy aportast son harnoys, et que Orson fust armé tout en telle maniere comme son propre corps estoit quant il ala pour combatre contre le Verd Chevalier. La chose fust faicte et acomplie, car le duc d'Acquitaine qui present fust de sa propre main aida a armer le sauvaige des armes de Valentin avec plusieurs barons qui la estoient. Et quant Orson fust armé il fust moult fort regardé des seigneurs et barons qui la estoient presens car moult bien il resembloit estre homme preux et hardy et chevalier de grant beauté plain, hault et bien formé en tous ses membres par droite mesure compassé. Il regarde le harnoys qui autour de luy reluyt, et puis fait signe des bras que devant qu'il fust midy [43recto]entre[2] ses mains il estrangleroit le Chevalier Verd par devant toute la court sans en avoir mercy ne pitié. Des mines et des gestes que faisoit Orson commencerent a rire tous ceulx de la compaignie. Et quant Orson eust prins congé du duc d'Acquitaine, il embraça Valentin et print congé de luy

---

[1] Text has *doubte*.
[2] *fiii* appears at bottom right corner of 43r.

the dignity of being a king's son, I know I was not raised thus in my babyhood. Therefore I can see nothing to preserve me from death in this case outside of calling upon the grace of my creator Jesus and His virgin mother, that they preserve me from this danger and keep me from ending my days most piteously."

Valentin spent the whole night awake, contemplating his situation, bemoaning his fortune, and fearing his fate. After thinking it all over, he had a divine inspiration concerning Orson the wild man whom he had conquered in the forest; it came to him that Orson might be able to help him, "for I believe that he never suckled a woman's milk, and it just might be that a queen gave birth to him in the forest."

While he was pondering all these things, the night finally came to an end and day dawned. Valentin arose, burdened by his melancholy thoughts, but he went to see Orson and made clear through signs that he wanted him to put on his armor, take his horse, and go fight the Green Knight. Orson was thrilled at this news, jumping and dancing for joy all around the room. He signaled through gestures that the Green Knight would never be able to escape him. While communicating thus he spied a massive heavy club. He placed this on his shoulder and, shaking his head, signaled that he need carry no other arm against the false pagan; not a horse, not a lance, nor any other type of weapon or equipment did he want to fight the giant.

"My friend," said Valentin, "you will not fight him thus. I want you to wear my armor, carry the coat of arms that King Pepin gave me, and ride the warhorse that I brought from France." Orson agreed to everything Valentin wanted, for above all else, as a loyal servant, he desired to obey Valentin and all his commands.

So Valentin ordered his equipment to be brought and Orson armed just as he himself had been when he had gone off to fight the Green Knight. The thing was soon accomplished, for the Duke of Aquitaine and several of his barons present in the room helped gird the wild man in Valentin's armor with their own hands. Once Orson was armed, everyone there gazed at him, for he looked brave and bold, like a tall, handsome knight, well-formed and well-proportioned in body and limb. He himself looked at the shiny armor enveloping his body and gestured to signify that before noon he would strangle the Green Knight without pity or mercy with his own hands in front of the entire court. His gestures and grimaces made everyone in the company laugh. After taking leave of the Duke of

en luy faisant signe que de riens il n'eust doubte, et que devant son retour ou mort ou vif le Verd Chevalier luy amenera.[1] Et Valentin en plourant a Dieu le commanda en priant bien devotement que contre le payen victoire il peust avoir. Et ainsi partit Orson.

Mais devant qu'il montast a cheval il s'avisa de la belle Fezonne de laquelle il n'avoit pas prins congé. Si monta au palays et entra en la sale ou estoit la dame et plusieurs aultres bien noblement acompaignee. Il courut devers elle et la voulut baiser, de quoy la dame et plusieurs aultres se prindrent moult fort a rire, car il luy faisoit signe que pour son amour avoir il s'en aloit combatre le Verd Chevalier. Et Fezonne qui de toute gracieuseté fut plaine, en soubzriant luy a fait signe qu'il se porte vaillamment, et que au retour de la bataille son amour elle luy donneroit.

Ainsi se partit Orson et monta a cheval, lequel moult notablement fust convoyé par le duc d'Acquitaine et plusieurs aultres barons et chevaliers jusques hors de la porte. Et quant ilz furent hors de la ville chascun s'en retourna en depriant Dieu qu'il luy voulsist donner victoire. Le bruit fut parmy la cité que le sauvage aloit combatre le Verd Chevalier. De laquelle chose chascun fust fort esmerveillé pour la bataille des deux champions.

Or s'en va Orson chevaulchant, vestu et armé des propres armes de Valentin, pour quoy le Verd Chevalier ja ne le cognoistera. Il n'a gaires aresté qu'il est venu au pavillon du Verd Chevalier, et sans dire mot du fer de sa lance l'a venu toucher[2] en signifiant qui luy baille deffiance. De laquelle chose le Verd Chevalier eust grant despit en son courage, et jura par ses dieux que son grant orgueil luy feroit humilier devant le jour passé. Il fust tantost armé puis monta a cheval et a prins la lance qui fut droite et forte. Puis est entré ou champ pour courir contre Orson, et Orson s'eslongna de luy. Si ont baissé leurs lances et tellement ont rencontré l'ung l'autre que chevaulx et hommes des deux par a terre sont tombéz. Et quant ilz furent bas tous deux se releverent et tirerent leurs espees pour assaillir l'ung l'autre moult rigoureusement. Mais le Chevalier Verd qui moult fust orgueilleux et plain d'ire frappa premier Orson ung coup si grant et si merveilleux que de son heaulme le sercle d'or luy couppa, et de son escu il en abatit ung grant quartier, et en telle maniere que l'espee qui fust pesante luy cheut a terre, et parmy le harnoys oultre passa tellement que de celuy coup Orson fut fort durement navré. Et quant il vit son sang aval son harnoys courir il fut plus fier que [43verso]ung liepart et orgueilleux comme ung lyon. Il tourne les yeulx et branle la teste et de l'espee fourbie a donné ung coup si grant sur le heaulme du geant que jusques a la teste le toucha et des che-

---

[1] Text has *amenrra*.

[2] This is a strange construction, perhaps emendable to *du fer de sa lance l'est venu toucher*, unless it is a rare instance of *venir*, here part of a two-verb construction with *toucher*, conjugated with *avoir* in the present perfect under the influence of the direct object pronoun placed before the auxiliary. I have not seen other examples elsewhere, however, and can find no reference to other instances of this kind of construction in studies of Middle French grammar.

Aquitaine, Orson embraced Valentin and took his leave from him, gesturing to him to have no fear, that he would bring the Green Knight back to him dead or alive. Valentin, for his part, commended him to God as he wept and prayed devotedly that he might have victory against the pagan. And so departed Orson.

However, before he mounted his horse, he spied the fair Fezonne from whom he had not yet taken leave. So he climbed up to the palace and entered the hall where the lady was with several of her noble attendants. He ran up to her to kiss her, which made the lady and her attendants start laughing, for he was gesturing to her how he was off to fight the Green Knight for her sake. But Fezonne, who was truly gracious, signaled to him (though she smiled as she did so) that he should conduct himself with valor, and that at his return she would grant him her love.

And so Orson departed, mounting his horse and being notably escorted out of the gate by the Duke of Aquitaine and several of his barons and knights. Once they were out of the city each turned back after praying God to grant him victory. The news spread throughout the city that the wild man was going to fight the Green Knight. Everyone marveled that there would be a battle between two such champions.

Orson was riding along, dressed and armed with Valentin's own weapons, for which reason the Green Knight did not recognize him. He did not tarry till he came to the Green Knight's pavilion, where, without saying a word, he touched it with the metal tip of his lance to signify that he challenged him. This irritated the Green Knight in his heart, and he swore by his gods that he would humble his opponent's great pride before the day was out. He armed quickly and mounted his horse, taking up his stout, straight lance. Then he entered the field to joust with Orson, who took up his position at some distance. Both men lowered their lances and clashed against each other so hard that men and horses fell to the ground. They rose quickly, drawing their swords to attack each other with vigor. But the Green Knight, fiercely proud and full of anger, struck Orson first with a blow so powerful and marvelous that he sent flying the circle of gold from his helmet and knocked off a full quarter of his shield, while the manner of the blow made the heavy sword continue its path to the ground, piercing Orson's armor and wounding him seriously. When he saw his blood running down his armor he grew more fierce than a leopard and prouder than a lion. He rolled his eyes and shook his head; then with his gleaming sword he smote the giant so hard on the helmet that the blow reached his head, casting a great quantity of hair and skin to the ground. But the blow continued past the helmet, and the

veulx de la peau a terre getta une grant partie. Et de celuy coup oultre le heaulme passa, et fut le Verd Chevalier navré au bras tant que le sang a grant puissance et randon commença a courir. Mais le Verd Chevalier de ceste playe n'en fist compte, car il print du baulme de quoy je vous ay devant fait mencion, et tantost qu'il a touché la playe elle a esté sanée et aussi sayne comme pardevant, de quoy Orson fust moult esmerveillé et bien se pensa que de glaisve ne pourroit son corps avoir quant sy tost estoit guarye la playe qui tant estoit grande et parfonde. Sur ceste matiere fust subtil et avisé; il getta son espee, cousteaux et harnoys a terre, puis est couru contre le Verd Chevalier et a force de bras tellement l'a sarré et tenu que dessoubz luy a terra l'a getté. Et quant il le tint dessoubz luy il luy osta le heaulme qu'i portoit pour luy coupper la teste. La fust le Verd Chevalier en telle subjection mis qu'il fust contraint par force de soy rendre a Orson et mercy luy prier. Mais Orson qui riens n'entend de son crier, il ne fist compte en maniere quelconques, et tant estroit le tient que sans nulle remission a ceste heure luy eust osté la vie se n'eust esté Valentin qui bien vit et cogneust les mines et gestes de Orson, et a force de cheval devers eulx acourut. Et quant il fust arrivé il fist signe a Orson que pas ne le tuast. Alors se trahyt Orson arriere quant il oÿt Valentin, mais tousjours tenoit le Verd Chevalier en sa subjection auquel Valentin parla en ceste maniere:

"Chevalier, a ceste heure vous pouez cognoistre et clerement sçavoir que vous n'avez force ne puissance de vous revencher ne de mort vous garder contre cestuy homme parquoy force vous est de mort endurer et deffiner voz jours treshonteusement, car ainsi que les aultres chevaliers ont esté par vous desconfis et en celuy hault arbre pendus. Tout ainsi vous serez vituperablement occys et au plus hault de tous les aultres ataché."

"Helas!" dist le Verd Chevalier, "vous me semblez bien estre homme de grant courtoisie et de noblesse guarny, et semble bien a vous veoir que de franche et loyalle gentillesse vous soyez extrait et descendu; pour laquelle chose il vous plaise de moy avoir pitié et ma vie sauver."

"Payen," dist Valentin, "ce ne feray je pas fors que par tel convenant que vous renoncerez la loy payenne et des faulx dieux que vous adorez en prenant la loy et creance de Jesucrist, le Dieu tout puissant, et en recepvant le sainct baptesme sans lequel nul ne peult avoir gloire pardurable. Et quant vous aurez cela fait, vous yrez en France et vous presenterez au roy Pepin et luy direz que Valentin et Orson vous envoyent par devers luy comme [44recto]chevalier[1] vaincu et par eulx conquis. Sy aiez avis et regard sur ce fait en moy donnant responce sur vostre intention et voulenté qui soit seure et certaine."

"Amy," dist le Verd Chevalier, "je vous donne telle responce. De ceste heure je regnye et renonce du tout et delaisse les faulx dieux et prens pour le demourant de ma vie pour maistre et servir le vray Dieu auquel vous avez creance, et en celle foy veul vivre et mourir. Et sy vous prometz que devers le roy Pepin comme vostre

---

[1] *f iiii* appears at bottom right corner of 44r.

Green Knight was so badly injured on his arm that blood began to flow in great abundance. But the Green Knight was unperturbed by the wound, for he took some of his balm, which I mentioned to you earlier, and, as soon as he touched it to the wound, it was healed and as whole as it had been before. Orson marveled at this, thinking to himself that he would never conquer him by the sword if his opponent could so quickly heal so deep and serious a wound. But Orson knew the clever and prudent thing to do; he threw aside his sword, knives, and weapons and, running up to the Green Knight, got a tight hold of him in his arms and flung him to the ground. Once he had him pinned under him, he wrested off the helmet he wore to cut off his head. The Green Knight, forced into subjection, had no choice but to give himself up and beg Orson for mercy. But Orson, who understood nothing of his cries, paid no attention to them whatsoever, continuing to hold him down so that without any pity he would have killed him then and there if Valentin had not seen and understood Orson's facial expressions and gestures, and galloped up to stop him. He immediately gestured to Orson not to kill him. Orson drew back as soon as he heard Valentin, but he continued to hold the Green Knight down while Valentin addressed him in the following manner:

"Knight, now you realize and understand that you do not have sufficient strength or force to protect yourself from death or take revenge against this man; rather you have no choice but to endure death and end your days most shamefully, just as did all the other knights whom you defeated and hanged from this tall tree. You will be killed ignobly and hanged higher than any of the others."

"Alas!" said the Green Knight, "you appear to me to be a man of great courtesy and nobility, descended from noble and loyal lineage; for that reason I beg of you to have pity on me and save my life."

"Pagan," said Valentin, "I will not do this unless you swear to renounce the pagan religion and the false gods that you worship and choose instead the faith and belief in Jesus Christ, the all-powerful God, and accept holy baptism without which no one can reach everlasting glory. And once you have done that, you will go to France and present yourself to King Pepin, telling him that Valentin and Orson send you to him as a knight vanquished by them. Be careful to give me a sincere answer concerning your intention."

"Friend," said the Green Knight, "I will give you just such a response. From this moment I forsake and renounce all the false gods and take the true God in whom you believe as my master for the rest of my life, and in this faith I will live

povre subgect et prisonnier au plus bref que je pourray de par vous je m'y rendray, et devant sa haulte majesté je me presenteray."

Quant le Verd Chevalier eust fait le serment et promis les choses dessusdictes acomplir, Valentin fist signe a Orson qu'i le laissast lever, et Orson, qui fust saige et bien avisé, luy osta ses armeures tant que il ne luy peust plus faire dommaige. Et quant le Verd Chevalier fust sur les piedz levé, il parla a Valentin en disant, "Sire chevalier, il me semble que vous estes celluy qui le jour passé eustes bataille avec moy et qui au jour d'uy deviez retourner. Et cestuy qui m'a conquis est celluy qui au palays du duc Savary contre la terre me getta."

"Il est vray," dist Valentin, "c'est bien cogneu a vous, la chose est veritable, mentir ne vous en fault."

"Or vous diray," dist le Verd Chevalier, "une chose de laquelle je vous prie que vous l'acomplissés—envoyez cestuy chevalier qui m'a conquis par devers ce hault arbre et sy peult oster l'escu et le blason lequel y est pendu, je pourray bien cognoistre que c'est celluy par qui je dois estre conquis et vaincu, car de nul aultre je ne puis en nul champ de bataille estre gaigné ne conquesté."

Adonc Valentin fist signe a Orson qu'il alast devers l'arbre pour querir l'escu qui pendu estoit. Orson tira celle part et tout aussitost qu'il aprocha de l'escu, il estendit son bras et l'escu luy saillit en la main, lequel il apporta au Verd Chevalier. Et quant il vit que Orson eust apporté l'escu et que de l'arbre l'avoit destaché sans y avoir fait force ne violence, il recogneust que c'estoit celuy qui estoit predestiné a le combatre et conquester. Il se getta a terre et luy voulut baiser les piedz, mais Orson qui fust saige et bien aprins par les signes de Valentin ne le souffrit ne le voulut, mais le print par les bras et le releva sus.

"Helas!" dist le Verd Chevalier, "bien m'apartient de vous porter honneur et reverence plus que a homme qui soit vivant. Car je sçay et cognoy clerement que [de] tous preux[1] et vaillans chevaliers vous devez avoir et emporter le bruit et le renon. Et entre les aultres je vous afferme et fay assavoir que celuy qui m'a conquis est le plus preux, le plus vaillant et hardy qui soit en tout le monde, et sy devez fermement croyre qu'il est filz de roy et de royne et si est tel que jamais [44verso]de femme ne fust nourry ne alaitté. Et qu'i soit verité par ma seur Esclarmonde je le vous puis prouver, car elle a une teste d'arain laquelle luy dist et declaire les aventures et fortunes qui a elle et a tous ceulx de sa generation peuent avenir. Dont ceste teste aura duree jusques a ce que le plus preux du monde entre en la chambre en quoy elle repose. Et quant il y sera entré de celle heure perdra sa force et sa vertu. Et celuy doit avoir ma seur Esclarmonde qui tant est belle et plaisante pour femme et pour espouse. Pour tant, chevalier, alez en celle part, car j'ay moult grant desir que celle vous ayez pour femme comme le plus preux chevalier de tout le monde, car tel vous peult on bien reclamer et nommer. Et affin de meilleure cognoissance avoir par devers elle, portez luy cestuy aneau

---

[1] Text has *peux*.

and die. I also promise you to go to King Pepin as soon as I can, to present myself to his exalted majesty as your poor subject and prisoner."

Once the Green Knight had taken this vow and promised to accomplish these things, Valentin gestured to Orson to let him up, and Orson, wise and prudent, took his weapons from him so that he could do no more harm. When the Green Knight was once more on his feet, he addressed Valentin saying, "Sir knight, it seems you are the one against whom I fought yesterday and who was supposed to return today. And this one who has vanquished me must be he who threw me down in Duke Savary's palace."

"It is true," said Valentin, "you've recognized us; that is who we are, I must not lie to you."

"I must beg you to do one thing," said the Green Knight. "Send this knight who vanquished me over to that tall tree, and if he can detach the shield hanging there, I will know that he is the one by whom I was destined to be conquered, for by no other may I be defeated in the field of battle."

So Valentin gestured to Orson that he go over to the tree to fetch the shield hanging there. Orson turned to go, but as soon as he approached and stretched out his arm, the shield leaped into his hand, and he brought it back to the Green Knight. Seeing that Orson had detached it from the tree without need of force or violence, he recognized that Orson was the one predestined to fight and conquer him. He threw himself to the ground, trying to kiss his feet, but Orson, well-behaved and well-instructed by Valentin's gestures, would not allow him to do so, rather taking him in his arms and raising him up.

"Alas!" said the Green Knight, "it is incumbent upon me to honor and revere you more than any man alive. For I see clearly now that of all hardy and valiant knights, you deserve the highest renown. Moreover, I confirm and announce that he who has conquered me is the bravest, boldest, and most valiant in all the world, and you should believe him to be the son of a king and queen, and never to have suckled woman's milk. I can prove the truth to you through my sister, Esclarmonde, for she possesses a brass head that can tell the events and fortunes that will happen to her and her family. And that head will last until the bravest man in the world comes into the chamber where it lies. And once he enters, at that very hour it will lose its force and powers. Moreover, that man will be the one to marry my sister, the fair and lovely Esclarmonde, and take her as his wife. Therefore, sir knight, go there; I want you to marry her, for you can surely claim to be the most worthy knight in all the world. And so that she will receive you properly, bring her this ring that she gave me on my departure. For my part, I

lequel au departir d'elle me donna. Et je m'en yray devers le roy Pepin, ainsi que promis vous ay, me rendre prisonnier et ma foy acquitter; et au retour de luy au chasteau de ma seur vers vous je me rendray. Et d'ores en avant serons mais qu'il vous plaise loyaulx et parfais amis, car jamais de vostre compaignie je ne veul departir."

Et quant le chevalier Valentin entendit que le Verd Chevalier avoit une seur qui tant estoit de grant beaulté plaine, par le vouloir de Dieu le tout puissant et par inclinacion de naturelle amour il fust d'elle frappé au cueur et esprins de sa beaulté tresardamment amoureux. Si a voué Dieu que jamais n'arrestera tant que il puisse veoir la belle de qui la beaulté est de renommee si excellente. Et apres ces choses le Verd Chevalier, qui de la Verde Montaigne estoit roy couronné et soubz luy tenoit grant paÿs et grans tenemens, fist cryer parmy son ost que tous payens qui a son mandement estoient venus pour le servir devant Acquitaine, de ceste heure s'en retournassent en leur païs sans la terre du duc Savary grever ne dommaiger en aulcune maniere. Ainsi departirent payens et Sarrasins qui pour la prinse du Verd Chevalier demenerent fort grant dueil et grant tristesse.

Et Valentin et Orson comme prisonnier le prindrent et le menerent en la cité d'Acquitaine. Si ne fault pas demander le grant bruit et le grant soulas et la grant joye et liesse qui parmy la cité de grans et de petis fust demenee. Et le duc Savary a toute sa baronnye saillirent devant les portes en moult grant honneur et triumphe a l'encontre de Orson qui le Verd Chevalier avoit conquis et vaincu.

Et quant le Verd Chevalier fust devers le duc d'Acquitaine et devant toute la chevalerie, il leur a dist en ceste maniere, "Seigneurs, bien devez porter honneur et reverence a cestuy chevalier lequel par force d'armes il m'a connquis et vaincu. Et sachés certainement que celuy est filz de roy [45recto]et de royne et jamais en sa vie de femme ne fut alaité, car si n'estoit ainsi jamais de moy conquerir il n'eust eu force ne puissance, car ainsi il estoit dit par la teste d'arain que ma seur Esclarmonde tient en sa chambre."

"Par ma foy," dist le duc d'Acquitaine, "assez bien vous en peult on croire, car il a bien monstré a l'encontre de vous la grant vaillance et proesse qui est en luy. Et puis que en luy je cognoys la noble hardiesse et le vaillant couraige qui est en luy, je luy veul porter honneur et reverence de toute ma puissance."

En disant ces parolles le duc d'Acquitaine avec toute sa court et le Verd Chevalier lequel Orson amenoit prisonnier sont entréz en la ville et montéz au palays. Et quant ilz furent dedens le duc manda sa fille Fezonne, puis a dit, "Ma fille, voy cy le Verd Chevalier lequel pour vostre corps conquerir et avoir vostre amour a longuement tenu la plus part de ma terre en sa subjection. Et combien qu'il ne soit pas de nostre creance, toutesfois fortune m'estoit contraire et dessoubz mon vouloir maistresse en telle maniere que forte et longue attente d'aultruy secours avoir avoient mon cueur contraint en telle chose acorder. Mais Dieu qui est vray juge sur ce fait a voulu remedier en telle maniere que de mon ennemy je suis vengé et venu au dessus par cestuy chevalier lequel par Valentin pour vostre corps secourir au congé et licence du roy Pepin deça vous a trammis et envoié. Or pouez

will go to King Pepin, as I promised you, to keep my word to give myself up as prisoner; then when I get back I will go find you at my sister's castle. From now on, if it please you, we will be perfect faithful friends, for I never wish to leave your company."

When Valentin heard that the Green Knight had such a beautiful sister, he was instantly smitten with ardent love, both because it was the will of almighty God and through natural inclination. He swore to God that he would never rest until he could see this lovely girl whose beauty was of such excellent renown. After this speech the Green Knight, who was the crowned monarch of the Green Mountain, possessing extensive lands and holdings, had it announced throughout his host that all the pagans who had come at his order to serve him in Aquitaine should at that hour return to their countries without doing any damage whatsoever to Duke Savary's land. Thus all the pagans and Saracens left, mourning sadly as they went the capture of the Green Knight.

Valentin and Orson took him prisoner and led him to the city of Aquitaine. No need to ask if there was much tumult and relief, extensive rejoicing and happiness throughout the city among its inhabitants both great and small. Duke Savary and all his barons issued forth from the gates to greet Orson, the vanquisher of the Green Knight, with great honor and triumph.

When the Green Knight stood before the Duke of Aquitaine and all the knights, he addressed them in the following manner: "My lords, you should honor and revere this knight who has conquered and vanquished me through force of arms. Know for certain that he is the son of a king and a queen and has never suckled a woman's milk, for if he were not so, he never would have had the strength or ability to conquer me, for so it was predicted by the brass head that my sister Esclarmonde keeps in her chamber."

"By my faith," said the Duke of Aquitaine, "one can certainly believe what you say, for he has surely shown what great valor and bravery he possesses through his battle with you. And since I recognize his noble daring and valiant courage, my first wish is to honor and revere him as much as I can."

While these words were spoken, the Duke of Aquitaine and the Green Knight, whom Orson led as prisoner, along with the entire court, entered the city and mounted up to the palace. Once there, the duke sent for his daughter Fezonne, to whom he said, "My daughter, here is the Green Knight who, in order to win you and your love, has long held my much of my land in subjection. And even though he is not of our faith, fortune was nevertheless against me, ruling against my wishes in such a way that for a long time, while waiting for help from someone, my will was constrained to accept such a thing. But God, who is a true judge, was willing to remedy the situation, so that I was avenged and triumphed over my enemy through this knight whom Valentin has brought to save you with the permission of King Pepin. Now you must realize that above all others is he

vous cognoistre que dessus tous les aultres il est preux, hardy et vaillant. Et si croy que pour vous conquerir Dieu le vous a transmis. Pour tant ma fille, ma seule esperance, en qui gist le seul espoir et confort de ma vie, avisez et prenez regard et consideration dessus ce cas, car ce seroit ma voulenté que celuy eussiez pour mary et espoux se vostre consentement et voulenté estoit au mien acordant, car nul aultre sa voulenté ne doit contraindre d'eviter en mariage ne prendre partie qu'il luy soit aggreable."

"Monseigneur," dist la pucelle qui moult fust bien endoctrinee et prouveue de responce, "vous sçavez que vous estes mon pere et je suis vostre fille, si n'est pas droit et rayson que moy, qui suis selon Dieu et nature a vous subjecte, face ma voulenté en quelconques chose, mais suis preste et appareillé de faire du tout vostre deliberation et se aultrement je vouloye faire je ne monsteroye pas que je fusse vostre fille naturelle, car vous sçavez bien que vous avez promis de moy donner en mariaige a celuy qui par force d'armes le Verd Chevalier pourroit conquerir. Or est venu celuy par qui la chose est acomplye du tout en tout, et lequel a acomply et parfait le contenu de vostre cry et denoncement que vous aviez fait faire et publier. Sy est bien rayson que celuy je doy prendre et que a celuy je soye donnee. Et se aulcunement prendre je ne le vouloye [45verso] je feroye vostre intention anichillee, qui a jamais seroit contre mon honneur reprouvee."

"Fille," dist le duc d'Acquitaine, "moult haultement avez parlé et bien me plaist vostre responce. Or fault il sçavoir du chevalier s'il vous vauldra prendre pour femme, et s'il en est content, je luy donneray pour le mariaige de vous d'Acquitaine la moytié."

La fut present Valentin qui par signes et paroles demanda a Orson sa voulenté et intencion. Et il luy a fait signe que jamais aultre ne veult avoir que la belle Fezonne. Ainsi furent les deux parties d'acord de laquelle chose. Ceulx qui le sçeurent en furent joyeulx. Le duc fit tantost venir ung evesque pour Orson et la belle Fezonne fiancer et leur faire promettre de l'ung l'autre espouser pour le temps a venir en loyal mariage demourer. Aultrement ne espouserent l'ung l'autre pour l'eure presente fors que foy promise. Et ne fault pas demander de la feste et de la grande triumphe ne exellente joyeuseté, ne tous esbas qui parmi Acquitaine furent fais, car le racompter seroit trop grant. Mais combien que Orson eust juré et promis de prendre la belle Fezonne, sy ne l'espousera il pas ne jamais a son costé elle ne couchera jusques a tant que par le vouloir de Dieu sçaura parler bon langaige, et que Valentin ait conquis la belle Esclarmonde. Desquelles choses je veul mencion faire cy apres tout au mieulx que mon entendement et petit engin le pourra comprendre et declairer.

bold, hardy, and valiant. I believe that God has sent him to win you. Therefore, my daughter, my only hope, in whom rests the only aspiration and comfort of my life, take heed and consider this situation, for it would be my will that you marry this man if your consent and will were in accord with my own, for no one should force another to marry against his will."

"My lord," said the girl, who was well-taught and well-spoken, "you know that you are my father and I am your daughter, thus it is not right or reason that I, who am subject to you according both to God and nature, should follow my own will in anything; rather I am ready and willing to do what you decide, and if I wished to do otherwise, I would not be showing myself as your natural daughter, for you know that you promised to give me in marriage to the one who could conquer the Green Knight through force of arms. Now the one who has accomplished this task through and through has come, and he has completely and thoroughly fulfilled the criteria of what you had proclaimed far and wide. Thus it is only reasonable that I take him and that I be given to him. And if ever I refused to take him, I would be abrogating your intention, which would always be a reproof to my honor."

"My daughter," said the Duke of Aquitaine, "you have spoken properly and your answer pleases me well. Now we need to see if the knight wishes to take you to wife, and, if he is happy about it, I will give him half of Aquitaine upon your marriage."

Valentin, who was present at this exchange, asked Orson through signs and words what was his will. And he signaled back that he wished never to have any other than the fair Fezonne. Thus the two parties came to an agreement. Everyone who learned of it was joyful. The duke sent for a bishop to pronounce the betrothal of Orson and the fair Fezonne, and to have them promise to marry and keep one another in faithful marriage forever. In other words, they did not marry each other at the present moment, only pledged their troth. And no need to ask about the excellent feasting, celebration, and great rejoicing, nor all the entertainments that took place throughout Aquitaine, for it would take too long to recount it all. But however much Orson had promised and sworn to take the fair Fezonne, he will not marry her nor ever lie at her side until by the grace of God he will learn how to speak properly, and until Valentin will have won the fair Esclarmonde. I will tell you all about these matters later on to the best of my ability.

[CHAPITRE 21]

Comment la nuyt que Orson eust juré la belle Fezonne l'ange s'aparut a Valentin; et du commandement qu'i luy fist. xxi. chap[itre].

Apres ce que Orson eust juré la belle fille du duc d'Acquitaine, c'est assavoir la tresplaisante Fezonne, en iceluy jour fust demené grant joye par tout le pays d'environ, car de l'assemblee furent joyeulx tous les seigneurs de la terre. En joye et en soulas passa le jour tant que la nuyt fust venue qui fust temps de prendre repos. Le duc d'Acquitaine se retrahyt devers sa chambre pour dormir et prendre son repos, et chascun s'en ala en son ordonnance aux chambres comme elles leur estoient ordonneez et determineez. Valentin et Orson s'en alerent en une belle chambre qui determinee leur estoit. En ung beau lit paré luy et Orson reposerent celle nuyt.

Et quant vint devers la minuyt par le vouloir de Dieu le tout puissant ung ange s'apparut a Valentin lequel luy a dist, "Valentin, saches que par moy Dieu te mande que demain au matin tu te partes de ceste terre et maine avecques toy Orson le sauvaige par lequel le Verd Chevalier a esté conquis, et sans nul sejour ne[1] dilation faire va au chasteau de Ferragu. Et la tu trouveras [46recto]la belle Esclarmonde par laquelle tu sçauras de quelle lignee tu es yssu et de quel pere tu es engendré et de quelle mere porté. Et si te commande en nom de Dieu que devant que ton compaignon espouse la belle Fezonne tu parfaices cestuy voyage."

De ceste vision fust Valentin en grant pensee et en grant mellencolie. En sousy passa la nuyt tant que le jour fust cler sans prendre nul repos. Et quant le jour fust venu il fist lever Orson et alerent au palais en la sale ou le Verd Chevalier avec les aultres barons et chevaliers estoit en attendant le bon duc Savary. Si ne demoura pas longuement que le duc entra en la sale.

Et tantost qu'il y fut, le Verd Chevalier a prinse la parole en le saluant en toute reverence deue puis luy a dist, "Franc duc, il est vray et certain que dedens le temps entre vous et moy assigné j'ay esté conquis et vaincu pour laquelle chose je n'ay occasion ne droit de riens demander a vostre fille. Mais de ceste heure la quitte et vostre pays veul delaisser en paix ainsi comme j'ay promis et pour mon serment acquitter. Je vous requiers et prie que me fachez donner le sacrement de baptesme affin que je puisse estre a Dieu le tout puissant plus aggreable."

"Chevalier," dist le duc, "bien avez parlé et a vostre requeste je veul du tout obeïr car a ceste heure presente vous serez baptisé." Le duc commanda que on feist venir ung prestre pour baptiser le Verd Chevalier. Et quant ce vint qu'i fist sur les fons pour le baptesme recepvoir, Valentin qui present fust parla devant

---

[1] Text has *de*.

CHAPTER 21

How the angel appeared to Valentin on the night Orson had pledged himself to the fair Fezonne; and concerning the order he gave him.

After Orson had pledged himself to the Duke of Aquitaine's beautiful daughter, that is to say, the most lovely Fezonne, there was great rejoicing throughout the country all around, for all the lords of the land were glad of their betrothal. The day was passed in delight and celebration until nightfall when it was time to rest. The Duke of Aquitaine retired to his chamber to sleep and take his rest, and all the others did likewise according to the distribution of rooms. Valentin and Orson went to a lovely chamber that had been provided them. That night they slumbered in a beautifully-adorned bed.

Towards midnight, by the grace of almighty God, an angel appeared to Valentin, saying to him, "Valentin, God has sent me to tell you to leave this country tomorrow morning, taking with you Orson the wild man, by whom the Green Knight was defeated, and, without rest or delay, go to the castle of Ferragu. There you will find the lovely Esclarmonde through whom you will discover from what lineage you are descended, what father engendered you and what mother bore you. Moreover, I command you in God's name to complete this voyage before your companion marries the fair Fezonne."

This vision caused Valentin much thought and melancholy. He lay wide awake all night in troubled thought until dawn. At the break of day he woke up Orson, and the two of them went to the hall in the palace where the Green Knight and all the other barons and lords awaited the good Duke Savary. Not long after the duke entered the hall.

As soon as he was there, the Green Knight spoke up, greeting him with all due respect, and said, "Noble duke, it is true and certain that I have been vanquished within the time agreed upon between us, for which reason I have no occasion or right to ask anything of your daughter. Rather from this time forward I relinquish all claim to her, desiring instead to leave your land in peace as I promised and as fulfills my pledge. I beg you to grant me the sacrament of baptism so that I may be more pleasing to almighty God."

"Sir knight," said the duke, "you have spoken well, and I desire nothing more than to grant your request and have you baptized right away." The duke ordered a priest to be brought to baptize the Green Knight. When it came to pass that he was at the font to receive his baptism, Valentin, who was present, announced to

tous disant haultement, "Seigneurs, qui cy estes assembléz, s'il plaist au vaillant duc de moy donner ung don, je luy requiers et prie que cestuy chevalier soyt nommé Pepin, car c'est le propre nom du noble et vaillant roy de France, qui moult doulcement m'a nourry et qui dessus tous princes est le plus vaillant et preux, par quoy je desire que cestuy chevalier en porte le nom."

A la demande de Valentin se consenterent et acorderent tous ceulx qui en la presence estoient. Et a sa requeste fust le Verd Chevalier appellé Pepin, lequel nom il porta de celle heure jusques a la fin de ses jours. Et apres qu'il fust baptisé le duc d'Acquitaine fist[1] venir Valentin et Orson pour espouser sa fille la belle dame Fezonne. Mais Valentin luy dist par maniere d'escusacion comment ilz avoient luy et Orson vouéz et promis d'aler en Jerusalem premierement et devant que nulle aultre chose feissent apres que le Verd Chevalier auroient conquis. Et soubz l'ombre de ceste excusacion le duc leur donna congé et licence par ainsi que Orson jura et promist de retourner en Acquitaine apres que son voyage auroit acomply et parfait, et au plustost que retourné seroit, sa fille Fezonne il la prendroit en mariage pour espouse. Et quant le vaillant et puissant duc Savary d'Acquitaine entendit le [46verso]veu et la promesse[2] que Valentin et Orson disoient avoir fait d'aler en Iherusalem, moult voulentiers leur ottroya.

Et le Verd Chevalier a celle heure print congé du duc d'Acquitaine pour aler en France vers le roy Pepin se rendre et sa foy acquiter. Et Valentin devant son departir luy demanda l'aneau qu'i luy avoit promis, lequel il devoit porter a sa seur Esclarmonde. Le Verd Chevalier luy bailla en luy disant, "Franc chevalier, gardez bien cestuy aneau, car la pierre qui dedens est enchassee est de telle vertu que celuy qui dessus luy la porte ne peult estre noyé ne par faulx jugement condempné."

Valentin print l'aneau et le mist en son doy. Atant prindrent congé, luy et Orson, pour faire leur voyage, et le Verd Chevalier print congé pour aler en France. Ainsi se departirent les trois chevaliers de la cite d'Acquitaine et prindrent leur chemin chascun vers sa partie.

Orson et Valentin monterent sur la mer et a force de voille tantost firent moult grant chemin, car la mer leur fust doulce et le vent aggreable. Ilz demanderent aux mariniers le chemin pour tirer vers le chasteau de Ferragu et ilz leur enseignerent, car bien le cognoissoient pour tant que celuy passaige estoit de coustume et d'usance que tous marchans payoient salaire et tribu. Or sont Valentin et Orson dessus la mer qui desirent moult fort a trouver le chasteau de Ferragu.

Et le Verd Chevalier chevaulche par les champs qui devers le pays de France a sa voye adressee, mais premier qu'il arrivast devant le roy Pepin, Blandimain l'escuier de Bellissant la royne, duquel j'ay devant fait mencion, qui par Valentin en habit de pelerin fust encontré, il salua le roy Pepin en grant honneur et reverence. Et quant le roy le veit en tel habit et la barbe ainsi flourie, il luy demanda s'il venoit du Saint Sepulchre ou de quel aultre voyage il estoit pelerin.

---

[1] Text has *fst*.
[2] Text has *peomesse*.

the assembly, "My lords, all you assembled here, if the duke would be pleased to grant me a boon, I request and pray him that this knight be named Pepin, for it is the very name of the noble and valiant king of France, who brought me up most generously, and who above all princes is the bravest and most worthy, for which reason I would like this knight to bear his name."

Everyone there agreed and consented to Valentin's request. Accordingly the Green Knight was named Pepin, which name he bore from that time forth until the end of his days. After his baptism the duke called for Valentin and Orson so that the latter could marry his daughter, the fair lady Fezonne. But Valentin excused them by explaining that he and Orson had taken a vow to go to Jerusalem first before doing anything else once the Green Knight had been conquered. In view of this excuse, the duke granted them leave with the pledge and promise on Orson's part to return to Aquitaine once his voyage was completed to take his daughter Fezonne in marriage. Once the valiant and powerful Duke Savary d'Aquitaine understood the vow and promise that Valentin and Orson said they had made about going to Jerusalem, he willingly allowed them to leave.

At the same time the Green Knight took leave of the Duke of Aquitaine to go to France to fulfill his promise to give himself up to King Pepin. But before his departure Valentin asked him for the ring he had promised him, the one he was to take to his sister Esclarmonde. The Green Knight handed it over to him saying, "Noble knight, take good care of this ring, for the stone embedded in it has the power to keep its wearer from drowning or condemnation by false judgment."

Valentin took the ring and placed it on his finger. Then he and Orson took their leave to begin their journey, and the Green Knight for his part took his leave to go to France. Thus departed the three knights from the city of Aquitaine, each wending his way to his destination.

Orson and Valentin set sail, traveling swiftly and steadily, for the sea was gentle and the wind favorable. They asked the sailors the way to the castle of Ferragu, and the sailors told them, for they knew it well, custom demanding that all merchants passing that way pay tribute. So Valentin and Orson are on the seas, impatient to find Ferragu's castle.

In the meantime the Green Knight was riding across fields on his way to the country of France, but before he arrived before King Pepin, Blandimain, Bellissant the queen's squire, whom I mentioned before and whom Valentin had met in a pilgrim's guise, greeted King Pepin with great honor and respect. When the king saw him in such a garment and with a flowing beard, he asked him if he was coming from the Holy Sepulcher or some other pilgrimage.

"Franc roy," dist Blandimain, "pelerin ne suis je pas, mais pour mon entreprinse plus seurement parfaire me suis mis en habit de pelerin, et sachez que je suis messaiger d'une haulte et puissante dame qui par trahyson et faulceté de son païs a esté degettee et en exil piteusement mise. Helas, sire, celle dame dont je vous parle est vostre seur, c'est assavoir Bellissant, la franche dame, laquelle a tort et sans cause par Alexandre, l'empereur de Grece, a esté vituperablement et honteusement dechassee, et qui en povreté et misere par faulte de secours piteusement languist. Bien avez le cueur dur, quant pour sa delivrance vous ne vous voulez aultrement employer, car vous estes le plus puissant roy qui soit en crestienté. Et pour tant, sire, veuillez a ce besoing monstrer vostre puissance et vaillance contre le faulx et mauldit empereur qui sans nulle cause ne rayson a la noble et franche dame Bellissant vostre seur tel deshonneur a [47 recto]fait, ou aultrement on ne vous doyt pas tenir pour loyal frere."

Quant le roy Pepin oÿt parler de sa seur Bellissant, moult tendrement il se print de cueur a souspirer et moult fort la regretta, car bien avoit xx. ans passés que d'elle n'avoit eu nouvelle.

"Amy," dist le roy, "dites moy ou est ma seur, car j'ay grant desir de sçavoir de son fait et comment elle se porte."

"Sire," dist Blandimain, "j'en sçay bien la verité, mais pour riens ne le vous diroie, car je luy ay promis que le lieu ou elle est point ne le declareray. Mais se de son fait vous estes doubteux et vous pensés qu'elle soit coulpable du fait par quoy elle est dechassee, je vous amenrray devant vostre presence tel homme qui pour sa querelle contre tous veult combatre et s'il est vaincu il veult estre pendu honteusement, et la dame s'oblige de souffrir mort piteuse et douloureuse."

"Helas!" ce dist le roy, "de la loyauté de ma seur je suis tout informé, ne je ne quiers jamais en avoir aultre experience que celle du faulx trahystre archevesque qui par le bon marchant a esté vaincu, et que par devant tous sa trahyson a confessee magnifestement. Je sçay bien que ma seur a tort est en exil. Je l'ay long temps fait serchier et querir, mais en nulle maniere d'elle je n'ay peu avoir cognossance. Et qui plus est au cueur me porte desplaisance, c'est que ma seur, que tant chierement j'aymoye, au temps de sa douloureuse fortune qu'elle fut dechassee par l'empereur de Grece a qui je l'avoye donnee, elle estoit grosse et enssainte d'enfant. Lors or ne sçay je quel enfant elle a peu enfanter ne en quelle maniere d'iceluy danger elle peult estre eschappee, car je sçay et cognoys que elle n'a pas eu a son besoing telle ayde ne confort comme il luy apartenoit."

"Sire," dist Blandimain, "pour parler de ceste matiere sachez que ma dame vostre seur en la forest d'Orleans sentit le mal d'enfant. Et quant le mal luy fust prins, elle m'envoya en ung villaige qui pres de nous estoit pour luy querir femme qui secours et ayde luy peust faire. Lors je feis la plus grande diligence que possible me fust de faire, mais oncques je ne sçeulx si tost retourner que la noble et franche dame avoit enfanté deux moult beaulx enfans, desquelz une ourse sauvaige furieusement et oultrageusement et ainsi que une beste enragee ung des ses enfans luy osta et emporta parmy le bois en telle maniere que la royne Bellissant,

"Noble king," answered Blandimain, "I am not a pilgrim — to assure the success of my undertaking I have traveled in a pilgrim's habit, but I am a messenger from the exalted and puissant lady who, through perfidy and treason, was cast out of her country and sent into piteous exile. Alas, sire, this lady of whom I speak is none other than your sister Bellissant, the noble lady, whom Alexander, the emperor of Greece, shamefully, ignominiously, wrongly, and without just cause banished, and who, for lack of succor, languishes forlornly in poverty and misery. You must have a hard heart not to make an effort to deliver her, for you are the most powerful monarch in Christendom. For that reason, sire, I beg you to demonstrate your authority and courage against the faithless and cursed emperor who, without any cause or reason, brought such dishonor on the noble and estimable lady Bellissant your sister, for otherwise no one should consider you a loyal brother."

When the king heard his sister Bellissant spoken of, he began sighing heartfelt sighs, and felt how much he missed her, for a good twenty years had passed since he had had news of her.

"Friend," said the king, "tell me where my sister is, for I have great desire to know what happened to her and how she is."

"Sire," said Blandimain, "I know the truth, but I wouldn't tell you anything, for I promised her to keep her whereabouts secret. But if you have doubts about her and believe her guilty of the charges that led to her banishment, I will bring before you a man who is willing to fight to defend her honor, and if he were vanquished, he would accept shameful hanging, and the lady is prepared to suffer piteous and painful death."

"Alas!" said the king, "I am well informed of the loyalty of my sister, nor do I require any proof other than that of the false traitor of an archbishop who was vanquished by the good merchant, and who confessed his treason openly in front of everyone. I know that my sister is in unjustified exile. I have searched for her a long time, but I could never get any word of her whereabouts. And what weighs even more heavily upon my heart is the fact that my sister, whom I loved so dearly, was pregnant at the time of her misfortune when she was banished by the emperor of Greece to whom I had given her. At present I know not what child she might have given birth to or how she might have survived her labor, for I am sure that she did not have such help and comfort as she needed and deserved."

"Sire," said Blandimain, "on this matter I can tell you that my lady your sister began her labor in the forest of Orleans. As the labor began, she sent me to a nearby village to seek a woman to help her. I went with the greatest possible speed, but I could not return before the noble lady had given birth to two beautiful children, one of which was carried violently away by a savage she-bear into the woods in such a manner that the queen Bellissant, who endeavored as much

qui de son corps et de sa puissance le cuida sauver et secourir mais elle ne sçeult qu'i devint. Et que tant par son enfant avoit souffert de peine et de douleur que je la trouvay parmy le bois dessus l'erbe couchee, piteusement aornee que mieulx sembloit morte que vive. Je la levay entre mes bras; de toute ma puissance je la resconfortay et quant elle fut revenue et que elle peust parler, en souspirant moult piteusement elle me compta la maniere comment elle avoit perdu [47verso]son enfant par la beste sauvaige, et comment elle avoit laissé l'autre dessoubz ung arbre. Et quant j'entendy ces paroles je le menay devers l'arbre ou je l'avoye laissé et la endroit fust sa douleur doublee et sa douloureuse destresse acrue, car elle ne trouva point l'enfant qu'elle y avoit laissee. Et ainsi furent les deux enfans de vostre bonne seur perdus en la forest, et aultres nouvelles je n'en sçay. Et se vous doubtez de ceste chose pour plus grant cognoissance en avoir, sachez, sire, que je suis Blandimain, et suis celuy qui tout seul fus baillé pour accompaigner ma dame Bellissant quant par l'empereur elle fut en exil envoyee."

"Helas, Blandimain," dist le roy, "vostre parler me donne tristesse et desplaisance quant de ma seur ne puis sçavoir le lieu ou elle demeure ne de ses deux enfans avoir certaine cognoissance. Mais puis que aultre chose je n'en puis sçavoir, dites moy s'il y a long temps que ma seur de ces deux enfans enmy la forest elle acoucha."

"Sire," dist Blandimain, "ce fust a celuy propre jour que vous me trouvastes dedens la forest d'Orleans et que je vous dy les piteuses nouvelles de l'exil et vituperable blasme de ma souveraine dame vostre seur Bellissant."

Quant le roy Pepin entendit les paroles de Blandimain, il fut moult pensif en son courage. Et ainsi qu'il estoit en pensee grande il luy ala souvenir de Valentin lequel a celuy jour il avoit trouvé dedens le bois, et de Orson qui par luy en celuy bois avoit esté conquis. Pour ceste chose fut en melencolye moult grande, et quant il eust consideré tout il cogneust par les ditz de Blandimain qu'ilz estoient filz de sa seur Bellissant. Il manda la royne Berthe sa femme et plusieurs aultres seigneurs et dames de sa court pour leur dire et declairer les nouvelles que Blandimain luy avoit aporté.

"Helas!" dist il, "seigneurs, j'ay tenu et nourry longuement en ma mayson ainsy que povres enfans et impourveux ceulx qui sont filz de roy et de royne et mes propres nepveux. C'est Valentin, lequel en la forest d'Orleans je trouvay que par ma seur Bellissant ou temps de sa fortune et aversité en celuy boys fust enfanté. Et si vous fay assavoir que Orson le sauvaige qui par luy a esté conquis, ainsi comme je puis entendre est son droit frere naturel."

De telles nouvelles oÿr fust la royne Berthe moult joyeuse, et aussi furent tous les seigneurs, barons et chevaliers de la court. La furent presens les deux ennemis mortelz de Valentin; c'estoient Hauffroy et Henry, qui de semblance monstroient chiere moult joyeuse, mais au cueur et en courage estoient tristes et

as she could in her state to rescue and save the child, couldn't find out what happened to it. She suffered such grief and pain for her child that I found her in a faint lying on the grass deep in the woods, in such a pitiful state that she seemed more dead than alive. I raised her in my arms; I did everything in my power to help her, and as soon as she came to and was able to speak, she recounted to me with pitiful sighs how she had lost her child to the wild beast, and how she had left the other under a tree. When I heard this, I brought her back to the tree where I had originally left her, and there was her pain doubled and her unbearable distress increased, for she did not find the child she had left there. That was how your good sister's two sons were lost in the forest, and that is all I know about it. If you doubt what I have told you, know, sire, that I am Blandimain, the sole person allowed to accompany my lady Bellissant when the emperor sent her into exile."

"Alas, Blandimain," said the king, "your story saddens and afflicts me, since I cannot know where my sister is nor know for sure what happened to her two children. But since I cannot find out anything more about that, tell me how long ago it is that my sister gave birth to those two boys in the forest."

"Sire," said Blandimain, "it was the very day that you saw me in the forest of Orleans, when I told you the sad news of her exile and the shameful blame laid on my sovereign lady your sister Bellissant."

When King Pepin heard what Blandimain had to say, he became very pensive. And as he was thinking, he remembered having found Valentin in the woods that day, and that Orson had been conquered by him later in those very same woods. This put him into a deep reverie, and the more he thought about it, the more likely it seemed, according to Blandimain's story, that these were the sons of his sister Bellissant. He sent for Queen Bertha his wife and many other lords and ladies of his court to impart to them the information Blandimain had brought him.

"Alas!" said he, "my lords, for a long time I raised and brought up in my own household as poor and penniless children those who turn out to be the sons of a king and queen and my very own nephews. I am speaking of Valentin, whom I found in the forest of Orleans, and whom my sister Bellissant gave birth to in those woods at the time of her adversity. Moreover, I believe that Orson the wild man, whom Valentin conquered, is his own natural brother."[1]

Queen Bertha was overjoyed to hear such news, as were likewise all the lords, barons, and knights of the court. But Valentin's two mortal enemies were also there — Hauffroy and Henry — who pretended to be as joyous as the others, but who were black with rage in their hearts, for more than anything else they

---

[1] Pepin speaks of having brought up "poor and penniless children," though, in fact, only Valentin was raised at court from babyhood. However, Orson's civilizing and conversion to chivalrous knight took place there, which is probably that to which Pepin is referring.

dolens, car sur toutes choses desiroient la mort de Valentin pour et afin que de Charlot leur petit frere ilz peussent faire a leur apetit et voulenté desordonnee, auquel ilz furent moult contraires comme vous orés apres.

Or fust Blandimain moult fort esmerveillé [48recto]quant il oÿt parler le roy Pepin du fait des deux enfans. Il luy demanda, "Sire, sçavez vous en quelle terre les deux enfans de quoy vous faictes mencion pourroyent estre trouvéz?"

"Amy," dist le roy, "j'en ay nourry ung en ma maison moult longuement en telle maniere que il est devenu grant, hardy, et puissant, et si a conquis l'autre qui a la forest d'Orleans comme beste sauvaige vivoit et faisoit au pays d'environ moult grant dommaige. Et quant il l'eust conquis, apres qu'ilz eurent long temps esté ensemble en ma court, de moy se sont departis et ont prins congé pour aler en Acquitaine contre ung vaillant et hardy champion qui le Verd Chevalier se fait appeller. Et depuis leur departement oncques nouvelles je n'en ay peu avoir."

"Sire," dist Blandimain, "selon que vous me dictes, je vous dy bien que au plus pres d'Acquitaine j'ay trouvé les deux enfans que vous me devisez, dont je suis moult desplaisant que il ne pleust a Dieu que je les peusse cognoistre. Car de toutes mes douleurs je eusse eu alors allegement."

De ceste matiere deviserent moult longuement. Et apres ces choses le roy commanda que Blandimain fust festoié et servy moult honnourablement en toutes choses que mestier luy feroyent. Lors fust prins Blandimain par les officiers du palais et fut mené entre les barons et chevaliers de la court qui en grant honneur et reverence le receurent et festoyerent.

Or avint que celuy jour le Verd Chevalier dont j'ay fait mencion arriva a la court du roy Pepin qui a Paris estoit. Et tantost qui fust descendu, il ala en la sale royalle en laquelle le roy Pepin avec ses barons estoit moult notablement acompaigné. Il salua le roy et moult grant reverence luy fist. Et quant le roy le vit vestu des armes verdes moult fust esmerveillé et luy demanda devant tous les chevaliers, "Dictes moy qui vous estes et quelle chose devers nous vous amaine, et pourquoy vous apportez telles verdes armes."

"Noble et honnouré roy," dist le chevalier, "sachez que de Sarrazinesme je suis extrait et natif, et de pere sarrasin suis engendré et de mere payenne ay esté enfanté. Si est vray que pour avoir a femme et a espouse la fille du duc d'Acquitaine qui est appellee Fezonne la belle, j'ay par ung an entier tenu le pays et la terre du duc tant en ma subjecion. Et ay fait que en la fin je luy ay donné six moys de triesves par tel convenant que s'il me bailloit chevalier qui par armes me peust conquerir en celuy temps durant je feray partir et vuider tout mon ost hors de son pays et de sa terre; et au cas que vaincu je ne seroye, il estoit tenu de moy donner sa fille, la belle Fezonne, pour femme et espouse. Or ay je esté devant la cité d'Acquitaine moult longuement attendant que je fusse combatu. Si sont venus a moy plusieurs vaillans chevaliers de divers païs et [48verso]diverses regions, lesquelz j'ay tous mis a mort et pendu a ung arbre, fors seulement deux vaillans chevaliers do[n]t l'ung a nom Valentin et l'autre Orson. Iceluy Valentin pour ung jour entier a moy print la bataille et tant fismes d'armes ensemble que la nuyt nous contraignit a departir, ainsi

desired Valentin's death so that they could carry out their evil designs on their little brother Charlot, whom they detested, as you will hear later on.

At first Blandimain was flabbergasted to hear Pepin speak thus of the two children. He asked him, "Sire, do you know in what country the two lads you speak of may be found?"

"My friend," said the king, "for a very long time I brought up one of them in my household until he became tall, strong, and bold, and afterwards he conquered the other who was living as a wild beast in the forest of Orleans, causing great damage to the country all around. Once Valentin had subdued him, and after they had both spent a long time here at my court, they took leave and departed for Aquitaine, there to fight a valiant and hardy champion called the Green Knight. Since their departure I have had no word from them."

"Sire," said Blandimain, "according to what you tell me, I believe I can tell you that I saw the two young men you describe near Aquitaine, which now upsets me, for it did not please God that I be able to recognize them. If only I could have, my sorrows would have been greatly abated."

They spoke of these matters for some time. Then the king commanded that Blandimain be feted and served most honorably with everything he needed. So the palace officials took Blandimain and led him to a seat among the barons and the knights of the court, who received him and feted him with great honor and respect.

Now it happened that very day that the Green Knight, whom I mentioned earlier, arrived at King Pepin's court in Paris. As soon as he got off his horse, he went to the royal hall where King Pepin sat nobly accompanied by his barons. He greeted the king and made him a deep bow. When the king noticed him dressed in green armor, he marveled greatly and asked him in front of all the knights, "Tell me who you are and what brings you to us, and why you are wearing green armor."

"Noble, honorable king," said the knight, "I am a native of Saracen lands, child of a Saracen father and pagan mother. The truth is that for an entire year I held in subjection the land of the Duke of Aquitaine in order to marry the duke's daughter, Fezonne the fair. I settled with him that I would give him six months' truce with the agreement that if he could find a champion who could conquer me, I would immediately withdraw my army from his land; but in the case whereby I would not be defeated, he was bound to give me his daughter, the fair Fezonne, as wife. I remained a long time just outside the city of Aquitaine, waiting to be fought. Many valiant knights from different countries and different regions came to me, but I put them all to death and hanged them on a tree, except for two stalwart knights, Valentin and Orson. Valentin battled me for an entire day, and we fought so long that nightfall forced us to part, weary and spent.

comme traveilléz et lassés. Et quant vint le lendemain au matin que le champ deust estre recommencé par nous deux, son compaignon Orson de son harnoys vestu et ses armes portoit, entra ou champ pour moy combatre et cuidoye bien que ce fust Valentin. Et quant celuy Orson fut dedens le champ entré, moult fierement il me fist signe de deffiance, lors je sailly hors contre luy, mais peu valut ma force, car je ne demouray pas longuement que par luy je fus conquis et vaincu. Sy m'eust osté la vie se n'eust esté Valentin qui a nous acourust, lequel me fist promettre de baptesme recepvoir et croyre en Jesucrist, et si me fist jurer que me viendroie rendre vers vous comme vaincu, et du tout submettant ma vie a vostre commandement et ordonnance. Et pour tant en acquitant ma foy et mon serment de par le chevalier Valentin a vous je me viens rendre comme a celuy qui de moy pouez faire vostre voulenté et qui apres Dieu apartient de ma mort aprocher ou prolonguer ma vie. Non pourtant, sire tresredoubté, je me rens devant vostre majesté royalle en demandant et esperant vostre misericorde en l'onneur d'iceluy Dieu de qui j'ay prins la creance. Car sachez que je suis crestien et croy en Jesucrist et d'ores en avant veul croyre de ferme et loyalle foy. Et quant je fus sur les sains fons baptisé, en l'onneur de vostre haulte et puissante renommee je fus appellé Pepin et Pepin suis nommé."

Quant le roy eust oÿ et entendu les parolles du Verd Chevalier il luy respondu doulcement devant tous les barons et chevaliers, "Bien soyez venu devers nous, car de vostre venue sommes joyeulx plus que de nulle aultre chose qui de long temps nous avint. Faictez chiere joyeuse et demenez liesse que pour l'amour de celuy qui devers nous vous envoye, je vous donne asseurance. Et si vous dy devant tous que devant bref de temps en mon royaulme je vous donneray grandes terres et possessions quant a mon service vous plaira a demener. Mais dites moy ou sont les chevaliers lesquelz vous ont conquis?"

"Sire," dist le Verd Chevalier, "ilz sont en Acquitaine avec le duc Savary et par dessus tous aultres les ayme et tient chiers."

Par les nouvelles de Blandimain et par le Verd Chevalier eut le roy Pepin nouvelles de sa seur et de ses deux nepveux lesquelz elle enfanta dedens la forest. Sy a promis a Dieu qu'il s'en yra en Grece pour dire et compter a l'empereur ces nouvelles et pour faire sa seur querir et serchier en telle maniere que trouvee elle puist estre, car sur toutes creatures il desiroit tresardamment a veoir sa seur Bellissant. Et quant il luy sou[49recto]venoit[1] du grant tort et injure qui luy avoit esté faicte des yeulx tendrement plouroit et au cueur en estoit moult fort triste et dolent.

---

[1] *g i* at bottom right corner of page.

Then, in the morning, when we were to pick up again where we had left off, his companion Orson, dressed in his armor and carrying his arms, entered the field to fight me, while I thought all the time it was Valentin. Once Orson was in the field, he made a fierce gesture of defiance, and I sallied forth against him, but my strength was for nought, for not long after was I conquered and vanquished by him. He would have taken my life had Valentin not come forward, making me promise to receive baptism and believe in Jesus Christ, making me swear to come give myself up to you in my defeat, submitting my life to your command. Thus, to acquit my faith and my oath to the knight Valentin, I come to render myself up to you, who may do with me as you like, and who, after God, has the power of life and death over me. Nevertheless, most respected sire, I give myself up to your royal majesty, asking and hoping for your mercy in honor of that God in whom I have placed my faith. For now I am a Christian and believe in Jesus Christ, and from now on I will believe with a firm and loyal faith. Moreover, when I was baptized in the holy fountain, in honor of your exalted and puissant glory, I was named Pepin, and Pepin am I called."

When the king had heard the Green Knight's story, he answered him gently in front of all his barons and lords, "We welcome you, for your arrival has given us more happiness than anything else that has occurred for a long while. Be happy and of good cheer, for I grant you your life for the sake of the one who sent you to us. Moreover, I declare in front of all assembled that once you choose to enter my service, I will speedily give you many lands and possessions from my kingdom. But tell me, where are the knights who vanquished you?"

"Sire," said the Green Knight, "they are in Aquitaine with Duke Savary who loves them above all others and holds them dear."

Through Blandimain and the Green Knight, King Pepin had news of his sister and of his two nephews to whom she had given birth in the forest. He promised God that he would go to Greece to recount all this news to the emperor and to go search for his sister until she might be found, for, more than any other creature, he desired most ardently to see his sister Bellissant. When he remembered the great wrong and injury done to her, he wept with much emotion, feeling great sadness in his heart.

[CHAPITRE 22]

Comment le roy Pepin partit de France pour aler vers l'empereur de Grece porter nouvelles de sa seur Bellissant; et comment devant son retour fist guerre au souldan qui avoit assiegé Constantinoble.
xxii. cha[pitre]¹

En celuy temps que le roy Pepin eut nouvelles de sa seur Bellissant, sans grant sejour et sans dilacion mist son ost sur les champs, et en grant puissance et excercite se partit de Paris pour aler en Constantinoble vers l'empereur de Grece porter nouvelles de sa femme ainsi que devant vous ay fait mencion. Il fist grant diligence tellement que en bref temps arriva en la cité de Romme. La fut receu de pape a grant honneur et reverence, car de la foy crestienne sur tous les aultres princes estoit vray deffenseur auxiliateur² propice. Au palays apostolique disna iceluy jour avec le pape qui luy compta nouvelles du souldan sarrasin qui la cité de Constantinoble avoit³ assiegé.

Et ainsi que de ceste matiere ensemble devisoient, arriva ung chevalier de Grece, lequel apres qu'il eust salué le pape, le roy et tous les assistens en moult grant reverence, il luy a dit, "Saint pape, qui estes Dieu en terre, sachez que⁴ Sarrasins a grant force et puissance d'armes ont assiegé et mys en subjection la terre et le pays de Constantinoble. Si vous mande l'empereur de Grece par moy que pour la foy crestienne garder et conserver, ainsi que par rayson faire, le devez vous luy envoyez par dela secours et confort, ou aultrement vous ferez cause de delaisser le pays perdre et la foy de Jhesucrist diminuer, car sans vostre aide et secours en ce grant besoing remedier n'y peut."

Quant le pape oÿt ces nouvelles il fut moult triste et desplaisant et demoura moult pensif, mais le roy Pepin qui la estoit present le resconforta grandement en luy disant, "Sainct pere, prenez en vous courage et ferme resconfort, car se bailler me voulez de vostre gent rommaine jusques a nombre suffisant, je les conduiray et menray devers Constantinoble avec mon armee, et tant feray a la grace de Dieu pour la foy crestienne que le souldan et son armee je metteray a vituperable confusion. Car nulle aultre chose je [49verso]n'ay si grant desir que pour la foy de Dieu soustenir contre payens combatre."

---

¹ Woodcut of king riding with attendants (repeat of woodcut on 18r).
² I have not found *auxiliateur* in any dictionaries of Old or Middle French. According to the Petit Robert, *auxiliaire* is first attested to in 1512. *Auxiliateur* may be a rare form derived from Latin that did not take hold in the language.
³ Text has *ovoit*.
⁴ Text has *que* twice.

CHAPTER 22

How King Pepin left France to bring news to the
emperor of Greece concerning his sister Bellissant; and
how before his return he made war against the sultan
who had besieged Constantinople.

At about the same time that he had news of his sister Bellissant, King Pepin gathered his army in the field without lingering or delay, and, with a great force and a great company, set out from Paris to go to Constantinople to the emperor of Greece to bring him news of his wife, as I recounted to you earlier. He traveled so quickly that he soon arrived in the city of Rome. There the pope received him with great honor, for, more than all other princes, he was the true defender and favored supporter of the Christian faith. That day he dined in the papal palace with the pope who told him of the Saracen sultan who had besieged the city of Constantinople.

While they were speaking thus together, a knight arrived from Greece, who, after greeting the pope, the king, and all the company with great reverence, spoke thus to the pope: "Holy pope, who is God on earth, know that Saracens have besieged and imperiled the land and country of Constantinople with a great army and show of force. The emperor of Greece has sent me to ask you to send him help and reinforcements in order to keep and preserve the Christian faith, which is only reasonable. Otherwise the country will be lost and the religion of Jesus Christ will diminish, for without your help and succor there is no other remedy for this great need."

When the pope heard this news he was sad and upset and remained thoughtful, but King Pepin, who was present there, comforted him greatly by saying to him, "Holy father, take courage and be comforted, for if you will lend me sufficient numbers of your Roman people, I will conduct and lead them to Constantinople along with my army, and there, by the grace of God, I will accomplish so much for the Christian faith that I will put the sultan and his army in absolute disarray. For I desire nothing else so much as to fight against pagans in order to sustain the true faith of God."

Quant le pape oÿt ainsi parler le roy Pepin et qui cogneust son courage, moult le remercia de tout son cueur et luy a dit, "Franc roy trescrestien, de Dieu soyez tu beneis, car de tous aultres roys tu es le plus puissant en fait et en courage. Et puis que telle chose tu veulx entreprendre, du païs de Romme feray venir gens a si grant nombre pour vous acompaigner que seurement pourrez aler et arriver en Grece contre les infideles et ennemys de la foy."

Le pape en celuy temps de tout le pays de Romme si grant peuple assembla et fist crier la croisee; c'est assavoir que tout homme qui vouldroit aler en ceste bataille en l'onneur de la passion de Jesucrist porteroit une croix et du pape prendre la benediction et pardon de tous leurs pechéz. En la cité de Romme en peu de temps s'asembla grant multitude de peuple pour passer oultre la mer avec le roy Pepin, et le pape au departir leur donna sa benediction et absolution de tous leurs pechéz. Ainsi print congé le roy Pepin du pape et des cardinaulx en soy recommandant aux prieres de saincte esglise.

Et avec xxx. mil Rommains et tous ceulx de son ost monta dessus la mer, et tant luy fust le temps aggreable que dedens peu de jours vindrent arriver a Constantinoble. Et la veirent que le souldan Moradin l'avoit de toutes pars enclose et assiegee. Et yceluy souldan avoit avec luy amené vint roys lesquelz pour destruire crestienté avec deux cens mil. payens avoit la mer passee. Et tant estoit celluy souldan pour sa force craint et redoubté que l'empereur de Grece de plusieurs chevaliers crestiens acompaigné dedens Constantinoble avoit son retrait prins, et si bien garda la cité que du payen ne peult estre prinse.

Tousjours en son courage desiroit et regrettoit sa femme Bellissant, et luy souvenoit du vitupere auquel il l'avoit livree a tort et sans rayson. A toutes pleurs et lamentations piteusement sa faulte cognoissoit et pensoit qu'elle fust du monde trespassee, car bien y avoit vint ans qu'il n'en avoit oÿ nouvelles. Mais tantost en ora parler par le roy Pepin qui tant naige sur mer que a deux lieues de Constantinoble est descendu et a fait tendre ses tentes et pavillons parmy les champs, et a fait ses gens mettre par moult belle ordonnance.

Adonc furent les coureux et chevaulcheurs de l'ost de Moradin le souldan moult espouventéz, qui en grant diligence vers son pavillon retournerent. Et luy ont dist ainsi que gens effroyéz et plains de paour, "Sire souldan, soyez certain que au jour d'uy sur ceste terre sont arrivéz Rommains a plus de deux cens mil combatans pour nous de ce pays chasser et expeller a honte et confusion. Si avisez sur ce fait, car la chose est doubteuse et si a peril tresgrant."

"Taisez vous," dist le souldan, "et de ceulx n'ayez doubte, car il n'est [50recto] pas[1] possible que du pays de Romme soient tant de gens descendus. Assez sommes puissans pour les attendre tous en bataille rengee, car j'ay ancores esperance que dedens bref temps je metteray en ma subjection et obeïssance tout le pays de Rommenie et celuy de France."

---

[1] *g ii* at bottom right corner of 50r.

When the pope heard King Pepin speak thus and understood what he wanted to do, he thanked him with all his heart and said, "Noble Christian king, may God bless you, for of all the kings you are the most powerful in heart and deed. And since you are willing to undertake this thing, I will get people to come from the country around Rome in such great numbers to accompany you that you will surely be able to go to Greece to confront the infidel enemies of our faith."

Right away the pope called together a large assembly of people from the entire country around Rome and declared a crusade; that is to say that every man willing to go to this battle for the honor of the passion of Jesus Christ would wear the cross, would be blessed by the pope, and would receive pardon for all his sins. A great multitude of people assembled in no time in the city of Rome to cross the sea with King Pepin, and at their departure the pope gave them his benediction and absolution of all their sins. Thus did King Pepin take his leave from the pope and the cardinals, commending himself to the prayers of holy church.

With the thirty thousand Romans in addition to his own army, King Pepin boarded his ships and set sail into such favorable weather that very soon they arrived in Constantinople. Immediately they saw how Sultan Moradin had surrounded and besieged it from all sides. Moreover, this sultan had brought with him twenty kings who had come over the seas with two hundred thousand pagans fully intent on destroying Christendom. This sultan was so dreaded and feared for his power that the emperor of Greece, accompanied by many Christian knights, had retreated into Constantinople, there guarding the city so well that it could not be taken by the pagan.

In his heart the emperor still desired and regretted his wife Bellissant, remembering to what blame he had delivered her, unjustly and unreasonably. Full of tears and piteous lamentations, he recognized his fault, thinking that she must have already died and left this world, for he had had no word of her for a good twenty years. But soon he will hear her spoken of by King Pepin, who made such speed on the sea that he has landed just two leagues from Constantinople, and has pitched his tents and pavilions in the fields, and has neatly arranged all his forces.

Alarmed at this sight, the couriers and scouts of Moradin the sultan's army hurried back to his pavilion. Worried and full of fear, they said to him, "My lord sultan, it is certain that the Romans have arrived here today with more than two hundred thousand soldiers to chase us out of this land and expel us with shame and confusion. Consider this matter carefully, for the situation is dangerous and presents a real peril."

"Quiet yourselves," said the sultan, "and have no fear of them, for it is not possible that so many men would have come from Rome. We are powerful enough to wait for them in our battle ranks, for I still hope soon to subject all the land of Rome and France to my control."

Il commanda par ses heraulx que tout son ost fust assemblé en telle maniere que a toutes heures fussent pres de recepvoir bataille. A celuy commandement furent paiens et Sarrasins obeïssans et de toutes pars s'assemblerent et arresterent en ung champ grant et large pour crestiens attendre. Et quant vint le lendemain au matin que le jour fust cler et luysant, le roy Pepin et toute son armee furent pres et en point de payens et Sarrasins assaillir. Adonc manda secretement le roy Pepin par une lettre close en la cité a l'empereur de Grece comme il estoit venu pour le secourir et qu'i a toute diligence par la cité ses gens d'armes face mettre en point et qu'i saillent sur les champs contre les payens et Sarrasins, car a ce jour de François et de Rommains ilz seroient secourus.

L'empereur fut moult fort joyeulx de la venue du noble roy Pepin; et selon le mandement de la lettre fist son ost mettre en point et ses gens d'armes armer. Puis sont saillis hors de la cité de Constantinoble pour aler contre payens et Sarrasins qui bataille attendoyent. Et tantost qu'i furent sur les champs ilz apperceurent les estandars, bannieres et enseignes et l'ost du roy Pepin qui celle part venoit a sy grant nombre de clarons et de tromppettes, qui sy grant bruit demenoient que c'estoit merveilles.

Bien veirent les payens que contre eulx venoit grant puissance de gens. Le souldan appella deux Sarrasins les plus vaillans et hardis et leur commanda qu'ilz alassent secretement regarder et nombrer l'ost des crestiens qui les venoient assaillir. Et quant ilz auroient ce fait ilz retournassent devers luy dire les nouvelles. Les deux Sarrasins, qui avoient nom l'ung Clarien et l'autre Vaudu, monterent a cheval et chevaulcherent vers l'ost du roy Pepin, mais n'eurent pas chevaulché longuement que le Verd Chevalier les vit sur une petite montaigne, et tout aussitost qu'il les apperceust il cogneust bien qu'ilz estoyent Sarrasins. Lors frappa son cheval et tout seul ala devers eulx, sa lance sur sa cuisse comme preux chevalier. Et quant les deux Sarrasins le veirent aprocher, pour tant qu'il estoit seul, ilz eurent honte de fuyr pour luy et dirent, "Par Mahon, ce seroit grant honte se cestuy crestien de nous deux eschappoit." Lors ont couché leurs lances et contre le Verd Chevalier sont venus a puissance en telle maniere que le harnoys et le cheval de l'ung des Sarrasins cheut a terre, et si n'eust esté Vaudu qui secourust son compaignon, le Verd Chevalier l'eust occis. Mais s'est[1] pris au Verd Chevalier et ce pendant Clarien se leva qui navré fust durement et monta a cheval [50verso]et a prins la fuitte et a laissé Vaudu qui secouru l'avoit. Sans nul semblant Vaudu est demouré qui au Verd Chevalier fierement s'est combatu, mais peu luy a valu sa force, car le Verd Chevalier luy a donné tel coup qu'i luy a rompu la cuisse et luy a osté la vie, et demoura la dessus la terre mor, et son compaignon s'en retourna qui moult fort estoit navré.

Bien vit le roy Pepin la vaillance du Verd Chevalier et aussi firent les aultres barons de quoy moult le priserent. A celle heure fist le roy drescher ses estandars et ses bannieres, puis a fait sonner tromppettes et clarons. Puis a grant puissance

---

[1] Text has *c'est*.

He ordered his heralds to assemble his entire army so that they would be ready at any moment for battle. Pagans and Saracens obeyed this order, assembling and arranging themselves to await the Christians in a large, broad field. And the next morning, when daylight arose, clear and shining, King Pepin and all his hosts were prepared and ready to attack the pagans and Saracens. At the same time King Pepin managed to get a secret message into the city to the emperor of Greece, informing him that he had come to help him, and requesting that he quickly arm his men throughout the city and that they sally forth into the field against the pagans and Saracens, for that day they would be helped by the French and the Romans.

The emperor was overjoyed with the coming of the noble King Pepin; in accord with the message, he prepared his army and had his knights armed. Then they burst forth out of the city of Constantinople to fight the Saracens who were waiting for battle. As soon as they reached the field they saw the standards, banners, and ensigns of King Pepin's army which was riding toward them with great numbers of clarions and trumpets, creating such a noise that it was astounding.

The pagans could see that a tremendous host was coming to attack them. The sultan called his two most valiant and hardy Saracens and commanded them to slip away secretly to observe and assess the size of the Christian army that was coming to assail them. This done, they were to return to report back to him. The two Saracens, named Clarien and Vaudu, mounted their horses and rode toward King Pepin's army, but they had not ridden long before the Green Knight saw them on a little hill, and as soon as he caught sight of them he realized they were Saracens. Then he spurred his horse and rode alone to them, his lance resting on his thigh like a doughty knight. When the Saracens saw him approaching, they were ashamed to try to escape, seeing as he was alone, and they said, "By Mohammed, it would be too great a shame if this Christian were to escape the two of us." So they couched their lances and came riding hard against the Green Knight in such a way that the armor and horse of one of the Saracens fell to the ground, and if Vaudu had not helped his companion, the Green Knight would have killed him. Rather he attacked the Green Knight, during which time Clarien, badly wounded, got up, mounted his horse, and fled, leaving behind Vaudu who had helped him. Nevertheless Vaudu remained behind and fiercely fought the Green Knight, but his strength was for nought, for the Green Knight landed him such a blow that it broke his thigh and took away his life, leaving him dead on the ground while his companion returned to camp badly wounded.

King Pepin observed well the valiance of the Green Knight, as did his other barons, for which they valued him greatly. At that juncture the King had his standards and banners unfurled, then had his trumpets and clarions sounded. Then, with a great show of arms, bravery, and courage, they attacked the army

d'armes, de meurs hardis et de couraige vaillant ont assailly l'armee du souldan Moradin. Sy fust de toutes pars le cry si grant que nul ne le sçauroit estimer. Sarrasins et crestiens l'ung l'autre assaillirent; maintz trais ilz ont tiré et maintes lances brisees, et d'une partie et d'aultre plusieurs a mort livréz.

La fust Millon d'Angler lequel entre les aultres vit le roy d'Acquille qui faisoit grant destruction de crestiens et piteuse occision. Et aussitost qu'il l'avisa il ala devers luy et d'une hache d'armes jusques au menton la teste luy fendit, et a deux ou trois payens a celle heure la vie toulit. Et tant fist vaillantes armes que le souldan Moradin qui tantost l'aperceust si cria haultement a ses gens qu'ilz assaillissent Millon d'Angler qui de Sarrasins si grant murtre faisoit. Au commandement du souldan fust Millon d'Angler de toutes pars assailly par paiens et Sarrasins et en telle subjection mis que a son cheval ilz coupperent une cuisse parquoy il fust contraint de choir a terre, et en celuy endroit fust mort et occys se n'eust esté le Verd Chevalier qui malgré Sarrasins se boutta en la presse et tant en abatit et rua par terre qu'il aprocha de Millon d'Angler et luy fist telle ayde qu'i luy bailla cheval et le monta dessus. A celle heure firent le Verd Chevalier et Millon d'Angler sy grant vaillance d'armes contre les payens que trop forte chose seroit de leurs grandes proesses racompter, car nul qui devant eulx se trouvoit jamais vif ne s'en retournoit.

Grande fust la bataille et moult dura. Pepin et ses gens ce jour firent des payens moult grant destruction. Mais nonobstant leurs vaillances le champ e[u]ssent perdu se n'eust esté l'empereur de Grece qui a tout son ost vaillamment acompaigné de l'autre part les payens tant et si fierement assailly que grant nombre a celle heure moururent. Bien cogneust le roy que l'empereur faisoit d'armes moult grant devoir. Il reprint force et courage et ses gens ralia, puis entra en la bataille plus ardamment que devant, et ainsi furent payens de deux pars assaillis fort rigoureusement.

Et tantost que le roy Pepin si aprocha de l'empereur il luy a dit, "Franc prince, or vous monstrez vaillant, car au jour d'uy par moy de vostre femme Bellissant aurez nouvelles."

A ces paroles fust l'empereur joyeulx et doubla [51recto]son[1] couraige et augmenta et acreust sa force trop plus fort que devant. Il crye "Constantinoble!" a ses gens, promet grans dons et grandes richesses mais qu'ilz soient fort vaillans. A ces motz est entré dedens la bataille d'ung courage si merveilleux que trop estoit hardy celuy qui l'atendoit. Et Pepin d'aultre part et le Verd Chevalier qui entrerent parmy payens en frappant dessus eulx de coupz si merveilleux que par tout ou ilz passoient ilz faisoient le chemin large par la grant proesse du Verd Chevalier. Bien le cuida cognoistre le souldan Moradin que ses armes regarda, car il estoit de bon lignaige pour tant qu'il estoit frere de Ferragu. Mais pour tant qu'il sçavoit que le Verd Chevalier estoit payen, jamais il ne sceust doubte qu'i fust venu celle part.

---

[1] *g iii* at bottom right corner of 51r.

of Sultan Moradin. The cry that rose up was so loud that no one could estimate its force. Saracens and Christians assailed each other; many arrows were launched and many lances broken, and on both sides many souls were delivered unto death.

Millon d'Angler was there in the thick of it, and spied the king of Acquille wreaking great destruction and killing many Christians. As soon as he noticed him, he rode in his direction, using his battle-axe to cleave his head down to the chin, and taking the life of two or three other pagans at the same time. He fought so dauntlessly that Sultan Moradin, who soon noticed him, shouted out to his men to attack Millon d'Angler who was murdering so many Saracens. At the sultan's command, Millon d'Angler was assailed from every direction by pagans and Saracens, and was overcome to the point that they managed to cut his horse's thigh, which forced him to fall to the ground. And Millon d'Angler would have been dead on that very spot had not the Green Knight forced his way despite the Saracens into the press of battle, striking and knocking down so many that he made his way to Millon d'Angler. Moreover, he was actually able to bring him a horse and help him mount it. The Green Knight and Millon d'Angler fought so brilliantly against the pagans that it would be too much to recount all their daring deeds, for not one who opposed them remained alive or returned from the battle.

Great was the battle and long did it last. Pepin and his men wreaked great destruction among the pagans. But despite their great prowess, they would have lost the field had it not been for the emperor of Greece, who, accompanied by his entire valiant army, assailed the pagans from the other side so fiercely that great numbers of them were killed that day. The king saw that the emperor was acquitting himself brilliantly in battle. He got a second wind and rallied his men, then reentered the battle more ferociously than before, so that the pagans were assailed relentlessly from two sides.

As soon as King Pepin could get close to the emperor, he said to him, "Noble prince, now is the time to show yourself valiant, for today I will give you news of your wife Bellissant."

The emperor was overjoyed at these words, and felt an even greater surge of courage and force. "For Constantinople!" he cried to his men, promising them generous gifts and great riches if they only showed themselves worthy. With these words he entered the thick of the battle with such marvelous daring that anyone opposing him was foolhardy. For their part, Pepin and the Green Knight entered into a crowd of pagans, raining on them blows so amazing that wherever they passed, the prowess of the Green Knight widened the path for them. Sultan Moradin, looking at his arms, thought he recognized him, for, as the brother of Ferragu, he was of high lineage. But since the sultan knew the Green Knight to be pagan, he never thought to find him involved in this battle.

Or furent payens et Sarrasins de celle heure mis en telle necessité que jamais ilz n'esperoient avoir de mort respit, mais prindrent tous la fuite quant le roy d'Esclavonnye, qui du souldan faisoit l'arriere garde, acompaigné de cinquante mil, saillit sur les crestiens en menant sy grant cry qu'il sembloit que tout deust fondre. Et quant l'empereur et le roy Pepin aperceurent leur venue, ilz veirent et considererent bien que leurs gens estoient travailléz, et les gens du roy d'Esclavonnie estoient frez et nouveaulx. Pour quoy fut deliberé entre eulx de non les attendre pour celle heure presente. Et apres le conseil prins, firent sonner tromppettes et clarons pour eulx retraire dedens Constantinoble, l'empereur et le roy Pepin a tout leur armee.

Et quant le souldan vit que les crestiens estoient entréz et reculéz dedens Constantinoble, il fist assieger la cité moult fort et de pres et tant il eut grant nombre de payens parmy toute la terre que l'empereur et le roy Pepin de dedens Constantinoble tant et en telle maniere que saillir dehors ne leur estoit possible. En ce point demourerent long temps en grant subjection et doubte de leurs ennemys qui de pres les tenoient en desirant leur mort et pourchassant la destruction et l'exil de toute la foy crestienne. Cy vous laray a parler de ceste matiere et vous parleray de Valentin et de Orson qui pour l'amour de Esclarmonde sont entréz en la mer ainsi que pardevant vous avez ouÿ racompter.

[CHAPITRE 23]

Comment Valentin et Orson arriverent au chasteau ou estoit la belle Esclarmonde; et comment pour la teste d'arain ilz eurent cognoissance de leur generation. xxiii. chap[itre].

Apres que Valentin et Orson eurent long temps esté dessus la mer ilz aviserent une isle en laquelle avoit ung chasteau moult fort et puissant et de grant beaulté plain. Iceluy chasteau estoit tout couvert de leton moult cler et reluisant. Et pour la grant beaulté de luy bien se pensa Valentin que c'estoit [51verso]le chasteau[1] ou le Verd Chevalier l'avoit envoyé pour sa seur Esclarmonde trouver. Il ala tantost celle part et descendit a terre a ung des pors de l'isle. Et quant il fust descendu il enquist et demanda a qui estoit cestuy chasteau qui tant estoit beau et entre les aultres poly et bien aorné. Et il luy fust respondu que icelluy chasteau estoit en la garde de Esclarmonde, seur du geant Ferragu, et que par ung Sarrasin moult riche avoit esté edifié. Lequel Sarrasin, entre les aultres noblesses excellentes qui sont en icelui chasteau, fist faire et composer une chambre moult belle et sur

---

[1] Woodcut of two men in a rowboat on a river passing a town.

Now the pagans and Saracens were in such dire straits that they no longer hoped to escape death, and were beginning to flee, when the king of Slavonia, responsible for the sultan's rear guard, suddenly burst upon the Christians with fifty thousand men, letting out such a battle cry that it seemed they would be overcome. And when the emperor and King Pepin saw them coming, they observed and considered the exhausted state of their men compared to the king of Slavonia's men, who were fresh and newly arrived. So they decided not to face them for the present. Rather, after taking counsel, they had their trumpets and clarions sound the retreat into Constantinople for the armies of the emperor and King Pepin.

When the sultan saw that the Christians had withdrawn and entered Constantinople, he besieged the city so tightly, with such a great number of pagans in the area around the city, that for the emperor and King Pepin inside Constantinople it was impossible to get out any which way. For a long time they remained subjected to and in fear of their enemies, who held them in a difficult position, desiring their death and attempting the death and destruction of all of Christendom. But for now I will leave off speaking of this matter and will instead talk to you about Valentin and Orson who, for love of Esclarmonde, have embarked, as I recounted to you earlier.

CHAPTER 23

How Valentin and Orson arrived at the castle where dwelt the fair Esclarmonde; and how they learned the truth of their birth from the bronze head.

After a long time on the sea, Valentin and Orson caught sight of an island with a castle on it, solid, strong and full of beauty. The castle was covered with bright shiny brass. Because of its splendor, Valentin thought it must be the castle to which the Green Knight had sent him in order to find his sister Esclarmonde. He headed immediately in that direction and landed at one of the gates of the island. Once he had disembarked, he inquired to whom this castle belonged which was so beautiful, being more splendid and magnificent than any other. They told him that this castle was in the hands of Esclarmonde, sister of the giant Ferragu, and that it had been erected by a very rich Saracen. This Saracen had ordered, among the other magnificent features of the castle, the construction and decoration of

toutes riche. (De laquelle chambre les richesses vous seront cy apres declairees.¹) Et oultre plus fust dist a Valentin que dedens celle chambre il y avoit ung pilier moult riche et excellent sur lequel avoit une teste d'arain, laquelle jadis si avoit esté par une faee fort subtillement et par art d'ingromance faicte et composee. Laquelle teste estoit de telle nature qu'elle rendoyt responce de toutes les choses que on luy demandoit.

Et quant Valentin entendit la declaration du chasteau, en son cueur fust moult fort joyeulx, car bien se pensa que c'estoit le lieu ou le Verd Chevalier luy avoit dist qu'il trouverroit sa seur Esclarmonde qui sur toutes aultres de sens et de beaulté estoit des grans et des petis renommee. Plus oultre n'en demanda pour celle heure presente, mais se mist en chemin luy et Orson pour aler en iceluy chasteau, et tant ont cheminé que ilz sont venus devant la porte pour entrer dedens.

Mais ilz ont trouvé dix hommes fors et hardys que de jour et de nuyt avoient de coustume de garder la porte.² Et quant ilz veirent Valentin et Orson qui dedens vouloient entrer ilz leur ont dit, "Seigneurs, retirez vous arriere, car dedens cestuy chasteau n'y entre nul tant soit de hault lieu venu sans le congé et licence de une pucelle a qui la garde en appartient qui sur toutes celles du monde est de beaulté garnye."

"Amy," dist Valentin, "alez vers la pucelle et luy demandez se c'est bien son plaisir de moy donner entree en son chasteau."

Lors le portier monta au dongon du chasteau et entra en la chambre ou la belle Esclarmonde estoit, puis a mis le genoul a terre et luy a dist, "Ma tresredoubtee dame, devant la porte de vostre chasteau y a deux hommes qui dedens veullent [52recto]entrer.³ Et semblent gens de fier couraige et de grant orgueil plains, et semble en leur maniere qu'ilz soient gens de mauvais couraige et affaire et contraires a nostre loy. Or dictes vostre voulenté et respondez aux gardes de la porte qui devers vous m'envoyent s'il vous plaist de les laisser entrer dedens ou non."

"Amy," dist la pucelle, "descendez en bas et je yray aux creneaux pour veoir quelles gens ce sont. Fay bien garder les portes car je veul a eulx parler."

Le portier descendit en bas et dist a ses compaignons que la porte fust bien gardee tant que la dame fust aux⁴ fenestres pour la responce donner. Lors Esclarmonde qui fust saige et bien aprinse, sur ung drap de fin or batu mist les bras sur une fenestre, et puis a dist a Valentin, "Qui estes vous que par si grant hardiesse voulez entrer dedens mon chasteau sans licence demander?"

"Dame," dist Valentin qui hardiment parla, "je suis ung chevalier qui passe mon chemin. Sy vouldroye bien s'il vous plaisoit parler a la teste d'arain qui a chascun donne responce."

---

¹ Text has *decliarees*.
² Text has *porter*.
³ *g iiii* at bottom right corner of 52r.
⁴ Text has *au*.

a beautiful room, more richly done up than any of the others. (The splendor of this chamber will be recounted to you later.) Moreover, they told Valentin that in this chamber there was a fabulous pillar supporting a brass head that a fairy had made and fashioned most cleverly with magic arts. The nature of the head was such that it answered any questions put to it.

When Valentin heard this description of the castle, he was overjoyed, for he was sure this was the place where the Green Knight had told him he would find his sister Esclarmonde, reputed by everyone to surpass all other women in beauty and intelligence. He asked nothing else for the present, but set out with Orson for the castle and soon arrived before the main entrance.

However, there were ten stout and hardy men in charge of guarding the gate day and night. When they saw Valentin and Orson who wanted to enter, they told them, "Withdraw, my lords, for no one enters this castle, however exalted he may be, without the permission and authorization of a maiden who has the keep of this castle, who is graced with more beauty than any maiden in the world."

"My friend," said Valentin, "go to this maiden and ask her if it is her pleasure to grant me entrance to her castle."

So the porter went up to the castle keep, entered the chamber where the fair Esclarmonde was to be found, knelt, and said to her, "My most respected lady, there are two men before the gate of your castle who wish to enter. They seem to be men with proud hearts, full of great arrogance; moreover, it seems from their manner that they mean to do harm, for they are not of our faith. Now tell me your will and send an answer to the gatekeepers who send me to you, whether it please you to let them in or not."

"My friend," said the maiden, "you go on down while I go up to the battlements to see what kind of men they are. Guard the gates well, for I want to speak to them."

The porter descended and told his companions to guard the gate well while the lady spoke from the windows. Then Esclarmonde, who was wise and well brought up, leaned out a window, her arms on a cloth of fine beaten gold, and said to Valentin, "Who are you, that with such presumption you wish to enter my castle without asking leave?"

"My lady," said Valentin, who spoke boldly, "I am a knight errant. If it please you, I would very much like to speak to the brass head that answers all questions."

"Chevalier," ce dist la dame, "ainsi n'y pouez vous pas parler se de l'ung de mes frerez ne m'aportez certaines enseignes. C'est du roy Ferragu ou du Verd Chevalier qui de Tartarie a la seigneurie et dominacion. Et se de l'ung des deux vous m'aportez enseigne ou certification je vous lasseray entrer ou chasteau a vostre bon plaisir et voulenté. Et sachez que par nulle aultre maniere n'y pouez vous entrer fors seulement par ung point que je vous diray. C'est que vous prenez congé du chastelain de ceste place lequel je vous donneray par tel convenant que devant que vous y entrez vous jousterez a luy cinq ou six coupz de lance. Si vous avisez lequel vous aymés plus chier, d'aler querir certaines enseignes de l'ung de mes freres comme je vous ay dist."

"Dame," dist Valentin, "faictes armer vostre chastellain, car j'ayme plus chier contre vostre chastellain combatre et par champ de bataille gaigner et deservir d'entrer en vostre chasteau que je ne fay par prieres, requestes ou flateries."

Ainsi parla Valentin a la belle Esclarmonde qui tant fut de couraige vallant et hardy que nonobstant qu'il portast du Verd Chevalier enseignes certaines — l'aneau d'or — il ayma mieulx la jouste pour son corps esprouver que l'aneau monstrer lequel a la belle Esclarmonde devoit presenter.

Et quant la dame veit la voulenté et hardy couraige dequoy il estoit plain, de celle heure elle fust de son amour esprinse par ung ardant desir qui au cueur luy toucha. Elle monta en la chambre ou estoit la teste d'arain et luy demande qui est celuy chevalier qui a si grant couraige d'entrer en ce chasteau.

"Dame," ce dist la teste, "du chevalier ne de son estat par moy riens non sçaurez jusques a ce que devant moy vous l'aurez amené."

Pour celle responce fust la belle Esclarmonde pour l'amour de Valentin en grant soussy. [52verso]Et quant elle eust consideré par elle le maintieng et le beau parler, hardiesse et contenance du plaisant Valentin, elle fust embrasee de son amour plus que de nul aultre que jamais elle eust veu.

"Vray Dieu, qui peult estre cestuy chevalier? Car dessus tous vivans il est digne d'estre aymé. Moult est plaisant et droit, et de beaulté corporelle tous les aultres passans. Et se la teste d'arain faisoit a mon vouloir jamais aultre de luy je ne prendroye."

Quant la belle Esclarmonde eust toutes choses dictes et pensees en son couraige, elle manda le chastellain et luy a dist les nouvelles du chevalier qui veult dedens le chasteau entrer.

"Par mon Dieu," dist le chastellain, "de grant folie se demente, car il n'y enterra ja sans son corps contre le mien esprouver. Et s'il est sy hardy de prendre a moy bataille je luy monsterray clerement devant tous que pour vostre amour avoir est trop tart arrivé."

"Chastellain," dist la dame, "puis que d'entrer au chasteau congé ne luy donnez, alez vous tost armer, car je vous fay assavoir que de luy vous aurez la bataille, et si ay moult grant doubte que trop tart ne vous repentez. Si vous conseilleroye que de vostre corps ne veuillez mettre en danger."

"Sir knight," said the lady, "you cannot speak to it if you haven't brought proof that you are sent by one of my brothers, that is to say, either from King Ferragu or from the Green Knight who rules over Tartary. If you bring me a token or a letter from one of them, I will let you enter the castle just as you wish and desire. But you must realize that there is no other way you may enter except by the one that I will explain to you. You must gain leave from the chatelain of this place with whom I grant you battle, so that before you may enter you will joust five or six lances with him. Think about which way you prefer, that or to go request tokens from one of my brothers, as I explained to you."

"Lady," said Valentin, "arm your chatelain, for I prefer to fight your chatelain to win and deserve the right to enter your castle than to do it by prayers, requests, or flattery."

So spoke Valentin to the fair Esclarmonde, for he had such a valiant and bold heart that despite the fact that he carried proof of having been sent by the Green Knight — the gold ring — he preferred to prove his mettle by the joust than to show the ring he was supposed to present to the fair Esclarmonde.

When the lady saw with what will and bold courage he was endowed, she fell in love with him on the spot, touched to the heart by an ardent desire. She went up to her chamber where the brass head was kept and asked him who this knight was who had such a great desire to enter her castle.

"Lady," said the head, "you will know nothing of this knight nor of his estate until you will have brought him before me."

After this response the fair Esclarmonde was very troubled out of love for Valentin. When she thought about his conduct and handsome speech, the boldness and bearing of the pleasing Valentin, she was inflamed with love for him stronger than any ever felt by her for anyone she had ever seen.

"Dear God, who can this knight be? For he is worthy to be loved more than any other man alive. He is so pleasing and upright, excelling all others in beauty. If the brass head carried out my wish, never would I have anyone other than him."

After having said these things to herself, the fair Esclarmonde sent for her chatelain to tell him about the knight who wished to enter the castle.

"My God," said the chatelain, "he must be mad, for he will never enter without proving himself against me. And if he is so bold as to fight me, I will show him without a doubt before everyone that he has arrived too late to win your love."

"Chatelain," said the lady, "since you do not give him leave to enter the castle, go arm yourself, for I tell you that you will have quite a battle, and I am afraid that you may repent too late. I would counsel you not to put yourself in danger."

"Dame," dist le chastellain qui moult fort fust orgueilleux, "laissez en paix telles parolles, car jamais devant que il y entre son corps l'achettera."

A ces motz se departit le chastelain qui s'en ala armer et monter a cheval. Et quant il fust monté il saillit hors de la porte, une lance en son poing moult grosse et moult bien ferree. Et la dame estoit aux fenestres pour regarder la bataille des deux vaillans champions qui sont dedens le champ entréz pour assaillir l'ung l'autre. Et quant Valentin a veu le chastellain qui de si fier courage contre luy est venu, il a baissé sa lance et frappé des esperons. Lors ont rencontré l'ung l'autre si droit que leurs deux lances sont volees par pieces, puis ont reprins nouvelles lances et si fierement sont l'ung sur l'autre arrivé que chevaulx et champions sont par terre tombéz. Mais le cheval de Valentin qui fust fort et puissant sans son maistre descendre sur ses piedz se releva. Et quant Valentin fust relevé il dist au chastellain moult doulcement, "Or vous relevez et montez a cheval tout a vostre ayse, car ja de moy vous n'aurez bataille jusques a tant que vous soyez a cheval, car peu me seroit de vaillance se en ce point vous combatoye."

Le chastellain fust moult joyeulx et prisa moult la gracieuseté de Valentin; sy monta dessus son cheval et puis a prins une lance, puis est venu contre Valentin moult despiteusement. Mais Valentin qui sceult a ceste heure de la lance jouer si grant coup luy donna que il luy osta le heaulme de la teste et getta bas a terre cheval et chastellain. Et quant il se veit abatu et en si grant danger, a Valentin dist, "Chevalier, je ne[1] sçay bien dont [53recto]vous estes, ne de quel pays, mais onques en jour de ma vie plus vaillant ne trouvay. Je me veul rendre a vous et vous laisseray entrer a vostre gré parmy le chasteau qui tant est beau et sumptueulx par tel convenant que sans mon congé et licence en maniere qu'il soit vous ne parlerez a la belle Esclarmonde."

"Par ma foy," dist Valentin, "de grant folie estes plain de dire telles paroles. Car tout pour l'amour d'elle ay je la mer passee et suis venu en ceste part, et combien que jamais je ne la veis, se suis je de elle amoureulx plus que de nulle aultre dame. Et vous fay assavoir que jamais d'icy ne me partiray tant que je aye parlé a elle et a la teste d'arain a mon plaisir."

Ainsi que Valentin et le chastellain ensemble devisoient, la belle dame Esclarmonde qui estoit aux fenestres de la franchise et courtoisie fut moult esmerveillee. "Helas!" dist elle a ses pucelles, qui avec elle estoient, "regardez comment cestuy chastellain est fol et malleureux de soy combatre contre ung si vaillant chevalier qui pieça l'eust occys se par sa franchise ne l'eust deporté. Filles, par le Dieu tout puissant, je me esmerveille moult qui peut estre celuy qui tant a grant desir de entrer en mon fort et puissant chasteau." En moult grant pensee fust la noble et belle dame Esclarmonde; en son couraige disoit que une foys elle auroit celluy chevalier pour amy, car de tant plus le veoit de tant plus estoit son amour en luy enracinee.

---

[1] Text is lacking the *ne* which is required by the sense of the rest of the sentence.

"My lady," said the chatelain, who was very proud, "don't say such things to me, for he will never enter without purchasing that right with his body."

With these words the chatelain left to arm himself and mount his horse. Once ready, he sallied forth out of the gate, in his grip a stout lance, well tipped with iron. The lady placed herself at the window to watch the battle between the two valiant champions who had just entered the field to attack each other. When Valentin espied the chatelain who had entered the field to fight him with such a fierce heart, he lowered his lance and spurred his horse. Soon they struck each other so hard that their two lances shattered into pieces; then each took up a fresh lance and came against the other once again with such ferocity that both horses and riders toppled over. However, Valentin's horse was powerful, and, without losing its master, it regained its feet. Once Valentin was up, he said generously to the chatelain, "Get up and remount your horse at your leisure; I will not attack until you are remounted, for it would be unchivalrous of me to fight you unhorsed like this."

The chatelain was overjoyed and greatly prized Valentin's graciousness; he remounted his horse, took another lance, and came riding defiantly against Valentin. But Valentin, who knew at that time how to use a lance, gave him such a blow that he knocked the helmet off his head, and threw both the chatelain and his horse to the ground. Realizing he was beaten and in great danger, he addressed Valentin: "Sir knight, I do not know who you are or what country you come from, but never in my life have I found anyone more valiant. I am willing to give myself up to you and will let you enter this beautiful and sumptuous castle as you wish, on the condition that you will not speak to the fair Esclarmonde in any way without my leave and permission."

"By my faith," said Valentin, "you are absolutely mad to say such things. For I have crossed the sea and come to this place out of love for her, and notwithstanding the fact that I have never seen her, I am more in love with her than I could be for any other lady. Moreover, I will have you know that I will never leave here before I have spoken to her and to the brass head at my pleasure."

As Valentin and the chatelain were thus speaking together, the fair lady Esclarmonde, who was watching all this from her window, was enchanted by [Valentin's] generosity and courtesy. "Alas!" said she to her maidens who were with her, "look how foolish and unfortunate this chatelain is to fight against such a valiant knight who would have killed him already a long time ago if not for his generosity. Young ladies, by almighty God, I wonder greatly who this man can be who has such an overwhelming desire to enter my strong and stout castle." The noble and fair lady Esclarmonde was thrown into deep thought; her heart murmured to her that she would have this knight as lover, for the more she saw him, the more love rooted itself deep within her.

Quant Valentin veit le grant orgueil du chastellain et sa grande oultrecuidance, il frappa des esperons et si grant coup luy donna parmy le corps que tout oultre le foye et le polmon passa et l'abatit mort par terre dont la belle dame Esclarmonde fust moult fort joyeuse. Adonc commanda aux portiers que ilz ouvrissent les portes et que Valentin luy fust amené en sa sale paree. Les portiers ont fait le commandement de la dame Esclarmonde et devers elle ont amené Valentin et Orson.

Et quant la dame vit Valentin elle ala a l'encontre de luy et luy dist, "Chevalier, bien soyez venu, car oncques plus vaillant ne plus hardy couraige en mon chasteau ne veys entrer. Bien monstrez par voz fais que de grant gentillesse vous soyez extrait et descendu."

"Dame," dist Valentin, "sachez que de mon propre nom suis appellé Valentin et suis ung povre aventureux que de ma generation ne de mon lignaige je n'eulx oncques cognoissance. Et si ne veis oncques le pere par qui je fus engendré ne la mere qui m'a porté, et aussi ne fist mon compaignon que vous voyez icy, car en ung bois fut nourry comme une beste sauvaige ou je le conquestay et gaignay a l'espee moult fort vaillamment. Et sachez que jamais en sa vie ne parla non plus comme vous voyez. Or ay je tant de chemin fait que a mon aven[53verso]ture en desirant de mon cueur que de mes amis avoir aulcune cognoissance que vostre[1] grant beaulté m'a fait la mer passer et venir en ceste part."

En disant ces paroles Valentin tira l'aneau que luy avoit baillé le Verd Chevalier et en soubzriant doulcement le bailla a la belle Esclarmonde laquelle fort bien le cogneust. Et a dist a Valentin, "Chevalier, beau sire, si vous m'eussiez monstré l'aneau quant devant mes portes arrivastes sans la jouste attendre et vostre corps mettre en danger de celle heure fussiez entré en mon chasteau sans nul contredit. Mais vous avez monstré la grant vaillance et noblesse qui sont en vous, quant avez mieulx aymé par vostre hardiesse ou chasteau entrer et devers moy venir que de nul aultre requerir."

Tantost que apres Valentin et la belle Esclarmonde eurent ainsi parlé les tables furent dreschés et fust la pucelle assise, et Valentin qui fust devant, qui ne print soulas ne plaisir fors seulement a celle qui devant luy fust assise.

"Helas! vray Dieu," dist Valentin en son courage, "veullez oster et delivrer mon cueur et delivrer briefment de ceste douloureuse destresse que pour l'amour de ceste dame suis au cueur si parfondement ataint que jamais jour de mon vivant en celle mellencolie ne fus. Hé, Dieu! elle est tant de grant beaulté garnye et de grant bonté plaine: les yeulx vairs, en riant arresté et rasis, le front cler et polly, et la face vermeille, et tous les aultres membres de son corps par droitte mesure naturellement composéz. Or suis je pour son amour si ardamment esprins que mieulx me seroit la mort aggreable que de faillir a ceste chose parfaire et acomplyr."

---

[1] Text has *voste*.

When Valentin saw the great arrogance and impudence of the chatelain, he spurred his horse and gave him such a blow through his body that it passed straight through his liver and lung, knocking him dead to the ground, which pleased the fair lady Esclarmonde. Right away she ordered her porters to open the gates and to bring Valentin into her reception hall. The porters followed the orders of the lady Esclarmonde and brought Valentin and Orson to her.

When the lady saw Valentin, she went straight up to him and said to him, "Sir knight, welcome, for I have never seen anyone more valiant or of stouter courage enter my castle. You have certainly demonstrated by your deeds that you are born and descended from great nobility."

"My lady," said Valentin, "you should know that I am called Valentin, and I am no more than a poor adventurer, knowing nothing of my parentage or lineage. Truly, I have never seen the father who engendered me or the mother who bore me, no more than has my companion whom you see here, for he was raised in the wood by a wild beast, and there I fought and vanquished him valiantly with my sword. Moreover, he has never spoken in his life a word more than you see him speak now. It so happens that I have come all this way on this adventure as much for the hope in my heart to discover some knowledge of my family as for the fact that your great beauty made me cross the sea and come here."

While pronouncing these words, Valentin took out the ring that the Green Knight had given him, and, smiling gently, offered it to the fair Esclarmonde, who recognized it right away. Then she said to Valentin, "Knight, fair sir, if you had shown me this ring when you stood before my gate, you could have entered my castle without dispute, and without needing to joust and put yourself in danger. However, you have demonstrated your great valor and nobility, for you obviously preferred to enter the castle and come into my presence by means of your prowess rather than through simple request."

Right after Valentin and the fair Esclarmonde had spoken thus, the tables were set up and the maiden took her seat, with Valentin across from her, taking no pleasure or comfort in anything except in seeing the one seated before him.

"Alas, dear God," said Valentin to himself, "I beg you to relieve my heart and deliver it as soon as you can from this painful distress which has assailed it so deeply owing to my love for this lady, such that never in my life have I ever been in such a melancholy. Oh, God! she is embellished with such beauty and full of such goodness: light-blue eyes, full of gaiety and serene, a clear and polished forehead, a rosy face, and all the other parts of her body perfectly made and proportioned. I am so smitten with ardent love for her that death would be more agreeable to me than to fail to gain her love."

En ceste maniere se complaingnoit le noble chevalier Valentin pour l'amour de la belle dame Esclarmonde. Et elle d'aultre part en regardant le chevalier souventes foys pour sa beaulté en changant et muant couleur perdoit maniere et contenance. En ceste grant mellencolie tout le plus fort honnestement qu'ilz peurent leurs contenances entretenir passerent le chevalier et la dame durant le disner.

Et quant les tables furent ostees, Esclarmonde print Valentin par la main et luy a dist, "Amy, tant avez fait que vous avez deservi de entrer en ma chambre secrepte en laquelle vous verrez la teste d'arain, laquelle de vostre lignaige vous dira nouvelles bonnes et trescertaines. Or vous en venez avec moy et amenez vostre compaignon car j'ay moult grant joye de oÿr la responce laquelle par la teste d'arain vous sera donnee."

Le noble chevalier Valentin fut moult fort joyeulx quant il oÿt la noble dame Esclarmonde ainsi parler. Ilz yssirent hors de la sale et s'en alerent devers la chambre ou la teste d'arain estoit moult richement aornee. Et tantost qu'ilz furent a la porte pour vouloir entrer dedens, ilz trouverent de l'une des pars ung merveilleux espoventable et fort horrible [54recto]villain, moult grant et ossu qui sur son col portoit une massue de fer qui estoit moult pesante. Lequel villain sembloit bien a veoir estre rebelle et plain de grant oultrage. Et d'aultre part de la porte il y avoit ung lyon moult grant, fier et orgueilleux. Ces deux estoient de tous temps ordonnéz pour deffendre et garder que nul n'entrast en la chambre sans le congé de la dame et sans combatre au villain et au lyon. Et quant Valentin aperceut le villain et le lyon, qu'ilz se drescherent contre eulx pour la porte deffendre, il demanda a la belle que telle chose vouloit dire ne signifier.

"Seigneurs," dist Esclarmonde, "ces deux que vous voyez icy sont pour garder la porte et n'y peult nul entrer que contre eulx ne se combate, pourquoy plusiers en sont mors sans plus oultre passer. Et au regard du lyon, il est de telle nature que jamais a filz de roy il ne fera mal ne oultraige."

"Belle," dist Valentin, "je ne sçay qu'il en aviendra, mais a l'aventure me metteray et en la garde de Dieu moy confiant combateray le lyon."

Lors s'aprocha de la beste orgueilleuse et a force de bras par le corps l'embrassa. Mais tout aussitost que le lyon sentit et odora le corps de Valentin, il le laissa aler et fust courtois et doulx sans luy faire nul oultrage. Et Orson fust de l'autre part qui le villain assaillit et devant qu'il eust levé la massue de fer, le print parmy le corps si rudement que contre le mur le getta. Puis luy osta sa massue et si grant coup luy donna qu'i l'abatit a terre par telle façon que se n'eust esté la belle Esclarmonde il eust tué et occys le villain en la place. Et ainsi fust le villain vaincu et le lyon conquis par les deux chevaliers.

Puis fut la porte ouverte et entrerent dedens la chambre qui de toutes richesses mondaines fust paree, car elle estoit painte de fin or et d'azur, par dedens semee et adornee de rubis et de saphirs sans aultre paremens; par toute la tapicerie

In such manner did the noble knight Valentin moan to himself over his love for the fair lady Esclarmonde. And she, for her part, stealing frequent glances at the knight, felt herself losing her composure and self-control as she blushed and changed color because of his beauty. In such a melancholic state the two of them tried to maintain their composure as best they could during dinner.

Once the tables were cleared, Esclarmonde took Valentin by the hand and said to him, "My friend, you have proved yourself worthy to enter my secret chamber where you will see the brass head that will give you good accurate information about your lineage. Now come with me, and bring your companion, for I will be very glad to hear the answer the brass head will give you."

The noble knight Valentin was overjoyed to hear the noble lady Esclarmonde speak thus. They left the hall and went to the room where the brass head was kept in rich adornment. Once they were at the door, ready to enter, they found there on one side an incredibly ugly and horrible churl, large and bony, carrying a heavy iron club on his shoulder. This churl looked mean-tempered and ready to brawl. On the other side of the door was a huge lion, proud and fierce. These two had long had the task of defending and guarding the room so that no one entered without permission of the lady and without fighting the churl and the lion. When Valentin saw the churl and the lion, that they were drawing themselves up to defend the door, he asked the fair lady what all this meant.

"My lords," said Esclarmonde, "these two that you see are here to guard the door, and no one may enter without fighting them, which is why many have died without ever passing inside. But as for the lion, his nature is such that he will never hurt or cause any harm to the true son of a king."

"Fair lady," said Valentin, "I know not what will happen, but I will take on this adventure and, putting my confidence in God, will fight the lion."

Then he approached the arrogant beast and gripped him tightly around his body. But as soon as the lion had a whiff of Valentin's body, he let him go and was courteous and gentle without causing him any harm.[1] Meanwhile, on the other side, Orson attacked the churl, and before he could even raise his iron club, Orson seized him roughly around his waist and threw him against the wall. Then he took away his club and gave him such a blow that he knocked him to the ground, and if Esclarmonde had not intervened, he would have killed the churl on the spot. Thus were both the churl and the lion vanquished by the two knights.

Then the door was opened and they entered a chamber ornamented with every worldly kind of opulence, for it was painted with fine gold and azure, sprinkled and adorned on the interior walls with rubies and sapphires without other

---

[1] Although this particular incident does not appear as an example in Stith Thompson's index of folklore motifs, it falls under the category index "H0-H199 Identity tests: recognition" in the third volume. The closest example in the index involving an animal is "H172, Animal will serve only certain man." See Stith Thompson, *Motif-Index of Folk-Literature*, vol. 3 (Bloomington: Indiana University Press, 1975-1976), 390.

de drap de fin or fust tendu, couverte de toutes pars de esmeraudes, dyamans et grosses perlles et de toutes aultre pierres precieuses. En celle chambre y avoit quatre pillers de jaspis a merveilles riches et de subtil ouvrage edifiéz, desquelz les deux premiers estoient jaunes plus que fin or, le tiers plus verd que herbe en may, le quart plus rouge que charbon enflambé. Et entre ces pillers il y avoit une armaire plus riche que dire ne pourroie, en laquelle la teste d'arain estoit sur ung riche piller moult richement enclose.

Valentin ouvrit l'armaire et regarda la teste en la conjurant que de son fait et estat luy voulsist la verité dire. Adonc parla la teste si clerement et si haultement que chascun l'oÿt et entendit en luy disant:

"Chevalier de grant renommee, je te dy que tu as nom Valentin, le plus hardy,[1] preux et vaillant qui oncques a nul jour du monde ceans entrast, et si es celuy a qui la belle Esclarmonde a [54verso]esté donnee et doit estre — ne jamais aultre que toy n'aura. Tu es filz de l'empereur de Grece et de la dame Bellissant, seur du roy Pepin, qui par luy a tort fust de sa terre dechassee. Ta mere est en Portingal ou chasteau de Ferragu,[2] lequel par l'espace de .xx. ans l'a gardee. Le roy Pepin est ton oncle, et celuy compaignon que tu maines avec toy est ton propre frere naturel. Vous deux fustes enfantéz de la royne Bellissant en la forest d'Orleans en pityé et en destresse douloureuse, et quant la royne vous eust sur terre mis, ton compaignon luy fust par une ourse sauvaige osté et emporté, et par elle a esté nourry au bois sans ayde ne confort de femme naturelle. Et tu fus celuy jour en la forest par le roy Pepin trouvé et emporté, lequel sans avoir de toy cognoissance moult fort doulcement t'a fait nourrir et eslever. Et sy te dy que ton frere qui est cy present jamais ne parlera jusques a tant que tu luy ayes fait coupper ung fillet lequel il a dessoubz la langue. Et quant tu luy aura fait coupper, il parlera aussi clerement que de tous pourra estre oÿ. Or pense de bien faire comme tu as commencé et tout bien te viendra, car puis que tu es entré en ceste chambre mon temps est achevé — ne jamais a creature ne donneray responce."

Quant la teste d'arain eust ces paroles dictes elle s'enclina bas et perdit le parler, et oncques depuis par elle ne fust parole proposee. Adonc Valentin, qui de joye fust transy, vint a Orson et en plourant moult fort tendrement le baisa en la bouche, et Orson d'aultre part l'embrassa et l'acolla en gettant grans souspirs et gemissemens.

"Helas," dist Esclarmonde a Valentin, "franc chevalier courtois, bien doy estre joyeuse de vostre venue, car par vous je suis hors de soussi et de moult grief martire ausquelz par plus de dix ans j'ay passé mon temps languissant en douleurs et en attendant celuy a qui je devoye estre donnee. Or estes vous celuy, je le voy clerement, car par nul aultre la teste d'arain ne devoit perdre son parler. Et puis qu'il est ainsi, que par vostre venue a sa rayson et loquence finee, je me donne et habandonne a vous comme a mon parfait et tresloyal amy, et celuy a qui je doy par

---

[1] Text has *gardy*.
[2] Text has *Ferrag*.

ornament; hanging everywhere were tapestries of fine gold, covered all over with emeralds, diamonds, large pearls, and all other kinds of precious stones. In this room there were four jasper pillars, marvelously rich and subtly made, of which the first two were more yellow than fine gold, the third was greener than grass in May, and the fourth redder than burning coal. Between these pillars was a cabinet more richly decorated than I could describe, in which the brass head was enclosed, sitting on a fancy pillar, also richly decorated.

Valentin opened the cabinet and gazed at the head, beseeching it to tell him the truth of his estate. Then the head spoke so clearly and so loudly that everyone heard it pronounce to him:

"Knight of great renown, I tell you that your name is Valentin, the boldest, bravest, and most valiant knight that ever walked upon this earth, and moreover you are the one to whom the fair Esclarmonde has been and must be given — no one else will ever have her. You are the son of the emperor of Greece and the lady Bellissant, King Pepin's sister, who was wrongly exiled by her husband from his land. Your mother is in Portugal at the castle of Ferragu who has kept her for twenty years. King Pepin is your uncle, and this companion with whom you are traveling is your own natural brother. Queen Bellissant gave birth to you both in the forest of Orleans in pitiful and painful distress, and once the queen had brought you into the world, your companion was seized and taken away by a wild she-bear, then nursed and brought up by her in the woods without the help or comfort of a normal woman. That same day you were found in the forest and taken away by King Pepin, who, without knowing who you were, brought you up and raised you most generously. Moreover, I declare to you that your brother here present will never speak until you snip the little thread under his tongue. Once it is cut he will speak so clearly that everyone will be able to understand him. Now take care to continue to do as well as you have begun and all good will come to you, for now that you have entered this chamber my time is over — never will I give any more answers to any creature alive."

Once the brass head had spoken these words, it bowed down and lost its power of speech, nor has it ever spoken a word since. Thereupon Valentin, overcome with joy, came to Orson and kissed him on the mouth as he wept tenderly, and Orson for his part hugged and kissed him as he sighed and moaned.

"Well then," said Esclarmonde to Valentin, "noble and courtly knight, I have every reason to be happy at your coming, for this relieves me from the worry and torment I have languished in these ten years, waiting and wondering to whom I should be given. You are the one, I see that clearly, for by the coming of no one else was the brass head to lose its power of speech. And since this is how it has turned out, that by your coming its reason and voice is ended, I give myself completely to you as my perfect and most loyal friend, as the one to whom I am by

droitte rayson estre ottroyee et donnee. Et d'ores en avant je vous jure et prometz de cueur, de corps et de biens, et de ma povre petit puissance vous loyallement et de couraige servir et a vostre plaisir faire."

"Belle," dist le chevalier Valentin, "de vostre bon vouloir treshumblement je vous remercye. C'est bien droit et rayson que sur toutes choses du monde je vous ayme et tienne chiere, car des devant Acquitaine vous me fustes donne[e] et ottroyee par le Verd Chevalier, lequel a l'ayde de moy et de mon frere Orson fust conquis et vaincu. Et quant il vous plaira de prendre la loy et la creance que vostre frere le Verd Chevalier a prinse, c'est assavoir [55recto]la loy de Jesucrist sans laquelle nul ne peult avoir pardurable salvacion [je vous espouseray]."[1]

"Sire," dist la pucelle, "telle chose veul je bien faire, car de tout mon courage suis preste et apparellee de tousjours vous complaire et a voz commandemens obeÿr plus que a nul homme vivant."

A celuy jour parmy le palais de petis et de grans joye fust demenee et disoient l'ung a l'autre que le chevalier estoit venu a qui la belle Esclarmonde devoit estre donnee, et par qui la teste d'arain avoit la parole perdue. Si grant fust la renommee du chevalier Valentin que par tout le pays d'environ le peuple en fust resjoy. Mais la grant joye et liesse de Valentin et de la belle Esclarmonde par la trahyson et mauvaistié de Ferragu le geant fust tantost muee en pleurs et en tristesse piteuse ainsi que je vous diray et declareray cy apres.

[CHAPITRE 24]

Comment par ung enchanteur lequel avoit nom Pacolet le geant Ferragu sceust les nouvelles de sa seur et du chevalier Valentin; et de la trahyson d'icelluy Ferragu. xxiiii. cha[pitre]

Au chasteau de plaisance de la belle dame Esclarmonde il y avoit ung nayn qu'elle avoit des son enfance gardé et nourry et mys a l'escolle. Iceluy nayn avoit nom Pacolet. De grant sens et subtil engin estoit plain, lequel a l'escole de Toullette tant avoit aprins[2] de l'art d'ingromance que par dessus tous les aultres estoit parfait et

---

[1] The sentence appears to be unfinished. It would be reasonable to assume that once Esclarmonde had agreed to convert, Valentin would ready to marry her. The Renaissance translator Henry Watson assumed the same and concluded the sentence with "I am content for to wedde you": Arthur Dickson, ed., *Valentine and Orson: Translated from the French by Henry Watson*, EETS o.s. 204 (London: Humphrey Milford / Oxford University Press, 1937), 141.

[2] Woodcut depicting messenger down on one knee, holding spear, handing a message to a standing robed and crowned figure, with one attendant partially seen behind him. Repeat of woodcut on 14v.

full rights granted and awarded. From now on I promise and swear to you with my heart, my body, and my goods to serve you and do your pleasure as loyally and bravely as my weakness allows."

"Fair one," said the knight Valentin, "I thank you most humbly for your good will. It is right and reasonable that I should love you and hold you more dear than anything in the world, for already in Aquitaine you were granted and given me by the Green Knight, who was vanquished by my brother Orson and myself. When you are ready to adopt the faith and belief that your brother, the Green Knight, took, that is to say, the religion of Jesus Christ, without which no one can gain enduring salvation, [then will I marry you]."

"Sire," said the maiden, "I am quite glad to do this, for with all my heart I am ready and willing always to please you and obey your commands above those of any man alive."

That day everyone throughout the palace, both great and small, rejoiced, saying to one another that the knight had arrived to whom the fair Esclarmonde was to be granted, and because of whom the brass head had lost its power of speech. So great was the reputation of the knight Valentin that all around the country the people were joyous at the news. But the great joy and gaiety of Valentin and of the fair Esclarmonde was soon to be turned to tears and piteous grief by the treason and evil-doing of the giant Ferragu, as I will explain to you below.

CHAPTER 24

How Ferragu found out about his sister and the knight Valentin from a magician named Pacolet; and concerning the treachery of this Ferragu.

In the fair lady Esclarmonde's pleasure castle there was a dwarf whom she had kept, brought up, and educated from the time of his childhood. His name was Pacolet. He was quite clever and cunning; moreover, at the school of Toledo he had learned so much of the magical arts that he excelled in it above all others.[1]

---

[1] See Dickson, *Study*, 219–20.

experimenté en telle maniere que par enchantement il fist et composa ung petit cheval de boys. Et en la teste d'iceluy cheval avoit fait et acomply artificiellement et par science subtille une cheville qui estoit tellement assise que toutes les fois qu'i montoit sur le cheval de bois pour aler quelque part, il tournoit la cheville qui en la teste de son cheval estoit devers le lieu ou il vouloit aler et tantost se trouvoit en la place sans nul mal et sans danger, car le cheval estoit de telle nature qu'il s'en aloit parmy l'air plus soudainement et plus legierement que nul oyseau ne sçait voler.

Celuy enchanteur Pacolet qui au chasteau de la belle Esclarmonde avoit esté nourry, tout le jour regarda et considera les manieres et façons du noble et vaillant chevalier Valentin. Adonc se pensa qu'il yroit en Portingal et [55verso]qu'i conteroit a Ferragu l'entreprinse de Valentin et la maniere de sa venue. Il est alé a son cheval de bois et monté dessus, puis a tourné la cheville par devers Portingal, et aussitost le cheval est monté en l'air et tant est alé que celle mesme nuyt il est arrivé en Portingal, et au roy Ferragu a compté les nouvelles. Quant Ferragu entendit le parler de Pacolet au cueur fust fort triste et dolent de sa seur Esclarmonde qui a ung chevalier crestien son cueur et son amour avoit donnee, dont trop amerement au cueur fust dolent et fort desplaisant, et jura son grant dieu qu'il en prendroit vengance. Mais devant Pacolet ne monstra pas sa fureur ne la voulenté de son courage, car homme qui trahison pense tient tousjours sa bouche secrete pour en mieulx parvenir a fin de son intencion.

Ainsi fist Ferragu lequel dist a Pacolet l'enchanteur, "Amy, retourne devers ma seur Esclarmonde et si dy au chevalier qui en mariage la doyt prendre que je suis de sa venue moult joyeulx, et que dedens bref de temps je yray veoir ma seur pour ses nopces faire, acompaigné de plusieurs grans et nobles barons, riches et puissans. Et sy luy donneray de ma terre et seigneurie tant et si largement qu'elle en sera bien contente."

"Sire," dist Pacolet, "je feray voulentiers le messaige tel que le m'avez dit et declairé."

Lors vint a son cheval, puis monta dessus et puis tourna la cheville et se leva en l'air tant et si legierement chevaulcha que il arriva au chasteau d'Esclarmonde. Quant il fut venu il salua la dame moult courtoisement, puis luy a dist, "Ma dame, je viens de Portingal et ay veu vostre frere Ferragu, lequel sur toutes les autres choses est moult fort joyeulx et resconforté du vaillant chevalier Valentin que pour mary vous devez avoir. Et sachez que sans grant sejour faire il vous viendra veoir a moult belle et noble compaignie pour faire en grant triumphe et magnificence les nopces et le mariaige de vous et du chevalier Valentin."

"Ha, Pacolet," dist la dame, "je ne sçay qu'il en aviendra, mais je doubte trop en mon couraige que mon frere Ferragu n'y pense quelque trahyson. Car je sçay et cognoys que jamais il n'aymera chevalier de France ne homme qui de Jesucrist tienne la creance, et d'aultre part je suis desplaisante que je ne sçavoye ton alee, si te fusses enquis d'une crestienne qui de long temps a demouré avec la femme de Ferragu mon frere."

In fact, with his magic he had formed and constructed a little wooden horse in whose head was inserted a pin fashioned with art and cunning knowledge. Thus, each time he mounted the wooden horse to go somewhere, he turned the pin in his horse's head in the direction of the place he wanted to go and soon found himself there without any harm or danger, for the horse was made in such a way that it flew through the air more quickly and lightly than any bird.

This magician Pacolet, who had been raised in the castle of the fair Esclarmonde, observed and examined all day long the manners and ways of the noble and valiant knight Valentin. Then he thought he might go to Portugal to tell Ferragu all about Valentin and how he had come. He mounted his wooden horse, turned the pin in the direction of Portugal, and right away the horse rose into the air, setting off so quickly that that very night he arrived in Portugal where he told King Ferragu the news. When Ferragu heard what Pacolet had to say, he was very upset that his sister Esclarmonde had given her heart and her love to a Christian knight — he was so bitterly upset and displeased that he swore to his great god that he would take vengeance on him. But he showed nothing of his furor or the intentions of his heart in front of Pacolet, for a man who is considering treason always keeps his mouth shut, the better to achieve his purpose.

Instead Ferragu said to the enchanter Pacolet, "My friend, return to my sister Esclarmonde and tell the knight who intends to take her in marriage that I am very glad at his coming, and that very soon I will go see my sister to prepare her wedding, accompanied by several important and noble barons, rich and powerful. Moreover, I will be so generous in granting her part of my land and holdings that she will be quite content."

"Sire," said Pacolet, "I will be most willing to transmit the message just as you have given it to me."

So he went to his horse, mounted it, turned the pin, and rose in the air, riding so lightly and quickly that in no time he arrived back at Esclarmonde's castle. Once there, he greeted the lady most courteously, saying to her, "My lady, I have just come from Portugal and have seen your brother Ferragu, who is pleased and delighted that you are to marry the valiant knight Valentin. Know that he plans without delay to come see you with a fine and noble entourage to celebrate the wedding between you and the knight Valentin with great jubilation and splendor."

"Ah, Pacolet," said the lady, "I'm not sure what will happen, but I do fear in my heart that my brother Ferragu is thinking of some bit of treachery. For I know well that he will never love a knight from France or a man who believes in Jesus Christ; moreover, I am very displeased not to have known you were going, for you should have inquired about a Christian woman who has stayed a long time with the wife of my brother Ferragu."

"Dame," dist Pacolet, "tantost je y seray retourné et demain devant midy en sçaurez des nouvelles."

"Par Dieu," ce dit Valentin, "ce ne pouez vous faire fors que par l'art de l'ennemy."

"Valentin," dist Esclarmonde, "delaissez le besongner et faire son mestier, car tant est bien aprins de son art que plus de cent lieues fera en ung jour."

Quant Valentin entendit que Pacolet sçavoit de tel art jouer moult fust esmerveillé et fort longuement pensa a luy mesmes dont cela [56recto]luy pouoit venir. Et tantost il appella Orson et le fist venir devant la dame Esclarmonde et a ceste heure luy osterent et luy coupperent le filet qu'il avoit dessoubz la langue. Et apres qu'il fust hors il se print a parler fort droit et moult plaisamment, et a celle heure leur dist et racompta comment il avoit esté long temps en la forest nourry de l'ourse sauvaige. Si cogneurent bien que la teste d'arain leur avoit dist et declairé de leur fait et de leur nacion la verité certaine. En parolles furent moult longuement et par grant partie de la nuyt. Esclarmonde escoutait moult voulentiers parler Orson qui plusieurs nouvelles racontoit.

Et quant vint le lendemain au matin Pacolet se trouva dedens la sale par devant le chevalier Valentin et luy dist, "Sire, je viens de Portingal et ay veu vostre mere laquelle est crestienne et croit en Dieu Jesucrist."

"Amy," dist Valentin, "tu soyes le tresbien venu, car c'est la chose que plus je desire, que d'elle oÿr parler. Et si n'ay de riens si grant desir que de la veoir et cognoistre, car tout le temps de ma vie en peine et en douleur je l'ay quise et serchee."

"Amy," dist Esclarmonde, "prenez en vous bon resconfort, car se mon frere ne vient en ceste part, vous et moy nous en irons en Portingal et vostre mere verrez que tant avez desiree."

"Dame," dist Pacolet, "sachez tout certain que vostre frere Ferragu en briefve espace de temps viendra par devers vous, car ainsi je luy ay oÿ dire et promettre."

"Helas!" dist la plaisante dame, "trop suis en mon cueur doubteuse que mon frere Ferragu ne face chose par quoy nostre joyeuse entreprinse ne soit tournee en dur desconfort. Car j'ay songé ung songe moult merveilleux, et moult me donne de sousy et de crainte la nuyt quant je me devoye reposer. Je songay que je estoye en une moult grande et merveilleuse eaue et parfonde a merveilles en laquelle je fusse noyee se n'eust esté une faee qui hors de l'eaue me tyra. Et puis me fust avis que je veis ung griffon yssir d'une nue, lequel de ses ongles agus et poingnans me print et emporta si loing que je ne sçavoye quelle part je estoye arrivee."

"Ha, m'amye," dist Valentin, "pour vostre songe ne prenez pas de mellencolie, car qui vouldroit en songe croire trop auroit a faire et a souffrir."

"Il est vray," dist la noble dame Esclarmonde, "mais garder ne m'en puis." A ces motz la belle dame Esclarmonde et Valentin entrerent en ung verger lequel de toutes herbes et fleurs estoit moult bien furny et garny. En celuy verger furent moult fort longuement parlant de leurs amours secretez et loyalles.

Or avint en celluy jour que le faulx geant Ferragu qui de trahyson fort plain arriva au chasteau de la belle dame Esclarmonde. Et quant la belle sçeut qu'il fust

"Lady," said Pacolet, "I can go back there right away and tomorrow at noon you will know what I found out."

"By God," said Valentin, "you can't possibly do that except with the devil's art."

"Valentin," said Esclarmonde, "let him work and use his skill, for he has learned his art so well that he can go more than a hundred leagues in a day."

When Valentin learned that Pacolet knew how to practice such art, he was amazed and wondered for a long time to himself how this had come about. But then he called for Orson and had him come present himself to the lady Esclarmonde, choosing that moment to have the thread under his tongue cut and taken out. As soon as it was gone he started to speak perfectly normally and quite pleasantly, telling them right then and there all about how he had been brought up in the forest for a long time by the wild she-bear. Then they knew for certain that the bronze head had recounted to them the absolute truth about their birth. They spoke long into the night, and Esclarmonde took great pleasure in listening to Orson, who told many stories.

The next morning Pacolet approached the knight Valentin in the hall, and said to him, "Sire, I have just come from Portugal and have seen your mother who is Christian and who believes in the Lord Jesus Christ."

"Friend," said Valentin, "you are certainly most welcome, for that is the thing I most desire, to hear all about her. And there is nothing I desire more than to see and know her, for I have sought and searched for her my whole life long in pain and sorrow."

"My beloved," said Esclarmonde, "be comforted, for if my brother doesn't come here, you and I will go to Portugal and you will see the mother you have so yearned for."

"My lady," said Pacolet, "know for certain that your brother will be here very soon to see you, for so I heard him say and promise."

"Alas!" said the pleasant lady, "I fear in my heart that my brother Ferragu may do something to turn our happy plans to cheerless woe. For I have been dreaming an extraordinary dream, and it worries and frightens me at night when I should be resting. I dreamt that I was in a vast and awesome sea, incredibly deep, in which I would have drowned had it not been for a fairy who pulled me out of the water. Then it seemed to me that I saw issue out of a cloud a griffon whose sharp and pointy claws seized me and bore me so far away that I had no idea where I had ended up."

"Ah, my dear," said Valentin, "do not be melancholy because of your dream, for he who would believe in dreams would suffer all the time."

"That is true," said the noble lady Esclarmonde, "but I cannot help myself." With these words the fair lady Esclarmonde and Valentin entered an orchard full of all kinds of plants and flowers. They spent a long time in this orchard speaking of their intimate and devoted love for each other.

As it happened, that very day the false giant Ferragu, full of treachery, arrived at the castle of the fair lady Esclarmonde. When that lovely maiden knew

arrivé, elle s'en ala devers luy pour luy faire la reverence et honneur. Il luy dist tres-doulcement, "Ma seur, sur [56verso]toutes creatures vivantes, j'avoye grant desir de vous veoir. Or me dites, je vous en prie, qui est le chevalier qui vous doit espouser."

"Beau frere, icy le pouez veoir." Adonc s'aprocha Valentin et se saluerent l'ung l'autre en grant reverence.

"Chevalier," dist Ferragu, "bien soyez venu par deça pour ma seur en mariage prendre, car tout ainsi que mon frere le Verd Chevalier, lequel qui par deça vous a envoyé apres que par vous a esté conquis et qu'il a prins de Jesucrist la creance, tout ainsi ay je ma voulenté et singulier desir de recepvoir baptesme et prendre vostre creance."

"Sire," dist Valentin, "de vostre vouloir soit Jesus mercié, car pour le sauvement de vostre ame faire et gloire eternelle acquerir, c'est le droit principal chemin."

Helas! Valentin pensoit bien que le trahytre Ferragu et de courage devot et a Dieu encliné telles paroles luy dist, car soubz doulces et humbles parolles de sainte loyauté trahyson mortelle luy pourchassoit. Et quant le geant Ferragu eut ainsi parlé a Valentin il[1] luy a dit, "Sire, on m'a dit et racompté que dedens vostre maison depuis l'espace de vingt ans ou environ vous tenés une crestienne laquelle de tout mon cueur je desire a veoir, car elle est ma mere et a[2] nom Bellissant, seur du roy Pepin et femme a l'empereur de Grece."

"Par ma foy," dist Ferragu, "vous dites verité, mais afin que d'elle vous soyez mieulx informé, vous viendrez en Portingal et verrez la dame. Et quant vous aurez parlé a elle vous pourrez sçavoir et cognoistre s'elle est telle que vous demandez."

"Grant mercys," dist l'enfant Valentin, "car de tel plaisir me faictes que de ma povre puissance je le deserviray."

Alors laissa Ferragu a parler, et pour son trahyson faire et acomplir[3] ala en la chambre de sa seur Esclarmonde, et par maniere de bonne amour et loyauté luy a dit, "Ma seur et ma seule esperance, je desire sur toutes choses vostre honneur et vostre avancement, et suis en mon cueur moult joyeulx de ce que vous avez trouvé si puissant et vaillant chevalier pour mary et espoux. Et pour sa grant vaillance je veul que vous et luy venez avec moy en Portingal afin que de toute ma puissance je puisse en triumphe excellente et magnifique[4] faire le jour de voz nopces ainsi comme il apartient."

Et quant Ferragu eust parlé en telle maniere a sa seur Esclarmonde, il fist ses navires et galees apareiller et ses gens monter sur la mer. Puis demanda Valentin lequel fust moult joyeulx d'aler en Portingal avec s'amye Esclarmonde, car bien pensoit que le geant Ferragu les menast par dela pour leur faire honneur, car il

---

[1] Text has *et*.

[2] Text has *a a*.

[3] Text has *Alors laissa ferragu a parler et a potur nahyson faire et acomplir*, a jumbled mess. I have attempted to emend to what the typesetter seemed to be trying to compose.

[4] Text has *et excellente magnifique*.

of his arrival, she went out to greet him with proper distinction. He spoke to her gently: "My sister, more than any other creature alive, I have been wanting to see you. Now tell me, I beg you, who this knight is who is to marry you."

"Dear brother, here he is." At that Valentin stepped forward and they greeted each other courteously.

"Sir knight," said Ferragu, "you are welcome here to take my sister in marriage, for just like my brother the Green Knight who sent you here after he was vanquished by you and who took the faith of Jesus Christ, so is it my wish and most particular desire to receive baptism and take your faith."

"Sire," said Valentin, "as to your wish, may Jesus be thanked, for it is the right road to save your soul and gain eternal glory."

Alas! Valentin really thought that the traitor Ferragu spoke to him this way out of a pious heart inclined toward God, for he carried off his mortal treason with sweet and humble words of holy faith. After the giant Ferragu had spoken thus to Valentin, the latter said to him, "Sire, it has been told to me that for the last twenty years or so you have had in your house a Christian woman whom I wish with all my heart to see, for she is my mother and her name is Bellissant, sister to King Pepin and wife of the emperor of Greece."

"By my faith," said Ferragu, "you speak the truth, but in order to know more, you must come to Portugal and see the lady. And when you have spoken to her you will be able to determine if she is the one you are seeking."

"Thank you very much," said the lad Valentin, "for you give me such pleasure that I will do whatever I can to requite you."

Then Ferragu ended that conversation to go to his sister Esclarmonde's room to carry out and execute his treachery, saying to her as if with true affection and loyalty, "My sister and my only aspiration, more than anything else do I desire your honor and your advantage. In my heart I am overjoyed that you have found such a mighty and valiant knight to be your husband. Because of his great valor, I want you and him to come with me to Portugal so that I may to the best of my ability give you a magnificent wedding in the superior style befitting the circumstances."

Once Ferragu had finished speaking thus to his sister Esclarmonde, he had his ships and galleys readied and his men mount aboard. Then he sent for Valentin, who was thrilled to be going to Portugal with his beloved Esclarmonde, for he truly believed that the giant Ferragu was bringing them there to do them

luy avoit promis de soy faire crestien et tous ceulx de sa court, parquoy Valentin fut trahy et son frere Orson, car tout aussitost que le mauldit Sarrasin fust sur la mer monté et qu'il eust dedens son bateau Valentin et Orson en sa subjection,[1] il pensa que jamais ne luy eschaperoient sans la mort [57recto]recepvoir.[2] Mais a l'entree de la mer beau semblant luy monstra et par faulces paroles et promesses decepvables les fist avec luy venir. Mais quant vint vers la minuyt que les deux chevaliers estoient aléz reposer le trahystre Ferragu fist secretement et en trahyson dedens leurs lis les prendre et lier estroitement et leur fist les yeulx piteusement bender, tout ainsi comme gens que par faulte criminelle publiquement sont a mort condempnéz.

Et quant la belle Esclarmonde veit son amy Valentin prins et lyé elle mena si grant dueil que trop avoit dur le cueur qui de plourer se tenoit.

"Helas!" dist elle, "chevalier Valentin, nostre joye et nostre soulas est en peu de temps tourné en dueil et en tristesse. Trop avez mon amour chierement achetee quant il fault que pour moy devez la mort souffrir. Mieulx amasse que pour vous jamais n'eusse esté nee, car en peine et en travail vous m'avez conquestee et en dueil et en tristesse je vous seray ostee. Trop est la mort chiere achetee, quant il fault pour aymer loyallement que vous endurez mort sans l'avoir deservi. Helas! helas! or doy je bien du cueur souspirer et des yeulx tendrement plourer quant il fault que pour mon amour le plus vaillant, le plus hardy, et le plus noble du monde soit a mort honteusement livré. Ha! Ferragu, mon beau frere, trop mal voulés ouvrer, car de tout le monde vous avez le plus hardy chevalier trahy et deceu. Et s'i fault que pour moy la mort luy soit livree, jamais jour de ma vie je n'auray joye au cueur, mais tout au plustost que je pourray de mort il ne me chault quelle ma vie soit, et mes jours abregeray et metteray a fin. Et sy vous fay assavoir que se les deux chevaliers vous faictes mourir une foys en aurez reproche villaine. Et pour tant laissez les a tant, car a leur mort pourchasser ne pouez avoir prouffit. Et se la mort leur voulez livrer, faites moy dedens la mer la premiere getter, car tant ne pourroy je vivre que je veisse devant mes yeulx tant vaillans et preux chevalier sans avoir fait offense estre mortellement puignis."

Tant fust la dame Esclarmonde au cueur parfondement attainte et navree que des l'eure elle se fust de ses deux mains a mort livree et en la mer pour soy noyer gettee, quant Ferragu son frere le fist par ses barons garder et retenir. Et si commanda que on la gardast en telle maniere que ung seul mot elle ne peust dire a nul des prisonniers. Ainsy demoura Esclarmonde en pleurs et souspirs moult piteulx.

Et Valentin et Orson furent des Sarrasins tenus et estroitement lyéz. Ilz reclamerent Dieu devotement que de celuy danger et peril ilz peussent eschapper:

"Helas!" dist Valentin, "or m'est bien Fortune contraire et a mon besoing perverse et desloialle. Or ay je toute ma vie en peine et en travail usee, ma jeunesse pour querir et trouver du lieu cognoissance dont [57verso]je fus extrait et

---

[1] Text has *subjectin*.
[2] *h i* at bottom right corner of 57r.

honor, for he had promised to become a Christian along with all of his court. But by this, Valentin and his brother Orson were betrayed, for as soon as the cursed Saracen was in open sea, having Valentin and Orson on his boat and in his control, he thought they would never escape him without being put to death. At the beginning of the voyage he pretended to be nice to them, using false words and deceptive promises to get them to come with him. But as midnight approached and the two knights retired for the night, the traitor Ferragu had them quietly and treacherously seized in their beds, bound tightly and blindfolded, as if they were condemned to death like common criminals.

When Esclarmonde saw her beloved Valentin seized and bound, she grieved so deeply that only the most hard-hearted person could keep from weeping.

"Alas!" said she, "sir knight Valentin, our joy and our solace have quickly turned into grief and distress. You have paid too dearly for my love when you must suffer death because of me. I would much prefer for your sake never to have been born, for you won me with pain and labor and now in grief and distress I will be snatched away from you. Death is dearly bought when for having loved faithfully you must endure death without meriting it. Alas, alas! I have every reason to sigh from the depths of my heart and weep bitter tears when for my sake the most valorous, the boldest, and the most noble man in the world is delivered up to a shameful death. Oh! Ferragu, my dear brother, you do wrong, for you have betrayed and deceived the doughtiest knight in the world. If he is given up to death on account of me, never for a single day in my life will I ever again have joy in my heart, rather, as soon as I may, by whatever means possible, not caring about death or that my life continue, I will shorten and end my days. And I tell you directly that if you kill these two knights, one day you will be severely criticized for it. So leave them be, for you can have no profit from procuring their death. But if you do deliver them unto death, have me cast into the sea, for I will not be able to live having seen with my own eyes such valiant and worthy knights mortally punished without ever having given offense."

So profoundly was the lady Esclarmonde struck through the heart with sorrow that she would have killed herself with her own two hands at that very moment and thrown herself into the sea to drown, but her brother Ferragu had her watched and guarded by his barons. Moreover, he ordered that she be guarded so closely that she would not be able to speak a word to any of the prisoners. Thus Esclarmonde remained drowned in tears and racked by the most piteous sighs.

In the meantime Valentin and Orson were held by the Saracens and very tightly bound. They appealed with great devotion to God that they might escape from this danger and peril:

"Alas!" said Valentin, "now Fortune is opposing me, acting perverse and disloyal when I need her. I have spent my entire life, all my youth, in effort and travail, searching for knowledge of where I come from and of the father and mother

du pere et de la mere par lesquelz au monde je suis mis. Et maintenant quant je suis pres[1] de ma douleur finer et convertir en joye, et que ma chiere mere que tant j'ay desiree j'esperoye avoir nouvelles tresprochainement et certaine cognoissance et en cuidant estre asseuré de mon entreprinse parfaire, mais aux lieux desloyaulx je suis maleureusement venu et cheu entre les mains de mes mortelz ennemys qui de ma vie sont envielx et de ma mort desirant. Helas! beau frere Orson, bien est nostre pensee et nostre intention en peu de temps changee et reversee, car jamais ne verrons ne parens ne amis."

En ce point se plaingnoient Valentin et Orson, et Sarrasins demenoient feste et joye. Et tant nagerent sur mer qu'ilz arriverent en Portingal ou chasteau Ferragu. Et aussitost que la royne Bellissant oÿt dire que Ferragu avoit amené deux crestiens prisonniers, elle saillit hors de la chambre pour les aler veoir. Quant elle vit Valentin et Orson lesquelz pas ne les cognoissoit elle leur demanda, "Enfans, de quel pays estes vous et en quelle terre fustes vous néz?"

"Dame," dist Valentin, "nous sommes du pays de France au plus pres de Paris, la royalle ville et cité."

Tantost que Ferragu vit la royne Bellisant qui aux enfans parloit il luy a dist moult fierement, "Dame, delaissez moy ce langaige et vous en alez en vostre chambre, car jamais ilz ne verront homme de leur lignaige. Je les feray mourir dedens ma chartre obscure de mort villaine s'ilz ne croient en Mahon, mon dieu, sur tous puissant."

Il appella le chartrier et luy commanda que les deux prisonniers fussent boutéz au plus parfont de la chartre et au lieu le plus obscur et que on ne leur donnast ne boire ne mengier fors du pain et de l'eaue. La furent les mauldis Sarrasins qui de gros bastons et de poings frappoient sur les deux enfans sans en avoir pitié non plus que de chiens. Et en une fosse et plaine d'ordure les getterent et devalerent. Et quant ilz furent en la prison ilz se mirent a genoulz, criant a Dieu mercy et en luy depriant que de leurs pechéz il leur voulsist faire pardon, car jamais ne pensoient de ce lieu en vie saillir.

Et apres que Ferragu eust ainsi fait enprisonner Valentin et Orson, il monta dessus en son palays et fist amener devant luy la belle Esclarmonde qui tant piteusement plouroit que des larmes qui de ses yeulx descendoient estoit toute sa face couverte et arrousee.

"Ma seur," dist Ferragu, "delaissez vostre plourer et changez vostre couraige, car par mon dieu Mahon trop avez longuement creu la teste d'arain quant vous voulez espouser et prendre en mariaige ung estranger et hors de nostre creance. Trop avez cueur variable et voulenté de femme quant celuy voulez aimer qui de vostre frere le Verd Chevalier s'est monstré ennemy mortel. Bien vous appartient d'avoir homme plus digne et de plus hault lignai[58recto]ge,[2] et se croire me voulez et ma voulenté faire je vous donneray pour mary le puissant roy Trompart

---

[1] Text has *prs*.
[2] *h ii* at bottom right corner of 58r.

who brought me into the world. And now, when I am close to ending my sorrow and converting it to joy, just when I hoped very soon to have news of and even to meet my dear mother, which I have wished for so much and was sure that I was about to achieve, instead I have come to this unhappy pass and fallen into the hands of my mortal enemies, jealous of my life and desirous of my death. Alas! dear brother Orson, in so little time our plans and intentions are upset and reversed, for we will never see either our family or our friends."

In this manner both Valentin and Orson lamented their fate while the Saracens celebrated. In the meantime the boat made such good progress that they soon arrived at Ferragu's castle in Portugal. As soon as the queen Bellissant heard it said that Ferragu had brought back two Christian prisoners, she left her room to go see them. When she saw Valentin and Orson, whom she did not recognize, she asked them, "Young men, from what country are you and in what land were you born?"

"Lady," said Valentin, "we are from France, near Paris, the royal seat and city."

As soon as Ferragu saw Queen Bellissant speaking to the young men he addressed her roughly, "Lady, leave off this speech and go to your chamber, for they will never again see anyone of their lineage. I will have them die a lowly death in my dark dungeon if they do not believe in Mohammed, my god, more powerful than any other."

He called his jailer and ordered him to throw the prisoners into the deepest and darkest part of the dungeon, and not to feed them anything other than bread and water. There the cursed Saracens beat the two young men with stout cudgels and their fists, having no more pity on them than they would on dogs. Then they cast and flung them into a filthy pit. Once in prison, they got on their knees, crying out to God for mercy and begging him to pardon them their sins, for they never believed they would get out of that place alive.

After Ferragu had thus imprisoned Valentin and Orson, he went up to the palace and had brought before him the fair Esclarmonde who was weeping so piteously that her entire face was covered and wet with the tears streaming from her eyes.

"My sister," said Ferragu, "you had better stop your crying and have a change of heart, for by my god Mohammed, you have believed in the brass head for much too long when you desire to marry a stranger outside of our faith. You have too flighty a heart and too much of a woman's caprice when you choose to love the man who showed himself the mortal enemy of your brother the Green Knight. You ought to have a worthier man of higher lineage, so, if you are willing to trust me and do my will, I will give you as a husband the powerful King

par lequel vous pourrez estre de tout temps de haulte vie et richement honnouree. Et pour tant oubliez les deux crestiens françoys et n'y ayez plus de fiance, car mourir je les feray et pendre par le col."

"Frere," dist Esclarmonde, "obeÿr me covient a vostre commandement, car il se fault deporter et passer legierement de la chose que on ne peult avoir; la ou force contraint droit n'a point de vertu, car necessité fait souvent mauvais marché prendre."

Apres ces parolles Ferragu se departit et la royne sa femme entra dedens la sale, laquelle en grant honneur a receu la belle dame Esclarmonde en luy disant, "Ma seur, bien soyez ceans arrivee, car de vous veoir je avoye grant desir et voulenté."

"Dame," dist Esclarmonde, "cent foys vous mercye, mais sachez que je suis moult doulente et desplaisante des deux chevaliers crestiens lesquelz mon frere Ferragu soubz umbre d'asseurance et de loyaulté a fait passer la mer et puis les a boutéz en une chartre obscure et villaine. Et par grant despit leur a la mort juree se ilz ne veullent leur loy renoncer. Helas! ma seur et chiere amye, il est vray que des deux chevaliers j'en devoye avoir ung en mariaige, qui dessus tous les hommes vivans est le plus beau, le plus vaillant et le plus hardy, et qui par force d'armes a mon amour conquise. Sy me veullez conseiller, dame, je vous en prie, car j'en ay bon mestier. Et vous plaise moy monstrer la crestienne laquelle vous avez en cest mayson sy longuement gardee."

"Belle seur," dist la royne, "icy la pouez vous veoir."

Lors parla Bellissant en disant, "Dame, que vous plaist il? Dictes vostre voulenté, car j'ay grant desir de vous oÿr parler."

"Helas, dame, je vous aporte nouvelles desquelles moult serez joyeuse et tantost apres doulente et desplaisante. Sachez pour certain que de vostre estat et de vostre vie je cognoy la verité certaine, car vous estes seur au roy Pepin et femme a l'empereur de Grece, lequel a tort et sans rayson de son royaulme vous a bannye et dechassee. Et tantost apres en une forest moult large vous enfantastes deux filz dont l'ung vous fust osté d'une ourse sauvaige. Vous ne sçavez comment l'autre fut perdu ne par quelle maniere. Or sont voz deux enfans encores en vie et je sçay le lieu ou trouver vous les pourrez."

A ces motz la royne Bellissant cheut a terre paulmee de joye et de pitié qu'elle eust. Et Esclarmonde la leva moult doulcement entre ses bras, et quant elle fut relevee elle demanda a la pucelle comment elle pouoit telles nouvelles sçavoir. Adonc luy compta Esclarmonde le fait et la maniere comment le roy Ferragu son frere par faulce et mauldite trahyson les avoit mis et detenoit en prison. Quant Bellissant la royne entendit que ses deux [58verso]enfans estoient en la prison il ne fault pas demander se elle demena moult grant dueil, car tant piteusement a pleuré ceste prinse que la femme de Ferragu est entree en la sale qui leur a demandé pourquoy elle demenoit si grant dueil. Et la belle Esclarmonde luy a compté de point en point la cause et la rayson.

"Or, dame," ce dist la femme de Ferragu, "apaisez vostre dueil et ne faictes de ceste chose maniere ne semblant, car se le roy Ferragu le sçavoit plus tost pourroit la chose empirer que amender."

Trompart, with whom you will have an exalted position and be richly honored. Forget these two Christian Frenchmen and trust them no longer, for I will put them to death, hanging them by the neck."

"Brother," said Esclarmonde, "I have no choice but to obey your command, since one must renounce and give up without regret the thing that one cannot have: there where force constrains, right has no virtue, and necessity often makes one accept a bad deal."

After these words Ferragu left and his wife the queen entered the hall, receiving the fair lady Esclarmonde with much honor and saying to her, "My sister, you are most welcome here, for I wished very much to see you."

"Lady," said Esclarmonde, "a hundred times I thank you, but know that I am most sorrowful and displeased concerning the two Christian knights whom my brother, under the pretext of security and loyalty, brought over the sea on his ship, subsequently casting them into a filthy, dark dungeon. Moreover, with great malevolence he has sworn to put them to death if they will not renounce their faith. Alas! my sister and dear friend, it is true that I was supposed to marry one of the two knights, who is handsomer than any man alive, more valiant and bolder as well, and who conquered my love through force of arms. Please advise me, my lady, I beg you, for I have great need of it. And would you also please show me the Christian lady whom you have kept so long in your household?"

"Dear sister," said the queen, "here she is."

Then Bellissant spoke saying, "Lady, what do you wish? Tell me your will, for I greatly desire to hear you speak."

"Alas, lady, I bring you news which will make you first very glad but afterwards sorrowful and upset. You should know that I am acquainted with the full truth about your rank and your life, for you are the sister of King Pepin and wife of the emperor of Greece, he who wrongly and without justification banished and exiled you from his kingdom. And soon after, when you were in the wide, deep forest, you gave birth to two sons, of whom one was taken away by a wild she-bear. You don't know how or in what manner the other one was lost. Now, your two children are alive, and I know the place where you can find them."

At these words, Queen Bellissant fell to the ground in a faint from the joy and emotion she felt. Esclarmonde lifted gently her in her arms, and, once she had risen, she asked the girl how she could know such things. Thereupon Esclarmonde recounted to her the way in which King Ferragu her brother, through false and damnable treachery, had thrown them into prison. There is no need to ask whether Bellissant the queen mourned most dolefully when she heard that her two children were in prison, for she wept so piteously over their capture that Ferragu's wife entered the room to ask why she mourned so. Then the fair Esclarmonde explained to her point by point the cause and the reason.

"Now, lady," said Ferragu's wife, "calm your grief and let no sign of it show, for if King Ferragu were aware of it, things could get worse rather than better."

Ainsi que les trois dames de ceste matiere parloient, l'enchanteur Pacolet entra dedens la sale lequel n'estoit pas venu par la mer avec Ferragu, mais estoit venu par l'air sur son cheval de bois. Et quant la belle Esclarmonde le veit dedens la sale elle s'escrye piteusement et dist, "Helas, Pacolet! que as tu empensé et quel mal t'ay je fait qui si honteusement m'as voulu oster et toullir mon soulas et ma joye? Las! je t'ay si doulcement nourry et tenu a l'escole. Que je t'ay fait aprendre tout le bien et la science que j'ai[1] peu, de quoy tu m'as bien mal reguerdonnee, quant de mon frere Ferragu tu ne m'as voulu dire ne declairer la cruelle entreprinse. Bien me disoit le cueur que doulente en seroye et bien cause y avoit, et penser y devoye quant sans mon congé et licence tu alas en Portingal porter les nouvelles."

"Dame," dist Pacolet, "contre moy ne soyez si fort couroucee, car par le grant dieu en qui je croy, de vostre frere Ferragu je ne sçavoye point la trahyson, ne de son couraige en riens ne m'avoit declairé fors que pour vostre bien et honneur et pour vous faire espouser au noble et vaillant chevalier Valentin. Il vous devoit venir veoir a tout moult belle compaignie. Mais puis qu'il est ainsi que par trahyson il a voulu ouvrer, je vous promettz par ma loy que je y metteray si bon remede[2] que de bref vous en serez bien vengee. Et si vous promettz et jure de ceste heure que vous et Valentin loyallement serviray tout le temps de ma vie."

"Amy," ce dit la dame Bellissant, "se tu povoyez tant faire que mes deus enfans hors de prison tu peusses mettre et degetter jamais jour de ma vie je ne te vouldroye faillir. Et si te promettz qu'ilz sont assez puissans pour te bien paier et guerdonner de ta peine et labour."

"Dame," dist Pacolet, "soyez toute joyeuse et prenez en vous bon resconfort, car en peu de temps je y besongneray et ouvreray si bien et si subtillemen de mon art que de ma personne vous serez toute contente."

[CHAPITRE 25]

Comment Pacolet par son sort et enchantement delivra Valentin et Orson des prisons du roy Ferragu; et comment il les mist hors de sa terre avec leur mere la belle Bellissant, et la belle et noble pucelle Esclarmonde. xxv. cha[pitre]

[59recto]Par[3] Pacolet l'enchanteur la belle Esclarmonde et la dame Bellissant furent de leur grant dueil resconfortees, et fit moult grant diligence. Quant le roy Ferragu et ceulx de sa court, qui de dancer et de jouer furent moult travailléz,

---

[1] Text has *ia*.
[2] Text has *bon si remede*.
[3] *h iii* at bottom right corner of 59r.

As the three ladies were discussing this matter, the enchanter Pacolet entered the hall, for he had not come by sea with Ferragu, but rather had come through the air on his wooden horse. When the fair Esclarmonde saw him in the hall, she cried out bitterly saying, "Alas, Pacolet! What were you thinking and what evil have I ever done to you that you have so shamefully desired to wrest from me my solace and my joy? Alas! I brought you up so gently and sent you to school. Why did I have you learn all the good and the knowledge that I could, as you have used it to repay me miserably, by not informing me of the cruel undertaking of my brother Ferragu? I knew in my heart, and with good cause, and I should have realized that I would suffer from your going to Portugal without my leave to bring him the news."

"Lady," said Pacolet, "don't be so angry with me, for, by the great god in which I believe, I had no notion of your brother Ferragu's treachery, nor did he say anything to me of his intentions other than what was intended for your well-being, your honor, and your marriage to the noble and valiant knight Valentin. He spoke of coming to see you with a goodly company. But since it is so that he really intended treachery, I promise you by my faith that I will soon find such a good remedy that you will be well avenged. Furthermore, I promise and swear to you that from this hour onward I will faithfully serve you and Valentin all the days of my life."

"Friend," said the lady Bellissant, "if you have the ability to bring my two children out of prison, I will never fail you any day of my life. And I promise you that they are capable of paying you well and rewarding you for your pains and your labor."

"Lady," said Pacolet, "be glad and of good comfort, for before long I will employ my art so cleverly and cunningly that you will be quite happy with me."

CHAPTER 25

How Pacolet used a spell to deliver Valentin and Orson from King Ferragu's prison; and how he helped them get away, along with their mother, the beautiful Bellissant, and the fair and noble maiden Esclarmonde.

The fair Esclarmonde and the lady Bellissant were much comforted in their great grief by the magician Pacolet, who then hastened to his task. When King Ferragu and his court, exhausted from dancing and celebrating, retired for the night,

alerent dormir et reposer, Pacolet ne dormit pas, mais fust moult esveillé. Il applica son sort pour jouer de son mestier, puis vint en une tour de laquelle les portes estoient de fin acier, grosses et espesses et fermement sarees. Mais tout aussitost que il a son sort getté les portes sont ouvertes et les sarrures rompues. Puis entre dedens jusques a l'uys de la fosse ou estoient les enfans, et tantost que il a touché l'uys il a esté ouvert et rompu comme l'autre porte. Et les enfans, qui en la fosse obscure estoient en grant danger et destresse, oÿrent ouvrir les portes. A joinctes mains et a deux genoux[1] a terre devotement a Dieu cryerent mercy, car bien cuidoient que le geant Ferragu les envoiast querir a celle hure pour les faire mourir.

Valentin se print a plourer tendrement, et Orson luy a dist, "Frere, prenez en vous resconfort et pacience. Il nous convient mourir et deffiner noz jours, je le voy clerement. Mais puis qu'il est ainsi que remede je n'y voy, devant que je seuffre mort je me pense venger du premier qui la main mettera sur moy."

Lors a prins une grosse barre qui au plus pres de luy estoit, et quant Pacolet les avisa il leur a dist, "Seigneurs, pour moy n'ayez nulle doubte; pour vostre delivrance suis ycy venu. Venez tost apres moy, car devant que le jour soit cler, je vous monsterray la mere qui vous a porté."

Moult fust joyeulx Valentin quant il oÿt Pacolet ainsi parler, mais Orson qui fierement le regarda ne si voulut fier. Et quant Pacolet vit Orson qui si fierement le regardoit, il se recula arriere[2] de luy de la grant paour et crainte qu'il eust, mais Valentin le resconforta moult doulcement et de son frere Orson luy donna asseurance, adonc Pacolet les mena et conduit jusques a la chambre ou estoient les dames doulentes et esplourees. Les portes estoient closes, mais bien les sceust ouvrir; puis sont entréz[3] dedens la maison ou Pacolet a getté son sort que tous ceulx de la maison a fait dormir sy fort que de leur venue nul n'a sceu nouvelles.

Et quant ilz furent dedens la chambre entréz les dames qui la estoyent coururent au devant et Bellissant la royne, qui les enfans regarda sans qu'elle sceust ung tout seul mot dire, a terre cheut paulmee.

Et la belle Esclarmonde a dist a Valentin piteusement, "Helas, chevalier, c'est vostre mere qui pour l'amour de vous a terre s'est paulmee."

Adonc Valentin l'embraça et la leva, et Orson doulcement entre ses bras l'acolla en disant, "Doulce mere, helas! parlez a moy." Lors le baisa la dame qui mot ne sceut dire. Et de pitié furent les trois tellement au cueur frappéz que a terre cheurent [59verso]paulmés moult longuement mors. Pour leur pitié ploura tendrement Esclarmonde, et getta maintz souspirs.

Et quant la dame Bellissant et les enfans furent relevéz, la mere leur a dist en plourant doulcement, "Helas, enfans, pour vostre amour j'ay souffert et enduré

---

[1] Text has *ge*. It occurs at the end of a line, and the typesetter apparently forgot to complete the word at the beginning of the next line.
[2] Text has *arrie*.
[3] Text has *entez*.

Pacolet did not follow them, but rather stayed completely awake. He prepared a spell according to his craft, then went to a tower whose doors were made of fine, thick steel, solid and carefully locked. But as soon as he cast his spell, the doors opened and the locks broke. He made his way to the opening of the pit where the young men had been thrown, and as soon as he touched the door it opened and broke like the other one. The youths, who were in great peril and distress in the dark pit, heard the doors open. On their knees with joined hands they cried out piously to God for mercy, for they believed that the giant Ferragu was sending for them at that moment to have them put to death.

Valentin began to weep bitterly, and Orson said to him, "Brother, calm yourself and be patient. We have no choice now but to die and end our days, I see that clearly. But since I find no help for it, before I suffer death, I plan to take vengeance on the first one to lay a hand on me."

Then he took hold of a stout rod near him, but when Pacolet caught sight of them, he told them, "My lords, have no fear of me; I have come to rescue you. Come with me right away, for before the day dawns, I will present you to the mother who bore you."

Valentin was overjoyed when he heard what Pacolet said, but Orson looked at him fiercely and didn't want to trust him. Seeing Orson looking at him so ferociously, Pacolet drew back, startled and afraid, but Valentin calmed him down gently and reassured him that his brother Orson would do him no harm, so Pacolet led them to the chamber where the ladies waited, anxious and weeping. The gates were closed, but he knew how to open them; then they entered the building where Pacolet cast a spell on everyone there, putting them so deeply to sleep that they were completely unaware of the intruders.

As soon as they entered the chamber the ladies ran up to them, but Bellissant the queen, who gazed at her children without being able to utter a single word, fell to the ground in a faint.

Then the fair Esclarmonde said to Valentin with much compassion, "Alas! sir knight, it is your mother who has fainted away out of love for you."

Thereupon Valentin embraced her and raised her up, and Orson hugged her gently in his arms saying, "Dear mother, alas! speak to me." Then the lady kissed him, for she could not utter a word. All of them were so overcome with emotion that the three of them fainted away as if dead. In keen sympathy Esclarmonde wept and sighed with deep feeling.

When the lady Bellissant and her children had recovered, their mother addressed them, sobbing softly: "Alas, my children, out of love for you I have

plus de peine, d'angoisse et de douleur que jamais povre femme pourroit soustenir. Et de tous mes regretz vous estes le seul et principal souvenir. Et puis que Dieu vous a par sa divine puissance en telle maniere sauvéz et conservéz que une foys en ma vie je puisse veoir et entre mes bras tenir, de toutes mes douleurs je suis resconfortee. Mais dictes moy et me declairez comment et par quelle maniere depuis le temps que je vous enfantay vous avez esté nourris et gouvernéz, et en quel pays et de quelles gens vous avez esté entretenus, car d'en sçavoir la verité j'en ay moult grant desir et grant voulenté en mon cueur."

Adonc Valentin, en regardant sa mere la royne Bellissant, en piteuses parolles il luy a dist et racompté de leur fait et gouvernement la verité, et comment au bois furent trouvéz, en luy declairant les fortunes et pereilleuses aventures ausquelles ilz avoient esté tout le temps de leur vie jusques a l'eure presente. Et quant Valentin eust la parolle finee, la royne Bellissant, qui cogneust clerement que c'estoient ses propres enfans, fust d'amour naturelle si parfondement esprins que plus fort que devant en grant habondance de larmes gettant a terre fut paumee.

Lors Pacolet, qui en la chambre estoit, leur a dist bien haultement, "Dame, laissez le plourer et pensez de partir de ce lieu, car il est temps de nous en aler hors de Portingal et se du roy Ferragu et de sa subjection voulez estre delivréz."

"Helas," dist Esclarmonde, "mon amy, Valentin, bien vous doit souvenir maintenant du serment et de la promesse que vous m'avez faicte. Tenez moy convenant, et me prenez a femme ainsi que m'avez promis."

"Dame," ce dist Valentin, "de ma loyaulté n'ayez doubte, car ce que de bon cueur vous ay promis veul loyaulment tenir, mais pour le present plus me touche au cueur l'amour naturelle de ma mere que j'ay tant quise que toutes les aultres plaisances du monde. Non pourtant, m'amye, ne vous doubtez car jamais je n'espoire ne je n'ay voulenté d'avoir aultre que vous pour femme et pour espouse."

Sur ces parolles vint Orson et dist a Pacolet que la chambre de Ferragu allast tantost ouvrir, et que de ses deux mains il l'occiroit et prendroit de luy vengance. "Orson," dist Pacolet, "a cela ne vous veul faillir. Or venez avec moy et vous portez vaillant, car tout a vostre voulenté en la chambre de Ferragu je vous feray entrer."

"Seigneurs," ce dist la belle Esclarmonde, "laissez vostre folle entreprinse, car jamais en jour de ma vie la mort de mon frere je ne vouldroye consentir. [60recto]Et[1] sy vous dy bien seurement que quant vous l'auriez fait mourir vous auriez perdu l'amour et l'acointance de mon frere le Verd Chevalier, lequel en plusieurs choses vous peult ayder et secourir."

"Par ma foy," dist Valentin, "vous dites verité et plus saigement que nous vous parlés, car de la mort de vostre frere vous ne devez estre coulpable."

A celle heure partirent de la cité, et Pacolet ala devant qui les portes leur ouvrit si doulcement que nul n'en sceut nouvelles. Et puis les mena hors de la dicte

---

[1] *h iiii* at bottom right corner of 60r.

suffered and endured more pain, anguish, and heartache than any poor woman could bear. Of all that I missed and regretted, you were the most important. But since God with His divine power has thus saved you and preserved you so that at least once in my life I may behold you and clasp you in my arms, I am comforted for all my sufferings. But tell me and explain to me how you were raised and brought up from the time I gave birth to you, in what countries and by what people you have been sustained, for I am anxious to know all about it."

Thereupon Valentin, gazing all the time at his mother Queen Bellissant, recounted to her the moving story of what had happened to them, such as how they had been found in the woods, and explaining their fates and the perilous adventures they had experienced throughout their lives up to the present hour. When Valentin finished speaking, Queen Bellissant, convinced that these were her very own children, was overcome so deeply by maternal love that she wept more violently than before and swooned.

Then Pacolet, present in the chamber, spoke up: "Lady, you must stop weeping and think about leaving this place, for it is high time we were far away from Portugal, if you wish to be delivered from subjection to King Ferragu."

"Well," said Esclarmonde, "Valentin, my love, now is the time for you to remember the vow and promise you made to me. Keep faith with me and take me as your wife as you have promised me."

"Lady," said Valentin, "have no doubt of my loyalty, for that which I promised you will I faithfully fulfill, but at the moment what touches my heart more than all the other pleasures of the world is the natural love I bear for my mother whom I sought for so long. Nevertheless, my love, have no fear, for I have no desire or hope ever to marry any other woman than you."

At these words Orson told Pacolet to go open Ferragu's room right away, and that he, Orson, would avenge himself on him by killing him with his own two hands. "Orson," said Pacolet, "I will not fail you. Come with me and show yourself valiant, for I will get you into Ferragu's chamber as you wish."

"My lords," said the fair Esclarmonde, "forget this mad undertaking, for never in my life would I consent to my brother's death. Moreover, I tell you that if you slay him, you will lose the love and friendship of my brother the Green Knight, who could help you in many things."

"By my faith," said Valentin, "you speak the truth and more wisely than we, for you should not be guilty of your own brother's death."

At that point they left the city, Pacolet going ahead to open the gates for them so quietly that no one was the wiser. Then he led them out of that city,

cité et tout droit les conduist et adressa tant que ilz arriverent sur le port de la mer et monterent sur une galee qui pour les recepvoir estoit preste et appareillee. Ilz eurent le vent a gré et fust la mer paisible et doulce que tantost arriverent au chasteau de Esclarmonde, et adonc prindrent terre pour eulx refreschir. Mais Valentin qui de Ferragu se doubtoit tousjours, dedens le chasteau n'a pas voulu longuement demourer. Mais est retourné vers le port et a dist aux mariniers que leurs galees fussent prestes et que de ce lieu il vouloit partir; et puis est retourné au chasteau sans faire nul semblant. Puis a dist a sa mere Bellissant et a la pucelle Esclarmonde qu'il vouloit aler en Grece devers Constantinoble pour veoir son pere l'empereur Alexandre, qui a tort et sans cause sa mere avoit d'avec luy bannye. A sa voulenté furent obeyssantes les deux dames, et aussi furent Orson et Pacolet. Adonc monterent sur la mer pour leur voyaige parfaire et acomplir.

Le jour fust cler et s'aprocha l'eure que le chartrier du chasteau Ferragu avoit de coustume d'aler veoir ses prisonniers. Il ala vers la grosse tour et porta pain et eaue pour leur donner a boire et a menger. Et quant il fust aux portes de la prison qui toutes ouvertes estoient, il veit que les prisonniers s'en estoient aléz. Lors retourna hastivement devers le roy Ferragu, et luy a dist en grant effroy, "Sire, mercy je vous demande, car en ceste nuyt j'ay perdu les deux chevaliers crestiens que vous m'aviez donné en garde."

En disant ces parolles il vint ung aultre messagier qui devant tous a dit haultement, "Puissant roy Ferragu, trop grant meschief est en ceste nuyt avenu, car tu as perdu ta crestienne que tant tu as gardee et nourrye si longuement en ta maison. Et qui plus est et plus te doit desplaire c'est qu'elle emmaine avec elle ta seur Esclarmonde que si chiere tu tenoyez."

Quant le geant Ferragu entendit ces nouvelles ainsi comme enrragé et hors du sens se print a cryer et ses habys derompre moult furieusement. Et en grant ire fist ses gens armer et saillirent hors des portes. Lors a prins une massue moult grande et pesante et devant tous les aultres est sailly hors des portes sans cheval, car tant estoit grant et pesant que a peine pouoit il trouver cheval qui le peust porter. [60verso]La teste avoit grosse et les cheveulx noirs et roides ainsi que pors sauvaiges, et les bras gros et ossus, et les espaules larges; de jambes et de corps portoit estature longue de treze piedz de long. Quant il fut hors de la ville il appella ses gens pour l'acompaigner et se mist en chemin pour Valentin trouver qui emmaine sa seur. Et a tous ceulx que il trouvoit parmy le chemin en demandoit nouvelles, mais nul ne luy en sçavoit riens dire, car Pacolet sçavoit tant bien jouer de son art quant il vouloit que par la ou il passoit, faisoyt les gens dormir. Et quant le roy Ferragu veit qu'il n'en pouoit avoir nouvelles, il a juré Mahon que le chasteau de sa seur Esclarmonde assiegera, car bien se pensa de les trouver dedens. Lors fist telle diligence que a l'aube du jour lendemain au matin au chasteau de sa seur Esclarmonde arriva pour cuider trouver Valentin et Orson avec les dames qui oultre son couraige de son chasteau s'en estoient escappeez. Mais quant il oÿt nouvelles que ilz estoient partis du lieu et montéz sur la mer, plus que devant fust enrragé et plain d'ire et de fureur,

directing them straight to the seaport where they boarded a galley rigged out and waiting for them. With a good wind and tranquil seas they soon arrived at Esclarmonde's castle, where they landed to refresh themselves. But Valentin was still worried about Ferragu and did not wish to remain long at the castle. Rather he returned to the port and told the sailors to keep their galleys ready for an imminent departure; then he went back to the castle without letting on what he had done. Subsequently he told his mother Bellissant and the maiden Esclarmonde that he wanted to go to Greece, to Constantinople, to see his father, the emperor Alexander, who had banished his mother wrongly and without justification. The two ladies were obedient to his will, as were Orson and Pacolet. So they set sail again on this new journey.

Day dawned and the hour approached when Ferragu's jailor customarily went to the dungeon to see his prisoners. He went to the stout tower, bringing bread for them to eat and water to drink. But when he saw the gates of the prison wide open, he knew the prisoners had escaped. So he hurried to King Ferragu and said to him in a fright, "Sire, I beg you for mercy, for this night have I lost the two Christian knights whom you gave me to guard."

Just as he was speaking, another messenger arrived who announced loudly, "Mighty King Ferragu, a terrible thing has happened this night, for you have lost the Christian woman whom you have guarded and kept so long in your household. And what is worse, and what will displease you even more, is that she has taken with her your sister Esclarmonde whom you hold so dear."

When the giant Ferragu heard these tidings, he became enraged; out of his senses, he began to howl and tear his clothes in his fury. Enraged, he ordered his men to arm and sally forth out of the gates. Then he took hold of a massive, heavy club and, before them all, burst out of the gates without a horse, for he was so big and heavy that he could hardly find a horse able to carry him. His head was huge, his hair black and stiff like that of a wild boar, his arms large and bony and his shoulders wide; his legs and his body carried a height of thirteen feet. Once they were out of the city, he called his men to follow him, and set out to find Valentin who had taken away his sister. He questioned everyone he met on the road, but no one could tell him anything, for Pacolet was so good at casting spells that he had caused everyone they had passed to fall asleep. When King Ferragu realized he couldn't get any information about them, he swore to Mohammed that he would besiege his sister Esclarmonde's castle, for he was sure to find them there. He applied such speed that by dawn the next day he arrived at the castle of his sister Esclarmonde where he thought to find Valentin and Orson with the ladies, all of whom had escaped his castle contrary to his wishes. But when he discovered that they had already left that place and sailed away, he was angrier and even more enraged than before, swearing to his gods that he would find Esclarmonde

et a juré tous ses dieux que il trouverra Esclarmonde et tous ceulx de sa compaignie, ou toute la crestienté en auroit moult a endurer et a souffrir.

[CHAPITRE 26]

Comment le roy Ferragu pour avoir vengance de Valentin et de sa seur Esclarmonde fist assembler tous ceulx de sa terre; et comment il descendit en Acquitaine. xxvi. chapitre[1]

Quant Ferragu le geant vit qu'il ne peult trouver Valentin et Orson, lesquelz sa seur et leur mere luy avoient osté et emmené hors de sa terre, il a juré et promis a ses dieux que il en prendra vengance dessus les crestiens. Et pour ceste cause manda par toute sa terre que tous ceulx qui estoient tenus de luy faire obeÿssance sans sejour ne dilation en armes et en point fussent appareilléz pour se comparoir devant luy, et pour monter dessus la mer pour aler sur les crestiens. Le cry fust tantost fait par toute la terre de Ferragu, et par ses heraulx et messaigiers fust de gens d'armes grant multitude assemblé, et en moult grant nombre a son ost amassé. Ilz monterent sur la mer et mirent le voille au [61recto]vent qui leur fust moult fort bon. Et quant ilz furent sur la mer montéz le roy Ferragu commanda aux gouverneurs des navires que ilz tyrassent vers la cité d'Acquitaine, car il pensoit bien en celluy lieu trouver ceulx par qui il estoit party. Ainsi firent les patrons et tant firent de chemin que ilz vindrent arriver sur la terre d'Acquitaine.

Valentin et Orson qui sur la mer estoient, ainsi comme devant vous avez ouÿ, entrerent dedens la dicte cité d'Acquitaine. Et sans faire mencion de leur estat a nul homme vivant, ainsy comme gens passans, en l'ostel d'ung moult riche bourgois se logerent. Et vouloit bien aler Valentin au palays du duc Savary, mais Orson, qui de grant subtilité fut plain et de grande cautelle, s'avisa et dist a son frere Valentin en ceste maniere, "Frere, je me suis avisé en pensant a par moy que la nature et voulenté d'une femme est de legier variable et tantost changee et muee. Et pour ceste cause je suis deliberé que nulle mencion ne soit faicte de nostre venue jusques a tant que je puisse cognoistre par aulcun signe evident de la belle Fezonne qui tant me reclamoit son chier amy aura changé couraige."

"Frere," dist Valentin, "vous ne dictes que bien; et se faire le pouez ce sera subtillement ouvré." Adonc s'abilla Orson en habit de chevalier qui quiert et serche ses aventures, et print avec luy pour escuyer le petit Pacolet. Puis ala vers le palais et entra en la sale du duc d'Acquitaine par la licence des gardes. Et quant il fut devant luy il le salua et luy fist la reverence telle qu'i luy appartenoit,

---

[1] Woodcut of king and attendants conferring. Repeat of woodcut on 13r.

and all those in her company, or all of Christendom would have much to suffer and endure.

CHAPTER 26

How King Ferragu assembled all those of his land in order to avenge himself against Valentin and his sister Esclarmonde; and how he traveled down to Aquitaine.

When Ferragu the giant realized that he couldn't find Valentin and Orson, who had taken his sister and their mother away from his land, he vowed to his gods to avenge himself on these Christians. For that reason he sent word throughout his land that all those owing him allegiance were immediately to come before him fully armed and ready to set sail to go attack the Christians. Heralds and messengers made the cry throughout Ferragu's land, assembling a great multitude of armed men, so that before long Ferragu had amassed a large army. They embarked, setting their sails into a good wind. Once at sea King Ferragu ordered all the ship captains to sail to the city of Aquitaine, for there he believed to find those whom he was seeking. Following orders, they made such good progress that soon they arrived in the land of Aquitaine.

Valentin and Orson, who were still at sea, as you heard earlier, entered that same city of Aquitaine. Without letting anyone know their true rank, they lodged with a rich burgher as if they were simply passing travelers. Valentin wanted to go to the palace of Duke Savary, but Orson, full of subtleties and a bit suspicious, thought better of it and addressed his brother Valentin in the following manner: "Brother, I have been considering and reflecting on the nature of women, how mutable they are and how easily they change their minds. For this reason, I have decided to make no mention of our return until I have a clear indication from the fair Fezonne, who previously proclaimed me her own dear love, as to whether she has had a change of heart."

"Brother," said Valentin, "what a good idea; if you can do it, it will be very cleverly done." Thereupon Orson dressed himself as a knight errant seeking adventures, and took little Pacolet with him as his squire. Then he went up to the palace, entering the hall of the Duke of Aquitaine with the permission of his guards. In his presence he greeted him, bowing with respect as he should, for

car pour telle chose faire il estoit saige et bien aprins. Et quant il l'eust salué, le duc le regarda fort et bien luy sembla Orson, mais pour tant qu'il parloit il ne le cogneust point et plus oultre n'y pensa, mais luy dist, "Chevalier, dictes moy qui vous maine."

"Franc duc," ce dist Orson, "je suis ung chevalier aventureux qui voulentiers trouverroye maniere de moy aventurer pour bon et loyal service de mon corps."

"Chevalier," dist le duc, "vous estes grant et beau, et me semble que vous devez estre en armes vaillant et hardy; et pour tant se vous me voulez servir loyaulment je vous donneray telz gaiges que vous serez content de moy. Et si pourrez tant faire a mon gré et plaisir devant que de moy departez sur tout vostre lignaige je vous feray riche et en honneur puissant."

"Grant mercis," dist Orson, "je le deserviray, et tant feray que vous pourrez cognoistre la loyaulté de moy et ma povre puissance."

"Chevalier," dist le duc, "de ma court je vous retiens et pour la grant fiance que j'ay en vostre bon service cent livres parisis devant que plus oultre me servez je vous feray delivrer."

Tant fut Orson saige et bien aprins en maniere et contenance que pour la prudence et saigesse de luy, en son palais a disner le retint avec ses chevaliers. Et quant il fust a table assis tant fust sa maniere fort plaisante et sa [61verso]contenance a tous aggreable que des barons et chevaliers fust moult regardé. Et sur toutes choses des dames et des damoiselles fust avisé. La fut la belle Fezonne laquelle estoit sa femme jurée. Pour la grant beaulté de luy fust en moult grant mellencolie, mais jamais ne se pensast que ce fust Orson, car changé estoit de habit et de langaige.

En ceste maniere se disna Orson a la court du duc Savary d'Acquitaine. Et quant vint apres disner le duc appella son tresorier et luy fist delivrer cent livres parisiz comme promis luy avoit. Et Orson print congé de luy pour ceste heure presente en luy remerchiant de sa noble largesse, en luy promettant sa foy, de le loyaulment servir en sa necessité, et puis s'en retourna au logis ou Valentin et les nobles dames estoient qui le attendoient. Et quant il fust devers eulx venu il leur dist et racompta comment le duc d'Acquitaine en grant honneur pour souldoyer l'avoit retenu et a ses gaiges, dont moult fort se prindrent a ryre et demener grant joye.

Or avint en celle sepmaine que le duc d'Acquitaine eust certaines nouvelles du roy Ferragu qui pour luy faire guerre estoit descendu. Il manda tous ses subgetz, barons et chevaliers qui pour le secourir tantost fussent venus tous pres et appareilléz de faire bataille se besoing en est. Puis de chair et de bledz fist la cité garnyr et remplir a moult grant habondance. Et fist les gens d'armes de tous ses pays venir et assembler pour son pays deffendre et la cité d'Acquitaine garder contre le roy Ferragu, lequel en ceste sepmaine mist et assist son siege devant Acquitaine au propre champ et a la propre place du Verd Chevalier son frere avoit son pavillon assis quant par Orson fust combatu.

he was now wise and well taught in these things. After the greeting, the duke looked at him closely, for it seemed to him that he resembled Orson, but since he could speak, the duke did not recognize him, nor did he think about it any longer, instead saying to him, "Sir knight, tell me what brings you here."

"Noble duke," said Orson, "I am a knight errant, seeking adventure and an opportunity to offer myself in loyal service."

"Sir knight," said the duke, "you are tall and handsome, and it seems to me that you must be valiant and bold in arms; for this reason, if you wish to serve me faithfully, I will give you such wages that you will be content with me. And if your deeds please me greatly, before you depart, I will make you richer and more honored than any of your lineage."

"Many thanks," said Orson, "I will endeavor to deserve it, and will accomplish such deeds as will allow you to judge my loyalty and the extent of my poor strength."

"Sir knight," said the duke, "I retain you for my court, and because of the great confidence I have in your good service, before you do anything I will have a hundred Parisian pounds sent to you."

Orson appeared so wise and well taught, as much in manners and countenance as in prudence and wisdom, that he retained him to dine at the palace with his knights. Once seated at table, his manner was so pleasing and his countenance so agreeable that all the barons and knights observed him. But, most of all, the ladies and maidens gazed at him. The fair Fezonne, who was his betrothed, was there among them. His great beauty made her very thoughtful, but she never dreamed that it was Orson, for he was so changed in habit and language.

In this fashion Orson dined at the court of Duke Savary d'Aquitaine. After dinner the duke called his treasurer and had a hundred Parisian pounds delivered to Orson as he had promised. Then Orson took leave from him for the present, thanking him for his noble generosity, pledging him his faith and loyal service in all his needs, and then returned to the lodging where Valentin and the noble ladies waited for him. When he arrived he recounted to them how the Duke of Aquitaine had retained him as a soldier with great honor and with wages, which produced much mirth and delight on their part.

That very week the Duke of Aquitaine received tidings that King Ferragu had descended upon him to wage war. He sent for all his subjects, barons and knights, who came right away to render him aid, fully outfitted and ready for battle if necessary. Next he had the city abundantly filled and stocked with meat and wheat. All armed men from his surrounding lands were assembled in order to defend his land and keep the city of Aquitaine out of the hands of King Ferragu, who that very week set up his siege in front of Aquitaine in the very field and very place where the Green Knight had erected his pavilion when he was trounced by Orson.

Grant et large a merveilles fut le siege des payens et Sarrasins; et moult grant dommaige porterent en la terre d'Acquitaine a leur arrivement et sy tindrent le pays en grant subjection et moult longuement par tout ou ilz peurent avoir domination, et bien pensoient de conquerir tout le pays et tous les crestiens destruire. Mais le noble duc d'Acquitaine, lequel fust moult hardy et vaillant, fist ses gens armer, et en grande et notable compaignie de barons et chevaliers pour payens combatre et leur siege lever hors d'Acquitaine saillit. Et entre les aultres furent Valentin et Orson avec le petit Pacolet qui sans grant bruit faire et sans faire a nul cognoissance entrerent parmy l'ost du duc d'Acquitaine.

Or furent celuy jour de la cité d'Acquitaine plusieurs nobles chevaliers crestiens sur les champs en armes pour le roy Ferragu combatre. Quant le bon duc d'Acquitaine veit l'ost des paiens qui estoit moult fort, grant et large, a Dieu se recommanda de tout son cueur que a ceste jour ne le voulsist ayder. Puis a fait ordonner ses batailles et sonner tromppettes [62recto]et clarons, et sur les Sarrasins est alé arriver qui fierement et de couraige fort orgueilleux encontre eulx fort marcherent.

A ce jour fust devant Acquitaine bataille moult piteuse. Il y mourut de vaillans chevaliers et gens de tous estas, tant que le sang par les champs couroit comme une riviere. Le geant Ferragu entra en la bataille au plus pres de son nepveu Dromadain qui sa banniere portoit. Autour de luy estoient Sarrasins a grant puissance pour le geant deffendre qui frapperent sur les chrestiens par si grans et si merveilleux assaulx que a celle heure ilz tuerent et mirent a mort six vaillans chevaliers, c'est assavoir Baudemain, Bauldry, Gaulthier, Galerann, Anthoine, le bon mareschal, et le hardy Gloriam, qui tous estoient prochains du duc d'Acquitaine. Tant furent crestiens par si merveilleux assaulx durement assaillis que ilz furent constrains de reculer et retraire, et le duc d'Acquitaine fust enclos entre ses ennemys, qu'i tout seul demoura sans nul secours avoir. Lequel faisoit telle vaillance d'armes que nul devant son coup n'osoit arrester. Il crye, "Acquitaine!" contre les faulx et mauldis Sarrasins, mais riens ne luy valut sa proesse, que Ferragu le geant tantost qu'il le cogneust, il ala devers luy et puis le print et l'emmena. Et quant il l'eust en sa subjection, il le fist moult estroitement lyer et devers son pavillon le fist mener, qui moult estoit riche et plaisant, et la le fist bien seurement garder. Puis retourna Ferragu en la bataille devers les crestiens.

Mais tant fust la journee pour les crestiens dolente et piteuse, que pour la perte de leur bon maistre, ilz vouloyent tous prendre la fuitte, quant Orson et Valentin leur vindrent au devant en cryant haultement, "Vaillans chevaliers d'Acquitaine! monstrez chevalerie! car de faillir a ce besoing reproche vous seroit moult grande. Ayez hardy couraige et Dieu vous aydera. Ayez bon cueur!"

Ainsi resconforterent les deux chevaliers le peuple d'Acquitaine, qui de paour estoient pres de fuyr, en telle maniere que crestiens sont contre Sarrasins retournéz et recommencerent la bataille plus forte que devant. Les nouvelles furent devant Acquitaine du duc qui estoit prisonnier, et grans et petis plourerent pour sa dolente et piteuse prinse.

Awesome and immense was the siege of the pagans and Saracens; moreover, they despoiled much of the land of Aquitaine when they arrived, and kept the surrounding area wherever they could dominate in terrible subjection for a long time, thinking to conquer the entire country and destroy all the Christians. But the noble Duke of Aquitaine, bold and valiant, armed his men and, with a large and notable company of barons and knights, set out to fight the pagans, lift their siege, and expel them from Aquitaine. Among them were Valentin and Orson and the little Pacolet who, quietly and without being recognized, slipped in among the hosts of the Duke of Aquitaine.

Now that day there were many noble Christian knights from the city of Aquitaine in the field, armed and ready to fight King Ferragu. When the good Duke of Aquitaine saw how strong and how vast the pagan army was, he commended himself to God with all his heart, praying for His aid that day. Then he placed his battalions in order, had the trumpets and clarions blown, and fell upon the Saracens who, puffed up with arrogant pride, already marched against them.

That day a piteous battle was fought before the gates of Aquitaine. So many valiant knights and men of all ranks died there that the blood ran through the fields like a river. The giant Ferragu entered the battle close to his nephew Dromadain, who was carrying his banner. All around him to protect the giant were gathered a mass of Saracens who assaulted the Christians so vigorously that they slew six valiant knights, namely Baudemain, Bauldry, Gaulthier, Galeran, Antoine the good marshal, and the stalwart Gloriam, all of whom were relatives of the Duke of Aquitaine. The Christians were set upon so severely that they were forced to fall back and retreat, while the Duke of Aquitaine found himself alone, surrounded by his enemies, without anyone to help him. Nevertheless he performed such feats of arms that no one within reach of his sword dared remain there. He cried out, "Aquitaine!" against the false and cursed Saracens, but his prowess was for nought, for as soon as the giant Ferragu recognized him, he rode up, seized him, and dragged him away. Once he had him in his power, he had him tightly bound and brought to his richly appointed and pleasant pavilion, there to have him guarded closely. Then Ferragu returned to the battle against the Christians.

So badly had the day gone for the Christians that they would all have taken flight after the loss of their good master, had not Orson and Valentin dashed up to them shouting, "Valiant knights of Aquitaine! show yourselves true knights! for to fail at this moment of need would be a great reproach to you. Embolden your hearts and God will help you. Be brave!"

Thus did the two knights encourage the people of Aquitaine, who had been close to fleeing out of fear, so that the Christians turned and recommenced their attack against the Saracens more vigorously than before. But the news circulated in the battlefield before the gates of Aquitaine that the duke had been taken prisoner, and everyone wept at the unfortunate and calamitous news of his capture.

Mais sur toutes aultres douleurs estoit incomparable et piteuse la complainte de Fezonne, qui en tordant ses mains et tirant ses cheveulx (plus que fin or luisans) disoit en souspirant du cueur, des yeulx gettant larmes de doleurs, "Las, povre dolente, que t'est il avenu? Or es tu la plus mal fortunee qui soit dessus la terre. Helas! mon treschiere pere, or vous fault il mourir, car des mains des faulx Sarrasins vous ne pourrez partir ne eschapper. Adieu, je vous dy, mon tresdoulx et treschier pere. Jamais ne vous verray, mais je demourray icy seullete [62verso]et despourveue comme povre orphenine, loing de toutes plaisances, pres de desconfort, amer et douloureulx. Helas! Orson, mon bon amy, vostre longue demouree me doit bien ennuyer au cueur, car se vous fussiez icy present par vous fust delivré mon pere qui tant est doulent." Et en cest maniere plouroit et gemissoit la plaisante Fezonne.

Et crestiens et Sarrasins sur les champs se combatent moult oultrageusement. La bataille tant longuement dura que de mors et de navréz[1] toute la terre fut couverte. Or y fut le chevalier Valentin a tout l'espee fourbie qui de Sarrasins faisoit si grant occysion que nul tant fust hardy devant luy n'osoit demourer. Et Orson fust de l'autre part lequel jura a Dieu et a ses sainctz que parmy la bataille il deffineroit ses jours ou il iroit querir le duc d'Acquitaine dedens les tentes du geant Ferragu. Pacolet fust aupres de luy qui bon confort luy a promis et bon secours et ayde, et luy a juré par son dieu que a son besoing ja ne luy fauldra.

Adonc Orson frappa des esperons et est entré parmy les Sarrasins si fierement et sans arrester que la bataille a rompue et tout oultrepassé. Et quant luy et Pacolet l'enchanteur eurent la bataille ainsi oultrepassé, ilz getterent leurs armes bas a terre et pendirent en leurs coulz escus de Sarrasins ou l'imaige[2] de Mahon estoit en signe. Puis s'en alerent ou pavillon du geant Ferragu sans que nul leur fist contredit, car Pacolet sçavoit bien parler leur langaige. Ilz entrerent aux tentes pour le bon duc d'Acquitaine ravoir, mais quant Pacolet veit que trop y avoit de payens qui le gardoient, il ala jouer de son sort si bien et si abillement que tous les a fait pour le temps coucher et endormir.

Et quant ilz furent endormis, Orson vint au duc d'Acquitaine et luy a dist, "Franc duc, venez avec moy et montez sur ce cheval sans faire nulle demouree, car des mains de Ferragu je vous deliveray. Je suis le chevalier qui dedens vostre sale vous demanday gaiges le jour que vous me donastes cent livres. N'ayez des payens nulle doubte, car sans danger en vostre ost vous menrray."

"Chevalier," ce dist le duc d'Acquitaine, "vous soyez le bien venu, qui hors de servaige me gettez et delivrez des mains de mes ennemis mortelz. Et pour le bon service que au jour d'uy vous me faictes pour guerdon et loyer je vous donneray ma fille la belle Fezonne en mariaige. Je l'avoye donnee il n'y a pas longtemps a ung chevalier qui estoit moult sauvaige que nul langaige ne parloit. Mais puis que il n'est devers moy revenu sa longue demouree luy portera dommaige. Je vous

---

[1] Text has a second *que* erroneously inserted at this point.
[2] Text has *le limaige*.

However, Fezonne's anguished sorrow was not to be compared with that of any other. As she twisted her hands and tore at her hair (brighter than the finest gold), sighing deeply from her heart while her eyes streamed with tears of woe, she said, "Alas, poor wretched one, what has happened to you? You are now the most unfortunate girl on earth. Alas! my most dear father, now you must die, for you will never be able to escape or get out of the hands of the false Saracens. Adieu, I must say to you, my gentle and most dear father. I will never see you again, but will have to remain here all alone and destitute, a poor orphan, removed from all pleasure, married to despair, bitter and grieved. Alas! Orson, my dear love, your long absence afflicts my heart, for if you were here, you would deliver my poor father." In this manner wept and moaned the lovely Fezonne.

In the meantime Christians and Saracens battled each other violently on the field. The combat lasted such a long time that the ground was covered with the dead and the wounded. Now the knight Valentin was there with his shining sword, slaughtering so many Saracens that no one, however bold, dared remain near him. And Orson was on the other side, swearing by God and all His saints that he would either end his days in this battle or go seek the Duke of Aquitaine in the tents of the giant Ferragu. Pacolet stayed near him, promising him help and aid, and swearing by his god that he would never fail him in his need.

At that point Orson spurred his horse and dashed headlong into the thick of the Saracens with such ferocity that he penetrated the battalion and passed on through. When he and Pacolet the magician had made it past the battalion, they threw down their arms and hung on their necks Saracen shields with the image of Mohammed as ensign. Then they went to the pavilion of the giant Ferragu without anyone opposing them, for Pacolet knew well how to speak their language. They entered the tents to find the good Duke of Aquitaine, but when Pacolet saw that there were too many pagans guarding him, he cast one of his spells which worked so well that they all lay down and fell asleep.

Once they were asleep, Orson approached the Duke of Aquitaine and said to him, "Noble duke, come with me and mount this horse without delay, for I will deliver you from the hands of Ferragu. I am the knight who asked you for wages in your hall the day you gave me a hundred pounds. Have no fear of the pagans, for I will bring you back to your army without danger."

"Sir knight," said the Duke of Aquitaine, "you are most welcome, for you bring me out of servitude and deliver me from the hands of my mortal enemies. For the good service that you render me today, I will repay you by offering you the hand of my daughter Fezonne in marriage. I had given her not long ago to a knight, a wild man unable to speak. But since he has not returned to me, his long absence will hurt him. I give my daughter to you, for you have certainly earned

donne ma fille, car bien l'avez gaigné, et si aurez avec elle pour don en mariaige la moitié de la terre d'Acquitaine."

"Grant mercys," dist le chevalier Orson, "tel don n'est pas a refuser. Mais au sourplus pensons de faire [63recto]dilligence pour eschaper de ce lieu et retourner en vostre hostaige."

Adonc les trois champions, le duc d'Acquitaine, Orson et Pacolet ont prins armes de Sarrasins et parmy l'ost ont passé sans que ilz ayent esté de nul cogneus et sont[1] a leur ost retournéz a sauveté.

Celuy temps durant que Orson ala devers le duc d'Acquitaine, Valentin qui estoit parmy la bataille demanda a plusieurs ou estoit son frere Orson, mais nul ne luy en sçavoit donner ne dire certaine responce ne cognoissance, dont Valentin fust moult dolent et au cueur courroucé, car il cuidoit qu'il fust demouré parmy la bataille mort, de quoy il getta maintz piteulx crys disant, "Helas! or suis je de tous poins sousprins de intollerable fortune et amere desplaisance; et bien sont toutes mes joies en souspirs et destresse changéz et convertis, quant j'ay perdu mon amy principal, la fleur de tout mon confort et l'espoir de toute ma vie. Helas! beau frere Orson, or vous ay je perdu par les faulx Sarrasins, car bien sçay que vostre vaillance et hardiesse a esté cause de vostre mort abregier. Car tant de vous je cognoys que plus chier avez par vaillance mourir que de vivre en vergongne. Las! vaillant frere Orson, en peine et en destresse au boys je vous conquis, et depuis vous ay gardé en peril et danger. Alors que je pensoie et proposoye de vous avoir liesse, soulas et confort, vous estes de moy separé et departy. Mais puis qu'il est ainsi que de vous je ne puis avoir nulles nouvelles en quelconques maniere, je jure et prometz a Dieu que de brief sçauray ou vous estes et vous trouverray ou mort ou vif, ou vostre amour sera cause de moy donner la mort porchaine."

A ces paroles douloureuses entra Valentin en la bataille, et ainsi que ung homme desconforté et chairgé de mellencolie, en sa main tint l'espee qui fust de fin acier et de son corps monstra telle chevalerie[2] que sans arrester nulle part cinq ou six Sarrasins a getté mort par terre. Et en faisant ceste proesse le geant Ferragu le cogneust et s'en ala tout aupres vers le bon chevalier Valentin, et de si pres le tint et tellement le contraingnit que devant tous avec luy l'emporta, car son cheval fust mort dessoubz luy.

Ferragu le geant fist radement loyer Valentin, et a juré tous ses dieux que il en prendra vengance. Mais il ne fist pas du tout a sa voulenté, car ainsi qu'il l'emportoit parmy le champ, Orson, Pacolet et le duc Savary d'Acquitaine l'encontrerent. Lors dist le vaillant duc, "Par Jesus, voyez le faulx payen qui nostre loy et noz gens veult mettre a destruction. Il emporte avec luy ung de noz chevaliers moult durement et estroitement lyé."

"Par Dieu," se dist Orson, "se nous sommes vaillans il ne nous doit pas eschapper." Lors frappa des esperons et ala devers le faulx payen et mauldit geant

---

[1] Text has *sort*.
[2] Text has *chvalerie*.

it, and moreover, with her, you will have as a wedding present half of the land of Aquitaine."

"Many thanks," said the knight Orson, "such a gift is not to be refused. But the important thing now is to get out of here quickly and return to your dwelling."

Thereupon the three champions, the Duke of Aquitaine, Orson, and Pacolet, took up Saracen arms and crossed through the army without anyone recognizing them until they were safely back with their own army.

While Orson went to find the Duke of Aquitaine, Valentin, in the thick of the battle, asked several men where his brother Orson was, but no one was able to give him definite information. Valentin was grieved and terribly upset, for he believed that he must be lying dead on the battlefield, for which he cried out piteously, saying, "Alas! now I have been overcome by intolerable misfortune and bitter affliction; now have all my joys been changed and converted to sighs and distress, for I have lost my best friend, the flower of all my comfort and the hope of all my life. Alas! dear brother Orson, now I have lost you to the false Saracens, for I am sure your valor and boldness hastened your death. For I know you preferred to die with valor than to live in shame. Alas! valiant brother Orson, I conquered you in the woods in pain and distress, and since that time I have kept you in peril and danger. Just when I thought and imagined having happiness, solace, and comfort from you, you are separated from me and gone. But seeing as how I can find no news of you whatsoever, I swear and promise to God that soon I will discover where you are and, dead or alive, I will find you, or else my love for you will be the cause of my imminent death."

With these impassioned words Valentin charged into the battle, and, like a man desperate and driven by misgiving, wielded his fine steel sword and demonstrated such prowess that, without a moment's respite, he quickly dispatched five or six Saracens. While carrying out these feats, he was recognized by the giant Ferragu, who dashed towards the good knight, pressing him so closely that he bore him away before everyone, for his horse was dead under him.

Ferragu the giant had Valentin quickly bound, and swore to all his gods that he would have vengeance. But he never got to satisfy his desire, for as he was carrying him across the field, Orson, Pacolet, and Duke Savary d'Aquitaine encountered him. "By Jesus," declared the valiant duke, "here is the false pagan who wishes to destroy our religion and our men. He is taking away one of our knights cruelly and tightly bound."

"By God," said Orson, "if we have any valor, he must not escape us." Then he spurred his horse and raced toward the false pagan and cursed giant, landing

auquel il bailla tel coup de lance que luy et Valentin a [63verso]getté contre terre. Et le geant qui fust fort et puissant sur ses piedz se releva et laissa Valentin qui de grant paour commença a fuyr. Et Orson luy a cryé, "Frere, retournez arriere et n'ayez nulle doubte!"

Adonc Valentin retourna vers son frere, lequel luy conquist ung cheval, et dessus le monta. Et Pacolet qui fust parmi l'ost en langage Sarrasin moult haultement crie "Portingal le meilleur!" et en ce cry faisant la bataille passa, et vint a l'ost des crestiens. Et ainsy furent tous mis hors des mains de leurs ennemys.

Et quant les crestiens veirent que leur duc estoit delivré leur couraige leur crust, et doubla leur force, et tant furent joyeulx que tous a une voys cryerent haultement, "Vive Acquitaine!" Et en menant ce bruit coururent sur payens et de si grant force et vigeur les assaillirent que le geant Ferragu, apres qu'il eust perdu grant nombre de ses gens par force d'armes, fust contraint de s'enfuyr et retraire et a son siege levé et reculé. On fist sonner haultement tromppettes et clarons et les gens d'armes retournerent dedens Acquitaine pour eulx refreschir et reposer. A celuy jour que crestiens et Sarrasins se combatirent il y eust si grande occysion et si grant murtre fait que de nombrer les corps seroit chose piteuse.

Au retourner de la bataille Valentin et Pacolet s'en retournerent en leur logis, et Orson s'en ala au palays avec le bon duc Savary et tous les aultres barons et chevaliers. Quant le duc Savary d'Acquitaine fust a son palays retourné il manda tous les princes et seigneurs de sa court et sa fille la belle Fezonne, puis appella Orson et luy demanda comment il avoit a nom. Et Orson fust subtil et dist, "Sire, j'ay nom Richief." Lors a dist le duc haultement devant tous, "Seigneurs, sachez de vray que sur tous chevaliers je suis tenu, et si veul que honneur soit faicte a cestuy que vous voyez icy en presence. Car par luy suis retourné en Acquitaine et ay esté delivré de mon aversaire et mortel ennemy. Et vous, ma fille, c'est mon desir et voulenté que vous aiez en mariaige cestuy vaillant chevalier, car sur tous les aultres je le tiens et puis tenir le plus vaillant et excellent. Et pour la grant proesse que vers moy il a monstré, je luy ay en guerdon vostre gent corps promis; et quant par loy de mariaige a luy serez espousee, bien le devez aymer pardessus tous les aultres quant tant a vostre pere aymé que la vie luy a sauvee."

A l'oppinion du duc furent consentans les barons et chevaliers[1] de la court et disoyent par ung commun acord que le chevalier estoit bien digne d'avoir la belle en mariaige qui si grant proesse avoit fait. Mais Orson qui fut en presence ne voulut sur ce fait son oppinion declairer jusques a tant qu'il eust essaié le couraige et la voulenté de la belle Fezonne ainsi que pardevant il avoit entreprins de faire.

---

[1] Text has *chvaliers*.

him such a blow with his lance that both he and Valentin were thrown to the ground. But the giant, of strong and powerful build, got back up and abandoned Valentin who out of fear began to flee. But Orson called out to him, "Brother, come back! fear not!"

Thereupon Valentin returned to his brother who snatched a horse for him and mounted him on it. And Pacolet, mixing among the enemy host, called out loudly in the Saracen tongue, "Victory to Portugal!" which allowed them to pass through the battle and get to the Christian side. Thus were they all safely out of their enemies' hands.

When the Christians saw that their duke was safely delivered, their courage rose, doubling in force, and so elated were they that their shouted out with one voice, "Long live Aquitaine!" With this cry they fell upon the pagans, assailing them with such force and vigor that the giant Ferragu, after having lost a significant number of his men to the attack, was forced to flee and withdraw, lifting the siege. Trumpets and clarions sounded on high as the soldiers returned to the city of Aquitaine to rest and refresh themselves. There was such a number of dead and dying men the day of that battle between Christians and Saracens that it would be too grievous a matter to count the bodies.

After the battle Valentin and Pacolet returned to their lodgings, while Orson went to the palace with the good Duke Savary and all the other barons and knights. When Duke Savary d'Aquitaine was back in his palace, he called together all the princes and lords of his court as well as his daughter Fezonne, then summoned Orson and asked him his name. Orson cleverly answered, "Sire, my name is Richard." Then the duke announced to everyone, "My lords, I declare to you that, more than any other knight, I am myself beholden, and thus I wish to honor this man whom you see here present. For it is thanks to him that I have returned to Aquitaine and have been delivered from my adversary and mortal enemy. And you, my daughter, it is my desire and will that you marry this valiant knight, for to me he is, more than any other knight, the most valiant and excellent. For the great feats he has accomplished for my sake, I have promised him your lovely self; and once you are wedded to him by the law of marriage, you must love him more than anyone else, since he saved the life of your beloved father."

The barons and knights of the court consented to the duke's intention, saying by common accord that the knight was certainly worthy to have the fair maid in marriage for having performed such an impressive deed. But Orson, who was present at all this, did not want to take a stance until he had had a chance to test the heart and resolve of the fair Fezonne, as he had undertaken to do.

[CHAPITRE 27]

Comment Orson voulut essayer la voulenté et loyaulté
de la belle Fezonne devant qu'il l'espousast.
xxvii. chapitre

[64recto]Orson[1] qui fust saige et subtil, devant qu'il espousast la belle Fezonne, il voulut sçavoir et essaier s'elle estoit pour sa foy garder ferme et loyalle, car bien souvent avoit oÿ dire que femmes pour bien peu leur serment et promesse, et pour petit de chose les rompent et faulcent. Mais combien que plusieurs soient de telle nature, toutesfois le vice des mauvaises ne doit point estre prins ne alegué pour corrumpre la loyalté des bonnes, car parmy ung buysson d'espines on trouve bien une rose flourie, et aussi entre plusieurs femes bien mauvaises, on en peult bien une bonne trouver, ainsi que fust Fezonne laquelle Orson trouva loyalle. Car pour l'essaier il a dist au duc en ceste maniere:

"Sire, de l'onneur que vous me fait[es] suis bien tenu de grace vous rendre. Mais au regard de vostre fille je vouldroye bien sçavoir sa voulenté et intencion, car bien luy apartient d'avoir homme de plus hault lieu que je ne suis. Et pour tant devant que je la prengne, je parleray a elle pour sçavoir son couraige, car mariaige fait oultre sa voulenté ne vient pas voulentiers a bonne perfection."

"Chevalier," dit le duc d'Acquitaine, "de ce vous avez bonne rayson et je le vous acorde. Or alez en sa chambre; si parlerez a elle affin que vous soyez de ce fait mieulx informé."

A ces motz Orson entra en la chambre de la belle Fezonne et se assist aupres d'elle dessus ung banc. Et puis l'a prins par la main et luy a dist doulcement, "Dame, la grant beaulté de vous m'a d'amours si fort esprins que sans vous je ne puis avoir nul confort ny alegement. Or soit Dieu loué quant il luy a pleu telle grace moy faire que pour feme vous me soyez donnee, car bien me pourray vanter que des aultres j'aray la plus belle pour amye. Et puis qu'il plaist au bon duc vostre pere que vous m'ayez pour mary, bien devez estre par rayson contempte, car je vous serviray et tiendray bonne et parfaite loyaulté durant tout le temps de ma vie. Sy vous prie, ma treschiere et tresaymee dame, que pour avoir l'ung de l'autre plus grant et plus ardant souvenir je vous requiers que a ceste heure presente vous me baisez et embraschés. Et ne me veullez pas [64verso]escondire ce dist l'amoureuse requeste, je vous prie, car puis que pour le temps a venir devons estre assembléz, de ma voulenté faire vous ne me devez refuser."

"Chevalier," ce respond la belle qui bien estoit aprinse, "de telle chose requerir vous devez retarder car vous perdez vostre peine. J'ayme tous chevaliers et gens de noble affaire en bien et en honneur. Mais dessus tous les aultres j'en ayme

---

[1] Woodcut of woman in wimple in conversation with two youthful male figures.

CHAPTER 27

How Orson wanted to test the will and loyalty of the fair Fezonne before marrying her.

Before marrying Fezonne, Orson, who was wise and clever, wanted to put her to the test to see if she would remain firm and true to her pledged troth, for he had often heard it said that women easily break faith and betray their promises and vows with the slightest temptation. But however many might have such a nature, the vice of those false ones should not be held against those who are loyal, for in the middle of a thorny bush one may certainly find a full-blown rose,[1] and similarly, among many bad women one can surely find a good one, as it was with Fezonne, whom Orson found loyal. In order to test her, he addressed the duke in the following manner:

"Sire, I owe you great thanks for the honor you offer me. But as regards your daughter, I would very much like to know her desire and intention, for she deserves to have a man of higher lineage than mine. For this reason, before I take her, I will speak with her to know her feelings on the subject, for marriage against one's will is rarely a success."

"Sir knight," said the Duke of Aquitaine, "that is a good idea, and I give you my permission. Go to her chamber and talk to her; find out what she thinks."

With these words Orson entered the fair Fezonne's chamber and sat next to her on a bench. Taking her by the hand, he addressed her gently: "Lady, your great beauty has so smitten me with love that without you I can have no comfort or happiness. May God be praised, since it has pleased Him to show me such favor as to allow me your hand in marriage, for now I can boast that I have the fairest woman in the world as my beloved. Moreover, as it pleases the good duke your father to make me your husband, you should be content, for I will serve you and remain loyal and true to you all the days of my life. Thus I beseech you, my most dear and beloved lady, to kiss and embrace me now as an ardent token of affection. Please don't reject this loving request, I pray you, for since we will soon be joined together, you must not refuse to do my will."

"Sir knight," answered the well-mannered lady, "you should refrain from asking for such things, for you are wasting your time. I have good and honorable affection for all knights and men of noble rank. But I love one above all others,

---

[1] Possible reference to Song of Songs 2:2.

ung et celuy veul aymer et a luy tenir foy et loyaulté, ainsi que je luy ay juré; ne jamais pour nul aultre je ne le doy changer ne oublier."

"Belle," ce dist Orson, "quant il plaist a vostre pere c'est bien rayson et droit que la chose vous plaise."

"Sire," dist la pucelle, "c'est bien rayson que je doy a monseigneur mon pere obeïr. Mais s'il avient que a telle chose me contraigne et qu'i me veulle a aultre donner que a celluy qui conquist le Verd Chevalier plus tost de luy me departiroye sans riens emporter que de ma foy passer."

"Par Dieu, dame," ce dist Orson, "je suis moult esmerveillé comment de celuy chevalier estes tant amoureuse. Car vous sçavez qu'il est de sauvaige nature et sy ne scet parler ne dire ung seul mot parquoy il vous puisse resjouÿr, ne sa voulenté dire."

"Sire," dist la dame, "vraye amour m'aprent a l'aymer naturellement, car on dist souvent que la chose qui plaist est a demy vendue. Pour tant, franc chevalier, a moy n'ayez plus d'esperance car jamais en ma vie celuy ne changeray a qui j'ay ma foy promise."

Moult fust joyeulx Orson du grant sens et de la sagesse de la belle Fezonne qui telle responce luy donna. Non pourtant il fist maniere que malcontent en estoit, et se partit de la chambre sans d'elle prendre congé. Et s'en ala vers le duc d'Acquitaine et luy a dist, "Franc duc, sachez que je viens de veoir vostre fille, mais elle m'a donné pour responce finalle que jamais jour de sa vie pour nul qui parler luy en sache aultre ne prendra pour mary que celuy qui le Verd Chevalier conquist."

"Chevalier," dist le duc, "de sa responce ne vous chaille, car en elle n'est pas de sa voulenté faire. Soyez ung petit attendant et ne vous ennuyez de riens, car au jour d'uy a ma fille plus avant je parleray."

"Grant mercys," dist Orson, "j'en suis a vous tenu."

Lors yssit Orson hors du palays et s'en ala au logis de son frere Valentin auquel il dist et compta la responce qui luy avoit esté faicte par la belle Fezonne.[1]

"Frere, vous avez bien ouvré et de tant vous doit bien souffire, car bien pouez cognoistre la grant leaulté et amour de quoy elle vous ayme. Mais je veul que nous alons ensemble, vous et moy, vers le palays, car tantost que le duc me verra je suis certain que moult bien serons receux."

"Frere," ce dist Orson, "vostre vouloir soit fait."

Lors s'abilla Valentin et se para richement, et Orson print le jaceran lequel il avoit vestu quant premier vint en Acquitaine, et alerent au palays; et avec eulx Pacolet qui en tou[65recto]tes[2] choses les suivoit. Ilz entrerent dedens la sale en laquelle estoit le duc parlant a sa fille devant plusieurs barons et nobles chevaliers.

"Fille," ce dist le duc, "dont vous vient celluy couraige que ma voulenté ne voulez acomplir et prendre en mariaige celuy vaillant chevalier que je vous veul donner en qui a tant de proesse et de renommee? Car par la vaillance de luy j'ay esté delivré et ma vie sauvee."

---

[1] Text has *Feyonne*.
[2] *i i* at bottom right corner of 65r.

and him will I love and with him will I keep faith as I swore to him; nor will I ever change or forget him for another."

"Fair one," said Orson, "when something pleases your father, it is only right and reasonable that it should please you as well."

"Sire," said the maiden, "it is true that I owe obedience to my lord father. But if it so happens that he tries to force me or wishes to give me to anyone other than to him who conquered the Green Knight, I would rather leave here penniless than break my faith."

"By God, my lady," said Orson, "I am amazed that you are so in love with this knight. For you know that he is of a wild nature and cannot speak or say one word to entertain you or tell you his will."

"Sire," said the lady, "true love teaches me to love him naturally, for they often say that the thing that pleases is already half sold. For that reason, noble knight, do not hope to win me, for never in my life will I change the one to whom I have pledged my troth for another."

Orson was delighted with the great good sense and wisdom of the fair Fezonne in answering him so. Nevertheless he pretended to be unhappy about it, leaving the room without saying goodbye. Then he went to the Duke of Aquitaine and said to him, "Noble duke, I have just seen your daughter, but she stated to me in no uncertain terms that never in her life under any circumstances will she have as husband anyone other than he who conquered the Green Knight."

"Sir knight," said the duke, "don't worry about her answer, for it is not for her to decide. Wait a little while and don't let this bother you, for I will speak again to my daughter."

"Many thanks," said Orson, "I am beholden to you."

Then Orson left the palace and went to his brother Valentin's lodgings, to whom he recounted the answer made him by the fair Fezonne.

"You have done well, brother, and this should suffice for you, for now you can see with what great loyalty and devotion she loves you. But I would like us to go together, you and I, to the palace, for as soon as the duke sees me, I am certain that we will be well received."

"Brother," said Orson, "we shall do as you say."

So Valentin dressed himself in his richest clothes while Orson put on the coat of mail he had worn when he first came to Aquitaine, and together they went to the palace. Pacolet, who followed them everywhere, went with them. They entered the hall where the duke was talking to his daughter in the presence of several barons and noble knights.

"Daughter," said the duke, "where does this obstinacy come from, that you refuse to fulfill my wish for you to marry this valiant knight of such prowess and renown? It was by his valor that I was delivered and my life saved."

"Helas! pere," dist la pucelle, "pourquoy m'en parlez vous? Car vous sçavez bien que j'ay baillé ma foy a celuy qui vous delivra de la main du Verd Chevalier. Or n'est il plus vaillant reproche a creature vivant que de rompre sa foy et briser ou faulcer son serment? Et s'il avient que par vous a telle chose je soy constrainte vous serez cause de mettre mon ame en danger qui vous sera reproche devant Dieu et devant le monde."

Et ainsi que le duc d'Acquitaine parloit a sa fille, il veit arriver Valentin et Orson lesquelz en grant humilité comme chevaliers courtois les recheut, et de grant joye les acolla et embraça. Et quant Orson eust le duc salué il ala devers la belle Fezonne qui de grant joye se print a soubzrire.

"Helas," dist elle, "amy, bien soyez vous venu, car vostre demouree m'a esté trop ennuyeuse, et se vous ne fussiez venu, mon pere me vouloit donner et marier a ung aultre chevalier que vous, qui pour moy avoir a prins moult grant peine. Et moult fort bien vous resembloit de nez et de bouche."

"M'amye," dist Orson, "j'en sçay la verité. Sachez que depuis que ne vous veis, j'ay aprins a parler, et suis celuy qui au jour d'uy en vostre chambre d'amours je vous ay prié." Lors fust la dame tant joyeuse que racompter ne le vous sçauroye. Et Orson est entré en une chambre qui cestuy habit changa et print robes et vestemens moult precieux qu'il avoit fait aporter par le petit Pacolet, puis entra en la sale. Et quant le duc le recogneust, il l'ala embracer doulcement et luy a dist, "Beaulx filz, veuillez moy pardonner de ce que je cudoiye donner ma fille a ung aultre que a vous, car bien pensoye que vous ne deussiez jamais retourner."

"Sire," dist Orson, "de bon cueur le vous pardonne."

Lors leur demanda le duc comment ilz s'estoyent portéz depuis leur departement. Et Orson a prins la parole et a compté devant tous les fortunes et aventures auxquelles ilz ont esté, et comment ilz sont filz a l'empereur de Grece, nommé Alexandre, et a la seur du roy Pepin, la belle Bellissant, laquelle ilz ont trouvee en Portingal. Quant le bon duc d'Acquitaine entendit que les deux vaillans et preux chevaliers estoient de si haulte maison extrait et de si noble generation venus, il eust au cueur telle joye que compter ne le vous sçauroye ne dire.

Lors a dist, "Chevaliers, moult estes fort dignes d'avoir moult grant honneur et grande renommee quant de tous les crestiens vous estes les plus nobles ex[65verso]trais et descendus. Mais d'une chose suis dolent et desplaisant — c'est de vostre pere l'empereur de Grece et de vostre oncle le roy Pepin qui sont dedens Constantinoble par payens et Sarrasins assiegés. Si a tant duré leur guerre que se Dieu de brief ne leur donne secours, par famine leur convient aux ennemys rendre, qui est chose moult piteuse."

Quant Valentin oÿt que son pere et son oncle estoient en tel danger il mena si grant dueil et si grant desconfort que nul de la maison ne le peult rapaiser. Et sur toutes choses plaingnoit le roy Pepin lequel l'avoit nourry plus fort que l'empereur. Lors Pacolet luy a dist, "Sire, laissés ce dueil, car se croire me voulez, devant qu'il soit demain vespre je vous metteray dedens la cité de Constantinoble."

"Alas! Father," said the maiden, "why do you speak to me about him? For you know well that I pledged my troth to the one who delivered you from the hands of the Green Knight. Now is there no greater reproach to any living creature than to break one's faith or betray one's oath? And if you end up forcing me to do this thing, you will be the cause of placing my soul in danger, which will be a reproach to you before God and before the world."

Just as the Duke of Aquitaine was speaking to his daughter, he saw Valentin and Orson, whom he received with great respect as courtly knights, embracing them with much joy. Once Orson had greeted the duke, he went over to the fair Fezonne who laughed with delight.

"Well, my love," she said, "you are most heartily welcome, for your long absence has been very hard on me, and if you had not come, my father would have given me and married me to another knight, who had taken great pains to possess me. Moreover, he rather resembled you in the nose and the mouth."

"My love," said Orson, "I know all about it. I must tell you that since I last saw you, I have learned to speak, and I am the one who beseeched you for your love today in your chamber." Then the lady was more delighted than I am able to recount to you. Orson retired to a chamber to change his clothes, putting on costly garments that little Pacolet had brought along, then reentered the hall. When the duke recognized him, he went over to embrace him gently, saying to him, "Fair son, please pardon me for having thought to give my daughter to someone other than you, but I really thought you would never return."

"Sire," said Orson, "I forgive you with all my heart."

Then the duke asked them how they had been since their departure. Orson spoke up, recounting to the company all the adventures that had befallen them, and how they were the sons of the emperor of Greece, named Alexander, and the sister of King Pepin, the beautiful Bellissant, whom they had found in Portugal. When the good Duke of Aquitaine heard that the two valiant and doughty knights were of such high and noble rank, he was thrilled beyond what I could ever describe.

Then he said, "Sir knights, you are both highly worthy of great honor and renown, since of all Christians you are of the noblest descent possible. But one thing saddens me, and that is the fact that your father the emperor of Greece and your uncle King Pepin are currently under siege by pagans and Saracens in Constantinople. Their war has gone on for so long that if God does not aid them soon, they will have to capitulate to their enemies from famine, which would be a terrible pity."

When Valentin heard that his father and uncle were in such dire straits, he was so grieved and upset that no one there could calm him. He was more particularly anxious about King Pepin, who had raised him, than about the emperor. Then Pacolet said to him, "Sire, leave off this grief, for, if you are willing to believe me, I can get you into the city of Constantinople before vespers tomorrow."

"Par Dieu," dist Valentin, "il est fol qui te croit ou il fauldroit que le dyable t'y portast."

"Sire," dist Pacolet, "se vous voulez monter dessus mon chevalet et faire ce que je vous diray, nous serons arrivéz en Grece demain devant jour failly."

"Pacolet," dist le chevalier Valentin, "a ces motz je me acorde, car de nulle aultre chose mon cueur ne desire tant que de veoir mon pere lequel je ne veis oncques."

A celle heure fust le chevalier Valentin disposé et deliberé de partir le lendemain au matin pour aler en Constantinoble, et pour l'amour de sa departie le duc d'Acquitaine fist premier espouser Orson a sa fille Fezonne. Et fist faire les nopces qui tant richement furent servies que le racompter seroit chose moult longue. Tant y eult de menestriez, de clarons, et de trommpettes que du bruit que ilz menoyent les Sarrasins l'oÿrent qui en leur ost estoient dont moult furent doulens et desplaisans. Le duc d'Acquitaine fist en moult grant honneur amener au palais les deux dames[1] Bellissant et Esclarmonde.

Lors y eust une espie qui veit l'assemblee et ala devers le geant Ferragu et luy a dist, "Sire, je viens de la cité d'Acquitaine ou j'ay veu la royne Bellissant, femme a l'empereur de Grece,[2] laquelle vous avez gardee, et vostre seur la belle Esclarmonde et les deux chevaliers qui de voz prisons sont saillis et le petit Pacolet lequel vous a mauvaisement trahy."

"Par Mahon," dist le geant Ferragu, "je doy bien estre dolent et desplaisant du trahystre garnement Pacolet qui ainsi m'a voulu faulcement et mauvaisement decepvoir et ma seur Esclarmonde[3] laquelle tant j'aymoye avec les crestiens emmener. Mais je jure mon dieu Mahon que bien brief je prenderay de luy et de tous ses aultres complices et ses adherens bonne vengance, car je les feray tous pendre et estrangler."

---

[1] Text has *amener les au palais deux dames*.
[2] Text has *geece*.
[3] Text has *eslcarmonde*.

"By God," said Valentin, "it is mad to believe you, or else it would have to be the devil carrying you there."

"Sire," said Pacolet, "if you are willing to get on my magic horse and do as I say, we will be in Greece before tomorrow nightfall."

"All right, Pacolet," said the knight Valentin, "I agree, for there is nothing my heart desires more than to see the father I have never seen."

At that moment the knight Valentin made the decision to leave the next morning to go to Constantinople, and, because of his departure, the Duke of Aquitaine arranged to have Orson wed his daughter Fezonne right away. The wedding was so elaborate that it would take too long to recount it. There were so many musicians, clarions, and trumpets that the noise they made was heard by the Saracens who were gathered in their camp, dejected and dispirited. The Duke of Aquitaine had the two ladies Bellissant and Esclarmonde brought to the palace with great honor.

At that time there was a spy who saw the whole assembly and returned to the giant Ferragu and told him, "Sire, I come from the city of Aquitaine where I saw Queen Bellissant, wife of the emperor of Greece, the one you were guarding, as well as your sister Esclarmonde, the two knights who escaped your prison, and little Pacolet who has betrayed you most foully."

"By Mohammed," said the giant Ferragu, "I have every reason to be aggrieved and angry at that miserable traitor Pacolet who has so falsely deceived me and led away my sister Esclarmonde, whom I love so, along with the Christians. But I swear to my god Mohammed that before long I will avenge myself on him and all his accomplices and helpers, for I will hang them all by the neck."

[CHAPITRE 28]

Comment le geant Ferragu pour avoir secours manda le Roy Trompart[1] et l'enchanteur Adramain; et comment Valentin partit d'Acquitaine pour aler en Constantinoble. xxviii. [chapitre]

[66recto]Ferragu[2] le faulx Sarrasin fust moult courroucé et plain d'ire quant il veit que de sa seur et des chevaliers il ne peult prendre vengance. Lors appella ung herault et print une lettre escripte que il avoit fait faire par laquelle il mandoit au roy Trompart que incontinent ces lettres veues il voulsist venir par devers luy en puissance et en armes tout au mieulx qu'il pourroit. Et s'il estoit ainsi que secours luy voulsist faire, il luy donneroit pour femme sa seur Esclarmonde, et avec ce il luy manda qu'il amenast l'enchanteur Adramain que de l'art de Toullette tant bien avoit aprins que de jouer d'ingromance estoit maistre passé. Ainsi furent les lettres faictes et baillees au messaiger lequel est mis au chemin pour faire son messaige.

Sy laisseray a parler de Ferragu et parleray de Valentin qui est dedens[3] Acquitaine ou il prent congé aux seigneurs et aux dames et a la belle Esclarmonde, laquelle de son partir estoit moult desplaisante. Et luy demanda, "Amy, quant m'espouserez[4] vous? Tenez moy loyal convenant, car en vous est ma seule fiance."

"Belle," dist Valentin, "de moy ne vous doubtez, car loyal je vous seray. Et sy vous jure et prometz ma foy que tout au plus tost qui plaira a Dieu le tout puissant que je retourne de Constantinoble, sans nul sejour ne alongnement je vous espouseray."

Lors a dit au duc d'Acquitaine et a son frere Orson, "Seigneurs, je vous laisseray m'amye Esclarmonde en garde comme a mes bons et principaulx amys, ou sur tous je me confie en vous suppliant que du plus tost que possible vous sera, vous luy fachez bailler et aministrer le sainct sacrement de baptesme. Et ne luy changez pas son nom pour aultre luy donner, car c'est ma voulenté que tel nom luy demeure."

"Valentin," dist le duc d'Acquitaine, "de elle n'ayez nul soussy, car tout et aussi chierement sera la belle Esclarmonde gardee que ma propre fille naturelle."

La endroit print congé Valentin du duc d'Acquitaine qui pour sa departie avoit le cueur piteux. Puis embraça la belle Esclarmonde et en prenant congé le[5] baisa doulcement, mais tant estoit la noble dame triste et douloureuse que parolle

---

[1] Text has *teompart*.
[2] *i ii* at bottom right corner of 66r.
[3] Text has *pedens*.
[4] Text has *mespouserz*.
[5] Another occurrence of *le* for *la*; see Chapter 8, p. 58, n. 1. Recurrence in next sentence.

CHAPTER 28

How the giant Ferragu sent for King Trompart and the magician Adramain for help; and how Valentin left Aquitaine to go to Constantinople.

Ferragu, the false Saracen, was furious and full of anger when he saw that he could not take vengeance on his sister and the two knights. So he called a herald and had a letter written in which he sent word to King Trompart to come to him with as large an armed force as he could muster as soon as he had seen the letter. Moreover, if he was willing to come to his aid, he, Ferragu, would give him his sister Esclarmonde to wed, and he was to bring with him the enchanter Adramain who was as well versed in the art of Toledo as he was a surpassing master in the magical arts. Thus was the letter composed and handed over to a messenger, who left right away to deliver it.

Now I shall leave off speaking of Ferragu and will speak instead of Valentin, who is still in Aquitaine where he is taking leave of the lords and ladies and the fair Esclarmonde, who is very upset at his going. She asked him, "My love, when will you marry me? Keep faith with me, for my only hope is in you."

"Fair one," said Valentin, "have no fear, for I will remain loyal to you. Moreover, I swear to you and pledge my troth that, as soon as it please God almighty that I return from Constantinople, I will wed you without any postponement or delay."

Then he said to the Duke of Aquitaine and to his brother Orson, "My lords, I leave my beloved Esclarmonde in your guard, for you are my dear and most important friends in whom I place the highest trust; and I beg you to have her administered the holy sacrament of baptism as soon as possible. But do not change her name for another, for I wish her to keep the name she has."

"Valentin," said the Duke of Aquitaine, "do not be anxious about her, for I will watch over the fair Esclarmonde as dearly as if she were my own natural daughter."

There Valentin took leave of the Duke of Aquitaine, whose heart was heavy at his departure. Then he embraced the fair Esclarmonde, gently kissing her goodbye, but so sad and afflicted was the noble lady that she couldn't utter a

ne luy peust dire. Valentin le layssa et se print a plourer. Et Orson print congé de luy qui moult doulcement luy dist, "Frere, je prie a Jesucrist qu'i vous veulle garder et conduire. Et entre les aultres choses je vous prie humblement que vous me recommandez a mon pere l'empereur de Grece et au roy Pepin, car si plaist a Dieu dedens brief temps je les yray veoir."

"Frere," dist Valentin, "je feray le messaige pour vous tout ainsi comme pour moy."

A ces motz se departirent les deux freres d'ensemble qui pour laisser l'ung l'autre avoient les cueurs dolens. Orson demoura au palays et Valentin retourna en son logis vers [66verso]sa mere Bellissant qui estoit pour son departement au cueur moult troublee. Et quant elle veit que prest il estoit de partir, elle l'embraça cuidant prendre congé de luy. Mais la vaillante dame le cueur eust si estraint qu'elle ne sceut ung seul mot dire a son filz. Valentin la tint entre ses bras en la resconfortant moult doulcement, car combien que il fust moult dolent, non pourtant il portoit sa tristesse le plus que il pouoit pour sa mere resconforter et resjouÿr, a laquelle il a dist en parolles doulces et amiables, "Mere, n'ayez pour moy ne douleur ne soussy, car s'il plaist a Jesucrist mon createur de brief me reverrez. Pensés et ayez tousjours vostre cueur en Dieu et priez pour moy, car en tous mes bienfais de vous il me souviendra. Et sur ce tout je vous recommande tant comme je puis la belle Esclarmonde laquelle en moy du tout se confie et loyaulté me veult garder."

"Helas, mon filz," dist la royne Bellissant, "je doy bien en mon cueur souspirer et porter douleur angoisseuse, car par toy et par ta vaillantise et hardiesse tu as tant fait que le jour viendra au vouloir de Jesus que de mon occasion et vitupere je seray trouvé innocente et pure. Et quant tu seras dedens la belle et noble cité de Constantinoble, salue de par moy ton pere, l'empereur Alexandre, et ton oncle le vaillant roy Pepin, mon frere, et leur dy de par moy que je prens sur la dampnation de mon ame que jamais a nul jour de ma vie du grant blasme et vitupere dont j'ay esté accusee coulpable je ne fus oncques. Et se a ce nul tant soit vaillant ou hardy veult entreprendre champ de bataille ou dire du contraire, combatez vous pour moy et prenez la querelle. Car se vaincu vous estes, je veul offrir mon corps a estre arse et brulee vituperablement et honteusement par devant tout le monde."

"Mere," dist le noble chevalier Valentin, "ne vous desconfortez point, car s'il plaist a Dieu le tout puissant et a la Vierge Marie en qui j'ay toute ma fiance, je feray tant pour vous que de brief vous serez renduee[1] et acordee a l'empereur Alexandre, mon pere, et que du tort que il vous a fait pardon et mercy il vous demandera et requerra."

A ces parolles partirent d'ensemble et menerent grant dueil et grans pleurs. Et au departir la dame requist au chevalier Valentin son filz que tout le plus tost qu'i pourroit qu'i luy renvoyast Pacolet pour sçavoir des nouvelles. Valentin luy

---

[1] The typesetter has a penchant for this double marking of the feminine gender. See *venuee* below.

word. Valentin left her and began to weep. When Orson took leave of him, he said to him with deep-felt emotion, "Brother, I pray to Jesus Christ that He keep and guide you. And more than any other thing I humbly beseech you to commend me to my father the emperor of Greece and to King Pepin, for if it please God, I will go see them before too long."

"Brother," said Valentin, "I will speak for you as I would speak for myself."

With these words the two brothers parted, heavy-hearted at this separation from each other. Orson remained in the palace, while Valentin returned to his lodging to find his mother Bellissant, whose heart was sorrowful at his departure. When she saw he was ready to leave, she embraced him, planning to say goodbye. But the valiant lady felt such a vise around her heart that she couldn't say a word to her son. Valentin held her in his arms, comforting her gently, for however dejected he was, he nevertheless hid his sorrow the best he could in order to comfort and cheer his mother, to whom he addressed these sweet and loving words: "Mother, don't be sad or anxious on my account, for if it please Jesus Christ my creator, you will soon see me again. Keep your heart and mind on God and pray for me, for in all my best deeds, I will think of you. And above all else, I entrust to you the fair Esclarmonde who has placed her trust in me and keeps faith with me."

"Alas, my son," said Queen Bellissant, "I have no choice but to sigh from the depths of my heart and bear this pain, for through you and your valor and boldness you have done so much that the day will come, should Jesus will it, that I will be found innocent and pure of the case of my blame. When you arrive in the lovely and noble city of Constantinople, greet your father, the emperor Alexander, for me, and your valiant uncle King Pepin, my brother, and tell them for me that I swear on the damnation of my soul that never any day of my life did I do any of the blameful and shameful acts of which I was declared guilty. And if anyone, however valiant or bold, wishes to undertake a challenge on the field of battle to prove the contrary, take up the quarrel and fight for me. For if you are vanquished, I am willing to offer my body publically and shamefully to be burned."

"Mother," said the noble knight Valentin, "do not upset yourself, for if it please God almighty and the Virgin Mary, in whom I place all my trust, I will defend you so well that soon you will return and be reconciled to the emperor Alexander, my father, who will beg your pardon and implore your forgiveness for the wrong he did you."

With these words they separated, all the while grieving and weeping. As he was leaving, the lady asked the knight Valentin her son to send back Pacolet to her as soon as he could so that she could have tidings of him. Valentin promised

promist que ainsi le feroit il. Puis entra en la chambre ou il trouva le petit Pacolet, lequel en l'attendant il avoit son cheval de bois appareillé.

"Or sus!" dist Pacolet, "il est temps de cheminer. Montez derriere moy et sans avoir paour ne crainte. Tenez moy fermement."

"Amy," dist le chevalier Valentin, "cela feray je bien."

Lors monterent sur le cheval et Pacolet tourna la cheville si bien et si a point que le cheval [67recto]parmy[1] l'air se leva. Et en celle nuyt tant fist et despecha de chemin qu'il passa oultre la mer et par dessus plusieurs bois, roches, villes et chasteaulx et grandes citéz. Et si bien ilz cheminerent que le lendemain devant midy ilz apperceurent Constantinoble. Il demanda a Pacolet quelle place c'estoit et il luy respondit que c'estoit la cité de Constantinoble "en laquelle vous avez si grant desir de arriver." Moult fust joyeulx le noble et vaillant chevalier Valentin quant il se vit si pres, car tant bien l'avoit conduit Pacolet que devant l'eure de vespres fut en la cité, et a l'eure que l'empereur et le roy Pepin estoient vers la sale imperialle assis pour souper. Pacolet qui Valentin amena se trouva dedens la sale dont Valentin fust moult esmerveillé quant il se veit devant telle compaignie.

Lors Blandimain et le Verd Chevalier qui en la sale estoyent cogneurent Valentin et moult grant feste luy firent. Et le roy Pepin qui Valentin avisa en souspirant dist a l'empereur, "Sire, ancores n'est pas failly vostre lignaige, car vous pouez icy veoir ung moult vaillant chevalier lequel est vostre propre filz."

Quant l'empereur oÿt ces parolles toute la couleur luy mua et perdit maniere et contenance. Il se leva de la table pour son filz venir baiser et embracer. Mais le Verd Chevalier tant fust joyeulx de la venue de Valentin que ce fust celuy qui premier le toucha ne acolla. Apres vint le roy Pepin son oncle qui l'enfant Valentin acolla, et puis fust l'empereur son pere qui de grant pitié, moitié de joie et moytyé de tristesse pour sa venue resjouÿ et pour la souvenance de sa femme piteulx et desconforté, son enfant print entre ses bras et moult doulcement le baisa. Et le vaillant Blandimain a la barbe flourie congneut le petit Pacolet, car il l'avoit veu en Portingal. Il vint par devers luy et luy demanda des nouvelles de la bonne dame Bellissant et luy compta la maniere comment tout avoit esté fait, et comment en plusieurs perilz et dangiers Valentin avoit eu de l'empereur et de sa mere cognoissance.

Grant joye et grant feste fust parmy tout le pays pour la venuee[2] du noble chevalier Valentin, le filz de l'empereur Alexandre. Chevaliers et barons de toutes pars arriverent pour veoir Valentin et luy faire reverence. Et ainsi que dedens la sale de l'empereur furent arrivéz plusieurs grans seigneurs, barons et chevaliers, Valentin, qui de grant hardiesse fut plain, parla en ceste maniere devant toute la compaignie:

"Seigneurs et chevaliers que icy estes presens, de l'onneur et de la reverence qu'i vous plaist a moy faire, je vous rens grace, et de ma puissance je vous remercye. Et dessus tous les aultres je remercye mon oncle le roy Pepin lequel jusques a ceste heure m'a nourry et mis sus, car plus suis tenu a luy et seray toute ma vie

---

[1] *i iii* at bottom right corner of 67r.

[2] Double marking of the feminine as noted previously with *renduee*.

her that he would. Then he entered the room where he found little Pacolet waiting for him with his wooden horse at the ready.

"Come now!" said Pacolet, "it is time to go. Get on behind me and don't be afraid. Hold on to me tight."

"Friend," said the knight Valentin, "I will do so."

So they got onto the horse and Pacolet turned the pin so well and so correctly that the horse rose into the air. That night they traveled so quickly that they crossed the sea and passed over woods, rocks, towns, castles, and great cities. So fast did they go that by noon the next day they saw Constantinople. He asked Pacolet where they were, and the latter responded that it was the city of Constantinople "which you so desire to reach." The noble and valiant knight Valentin was delighted when he saw himself so close, for so quickly did Pacolet bring him there that before the hour of vespers he was in the city, at the hour when the emperor and King Pepin were in the imperial hall seated for supper. Pacolet led Valentin into the hall, where Valentin felt rather overwhelmed, seeing himself before such a company.

At that moment Blandimain and the Green Knight, who were in the hall, recognized Valentin and greeted him joyfully. Then King Pepin, who caught sight of Valentin, said to the emperor with a sigh, "Sire, your lineage has not yet failed, for here you see a most valiant knight who is your very own son."

When the emperor heard these words, he went pale and lost his composure. He rose from the table to go kiss and embrace his son. But the Green Knight was so delighted to see Valentin that he was the first to reach him and hug him. After that was King Pepin his uncle who hugged the young man Valentin tightly, and then it was the emperor his father who took his child in his arms and kissed him gently, full of emotion, half joy, half sorrow, for he was delighted at his coming but saddened at the memory of his wife. Then the valiant Blandimain, now white-bearded, recognized little Pacolet, for he had seen him in Portugal. He went up to him and asked him news of the good lady Bellissant, and Pacolet recounted how everything had occurred, and how Valentin had passed through many perils and dangers to find out about the emperor and his mother.

There were great joy and festivities throughout the country for the coming of the noble knight Valentin, son of the emperor Alexander. Knights and barons gathered from all sides to see Valentin and pay their respects. But just as several great lords, barons, and knights were assembled in the emperor's hall, Valentin, who was full of daring, spoke in the following manner before the entire company:

"My lords and knights here present, for the honor and respect you are pleased to show me, I thank you and express my deepest appreciation. But, more than any other, I thank my uncle King Pepin, who, up to this very hour, has raised and brought me up; thus I am and will be beholden to him all my life long more

que a nul [67verso]homme qui soit sur la terre. Nonobstant que souvent on dit que jamais on ne peut estre tant subject ne tenu comme a pere et a mere, mais sauf l'onneur de mon pere qui cy est present, je doy par rayson estre et me nomme de mon pere bien orphenin, et de tout bien d'aultrui par charité et aumoisnes nourry et eslevé. Et sont des biens et des graces mon oncle le roy Pepin qui comme son enfant, sans de moy avoir cognoissance, la de clarté remply et de grace divine inspiré, m'a doulcement nourry. Et se celuy n'eust esté, je devoye bien par droit et par rayson piteusement et douloureusement mourir sans jamais avoir cognoissance de nul de mes parens et amis, et sans recepvoir le saint sacrement de baptesme le jour que de ma mere je nasqui dessus la terre. Car de mon pere avoir confort ne ayde estoit chose moult fort difficille, quant par ung seul faulx et mauvais raport avoit a moult grant honte et vitupere villainement deboutee, deschassee et bannye celle qui en ses flans doulcement neuf moys me porta — c'est ma mere la royne Bellissant, qui par le faulx, mauldit et desloyal archevesque a esté faulcement et mauvaisement trahye et deceue, tant que la douloureuse fortune par l'espace de vint ans en pleurs douloureux et gemissemens angoisseulx a esté constrainte de user et passer piteusement ses jours. Pour monstrer que elle est du fait innocente et de loyaulté plaine, moy, comme son filz naturel et legitimement engendré, veul contre le faulx et mauldit archevesque que faulcement et decepuablement l'a accusee en champ de bataille mon corps offrir jusques a la mort, et aussi contre tous aultres qui pour ma mere accuser se vouldroyent presenter en quelconques maniere."

Quant l'empereur Alexandre oÿt son filz le chevalier Valentin qui de si grant couraige pour la grant honte et la grant deshonneur de sa douloureuse mere se vouloit combatre, il se print piteusement[1] a plourer, et en parolles piteuses a dist doulcement a son filz Valentin, "Helas, mon chier filz et enfant, je sçay et cognoy clerement que tu es[2] mon filz legitime et que a bon droit tu te veulz pour ta mere combatre, laquelle par ung faulx et mauvais raport et legiere creance j'ay mise et envoyee en exil. Mais de champ de bataille pour son fait prendre ou attendre il n'en est nul besoing, car le faulx et mauldit archevesque qui l'avoit accusee a esté combatu et honteusement vaincu et mis a mort vituperablement par ung vaillant marchant. Lequel en la presence du roy Pepin ton oncle et de moy et devant toute l'assistence de plusieurs princes, barons et chevaliers, devant sa mort a dist et confessé comment a tort et a mauvaise cause par envye et diabolicque temptation il avoit la bonne dame devers moy accusee. Et quant j'entendis sa confes[68recto]sion[3] je fus au cueur si amerement navré que de ma doleur trop forte chose seroit[4] a racompter. Et depuis celuy temps j'ay envoyé plusieurs messagiers en diverses contrees et regions en esperant avoir de ma femme aulcunes certaines nouvelles.

---

[1] Text has *piseusement*.
[2] Text has *et es*.
[3] *i iiii* at bottom right corner of 68r.
[4] Text has *seroir*.

than to any man on earth. In spite of the frequent saying that one is never more beholden than to one's father and mother, nevertheless, with all due respect to my father here present, I must by reason call myself a fatherless orphan, since I was raised and brought up by another's benevolence and alms. For it is my uncle King Pepin, through kindness and generosity, filled with light and inspired by divine grace, who raised me tenderly like his own child, without knowing anything about me. Had it not been for him, by right and by reason, I would have died pitifully and sorrowfully the day my mother brought me into the world, without ever knowing anything of my relatives and friends, and without receiving the blessed sacrament of baptism. For to have aid or comfort from my father was impossible, since, based solely on a false and evil report, he had shamefully and dishonorably cast out, exiled, and banished the one who carried me gently in her loins for nine months — that is, my mother Queen Bellissant, who was falsely and deliberately betrayed and deceived by the false, cursed, and faithless archbishop, so that for twenty long years it has been her unhappy fate to live out her days piteously in wretched tears and anguished moans. In order to demonstrate that she is innocent of this charge and full of loyalty, I wish, as her natural son legitimately engendered, to offer myself to fight to the death this perfidious and cursed archbishop who has accused her falsely and deceitfully, as well as any others who would wish to present themselves to accuse my mother in any manner whatsoever."

When the emperor Alexander heard his son, the knight Valentin, propose so courageously to fight because of the terrible shame and dishonor cast on his unhappy mother, he began to weep piteously, and said gently to his son with heart-felt words, "Alas, my dear son and child, I do know absolutely that you are my legitimate son, and that you have every reason in the world to want to fight for your mother, whom I did indeed exile based on a false and evil report and my too gullible belief in it. But there is no need for you to defend her on the field of battle, for the false and cursed archbishop who had accused her was fought, vanquished shamefully, and put to a dishonorable death by a valiant merchant. Before he died the archbishop spoke up in the presence of your uncle King Pepin and myself, and before an audience of several princes, barons, and knights, confessing how he had wrongly and unjustly denounced the good lady to me. When I heard his confession, I was so bitterly wounded in the heart that my pain would be too difficult to describe. Since that time I have sent multiple messengers to many different countries and regions, hoping to have some tidings of my wife.

Mais je n'ay tant sceu faire que de elle j'aye peu avoir aulcune cognoissance. Et pour tant mon filz et ma seule esperance, se tu sçavoyez riens de ta mere ne le me veullez point celer, car sur tous mes desirs j'ay voulenté singuliere de sçavoir des nouvelles."

"Sire," dist Valentin, "pour parler de ma mere sachez pour tout certain que arssoir vers la minuyt je la veis et parlay a elle dedens la cité d'Acquitaine."

"Beau filz," dist l'empereur, "comment est il possible que dedens si peu de temps ayez tant de chemin fait?"

Adonc luy compta Valentin comment Pacolet par sa science et art subtil l'avoit en si peu de temps amené, de laquelle chose l'empereur son pere fut moult fort esmerveillé de la venue de Valentin. Fust parmy la cité de Constantinoble grant joye demenee et tant en fut l'empereur Alexandre resjouy que il commanda a sonner toutes les cloches parmy la cité. Et quant les Sarrasins et payens oÿrent la grant joye que ceulx de la cité faisoient, ilz coururent aux armes et en grant diligence furent arméz et en point mis. Et quant ilz furent tous pres et arméz, le souldan Moradin, acompaignié de trente roys fors et puissans, fist assaillir la cité de Constantinoble, laquelle estoit sy fort plaine de peuple que mors estoient les chevaulx de fain. Et aussi plusieurs hommes et femmes et petis enfans de jour en jour par faulte de naturelle substentation parmy les rues mouroyent et deffinoient piteusement leur jours.

Et quant Valentin avisa et cogneut la grant multitude de payens et Sarrasins et la necessité et indigence de la cité de Constantinoble, il parla devant tous les seigneurs et les capitaines disant en ceste maniere, "Seigneurs et chevaliers, vous sçavez et cognoissez que dedens ceste cité vous estes en grant necessité de vivrez, et si n'en pouez recouvrer ne estre furny sinon par vostre vaillance les alez conquerir sur voz ennemys. Sy seroye d'oppinion que on fist saillir certain nombre de gens d'armes pour conquerir des vivres, et moy tout le premier suis pres et appareillé de conduire de tout mon petit pouoir au mieulx que ma puissance se pourra estendre tous ceulx qui de la cité vouldront sayllyr avec moy."

A celuy conseil furent consentans tous les capitaines et gouverneulx de toute l'armee. Et saillirent hors de la cité avec le chevalier Valentin vint mil combatans, et sy y a grant multitude de menu peuple qui pour l'indigence et la grant necessité ou ilz estoient voulentiers les suivyrent. Et quant ilz furent dehors les portes coururent sur les Sarrasins [68verso]et payens[1] si fierement et si vaillamment que en peu d'heure et en peu de temps gaignerent et leverent troys cens charios de vivres. Mais ainsi que ilz les amenoient devers la cité de Constantinoble, le souldan, qui de ceste perte fust douloureux, avec fort grant multitude de payens et Sarrasins, a grant puissance d'armes, entre les crestiens et la cité pour les vivres recouvrer et oster, s'en vint mettre en bataille. Et quant le roy Pepin veit que ilz luy avoient sarré le passage, il frappa des esperons et mist la lance en l'arrest et si

---

[1] Text has *Sarrasins et Sarrasins*, a mistaken (I believe) departure from the usual formula of "payens et Sarrasins," owing, most probably, to the page break.

But I have never been able to find out anything about her. For that reason, my son and only hope, if you know anything about your mother, please don't hide it from me, for, more than anything else, I desire to have news of her."

"Sire," said Valentin, "as regards my mother, know that last night towards midnight I saw and spoke to her in the city of Aquitaine."

"Fair son," said the emperor, "how is it possible that you traveled so far so fast?"

Thereupon Valentin recounted to him how Pacolet had brought him in so little time through his skill and magic arts, a way of traveling that thoroughly impressed the emperor his father. Great joy spread throughout the city of Constantinople, and the emperor Alexander was so delighted that he ordered all the bells to be rung throughout the city. But when the pagan Saracens heard the great joy of those in the city, they ran to their weapons and quickly armed and prepared themselves. Once they were ready, Sultan Moradin, accompanied by thirty strong and powerful kings, attacked the city of Constantinople, which was already so full of people that horses were dying of hunger. Moreover, many men, women, and little children were dying every day in the streets, ending their days most pitifully for lack of normal sustenance.

When Valentin saw the great multitude of pagans and Saracens, and realized the want and indigence of the city of Constantinople, he spoke before all the lords and captains, saying, "My lords and knights, you are fully aware that you are in great need of provisions in this city and that you cannot get them or be supplied if you do not go conquer them from your enemies through your own valor. I believe a certain number of armed men should issue forth to seize provisions, and I am ready to lead them to the best of my ability with whatever strength I have, if it can be joined to that of those from the city willing to sally forth with me."

All the captains and leaders of the army agreed with this advice. So twenty thousand fighters issued forth from the city with the knight Valentin, along with a multitude of townspeople who followed them willingly, so starved were they. Once outside the gates, they fell upon the pagan Saracens so ferociously and so valiantly that in a short space of time they took possession of and carried away three hundred cartloads of food. But just as they were approaching the city of Constantinople, the sultan, who was distressed at this loss, threw himself into the battle with a great multitude of pagans and Saracens, coming between the Christians and the city in order to recover the victuals and wrest them back by armed force. When King Pepin saw that they had blocked the passage, he spurred his horse and lowered his lance into position, attacking so valiantly that

vaillamment a fait que devant le souldan il abatit mort par terre le fier et orgueilleux Maragon, lequel de Capharnaon estoit roy. Puis a trayte l'espee et en ferit Arcillon, qui moult estoit fort et puissant payen, tellement que de l'arson de la selle il le getta a terre.

Et quant Valentin et le Verd Chevalier veirent les armes et vaillances que le roy Pepin faisoit, ilz entrerent en la bataille et sans laisser l'ung l'autre ont tant fait a force d'armes que devant le souldan ont abatu et rué par terre l'esta[n]dart des payens et mauldis Sarrasins. Quant l'estandart fust bas Valentin passa oultre contre le maldit souldan et si grant coup de lance luy donna que de dessus l'olifant ou il estoit monté a terre le getta et abatit. A celle heure tant furent de vaillances faictes par Valentin et le Verd Chevalier que Moraldos fut mort et l'admiral prins par le Verd Chevalier. Et Valentin malgré tous les payens et Sarrasins a getté et abatu a terre quatre roys sarrasins et si a osté les deux bras a l'admiral d'Ombrie. Mais les deux bons chevaliers celuy jour de conquerir proesse furent trop ardans, et trop avant entrerent dedens l'ost des payens, car quant ilz cuiderent retourner ilz furent enclos et prins des Sarrasins si fort et si estroitement que leurs corps furent menéz ainsy comme prisonniers, moult durement lyéz, devant le souldan, lequel ausytost que il les veit il a juré son grant dieu que jamais vers les crestiens ilz ne retourneront, "mais feray faire ung gibet devant la cité de Constantinoble et si hault les feray pendre et estrangler que de tous leurs amys pourront estre veux." Valentin et le Verd Chevalier qui jamais n'ont esperance de leur vie sauver. . . .[1]

Et les crestiens sont retournéz dedens la cité malgré payens et Sarrasins, et emmenerent des vivres en si grande habondance et largesse que tout le peuple de la cité en fust repeu et resconforté. Mais premier que ilz arrivassent dedens la cité ilz eurent par les payens et Sarrasins piteuse rencontre et tant grande bataille que bien cuidoient les crestiens de jamais retourner dedens la cité de Constantinoble. Lors ceulx de la cité qui bien veirent la necessité de leur gens firent cryer parmy la ville sur peine de perdre la vie que tous hommes, prestres, clers, femmes et enfans, chanoines et [69recto]moysnes sy portent la croyx devant eulx en l'onneur et reverence de la passion de Nostre Seigneur Jesucrist pour saillir dehors sur les payens. Lors fut le nombre si grant du peuple qui saillit de la cité que l'estimacion montoit a xl.mil. Et quant les payens et Sarrasins veirent le grant nombre de gens qui de la cité Constantinoble a l'encontre d'eulx estoient saillys ilz se reculerent arriere en leur ost le plus tost que ilz peurent et laisserent aux crestiens les vivres emporter.

Mais devant que nul des payens et Sarrasins peussent en leurs tentes retourner la bataille fust si grande des deux pars que quatre mil crestiens y finerent leurs jours qui fut chose piteuse a ceulx de la cité, moult grifve et dommaigeuse. Moult fust dolent l'empereur de Grece de plusieurs barons et vaillans chevaliers qui en la bataille estoient demouréz. Mais sur tous les aultres en son cueur fust moult dolent et amerement desplaisant de son filz le vaillant chevalier Valentin et

---

[1] This appears to be a sentence fragment. Since it is impossible to imagine what completion was intended, I have translated it as if the relative pronoun *qui* were not there.

he killed the proud and arrogant Maragon, king of Capharnaon, right in front of the sultan. Then he drew his sword and struck Arcillon, a strong and powerful pagan, with such vigor that he knocked him from his saddle to the ground.

When Valentin and the Green Knight saw the valiant deeds King Pepin was doing, they entered the thick of the battle, and, without leaving each other's side, performed such feats of arms that right in front of the sultan they struck down to the ground the standard of the cursed pagans and Saracens. Once the standard was down, Valentin rode towards the cursed sultan, giving him such a blow with his lance that he knocked him off his elephant and onto the ground. Such great feats of arms were performed then by Valentin and the Green Knight that Moraldos was killed and the emir captured by the Green Knight. Then Valentin, despite all the pagans and Saracens, smote four Saracen kings and struck off the arms of the emir of Ombrie. But the two good knights were too ardent that day in their quest to excel, riding too far into the pagan host, for, when they tried to return, they found themselves so closely enclosed and overwhelmed by the Saracens that they were led as tightly bound prisoners before the sultan, who, as soon as he saw them, swore to his great god that they would never return to the Christians, "but rather I will have a gallows built before the city of Constantinople, and I will have you hanged by the neck at such a height that all your friends will be able to see you." Valentin and the Green Knight lost all hope of saving their lives.

The Christians returned to the city in spite of the Saracens, bringing back provisions in such abundance that all the townspeople were relieved of their hunger. But before they were able actually to enter the city, they had such a devastating battle with the pagans and Saracens that the Christians were afraid they would never get back into the city of Constantinople. Then those in the city, seeing how great was the need of their men, had it cried throughout the town that, on pain of losing their life, all men, priests, clerks, women and children, canons, and monks were to carry the cross before them in honor and reverence for the passion of Our Lord Jesus Christ and fall upon the pagans. So great a number of people burst out of the city that the estimate reached forty thousand. When the pagans and Saracens saw the great number of people from Constantinople coming to attack them, they withdrew with their forces as quickly as they could and allowed the Christians to carry off the victuals.

But before any of the pagans and Saracens were able to return to their tents, the battle raged so fiercely on both sides that four thousand Christians ended their days in it, which was a piteous and grievous thing for the townspeople. The emperor of Greece was doleful over the loss of several barons and valiant knights in the battle. But, above all, his heart, like that of King Pepin of France, was heavy and bitterly upset over the loss of his son, the valiant knight Valentin, and

du Verd Chevalier qui tant de proesses et vaillances avoyent faictes, et aussi fust le roy Pepin de France. Ces deux demenerent moult grant destresse en gettant grans cris et lamentacions pour l'enfant Valentin qui sy tost l'avoyent perdu.

Mais le petit Pacolet moult bien les conforta disant, "Seigneurs, laissez vostre plourer et desconfort, car de Valentin vous serez joyeulx et de luy aurez bonnes nouvelles plus tost que vous ne pensés."

"Amy," dist l'empereur, "Dieu t'en veulle oÿr et donner la puissance, car se tant peulx faire de l'amener devers moy et de l'oster des mains du souldan qui sa mort a juree, peulx seurement dire que dessus tous les aultres en honneur te metteray et esleveray."

"Sire," dist Pacolet, "attendez vous a moy, car de brief vous cognoisterrez de quelle amour je vous ayme et vostre filz Valentin."

Alors Pacolet print son cheval de bois et sans aultres parolles dire partit pour aler en l'ost des payens. Et le souldan estoit dedens son tref, lequel pour Valentin et le Verd Chevalier faire juger a mort avoit fait venir tous les plus grans de son ost. Mais de son entreprinse fust fait tout au contraire comme[1] icy apres vous le pourrez oÿr et declairer.

[CHAPITRE 29]

Comment l'enchanteur Pacolet delivra Valentin et le Verd[2] Chevalier de la prison au souldan Moradin, et comment il deceut ledit souldan Moradin. xxix. chapitre

Quant le souldan Moradin fust en son ost retrayt il fist venir devant son pavillon l'enfant Valentin et le Verd Chevalier en la presence de tous les plus grans barons et chevaliers[3] de sa court. Il a dist en ceste maniere, "Seigneurs, a ceste heure vous pouez bien veoir et cognoistre les deux du monde qui plus nous portent et [69verso]font[4] de grief dommaige et qui plus ont fait de desplaisir et de oultraige au vaillant roy Ferragu. Et entre les aultres choses cestuy Verd Chevalier a nostre loy laissee et s'est fait crestien pour plus nous porter de nuysance et exil dommaigeulx. Il me semble que bon seroit de les envoyer audit roy Ferragu, car bien sçay que il prenderoit de eulx vengance et qu'i les feroit mourir de mort mauvaise, honteuse et villaine tout et en telle maniere comme ilz l'ont bien deservy."

---

[1] Text has *commme*.
[2] Text has *vrrd*.
[3] Text has *chvaliers*.
[4] Woodcut of armed knights leaving walled encampment of tents.

the Green Knight, both of whom had performed such daring feats. The two of them grieved violently with much wailing and lamentation for the young man Valentin whom they had lost so soon.

But little Pacolet comforted them saying, "My lords, no need to weep and mourn, for you will have good tidings of Valentin and will delight in him sooner than you think."

"My friend," said the emperor, "my God hear you and give you strength, for if you can wrest him from the hands of the sultan who has sworn to kill him and bring him back to me, I can tell you that I will raise you up and honor you above all others."

"Sire," said Pacolet, "trust me, for soon you will see how much I love you and your son Valentin."

Then Pacolet took his wooden horse and, without saying anything else, left for the pagan camp. The sultan was in his tent, where he had gathered all the great lords of his army to condemn Valentin and the Green Knight to death. But his plans were completely overturned, as you will soon hear explained.

CHAPTER 29

How Pacolet delivered Valentin and the Green Knight from the prison of Sultan Moradin; and how he deceived the sultan.

Once Sultan Moradin had retreated into his camp, he had the youth Valentin and the Green Knight brought before his pavilion in the presence of all the greatest barons and knights of his court. He declared in the following manner: "My lords, now you can see and know the two men in this world who cause us the greatest damage, and who affronted and outraged valiant King Ferragu. Moreover, among other things, this Green Knight has deserted our faith and become a Christian in order to hurt and damage us all the more. It seems to me that the best thing to do is send them to King Ferragu, for I know he will take proper vengeance on them, making them die an evil, shameful, and villainous death, just as they deserve."

"Syre," dirent les payens et Sarrasins, qui de la mort des crestiens avoient grant envye, "il n'est ja mestier de tant sejourner, mais faictes sur les champs une fourche lever pour demain au plus matin faire pendre et estrangler les deux faulx et mauvais garnemens qui tant vous ont fait et porté de dommaige et d'encombrier."

"Seigneurs," dist le souldan Moradin, "vostre conseil est bel et bon et de tel je veul user, que par le dieu Mahon je vous jure et prometz que demain au plus matin si hault je les feray pendre et estrangler que tous ceulx de la cité de Constantinoble les pourront veoir et a leur mort prendre exemple."

Apres ces parolles dictes ainsi que le souldan entra dedens sa tente pour s'en aler soupper, le petit Pacolet se trouva devant luy, lequel de par Mahon le salua moult haultement. "Pacolet," dist le payen, "bien soyez tu arrivé. Or me dy legierement, comment se porte le fait du roy Ferragu qui dessus tous les aultres est mon parfait amy?"

"Sire," dist Pacolet, "il se porte tres bien et sur tous a vous se recommande. Et par moy vous envoye nouvelles qui sont moult secretes lesquelles je vous diray s'il vous plaist a les escouter."

"Amy," dist le souldan, "moult voulentiers et de bon cueur escouteray vostre messaige."

Lors le tira a part pour luy dire son secret. Et Pacolet luy a dist tout bas, "Sire, sachez que je viens de Portingal et suis icy transmis et envoyé de par ma redoubtee dame, la femme Ferragu, laquelle de tout son cueur a vous se recommande trop plus hardiment que dire ne le vous sçauroye. Et que il soit vray je le vous fay assavoir que dessus tous les hommes du monde elle est de vous tant et si fort amoureuse que pour avoir vostre[1] amour elle ne peult reposer ne dormir de nuyt ne de jour tant est fort esprinse de vostre amour. Or est il vray que celle laquelle du tout en [70recto]moy se confie m'a devers vous transmis et envoyé et vous mande sy expressement sur l'amour que peuent avoir deux loyaulx amans que sans sejourner ne differer vous le[2] venés veoir, car le roy Ferragu pour le present est devers Acquitaine. Si pourrez tout a vostre plaisir et voulenté de la plaisante dame, qui dessus toutes les aultres de beaulté reluyt, faire vostre plaisir et voulenté. Et pour tant, sire, venez vous en avec moy, car dessus mon chevallet je vous y conduyray sy bien et en telle maniere que demain au plus matin en Portingal devant la noble et belle dame je vous renderay."

"Ha, Pacolet," dist le souldan Moradin, "tu me donnes au cueur liesse et resconfort plus grant que nul aultre jamais me pourroit donner. Car sur toutes les femmes du monde je suis et ay longuement esté de la femme du roy Ferragu amoureulx. Mais tant il y a que jamais a nul jour je ne me puis vers elle trouver en maniere que je puisse ma voulenté acomplir ne dire mon secret. Mais ores endroit acomplyray le desir de mon cueur que tant et si longuement j'ay attendu.

---

[1] Text has *vossre*.
[2] Another occurrence of *le* for *la*; see Chapter 8, p. 58, n. 1.

"Sire," said the pagans and Saracens, who greatly desired the death of the Christians, "there is no need to wait so long; have a gibbet built so that tomorrow morning at dawn you can have these two false and evil miscreants, who have caused you so much trouble, hanged by the neck."

"My lords," said Sultan Moradin, "your counsel is fair and good and I will follow it; thus, by the god Mohammed, I swear and promise that early tomorrow morning I will have them hanged by the neck so high that everyone in the city of Constantinople will be able to see them and take their death as an example."

After this pronouncement, just as the sultan was entering his tent to eat supper, little Pacolet suddenly appeared before him, greeting him loudly in Mohammed's name. "Pacolet," said the pagan, "I am glad to see you. Now tell me quickly, how goes it with King Ferragu, who is, above all others, my true friend?"

"Sire," said Pacolet, "he is well and commends himself to you above all others. He sends you news most secret by way of me, which I will tell you if it please you to listen."

"My friend," said the sultan, "I will listen to your message most willingly and with an eager heart."

Then he took him aside so that he could reveal his secret. Pacolet spoke to him in a low voice: "Sire, know that I come from Portugal and was sent here by my most respected lady, Ferragu's wife, who commends herself to you with all her heart more fervently than I can say. And I make known to you that it is true that she loves you so much more than any man in the world that, wondering how to have your love, she cannot rest or sleep day or night, so smitten is she with love of you. Now the truth is that she, trusting me completely, has sent me to you expressly to request, in the name of the love that two loyal lovers can have for one another, that you come see her without deferral or delay, for King Ferragu is presently in Aquitaine. Thus you will be able to enjoy at your leisure and as you will the pleasant lady who sparkles with beauty above all others. For that reason, sire, come with me, for I will convey you so quickly on my magic horse that early tomorrow morning you will be in the presence of the noble and beautiful lady."

"Ah, Pacolet," said Sultan Moradin, "you put joy in my heart like no other has ever done. For I am and have long been enamored of King Ferragu's wife more than of any other lady in the world. But for such a long time there has been no opportunity where I could satisfy my wish or tell my secret. But soon I will attain the

Car je te prometz que demain au plus matin avec toy je m'en yray et acompliray mon desir et ma voulenté."

A celle heure (que je vous compte) le souldan Moradin se assist a table et fist servir l'enchanteur Pacolet tout le plus honnestement que il peust, car sy fort joyeulx estoit des nouvelles que l'enchanteur Pacolet luy avoit aporté que le cueur de son ventre tout de joye tressailloit et menoit grant deduit. Et Pacolet, qui bien vit que le souldan Moradin estoit en grant joye, dist bassement tout par luy, "Je suis bien festoyé et bien ayse tenu, mais devant qu'il soit demain vespre tel me donne de son pain a menger que il mauldira l'eure que je fus né."

Or estoient Valentin et le Verd Chevalier en la tente et pavillon du souldan Moradin qui estoient bien estroitement lyéz et tenus. Bien cogneurent Pacolet dont furent joyeulx en leur couraiges en disant et pensant en leur cueur que pour leur delivrance il estoit la arrivé, mais nul semblant n'en firent. Et Pacolet en monstrant fort grant chiere et semblant au souldan Moradin en regardant les prisonniers a dist tout haultement, "Sire, comment estes vous si courtois de tenir et garder le Verd Chevalier en voz prisons sans le faire mourir? Car sur tous les vivans il a porté dommaige a son frere[1] Ferragu, et pour plus luy nuyre il a renoncé Mahon, et trouvé chemin et maniere de luy toullyr sa seur la belle Esclarmonde pour la donner a ung crestien. Si me semble que trop estes simple quant luy et tous les aultres de sa sorte et compaignie vous ne les faictes tous mourir sans en avoir aulcune pitié ne mercy."

"Amy," dist le souldan Moradin, "ce est bien ma voulenté et intention, car je suis du tout deliberé de les faire [70verso]demain au matin en une aultre fourche pendre et estrangler."

Tant fust Pacolet saige et bien aprins que jusques a heure de dormir en bourdes et en falaces entretint le souldan. Et quant l'eure fut venuee que on deust aler reposer le souldan commanda que les prisonniers fussent gardéz tant et si estroittement et sur peine de la vie on luy en sceust lendemain rendre compte. Et ainsi se retrahyt en sa chambre et laissa en garde Valentin et le Verd Chevalier pour celle nuyt a ung grant tas de Sarrasins et de payens qui sur tous les aultres de leur mort estoient convoiteulx. Or fut l'eure venue que chascun fust retrayt fors le petit Pacolet; lequel pas ne dormit, mais si bien et en telle maniere parmy le palays a getté son sort que tous ceulx qui furent dedens pour lesdis prisonniers garder cheurent a terre tous endormis que se toutes les tentes eust abatu pas ne se fussent reveilléz.

Adonc est venu au chevalier Valentin et au Verd Chevalier et leur a dist, "Seigneurs, a ceste heure vous osteray et delivreray des mains du faulx souldan Moradin."

Cy ne fault pas demander se a celle heure furent joyeulx et de tous leurs maulx consoléz. Ilz saillirent hors de la sale sans plus longuement sermoner ne

---

[1] Text has *fre*.

desire of my heart that I have so long awaited. For I promise you that early tomorrow morning I will go with you to accomplish my desire and my will."

At that hour (that I am recounting to you) Sultan Moradin sat down at table and had the enchanter Pacolet served as honorably as he could, for he was so thrilled by the news that the magician Pacolet had brought him that the heart inside him rejoiced and trembled with delight. Pacolet, fully aware of Sultan Moradin's joy, said softly to himself, "I am well feted and well treated, but, before vespers tomorrow, he who now feeds me his bread will curse the hour I was born."

Now Valentin and the Green Knight were in the pavilion of Sultan Moradin, both tightly bound up. They recognized Pacolet, which gladdened their hearts, for they thought to themselves that he had surely come there to rescue them, but they made no outward sign of this. Then Pacolet, outwardly making good cheer with Sultan Moradin, looked over at the prisoners and said loudly, "Sire, how is it that you are so courteous as to hold and guard the Green Knight a prisoner without having him executed? For above all living men, he has caused harm to his brother Ferragu, and, to hurt him all the more, he has renounced Mohammed and found a way to take away from him his sister, the fair Esclarmonde, to give her to a Christian. It seems a bit naive to me for you not to kill him and anyone in his company without pity or mercy."

"My friend," said Sultan Moradin, "that is indeed my desire and intention, for I have already decided to hang them on a gibbet tomorrow morning."

Pacolet was so clever that he kept the sultan entertained with fibs and lies until bedtime. And when it was time to retire, the sultan ordered the prisoners to be so well and so closely guarded that, on pain of death, a good account of them could be made the next morning. Then he retired to his chamber, leaving that night's guard of Valentin and the Green Knight to a large group of Saracens and pagans who wished for their deaths more than anything else. Now the time came that everyone had retired except little Pacolet; he did not sleep, rather he cast such a spell throughout the palace on those who were there to guard the prisoners that they all fell to the ground in a sleep so deep that, had their tents fallen, they would not have woken up.

Thereupon he came to the knight Valentin and the Green Knight, saying to them, "My lords, now I will take you away and deliver you from the hands of the false Sultan Moradin."

No need to ask if they were overjoyed at that moment and consoled for all their pain. They left the hall without any more discourse or talk, for Pacolet hur-

parler en aulcune maniere, car Pacolet les hasta le plus fort qu'il peust, car il veoit que l'heure estoit fort tardive et du souldan fort se doubtoit, et en la plus grant diligence que il peut les mist hors. Et sy bien les enseigna que sans avoir nul empeschement de Sarrasins ne de payens ilz passerent tref, tentes et pavillons, et vindrent a leur ost.

Et Pacolet, qui nul semblant n'en fist, quant vint vers l'aube du jour entra en la tente du souldan et luy escrya tout en hault, "Ha! sire! tres mal va de nostre fait et mal vous monstrez de la femme Ferragu que tant vous desire a veoir quand vous demourez[1] tant de faire diligence de sa voulenté acomplir. Levez vous et ne tardez plus et vous monstrez loyal, car cueur qui veult loyaument aymer ne doyt point au lit dormir si longuement."

Quant le souldan oÿt Pacolet qui si fort le crye il s'esveilla souldainement comme tout esmerveillé, puis a dist a Pacolet, "Amy, par Mahon le tout puissant tu as bien fait de m'esveiller car tu m'as osté de grant peine, car je songoye ung songe merveilleux. Et en songant m'estoit avis que une cornille m'emportoit et faisoit voler parmy l'air moult fort loing. Et en volant parmy l'air venoit a moy ung si grant oyseau qui de son becq me frappoit tant fort que le sang en faisoit courir dessus la terre a moult grant habondance. Si ne sçay que veult dire ne en quelle maniere cestuy songe se veult exposer. Et suis en moult fort grant doubte que le roy Ferragu ne saiche ceste entreprinse."

"Sire," dist Pacolet, "vous avez trop lache couraige quant pour ung seul songe vous [71recto]voulez laisser l'amoureuse entreprinse et a celle faillir, laquelle en vous a tant languy et souspiré d'amours."

"Par Mahon," dist il, "Pacolet, tu dis verité." Lors appella son chambrelan et sy se fist mettre en point. Puis luy a dist, "Amis,[2] garde que tu me soyez secret et loyal. Et se mon oncle Bruant me demande, tu luy diras que je me suis alé ung petit esbatre avec Pacolet."

"Sire," dist le chevalier, "alez la ou vous vouldrez, car de vostre fait je ne me veul enquerir, mais je veul bien celer et vous estre secret."

Lors monta Pacolet a cheval et fist monter le souldan Moradin derriere luy et l'embraça bien serremement par le corps. Et quant ilz furent montéz Pacolet tourna la chevillete et le cheval se leva si hault en l'air si impetueusement que tout aussi tost furent en la cité de Constantinoble au palays de l'empereur Alexandre. Et quant le souldan Moradin veit que Pacolet estoit arresté il luy a dist, "Amy, devons nous icy logier?"

"Oy," dist Pacolet, "n'ayez de riens doubte ne crainte, car nous sommes dedens Portingal au palays du puissant roy Ferragu."

"Par Mahon en qui je croy," dist le souldan Moradin, "je suis moult fort esmerveillé comment le dyable t'y a sy tost peu apporter."

---

[1] Text has *demoueez*.

[2] Another infrequent example of the *s* of the Old French nominative in Middle French. It occurs with the same word below on p. 272. See p. 153, n. 1.

ried them as fast as he could, for he saw that the hour was very late and he feared the sultan, so, with all possible speed, he directed them out. So well did he guide them that they glided past tents and pavilions without interference from Saracen or pagan and made it back to their own encampment.

Then Pacolet, as if nothing had happened, entered the sultan's tent at dawn, booming out, "Ah, sire, this will not do — you make a poor impression on Ferragu's wife, who so much desires to see you, dragging your feet like this in carrying out her will. Get up, don't waste time, show yourself loyal, for a heart that wishes to love faithfully mustn't linger in bed."

When the sultan heard Pacolet calling so loudly, he awoke suddenly in a daze, saying to Pacolet, "My friend, by almighty Mohammed, you did well to wake me — you have delivered me from great pain, for I was dreaming an amazing dream. As I dreamed it seemed to me that a crow was carrying me far away as he flew through the air. While we were flying thus, a huge bird came to me and began pecking me so hard that blood streamed abundantly to the ground below. I have no idea what the dream means or signifies. I am terribly afraid that King Ferragu has found out about this affair."

"Sire," said Pacolet, "you have a faint heart indeed if you are willing because of a mere dream to give up this amorous enterprise and fail this lady who has languished and sighed so long for your love."

"By Mohammed," he said, "you speak true, Pacolet." Then he called his chamberlain and got ready. Then he said to the latter, "My friend, take care to remain discreet and trustworthy with me. And if my uncle Bruant asks for me, you will tell him that I have gone to amuse myself a little with Pacolet."

"Sire," said the knight, "go where you like, for I have no desire to pry into your affairs, but rather will keep quiet and discreet."

Then Pacolet mounted the horse and had Sultan Moradin get on behind, holding on to him tightly around the middle. Once they were both mounted, Pacolet turned the pin and the horse rose so high and so quickly in the air that they were almost immediately in the city of Constantinople at the palace of the emperor Alexander. When Sultan Moradin saw that Pacolet had stopped, he said to him, "My friend, are we to lodge here?"

"Yes," said Pacolet, "have no fear, for we are in Portugal, at the palace of the powerful King Ferragu."

"By Mohammed in whom I place my faith," said Sultan Moradin, "I am amazed how the devil has brought you here so quickly."

"Or avanchez vous," ce dist Pacolet, "entrez en ceste sale et je m'en voy en la chambre de la plaisante dame, la femme du roy Ferragu, et tout a ceste heure je vous feray ouvrir la chambre et avecques elle coucher."

"Amy," dist le souldan Moradin, "de grant joye tu me fais ryre.[1] Or va de par Mahon qui te veulle conduire."

Pacolet l'enchanteur laissa le souldan Moradin dedens la sale laquelle de toutes pars fut moult fort bien sarree et fermee tellement qu'il n'eust peu saillir dehors. Puis ala devers la chambre de l'empereur Alexandre et donna sy grant coup contre la porte que le chambrelan l'ouÿt et s'escrya fierement en demandant, "Qui estes vous qui a ceste heure si hardiment en la chambre imperiale venez frapper et mener tel bruit?"

"Amy," dist Pacolet, "de riens ne vous doubtez. Je suis Pacolet, qui viens de l'ost du souldan et Valentin et le Verd Chevalier ay fait delivrer des mains des Sarrasins qui a mort les avoient jugéz et condempnéz. Et oultre plus, dictes a l'empereur que j'ay en ce palays avec moy amené le souldan Moradin, lequel croit fermement estre en Portingal. Or fault il sans nul sejour le prendre et escorcher tout vif car bien l'a deservy."

Quant le chambrelan oÿt les nouvelles, il ala devers l'empereur et le roy Pepin, lesquelz pour veoir le souldan avec grant nombre de barons et chevaliers se abillerent. Et le souldan estoit en la sale, lequel en cryant hideusement a commencé a dire, "Ha, faulx trahystre, Pacolet, Mahon te puisse mauldire! Je t'ay bien entendu et ouÿ parler; tu m'as par ta faulce cautelle mauvaisement et honteusement trahi. Mais par [71verso]la loy que je tiens encores je t'en feray repentir."

Alors a traytté son espee et comme homme enrragé et hors du sens s'est prins a courir par la sale en frappant les murs et les pierres sy tresfierement que des pierres de mabre[2] faisoit le feu saillir. Et ainsi que parmy la sale a par luy se combatoit, l'empereur et le roy Pepin a torchez et a phaloz de plusieurs gens acompaignéz sont venus devers luy et quant il les aperceust il se mist en deffence moult oultrageusement en telle maniere que devant le roy Pepin ung escuier tua qui prendre le vouloit. Et le roy, qui de desplaisance en fust fort courroucé, s'avança contre le souldan et si grant coup luy baille que a terre l'abatit. Puis fut prins et lyé moult fort et moult estroit a tant fust le jour venu. Valentin et le Verd Chevalier, qui de l'ost du souldan venoyent par l'ayde de Pacolet, furent devant les portes. Ilz trouverent le souldan dont moult furent joyeulx. L'empereur et le roy Pepin pour la delivrance de Valentin menerent feste et joye et aussi firent ilz pour le Verd Chevalier car moult estoit prisé et aymé. L'empereur mercya moult grandement le petit Pacolet pour son filz le vaillant chevalier Valentin. Et le roy Pepin luy a dist, "Pacolet, beau sire, il fault que tu me monstres ung tour de ton chevalet."

---

[1] Text has *ryee*.

[2] This spelling of 'marbre' recurs, thus it appears to be particular to this text and not an error of typesetting.

"Now go on in," said Pacolet, "enter this hall while I go to the chamber of the pleasant lady, the wife of King Ferragu, and very soon I will open her chamber to you and get you into her bed."

"My friend," said Sultan Moradin, "you make me laugh with joy. Now go and may Mohammed guide you."

Pacolet the magician left Sultan Moradin inside the hall, which was closed and locked so well from all sides that he could not get out. Then he went to the chamber of the emperor Alexander, knocking so loudly on the door that the chamberlain heard him and cried out fiercely, "Who are you to come knocking so boldly at the imperial chamber, making such noise at this hour?"

"My friend," said Pacolet, "do not be afraid. I am Pacolet, and have just come from the Sultan's camp where I delivered Valentin and the Green Knight from the hands of the Saracens who had condemned them to death. Moreover, tell the emperor that I have brought Sultan Moradin back with me to the palace, and he firmly believes himself to be in Portugal. Now he must be taken and skinned alive without delay, for that is what he deserves."

When the chamberlain heard these tidings, he went straightaway to the emperor and King Pepin, both of whom dressed to come see the sultan with a great number of their barons and knights. Meanwhile the sultan in the hall was beginning to yell horribly, saying, "Ah, false traitor, Pacolet, may Mohammed curse you! I listened to you, but you have wickedly and shamefully betrayed me with your perfidious trickery. Yet, by the faith that I hold to still, I will make you repent."

Then he drew his sword and began to dash about the room like a crazed man, completely out of his senses, striking the walls and stones so forcefully that sparks flew from the marble stone. As he was thus fighting alone in the hall, the emperor and King Pepin came to him with torches and lanterns, well accompanied by several men. When he saw them, he leapt to a violent defense, and, right in front of King Pepin, killed one of the squires trying to take hold of him. The king, upset and angry, advanced on the sultan, giving him a blow that knocked him down. Then he was seized and very tightly bound before the day dawned. Valentin and the Green Knight, who had escaped the sultan's camp with Pacolet's help, were before the gates. Finding the sultan there, they were overjoyed. The emperor and King Pepin, for their part, were thrilled and delighted at Valentin's escape, and just as happy to see the Green Knight whom they also prized and loved. The emperor thanked little Pacolet heartily for liberating his son, the valiant knight Valentin. Then King Pepin said to him, "Pacolet, fair sir, you must show me how your magic horse works."

"Sire," dist Pacolet, "montez derriere moy et je vous porteray sans arrester jusques dedens enfer."

"Amy," ce dist le roy Pepin, "Dieu m'en veulle garder!"

Or ce dist Pacolet, "Seigneurs, faictes diligence de ce faulx souldan mourir, car se jamais il vous eschappe, pensés que mal en aviendra."

A celle heure furent dedens le palays assembléz plusieurs grans seigneurs pour veoir le souldan par le conseil et deliberation desquelz il fut jugé et condempné que ledit souldan seroit pendu et estranglé aux creneaulx du palays affin que des payens et Sarrasins il peust estre veu et regardé. Et tel fust le jugement donné et la chose ainsi faicte et acomplie. Et quant les payens et Sarrasins veirent le souldan qui la estoit pendu moult furent esmerveilléz par quelle maniere pouoit avoir esté mené dedens la cité. Bruant leur compta comment il avoit esté par Pacolet deceu.

Grant cry et grant doleur fust parmy l'ost des payens et Sarrasins demené pour l'amour du souldan, lequel ilz avoient perdu et si ne sçavoient par quelle maniere ne façon, car moult estoit vaillant homme et des crestiens grant persecuteur. Et apres que ilz eurent fait grant cry et grandes complaintes ilz assemblerent leur conseil et esleurent pour leur souldan Bruant qui fust oncle de Moradin. Celuy jour furent dolens Sarrasins et payens, et les crestiens parmy la cité demenerent moult grant feste et grant joye pour la mort du souldan et aussi pour les vivres que ilz avoient recouvrés et gaignéz.

Et puis apres toutes ces choses [72recto]ainsi faictes, Pacolet print congé de l'empereur et de toute sa court pour retourner en Acquitaine vers la belle dame Esclarmonde ainsi comme promis luy avoit. Adonc Valentin vint vers luy et luy a dist, "Amis[1] Pacolet, puis que vous alez en Acquitaine, saluez moy doulcement ma mere la royne Bellissant, et m'amye Esclarmonde, et mon beau frere Orson, et le bon duc d'Acquitaine, et tous les aultres barons et chevaliers. Et baillez ceste lettre a ma dame ma mere par laquelle elle pourra cognoistre et sçavoir clerement des nouvelles de par deça."

"Sire," dist Pacolet, "le messaige feray voulentiers." Adonc a prins son chevalet et est monté dessus une fenestre de mabre, puis a tourné la chevillette et saissit sur le dos de son chevalet et s'en va par l'air ainsi comme devant. L'empereur et le roy Pepin estoient aux fenestres que moult fort le regardoyent.

"Par Dieu," se dist le roy Pepin, " pour tout l'or du monde, je ne vouldrois[2] estre la!"

Or s'en va Pacolet par si grant diligence que le lendemain au matin il arriva en Acquitaine et trouva le bon duc qui la cité gardoit, Bellissant, Orson, et la belle Esclarmonde. Et les salua tous de par Valentin moult honnourablement.

"Amy," dist Orson, "comment se porte le fait de mon pere?"

---

[1] See p. 152, n. 1.
[2] Text has *vouldroit*.

"Sire," said Pacolet, "get on behind me and I will take you all the way to hell without stopping."

"My friend," said King Pepin, "may the Lord preserve me!"

Then Pacolet said, "My lords, don't delay executing this false sultan, for if ever he escapes you, be sure that evil will follow."

That day several important lords gathered in the palace to see the sultan; through their counsel and deliberation, the sultan was judged and condemned to be hanged by the neck on the highest tower of the palace so that the pagans and Saracens could see him well. Just as the judgment was given, so was it carried out. When the pagans and Saracens saw the sultan hanging up there, they were astounded as to how he could have been brought into the city. Bruant recounted to them how he had been tricked by Pacolet.

A great cry and great mourning spread throughout the camp of the pagans and Saracens for love for the sultan, whom they had lost without really understanding how it had happened, for he was a brave man and a great persecutor of Christians. After their loud mourning they assembled their council and elected Bruant, Moradin's uncle, as their sultan. That day the pagan Saracens were full of grief, while the Christians within the city celebrated the joyous occasion of the death of the sultan and their new supply of victuals.

After all these events, Pacolet took his leave of the emperor and all his court to return to Aquitaine to the fair lady Esclarmonde, just as he had promised her. Thereupon Valentin came to him and said, "Friend Pacolet, since you are going to Aquitaine, give a tender greeting to my mother Queen Bellissant, to my beloved Esclarmonde, to my dear brother Orson, to the good Duke of Aquitaine, and to all the other barons and knights. Moreover, deliver this letter to my lady mother, which will explain to her all the news from here."

"Sire," said Pacolet, "I will deliver your message willingly." Then he took his magic horse, climbed up on a marble windowsill, turned the pin, and, settling himself on its back, took off into the air just as he had done so previously. The emperor and King Pepin watched him with fascination from the windows.

"By God," said King Pepin, "I wouldn't want to be on that thing for all the gold in the world!"

Now Pacolet traveled with all speed so that the following morning he arrived in Aquitaine and found the good duke, who guarded the city, along with Bellissant, Orson, and the fair Esclarmonde. He greeted them most properly on Valentin's behalf.

"My friend," said Orson, "how goes it with my father?"

"Sire," dist Pacolet, "il se porte tresbien, mais pour sçavoir des nouvelles vecy unes[1] lettres que je apporte a ma redoubtee dame Bellissant de par vostre frere Valentin."

La dame print les lettres qui moult en fust joyeuse, puis appella ung secretaire pour les faire lire. "Dame," dist le secretaire qui les lettres regarda, "sachez que le vaillant chevalier vostre filz Valentin vous mande par ceste lettre que le puissant[2] empereur, lequel vous verroit voulentiers, humblement de tout son cueur vous salue. Lequel depuis le temps de vostre departement en peine et en travail longuement vous a quise et fait querir. Et vous mande comment tantost apres que par luy fustes dechassee, il eust clere cognoissance de vostre loyaulté et de la trahyson et entreprinse du faulx archevesque lequel par ung marchant a esté combatu et mis a telle subjection que devant sa mort publiquement a confessé sa faulce et dampnable deception. Pour lesquelles choses le bon empereur vostre mary de jour en jour desire de vous veoir et avoir avec luy. Tant que il vous revoye jamais au cueur joye n'aura. Et si saichez que au plus tost que il sera despeché des faulx ennemis de la foy crestienne lesquelz en grant puissance d'armes ont la cité de Constantinoble assiegee, il viendra devers vous et amenera le Verd Chevalier lequel par Orson vostre filz devant Acquitaine fust conquesté. Ainsi le vous mande et rescript le vostre humble et loyal filz Valentin par le teneur de ceste lettre."

Quant la dame oÿt les nouvelles elle eust au cueur si grant joye qu'elle se paulma, et Orson l'embraça et print entre ses bras moult doulcement.

[72verso] "Mon enfant," dit la royne, "bien doy Dieu mercier et au cueur estre fort joyeuse quant l'empereur de Grece a certaines nouvelles que je suis innocente et pure de l'infameté et crisme abhominable lesquelz par faulce trahyson m'avoyent esté imposeez. Or me doinst Dieu la grace que de bref devant l'empereur je me puisse trouver, car se une foys en ma vie de mes yeulx le puis veoir plus ne demande a Dieu ne au monde demourer quant telle grace m'a fait, que a l'onneur de moy et de tout le sang de France il a monstré la trahyson du[3] mauldit et irregulier archevesque lequel a recogneu son grant malefice."

---

[1] Text has *une*.
[2] Text has *puistant*.
[3] Text has *du du*.

"Sire," said Pacolet, "he is very well, but, for the news, here is a missive from your brother Valentin that I carry to my respected lady Bellissant."

The lady took hold of the letter with much delight, then called a secretary to read it aloud. "Lady," said the secretary as he looked at the letter, "know that the valiant knight, your son Valentin, sends you word by this letter that the mighty emperor, who is eager to see you, sends you humble salutations with all his heart. From the time of your departure, with much effort and labor, he has striven to search for you. He wants you to know that soon after you were expelled by him, he had clear knowledge both of your loyalty and of the treason and plotting of the false archbishop by means of a merchant who fought him and defeated him so that, before he died, he publicly confessed his evil and damnable deceit. For this reason, the good emperor your husband desires to see you and have you with him every day. Until he sees you again he can never be happy. Know, moreover, that as soon as he will have dispatched the false enemies of the Christian faith, who have besieged the city of Constantinople with great force of arms, he will come to you and will bring along the Green Knight who was conquered by Orson your son before Aquitaine. Such is the message from your humble and faithful son Valentin in this letter."

When the lady heard the news she had such joy in her heart that she fainted, and Orson embraced her, holding her most tenderly in his arms.

"My child," said the queen, "I must thank God and have a joyful heart now that the emperor of Greece has clear evidence that I am innocent and pure of the infamy and abominable crime imputed to me by false treason. Now may God grant me the favor to see the emperor before too long, for if just once in my life I may see him with my own eyes, I will never ask for anything else from God, not even to remain in the world once He has granted me such a favor, namely that of demonstrating, for the sake of my honor and that of all the royal blood of France, the treason of the cursed and irregular archbishop who recognized his great evil-doing."

[CHAPITRE 30]

Comment le roy Trompar vint et arriva devant
Acquitaine pour secourir Ferragu et amena avec luy
Adramain l'enchanteur par qui Pacolet fust trahy.
xxx. chapitre[1]

A celuy jour que Pacolet arriva dedens Acquitaine, le roy Trompar vint et arriva dedens l'ost de Ferragu a grant puissance de combatans pour luy faire secours contre les crestiens, et en grant honneur les receut le geant Ferragu. Et pour l'amour de sa venue il fist faire feste et joye parmy l'ost.

"Franc roy," dist le geant, "de vostre venue je me doy bien resjouÿr, car j'ay esperance que par vous auray de ceulx vengance qui ma seur Esclarmonde ont trahye et deceue. Or say je bien de vray qu'elle est dedens Acquitaine et que on luy a veue, dont je prise petit ma puissance se je ne la puis avoir. Et s'il est ainsi que par vostre puissance, moyen et ayde elle puisse estre conquestee, de ceste heure la vous donne pour femme et pour espouse."

"Ferragu," dist le roy Trompar, "de ce ne vous doubtez, car j'ay avec moy amené Adramain l'enchanteur, lequel aura tantost trahy et deceu Pacolet, car plus scet d'art d'ingroma[n]ce que tous les vivans."

"Par Mahon," dit Ferragu, "je suis joyeulx de sa venue et se tant me peult faire que Pacolet me rende je le feray de tous le plus riche et puissant."

"Sire," dist Adramain, "aiez en moy fiance, car si bien vous serviray que de brief en aurez cognoissance."

Lors se partist Adramain et habilla son sort pour jouer de son mestier, puis s'en ala vers la cité d'Acquitaine et affin de plus seurement entrer dedens il s'est chargé de vivres. Or a tant fait par son engin qu'il est venu devant [73recto][2] les portes et a demandé entree pour ses vivres vendre et despecher. Il fut subtil et cautelleux et a ceulx de la cité sceut bien parler. Si luy furent les portes ouvertes pour l'amour des vivres qu'il portoit. Il entra en la cité puis ses vivres vendit puis trouva maniere d'aler vers le palays. La trouva Pacolet qui moult bien le cogneut car aultreffois l'avoit veu.

"Adramain," dist Pacolet, "bien soyez arrivé. Or me dictes s'il vous plaist de quel lieu vous venez et qui a ceste heure par deça vous amaine."

"Pacolet," dist Adramain, "vous sçavez que j'ay servy longuement le roy Trompart. Si avint l'autre jour que par ung de ceulx de sa court je fus feru et oultragé moult villainement pour cause que je ne luy vouloye aprendre de mon mestier le secret. Et quant je me veis feru j'en eulx despit en mon couraige et d'ung

---

[1] Woodcut of armed knights approaching a city under siege (at right), with walled encampment of tents to left.

[2] *k i* at bottom right corner of 73r.

CHAPTER 30

How King Trompart came to Aquitaine to help Ferragu, bringing with him Adramain the magician by whom Pacolet was betrayed.

The same day that Pacolet arrived in Aquitaine, King Trompart joined Ferragu's host with a large contingent of warriors to help him against the Christians, and he was received with great honor by the giant Ferragu. In honor of his coming, he held celebrations throughout the camp.

"Noble king," said the giant, "I am very glad of your coming, for I hope with your help to take vengeance on those who have betrayed and deceived my sister Esclarmonde. Now what I know for certain is that she is in Aquitaine and that she has been seen, for which reason I deem my power puny if I cannot get her back. And if she can be conquered with your strength and aid, I offer her to you from this time forward as wife and spouse."

"Ferragu," said King Trompart, "you need have no doubts, for I have brought with me Adramain the enchanter who will soon trick and betray Pacolet, for he knows more of the art of magic than anyone alive."

"By Mohammed," said Ferragu, "I am glad of his coming, and if he can manage to render me Pacolet, I will make him richer and more powerful than anyone."

"Sire," said Adramain, "trust me, for so well will I serve you, you will soon see the results."

Adramain left them to prepare his enchantment according to his craft, and then went to the city of Aquitaine, loading himself with provisions, the better to assure his entry. So cleverly had he thought it out that he came before the gates, asking for entry to sell his victuals. He was subtle and sly and knew well how to talk to the townspeople. So they opened the gates to him for the sake of the provisions he was carrying. He entered the city, sold his provisions, and then found the way to the palace. There he located Pacolet who knew him well, for he had met him in the past.

"Adramain," said Pacolet, "welcome. Tell me please whence you come and what brings you here now."

"Pacolet," said Adramain, "you know that I have long served King Trompart. It happened one day that I was villainously attacked and struck by someone in his court because I did not want to teach him the secret of my craft. When I saw myself hit in this way, I was outraged and stabbed him so with my knife that

cousteau le frappay tant qu'il fut mort. Quant j'eulx fait le coup pour doubte de mourir je suis de la court yssu, et en ce point du service du roy Trompart getté et dechassé. Si suis venu par devers vous pour la loyaulté et fiance que je pense vers vous trouver. Et d'ores en avant je veul estre et demourer avec vous comme loyal compaignon s'il vous plaist que je le soye."

"Adramain," dist Pacolet, "j'en suis bien d'acord. Faictes joyeuse chiere et de riens ne vous doubtés."

Lors Pacolet le fist bien servir et moult honnestement recepvoir ainsi comme compaignon qui de sa venue est joyeulx. Et en faisant chiere ensemble Adramain veit la belle Esclarmonde passer par le palays. Si demanda a Pacolet qui estoit ceste dame tant belle et tant gracieuse.

"Amy," ce dist Pacolet, "c'est la belle Esclarmonde, la seur du roy Ferragu, laquelle doit estre moult richement mariee a ung moult hault riche et vaillant chevalier."

A celle heure arriva Orson devers les deux compaignons et leur a dist, "Seigneurs, jouez ung petit entre vous deux de vostre mestier affin de consoler[1] ung peu et resjouÿr la compaignie."

Adonc Adramain leva une couppe par dessus ung pilier et en itel sort que il sembla et fust avis a ceulx qui la furent presens que parmy la place couroit une riviere moult grande et terrible. Et en icelle riviere sembloit avoir poissons grans et petis a moult fort grant habondance. Et quant ceulx du palays veirent l'eaue si grande, ilz commencerent tous a lever leurs robes et a cryer moult fort comme ceulx qui avoient paour de noyer. Et Pacolet qui l'enchantement regarda commença a chanter, et fist ung sort sy subtil en son chant que il sembla a tous ceulx du lieu que parmy la riviere couroit ung cerf moult grant et cornu qui gettoit et abatoit a terre tout ce que devant luy trouvoit. Puis leur fut avis qu'i veoient les chasseurs et veneurs apres le cerf courir a grant nombre et puissance de levriers et braches. Lors y eult plusieurs de la compaignie qui saillir au devant pour le cerf [73verso]atrapper et cuider prendre, mais Pacolet fist tost le cerf faillir.

"Par ma foy," dist Orson, "moult bien avez joué et bien sçavez de vostre art user."

A ces motz se leverent les deux enchanteurs et Pacolet, qui tout bien y pensoit, mena Adramain en sa chambre pour celle nuyt dormir et reposer dont depuis fut moult dolent et courroucé, car quant vint a la minuyt Adramain getta ung sort parmy tout le palays que grans et petis furent endormis si fort que pour cry ne pour bruit esveiller ne se pouoient jusques au soleil levant, et si fist dormir Pacolet tout ainsi comme les aultres. Puis ala vers le chevalet lequel il avoit bien veu en la chambre, mais nul semblant n'en avoit fait. Et quant il eut le cheval il ala en la chambre de Esclarmonde et par son subtil art en dormant la fist vestir et habiller. Puis la monta avec lui sur le cheval et vint a une fenestre et a tourné

---

[1] Text has *confoler*.

he died. Having committed that deed, I left the court in fear for my life, and thus I am cast off and expelled from the service of King Trompart. I have come to you out of the loyalty and trust I hope to find in you. From now on I wish to remain here with you as a loyal companion, if that please you."

"Adramain," said Pacolet, "of course it does. Make good cheer and don't worry about anything."

Then Pacolet had him served and received most honorably as a companion whose coming pleased him. While they were making cheer together, Adramain saw the fair Esclarmonde passing through the palace. He asked Pacolet who was this lady so fair and gracious.

"My friend," said Pacolet, "that is the fair Esclarmonde, sister of King Ferragu, who is to be married with great pomp to a very rich and valiant knight."

At that moment Orson came to the two companions and said to them, "My lords, perform a little of your craft before us in order to gladden and entertain the company a bit."

Thereupon Adramain raised and placed a cup on a high pillar, and in this spell it seemed to everyone there that a great and terrible river ran from it. In this river there even appeared to be a great abundance of fish, both large and small. And when the palace folk saw such a flow of water, they all began to raise the hems of their robes and to cry out like people in fear of drowning. But Pacolet, who watched this bit of magic, began to sing, casting so subtle a spell in his song that it seemed to everyone present that, in the middle of the river, a huge horned stag was running, throwing and knocking over everything in his path. Then it seemed to them that they saw huntsmen and veneders chasing after the stag with a great number of greyhounds and hunting dogs. Then there were several in the company thinking to jump forward to catch the stag and take it, but Pacolet made it suddenly disappear.

"By my faith," said Orson, "you have done well, and certainly know how to use your skills."

With these words the two magicians arose, and Pacolet, suspecting nothing, led Adramain to his chamber to sleep there that night. Later he was very sorry to have done so, for when midnight came, Adramain cast a spell over the entire palace so that everyone, great and small, slept so soundly that no cry or noise could wake them until sunrise, Pacolet along with the others. Then he went to the magic horse, which he had certainly seen in the room, though without taking obvious notice of it. With the horse in his possession, he went to Esclarmonde's chamber, where, while she slept, he used one of his subtle charms to get her dressed. Then, mounting her on the horse with him, he went to the window,

la cheville (car il en sçavoit bien l'art) et tant a fait que sans sejourner il est arrivé au pavillon du roy Trompart a tout la belle Esclarmonde.

Lors s'escrie Adramain, "Sire, roy Trompart, ne veullez pas dormir mais levez vous tantost sus! Car icy vous pouez veoir la plaisante Esclarmonde laquelle j'ay desrobé par dedens Acquitaine, et sy ay tant bien fait et subtillement besongné que de Pacolet j'ay le chevalet robé."

"Adramain," dist Trompart, "a ceste heure cognois que tu es amy loyal et que dessus tous aultres je suis a toy tenu. N'esse pas la fille au grant roy Justaumont que est seur du roy Ferragu?"

"Oy," dit Adramain, "je l'ay bien sceu subtillement avoir et Pacolet l'enchanteur trahy, car de son chevalet jamais il n'aura le gouvernement."

"Adramain," dist le roy Trompart, "en sçais tu bien jouer?"

"Oy," ce dist l'enchanteur, "de long temps j'ay aprins." Adonc luy a monstré la maniere de la chevillette tourner et du cheval gouverner. Et quant Trompart a veu la subtilité il s'est avisé et pensé en luy mesmes que sur le chevalet la belle Esclarmonde en son pays l'emportera et l'espousera et prendera a femme. Lors a embrassé la belle Esclarmonde qui encores dormoit pour le sort de Adramain, et avec luy sur le chevalet de bois l'a mise.

Et Adramain le regarde et lui a dit, "Monseigneur, se vous faillez a jouer du chevalet en danger et peril vous mettez vous et la dame."

"Nennil," ce dist Trompart, "de ce n'ayez doubte." Et alors tourna la chevillette droitement a son tour et parmy une nue s'en est alé si loing que plus de cent lieues eust fait devant le jour. Et a celle heure s'esveilla la belle Esclarmonde qui tant fut dolente et desconfortee de se veoir en[1] tel estat que de douleur paulma, dont Trompart fut moult esbahy et au cueur moult effroyé, car il cuida qu'elle fust morte. Il tourna la chevillette et arresta le cheval dedens ung pre herbu aupres d'une fontaine qui moult estoit belle et clere. Et quant il eust la da[74recto]me[2] descendue sur l'erbe, il print de l'eaue de la fontaine et sur la face luy getta pour veoir s'elle pourroit revenir. Et la plaisante dame pour la froideur de l'eaue ung petit ouvrit les yeulx et se print a getter si piteulx cry et dolente complaintes que bien cuida le roy Trompart que le cueur luy deust partir, dont grant pitié luy en print. Et ne trouvoit maniere de luy faire secours fors[3] que par ung pasteur qui au plus pres d'eulx estoit auquel il demanda du pain. Et le pasteur luy en bailla ung quartier duquel il en emporta a la belle Esclarmonde et luy en mist en la bouche. La pucelle en menga ung petit et de l'eaue de la fontaine sa gorge en a arousee.

---

[1] Text has *in*. Since this recurs nowhere else, I have emended it. Although *in* for *en* occurs in the very early OF text of Sainte Eulalie, there is no reason to think here it is anything more than a typesetting error. See C.W. Aspland, *A Medieval French Reader* (Oxford: Clarendon Press, 1979), 6 (v. 25) for the example from the Sainte Eulalie sequence.

[2] *k ii* at bottom right corner of 74r.

[3] Text has *fort*.

turned the pin (for he well knew how to do it), and very soon arrived in the pavilion of King Trompart with the fair Esclarmonde.

Then Adramain called out, "Sire, King Trompart, don't sleep now — arise! For here is the lovely Esclarmonde whom I have stolen away from Aquitaine, and so well and so shrewdly have I done my work that I also snatched Pacolet's magic horse."

"Adramain," said Trompart, "now I can see what a loyal friend you are; I am beholden to you more than any other. Is this not the daughter of the great King Justaumont and sister of King Ferragu?"

"Yes," said Adramain, "I have managed to spirit her away and trick Pacolet the enchanter, for never again will he have possession of his magic horse."

"Adramain," said King Trompart, "do you know how to operate it?"

"Yes," said the magician, "I learned a long time ago." Thereupon he showed him how to turn the pin and control the horse. When Trompart saw how cleverly it was constructed, he thought to himself that he would carry the fair Esclarmonde to his country on the magic horse and there would marry her and take her as his wife. So he embraced the fair Esclarmonde who was still asleep through Adramain's spell, and placed her on the magic wooden horse with himself.

But Adramain saw what he was doing and said, "My lord, if you fail to operate the magic horse just right, you are putting yourself and the lady in great peril."

"No, no," said Trompart, "have no fear of that." So now in his turn he twisted the pin straight ahead, taking off so swiftly through a cloud that before daylight he had covered more than a hundred leagues. At that moment the fair Esclarmonde woke up, who, despairing to see herself in such a situation, fainted from grief, which alarmed Trompart and frightened him greatly, for he thought she must be dead. He turned the pin, stopping the horse in a grassy meadow near a lovely clear spring. After lowering the lady onto the grass, he took water from the spring and splashed it on her face to see if she would come to. The cold water did open the eyes of the pleasant lady a little, but then she began to cry out so bitterly and make such mournful lamentations that King Trompart believed her heart would break, which filled his own with pity. He could find no means to help her except to ask for bread from a shepherd nearby. The shepherd gave him a quarter loaf which he brought to the fair Esclarmonde, placing some in her mouth. The maiden ate a little bit of it and wet her throat with water from the spring.

Et quant le cueur luy fut ung petit revenu et la parolle enforcie, elle se print a plourer en disant, "Lasse, chaistive, sur toutes doloureuse, que m'est il avenu? Or ay je du tout perdu mon soulas et ma joye par fraude maleureuse et trahyson mauldicte. Helas! mon amy Valentin, or vous ay je perdu. De Dieu soit il mauldit qui ainsi nous depart!"

Quant le roy Trompart oÿt les regretz que la belle Esclarmonde pour son amy Valentin faisoit, il luy a dist moult rudement, "Dame, laissés telles parolles et du garson crestien jamais n'en parlez devant moy, ou par mon dieu Mahon du corps vous osteray la vie. Bien est droit et rayson que plus tost je vous espouse et soyez a moy donnee qui ay mon royaulme soubz ma dominacion et seigneurie que de prendre celuy malleureux qui n'a point de terre ne de seigneurie."

En disant ces parolles s'enclina vers la dame et la voulut baiser, mais la noble dame qui de son amour estoit peu curieuse luy bailla du poing sur les dens tant que le sang en fist saillir, dont le roy Trompart fut dolent et au cueur desplaisant que par fureur et grant ire la mist sur le chevalet pour partir de la place et pour aler en son païs. Mais on dist communement qui fait mal cuider estre maistre du maistier dont on ne sçait riens. Ainsi en print il au roy Trompart qui du chevalet de Pacolet cuida bien sçavoir jouer, car si mal apoint tourna la chevillette que de son chemin se eslongna et faillit de plus de cent lieues. Et ainsi qu'il pensoit sur sa terre arriver, il vint et arriva en Inde la Major et en une moult grande place ou pour celuy jour on tenoit le marché. Et voiant toute la gent dessus son chevalet avec la dame Esclarmonde a terre descendit.

Desquelles choses moult furent esmerveilléz tous ceulx qui presens estoient et fort esbahys. Et a celle heure la dame Esclarmonde cogneut le chevalet, car pour la douleur en quoy elle avoit esté toute la nuyt passee elle ne s'en estoit donné de garde.

"Helas! Pacolet," ce dist la dame Esclarmonde, "or suis je faulcement trahye et vous premierement desrobé. Or puis je bien a ceste heure commander a Dieu mon amy Va[74verso]lentin, des aultres le plus doulx et le plus courtois."

"Par Mahon," dit le roy Trompart qui en son pays cuidoit estre, "se jamais vous me parlez de celuy garson crestien de brief verrez et cognoisterrez de quelle amour je l'ayme, car de mon espee trenchant je vous feray la teste partir jus des espaules."

Or est deceu Trompart qui cuidoit estre ailleurs et qui pour la belle Esclarmonde avoit cuidé jouer d'ingromance, et est arrivé au lieu ou il conviendra que il deffine ses jours, car apres que de plusieurs eust esté en la place regardé et avisé, desquelz les ungz disoient entre eulx que c'estoit le grant dieu Mahon qui en chair et en sang pour son peuple viseter estoit du chiel descendu.

But when she had somewhat revived and could speak, she began to weep, saying, "Alas, wretched one, of all women the most miserable, what has happened to me? Now have I lost my solace and my joy through unhappy fraud and cursed treason. Alas! my beloved Valentin, now have I lost you. May the one who parts us be damned by God!"

When King Trompart heard the regrets of the fair Esclarmonde for her beloved Valentin, he spoke to her brusquely: "Lady, leave off such speech and never speak of that Christian boy again in my presence, or, by my god Mohammed, I will kill you. It is right and proper that as soon as possible I marry you and that you be given to me, I who have a kingdom under my domination and lordship, rather than to take that wretch who has neither land nor lordship."

While saying these words, he bent over the lady, trying to kiss her, but the noble lady, having little interest in his love, hit him so hard in the teeth that blood streamed forth. King Trompart was so hurt and displeased by this reaction that, in a great fury, he forced her back on the magic horse to leave that place and go to his own country. But, as everyone says, it is a mistake to think oneself master of a craft of which one knows nothing.[1] So it was with King Trompart, who thought he knew just how to control Pacolet's magic horse, for so badly did he aim the pin that he miscalculated his route by more than a hundred leagues. And just as he thought he was arriving in his own land, he came instead to India Major, landing in a large square in the middle of market day. Seeing all the people from his magic horse, he descended to the ground with the lady Esclarmonde.

Everyone there was absolutely amazed and astounded to see such a thing. Only at that moment did Esclarmonde recognize the magic horse, for she had passed the night in such distress that she had not noticed it.

"Alas! Pacolet," said the lady Esclarmonde, "now am I falsely betrayed and you most of all robbed. Now I have no choice but to commend to God my beloved Valentin, the gentlest and most courteous of men."

"By Mohammed," said King Trompart, who thought he was in his own country, "if you ever again speak to me of that Christian boy, you will quickly discover how much I care for him, for with my own sharp sword I will cut your head from your shoulders."

But Trompart, who thought himself elsewhere than where he actually was, and who, for the sake of the fair Esclarmonde, had thought he could play the magician, was quite deceived, and had arrived in the place where he was to end his days, for once several local people saw him, some said among themselves that it must be the great god Mohammed who had descended from heaven in flesh and blood to visit his people.

---

[1] Although I could find no proverb with a similar wording in the standard collections, the didactic sense of this proverb is contained in two others: "En un mui de cuidier n'a pas plaing poing de savoir" (Morawski, *Proverbes*, 25 [no. 702]), and "Nus ne doit fes emprendre qu'il ne puisse porter" (Morawski, *Proverbes*, 51 [no. 1407]).

Les nouvelles de ceste vision vindrent au roy d'Inde lequel commanda que par devant luy il fust amené. Or fut mal arrivé le roy Trompart, car tout aussitost que le roy d'Inde le veit devant luy, il le cogneust moult bien, et luy a dit, "Trompart, vous soyez le tresbien venu, car maintenant est venu le temps que de la mort de mon frere je prendray vengance, lequel par vostre fier couraige vous avez par l'espace de sept ans contre luy mené guerre. Et puis vous l'avez en la fin en tourment et douloureux martire fait mourir et definer ses jours honteusement. Sy veul a mon frere monstrer que en sa vie je l'ay loyaulment aymé et apres sa mort de ses ennemys je l'ay vengé."

Adonc le roy d'Inde sans aultre deliberation a celle heure presente[1] fit au roy Trompart la teste coupper. Et apres la justice faicte il fit prendre la belle Esclarmonde avec le chevalet de boys. Et pour la bonté de la dame la fist en son palays mener et moult fort honnourablement garder et servir. Puis est entré en son palays et devant luy l'a fait amener par les plus prochains de sa personne. Et quant elle fut devant luy moult voulentiers l'a regardee, et pour la maniere et doulce contenance de la dame qui de beaulté corporelle toutes les aultres passoit.

Il luy a dist moult doulcement, "Dame, je ne sçay qui vous estes ne de quel lieu vous estes venue, mais le sens et la beaulté qui sont en vous me font de vostre amour estre esprins et embrasé trop plus ardamment que jamais de dame je ne fus. Je suis deliberé de vous prendre pour femme et espouse, et de vous faire royne et maistresse de toute la[2] terre d'Inde la Major."

"Sire," ce dist la dame Esclarmonde qui bien sceut respondre, "vous parlez tressaigement et vous me promettez et presentez de biens plus que je ne suis digne d'avoir. Mais quant au regard de vous prendre pour mary et espoulx pour ceste heure presente vous plaise a moy pardonner, car j'ay fait serment et voué devant l'ymage de Mahon pour certaines necessités esquelles je me suis trouvee que de cy ung an entier nul homme ne prendray pour mary [75recto][3] ne espoux. Et pour tant, sire, s'i vous plaist ma promesse vous me laisserez tenir et acomplir jusques au terme d'ung an, et quant le terme sera passé si me prenez pour femme et espouse ou faictes de moy a vostre voulenté."

"Par Mahon," dist le roy, "vous ne dites que bien. Et puis que vous l'avez ainsi entreprins et voué a nostre dieu Mahon, je suis d'acord et content d'attendre jusques au temps que la fin de vostre serment sera acomply."

Ainsi demoura la dame au palays du roy d'Inde la Major, lequel pensoit bien dedens l'an acomply sa voulenté parfaire. Et commanda que la belle dame Esclarmonde fust sur toutes les aultres bien servie et chierement tenuee, et luy fist bailler et delivrer chambre moult belle et moult richement adornee en laquelle la plaisante[4] dame fist porter le chevalet de boys et au lieu le plus secret le mist

---

[1] Text has *piesente*.
[2] Text has *la la*.
[3] *k iii* at bottom right corner of 75r.
[4] Text has *plaisant*.

The tidings of this supposed vision came to the king of India, who ordered him to be brought before him. Now King Trompart was in a sorry state, for as soon as the king of India saw him, he recognized him and said, "Trompart, you are most welcome, for now the time is come for me to avenge the death of my brother against whom in your arrogance you waged war for seven long years. Then in the end you put him to death in torment and painful martyrdom, ending his days in shame. It is my wish to demonstrate to my brother that during his life I loved him loyally and after his death I avenged him."

Thereupon the king of India, without further deliberation, had King Trompart's head cut off right then and there. Once the execution was carried out, he took possession of the fair Esclarmonde and the wooden horse. Because of the lady's qualities, he had her led into his palace, where she was kept and served most honorably. Once back in his palace, he had her brought before him by those closest to him. When she was before him, he gazed at her most willingly, both for the lady's manner and her sweet countenance, for she surpassed all other women in corporeal beauty.

He spoke to her quite gently: "Lady, I know not who you are nor from what place you have come, but the sense and beauty I see in you inflame me, making me burn for your love more ardently than I ever have for any other lady. I have decided to take you as wife and spouse, making you queen and mistress of all the land of India Major."

"Sire," said the lady Esclarmonde, who knew well how to respond, "you speak graciously, and you promise me and offer me more favor than I am worthy of receiving. However, as regards taking you as my husband and spouse, for now you must excuse me, for I have sworn an oath and vowed before the image of Mohammed, because of certain needs I found myself in, that for an entire year I would take no husband or spouse. For that reason, sire, I beg you to allow me to keep my vow for one year, and when that term is up, you may take me as wife and spouse or do with me as you will."

"By Mohammed," said the king, "you speak wisely. Since you have undertaken this and made a vow to our god Mohammed, I must agree and am content to wait until such time as the term of your vow is completed."

So the lady remained in the palace of the king of India Major, who really thought to accomplish his desire in a year's time. He ordered that the fair lady Esclarmonde be well kept and well served above all others, and gave her a beautiful and richly adorned chamber to which the pleasant lady had the wooden horse brought, hiding it in the most secret spot she could find under her wardrobe. But

dessoubz sa garderobe. Et quant la dame veit le chevalet en regrettant Pacolet des yeulx tendrement plouroit en priant a Dieu doulcement que de ce danger la voulsist delivrer.

"Helas!" dist la dame, "vray Dieu tout puissant, en qui est ma seule creance, veullez vostre grace benigne dessus ceste povre femme estendre ou aultrement je suis et demourray dolente esgaree, de tous mes amis separee, et entre les aultres la plus dolente. Et aux mains de mes ennemis me fauldra le demourant de ma vie user et passer mes jours. Helas! vray Redempteur qui pour nous a souffert mort et passion, veullez moy delivrer de ceste tribulation amere en laquelle je suis, et fay par ta puissance que devant la fin de mes jours je puisse veoir de mes yeulx le plaisant Valentin a qui je suis donnee, car mieulx ayme mourir et souffrir mort honteuse que de mon corps habandonner a nul aultre que a luy."

La dame est en Inde la Major laquelle nuyt et jour en larmes et en pleurs, Dieu devotement priant qui la voulsist de ce danger mettre hors et la rendre saine au chevalier Valentin auquel sur tous les aultres sa foy luy avoit baillee et de cueur et de couraige loyaulté promise. Or laisseray a parler d'elle et du roy d'Inde et pour ma matiere entretenir je vous parleray de Pacolet et du grant dueil qui pour Esclarmonde la belle et plaisante fut demené en la noble cité d'Acquitaine.

[CHAPITRE 31]

Comment Pacolet print vengance de l'enchanteur Adramain lequel avoit trahy et desrobé la belle Esclarmonde. xxxi. chap[itre]

Apres que la nuyt fust passee en laquelle Adramain avoit trahy Pacolet et emmena Esclarmonde, parmy la cité d'Acquitaine fut grant cry demené pour la perte de la dame, car les gardes du palays lesquelz au matin la trouverent perdue getterent grandes lamentacions et firent si grant bruit que parmy toute la cité en furent les nouvel[75verso]les. Et quant Pacolet cogneust qu'i s'en estoit party, de trahyson se doubta; lors regarda parmy la chambre et tantost veit que son chevalet avoit perdu.

Si se detort les bras et tire les cheveulx en cryant haultement, "Ha! faulx Adramain, par toy je suis deceu! Car mon chevalet faulcement as desrobé, et ma dame Esclarmonde dessus a emportee. Bien doy haïr ma vie quant par toy suis ainsi trahy et despourveu et mis hors de la chose que plus je aymoye. Or viens a moy, Mort, pour moy hors du monde getter, car plus n'ay espoir de confort ne consolacion avoir."[1]

---

[1] Text has *ne confort de consolacion avoir.*

when the lady saw the magic horse, she began to weep tender tears, missing Pacolet, and praying sweetly to God that He deliver her from this danger.

"Alas!" said the lady, "true God all-powerful, in whom I place my sole belief, please extend your beneficent grace to this poor woman, for otherwise I am and will remain a sorrowful wanderer, separated from all my friends, and more wretched than any other. I will have to spend the rest of my life and pass my days in the hands of my enemies. Alas! true Redeemer who suffered death and passion for us, deliver me from this bitter tribulation in which I find myself, and allow me, through your power, before I die, once again to see with my own eyes the pleasing Valentin to whom I was given, for I prefer to die and suffer a shameful death than to abandon myself to anyone other than him."

The lady in India Major spent that night and day in tears and weeping, praying devoutly to God that He release her from this danger and return her safely to the knight Valentin to whom, above all others, she had pledged her troth and promised loyalty of heart and mind. Now I will leave off speaking of her and of the king of India, and, to keep up with my story, I will tell you about Pacolet and of the great mourning that went on in the noble city of Aquitaine for the fair and pleasant lady Esclarmonde.

CHAPTER 31

How Pacolet took vengeance upon the magician Adramain, who had betrayed him and kidnapped the fair Esclarmonde.

When the night during which Adramain betrayed Pacolet and took away Esclarmonde was concluded, a great cry went up throughout the city of Aquitaine for the loss of the lady, for the guards of the palace made such a noise of lamentation when they found out she was gone that the news spread quickly throughout the city. And when Pacolet realized that Adramain had left, he suspected betrayal; so he searched his room and saw right away that his magic horse was gone.

Then he wrung his hands and tore his hair, crying loudly, "Ah! false Adramain, I am deceived by you! For you have stolen my magic horse perfidiously and carried away my lady Esclarmonde on its back. I have no choice but to hate myself, seeing myself thus betrayed and destitute and separated from what I loved best. Now, Death, come to me, cast me out of this world, for I have no more hope to have comfort or consolation."

Tant fust triste et douloureux Pacolet pour la belle Esclarmonde que se n'eust esté Orson qui vers luy arriva d'ung cousteau se fust tué. De toutes pars du pays furent oÿ souspirs angoisseux et plaintes douloureuses. Bellissant[1] la royne haultement crye et pleure, et la belle Fezonne demena si grant dueil que ses riches habis a desrompu pour l'amour d'Esclarmonde qui frauduleusement fut emmenee et robee. Et menerent dueil et tristesse innumerable tous ceulx de la cité d'Acquitaine, et entre tous les aultres fut piteuse a ouÿr la complainte et lamentacion du bon duc d'Acquitaine.

Et quant Pacolet veit le grant dueil que chascun demenoit il leur a dist, "Seigneurs, je jure a Dieu qui tout le monde a fait que jamais je n'auray jour de ma vie joye ne confort jusques a ce que j'aye prins vengance du trahystre et desloyal Adramain par qui nous sommes ainsi trahys et deceus."

A ces motz s'est party, dolent et courroucé, et a osté sa robe et a prins habillement de femme ainsi comme une jeune pucelle. Fort moult gentement s'est paré et habillé, et en celuy estat s'est party de la cité d'Acquitaine et s'en est alé en l'ost du roy Ferragu. Et tantost qu'il fust en l'ost des payens et Sarrasins, et devers luy en vint ung qui moult fort le pria d'amours. Et moult luy sembla belle pucelle pour tant que Pacolet par son sort avoit sa face lavee d'une eaue tressubtille et en telle maniere que tous ceulx qui la regardoient entre eulx disoie[n]t que jamais n'avoyent veu plus belle ne plus gracieuse. De plusieurs payens et Sarrasins fut regardee et requise, mais de tous se escusa en leur disant, "Seigneurs, pardonnez moy, car pour ceste fois je suis promise et ay convenant a l'enchanteur Adramain, lequel m'a retenue."

"Belle," ce dirent les aultres, "or alez vostre voye."

Et ainsi Pacolet print le chemin pour aler devers l'enchanteur Adramain qui estoit en la tente. Et quant Adramain la[2] veit il fust si enchanté que Pacolet luy sembla estre la plus[3] belle femme que oncques Dieu crea. Et tant en fut amoureux que pour dormir celle nuyt avec elle la retint. Pacolet s'i accorda moult voulentiers.

"Monseigneur, sachez que de plusieurs j'ay esté requise. Mais sur tous les aultres vous me semblez estre le plus digne d'estre servy."

[76recto]"Fille,"[4] dist Adramain, "de riens ne vous doubtez, mais faictes bonne cheiere, car j'ay bien voulenté de vous servir et faire du bien et payer largement."

Lors commanda Adramain a ung sien serviteur qu'il gardast bien la fille et qu'elle fust au soupper servie de toutes viandes et de vin a sa plaisance. Or est l'enchanteur Pacolet au logis Adramain bien servy et honnestement receu. Et Adramain est parmy l'ost Ferragu a servir.

---

[1] Text has *Bessissant*.

[2] There are several instances in which the feminine third person direct object pronoun *la* is used to represent Pacolet in a woman's disguise. I have translated accordingly.

[3] Text has *qlus*.

[4] *k iiii* at bottom right corner of 76r.

Pacolet was so sad and grief-stricken over the fair Esclarmonde that had Orson not come to him just then he would have stabbed himself with a knife. From every part of the country were heard anguished sighs and doleful lamentations. Bellissant the queen cried and wept bitterly, and the fair Fezonne mourned so violently that she tore her rich garments out of love for Esclarmonde who had been so perfidiously kidnapped and carried away. Everyone in the city of Aquitaine mourned and grieved, most of all the good Duke of Aquitaine, whose complaint and lamentation were pitiful to hear.

When Pacolet saw everyone's deep mourning, he said to them, "My lords, I swear to God, who created the entire world, that I will never have joy or comfort a day in my life until I have taken vengeance upon the traitorous and disloyal Adramain by whom we have been betrayed and deceived."

With these words he left, still upset and angry. He took off his robe and put on woman's clothing, like that of a young maiden. He dressed up and adorned himself very elegantly, and in this disguise left the city of Aquitaine to go to King Ferragu's camp. Once arrived at the camp of the pagans and Saracens, someone approached him to ask insistently for love favors. He believed he was talking to a beautiful young girl because Pacolet had bathed his face in a special charmed water: thus all who looked at him said to each other that they had never seen a more beautiful or more gracious woman. He was eyed and applied to by several pagans and Saracens, but he excused himself from them all by saying, "My lords, pardon me, because for the moment I am promised and have an appointment with the enchanter Adramain who has retained me."

"Fair one," said the others, "then go on your way."

And so Pacolet found his way to the enchanter Adramain who was in his tent. When Adramain saw her, he was so entranced that Pacolet appeared to him to be the most beautiful woman ever created by God. He was so in love with her that he retained her to sleep with him that night. Pacolet agreed to this willingly.

"My lord, know that several asked for my company. But you seem to me of all the others the worthiest to be served."

"My girl," said Adramain, "don't worry about anything, rather make yourself at home, for I wish to serve you well, to do you good, and to pay you generously."

Then Adramain ordered one of his servants to guard the girl well and to have her well served at supper with all possible meats and wines according to her pleasure. Now is the magician Pacolet well served and honorably received in Adramain's lodging. In the meantime Adramain is off serving in Ferragu's camp.

"Amy," dist Pacolet au varlet de Adramain, "ou est le roy Trompart qui tant est puissant et renommé?"

"Par Mahon," dist il, "ma dame, je croy qu'il s'en est retourné en son pays, et maine avec luy la belle Esclarmonde dessus ung chevalet de bois que mon maistre luy a donné."

Quant Pacolet oÿt ces motz ne demandez point s'il fust dolent, mais nul semblant n'en monstra. Adonc est entré Adramain dedens la tente qui vin et espices presente a Pacolet. Puis luy a dit, "Ma fille, temps est d'aler reposer. Voycy le lyt en quoy vous et moy dormirons et ferons nostre voulenté."

"Seigneur," dist Pacolet, "vostre voulenté soit faicte."

Et lors Adramain se desvetit et entra en la couche pensant que la fille au plus pres de luy se couchast. Mais tout aussitost que dedens le lit fut, Pacolet tellement l'enchanta et si fort le fist dormir que pour chose que l'on sceust faire, jusques a lendemain matin ne se pouoit esveiller. Et quant il l'eust ainsi endormy il gette son sort parmy toute la tente tant que tous ceulx de l'environ ainsi comme Adramain a fait dormir. Et quant ilz furent tous endormis Pacolet a desvetu tous ses habis de femme et des plus riches habillemens de Adramain s'est revestu et paré. Puis a prins une espee qui en la chambre pendoit, et la teste de Adramain couppa et avec luy l'emporta sur la poincte de son espee. Et quant il eust ce fait il vint au tref de Ferragu qui de nul ne se doubtoit et n'avoit garde de nul Sarrasin. Et tant a sceu jouer de son art que tous a terre les a fait cheoir et endormir. Puis entra en la tente ou Ferragu dormoit, lequel l'a tant enchanté que de son lyt l'a fait saillir et courir en la place. Adonc Pacolet a prins sa sainture et au col luy a atachee en telle maniere que tout ainsi que une beste il le maine et fait courir apres luy jusques aux portes d'Acquitaine.

Et quant Pacolet fust aux portes de la cité d'Acquitaine, il trouva le duc Savary acompaigné de plusieurs seigneurs et barons qui avoient moult grant desir de sçavoir de celle entreprinse. Et aussitost que ilz ont veu Pacolet, ilz luy ont demandé, "Amy, ou est Esclarmonde? Que ne la ramenez vous?"

"Seigneurs," dist Pacolet, "ayez ung peu de pacience, car tout au premier coup de l'ache n'est pas l'arbre abatu. Sachez que de Adramain je suis vengé, car voyez en icy la teste. Et si ay tant fait par mon art que je maine avec moy le geant Ferragu lequel tout en dormant ay fait [76verso]courir apres moy parmy les pres."

"Par ma foy," dist Orson, "bien avez besongné."

"Messeigneurs," dist Pacolet, "ancores ay je fait plus fort, car en tout l'ost de Ferragu n'y a paien ne Sarrasin qui ne soient soubz les arbres couchéz et moult fort endormis. Pour tant se vous voulez avoir sur eulx victoire, a ceste heure vous les pourrez tous confundre et mettre a mort."

"My friend," said Pacolet to Adramain's valet, "where is King Trompart, the powerful and renowned?"

"By Mohammed, my lady," he said, "I believe that he has returned to his country and brings with him the fair Esclarmonde on a wooden horse that my master gave him."

When Pacolet heard these words, he was very upset, needless to say, but he gave no outward sign of it. Thereupon Adramain entered the tent, bringing wine and spices to Pacolet. Then he said to him, "My girl, it is time to rest. Here is the bed in which you and I will sleep together and do as we like."

"My lord," said Pacolet, "may your will be done."

Then Adramain disrobed and got into bed, thinking that the girl would lie down next to him. But as soon as he was in the bed, Pacolet put a charm on him, making him sleep so deeply that, whatever one might do to him, he would not be able to awake till the next morning. Once he had him thus slumbering, he cast his spell throughout the tent so that everyone there slept as deeply as Adramain. Once that was done, Pacolet took off his woman's clothes and dressed and adorned himself again in Adramain's richest garments. Then he took a sword hanging in the room and cut off Adramain's head, carrying it away with him on the point of his sword. Having done that, he headed to the tent of Ferragu who suspected no one nor was on guard against a Saracen. So well did he employ his craft that he caused everyone to collapse in deep sleep. Then he entered the tent where Ferragu lay sleeping, spinning such a spell on him that he leapt from his bed and began running around. Then Pacolet grabbed his belt and attached it around his neck in such a way that he was able to lead him like a beast. He made him run behind him all the way to the gates of Aquitaine.

When Pacolet arrived at the gates of the city of Aquitaine, he found Duke Savary accompanied by several lords and barons who wanted to know what Pacolet had managed to do. As soon as they saw Pacolet, they asked him, "Friend, where is Esclarmonde? Why aren't you bringing her back?"

"My lords," said Pacolet, "you must have some patience, for the tree is not felled by the first stroke of the ax.[1] I can tell you that I have avenged myself upon Adramain, for here is his head. Moreover, I have put my craft to the task of bringing with me the giant Ferragu, whom I made run behind me through the fields while he sleeps."

"By my faith," said Orson, "you have done well."

"My lords," said Pacolet, "I have done even better than that, for there is not a pagan or Saracen among all the host of Ferragu who is not sprawled under the trees fast asleep. So, if you want to have victory over them, now is the time for you to destroy them and put them all to death."

---

[1] Cf. Morawski, *Proverbes*, 7 (no. 189).

"Messeigneurs," dist Orson, "Pacolet dit bonnes nouvelles et me semble qu'il feroit bon de saillir hors de la cité et courir dessus tous les payens qui tellement sont endormis." Ainsi fut le conseil ordonné et la chose deliberee.

Lors firent mettre en une chartre obscure Ferragu jusques a leur retour. Puis a xv. ou a xvi. mille combatans saillirent de la cité d'Acquitaine. Et si secretement sont entréz en l'ost des Sarrasins que devant soleil leva[n]t les ont tous vaincus et mis a mort. A celle heure fust si grant occision de payens que de leurs corps fust toute la terre couverte. Et apres la destrousse les crestiens coururent parmi leurs tentes et prindrent toute leurs richesses et joyaulx. De l'ost des Sarrasins a moult grant joye et liesse retournerent vers Acquitaine.

Et quant le duc fust en son palays avec tous ses barons, il fist devant luy amener le geant Ferragu. Lors Ferragu qui esveillé fut tant dolent et courroucé que du cry qu'i faisoit sembloit homme enrragé. Lors luy dist le duc d'Acquitaine, "Le desespoir ne vous vault riens. Mais se baptiser vous voulez et prendre de Jesucrist la loy je vous sauveray la vie et vous feray en mon palays honnourer."

"Par Mahon," dist Ferragu, "j'aime mieulx mourir que renoncer mon dieu Mahon auquel j'ay longuement servy."

Lors commanda le duc d'Acquitaine que on luy trenchast la teste sans plus d'alongnement. Ainsi mourut Ferragu le geant. Pour laquelle mort furent tous joyeulx ceulx de la cité et tous les aultres crestiens qui de luy avoient cognoissance.

Moult pensa Orson par luy comment Pacolet pouoit avoir tant de science en luy et a dit a Pacolet, "Je cognoy que tu es ung serviteur loyal et que pour l'amour de moy tu t'es bouté et mis en plusieurs dangiers, et pour tant se c'est ton vouloir tout le temps de ta vie avec moy seras, de toute ma puissance bon guerdon te renderay."

"Sire," dist Pacolet, "je vous en remercye et vous prometz bien et afferme que tant que j'auray vie en tous les lieux ou je seray me trouverrez loyal."

Apres toutes ces choses acomplies et que la cité d'Acquitaine fut delivree et dehors de subjection des payens et Sarrasins par lesquelz elle estoit assiegee, Orson voulut prendre congé du duc d'Acquitaine pour aler en Constantinoble pour l'empereur[1] son pere secourir et son oncle le roy Pepin. Il est venu devant le duc et luy a dist, "Sire, puis que Dieu vous a fait telle grace que de voz ennemis vous estes vengé et que vostre terre est delivree, s'i plaist a vo[77recto]stre haulte seigneurie vous me donnerez congé pour aler en Constantinoble. Car sur toutes mes entreprinses, le plus grant desir de mon cueur est de veoir mon pere et de luy remener la royne Bellissant, ma mere, qui par mauldicte envye a esté si longuement de luy separee. Et avec les aultres choses vous sçavez que la cité de Constantinoble et tous les crestiens qui dedens sont seuffrent et endurent trop de douleurs et aultres tribulations a l'occasion des infideles et ennemis de nostre foy, lesquelz pieça et de long temps les ont durement assiegéz."

---

[1] Text has *lpeemrer*.

"My lords," said Orson, "Pacolet brings good news, and it seems to me that we should charge forth from the city right now and descend upon all these slumbering pagans." Thus was the project arranged and the thing decided.

First they had Ferragu put into a somber prison to await their return. Then with fifteen or sixteen thousand warriors they issued forth from the city of Aquitaine. So furtively did they infiltrate the Saracen army that before sunrise they had vanquished them all and put them to death. There was such a great massacre of pagans that the entire ground was covered with their bodies. After that attack, the Christians ransacked their tents, taking all their gold and jewels. With much joy and delight did they return from the Saracen host to Aquitaine.

Once the duke was back in his palace among his barons, he had the giant Ferragu brought before him. When Ferragu was awakened, he was so upset and enraged that he seemed, by the howl he made, a man out of his senses. The Duke of Aquitaine addressed him: "Despair avails you nothing. However, if you are willing to undergo baptism and take on the faith of Jesus Christ, I will spare your life and have you honored in my palace."

"By Mohammed," said Ferragu, "I prefer death to renouncing my god Mohammed, whom I have long served."

Thereupon the Duke of Aquitaine sentenced him to immediate decapitation, and so died Ferragu the giant. Not only the inhabitants of Aquitaine but Christians everywhere who knew of him rejoiced in his death.

Orson, considering the knowledge Pacolet possessed, said to him, "I recognize that you are a loyal servant and that for my sake you have placed yourself in many dangerous situations; for that reason, if you are willing to stay with me for the rest of your life, I will do my utmost to repay you fittingly."

"Sire," said Pacolet, "I thank you for your offer and promise you most sincerely that, as long as I live and wherever I may go, you will find me loyal."

After all these events, with the city of Aquitaine freed from the yoke of the pagans and Saracens by whom they had been besieged, Orson wished to take leave of the Duke of Aquitaine in order to go to Constantinople to help his father the emperor and his uncle King Pepin. He came before the duke and said, "Sire, since God has graced you with vengeance over your enemies and the deliverance of your land, may it please your lordship to grant me leave to go to Constantinople. For of all possible undertakings, the greatest wish of my heart is to see my father and to bring back to him my mother Queen Bellissant who has been separated from him for so long owing to cursed envy. And, above all, you know that the city of Constantinople and all the Christians within it suffer and endure a great many sorrows and other tribulations because of the infidels and enemies of our faith who have long besieged them."

"Orson," dist le duc d'Acquitaine, "vous parlez bien et saigement. Puis que vous estes deliberé de ainsi faire, je suis de ma part deliberé d'aler en vostre compaignie et d'entrer sur la mer a force et a grant puissance d'armes pour aler ayder et secourir vostre pere l'empereur de Grece et vostre oncle le roy Pepin."

Moult fut joyeulx Orson et moult mercya le bon duc d'Acquitaine. Si ne demoura pas longuement que le duc fit ses gens assembler, et apres qu'il eust baillé sa cité en garde a ung moult noble chevalier, ilz entrerent sur la mer pour acompaigner Orson, lequel avec luy mena sa mere la royne Bellisant et sa femme la belle Fezonne. Moult bien furent garnis de gens et de vivres et nagerent tant sur la mer de Grece que en brief temps veirent la noble cité de Constantinoble dont moult furent resjouys, et entre les aultres la royne Bellisant qui moult piteusement commença a plourer en faisant regretz, lamentacions et complaintes quant de son mary l'empereur et de sa fortuneuse tribulation luy souvenoit.

"Mere," ce dist Orson, "prenez en vous confort, car s'il plaist a Dieu de brief vous verrez celuy que vous desirez, et de la trahyson par laquelle vous fustes accusee aurez nouvelles a vostre proffit et honneur. Mais je suis moult pensif comment dedens Constantinoble pourrons entrer."

"Sire," dist Pacolet, "de ce n'ayez nulle doubte, car de brief je trouverray maniere que dedens la cité vous aurez entree, car je iray dedens la ville et leur compteray vostre venue et entreprinse."

"Amy," ce dit Orson, "de ce je te veul bien prier. Et si diras a Valentin la piteuse aventure et fortune de la belle Esclarmonde."

"Par ma foy," dist Pacolet, "de ce me pardonnerez, car trop a temps vient qui mauvaises nouvelles aporte."

Tantost apres ces motz Pacolet yssit hors de la nef pour aler en Constantinoble. Mais premier que il arrivast en Constantinoble il entra premier en l'ost des Sarrasins pour Valentin et le Verd Chevalier delivrer des prisons du souldan qui en iceluy jour par les Sarrasins avoient esté prins devant Constantinoble comme cy apres il est declairé.

"Orson," said the Duke of Aquitaine, "you speak wisely and well. Since you are determined to act thus, I am, for my part, determined to go in your company and cross the sea with a great force of arms to bring help and succor to your father the emperor of Greece and to your uncle King Pepin."

Orson was overjoyed and thanked the good Duke of Aquitaine profusely. Before long the duke had his men assemble, and, after having handed the city over to the keeping of a very noble knight, he embarked with Orson, who took with him his mother Queen Bellissant and his wife the fair Fezonne. They were well furnished with men and supplies, and crossed the Greek sea so swiftly that before long they saw the noble city of Constantinople, a sight which gladdened many of them, especially Queen Bellissant, who began to weep most piteously, remembering with regrets, lamentations, and plaints her husband the emperor and her unfortunate tribulations.

"Mother," said Orson, "be comforted, for if it please God, you will soon see the one you desire, and, concerning the treason of which you were accused, you will have tidings to your advantage and honor. But I am worried how we will manage to enter Constantinople."

"Sire," said Pacolet, "have no fear; I will soon find a way for you to enter the city, for I will get into the town and will recount to them your coming and your mission."

"Friend," said Orson, "please do so. And tell Valentin the sad adventure and misfortune of the fair Esclarmonde."

"By my faith," said Pacolet, "you must spare me that, for he who brings bad tidings always comes too soon."

Right after this exchange, Pacolet left the ship to go to Constantinople. But before entering the city, he went first to the Saracen camp to deliver Valentin and the Green Knight from the sultan's prison, for they had been taken that very day in front of Constantinople, as will be explained below.

[CHAPITRE 32]

Comment les crestiens pour avoir des vivres saillirent de Constantinoble et comment Valentin et le Verd Chevalier furent prins par les Sarrasins. xxxii. [chapitre]

[77verso]L'empereur[1] de Grece et le roy Pepin lesquelz dedens Constantinoble estoient par les ennemis de la foy assiegéz, et ne sçavoient riens de la venue du duc d'Acquitaine qui pour les secourir avec Orson a grant nombre de navires dessus la mer estoient. En ladite ville estoyent l'empereur et le roy Pepin qui d'avoir secours n'avoient esperance. La estoient plusieurs vaillans champions crestiens et gens de tous estas en grant destresse et indigence de vivres. A cogneu Valentin leur grant necessité, pour laquelle chose luy, de grant hardiesse et vaillantise plain, acompaigné du Verd Chevalier et de vint mille combatans chevaliers, pour avoir et conquerir des vivres saillyrent[2] hors de la cité de Constantinoble. Et des vivres des payens et Sarrasins chairgerent trois cens charretees et tuerent et mirent[3] a mort tous ceulx qui les conduisoient.

Mais ainsi que devers la ville cuiderent retourner pour les vivres emmener, a l'encontre des crestiens vindrent d'une part le souldan[4] et d'aultre part le roy d'Arappe et le roy Affricant. La fut moult grande destruction de payens et de Sarrasins et moult piteuse occysion de crestiens. De la proesse et de la vaillantise du noble chevalier Valentin il n'en fault riens parler, car a cest assault il tua le roy Dramagant avec le chevalier Clarien et plusieurs aultres dequoy les noms nous sont incogneus. Et le Verd Chevalier au roy de Morienne d'ung coup luy abatit le bras et l'escu, et devant luy tua son frere Abillant avec dix chevaliers payens moult fors. Mais nonobstant leurs forces, puissances et hardiesse, mal furent secourus et doubteuse aventure dont fut moult grant pitié.[5] Car de leurs ennemis mortelz furent prins prisonniers et au mauldit souldan menéz, lequel en demena moult grant feste et grant joye. Et pour les faire mourir et juger a honteuse mort il fist assembler quinze roys payens qui pour le secourir en l'ost estoient venus. Moult grant couroux fust parmy la cité de Constantinoble de l'empereur et du roy Pepin pour la perte de Valentin et du Verd Chevalier, car ceulx qui en la cité retournerent fuyans si raporterent les nouvelles que sans nulle remission estoient mors en la bataille.

---

[1] Woodcut of battle scene.
[2] Text has *saillyrens*.
[3] Text has *nirent*.
[4] Apparently a new sultan, as Moradin was captured and executed in Chapter 29.
[5] There seems to be a verb missing. The latter part of the sentence should perhaps read, "...et [eurent] doubteuse aventure dont fut moult grant pitié."

CHAPTER 32

How the Christians rode forth from Constantinople to find provisions; and how Valentin and the Green Knight were taken by the Saracens.

The emperor of Greece and King Pepin, besieged within Constantinople by the enemies of the faith, knew nothing of the Duke of Aquitaine's coming and his having set sail with Orson and a great number of ships in order to help them. The emperor and King Pepin were caught in that city without any apparent hope of outside aid. Many valiant Christian champions were there, as well as people of every estate, all in great distress for lack of food. Valentin, full of boldness and valor, was aware of their great need, for which reason he rallied the Green Knight and twenty thousand soldier knights to sally forth out of the city of Constantinople to seize provisions. And they fell upon three hundred wagons of food for the pagans and Saracens, after killing and putting to the sword all those conducting them.

However, just as they were returning to the city with the provisions, the Christians were attacked on one side by the sultan and on the other by the king of Arabia and King Affricant. There was great destruction among the pagans and Saracens, but also much piteous killing of Christians. One can hardly describe the prowess and valiance of the noble knight Valentin, for in this assault he slew King Dramagant, along with the knight Clarien, and many others whose names are unknown. For his part, the Green Knight sliced off with one stroke the arm and shield of the King of Morienne, and before him slew his brother Abillant along with ten powerful pagan knights. Yet notwithstanding their force, strength, and boldness, they were badly supported and got caught in a dangerous adventure, which was a great pity. For they were taken prisoner by their mortal enemies and brought before the cursed sultan, who gloated in his joy. In order to have them sentenced to a shameful death and executed, he assembled fifteen pagan kings who had joined his host to come to his aid. Meanwhile, great sorrow spread throughout the city of Constantinople and in the hearts of the emperor and King Pepin for the loss of Valentin and the Green Knight, for those who returned in flight to the city brought back news that they had been without doubt killed in the battle.

Or furent Valentin et le Verd Chevalier dedens les tentes du souldan estroitement lyéz et rigoureusement tenus dont Valentin ploura disant a voix fort piteuse, "Helas! belle Esclarmonde, jamais ne vous verray dont j'ay le cueur triste et dolent. Par long temps m'avez attendu, et en peine et en travail de mon corps longuement vous ay quise comme celle qui du vouloir de Dieu pour moy espouser estoit determinee. Et quant le temps estoit venu que de mes maulx je devoie avoir alegance et de mes doleurs resconfort et consolacion, je suis de tout plaisir desvetu et separé de mes amis, et aux mains de mes ennemis qui ma mort ont juree. Adieu mon pere, noble empereur de Grece, car en moy vous n'aurez plus d'enfant. Adieu la noble Bellissant ma mere redoubtee, car oncques pour moy vous n'eustes petit de plaisir et de confort, et jamais plus vous n'aurez que doleur et tristesse. Adieu mon vaillant frere Orson, que tant de bon cueur vous m'avez aymé et loyallement servy, car l'esperance que j'avoye de passer et finer noz jours avec pere et mere le demourant de nostre vie est[1] par ung cas infortuné soudainement tourné."

Quant le Verd Chevalier veit que Valentin si piteusement se complaingnoit en regrettant ses amis il luy a dist, "Sire, pour Dieu, oublions[2] pere et mere, tous amys et parens et faisons priere a Dieu qui de nous veulle avoir mercy et noz ames en son paradis recepvoir. Prenons congié de ceste vie et en gré la mort pour la saincte foy soustenir, et ayons fiance en Dieu qui pour nous voulut souffrir mort et passion."

Or fut le souldan assis en une chaiere paree, en grant orgueil et en grandes pompes, moult richement vestu et adorné, lequel dit devant tous, "Seigneurs, j'ay fait serment au dieu Mahon que ces deux faulx crestiens, lesquelz de present et aultreffois se sont perforcéz de nous porter dommaige et de mes gens destruyre, mourront villainement. Si veullez aviser par entre vous de quelle mort honteuse je les feray mourir."

En disant ces parolles Pacolet se getta en la presse, lequel getta ung tel sort que, jassoit ce que aultre foys l'eussent veu du temps que par luy le souldan Moradin fust prins, pour tant a celle heure il ne fut de nul cogneu. Il entra dedens la tente ou se faisoit le jugement des deux chevaliers crestiens, et tantost que il aperceut Valentin et le Verd Chevalier il se mist a deux genoulx et en langaige sarrasins de par Mahon salua le souldan puis luy a dist, "Trespuissant sire, entendez mon messaige. Sachez que je suis messaiger de vostre frere Groant le puissant roy d'Argie, lequel pour vostre secours et pour les crestiens confundre, vient par devers vous, acompaigné de quatre roys fors et puissans, avec grant nombre de capitaines lesquelz ont de plusieurs puissans chevaliers et de vaillans combatans

---

[1] Text has *et*.

[2] Text has *omblions*. This (mis)spelling of the verb *oublier* recurs in this chapter and elsewhere. Since the *n* and *u* are often substituted one for the other in the typesetting of this volume, such a spelling may be a confusion of *m* for *n*. It will be emended and noted at each occurrence.

Now Valentin and the Green Knight were being held tightly bound in the tents of the sultan. Valentin wept, saying in a piteous voice, "Alas! fair Esclarmonde, my heart breaks, for I will never see you again. You have waited so long for me, and with much pain and travail did I long seek you, as the one whom God had ordained me to marry. And when the time had come that I was to have some alleviation of my trials and receive comfort and consolation for my sorrows, here I am divested of all pleasure, separated from my friends, and trapped in the hands of my foes who have sworn my death. Goodbye, my father, noble emperor of Greece, for you will no longer have a child in me. Farewell, noble Bellissant, my respected mother, for you will never have from me the least pleasure or comfort, only sorrow and sadness. Farewell, my valiant brother Orson, you who have loved me with such a good heart and served me faithfully, for the hope I had of spending and ending our days with our father and mother for the rest of our life is suddenly rendered hopeless by an unfortunate turn of events."

When the Green Knight saw Valentin complaining so bitterly, regretting his loved ones, he said to him, "Sire, for God's sake, let us forget father and mother, all friends and relatives, and let us pray to God to have mercy on us and receive our souls into His paradise. Let us take leave of this life and accept our death as sustaining the holy faith, and let us put our trust in God who was willing to suffer death and passion for us."

In the meantime, the sultan, richly dressed and adorned, was seated in an ornate chair, surrounded in his great pride with all kinds of pomp. Now he spoke before all: "My lords, I have sworn to the god Mohammed that these two false Christians shall die ignominiously, for they have committed great violence against us and caused destruction among my men both in the past and in the present. Confer among yourselves as to by what shameful method I shall put them to death."

As he spoke these words, Pacolet slipped into the press of men, casting such a spell that, even though they had seen him before when he had captured Sultan Moradin, they nevertheless did not recognize him at that moment. He entered the tent where judgment was being pronounced on the two Christian knights, and, as soon as he perceived Valentin and the Green Knight, he went down on both knees and spoke in the Saracen tongue, greeting the sultan and saying to him, "Most puissant sire, hear my message. Know that I am a messenger from your brother Groant, the powerful king of Argie, who, in order to bring you aid and destroy the Christians, is coming to you, accompanied by four strong and doughty kings, along with a great number of captains who have many stout knights and valiant soldiers, all of whom bring you aid. Through me they ask that

lesquelz vous feront aide. Et par moy vous mande [78verso]que se vous luy faictes sçavoir le quartier et la place ou vous vouldrez que son siege soit mis, et se vous avez aulcuns prisonniers des faulx crestiens, que vous les luy transmettez et il les fera mener en son pays pour tyrer a la charrue et labourer les terres ainsi comme bestes mues. Si me semble que j'en voy icy deux qui moult y seront dignes et propices de telle peine souffrir, desquelz vostre frere seroit moult fort joyeux."

Et en disant ces parolles Pacolet soufla contre le souldan et fist ung sort si subtil que de tout ce que il disoit il estoit creu. Moult fut joyeulx le souldan des nouvelles de Pacolet, car il pensa que il luy deist verité. Il le fist moult richement servir au disner, et commanda que pour ceste nuyt fust retenu et que de sa peine il fust guerdonné et payé richement.

Grant joye demenerent Valentin et le Verd Chevalier en leur cueur quant ilz veirent Pacolet, mais nul semblant n'en firent. Or fut la nuyt venue que chascun fut retrait pour dormir et reposer fors que deux cens Sarrasins qui estoient en armes et en bastonnéz, lesquelz pour les prisonniers garder celle nuyt furent esleuz. Mais mauvaise garde en firent pour eulx car quant vint vers la minuit Pacolet qui son mestier n'avoit pas oublié[1] vint par devers eulx, et en parlant aux faulx et mauldis Sarrasins de par Mahon les salua. Puis a getté son sort par si habille maniere que tous a la terre se sont couchéz et endormis, tout ainsi que des aultres desquelz est mencion faicte. Puis a prins deux chevaulx et est venu aux prisonniers lesquelz contre ung pillier moult fort estroitement estoient lyéz. Et apres que il les eust destachéz souldainement et sans demouree les a fait a cheval monter. Et en ce point les a delivréz et hors des mains de leurs ennemis mortelz aménéz sans que de nul puissent avoir esté veuz ne cogneus.

Et quant ilz furent aux champs hors de leurs ennemis et loing de tous dangiers Pacolet leur a dit, "Seigneurs, menez chiere joyeuse et prenez en vous resconfort, car sachez que sur ceste terre sont venus le bon duc d'Acquitaine et le vaillant chevalier Orson qui pour vostre secours et ayde plusieurs vaillans capitaines a grant nombre de combatans ont fait la mer passer. Et si vient en leur compaignie la noble royne Bellissant et la belle Fezonne."

"Amy," dit Valentin, "que ne vient la belle Esclarmonde?"

"Par ma foy," dist Pacolet, "moult voulentiers elle fust venue et grant desir en avoit mais sachez que tout aussitost que elle fust montee dessus la mer pour l'odeur de l'eaue si tresgrant mal au cueur luy print que force fust de la remener en la cité d'Acquitaine."

Le chevalier Valentin le creut et nulle aultre enqueste n'en fist pour celle heure presente, car bien cuidoit le vaillant Valentin qu'il deist verité. Lors a dist Pacolet, "Seigneurs, alez en Constantinoble [79recto]et faictes demain au matin en maniere que vous saillez hors de la ville tant et en si grant puissance comme possible vous sera pour aler a l'encontre de voz ennemis. Et je feray en telle maniere

---

[1] Text has *omblie* (see p. 298, n. 2).

you let him know where you want him to mount his siege, and if you have any false Christian prisoners, that you send them to him, and he will bring them to his country to pull the plow and labor in the fields like mute beasts. It seems to me that I see two right here who merit such a punishment, which would make your brother quite happy."

While saying these words Pacolet blew lightly on the sultan and cast such a subtle spell that everything he said was believed. The sultan was overjoyed by Pacolet's tidings, for he thought he was telling him the truth. He had him served sumptuously at dinner, ordering that he be retained for that evening and generously paid and compensated for his trouble.

Valentin and the Green Knight were inwardly filled with joy when they saw Pacolet, but they gave no outward sign at all. When night fell, everyone retired for sleep and rest except for two hundred Saracens who remained armed, having been chosen to guard the prisoners that night. However, they mounted a poor guard, for when midnight came, Pacolet, who had not forgotten his craft, came to them, greeting the false and accursed Saracens in the name of Mohammed. Then he cast a spell on them in so clever a manner that they all immediately sank to the ground in a deep sleep, just as others had done as I mentioned before. Then he found two horses and came to the prisoners who had been very tightly bound to a pillar. Quickly untying them, he mounted them without delay. Thus did he deliver and free them from the hands of their mortal enemies without anyone having seen or recognized them.

Once they were in the fields far away from their enemies and all danger, Pacolet spoke: "My lords, be joyous and take comfort, for I tell you that the good Duke of Aquitaine and the valiant knight Orson have come to this land, bringing with them over the sea many stalwart captains and a great number of soldiers to bring you aid. In their company came also the noble queen Bellissant and the fair Fezonne."

"Friend," said Valentin, "why hasn't the fair Esclarmonde come as well?"

"By my faith," said Pacolet, "she would have come most willingly, and greatly did she desire to do so, but as soon as she was at sea, such terrible seasickness came over her that we were obliged to bring her back to the city of Aquitaine."

The knight Valentin believed him and made no other inquiry for the present moment, for the valiant Valentin really thought he spoke the truth. Then Pacolet said, "My lords, go to Constantinople, and make sure that you sally forth out of the city tomorrow morning with as great a force as possible against your enemies. For my part, I will make sure that the entire army of the Duke of Aquitaine, who

que toute l'armee du duc d'Acquitaine qui est venue d'aultre part les assauldra, et a celle heure cuidera le souldan que ce soit secours qui luy viengne. Car je luy ay fait entendant que le roy d'Argie son frere est arrivé et acompaigné de quatre roys lesquelz demain au plus matin se doivent en son ost trouver et assembler."

"Pacolet," ce dist le chevalier Valentin, "tu parles saigement et tout ainsi sera fait."

A ces motz[1] prindrent congé l'ung de l'autre Valentin et Pacolet. Pacolet retourna devers le duc d'Acquitaine lequel sur le port de la mer estoit avec toute son armee. Et luy compta comment il avoit esté dedens l'ost du souldan et avoit illec delivré Valentin et le Verd Chevalier. Puis leur a dist la maniere comment il avoit par son sort fait a croire au souldan que son frere le roy Groan lendemain le devoit venir secourir.

"Pacolet," ce dist Orson, "vous estes moult a prisier quant telles choses vous sçavez bien faire."

"Sire," dist Pacolet, "une aultre chose il y a. C'est que demain au plus matin nous alons contre les payens et Sarrasins frapper dessus leur ost, car ceulx de Constantinoble a grant puissance d'armes de leur part si les doivent assaillir, et par ainsi seront tous mors et desconfiz. Car de toute l'armee de par deça cuidera le souldan que soyons payens et Sarrasins par la façon et le subtil langaige de quoy je l'ay enchanté."

De ceste entreprinse fust joyeulx et moult esmerveillé le duc d'Acquitaine et tous ceulx de sa court. Il fist ses gens armer et appointer pour la chose parfaire et acomplir. Et toute la nuyt entour de luy fist mettre bon gait et seures gardes.

Les nouvelles furent tantost parmy la cité de Constantinoble du delivrement de Valentin et du Verd Chevalier; en iceluy jour en la cité arriverent. De la joye et de la liesse de l'empereur de Grece et du roy Pepin pour l'amour de Valentin je ne vous sçauroye que dire ne que racompter, car tant furent de joye au cueur parfaictement touchéz que ris et pleurs ensemble procedoient. Le vaillant chevalier Valentin vint devant les deux vaillans princes qui moult fort doulcement entre leur bras le baiserent et acolerent. Puis leur dist comment et compta ledit Valentin toute la maniere de sa dolente prinse et comment ilz avoient esté, luy et le Verd Chevalier, par Pacolet delivréz et degettéz hors des mains du souldan qui leur mort avoit juree. Et si leur racompta la venue du duc d'Acquitaine et de son frere Orson qui pour les venir secourir estoient venus et passéz oultre la mer. Et finablement leur a dit toute l'entreprinse qui estoit faicte des payens et Sarrasins assaillir tout ainsi que par [79verso]Pacolet avoit esté deliberé.

Quant l'empereur de Grece et le roy Pepin oÿrent les nouvelles dilligamment et sans nulle prolongacion toute la nuit firent leurs gens armer et mettre en point. Et de leur armee ilz firent ordonner cincq batailles. La premiere fut baillee a Valentin, la secunde au Verd Chevalier, la tierche au roy Pepin, la quarte a Millon

---

[1] Text has *mortz*.

has come, will attack them from the other side, but at that moment the sultan will believe help is coming to him. For I led him to believe that the king of Argie his brother has arrived, accompanied by four kings, who are supposed to find his army and assemble with them in the early morning."

"Pacolet," said the knight Valentin, "you speak wisely, and we shall do as you say."

With these words Valentin and Pacolet took leave of each other. Pacolet returned to the Duke of Aquitaine, who was still in port with his entire army. He recounted to him how he had gotten into the sultan's camp and had there delivered Valentin and the Green Knight. Then he told him the way in which he had used a spell to make the sultan believe that his brother Groant was supposed to come bring him help the next day.

"Pacolet," said Orson, "you are to be highly prized for such marvels."

"Sire," said Pacolet, "there is something else. Early tomorrow morning we are attacking the pagan and Saracen host, for the men of Constantinople are supposed to assail them from their side with great strength, and thus, attacked on both sides, they will all be routed and killed. For the sultan will believe that all the army on this side is pagans and Saracens because of the way I enchanted him with magical language."

The Duke of Aquitaine, as well as his entire court, was thrilled and full of wonder at this development. He had his people arm themselves and get ready to carry out the plan. That night he had a careful watch set up all around with his best guards.

The day Valentin and the Green Knight arrived in the city of Constantinople, tidings of their liberation soon made the rounds of the city. I could never recount to you the joy and delight of the emperor of Greece and King Pepin because of their love for Valentin, for their hearts were so elated that laughter and tears mixed together. The dauntless knight Valentin came before the two valiant princes, who both clasped him in their arms to kiss and hug him. Then Valentin recounted to them the story of their unfortunate capture, and how he and the Green Knight had been delivered and rescued by Pacolet from the hands of the sultan who had sworn their deaths. Next he told them of the coming of the Duke of Aquitaine and his brother Orson, who had crossed the sea to come to their aid. Finally he explained the plan to assail the pagans and Saracens, just as Pacolet had set it up.

When the emperor of Greece and King Pepin heard the tidings, diligently and without any delay they spent the night readying their men for battle. They set up five battalions in their army. The first was given to Valentin to lead, the second to the Green Knight, the third to King Pepin, the fourth to Millon d'Angler,

d'Angler, la quinte fut baillé a Sanson d'Orleans qui portoit en sa banniere ung ours d'argent. Et ainsi ordonna ses batailles le puissant empereur de Grece qui puissant fut en guerre et en armes bien subtil.

Et quant vint a l'aube du jour saillirent de la cité pour aler Sarrasins assaillir et combatre. Et quant ilz furent sur les champs, chascun en son endroit fit trommpettes sonner, clarons et busines, et a grans cours d'oliphant dont le bruit fut si grant que Sarrasins et payens tout a celle heure crierent a haulte voix alarme, et de leurs tentes fierement ilz saillirent a si grant multitude que toute la terre en estoit couverte. A celle heure furent assaillis payens et Sarrasins de par l'empereur de Grece et du bon roy Pepin. Piteuse fust la bataille pour les crestiens celluy jour et pour les payens et Sarrasins cruelle et dommaigeuse desconfiture, car a celluy assault moururent villainement et a moult grant honte grant nombre de Sarrasins et de infideles de la foy crestienne jusques a nombre de cinquante mil et plus.

La fust le roy Pepin lequel en donnant couraige et hardiesse a ses gens a haulte voix criant "Moultjoye!" Lors il y eust ung Sarrasin qui a haulte voix crya, disant au souldan, "Ha! sire, reculez arriere et pensons de sauver la vie, car en ceste nuyt avez perdu les deux prisonniers que tant faisiez estroitement garder. Et d'aultre part nous avons veu ung bannyere soubz laquelle il y a grant multitude de gens qui contre nous fierement courent."

"Par Mahon," dist le souldan, "je cognoy clerement que nous sommes trahys, mais non pourtant ayons bonne fiance en noz dieux et pensons de nous deffendre, car j'ay bonne esperance a l'ayde de Mahomment que au jour d'uy par nous seront les crestiens destruis."

A celle heure prindrent les payens si grant couraige de combatre que par force contraingnirent les crestiens a reculer. Mais petit leur valut leur orgueilleux couraige, car sur eulx vindrent frapper le duc d'Acquitaine et Orson qui si estroitement les suivirent et assaillirent de toutes pars qu'i furent si court tenus que sans nulle remission deffinerent leur jours villainement tant et si grant nombre que de toute leur puissance n'en eschappa que xxiii. et ainsi par le vouloir de Jesucrist et par la grant vaillance des preux et grans princes. A celuy jour furent les mauldis payens et Sarrasins desconfis devant Constantinoble.

Et quant la bataille eust prins fin et que les crestiens tous ensemble furent la liéz, Valentin et son frere Orson [80recto], lesquelz l'ung l'autre avoient cogneu, vindrent devant l'empereur de Grece en moult grant reverence.

"Pere," dist Valentin, "vous pouez icy veoir mon frere Orson, lequel jamais vous ne veistes, et par lequel en ceste journee vous avez esté notablement conforté et secouru."

Lors l'empereur embraça son filz Orson en plourant moult piteusement, et aussi fist le roy Pepin.

"Beau filz," dist l'empereur, "bien soyez tu venu, car par toy est ma joye doublee et mon espoir fortifié."

"Orson," ce dist le roy Pepin, "ne vous souvient-il pas quant vous me abatistes de dessus mon cheval a terre ou boys auquel je vous chassoye?"

and the fifth to Samson d'Orleans, whose banner displayed a silver bear. Thus did the puissant emperor of Greece, mighty in battle and clever in war, order his battalions.

As day dawned, they issued forth out of the city to assail and combat the Saracens. Once they reached the fields, each one from his emplacement had the horns, trumpets, and clarions sounded, and at the terrifying noise of the great elephant-ivory horns, all the pagan Saracens cried the alarm loudly, streaming fiercely out of their tents in such a multitude that the entire earth seemed covered with them. At that very moment the pagans and Saracens were attacked by the emperor of Greece and the good King Pepin. The battle was piteous for the Christians that day, but for the pagans and Saracens it brought cruel and devastating defeat, for, in that first assault, great numbers of Saracens and infidels to the Christian faith died basely and shamefully, up to fifty thousand and perhaps more.

There in the thick of it was King Pepin, inspiring courage and boldness in his men as he cried, "Montjoy!" Then there was a Saracen who called out loudly to the sultan, "Ah, sire, withdraw and let us try to save our lives, for this night you have lost the two prisoners on whom you had set such a close guard. Moreover, we have seen the banner of a great multitude of men who are about to attack us fiercely."

"By Mohammed," said the sultan, "I can see clearly that we are betrayed, but nevertheless let us trust in our gods and think to defend ourselves, for I have great hope that with Mohammed's aid we will destroy the Christians today."

At that moment the pagans mustered so well their courage to fight that they forced the Christians to fall back. But little did their arrogant daring avail them, for the Duke of Aquitaine and Orson struck at them, hounding and assailing them so closely from every side that they could find no escape, and without any remission such huge numbers ended their days ignominiously that of all their original strength only twenty-three survived, all of which is due to the will of Jesus Christ and the great valor of the grand and bold princes. That day the accursed pagans and Saracens were defeated on the field before Constantinople.

When the battle was over and the Christians were celebrating, Valentin and his brother Orson, who had found each other, came before the emperor of Greece and greeted him with great ceremony.

"Father," said Valentin, "here is my brother Orson, whom you have never seen, and from whom today you received splendid help."

Thereupon the emperor, weeping piteous tears, embraced his son Orson, as did King Pepin.

"Fair son," said the emperor, "you are most welcome, for by you is my joy doubled and my hope fortified."

"Orson," said King Pepin, "do you remember when you knocked me off my horse to the ground in the wood where I was hunting you?"

"Beaulx oncle, de ce me doit il bien souvenir, et de plusieurs aultres choses par moy faictes. Mais pour le present ne devons aultre chose penser fors que de louer Dieu et regracier de la victoire laquelle par luy nous a esté au jour d'uy donnee contre les faulx ennemis de la foy crestienne. Car de toute nostre puissance nous devons cueur et couraige appliquer pour venger Jesucrist lequel en la croix souffrit mort et passion pour nous."

De ces parolles oÿr furent joyeulx tous ceulx qui en la presence estoient, et moult priserent et aimerent Orson qui tant sagement avoit parlé.

Adonc s'assemblerent l'empereur et le roy Pepin, Valentin et Orson et le Verd Chevalier, Blandimain et Guygard le marchant par qui l'archevesque fut pieça combatu, et en grant honneur et triumphe sont aléz veoir les tentes de la royne Bellissant et de la belle Fezonne, lesquelles en attendant la desconfiture des Sarrasins estoient en ung pavillon, honnestement acompaignees. Dieu devotement deprioyent qu'il voulsist garder et deffendre l'empereur et toutes ses gens des payens et Sarrasins qui leur mort desiroient.

Et quant Bellissant sceut que la bataille estoit gaignee elle a dist a Fezonne, "M'amye, faictes bonne chiere car vous verrez tantost l'empereur mon mary lequel est pere de Orson qui pour femme vous a prinse."

"Dame," ce dist Fezonne, "Dieu en soit mercié, car de telle chose veoir j'en ay moult grant desir."

En disant ceste parolle arriva devant leur pavillon l'empereur et sa compaignie, et quant l'aperceurent elles saillirent au devant. Lors l'empereur quant il avisa Bellissant il saillit bas de son cheval, en plourant et souspirant, sans parolles pouoir dire, vint embracer la dame laquelle a deux genoulx a terre se getta. La endroit s'assemblerent l'empereur et la bonne dame qui par l'espace de xx. ans et plus d'ensemble avoient esté separéz. Or ne fault il pas enquerir se de se[1] trouver l'ung l'autre eurent bon soulas et se de pitié parfonde eurent les cueurs touchéz et estrains que d'amour naturelle entre les bras l'ung de l'autre a la terre cheurent paulmés.

Et quant Valentin et Orson veirent la grant pitié de leur pere et de leur mere, moult tendrement et piteusement commencerent a plourer et au plus pres d'eulx cheurent tous paulmés. [80verso]Le roy Pepin et plusieurs aultres barons et chevaliers qui ceste chose regarderent moult tendrement commencerent a plourer.

Et apres que l'empereur et sa femme Bellissant eurent leurs douleurs moderees, et que ilz furent venus hors de paulmoison, l'empereur si parla a la royne en telle maniere, "Helas! m'amye, moult me doit fort au cueur desplaire de la douleur et de la peine ou vostre corps a esté par longue espace livré a cause de l'exil en quoy je vous ay mise par envye mauvaise et legiere credence. Car je sçay de certaine que a tort et sans rayson de moy vous fustes chassé, dont depuis j'ay esté en peine et en soussy, vostre corps regrettant et plourant ma doloureuse

---

[1] Text has *ce*.

"Dear uncle, I have no choice but to remember that and many other things I did. But for now, we should think only of praising God and thanking Him for the victory He granted us today against the false enemies of the Christian faith. For with all our strength we must set our hearts and minds on avenging Jesus Christ, who suffered death and passion for us on the cross."

Everyone there rejoiced to hear these words, and they loved Orson and valued him for his wise words.

Then the emperor and King Pepin, Valentin and Orson with the Green Knight, Blandimain and Guygard, the merchant who had fought the archbishop so long ago, assembled together, and with great honor and triumph they went to the tents to see Queen Bellissant and the fair Fezonne, who, properly attended, had awaited the defeat of the Saracens in a pavilion. They had been praying devoutly to God to keep and defend the emperor and all his people against the pagans and Saracens who desired their death.

When Bellissant found out that the battle had been won, she said to Fezonne, "My friend, be happy, for soon you will see the emperor, my husband, who is the father of Orson, who has taken you as wife."

"Lady," said Fezonne, "may God be praised, for I have great desire to see him."

While she was speaking thus, the emperor and his company arrived at the pavilion, and when they noticed them, the ladies issued forth. As the emperor caught sight of Bellissant, he leapt from his horse, weeping and sighing, unable to utter a word, and came to embrace the lady, who, for her part, threw herself to her knees before him. There came together the emperor and the good lady who had been separated from each other for more than twenty years. It goes without saying that their meeting caused them great joy, but such deep emotion touched and clutched their hearts that from natural love they fell in a faint to the ground in each other's arms.

When Valentin and Orson saw the intensity of their father's and mother's feelings, they too began to weep tenderly and piteously, each falling in a swoon next to them. King Pepin and many other barons and knights watching this scene were themselves moved to tender tears.

When the emperor and his wife Bellissant had managed to calm their emotions somewhat and come out of their swoon, the emperor addressed the queen in the following manner: "Alas! my dear, my heart grieves for the pain and sorrow you endured so long in the exile I forced upon you through evil motivation and a too easy credulity. For I know for certain that I banished you wrongly and without just cause, for which reason I have long suffered, not only missing you yourself, but also

faulte et la peine et grief martire ausquelz je premeditoie que vous fussiez. Mais sur toutes choses vous me pardonnerez, s'il vous plaist, car a grant peine se peut nul de trahyson garder."

"Mon amy," dist la bonne dame, "de la tribulation en laquelle j'ay esté plus ne vous soussiez, car de l'eure que je vous ay veu de toutes mes douleurs j'ay eu alegance et confort. Mais d'une chose je vous prie — c'est qu'i vous plaise de moy monstrer[1] le bon marchant par lequel la trahyson a esté cogneue et le faulx archevesque combatu."

"M'amye," dist l'empereur, "icy le pouez regarder, car veez icy le bon Guygard par lequel la chose a esté cogneue et vostre honneur esprouvee."

"Amy," ce dit la dame au marchant, "bien estes digne de aymer et de estre chier tenu entre les aultres, car pour le grant prouffit et honneur que vous avez fait a l'empereur de Grece et au noble sang de France de icy en avant je vous retiens mon chambrelan. Et avec ce veul que vous ayez pour voz peines et labours mille mars d'or fin."

"Dame," dist le marchant, "de ce vous doy bien remercier et toute ma vie loyallement je vous serviray, combien que pas je ne la deservy que si grant don vous me donnez. Mais a Dieu soyent les graces et les louenges lesquelles en vostre aversité vous a voulu consoler et conforter, et vostre bonne renommee et loyalle preudommie conserver et deffendre."

Lors parla Valentin a la bonne dame sa mere en luy disant, "Ma dame, plaise vous parler a moy, et me dictes de ma bonne amye Esclarmonde nouvelles, comment elle se porte."

"Ha, beau filz," dist la dame, "prenez en vous confort et pacience, car la belle Esclarmonde faulcement et mauvaisement en la cité d'Acquitaine a esté desrobee et livree au roy Trompart qui pour les payens secourir estoit devant la cité d'Acquitaine venu."

Quant Valentin oÿt ces nouvelles il regarda Pacolet moult furieusement comme celuy qui pensast que par luy fust deceu. Et par couraige souldain et despiteulx voulut dessus luy frapper d'ung glaisve moult trenchant et dangereux. Et adonc Pacolet qui sa fureur cogneut a deux genoulx se getta et luy a dist que pour Dieu il ne veulle estre contre luy courroucé, "car de ma faulte il [81recto]n'y[2] a chose par quoy mains vous me doyez aymer. Mais sachez que moy mesmes j'ay esté trahy et deceu mauvaisement par ung enchanteur que le mauldit Trompart avoit avec luy amené. Et qu'i soit vray, iceluy encha[n]teur desroba mon chevalet que tant je tenoie chier; mais nonobstant son art et son enchantement de luy j'ay prins telle vengance que la teste je luy ay coupee."

Quant Valentin entendit que par trahyson il avoit perdu la belle Esclarmonde et que Pacolet et tous les aultres en estoient innocens, il getta ung cry si piteulx et si grant signe de douleur que tous ceulx qui le regardoient par piteuse

---

[1] Text has *monstre*.

[2] *l i* at bottom right corner of 81r.

bewailing my bitter mistake and the pain and grievous martyrdom you suffered because of me. But if it please you, you will pardon me for these things, for even with great effort no one can guard himself entirely against treason."

"My dear," said the good lady, "for the tribulation I suffered, think no more on it, for from the moment I saw you, I felt lightened and relieved of all my sorrow. But one thing I do pray you — and that is to introduce me to the good merchant by whom the treason was known and the false archbishop defeated."

"My dear," said the emperor, "you may see him at once, for here he is, the good Guygard by whom the thing was known and your honor proven."

"Friend," said the lady to the merchant, "you are indeed worthy to be loved and held dear among all others, and for the great good and honor that you have rendered to the emperor of Greece and to the noble blood of France, from now on I retain you as my chamberlain. Morever, I would like you to receive a thousand marks of fine gold for your pain and labor."

"Lady," said the merchant, "I am most beholden to you and will serve you loyally all my life, and yet I do not deserve such a generous gift from you. Rather may God receive the praise and thanks for having consoled and comforted you in your adversity, and for having kept and defended your good reputation and true virtue."

Then Valentin spoke to the good lady his mother, saying, "My lady, may it please you to speak to me and give me news of my dear beloved Esclarmonde and of how she is."

"Ah, dear son," said the lady, "you must take comfort and be patient, for the fair Esclarmonde was falsely and wickedly kidnapped from the city of Aquitaine and handed over to King Trompart, who had come to the aid of the pagans before the city of Aquitaine."

When Valentin heard these tidings, he looked in fury at Pacolet, for he believed himself tricked by him. With a sudden violent anger, he moved as if to strike him with a very sharp and dangerous sword. Thereupon Pacolet, who understood his fury, threw himself upon his knees and begged him for God's sake not to be so angry at him, "for I know my fault is such that nothing could make you love me less than this has. But I want you to know that I was wickedly betrayed and tricked by a magician that the cursed Trompart had brought with him. That magician stole the magic horse I held so dear, which shows you my story is true; but in spite of his art and his spells, I took such vengeance upon him that I cut off his head."

When Valentin understood that he had lost the fair Esclarmonde through treachery and that Pacolet and all the others were innocent, he cried out so pitifully, seemingly in so much pain, that everyone there regarded him with deep

compassion estoient contrains a plourer. Au cueur fut moult dolent et courroucé sans que nul semblant en monstrast, mais comme saige et bien aprins sa douleur deporta et amodera.

A celle heure prindrent chemin princes, barons et chevaliers pour aler en Constantinoble. Et les prestres et les clers en grant devocion firent procession generalle en laquelle firent aler toutes manieres de gens, femmes et enfans a l'encontre des vaillans princes lesquelz avoient payens conquis et desconfis. Et en chantant hymnes et louenges de Dieu jusques a la grant esglise, les acompaignerent de grant joye et de grant pitié plouroient tant grans comme petis. Et apres que dedens ladicte esglise eurent fait leurs devocions et rendu graces a Dieu, l'empereur et le roy Pepin alerent au palays imperial, lesquelz menerent si grant feste que par six jours entiers firent tenir table ronde a tous venans plainiere. Si ne fault pas demander ne enquerir des pompes et honneurs ne des triumphes et services que adonc furent fais. Car tous furent joyeulx et menerent chiere lie par la tresgrant grace que Dieu leur avoit donné contre leurs ennemis. Moult longue fust la feste par la cité de Constantinoble. Et apres certains jours plusieurs princes et barons prindrent congé de l'empereur pour retourner en leur pays, desquelz je ne pense pas vous faire plus de mencion fors seulement du noble et puissant roy Pepin pour cause que de celuy est nostre matiere, subjecte et premierement commencee.

[CHAPITRE 33]

Comment le roy Pepin print congé de l'empereur pour retourner en France; et de la trahyson de Henry et de Hauffroy a l'encontre de Orson. xxxiii. chapitre[1]

[81verso]Apres la destruction des ennemis de la foy crestienne, lesquelz pour nostre foy diminuer et crestiens destruire avoient assiegé Constantinoble, le roy Pepin print congé de l'empereur de Grece pour retourner en France. Et quant Orson vit que le roy s'en retournoit en son païs il luy a dist, "Sire, j'ay voule[n]té et couraige de m'en aler avec vous en France et de passer et user mes jours en vostre service sans vous changer jamais pour nul aultre servir."

"Orson," ce dit Pepin, "de ce suis content. Et puis que tant avez de couraige de moy loyallement servir sachez que je vous emmerray en France, et dessus tous les aultres pour mon royaulme gouverner je vous feray mon connestable. Et se il avenoit ainsi que du vouloir de Dieu mon petit filz Charlot deffinast sa vie et ses jours durant ma vie et mon temps, je vous feroie et constituroye roy de France."

---

[1] Woodcut of robed and capped standing figure at left addressing group of armed standing knights, lead knight holding a halberd.

compassion, and wept in sympathy. His heart was pierced with sorrow, but he tried to show no sign of it, controlling and moderating his grief like a sensible man.

At that point the princes, barons, and knights headed into Constantinople. With great devotion the priests and clerks formed a general procession of all sorts of men, women, and children to meet the valiant princes who had vanquished the pagans. Singing hymns and praises to God, the exalted and the humble accompanied them all the way to the mighty church, weeping from great joy and full hearts. Then, after having made their devotions and rendered thanks to God, the emperor and King Pepin went to the imperial palace, and held such a huge feast that for six whole days they kept a round table open to all comers. It goes without saying that there was pomp and circumstance, honor and service of the most gracious kind. Everyone rejoiced and celebrated the victory that God had given them over their enemies. The feasting went on for a long time in the city of Constantinople. After a certain number of days, some of the princes and barons took leave of the emperor to return to their countries, but I think I will speak no more of them, except concerning the noble and powerful King Pepin, because he is the main topic with which we began.

CHAPTER 33

How King Pepin took leave of the emperor to return to France; and concerning Henry and Hauffroy's treachery towards Orson.

After the destruction of the enemies of the Christian faith, those who had besieged Constantinople in order to harm our religion and destroy Christians, King Pepin took leave of the emperor of Greece to return to France. When Orson saw that the king was to return to his country, he said to him, "Sire, I have a great desire to go with you to France, to spend all my days in your service, never to serve another."

"Orson," said Pepin, "that would make me very happy. Since you wish so much loyally to serve me, I will take you with me to France, and above all others I will appoint you as my constable to govern my kingdom. And if it so happens that it is God's will that my young son Charles end his days during my lifetime, then I will make you king of France."

"Sire," dist Orson, "mille mercis vous rens, car puis que vostre voulenté est de moy recepvoir en vostre service loyal, sachez que je emmenrray Fezonne. Et du tout vous veul estre loyal et a l'espee trenchant vostre bo[n] droit deffendre."

Atant partirent de Constantinoble le roy Pepin et Orson et moult grande chevalerie a puissance. Pour la departie de Pepin plourerent tendrement l'empereur et la bonne dame Bellissant et aussi firent tous les aultres, tant grans que petis. Orson baisa son frere Valentin et le recommanda a Dieu de piteux pleurs et souspirs plain. Et de sa mere Bellissant ne peut pas congé prendre pour la grant pitié qu'il avoit de laisser sa mere fors seullement qu'i l'embraça et la baisa doulcement.

Apres le congé prins a grans et a petis le roy monta sur la mer, luy et sa compaignie, et l'empereur et ceulx de sa court lesquelz jusques au port les avoient convoyéz retournerent plourant moult piteusement en Constantinoble. Mais avec la douleur du departement au roy Pepin plus que nul des aultres fut au cueur desplaisant l'enfant Valentin, et pour l'amour d'Esclarmonde laquelle il avoit perdue il dist a l'empereur en gettant grosses larmes, "Chier et redoubté pere, veullez moy pardonner se congé prens de vous, car jamais en ma vie je n'auray joye ne repos tant que je saiche nouvelles certaines que m'amie est devenue, car je l'ay a danger de mon corps conquise et gaignee parquoy je la doy bie[n] desirer et regretter."

Quant la royne sa mere entendit que son enfant s'en vouloit aler a terre cheut paulmee. "Mere," dist Valentin, "laissez vostre plourer, car jusques a la mort je veul celle que tant aimoie sercher et querir. Et se ainsi il avient que je ne la puisse trouver jamais jour de ma vie je n'auray liesse, mais je desire la mort pour mes jours abreger et terminer mes desconfors et mes pleurs douloureux." Lors appella Pacolet et luy a dist, "Amy, s'il vous plaist moy servir en ceste necessité et venir avec moy, jamais jour de ma vie pis que moy vous n'aurez."

"Sire," dist Pacolet, "pour tant ne demourra la chose, car je [82recto][1]suis pres et appareillé de vous suivir en toutes places a vostre voulenté parfaire." Ainsi fut Pacolet deliberé d'aler avec Valentin.

Et Valentin fust pour l'amour d'Esclarmonde en tel point demené qu'i delaissa pere et mere et ne luy chalut. Et sans nul aultre sejour ne appointement fit Pacolet appareiller[2] et luy quatriesme. De la noble cité de Constantinoble partit pour celle trouver de laquelle son cueur estoit triste et dolent. Du dueil a l'empereur de Grece et a la royne Bellissant ne pourroit homme racompter[3] la moitié, car en tel point estoient que sans parolle dire en leur chambre entrerent piteusement desconfortéz. Et Valentin, qui le couraige avoit ferme et entier de son entreprinse parfaire, monta a cheval pour aler vers le port. Il monta sur la mer, luy et sa compaignie.

---

[1] *l ii* at bottom right corner of 82r.

[2] There seems to be some text missing here, a reference perhaps to two other squires or servants accompanying him, which would make himself the fourth of the group.

[3] Text has *racomprer*.

"Sire," said Orson, "I render you a thousand thanks, and as it is your desire to receive me into your loyal service, I will bring along Fezonne. And more than anything else, I desire to be faithful to you, and defend your right with my keen sword."

Soon after, King Pepin and Orson left Constantinople with a great number of knights. The emperor and the good lady Bellissant wept tenderly at Pepin's departure, as did everyone else, both great and small. Orson, full of piteous tears and sighs, kissed his brother Valentin, commending him to God. And he could not speak his farewell to his mother Bellissant at all, so overcome was he by sorrow at leaving his mother, but he embraced and kissed her tenderly.

After taking leave of everyone, great and small, king and company set sail, while the emperor and his court, who had accompanied them to the port, returned in sorrowful tears to Constantinople. But in spite of the sadness caused by Pepin's departure, no one's heart was as grieved as that of the young man Valentin, and because of his love for Esclarmonde, whom he had lost, he said, weeping copiously, to the emperor, "Dear respected father, please pardon me if I take leave of you, for never in my life will I have joy or repose until I know what has happened to my beloved, for at great danger to my person did I conquer and win her, for which I have much reason to want her and miss her."

When the queen his mother heard that her child wanted to leave, she fell to the floor in a faint. "Mother," said Valentin, "do not weep, for until I die I will search, seeking the one I love. And if it so happens that I cannot find her, not a day in my life will I have joy; I would prefer then for death to shorten my days, putting an end to my distress and doleful tears." Then he called Pacolet and said, "Friend, if it please you to serve me in my need and come with me, never a day in my life will you have worse than myself."

"Sire," said Pacolet, "that would never stop me, for I am ready and willing to follow you anywhere to do your will." Thus did Pacolet decide to go with Valentin.

Valentin was so driven by his love for Esclarmonde that he left father and mother with nary a care. And without any delay, he first had Pacolet [and two squires] get themselves ready, then himself the fourth. They set out from the noble city of Constantinople to find her for whom his heart was sad and mournful. No one could recount even half the sorrow of the emperor of Greece and Queen Bellissant, for they were upset to such a point that without saying a word they entered their chamber in piteous distress. But Valentin, whose heart was set on accomplishing his goal, mounted his horse to ride to the port. There they set sail, he and his company.

Or me tairay atant de[1] luy et parleray du roy Pepin lequel arriva a Paris et fust receu en grant honneur et reverence, que de toutes les esglises saillirent processions en grant multitude de prestres et de clers, et de gens de tous estas alerent au devant moult loingz hors de la ville. Entre les aultres fut la royne Berthe lequel moult doulcement en la bouche le baisa et Charlot son petit filz qui fust saige et bien aprins. A son pere fist la reverence, lequel entre ses bras le print et le baisa. Puis entra le roy au palays et a grant honneur moult richement acompaigné. Et pour l'amour de sa venue fust grant feste demenee et plusieurs grans offices departis et donnéz.

Mais dessus tous les aultres fust en honneur monté et eslevé le vaillant chevalier Orson, tant et en telle maniere que tout ce que il vouloit dire et commander il estoit fait et tenu. Tant fust de sens et de sçavoir remply que par luy estoit toute la court gouvernee, les malfaiteurs pugnis et les bons eslevéz en honneur. Nul qui devers le roy eust affaire aultre moyen que Orson ne demandoit, pour lesquelles choses Hauffroy et Henry, desquelz j'ay devant mencion faicte, eurent encontre du bon Orson envye si grande que a l'encontre de luy machinerent trahyson mortelle a toute leur puissance et dirent l'ung a l'autre que trop leur estoit chose vituperable et dommaigeuse quant Orson par dessus eulx estoit honnouré et prisé.

"Par Dieu," dist Hauffroy a son frere Henry, "bien peu devons priser nostre puissance de celluy sauvaige Orson que vengance n'en sçavons prendre. Car si regne plus longuement ancores verrons nous le temps que par luy nous serons degettéz hors du royaulme de France."

"Frere," dist Henry, "vous estes saige et avez dit verité. Or ne sommes nous que deux freres germains, si devons l'ung l'autre conforter et ayder encontre noz ennemis. Mais sur ceste matiere je ne sçay que penser."

"Henry," ce dist Hauffroy, "entendez ma rayson: nous avons deux nepveurs, filz de nostre seur aisnee, c'est assavoir Florent et Guernié, lesquelz sont moult hardis [82verso]et fiers. Et me semble que par ces deux pourra estre de legier une trahyson faicte et brassee plus tost que de par nous," car bien sçavoient de vray que le roy ne les aymoit point, et que "plus tost croira et aura fiance au parler d'aultruy que au nostre. D'aultre part l'ung est boutiller du roy et l'autre est huyssier de la chambre en laquelle il dort, et par le moyen d'eux pourrons entrer en la chambre de Pepin nostre pere et en son lit le tuer. Chascun diroit que ce auroit esté Orson, car dessus tous les aultres il est garde du corps du roy et en luy il se fie. Et par ainsi seroit ledit Orson condemné a mourir et demourroit du tout le royaulme a nostre deliberacion car Charlot nostre frere n'est pas ancores assez puissant pour nous contredire."

"Hauffroy," dist Henry, "vous avez fort bien avisé. Mais pour ceste chose parfaire et acomplir il y convient bien mettre dilligence."

---

[1] Text has *le*.

I shall now leave off speaking of him and will speak instead of King Pepin, who arrived in Paris where he was received with great honor and reverence. Great multitudes of priests and clerks issued forth in procession from all the churches, and people from all levels of life marched out of the city to greet him. Among them were Queen Bertha, who kissed him gently on the mouth, and his young son Charles, who was wise and well taught. He bowed to his father, who took him in his arms and kissed him. Then the king, richly accompanied, entered the palace with great pomp and circumstance. There was much celebration in honor of his arrival, and much patronage was given out and distributed.

But more than anyone else, Orson the valiant knight was raised in honor, so much so that anything he desired to say or command was immediately executed. So full of good sense and knowledge was he that he had charge of the entire court, punishing criminals and raising the good in honor. Anyone who had business with the king could reach him through no other channel than Orson, for which reason Hauffroy and Henry, whom I mentioned previously, were so terribly envious of Orson that they garnered all their might to plot mortal treason against him, saying to each other that it was too horrible a thing that Orson should be honored and prized above themselves.

"By God," said Hauffroy to his brother Henry, "we should have a low opinion of our abilities if we cannot find a way to take revenge on this wild man Orson. For if he reigns much longer, we will see the time come when he expels us from the kingdom of France."

"Brother," said Henry, "you are wise and speak the truth. Now we are but two blood brothers, thus we should comfort and help each other against our enemies. But I am not sure what to think about this matter."

"Henry," said Hauffroy, "listen to my idea: we have two nephews, the sons of our elder sister, that is, Florent and Guernier, who are quite bold and fierce. It seems to me that we could more easily accomplish some treachery through them than by our own means," for they knew well that the king loved them not at all, and that "he would more easily believe and have more confidence in the word of others rather than in ours. Moreover, one of them is the king's cupbearer and the other guards the chamber where he sleeps, so through them we will be able to enter the bedchamber of Pepin our father and kill him in his bed. Everyone will say it must have been Orson, for he has been placed above all others as the king's personal bodyguard, and he trusts him thoroughly. Thus would Orson be condemned to death and the entire realm would be in our hands, for our brother Charles is not yet powerful enough to counter us."

"Hauffroy," said Henry, "that is an excellent idea. But in order to accomplish this thing, we must move quickly and carefully."

En ce point machinerent les deux mauvais trahystres la mort du noble et puissant roy Pepin lequel estoit leur pere naturel. Et de si malle heure les avoit engendrés que du sauvement de leurs ames guaires ne leur challoit. Ilz manderent les deux aultres mauldis trahystres, c'est assavoir Flourent et Guernyer lesquelz sont moult vaillans et hardis. Et quant ilz furent venus devant eulx Hauffroy print la parolle et dit en ceste maniere, "Seigneurs," dist il, "entendez nostre intencion, car nous sommes deliberéz, mon frere et moy, de faire chose pour laquelle nous aurons prouffit et vous monterons et esleverons en honneur plus que ne fustes jamais, en laquelle je desire pour cause que vous estes mes propres nepveux et de mon propre sang, et doy plus vostre bien desirer que nul aultre, et pour venir a fin, je vous veul dire mon intencion et declairer.

"Vous sçavez que le roy Pepin, combien qu'il soit nostre pere, jamais jour de sa vie de bon cueur ne nous ayma. Tousjours de sa puissance les estrangiers a eslevé et mis en hault, et en toutes offices et dignitéz a avancé plus que nous; pour quoy, toutes ces choses considerés, mon frere Henry et moy, qui sommes voz oncles legitismes, voulons et consentons et sommes deliberéz[1] de faire mourir le roy Pepin. Et apres sa mort nous quatre gouvernerons et tiendrons son pays et sa terre a nostre voulenté. Mais il convient que la chose soit faicte et acomplye par l'ung de vous deux, et me semble que vous Guernyer estes le plus propice a ceste chose entreprendre, car vous avez office a ce faire convenable et decente plus que nul aultre, attendu que vous estes maistre huysser et garde principalle de la chambre du roy. Et pouez cognoistre de jour et de nuyt qui entre dedens la chambre. Vous irez mucer en quelque lieu secret, et quant le roy Pepin sera en son lit endormy subtillement et sans mener bruit viendrez a luy et l'occyrez. [83recto]Puis[2] viendrez en la chambre ainsi comme bien vous le sçaurez faire. Et quant le lendemain au matin les nouvelles seront que le roy sera mort, la chairge et la coulpe en sera baillee a Orson a cause que toute la nuyt il dort et repose tout au plus pres de son corps, et par ainsi sera fait et condempné a mourir. Et apres ces choses au petit Charlot osterons la vie de legier, et pour tant nous demoura le royaulme et la succession a departir tout a nostre voulenté."

"Oncle," ce dist Guernyer, "de tout ce fait ne vous esmayez ja, car vostre pere le roy Pepin perdra la vie."

Or fut la trahyson ordonnee contre le roy Pepin qui a nul mal ne pensoit par les deux mauvais enfans lesquelz en eulx n'avoyent pitié de leur pere faire mourir. De male heure est l'enfant né qui a l'encontre de son pere veult telle mort pourchasser, et de male heure furent oncques engendréz Hauffroy et Henry quant par eulx fut trahyson faicte et mains païs gastéz. Par eulx fust le nepveu Guernyer de si mauvaise voulenté plain que tantost apres que la trahyson fust devisee il espia et avisa une nuyt que le roy estoit au soupper assis. Si print ung cousteau moult pointu et taillant, et subtillement entra en la chambre royalle, et derriere

---

[1] Text has *deliberz*.
[2] *l iii* at bottom right corner of 83r.

Thus did the two evil traitors plot the death of the noble and puissant King Pepin, who was their natural father. But woe unto him that he had sired them, for they had nary a care for their mortal souls. They sent for the two other cursed traitors, that is, Florent and Guernier, both fearless and bold. When they had arrived before them, Hauffroy addressed them thus: "My lords," he said, "listen to our plan, for we have decided, my brother and I, to undertake something which will profit us well and which will raise you more in honor than you ever were, which I wish to do because you are my own nephews and of my very blood, and thus must I desire your well-being more than that of any others, and so I will explain to you my plan.

"You know that King Pepin, despite the fact that he is our father, has never really loved us. He has always used his power to elevate strangers to high position, advancing them in offices and dignities more than us; for this reason, having considered all these things, my brother Henry and I, who are your legitimate uncles, have decided in concert to kill King Pepin. And after his death, we four shall take possession of his country and govern his lands as we will. But it makes sense for the thing to be carried out and accomplished through one of you two, and it seems to me that you, Guernier, are the most likely one to undertake this, for your position is the most convenient, as you are the chief officer and principal guard of the king's chamber. Thus you know day and night who enters the chamber. You will go hide in some secret place, and when King Pepin is asleep in bed, you will sneak up to him, making no noise, and kill him. Then afterwards, you will come into the room as you normally would. Then when the news spreads the next morning that the king is dead, the burden and the blame will fall on Orson, since he sleeps all night right next to the king; thus he will be done for, condemned to die. After these events it will be easy to take little Charles' life, and subsequently the kingdom and the succession will be left to us to distribute according to our will."

"Uncle," said Guernier, "have no worries about any of this, for your father King Pepin shall surely die."

Now the plot was hatched against King Pepin, who imagined no harm coming from these two evil children who themselves felt no remorse about killing their father. In an evil hour is the child born who seeks such a death for his father, and in a most evil hour were Hauffroy and Henry sired, when by them such treason was committed and so many lands wasted. It was owing to them that their nephew Guernier was filled with such malevolence that, soon after this plot was hatched, he spied out and chose a night when the king was seated at supper. Then he took a very sharp-pointed knife and slipped into the royal chamber,

une tente du lit se muça si secretement que de nul ne peut estre aperceu. Et quant l'eure fut venue que le roy deust aler reposer, par les gardes et chambrelans fut mené ou lyt, et ainsy que la coustume estoit de faire, le roy entra dedens son lit lequel a Dieu se recommanda moult devotement. Et tous saillirent de la chambre excepté Orson, et pour luy faire passer temps jusques au dormir de plusieurs choses luy parla. Mais adonc quant Orson veit que le roy vouloit reposer, sans plus faire de bruit le laissa, et au plus pres de luy en une couche se mist.

Et quant vint entour la minuit le trahystre Guernier sallit hors de son lieu, et en portant le cousteau en sa main ala au lit du roy pour son entreprinse parfaire. Mais quant il fust aupres de luy et qu'i leva le bras pour la mort luy livrer, il luy sembla que le roy se vouloit esveiller dont si grant paour luy print que de costé le lyt se laissa cheoir au bas ou il fut longuement sans soy oser remouvoir. Puis apres se leva pour frapper secondement le roy Pepin, mais ainsi que le coup luy vouloit donner, si grant paour luy print que tout le corps luy faillit, et commença a trambler le corps et tous les membres tellement qu'il ne sceut faire son entreprinse,[1] et bouta le cousteau dedens le lyt, puis s'en retourna mucer en son lieu tout tramblant et attendant le jour et si effroié que bien eust voulu estre cent lieues oultre la mer.

Et Orson estoit en son lit qui du fait ne se doubtoit pas, et songa ung songe merveilleux, car il luy fut avis en son dormant que on luy vouloit oster l'onneur de sa femme Fezonne et que au pres de elle es[83verso]toient deux larrons qui machinoient une trahyson a l'encontre de luy. Puis il luy sembla que dessus ung estang il veoit deux harons moult grans qui combatoient encontre ung esprivier et de toute leur puissance ilz se perforçoient de l'occyrre. Mais si vaillamment se deffendoit l'esprivier que les deux harons travailla et tous deux fussent mors se n'eussent esté une grande multitude de petis oyseaulx qui descendirent sur l'esprivier et tantost l'eussent tué se ne fust ung aigle moult grande que l'esprivier secourust. En ce songe s'esveilla Orson qui de ce songe fust esmerveillé.

"Ha! vray Dieu, veullez moy garder de trahyson et veullez conforter mon frere Valentin en telle maniere que de la belle Esclarmonde il puisse avoir nouvelles certaines."

A celle heure apparut le jour et Orson se leva qui secretement s'en yssit de la chambre de paour du roy esveiller. Et quant Guernyer vit que Orson estoit dehors tout au plustost qu'il peust il saillit dehors de la chambre et s'en ala en son hostel fort vistement courant. La trouva les deux freres, Hauffroy et Henry, et Florent avec eulx, qui avoyent grant fain de sçavoir des nouvelles de leur mauldicte et desloyalle trahyson.

"Gardés vous, Guernyer, que vous diez comment il va de nostre entreprinse."

"Seigneurs," ce dist Guernyer, "par le Dieu tout puissant qui tout le monde a fait et creé, pour tout l'avoir de France je n'en feroyes pas ancores autant que

---

[1] Text has *entreprnse*.

hiding so well behind the bed hangings that no one could see him. When the hour had come for the king to go for his nightly rest, his guards and chamberlains accompanied him to the bed, and, as was his custom, he climbed into bed, commending himself into God's hands most devoutly. Then everyone left the chamber except Orson, and, to pass the time before sleep, they chatted about different things. But when Orson saw that the king wished to rest, he left him alone without making any noise and lay down nearby on a cot.

Around midnight the traitor Guernier sneaked out of his hiding place, and, gripping his knife in his hand, approached the king's bed to carry out his mission. But as he drew close to him and raised his arm to deal him his death, it seemed to him that the king was about to awaken, which frightened him so much that he dropped to the floor next to the bed, where he remained a good while without daring to make a move. Then, a little later, he rose a second time to attack King Pepin, but just as he was about to deal him the blow, such fear took hold of him that his body failed him, and he began to tremble so in all his limbs that he could not carry out his plan. So he thrust the knife into the bed, and returned to his hiding place all in a tremble to wait for daybreak, so affrighted that gladly would he have been a hundred leagues away across the sea.

In the meantime, Orson lay unsuspecting in his bed, dreaming a marvelous dream, for it seemed to him while he slept that someone was trying to violate his wife Fezonne's honor while two felons nearby were scheming treachery against him. Then it seemed to him that he saw two enormous herons fighting a sparrow-hawk above a pond, trying with all their might to kill it. But the sparrow-hawk defended itself so valiantly, harassing the two herons, that they would have been dead had not a great number of little birds descended on the sparrow-hawk. They would have slain him if a huge eagle had not come to the aid of the sparrow-hawk. At this point Orson woke up, amazed by his dream.

"Ah! true God, defend me from treachery, and comfort my brother Valentin so that he may have some good news of the fair Esclarmonde."

Then day broke and Orson arose, creeping quietly out of the chamber in order not to awaken the king. When Guernier saw that Orson had gone out, he also left the chamber as quickly as he could, running swiftly to his lodging. There he found the two brothers, Hauffroy and Henry, and Florent with them, all eager to know the outcome of their damnably disloyal treason.

"Take care, Guernier, that you tell us exactly how it went."

"My lords," said Guernier, "by almighty God who made and created the entire world, I would not for all the wealth of France do again as much as I did. As

j'ay fait. Et au regard du roy, saichez que il est ancores en vie, car ainsi que je le cuidoye de mon cousteau occirre je fus si effroyé que le cueur me faillit et n'eusse eu courage de son corps dommaiger pour tout l'avoir du monde. Mais d'une aultre trahison je me aviseray, car le cousteau que je portoye mucer je l'ay laissé dedens le lyt du roy. Sy me suis pensé que pour tant nous accuserons Orson de trahyson. Et dirons au roy que ilz sont quatre tout d'ung appointement que tous sont deliberéz de faire le roy mourir, desquelz Orson est le principal, et dirons ainsi que ilz veullent faire mourir Charlot pour avoir par entre eulx quatre le royaulme de France avec les appartenances. Et pour nostre fait mieulx esprouver et estre creu de ceste chose, nous dirons comment Orson a son fait apresté et le cousteau tout prest lequel il a mucé dedens le lyt. Et qui nous demandera comment nous le sçavons nous dirons que ilz estoyent en une chambre parlant de ceste matiere et l'ung de nous estoit tout au plus pres de la porte qui leur secret entendit."

"Guernyer," ce dist Hauffroy, "vous estes moult subtil et parlez moult saigement, et se il avenoit que Orson voulsist dire du contraire vous et vostre frere Florent contre luy prendrez champ de bataille. Sy sçay de certain que de vous desconfire il n'aura pas de puissance. Et se d'aventure il avenoit que dessus vous [84recto]tournast[1] le pire, nous serons, mon frere Henry et moy, bien pourveuz de gens a grant nombre et malgré tous les aultres vous yrons secourir."

"Seigneurs," dirent Guernier et Florent, "vostre deliberation est tres bonne, et bien avons en couraige de la chose parfaire."

Ainsi fut la trahyson secondeme[n]t et de rechief a l'encontre de Orson pensee et machinee, lequel de tout ce fait estoit pur et innocent.

Le jour fust cler et l'eure venue que le roy, apres ce que il eust oÿ messe, il entra en sa sale royalle et au disner fust assis. La furent Hauffroy et Henry qui devant luy servirent, lesquelz a Orson faisoient honneur et monstroient beau semblant, mais de cueur luy pourchassoient trahison mortelle de toute leur puissance. Et quant Guernier vit que il estoit temps de parler il entra en la sale et vint devant le roy lequel il salua et moult grant reverence luy fist. Puis luy a dist, "Redoubté sire, il est vray que de vostre[2] benigne grace m'avez fait chevalier, et baillé office en vostre palays plus honneste que a moy n'appartient, et pour cause que par vous tant d'onneur m'avez fait de moy entretenir en vostre service, je ne dois par rayson estre en lieu ne en place ou vostre dommaige soit pourchassé. Si suis par devers vous venu dire une trahyson laquelle contre vous a esté faicte, et affin que du danger vous vous puissez garder et voz ennemis pugnir."

"Guernier," ce dit le roy, "or dictes vostre couraige car tresvoulentiers je vous escouteray."

"Sire," ce dist Guernier, "faictes tenir Orson affin qu'il ne s'enfuye, car dessus luy tournera la perte et le dommaige. C'est le trahystre par qui la chose est commencee et doit estre a fin menee. Et se vous voulez sçavoir la maniere, sachez

---

[1] *l iiii* at bottom right corner of 84r.
[2] Text has *vostrre*.

to the king, know that he is still alive, for just as I was about to stab him with my knife, I took such fright that my heart failed me and I didn't have the wherewithal to harm him for all the wealth in the world. But I will tell you of another plot, for I left the knife I was carrying hidden in the king's bed. It occurred to me that, in this way, we will accuse Orson of treason. And we will say to the king that there are four men, of whom Orson is the leader, who have conspired to kill the king in order to share out among them the kingdom of France and all its dependencies. The better to prove our story and be believed, we shall tell how Orson prepared his deed by hiding the knife in the bed to have it ready. And to anyone who asks how we know about this, we will say that they were speaking of this in a room, and one of us was near the door and heard their secret."

"Guernier," said Hauffroy, "you are very clever and speak wisely, and if it so happens that Orson chooses to contradict, you and your brother Florent will take the field of battle against him. I am certain that he will be incapable of defeating the two of you. And if by chance it happens that it turns out badly for you, we, my brother Henry and I, will be accompanied by many men and will come rescue you despite any opposition."

"My lords," said Guernier and Florent, "yours is a good decision, and we are ready and willing to carry out this deed."

Thus was hatched a second plot against Orson, who was completely unaware of it and quite innocent.

It was broad daylight, and the hour had come that the king, having heard mass, entered the royal hall for dinner. Hauffroy and Henry were there serving him, pretending to honor Orson and showing him respect, while in fact they harbored a mortal hatred of him in their hearts. When Guernier saw that it was time to speak, he entered the hall and came before the king, greeting him and making a proper bow. Then he said, "Respected sire, it is true that in your benevolence you have made me a knight, granting me a position in your palace more honorable than I deserve, and since you have done me such honor by taking me into your service, I must never do anything to cause you harm. Thus I have come to tell you about a plot that has been hatched against you, so that you may keep yourself out of danger and punish your enemies."

"Guernier," said the king, "tell me what weighs on your heart, for I will listen to you attentively."

"Sire," said Guernier, "have Orson detained so that he may not escape, for the harm and the loss turn on him. He is the traitor who started this thing and was to carry it through. And if you wish to know by what means this was to be

qu'i sont quatre des plus grans de vostre court lesquelz sont deliberéz de vous faire mourir, desquelz Orson est le principal qui dedens vostre lit vous doit faire mourir et d'ung cousteau au cueur vous frapper quant vous serez endormy. Et affin que mieulx vous me croyez, ainsi que leur acord faisoient au jour d'uy j'estoie en ung certain lieu ou pas ne me sçavoyent et ay entendu comment Orson disoit aux aultres que le cousteau de quoy vous devez estre occis est dedens vostre lit mucé. Et s'il vous plaist de y aler ou de aulcun y envoyer vous trouverrez la chose veritable."

"Sire," ce dist Florent qui fut de l'autre part, "mon frere dist verité dont je suis triste et dolent dont ceulx a qui vous avez fait tant de bien veullent vostre mort pourchasser."

Moult fut le roy de telle parolle esmerveillé et en maintes manieres et contenances regarda Orson. "Faulx et desloyal homme, comment avez vous eu telle pensee de ma mort desirer, moy qui tout le temps de ma vie vous ay si chier tenu et plus que les enfans que j'avoye engendréz prisé et honnouré?"

"Ha! sire, ne veullez croire contre moy si legierement, car jamais en jour de ma vie trahyson ne pensay, mais je suis [84verso]accusé de ce fait et par leur faulce envye."

"Or n'en parlez plus," dit le roy, "car se le cousteau est ou lit trouvé je vous tiens coulpable du fait, ne aultre preuve je n'en demande." Lors appella ses barons et leur dist, "Seigneurs, par Jesucrist[1] je ne fus oncques plus esmerveillé que je suis de ceste trahison."

"Sire," ce dist Millon d'Angler, "je ne sçay comment il en va, mais a peine pourroy je croire que Orson eust voulu une telle chose entreprendre contre vostre royalle majesté."

"Voyre," ce dist le roy, "mais se nous trouvons dedens le lit le cousteau, bien est signe evident que la chose doit bien estre de croire."

"Or pour Dieu," ce dist Millon d'Angler, "alons veoir ceste experience."

Lors ala le roy en sa chambre avec plusieurs de ses barons et chevaliers et ainsi que ilz furent aupres du lit ilz ont le cousteau trouvé par ainsi que Guernyer le trahystre leur avoit dit.

"Helas!" ce dist le roy, "en qui peult on avoir fiance quant mon propre nepveu qui j'ay tant chier tenu est de ma mort convoiteulx et de ma vie envieulx? Mais puis que le fait est tel je jure et prometz a Dieu que jamais il n'aura jour de respit que je ne le face pendre et estrangler!"

Lors ung vaillant chevalier lequel estoit appellé Symon courut devers Orson car moult l'aymoit, si luy dist, "Helas, beaux amys, fuyez vous ent d'icy et pensez d'eschapper, car le roy a trouvé le cousteau dedens le lit ainsi comme Guernyer luy avoit dict, dont le roy si a juré de vous faire par le col pendre et estrangler au plus tost que il sera venu."

---

[1] Text has *ieucrist*.

done, know that four of the highest lords of your court decided to kill you, Orson being the principal among them who was to kill you in your bed, stabbing you through the heart with a knife while you slept. And this will convince you all the more: as they were plotting this today, I was placed nearby where they couldn't see me, and I heard how Orson was saying to the others that the knife with which you were to be killed was hidden in your bed. And if it please you to go there or send someone there, you will find the matter to be true."

"Sire," said Florent who was next to him, "my brother speaks the truth, which saddens me greatly, that those for whom you have done so much would pursue your death."

The king was astounded by this account and looked askance at Orson. "False and disloyal man, how could it have entered your mind to desire my death, I who have always held you dear, honoring and prizing you even more than the children I have engendered?"

"Oh, sire, please do not suspect me so easily, for never a day in my life have I ever even considered treason, rather I am accused of this deed through their false envy."

"There is no point in talking about it," said the king, "for if the knife is found in the bed, I hold you guilty, nor do I seek other proof." Then he called for his barons and said to them, "My lords, in the name of Jesus Christ, I have never been so astonished as I am by this treason."

"Sire," said Millon d'Angler, "I have no idea exactly what is going on, but I can hardly believe that Orson would want to do any such thing against your royal majesty."

"Indeed," said the king, "but if we find the knife in the bed, it is a clear sign that the thing must be believed."

"Well, then, for God's sake," said Millon d'Angler, "let's go see."

So the king went to his chamber with several of his barons and knights, and upon reaching the bed they found the knife, just as Guernier the traitor had predicted.

"Alas!" said the king, "in whom can one place trust when my own nephew, whom I have held so dear, is jealous of my life and desires my death? But as it is so, I swear to God that I will have no rest until he hangs by the neck till he is dead!"

Then a valiant knight named Simon ran to find Orson, for he loved him much, and said to him, "Alas, dear friend, you must flee from here, for the king has found the knife in the bed just as Guernier described it, for which the king has sworn to have you hang by the neck as soon as he arrives."

"Or ne vous chaille," ce dist Orson, "car j'ay bonne fiance en Dieu qui mon bon droit me gardera."

A tant entra le roy dedens la sale ou Orson estoit tenu de quinze puissans et fors hommes moult estroitement. Puis manda et fit appeler plusieurs grans chevaliers et advocas de son palays pour juger et condempner Orson, mais Dieu, qui ses bons amys au besoing n'oublie, contre les faulx et mauldis trahystres le garda et deffendit tellement que leurs jours honteusement fineront — les trahystres desloyaulx! — et fera leur mauldicte trahyson descouverte.

[CHAPITRE 34]

Comment Orson quant on le vouloit juger mist opposition et demanda champ de bataille contre ses accusateurs, laquelle chose par lé douze pers luy fust ottroyé. xxxiiii. cha[pitre][1]

[85recto]Quant Orson fust devant le roy et devant les juges de son palays, qui pour le condempner estoient assembléz, il parla devant tous moult haultement et en grant hardiesse disant, "Sire tresredoubté et vous seigneurs, docteurs, barons et vaillans clers, vous sçavez que il n'est homme qui de trahyson se puisse garder ne fuyr de la fortune quant elle luy vient. Et puisque ainsi est que je suis accusé de crisme contre la majesté, c'est de la mort du roy, et que vous estes icy assembléz pour faire de moy jugement et que de ma parolle je ne puis estre creu contre mes ennemis, je demande devant tous le droit et la loy de vostre palays qui est telle que quant ung chevalier est accusé ou occupé de murtre ou trahison et il se veult deffendre en champ de bataille il doit estre receu. Or suis je chevalier qui me tiens sans reproche et du cas innocent. Si veul par l'ordonnance dessusdicte estre receu en mes deffences se par l'assistence de toute vostre court il m'est adjugé et ordonné. Et affin que nul ne pense que ceste chose je ne veulle poursuivir et mon corps offrir en bataille, voyez icy mon gaige lequel devant toute vostre puissance je bataille et le delivre. Et se je suis en la bataille vaincu, faictes de mon corps justice ainsi comme le droit le requiert."

"Orson," ce dist Guernyer, "de telle chose vous pouez vous bien taire, car ja ne desplaise a Dieu que de chose prouvee je prengne contre vous bataille."

"Ha, trahystre!" ce dist Orson, "point n'est chose prouvee se n'est quelque homme qui ne doubte son dampnement et ayme son honneur, qui pour tel cas ne peult a mort juger quant je veul champ avoir en deniant le cas. Sans le confesser condempné ne doit estre."

---

[1] Woodcut of two knights on horseback, one at left with lance charging retreating knight at right.

"Now don't worry," said Orson, "for I have complete trust in God that He will see justice done me."

At that moment the king entered the hall, where he had Orson seized by fifteen stout and stalwart men. Then he called for several great knights and lawyers of his palace to judge and condemn Orson, but God, who never forgets His true friends, kept him from these false and cursed traitors — the treacherous villains! — defending him so well that their days will end shamefully and their wicked treason be discovered.

CHAPTER 34

How Orson opposed a trial, asking instead for judicial battle against his accusers, which was granted him by the Twelve Peers.

When Orson was brought before the king and the judges of the palace, assembled to condemn him, he spoke up proudly, saying with great boldness, "Most venerable sire, and you, my lords, masters, barons, and gallant clerks, you know that there is no man who can completely avoid treachery or flee from misfortune when it comes. And since I am here accused of a crime against His Majesty, namely of attempted regicide, and you are assembled here to pass judgment on me, and there is no way my word will be taken against that of my enemies, I thereby request, in the presence of all, the lawful right of your palace that allows a knight accused of murder or treason to defend himself on the field of battle. Now on my honor as a knight, I hold that I am completely innocent of this charge. Thus I wish, according to the above-cited rule, to be allowed to defend myself, if those of your court will so judge and ordain. And if anyone doubts my willingness to follow through and offer myself up to battle, mark well that here I throw down my gauntlet for all to see. And if I be vanquished in battle, render justice on me as you will and as the law requires."

"Orson," said Guernier, "you might as well save your breath, for may it never please God that I take up battle against you for a matter already proven."

"Ah, traitor!" said Orson, "the matter is not proven if there be a man who has no fear for his own damnation and loves his honor — he cannot rule death in such a case, when I request judicial battle to deny the accusation. Without confessing the deed one cannot be condemned."

Sur ces parolles firent les douze pers de France oster et mener hors du lieu Orson et ses deux aversaires pour la chose entre eulx disputer et considerer les raysons des deux parties. Si fut par eulx adjugé que la demande de Orson estoit raysonnable et qu'i devoit estre receu et oÿ en ses raysons. Et lors firent venir Guernier et son frere en la presence du roy, et le duc Millon d'Angler demanda a Guernyer qui estoient les quatre qui de la mort du roy estoient consentans.

"Seigneurs," ce dist Guernier, "de ce n'en querez plus, que pour tout l'or de France je ne vous diray."

"Guernier," ce dist le juge qui ordonné estoit, "pour tant vous condempnons a recepvoir le gaige lequel Orson vous livre a vous et a vostre frere. Encontre luy combaterez, car puisque ne voulez declairer ceulx qui de la chose sont coulpablez il est de legier a croire que en vostre fait a malice."

Joieulx fust Orson d'iceluy appointement, et aux deux trahystres getta son gaige en disant, "Seigneurs, voyez icy mon gaige, lequel je vous delivre par tel convenant que se je ne puis vaincre et combatre les deux trahystres, Guernyer et son frere Florent, je habandonne mon corps [85verso]a estre pendu honteusement devant tous."

"Or avant," dist le roy, "la chose est acordee et le jugement fait. Mais pour l'entreprinse menee a fin il vous convient gaige et fiance pour vous ou par aulcuns pour vostre corps presenter a la journee laquelle asignee vous sera."

Adonc Hauffroy et Henry demourerent et offrirent leurs corps pour Florent et Guernyer, et Millon d'Angler, Sanson, Galeran et Gervaiz offrirent leurs corps et demourerent pour Orson, et promirent le rendre au jour qu'il sera assigné a ung mois en suivant. Et quant la fin du mois fust venue et le jour que on devoit combatre, le duc Millon d'Angler, Sanson, Galeran et Gervaiz armerent Orson car moult estoit de eulx aymé. Et quant il fust armé et monté a cheval a son col mist l'escu richement armoyé, puis chevaulcha parmy la ville moult noblement acompaigné. Et ala tout droit ou champ que on avoit ordonné hors des murs de la ville dessus l'eaue de Saine, et la en attendant ses ennemis mist le fer de sa lance en terre et dessus l'arrest se apuya. Si ne demoura pas longuement que tantost entrerent au champ Hauffroy et Henry qui leurs deux nepveux amenerent armés tresfort et richement. Moult redoubtoient Guernyer et Florent leur aversaire Orson, mais Hauffroy et Henry tousjours les reconfortoyent et promettoient les secourir.

Et ainsy comme ilz furent entréz dedens le champ l'evesque de Paris ala devers eulx et leur fit faire les sermens qui estoient acoustumés de faire, puis vindrent les heraulx et les gardes du champ que tous ceulx qui estoyent dedens firent vuider fors que les troys combatans. Or avoit appointé Hauffroy troys cens hommes que il avoit mis dedens une maison au plus pres de la plaice, et leur avoit dit et commandé que tout aussitost que ilz oroient sonner son cor que ilz venissent vers luy.

Upon these words, the Twelve Peers of France[1] had Orson and his two adversaries brought outside to discuss the matter and consider each side's position. They judged Orson's request to be reasonable and he himself deserving of being received and heard. So they had Guernier and his brother brought before the king, and Duke Millon d'Angler asked Guernier who were the four who agreed to the regicide.

"My lords," said Guernier, "ask no more about this, for I will not tell you for all the gold in France."

"Guernier," said the appointed judge, "then I order you to accept the gauntlet Orson has thrown down to you and your brother. You will fight him, for, since you are not willing to denounce all the guilty parties, one may easily believe there to be malice in your accusation."

Orson was thrilled with this arrangement, and he threw his gauntlet at the two traitors, saying, "My lords, here is my gauntlet, which I cast down before you with the understanding that if I cannot fight and vanquish these two traitors, Guernier and his brother Florent, I give myself up to be hanged shamefully before all."

"Well then," said the king, "the matter is agreed upon and judgment is given. But in order for the matter to be settled, you must provide a guarantee that you will present yourselves on the day assigned to you."

Thereupon Hauffroy and Henry agreed to remain at court and offer themselves for Florent and Guernier, while Millon d'Angler, Samson, Galeran, and Gervais offered the same for Orson, promising to render him up the day assigned for the following month. And when the month was up and the day had come that they were to fight, Duke Millon d'Angler, Samson, Galeran, and Gervais armed Orson, for they loved him dearly. Once he was armed and mounted, he placed a richly armored shield around his neck and rode through the city accompanied by many noble knights. He went straight to the field chosen outside the walls of the city on the banks of the Seine, and once there, awaiting his enemies, he thrust his lance into the ground and leaned on his lance rest. He hadn't remained there long before Hauffroy and Henry entered the field leading their two well- and richly-armed nephews. Guernier and Florent were in great fear of their adversary Orson, but Hauffroy and Henry comforted them and promised to help them.

As they came into the field, the bishop of Paris approached them and had them swear the customary oaths. Then the heralds and field guards came to empty the field of everyone except for the three combatants. Now Hauffroy had arranged for three hundred men to be placed in a house nearby, ordering them to come to his aid as soon as they heard him sound his horn. In that way they

---

[1] The term "the Twelve Peers of France" traditionally refers to the legendary twelve vassals of Charlemagne's inner circle, whose names appear in *La Chanson de Roland*. The term is being used here to refer to Pepin's closest circle of vassals. Later they will accompany Pepin on his pilgrimage to Jerusalem (Chapters 48, 51). They are not named.

Bien pensoyent les trahystres secourir et deffendre en leur necessité, mais petit luy valut toute son entreprinse, car aussytost que les gardes commanderent aux champions de faire leur devoir, Orson baissa la lance et a pointe d'esperons s'en vint contre ses ennemys. Par moult grant couraige vint tout premier frapper Guernier et si grant coup luy donna que l'escu et le harnoys tout oultre luy passa. Et Florent fust de l'autre part que moult fierement frappa Orson ung moult grant et horrible coup, mais autant en tint de compte comme s'il eust frappé sur une tour.

"Faulx, mauldit et desloyal trahystre, a tord et sans cause vous m'avez accusé! Mais au jour d'uy je vous monsterray ou loyaulté repose."

A ces motz de l'espee flamboiante a tellement feru Guernyer que l'arçon de sa selle abatit a terre et aussy tout subitement le heaulme luy osta de la teste. Puis apres luy eust couppee se n'eust esté son frere Florent [86recto]qui frappa Orson moult durement. Lors Orson se retourna et tellement ferit Guernier que l'oreille senestre luy abatit a terre, puis luy a dit, "Beau maistre, homme qui trahison pourchasse ne doit point gaigner au marché." La commença forte bataille entre les trois champions. Guernier reconquist son heaulme et en sa teste le remist. Puis vint vers Orson et de toute sa puissance s'esforça de le dommaiger, mais tantost eust esté desconfit se ne fust Florent son frere qui souventesfoys le secourust.

Moult eust Orson de peine et de travail pour les deux mauldis et desloyaulx trahystres[1] combatre, car fort estoient armés et si prenoyent courage pour Hauffroy et Henry lesquelz leur avoient promis secours et aide. Et tant fit Orson entour Guernier que moult durement le navra, et quant il se sentit navré il descendit a terre et le cheval habandonna. Puis vint contre Orson et frappa son cheval par telle façon et maniere que une jambe luy couppa et a terra l'abatit. Mais Orson, qui fut diligent et fort, quant son cheval sentit verser, les deux piedz mist hors des estriers et a terre saillit. Puis est venu a Guernyer et si estroitement entre ses bras l'a prins que l'escu et le blason luy osta et a terre l'abatit. Mais ainsy que ung estoc ou ventre luy voulut frapper, Florent frappa des esperons pour secourir son frere et dessus le heaulme de Orson si grant coup luy donna que tout le fit chanceler. Orson ala vers luy qui eust grant despit et le frappa par ung si grant couraige que le cheval abatit mort et a Florent osta le heaulme de la teste, dont fust moult esmerveillé, et ne trouva remede fors de fuyr et de courir parmy le champ en soy couvrant la teste de son escu, et Orson courut apres par moult grant couraige qui de le veoir fuir avoit plaisir.

"Ha, Florent," dist Guernier, "pourquoy fuyez vous tant? Retournez vous arriere et pensez de vous deffendre car se vous avez bon couraige au jour d'uy par nous sera vaincu!"

A ces motz assaillirent les deux trahistres le vaillant Orson moult durement et de leurs espees taillantes et fortes tant de coupz luy donnerent que parmy son harnoys les coupz entrerent et le sang firent saillir a grant randon. Lors Orson

---

[1] Text has *trrhystres*.

thought they could help and defend the traitors if they needed it, but their efforts were in vain, for as soon as the guards ordered the champions to do their duty, Orson lowered his lance and spurred his horse to attack his enemies. With tremendous zeal he attacked Guernier first, landing him such a mighty blow that it pierced shield and harness right through. In the meantime Florent set upon Orson fiercely with a monstrous blow, which had about as much effect as if it had struck a tower.

"False, damned, and faithless traitor, wrongly and without cause have you accused me! But today I will show you where true loyalty lies."

At these words he whacked Guernier so hard with his flashing sword that he knocked him from his saddle to the ground, immediately wrenching his helmet from his head. He would thereupon have lopped off his head, had it not been for Florent his brother who set hard upon Orson. Then Orson turned back and lopped off Guernier's left ear, saying to him, "Fair master, he who pursues treason must not gain by the bargain." There began a terrible battle among the three champions. Guernier recovered his helmet and thrust it back on his head. Then he came towards Orson and tried with all his might to harm him, but he would himself have been overthrown had not his brother Florent come repeatedly to his aid.

It cost Orson much effort and many pains to fight the two wicked and faithless traitors, for they were well armed and, moreover, they took courage from the fact that Hauffroy and Henry had promised to come to their aid. Nevertheless, Orson wounded Guernier so badly that, upon realizing his hurt, he slipped from his horse and abandoned it. Then he set upon Orson, striking his horse in such a way that he cut off one of its legs and forced it to the ground.[1] But Orson, ever diligent and quick, pulled his feet from the stirrups and jumped to the ground just as he felt his horse falling. Then he approached Guernier, grasping him so tightly in his arms that he wrenched his shield from him and cast him to the ground. But just as he was about to gouge him through the belly with his sword, Florent spurred his horse to go rescue his brother, and gave Orson such a blow on the helmet that he sent him reeling. Orson came back at him full of wrath, striking with such zeal that he killed his horse and wrenched Florent's helmet from his head. Florent was so staggered by this that he could do no better than to run away across the field, covering his head with his shield, with Orson, who took great pleasure in seeing him flee, in hot pursuit.

"Ah, Florent," cried Guernier, "why are you running away like that? Come back here and defend yourself, for if you show good courage today, we will beat him!"

With these words, the two traitors assailed the valiant Orson most fiercely, landing such a number of blows with their keen swords that they struck through

---

[1] Purposefully injuring one's opponent's horse was considered perfidious. Paul Bancourt, *Les Musulmans dans les chansons de geste du cycle du roi*, vol. 2 (Aix-en-Provence: Université de Provence, 1982), 283–84.

qui frappé se sentit Dieu devotement reclama et la Vierge Marie, et sur Florent frappa ung coup si grant que le poing et l'espee luy abatit a terre.

A celle heure fut la bataille moult grande et merveilleuse, et durant celuy temps la belle Fezonne estoit en une esglise laquelle moult tendrement plouroit en depriant a Dieu devotement qu'i luy voulsist son bon amy Orson garder et deffendre et luy donner victoire contre ses ennemis.

Moult fut le peuple esmerveillé de la grant proesse de Orson et des armes que il faisoit. Dolent et esbahy fust Florent quant le bras eust perdu; non pourtant il ne layssa point de assaillir Orson a [86verso]toute sa puissance. Et quant Orson l'a veit venir il fist semblant de ferir Guernyer, puis retira soudainement son coup et frappa Flourent en telle maniere que tout mort a terre l'abatit.

Puis a dit a Guernier, "Trahystre! apres vous fault passer, ou vous cognoisterez devant tous la trahyson que vous avez brassee."

"Orson," ce dit Guernyer, "aultrement en ira, car se mon frere avez occis, au jour d'uy j'en prendray vengeance."

"Hauffroy," ce dit Henry, "de nostre fait va mal a point, car Orson a ja tué et deffait nostre nepveu Florent, et si verrez de brief qu'il vainquira Guernyer et luy fera la trahyson confesser, parquoy nous ferons a tousjours mais deshonnouréz et en danger de mort se ne trouvons maniere de fuyr et eschapper."

"Frere," ce dist Hauffroy, qui de trahyson fust plain, "je vous diray que nous ferons. Tout aussitost que nous verrons que Guernier sera vaincu et premier qu'i confesse la trahyson, nous enterrons dedens le champ, et en signe de maintenir Orson a nostre nepveu nous coupperons la teste. Et pour tant ne pourra jamais la trahyson estre cogneue."

"Par Dieu," ce dist Henry, "on ne pourroit pas mieulx dire ne aviser." Et ainsi pensoient les deux mauldis et desloyaulx traistres nouvelles trahysons pour les vielles couvrir.

Et les deux champions sont dedens le champ qui moult fort durement assaillent l'ung l'autre. "Guernyer," ce dit Orson, "bien voyez que contre moy ne vous fault deffendre. Et pour tant pensez de vous rendre et de confesser vostre mauldite trahyson et je vous prometz de vous sauver la vie et faire vostre paix devers le roy Pepin; et vous envoyeray a l'empereur de Grece, mon pere, qui pour l'amour de moy de sa court vous retiendra et grant gaiges vous donnera."

"Garson," ce dit Guernyer, "de riens ne me sert ta promesse. Car plus que j'ay une oreille perdue jamais en nul lieu je ne seray prisé ne honnouré; si ayme mieulx contre toy mourir vaillamment ou ton corps conquerir et toy livrer a mort honteuse pour mon honneur en vergongne."

"Par ma foy," ce dist Orson, "tresbien vous acorde. Et puis que de mourir avez envye, en moy aurez trouvé bon maistre. Pensez de vous deffendre car voycy vostre dernier jour." A ces motz est alé vers Guernier et a force de bras dessoubz luy l'a getté a terre et de la teste le heaulme luy a osté. Lors Hauffroy qui bien vit que plus n'y avoit de remede s'escria moult hault, "Orson! ne le veullez tuer, car

his armor and made the blood run freely. Then Orson, feeling himself wounded, called devoutly on God and the Virgin Mary, turning again to strike Florent with a blow that severed fist and sword.

While at that moment the battle was hot and marvelous to behold, the fair Fezonne was in church, weeping tenderly and praying devoutly to God to keep and defend her beloved Orson, and to give him victory over his enemies.

The people were all amazed by Orson's great prowess and feats of arms. Florent was pained and stupefied to have lost his arm; nevertheless, he continued to assail Orson with all his strength. Although Orson saw him coming, he pretended to strike Guernier, pulling suddenly back and instead striking Florent dead to the ground.

Then he said to Guernier, "Traitor! You are next, unless you confess before everyone the treason you plotted."

"Orson," said Guernier, "it will go otherwise, for if you have killed my brother, today I will take my vengeance."

"Hauffroy," said Henry, "our plan goes badly, for Orson has already killed and undone our nephew Florent, and see, he will soon vanquish Guernier and make him confess the plot, by which we shall be forever dishonored and in danger of death, if we cannot find some means to flee or escape."

"Brother," said Hauffroy, who was full of treachery, "I will tell you what we shall do. As soon as we see that Guernier has been defeated and before he confesses the plot, we will enter the field, and to show that we wish to support Orson, we will cut off our nephew's head. That way the conspiracy will never be known."

"By God," said Henry, "no one could give better advice." Thus the two wicked and faithless traitors thought up new treachery to cover the old.

In the meantime the two champions were still hard at it, assailing each other in the field. "Guernier," said Orson, "you see that you can't defend yourself against me. Therefore consider giving yourself up and confessing your wicked treason, and I promise to spare your life and help you make your peace with King Pepin; moreover, I will send you to my father, the emperor of Greece, who for love of me will retain you at his court and pay you handsome wages."

"Boy," said Guernier, "your promise is worth nothing to me. For since I have lost an ear, I will never be honored or found worthy anywhere;[1] therefore I prefer to die fighting you valiantly, or conquer you and give you up to a shameful death, rather than cover my honor with shame."

"By my faith," said Orson, "I grant you your wish. Since you desire death, you will find me a ready master. Defend yourself, for today is your last." With these words he strode towards Guernier and, with no more than the strength of his arms, he threw him to the ground and wrenched his helmet from his head. When Hauffroy saw that there was no more help for it, he cried out aloud,

---

[1] Ear-cutting was used to punish and mark a criminal. See Esther Cohen, *The Crossroads of Justice: Law and Culture in Late Medieval France* (Leiden: Brill, 1993), 168.

bien cognoissons que a grant tort accusé vous a. Si en voulons faire la justice ainsi que au trahytre appartient; jamais ne le voulons laisser vivre ne tenir a parent."

Il entra dedens le champ et dist a Guernier, "Beau maistre, confessez vostre cas et la maniere de la trahyson et nous ferons tant au roy que vous aurez pardon de vostre faulte."

"Seigneurs," ce dist le trahystre Guernier, "j'ay faicte la trahyson et bouté le cousteau dedens le lyt."

En [87recto]disant ces parolles Hauffroy, qui fut subtil et cautelleux, tira son espee et affin que de ceste chose plus avant il ne parlast a celle place le frappa et l'abatit mort, et puis a dist, "Seigneurs, or soit ce trahystre prins et mené au gibet, car bien l'a deservy." Puis vint devers Orson et luy a dist, "Cousin, je suis moult joyeulx de la victoire que vous avez heue, car bien a Dieu monstré que vous estes loyal et preudomme, et que la loyaulté vous voulez garder et maintenir. Et puis que Guernyer estoit mon nepveu, si ne le veul je jamais pour parent reclamer ne tenir puis que de trahyson faire s'est voulu dementer."

Tantost vint la belle dame Fezonne qui moult fort doulcement acola Orson, et Pepin luy demanda, "Beau nepveu, avez vous playe sur vostre corps qui soit fort dangereuse?"

"Oncle," ce dist Orson, "nennil, la mercy Dieu. J'ay vaincu ces deux mauvais et desloyaulx trahystres desquelz Hauffroy a fait confesser la trahyson a Guernyer, et puis comme preudomme devant tous luy a osté la vie."

"Ha! beau nepveu, ne le croyez pas trop de legier, car quelque semblant que il vous face il est participant de la trahyson, mais atant m'en veulx taire pour l'eure presente."

Le roy et les barons retournerent en la cité de Paris, lesquelz moult furent joyeulx de la victoire et de l'onneur que Orson avoit acquise. Et Hauffroy et Henry en icelluy jour moult de bien en disoient de bouche et du cueur sa mort desiroient. Mais tantost apres vint le temps que leur faulce, mauldicte et desloyalle trahyson fut aperceue et cogneue, et que de leurs maulx furent pugnis comme bien l'avoyent deservy. Sy veul laisser atant ceste matiere et vous parleray du chevalier Valentin lequel par le pays chevaulchoit moult dolent et desconforté pour s'amye la belle Esclarmonde recouvrer. Laquelle estoit en Inde la Major ou le roy le faisoit garder pour l'espouser et prendre en mariaige a femme ainsi que devant vous avez oÿ faire mencion.

"Orson! Don't kill him, for we see that he accused you wrongly. Thus we wish to render justice as this traitor deserves; never do we wish to let him live or keep him as a relative."

He entered the field and said to Guernier, "Fair master, confess your deed and what treason you plotted, and we will do all in our power to persuade the king to pardon you your fault."

"My lords," said the traitor Guernier, "I carried out the plot and hid the knife in the bed."

As he spoke these words, Hauffroy, subtle and sly, drew his sword and, not wanting him to say any more on the matter, struck off his head on the spot, then said, "My lords, now let this traitor be taken and hanged on the gallows, for he has well deserved it." Then he came up to Orson and said, "Cousin, I am overjoyed at your victory, for God has demonstrated that you are honest and true, and that you desire only to keep and maintain fealty. And despite the fact that Guernier was my nephew, I have no wish to claim him as family, since he was willing to stoop to treason."

Soon after, the fair lady Fezonne came to embrace Orson most sweetly, while Pepin asked of him, "Fair nephew, have you any dangerous wound on your body?"

"No, Uncle," said Orson, "thanks be to God. I have vanquished these two faithless, evil traitors. Hauffroy made Guernier confess the plot, and then like an honest man, in the presence of all, he killed him."

"Well, fair nephew, do not believe him so easily, for however he might dissemble before you, he participated in the plot, but for now I prefer to say no more."

The king and his barons returned to the city of Paris, thrilled by the victory and the honor that Orson had achieved. But Hauffroy and Henry, while they said much good of him with their mouths, in their hearts desired his death. Later on, however, the time came that their false, accursed, and faithless treachery was discerned and known, and their evil deeds punished as they well deserved. But for now, I wish to leave off speaking of this matter in order to speak to you about the knight Valentin, who was riding through the country, most upset and troubled about how to recover his beloved, the fair Esclarmonde. She was in India Major, where the king kept her under close guard in order to marry her and take her to wife, as I explained to you before.

[CHAPITRE 35]

Comment Valentin en querant Esclarmonde[1] arriva en Antioche; et comment il combatit et vainquist le serpent.xxxv. [chapitre][2]

Valentin, qui sur la mer estoit monté pour recouvrer la belle et plaisante Esclarmonde sa femme,[3] tant fist par la grace de Dieu qu'il arriva en la cite d'Antioche. Et quant il fust en ladicte cité Paco[87verso]let, qui bien sçavoit parler sarrasin, pour luy print logis en ung moult riche hostel. Mais l'oste de la maison, qui fut moult cautelleux et subtil, quant ilz furent en leur chambre retrays, il les ala escouter. Sy entendit Valentin qui de Jesus et de la Vierge Marie parloit par quoy bien se doubta que ilz estoient crestiens. Et toute a celle heure partit et s'en ala vers le roy d'Antioche et luy a dist, "Chier sire, sachez que en ma maison sont logéz quatre crestiens lesquelz sans nul tribu payer sont entréz et descendus sur vostre terre et seigneurie. Et affin que nul reproche ne me puissez donner de les avoir receulx je le vous viens dire et notifier."

"Amy," ce dist le roy, "ainsi dois tu faire." Or avant tost dist il a ses gens, "Alez les moy querir, et faictes que expressement devant moy soyent amenéz." Lors partirent plusieurs sergens et officiers pour aler avec l'oste querir Valentin et ceulx de sa compaignie, lesquelz furent amenéz au palays devant le roy d'Antioche.

Et quant Valentin le veit moult haultement le salua en disant, "Sire roy, Mahommet auquel vous croyez de telle puissance qu'il a vous veulle garder et deffendre. Et celuy Dieu qui pour nous en la croix souffrit mort et passion en mon aversité me veulle donner confort de la chose que je requiers."

"Crestien," ce dist le roy, "bien tu te monstres hardy quant devant ma presence tu me fais memoire de ton Jesus, lequel je n'aymay oncques ne jamais ne feray. Si te fay assavoir que de deux choses l'une te convient faire ou la mort recepvoir."

"Roy," ce dist Valentin, "or dictes vostre voulenté, car plusieurs choses vouldroye bien faire plustost que la mort endurer, combien que j'avoye oÿ dire que dedens vostre royaulme il y avoit respit pour les crestiens de payer tribu."

"Par ma loy," dist le roy d'Antioche, "le contraire est vray. Et puis que sans mon congé vous y estes entréz et de mort vous voulez eschapper, il vous fault renoyer vostre Dieu Jesus. Et se faire ne le voulez il vous fault combatre a ung serpent moult grant et horrible qui par l'espace de sept ans a esté devant ceste ville et tant de gens a devouré et fait mourir que le nombre est inestimable et incogneu. Si avisez des deux choses lequel vous voulez faire et acomplir, car par nulle aultre maniere ne pouez vostre vie sauver."

---

[1] Text has *esmonde*.
[2] Woodcut of mounted figures crossing drawbridge and entering castle gate.
[3] They have not yet married at this point.

CHAPTER 35

How Valentin, in search of Esclarmonde, arrived in Antioch; and how he fought and vanquished the serpent.

Valentin, who had set sail to recover the fair and pleasing Esclarmonde, his beloved, traveled so quickly, thanks to God, that he soon arrived in the city of Antioch. Once there, Pacolet, who spoke the Saracen language quite well, secured rich lodgings for him. But the host of the house, who was most subtle and sly, went to eavesdrop on them after they had settled in their room. Thus he heard Valentin speaking of Jesus and the Virgin Mary, which made him suspect they were Christians. He immediately rushed to the king of Antioch and told him, "Revered sire, you should know that four Christians, who have entered your lands and strongholds without paying any tribute, are lodged in my house. I have come to notify you of this so that you may have no reason to reproach me for having received them."

"Friend," said the king, "you have done just as you should." Then he addressed his men: "Go find them for me, and take care to bring them to me directly." So several sergeants and officers left with the host to find Valentin and his companions, who were brought to the palace before the king of Antioch.

When Valentin saw him, he greeted him, saying, "Sir king, may Mohammed, in whom you believe, keep and defend you with such power as he possesses. And may God, who suffered death and passion on the cross for us, give me comfort in my adversity and in the thing I seek."

"Christian," said the king, "you show yourself rather bold, making mention in my presence of your Jesus whom I have never loved nor never will. However, I inform you that you must do one of two things or face death."

"King," said Valentin, "tell me now your will, for there are many things I prefer to death, although I had heard that in your kingdom there was safe passage for Christians who paid tribute."

"By my law," said the king of Antioch, "the opposite is true. And since you entered without my permission yet wish to escape death, you must deny your God Jesus. And if you are not willing to do this, then you must fight a great and horrible serpent that has stalked just outside the city for seven years, eating and killing an untold number of people. Therefore you must decide which of these two things you will carry out, for by no other manner may you save your life."

"Quant par force le me fault faire le jeu est mauvais pour moy a departir. Non pourtant dictes moy s'i vous plaist se vous avez veu la beste et de quelle forme et estature elle est, et quelles sont ses manieres et façons."

"Crestien," ce dist le roy d'Antioche, "je te dy que la beste ay bien veue et regardee, et saichez que elle est moult layde et hydeuse et plus grande de corps que ung cheval. Et si a les alles moult fort, grandes et empennees a la mode et maniere d'ung griffon, et porte la teste de serpent et le regard fort ardant. [88recto]La peau a couverte d'eschailles moult dures et espesses ainsi comme poisson qui naige par la mer, et porte piedz de lyon moult poingnans et agus plus que cousteau d'acier."

"Par mon Dieu," dist Valentin, "a ce que vous comptez est moult hideulx et horrible. Mais nonobstant toute sa force, se voulez croire en Jesucrist et me promettre de recepvoir baptesme au quel cas que la beste pourray occire et mettre a mort, je m'en iray assoir contre elle et a la garde de Dieu je metteray mon corps en danger sans nul homme vivant mener avec moy."

"Crestien," dit le roy, "je te jure par ma loy que se tu la peulx destruire moy et toutes mes gens renoncerons Mahon et toute ta voulenté ferons. Mais tant te veul dire que de toy n'a garde ne danger, car jamais nul n'y ala que par elle ne fust devouré."

"Sire," ce dist Valentin, "laissez moy faire contre elle, car tant me fie au doulx Jesus qui me sera escu et garde contre la faulce beste par tel convenant que promesse vous me tiendrez."

"Oy," ce dist le roy, "pensez de bien ouvrer, car se de la beste tu me peulx delivrer je te jure mon dieu Mahon que ta loy et ta creance prenderons et laisserons la nostre."

"Or bien," dist Valentin, "je y metteray peine." Lors il demanda les ouvriers de la cité et fit faire ung escu moult subtillement composé et en iceluy escu fist estacher plusieurs broches de fin acier plus poingnans que aguilles, et fortes, et formement assises et d'ung pied de long. Et quant l'escu fut ainsi fait il vestit son harnoys et son heaulme mist en sa teste, puis a prins son espee et en l'onneur de Jesucrist la croix souvent a baisee. Puis print congé de ses hommes et monta a cheval et pour la beste combatre yssit hors de la cité. Grans et petis monterent sur les murs, tours et creneaulx pour Valentin regarder. Et quant ilz fust hors de la ville les portiers si fermerent les portes apres luy, car bien pensoient de vray que jamais il n'en deust retourner.

Or estoit la beste de telle condicion que tous les jours il luy convenoit livrer pour sa proye quelque beste ou personne, et qu'i failloit a luy bailler il n'estoit homme que de la cité osast saillir. Mais tout aussitost que de la cité on luy avoit livré et baillé sa proye elle s'en retournoit en son lieu et la se tenoit et nul mal ne faisoit a personne. Et pour tant estoit de coustume par toute la terre d'environ que larrons et murtriers et toutes mauvaises gens qui par sentence et jugement estoient condempnéz a mourir dedens la cité d'Antioche estoient rendus et ameneź pour bailler et delivrer au serpent mauldit et venimeuse beste. Et avec ce il y avoit certaines gens qui parmy les pors de mer aloyent sercher et querir les crestiens et les amenoyent en ladicte ville et cité d'Antioche pour les faire devourer au serpent.

"When my hand is forced, it is a bad game for me from the beginning. Nevertheless, tell me, if you please, whether you have seen the beast yourself, what size and shape it is, and what its habits and ways are."

"Christian," said the king of Antioch, "I tell you that I have certainly seen the beast and watched it, and know that it is hideously ugly and larger than a horse. It has powerful wings, huge and plumed like that of a griffon, a head like that of a serpent, and it breathes fire. Its skin is covered with hard, thick scales like those of a fish swimming in the sea, and it has the feet of a lion, pointy and sharper than a steel blade."

"By my God," said Valentin, "from what you say, it indeed sounds hideous and horrible. Yet, notwithstanding all its strength, if you are willing to accept Jesus Christ and promise me to receive baptism if I can kill and destroy this beast, I shall assail it, and, placing myself in God's keeping, I shall face this danger alone, bringing no living man with me."

"Christian," said the king, "I swear to you by my faith that if you can destroy it, I and all my people will renounce Mohammed and will act according to your will. But I must say to you that nothing can avail you, for no one has ever approached it without being devoured."

"Sire," said Valentin, "let me try myself against it, for I trust so much in gentle Jesus, who will be my guard and my shield against the foul beast, that, concerning this agreement, you will keep your promise to me."

"Yes," said the king, "do your best, for if you are able to deliver me from the beast, I swear upon Mohammed that we shall take up your faith and beliefs and leave off our own."

"Well, then," said Valentin, "I shall strive my best." Then he called for workmen in the city to make him a specially fashioned shield, and on this shield he had them attach multiple spikes, each a foot long, of strong, fine steel, sharper than needles and well set in the shield. When the shield was ready, he put on his armor, placed his helmet on his head, took up his sword, and kissed its cross many times in honor of Jesus Christ. Then he took leave of his men, mounted his steed, and issued forth from the city to go fight the beast. Everyone great and small climbed up on the walls, towers, and ramparts to watch Valentin. Once he was out of the city, the porters closed the gates behind him, for they never really thought to see him return.

Now the beast was such that every day they had to deliver it some animal or person as its prey, and when they failed to feed it, no man dared leave the city. But as soon as they provided its prey from the city, it returned to its lair where it stayed and harmed no one. So it had become the custom throughout the region to deliver to the cursed and venomous beast all sorts of thieves, murderers, and criminals given the death penalty in the city of Antioch. In addition, certain people looked for Christians in the port cities to bring back to Antioch for the serpent to devour.

Et quant le serpent aperceut Valentin devers luy venir il commença a baisser lé alles moult fierement [88verso]en gettant grant fumee et grant feu par la gulle. "Ha, Dieu!" dist Valentin, "veullez moy secourir et preserver d'entrer en celuy ort passaige, et me donnez force et puissance que je puisse vostre loy exaucer et acroistre."

Lors descendit du cheval et a l'arçon de sa selle laissa sa hache trenchant et ala vers le serpent qui moult fust orgueilleux. Aussitost qu'il aprocha de luy pour le cuider frapper, le serpent leva la pate qui fut grosse et large et a merveilles poingnante pour frapper Valentin. Mais il getta son escu au devant tellement que la beste frappa dessus les broches qui estoient pointues. Sy getta ung cry moult grant en soy tirant arriere, et Valentin le suivit qui le couraige eust hardy. Mais quant la beste le vit aprocher elle se leva toute droite dessus les piedz de derriere et des peidz de devant cuida Valentin abatre a terre, lequel de l'escu fust couvert et pour la doubte des broches se retira la beste.

"Par Mahon," ce dist le roy d'Antioche qui en une haulte tour estoit, "voyez le chevalier moult vaillant et bien digne d'estre prisé." D'aultre part fut la royne laquelle avoit nom Rozemonde qui pour la beaulté de Valentin et sa hardiesse fust au cueur touchee d'amours moult fort.

Hors de la cité si grande fut la bataille du serpent et de Valentin car se n'eust esté l'escu poingnant que la beste redoubtoit et craingnoit moult tost eust Valentin a la terre getté. Mais il tenoit l'escu dont bien se sçavoit ayder et a l'autre bras il tenoit l'espee dont frappa le serpent au plus pres de l'oreille ung coup moult grant et fort, mais tant fust la peau dure que l'espee rompit.

"Vray Dieu," dist Valentin, "veullez moy ayder et secourir contre cestuy ennemy qui tant est horrible et fier!" En grant danger fut Valentin qui son espee eust perdue car le serpent se print a eschauffer, et d'une de ses pates le frappa tellement d'une de ses ongles que le harnois luy rompit et la chair luy entamma. Et Valentin se tira arriere; si tira hors ung glaisve moult pointu et le getta a la beste si droit que en la gulle bien demy pied luy entra dont le serpent conte n'en fist. Et Valentin se tira arriere et courut devers son cheval, si print la hache qui a l'arçon de la selle pendoit, et a la beste est retourné en faisant le signe de la croix. En demandant a Dieu confort il s'aprocha de la beste qui moult fort le guettoit, et de la hache tranchante sur la queue le frappa tellement que la peau jusques a l'os luy couppa, et fist a grant randon de sang a la terre courir. Esmerveilléz furent payens et Sarrasins qui sur les murs estoient de la proesse et vaillantise du chevalier hardy.

Et Rozemonde la royne qui moult voulentiers le regarda a par elle dist tout bas, "Ha! chevalier, beau sire, Mahommet te veulle garder et ramener a joye, que par Mahon en qui je croy de tous les chevaliers qui oncques regarday, mon cueur ne fust d'amours si ardamment esprins." Ainsi disoit la dame qui d'amours fut [89recto]tant[1] embrasee.

---

[1] *m i* at bottom right of 89r.

When the serpent saw Valentin coming towards it, it began to lower its wings fiercely as it belched great plumes of smoke and fire from its mouth. "Dear God!" said Valentin, "help me and preserve me from that foul gullet; give me strength and force to glorify your religion and cause it to increase."

Then he got off his horse, leaving his keen-edged ax hanging from his saddlebow, and went toward the proud serpent. As he approached it, about to strike, the serpent raised one huge and marvelously sharp-clawed paw in order to smite Valentin. But Valentin hoisted his shield before him so that the beast stabbed itself on the pointy spikes. It let out a great cry as it retreated, but stout-hearted Valentin followed it. When the beast saw him approach, it raised itself up on its hind legs, preparing to knock Valentin to the ground with its front paws, but Valentin protected himself with the shield and the beast retreated in fear of the spikes.

"By Mohammed," said the king of Antioch watching from a high tower, "see how valiant and worthy of praise is this knight." Listening nearby was the queen, whose name was Rozemonde, and whose heart was already smitten with love by Valentin's beauty and boldness.

Outside the city the great battle between Valentin and the serpent wore on, for had it not been for the sharp spikes of the shield that the beast doubted and feared, it would soon have beaten Valentin to the ground. But Valentin wielded the shield wisely, and, with his other arm, grasped his sword with which he struck the serpent a mighty blow near its ear, yet its skin was so hard that it broke the sword.

"True God," said Valentin, "help me against this horrible and fierce enemy!" Valentin was in great danger after having lost his sword, for the serpent grew wilder, and with one of its paws it smote him such that one of its claws pierced his armor and his flesh. Valentin drew back, then brought forth a keen dagger and threw it at the beast so straight that it penetrated its mouth a good half a foot, which the serpent seemed hardly to notice. Then Valentin fell back again and ran to his horse, taking the ax where it hung on the saddlebow, then returned to the beast, making the sign of the cross. While praying God for help, he approached the beast, who was watching him warily, and smote it so hard on the tail with his keen-edged ax that it cut through the skin to the bone, causing a river of blood to flow to the ground. Pagans and Saracens watching on the walls were amazed at the prowess and valor of this bold knight.

In the meantime, Rozemonde the queen watched him with great pleasure, saying to herself, "Ha, knight, fair sire, may Mohammed keep you and bring you back in joy, for by Mohammed in whom I believe, of all the knights I have ever seen, my heart was never smitten with such ardent love." Thus said the lady inflamed by love.

Et Valentin se combat encontre le serpent qui sa queue grosse et pesante maintesfois luy a getté dont si fort la travaille que a peu que a terre ne l'abatit. Mais il tenoit la hache asseuree de laquelle sçavoit moult bien jouer si que au cruel serpent ung quartier de la queue luy couppa. Et adonc getta ung si grant cry que toute la ville en retentist et sonna. Puis a frappé des alles et en l'air est voulé pardessus Valentin lequel il a frappé de ses pattes poingnantes si grant coup par la teste que le heaulme luy arracha et le bon chevalier a la terre abatit. Mais par sa diligence fust tost relevé, dolent et courroucé de ce qu'il avoit la teste nue. Dieu et la Vierge Marie se print a reclamer en regrettant souvent la belle Esclarmonde. Et quant ceulx de la cité veirent qu'il avoit le heaulme perdu moult bien penserent que jamais il ne deust eschapper.

"Par mon dieu," dist le roy, "bien se peult maintenant dire que le chevalier crestien jamais deça ne reviendra."

Or fut Pacolet moult dolent et moult piteusement se print a plourer[1] pour l'amour de Valentin. "Helas! seigneurs, faictes moy les portes ouvrir et me delivrez ung harnoys, car je veul au jour d'uy avec mon maistre vivre et mourir. Et si me baillez ung heaulme car je luy veue porter pour sa teste couvrir." Pacolet fust tantost armé et luy fust donné ung heaulme et les portes ouvertes. Il se recommanda a Dieu et ala courant vers le champ. Bien le veit venir Valentin, mais point ne le cognoissoit, quant Pacolet luy escria, "Sire! je suis vostre servant qui par longtemps vous ay servy et qui pour vostre corps secourir a l'encontre du faulx ennemy je suis icy venu par devers vous."

"Helas! amy," dist Valentin, "icy mourir me convient, car de toutes mes aventures et fortunes j'ay au jour d'uy trouvé la plus dangereuse. Pour Dieu saluez mon pere et madame ma mere, avec Orson mon frere que j'ay si chierement aymé, et la belle Esclarmonde aussi se jamais vous la pouez veoir. Pour Dieu alez vous en d'icy et ne revenez plus, car quant vous mourriez avec moy je n'y puis avoir secours ne proffit."

Ainsi que Pacolet s'approcha de Valentin pour luy bailler le heaulme le serpent a bien veu et aperceu que pas il ne portoit de escu comme l'autre, si vint a Pacolet, et par la senestre jambe le print et soubz luy l'abatit en luy donnant si grant coup de sa poingnante patte que oultre son harnois durement le navra. Et la l'eust tué se n'eust esté Valentin qui de sa hache le ferit tant que le nez luy couppa tout oultre et l'ung des yeulx luy creva. Le serpent crie et brait comme une beste enrragee. Il bat ses alles et est en l'air monté sur une haulte roche ou il se retrait. Lors Valentin vint a son heaulme pour le mettre en sa teste mais ainsi que prendre le cuida il vit venir la beste. Lors a prins son blason pour sa teste couvrir, et le serpent s'en retourne [89verso]assoir sur ladicte roche. Adonc Pacolet en la teste de Valentin bouta ledit heaulme.

---

[1] Text has *plourerer*.

Valentin continued to fight the serpent who kept batting at him with its huge, heavy tail and setting it about him so stoutly that it almost knocked him to the ground. But he grasped his ax with assurance, wielding it so well that he cut off a good quarter of the cruel serpent's tail. It let out such a cry that the whole city echoed with the sound. Then it flapped its wings and flew into the air above Valentin, whom it dealt such a blow with its sharp-clawed paws that it wrenched the helmet from his head and knocked the good knight to the ground. However, he promptly sprang up again, angry and worried to have his head so exposed. He began to call upon God and the Virgin Mary, regretting as well the fair Esclarmonde. And when the people in the city saw that he had lost his helmet, they were sure that he would never escape.

"My god," said the king, "now it seems for sure that the Christian knight will never make it back from there."

Pacolet was deeply grieved and began to weep most piteously for love of Valentin. "Alas! my lords, open the gates for me and bring me a set of armor, for I wish to live and die today with my master. And give me a helmet, for I wish to bring it to him to cover his head." Pacolet was immediately armed while a helmet was brought him and the gates opened. He commended himself to God and rushed to the field. Valentin saw him coming, but he didn't recognize him until Pacolet called out, "Sire! I am your servant who has served you a long time — I have come here to help you against this wicked enemy."

"Alas, my friend," said Valentin, "here must I die, for, of all my exploits and adventures, today I have discovered the most perilous. For God's sake, give my final salutation to my father and to my lady mother, along with Orson my brother whom I have loved so dearly, and also to the fair Esclarmonde if ever you succeed in finding her. For God's sake, go away and don't come back, for if you were to die with me I would have no succor or profit."

Just as Pacolet approached Valentin to give him the helmet, the serpent saw and understood that he was not carrying a shield like the other man, so it came toward Pacolet, seizing him by his left leg, knocking him under itself, and striking him so hard with its sharp paw that it hurt him badly wherever his armor couldn't protect him. It would have killed him right on the spot had not Valentin smote it so with his ax that he cut off its nose and gouged out one of its eyes. The serpent cried and brayed like an enraged beast. It beat its wings and rose in the air, settling on a high rock. Then Valentin came to get his helmet to place it on his head, but just as he was about to do so he saw the beast coming. He grabbed his shield to cover his head, and the beast returned to alight on the same rock. Then Pacolet thrust the helmet onto Valentin's head.

"Sire," ce dist Pacolet, "moult fort je suis navré au corps, sy me fault retourner en la cité pour ma playe garir, car j'ay tant de mon sang perdu que le cueur me fault." Ainsy a prins congé et se mist en la voye, mais tout aussitost que le serpent le veit eslongnier il ouvrit ses grandes alles et devers luy vola. Et Pacolet qui l'aperceut venir tantost il retourna a son maistre, et le serpent ala Valentin assaillir, et en volant par dessus luy par la teste le cuida frapper. Mais Valentin getta la hache si a point que de son coup une alle luy couppa et abatit, de quoy la beste ung si merveilleux cry getta que tous ceulx qui l'oÿrent en furent espauentéz. Dolent fut le serpent qui son alle eust perdue, car jamais il ne peult voler. Sur les piedz se leva pour Valentin abatre, mais tant aprocha pres de luy le bon chevalier que a ce coup luy abatit l'autre alle.

La endroit fut la bataille si grande entre eulx deux que Valentin ne pouoit entour de la beste tourner ne sa hache lever tant fust lasse et travaillé, et fit tant que sur ung arbre monta pour soy reposer. Et la beste qui plus voler ne peut moult cruellement le regarda en gettant par la gueulle feu horrible et puant.

"Sire," dist Pacolet, "prestez moy vostre escu et je m'en iray vers la beste aventurer."

"Amy," dist le franc chevalier, "retournez en la cité pour voz playes mediciner, car ja s'il plaist a Dieu le Pere la beste ne sera par aultre desconfite que par moy. Si requiers a Dieu par sa grace qu'i la me doinst de brief gaigner et conquerir, et que je puisse tant faire que le roy d'Antioche et tout le peuple incredule laisse la loy dampnable de Mahon et prengne la foy catholique de Nostre Seigneur Jesucrist."

Apres qu'il eust dit ces parolles il descendit de dessus l'arbre, et en faisant le signe de la croix ala devers le serpent qui contre luy courut gettant feu et flamme moult despiteusement. Valentin mist l'escu devant luy que le serpent doubtoit, et de la hache d'acier tellement le frappa qu'i luy couppa la cuisse senestre et l'abatit a terre. Le serpent brait et crie a voix merveilleuse et plus horrible que devant. Et Valentin qui fust hardy de son coup poursuivyr vint sur elle arriver tant que dedens la gueule la hache si avant luy bouta que a celle heure l'abatit mort, en gettant telle fumee que tous ceulx qui la regardoient en estoient moult grandement esmerveilléz. Et a l'eure que le serpent fut mort, chayt et trebucha dedens Antioche une grosse tour quarree et des creneaulx a l'environ jusques a demy trait d'arbalaistre rompirent et cheurent bas. Esbahys furent payens de ceste grande aventure, et disoient l'ung a l'autre que c'estoit l'ame du dyable qui par la estoit passee.

Quant le roy fust au pres de luy il l'acola moult doulcement en luy disant, "Franc chevalier, de tous les aultres [90recto]estes[1] le plus vaillant et hardy. Et bien a vostre Dieu monstré qu'i vous veult aymer et chier tenir quant par vostre grande proesse nous avez de l'ennemy delivré qui tant avoit nostre terre dommaigee et de toutes pars exillee."

---

[1] *m ii* at bottom right corner of 90r.

"Sire," said Pacolet, "I am gravely wounded in my body; I must return to the city to have my wounds looked to, for I have lost so much blood that my heart fails me." Thus he took leave and started back, but just as soon as the serpent saw him leaving, it opened its huge wings and flew toward him. Pacolet, who saw it coming, returned immediately to his master, while the serpent headed instead toward Valentin, thinking to attack him from above. But Valentin heaved his ax at it with such precision that he sliced off one of its wings, at which the beast let out such an astounding wail that everyone who heard it was terrified. The serpent was anguished at the loss of its wing, for it could never again fly. It drew itself up on its feet to attack Valentin, but the good knight moved right in and sliced off the other wing.

The terrible battle continued between them until Valentin could no longer find the strength to maneuver around the beast or raise his ax, so exhausted was he, but he managed to climb a tree to rest himself a while. The beast, which could no longer fly, glared at him with cruel intent, breathing horrible stinking fire from its mouth.

"Sire," said Pacolet, "lend me your shield and I will try my strength against the beast."

"Friend," said the noble knight, "go back to the city and have your wounds looked to, for may it never please God the Father to let the beast be defeated by anyone other than myself. Thus I pray that God by His grace will soon grant me the wherewithal to conquer it, so that I may thereby cause the king of Antioch and all his unbelieving people to leave off the damnable religion of Mohammed and take up the catholic faith of Our Lord Jesus Christ."

Having said this, he came down from the tree and, making the sign of the cross, approached the serpent, who rushed toward him, spitting out streams of fire and flame. Valentin placed the shield that the serpent feared before him, and smote it such a blow with his steel ax that he cut off its left thigh and brought it to the ground. The serpent brayed and let out a piercing cry more hideous than before. And Valentin, who was quick to follow up his stroke, came up close, thrusting the ax so deep in its throat that he killed it forthwith, and it went down emitting such smoke that everyone watching was astounded. At the very moment the serpent expired, a huge square tower inside Antioch trembled and fell, and battlements all around within half a bowshot broke and collapsed. The pagans were amazed by this adventure, and said to one another that the soul of a devil had passed by there.

When the king came up to him, he embraced him gently, saying to him, "Noble knight, among all others you are the most valiant and bold. Your God has truly demonstrated that He loves you and holds you dear, when by your great prowess you have delivered us from the enemy that had caused us so much harm and ravaged our land."

A ces parolles entrerent dedens la cité et monterent au palays royal ou tout le jour et la nuit ensuivant demenerent grant feste et grant liesse Sarrasins et payens pour la mort[1] du serpent. Le roy fit chierement garder Valentin et ses playes mediciner, grandes et petites.

Et luy pourtoit honneur et reverence la reine Rozemonde, et de parler a luy avoit grant affection et voulenté, car tant en estoit amoureuse que de l'eure que premierement le veit son cueur n'arresta. Et pour l'ardeur de son amour voulut pourchasser la mort du roy d'Antioche son mary ainsi comme vous orés cy apres.

[CHAPITRE 36]

Comment le bon chevalier Valentin, apres ce que il eust conquis le serpent, il fist baptiser le roy de Antioche et tous ceulx de sa terre; et de la royne Rozemonde qui de luy fut amoureuse. xxxvi. chapitre

Quant le bon chevalier Valentin dedens la cité d'Antioche eust ung petit prins de repos pour soy refreschir et ses playes mediciner, il ala devers le roy et luy a dist, "Sire, vous sçavez bien que vous m'avez promis de croyre en Jesucrist et vostre peuple aussi, se tant avenoit que du serpent je vous peusse delivrer. Or m'a Dieu donné grace que je l'ay mis a mort. Et pour tant, sire roy, je vous appelle de serment non pas par contrainte vous devez convertir, mais le miracle est grant et evident que Jesus mon createur a devant vous voulu faire et monstrer. Car bien pouez sçavoir et cognoistre que par force corporelle pas ne le conquis, mais a esté par la vertu de Dieu en qui je croy et en qui j'ay toute ma fiance et esperance singuliere."

"Franc chevalier," dist le roy, "sachez que je vous veul ma promesse tenir, et est ma voulenté de renoncer mahommerie et croyre en Jesucrist." Lors fit cryer par toute sa terre que grans et petis creussent en Jesucrist et delaississent la loy Mahommet sur peine d'avoir la teste couppee. Lors furent Sarrasins et payens tant de grace inspiréz que celuy temps que je vous compte que a la saincte foy par Valentin furent tous convertis.

Et tout au plus tost que la royne peult elle manda Valentin en sa chambre secrete, lequel par devers elle voulentiers vint. "Dame," dist Valentin qui bien fust aprins, "vous m'avez mandé et je viens devers vous comme celuy qui est du tout prest et appareillé de vostre voulenté parfaire et acomplir."

"Ha!" ce dist la dame, "l'onneur, le sens et le sçavoir, la force, vaillantise, beaulté et hardiesse qui sont en vous font vostre grant noblesse sur tous les [90verso]vivans loer, priser et honorer. Et pour les vertueulx fais qui sont en

---

[1] Text has *lamour* (l'amour), which appears to be a confusion with *lamort* (la mort), the latter being the more likely choice, given the context.

With these words they entered the city and mounted up to the royal palace, where the following day and night the pagan Saracens held great feasts and celebrated the death of the serpent. The king had Valentin looked after with great care and had all his wounds, great and small, tended to.

And Queen Rozemonde held him in much honor and reverence, and had an urgent desire to speak to him, for she was so enamored of him that from the first moment she saw him her heart had fixed on him. And because of her passion for him, she desired the death of the king of Antioch, her husband, as you shall hear below.

CHAPTER 36

How the good knight Valentin, after defeating the serpent, had the king of Antioch and everyone in the land baptized; and concerning Queen Rozemonde, who fell in love with him.

After the good knight Valentin had taken some rest to revive himself and had had his wounds tended to in the city of Antioch, he came to the king and said, "Sire, you know that you made a promise to me to accept Jesus Christ, along with your people, if I were able to deliver you from the serpent. Now God has graced me with that victory. And for that reason, sir king, I call upon you by your oath, not by constraint, to convert, for the miracle is great, and it is clear what Jesus my creator has placed before you as evidence. For you can clearly see that I didn't conquer it by my own bodily strength, but by the power of God in whom I believe and in whom I place all my trust and hope."

"Noble knight," said the king, "know that I wish to keep my promise, and it is my desire to renounce Mohammedanism and believe in Jesus Christ." Then he had it announced throughout his land that everyone, both great and humble, was to believe in Jesus Christ and to leave off the religion of Mohammed on pain of decapitation. Then were the pagan Saracens inspired by such grace that, in the time it takes me to tell this to you, everyone was converted to the sacred faith by Valentin.

As soon as she could, the queen sent for Valentin to come to her secret chamber, and he went to see her willingly. "Lady," said Valentin, who had been properly taught, "you have sent for me and I come to you as one ready and willing to carry out your bidding."

"Well!" said the lady, "the honor, good sense, and knowledge, the strength, valiance, beauty, and boldness that you possess mean that your great nobleness is to be praised, prized, and honored above that of all other living men. With such virtues as you possess, the lady who would be loved by you would well be able

vous, la dame qui en seroit aymee pourroit bien dire que de tous chevaliers elle auroit le plus vaillant, le plus noble et le plus beau. Or pleust a Dieu que je peusse ma voulenté parfaire et que a nul je ne fusse subjecte. Je prens sur l'ame[1] de moy que jamais aultre que vous mon cueur n'aymeroit, se tant de grace vous plaisoit a moy faire que mon amour vous fust aggreable."

"Dame," dist Valentin, "de tant je vous en remercye. Mais vous avez espousé ung roy moult hardy et redoubté, lequel sur tous les aultres vous devez aymer et chier tenir."

"Chevalier," dist la dame, "je l'ay longtemps aymé, mais depuis le jour que je vous veis mon cueur de vous ne departit."

Quant Valentin aperceut que la dame avoit tel couraige tout au plus doulcement que il peult devers la dame s'escusa de son amour. "Dame," dit Valentin, "se le roy vostre mary[2] le sçavoit jamais a nul jour n'arresteroit tant comme il m'eust a mort livré. Or est il viel et ancien et vous estes belle dame et moult joyeuse. Si vous fault ung petit attendre jusques au retour de mon voyage que j'ay entreprins d'aler en Hierusalem viseter le Sainct Sepulchre de Nostre Seigneur Jesucrist qui fust mis en la croix pour nous. Et au retour s'il avient que le roy ne soit en vie alors je parferay toute vostre voulenté."

La royne Rozemonde ne respondit parolle, mais fut au cueur de l'amour de Valentin si fort frappee que de la mort du roy fust convoiteuse et de sa vie ennemie, comme souvent avient que par folle amour plusieurs hommes tuent et murtrissent l'ung l'autre, et plusieurs femmes pourchassent la mort de leur mary pour leur voulenté parfaire. Si a grant danger de follement aymer la chose par quoy tant de mal en peult venir, comme fut Rozemonde la royne, qui pour avoir Valentin a son plaisir, la nuyt quant le roy se deult coucher et que le vin luy fust apporté, la dame print la couppe et dedens mist tel venin que nul homme qui en eusse beu de mort n'eust peu eschapper. Puis en monstrant signe de grant amour au roy le presenta qui moult fust saige et de devocion plain. Et en beneissant le vin au nom de Jesucrist fist le signe de la croix et tantost aperceut le vin qui devint troublé et cogneut les poysons qui dedens estoient.

"Par ma foy, dictes, dame! Vous y avez failly, mais je prometz a Dieu, qui tout le monde forma, que tel vin que vous m'avez brassé a ceste heure vous feray boire ou vous me direz la rayson pour quoy telle chose avez entreprinse."

"Helas! sire," ce dist la dame qui a terre se getta, "je vous requiers mercy et pardon. Sachez que Valentin pour mon amour avoir m'a fait ceste chose entreprendre."

"Par Dieu, dame," dist le roy, "assez bien vous en croy; mais par mon ceptre royal puis que par mauvais [91recto]conseil[3] ceste chose avez faicte, je vous en donne pardon et plus ne vous en doubtez."

---

[1] Text has *larme* (l'arme).

[2] Text has *pere*, which doesn't make sense in the context of the rest of Valentin's speech.

[3] *m iii* at bottom right corner of 91r.

to say that of all knights she had the most valiant, the most noble, and the most handsome. Would it please God that I might achieve my desire and not be subject to any other man! I swear on my very soul that my heart would never love another if it pleased you to grace me by accepting my love."

"Lady," said Valentin, "I thank you for so such favor. But you have married a bold and doughty king whom above all others you are obligated to love and hold dear."

"Sir knight," said the lady, "I have loved him a long time, but since the first day I saw you, my heart has not let go of you."

When Valentin saw how the lady felt, he extricated himself from her love as gently as he could. "Lady," said Valentin, "if the king your husband knew, he wouldn't wait a single day to have me put to death. Now he is old and ancient, while you are a beautiful and lively lady. You must wait awhile until I return from the voyage I have undertaken to go to Jerusalem to visit the Holy Sepulcher of Our Lord Jesus Christ who was nailed to the cross for us. If, upon my return, it comes about that the king is no longer alive, then I will fulfill all your desires."

Queen Rozemonde made no reply, but her heart was so impassioned with love of Valentin that she longed for the death of the king and was an enemy to his life, as often happens when mad love causes men to murder each other and when women plot their husbands' death in order to fulfill their desires. Thus there is great danger in loving someone so madly, for it leads to much evil, as it did Rozemonde the queen, who, in order to have Valentin at her pleasure, took up the cup that night when the wine was brought as the king was to go to bed, and she put in it a poison such that any man who drank of it would be unable to escape death. In her most loving manner she presented it to the king, who was wise and full of devotion. Then, as he blessed the wine in the name of Jesus Christ, he made the sign of the cross, and right away he noticed that the wine became cloudy and understood that there was poison in it.

"By my faith, speak, lady! You have failed, but I swear to God, who made the world, that I will make you drink this wine you have brewed for me right now if you do not tell me why you have done this thing."

"Alas, sire," said the lady, throwing herself on the ground, "I beg your mercy and pardon. Know that Valentin made me do this in order to have my love."

"By God, lady," said the king, "I am inclined to believe you; in fact, by my royal scepter, since you have done this thing because of bad counsel, I pardon you and don't worry about it any longer."

Celle nuyt coucha le roy avec Rozemonde laquelle en la baisant et acolant toute la nuyt luy disoit, "Sire, je vous requiers pour Dieu que vous fachez Valentin occirre, cestuy estranger que ainsi m'a voulu trahyr."

"Ne vous doubtez," ce dist le roy, "car je l'ay bien en pensee."

Quant la royne l'oÿt elle en fut dolente et tant fit celle nuyt que elle parla a une chambriere laquelle sur toutes les aultres elle tenoit secrepte. Si l'envoya devers Valentin pour luy dire la voulenté et le couraige que le roy avoit contre luy, et comment elle avoit failly a luy faire boire le venin et par force avoit confessé que Valentin luy avoit fait faire.

La chambriere fist le messaige moult tost et secretement. Et quant Valentin oÿt les nouvelles qu'il estoit occuppé de la chose dont il estoit innocent, de grant merveilles plusieurs foys se seigna en disant, "Doulce dame! qu'esse de couraige de femme? Or me fault il pour l'amour de la royne comme trahystre partir se je ne veul devant tous descouvrir son deshonneur. Si ayme mieulx partir et le paÿs laisser que pour l'amour de moy son deshonneur fust cogneu."

A celle heure a fait ses gens mettre en point et a fait seller ses chevaulx; devant le jour fist les portes ouvrir, car aymé estoit et cogneu. Il saillit hors de la cité et tant bien chevaulcha que il arriva en ung port de mer et trouva la une nef d'ung marchant qui la mer vouloit passer. Il entra en la mer et se mist avec eulx en priant a Dieu devotement que tant puisse aler par mer ou par terre que de la bonne dame Esclarmonde puisse avoir nouvelles.

Lendemain au plus matin que le roy fut levé il entra dedens son palays et fist ses barons assembler et leur dist, "Seigneurs, moult suis en mon cueur desplaisant quant par l'omme du monde en qui plus je me fioye je me trouve trahy et deceu. C'est le faulx Valentin lequel par sa malice et desordonnee voulenté a la royne ma femme de deshonneur requise, et luy a en courage mis de moy par poysons vilainement[1] faire mourir. Si me veullez conseiller quel jugement je doy de luy faire et de quelle mort je le doy faire mourir."

"Sire," ce dist ung moult saige baron qui la estoit, "de le condempner a mort en son absence ne seroit pas raison ne justice loyalle. Ne il n'est homme tant soit mauvais qui ne doye estre oÿ en ses raysons qui veult faire bonne justice."

Atant commanda le roy d'Antioche que Valentin luy fust amené. Lors vint son hoste au palais lequel luy dist que Valentin devant l'aube du jour estoit de son hostel party. Dolent en fut le roy et fist ses gens armer pour le suivyr, mais de tant ilz perdirent leurs peines, car sur la[2] mer estoient monté ainsi comme je vous ay dist.

---

[1] Text has *vaillamment*, an unlikely and highly illogical word choice. I have assumed it to be a mistake on the part of the typesetter and have emended it to "vilainement."

[2] Text has *la la*.

That night the king slept with Rozemonde, who, while he was kissing and embracing her all night long, was saying to him, "Sire, for God's sake, I beg you to have Valentin executed, this foreigner who wanted to betray me thus."

"Have no fear," said the king, "for I have a good idea what to do."

When the queen heard him, she was quite upset, but she managed that very night to speak to a chambermaid in whom, above all others, she could confide. She sent her to Valentin to tell him what the king was planning to do to him, and how she had failed to get him to drink the poison and had been forced to confess that Valentin had made her do it.

The chambermaid got the message to him quickly and discreetly. And when Valentin heard the news that he was being blamed for something of which he was innocent, he crossed himself several times in his amazement, saying, "Good heavens! what is the heart of woman? Now, because of the queen's love, I am forced to sneak away like a traitor, if I don't want to make her own dishonor publicly known. Well, I prefer to depart, leaving this country behind, than let her be shamed out of love for me."

Right away he had his men get ready and saddle their horses; before dawn they opened the gates for him, for he was known and loved. He left the city and rode swiftly until he came to a seaport where he found a merchant ship about to depart. He boarded and set sail with them, all the time praying God devoutly that either by land or by sea he might have tidings of the good lady Esclarmonde.

The next morning the king rose early, entered his palace, and assembled his barons, saying to them, "My lords, I am very unhappy to find that I have been deceived and betrayed by the one man in the world in whom I most trusted. I am speaking of the false Valentin who, through his malice and wicked desire, tried to seduce my wife the queen, and put it in her mind to try villainously to kill me by poison. So please advise me how to judge him and by what death he should be executed."

"Sire," said a very wise baron who was there, "to condemn him to death in his absence would be neither right nor true justice. There is no man so wicked that he shouldn't be allowed by one who dispenses proper justice to explain his reasons."

Thereupon the king of Antioch ordered that Valentin be brought to him. Then the man who had lodged Valentin came into the palace to tell him that Valentin had left his lodgings before day had dawned. The king was furious and had his men arm themselves in order to follow him, but their efforts were for naught, for they had already set sail, as I just explained to you.

[CHAPITRE 37]

[91verso]Comment le roy d'Antioche pour tant qu'il avoit renoncé la loy de Mahon fust par Brandiffer le pere de sa femme mis a mort; et comment l'empereur de Grece et le Verd Chevalier furent par ledit Brandiffer prins devant Cretophe.[1] xxxvii. chapitre[2]

Tantost apres que le roy d'Antioche fut a la sainte foy converty, le[3] pere de Rozemonde, sa femme, lequel avoit nom Brandiffer, payen et entre les aultres prince du pays, de guerre estoit convoiteux et aux armes hardy, du roy eust grant despit qui sa loy avoit laissee, si luy manda tout court que sa fille Rozemonde il luy envoyast. De laquelle chose le roy d'Antioche plainement l'escondit, et pour iceluy refus Brandiffer, qui fust syre de Falizee, a cent mille payens vint assieger le roy d'Antioche dedens sa cité, et tant fist par ses armes que dedens quatre mois luy fut la cite delivree par ung faulx trahystre. Et la fust le roy prins de ses ennemis, lequel pour tant qu'il ne voulut renoyer la loy de Jesus, Brandiffer le fist mourir de mort honteuse au milieu de la ville. Puis renvoya sa fille Rozemonde en sa terre et du royaulme d'Antioche se fist roy couronner.

Apres lesquelles choses ainsi faictes se bouta sur la mer pour retourner en son païs, mais par fortune de temps et subtil oraige fut constraint de descendre en la terre de Grece au plus pres d'une cité que on appeloit Crethophe, laquelle estoit moult grande et large. Or avint que en celle cité pour certaines causes et raysons l'empereur de Grece nouvellement estoit arivé. Si fut la fortune si grande que luy, qui de la venue des paye[n]s riens n'en sçavoit, par ung matin a heure de prime, acompaigné du Verd Chevalier et de plusieurs aultres hommes fors et vaillans, de Cretophe saillirent pour leur plaisir et esbatement. Mais de malle heure saillirent sans garde ne sans gait, car par les gens Brandiffer dont nul ne sçavoit nouvelles, furent l'empereur prins et le Verd Chevalier et tous ceulx de leur compaignie mors et desconfis. Et a celle heure coururent paiens jusques aux portes de Cretophe ou leur peine perdirent, car la cité fut forte et de telles gens garnie que souldain ilz leur convint retourner.

Courroucéz et dolens furent ceulx de Cretophe de la perte de l'empereur et du Verd Chevalier pour laquelle chose firent une lettre et par ung herault [92recto]la[4] transmirent a la royne Bellissant, femme dudit empereur, luy mandant des

---

[1] Identified as Christopolis by Dickson in *Study*, 228–29. Medieval Christopolis is identified with Kavala or Neopolis in modern Greece.

[2] Woodcut of a stern-faced standing king observing a kneeling king about to be beheaded by a figure wielding a sword.

[3] Text has *au*.

[4] *m iiii* at bottom right corner of 92r.

[CHAPTER 37]

How the king of Antioch was put to death by Brandiffer, his wife's father, for having renounced the faith of Mohammed; and how the emperor of Greece and the Green Knight were captured by Brandiffer before the walls of Christopolis.

Soon after the king of Antioch was converted to the holy faith, his wife Rozemonde's father, named Brandiffer, a pagan and noble prince of the land, bold at arms and greedy for war, was full of wrath against the king for having rejected his religion, and so ordered him immediately to send back to him his daughter Rozemonde. The king of Antioch dismissed this demand out of hand, and because of this refusal, Brandiffer, who was lord of Falize, came with a hundred thousand pagans to lay siege to the king of Antioch in his very city, and succeeded so well that, within four months, the city was delivered to him by a false traitor. There the king was taken by his enemies, and since he refused to abjure the religion of Jesus, Brandiffer had him put to a shameful death in the center of the city. Then he sent his daughter Rozemonde back to his country, and had himself crowned king of the realm of Antioch.

Following these events he set sail to return to his own country, but owing to the fortunes of weather and storm, he was forced to land in the territory of Greece near a city called Christopolis, which was quite large and spread out. Now it just so happened that the emperor of Greece had recently arrived in that city. And it was just his luck that, knowing nothing of the coming of the pagans, he, the Green Knight, and several other strong, valiant men issued forth from the city of Christopolis early one morning to take their ease. But woe unto them that they went out without any guard or watch, for the emperor and the Green Knight were taken by Brandiffer's men, of whom they had had no warning, while all the men of his company were killed and destroyed. Immediately thereafter the pagans hastened up to the gates of Christopolis, but there they wasted their efforts, for the city was strong and defended by such men that they had to abandon their attempt.

However, the people of Christopolis were dismayed and distressed by the loss of the emperor and the Green Knight, for which reason they wrote a letter and sent it with a herald to Queen Bellissant, the wife of the emperor, bearing

nouvelles de la prinse d'iceluy et demandant secours contre leurs ennemis pour et affin que les payens ne ammenassent l'empereur en leur païs. Dolente fut la dame de la prinse de son loyal mary et moult fort ploura la prinse. Ses capitaines manda et ses gens fist assembler par le pays de Grece a moult grant diligence; et d'aultre part elle manda heraulx vers le païs de France pour avoir de son frere le roy Pepin et de son filz Orson a son besoing secours et en son aversité confort.

En peu de temps de la cité de Constantinoble saillit moult grande armee de ceulx du pays de Grece pour aler en Cretophe secourir l'empereur contre Brandiffer. Mais celuy Brandiffer, qui fut subtil et malicieux, avoit mis par le pays chevaulcheurs et grans gardes par lesquelz il sceut l'entreprinse des Gregoys. Et pour la doubte de leur grande puissance et de perdre ses prisonniers et toute son armee, rentrerent sur la mer et tant nagerent en peu de temps que ilz arriverent en Falize. La endroit prindrent terre et alerent a ung chasteau fort qui estoit ainsi appellé auquel il faisoit garder moult precieusement ses deux filles, c'est assavoir Rozemonde et Galasie, qui toutes les aultres en beaulté passoit, et pour la grant beaulté de elle avoit esté en iceluy an a Brandiffer demandee pour mariage de xiiii. roys payens moult riches et puissans. Et pour tant que Brandiffer ne la vouloit pas ancores marier, mais la garde et tient fort, songneusement enfermee l'avoit en celuy chasteau, pour tant que de tous les aultres de la terre c'estoit le plus fort et le plus seur. Celuy chasteau estoit a merveilles hault et de tours espesses quarrees moult fort fortiffié. Au milieu d'iceluy chasteau avoit ung donjon de fin leton; il avoit une porte double de fer espesse et forte. De fosses larges et parfons, plains et remplis d'eaue courant estoit le chasteau environné. Et ou millieu du chasteau et des fosses il y avoit ung pont si subtillement composé qu'i n'y pouoit passer que ung homme seul, et se deux y vouloyent passer ilz tresbuchoient en l'eaue courant, et la estoient ilz mors et noyéz. Et au bout d'iceluy pont il y avoit deux lyons moult terribles et fors qui l'entree du chasteau gardoient. Au donjon d'iceluy chasteau estoit la pucelle Galasie gardee, et dessoubz lequel donjon y avoit une fosse moult grande, parfonde et obscure en laquelle furent boutéz l'empereur et le Verd Chevalier avec dix aultres crestiens lesquelz moult longuement en peine et en doleur avoient esté tenues.

Si vous laisseray a parler de ceste matiere et parleray d'Esclarmonde laquelle le roy d'Inde la Major tenoit en ses prisons ainsi que par devant vous ay fait mencion.

her the tidings of his capture and begging for aid against their enemies so that the pagans not be able to carry away the emperor to their own country. The lady was distraught by the capture of her devoted husband and bewailed his seizure. She sent for his captains and quickly had them assemble his men from throughout the country of Greece; moreover, she sent a herald to the country of France in order to get help in her need and comfort in her adversity from her brother King Pepin and from her son Orson.

In very little time, a large army of Greeks sallied forth from the city of Constantinople to go to Christopolis to come to the emperor's aid against Brandiffer. But Brandiffer, who was sly and malicious, had placed scouts and guards throughout the country who informed him of the Greeks' plan. So, fearful of their great numbers and of losing his prisoners and all his army, he set sail, making such good time that he soon arrived in Falize. There he disembarked and headed to a castle fortress that was called Chastel Fort, where he had his two daughters closely guarded, namely Rozemonde and Galasie, the latter daughter exceeding all others in beauty. Because of her great beauty, fourteen wealthy and powerful pagan kings had requested her hand in marriage from Brandiffer just that year. But Brandiffer did not wish to marry her off yet; rather, he kept her under close guard, carefully enclosing her in that castle, for it was the strongest and safest one in that land. This castle was marvelously high and fortified with thick square towers. In the middle of the castle was a keep constructed of fine brass with a double door of thick strong iron. Wide, deep moats filled with rushing water surrounded the castle. In the middle of the fortress and the moat was a bridge so cleverly fashioned that only a single man could pass over it, and if two tried to pass, they fell into the rushing water and there drowned. At the end of this bridge were two mighty and terrifying lions who guarded the entrance to the castle. In the castle keep was kept the maiden Galasie, and under this keep was a large dungeon, deep and dark, where the emperor and the Green Knight were cast along with ten other Christians who had long been imprisoned there in pain and despair.

Now I will leave off speaking of these matters, and will tell you about Esclarmonde, whom the king of India Major kept in his prison, as I mentioned to you before.

[CHAPITRE 38]

Comment la belle Esclarmonde apres que l'an fut
acomply contrefit le ma[92verso]lade affin que le roy
d'Inde Major ne l'espousast; et du roy Lucar qui voulut
venger la mort du roy Trompart son pere a l'encontre du
roy d'Inde la Major. xxxviii. chap[itre]

Or avez vous bien oÿ reciter et dire comment le roy d'Inde, apres ce qu'il eust fait mourir le roy Trompart lequel sur le cheval de Pacolet Esclarmonde avoit emportee, iceluy roy d'Inde voulut prendre et avoir a femme ladite dame Esclarmonde, laquelle comme subtille, sage et bien aprinse, luy fit entendant que elle avoit serment et voue aux dieux de non avoir habitacion d'omme jusques a ung an, et celuy terme luy donna le roy qui le temps durant la fist garder chierement et honnourablement. Or avoit la dame ceste chose pensee et avisee pour dissimuler et eslongner la fortune douloureuse, et esperant que par aulcune maniere elle peust avoir ayde et secours, mais de son esperance fust bien loing et deceu, car de nul n'eust confort ce terme durant.

Ainsi fust l'an passé et le terme finy. Si vous diray de quoy elle s'avisa pour mieulx sa foy garder et loyaulté tenir a son amy Valentin. Quant la belle Esclarmonde vit et aperceut que le terme estoit passé et que nulle excusacion elle ne pouoit plus trouver devers le roy d'Inde, moult fut au cueur durement frappee et trop amerement courroucee. Valentin desiroit et regrettoit en gettant souspirs piteux et larmes douloureuses. Et quant elle eust pensé et consideré sa fortune dolente et piteuse aventure, pour plus honnestement son honneur maintenir et fuyr et eslongner vitupere, vergongne et blasme, par ung matin se tint et demoura en son lit sans soy levee et faignit et contrefit le malade en plangnant la teste moult piteusement.

Au roy d'Inde Major vindrent tantost les nouvelles que la belle Esclarmonde estoit malade, de laquelle chose il fut moult desplaisant. Et tout incontinent vint en la chambre pour la belle viseter, mais ainsi qu'i vouloit mettre sa main sur son chief pour la belle viseter et conforter, elle luy print le bras et leva hault la teste en faisant maniere de le vouloir mordre, dont le roy fut moult fort esmerveillé. Puis tourna la dame les yeulx en la teste en froncissant la face et menant layde vie tellement que de sa maniere regarder fut le roy d'Inde trop esbahy. Et de la grant paour que il eust saillit hors de la chambre, et fît venir les dames pour la belle viseter, et leur a dist, "Pour dieu, pensés bien de m'amye Esclarmonde, car par Mahon je me doubte trop que elle ne viengne enrragee et du tout forcenee."

En ce point s'entretint et maintind la dame moult longuement, et si bien le sceut faire que dedens quinze jours elle sembloit mieulx beste que femme raysonnable. Tant fust de fole contenance et cruelle maniere que tous [93recto]les serviteurs, petis et grans, dames et damoiselles, l'abandonnerent et sans compaignie demoura. Aux dens et aux ongles court a tous et esgraffigne tous ceulx qui de elle

CHAPTER 38

How, once the year was up, the fair Esclarmonde
pretended to be ill so that the king of India Major
would not marry her; and concerning King Lucar, who
wanted to take vengeance on the king of India Major
for the death of King Trompart his father.

Now you have heard tell how, after executing King Trompart (who had borne Esclarmonde away on Pacolet's horse), the king of India wanted to take to wife the lady Esclarmonde, but she, clever and wise and well taught, had made him believe that she had taken a vow and sworn to the gods not to cohabit with a man for a full year, and the king granted her this period during which he had her guarded properly and honorably. Of course the lady had fabricated this story to dissimulate and to distance the unfortunate event, hoping that by some means aid and rescue would come her way, but her hopes were dashed, for no help came all during this time.

Thus did the year pass and the term granted end. And so I will tell you what she concocted, the better to keep her faith and pledge to her beloved Valentin. When the fair Esclarmonde realized that her time was up and that she could find no other pretext to fend off the king of India, she was heartsick and bitterly upset. She wept and sighed piteously, desiring Valentin's presence and missing him in his absence. Then, after considering her sad fate and terrible luck, she came up with a plan to maintain her honor, avoid insult, and ward off shame and blame. One morning she remained in bed without getting up, feigning illness and complaining of terrible headache.

The news soon came to the king of India that the fair Esclarmonde was ill, a piece of news he found most displeasing. Right away he came to her chamber to see how the fair one was doing, but just as he tried to lay his hand on her head to examine her and comfort her, she seized his arm and raised her head as if she meant to bite him, which greatly startled the king. Then the lady rolled her eyes back in her head, wrinkling up her face and generally acting in such a repulsive manner that, seeing this, the king was completely alarmed. He dashed out of the room in fear, and called for ladies to examine the fair one, saying to them, "For heaven's sake, take good care of my beloved Esclarmonde, for by Mohammed, I am afraid she has gone completely mad."

The lady continued to behave like this for a long time, and she did it so well that within fifteen days she seemed more a beast than a reasonable woman. She manifested such a wild temperament and ferocious manners that all the servants, great and humble, ladies and maidens, abandoned her, leaving her without company. She would run up to everyone with her teeth bared and nails ready to scratch anyone who dared approach her. Because of her ferocity,

veullent approcher, et pour sa grande crudelité fust toute seule en sa chambre enfermee et par une fenestre on luy bailloit a boire et a menger comme a une beste. De jour en jour faisoit maniere que sa maladie croissoit, et toutes ses robes deschiroit et desrompoit. Sa chemise vestoit dessus sa robe une foys a droit, l'autre foys ce dessus dessoubz. En une cheminee froitoit ses mains et puis en froitoit son visaige en telle maniere que sa plaisante face blanche et coulouree estoit devenue noire et enfumee.

En iceluy estat vint le roy la veoir; au cueur moult courroucé fust de son piteux maintien. "Helas, dame," dist il, "trop mauvaisement me va quant en ce point je vous voy. Car maintenant estoit venu le temps que de vous je devoye avoir tout soulas, tout plaisir et toute liesse. Dame, prenez en vous aulcun peu de confort et ne soyez de maniere en vostre maladie si dissolue."

Quant la dame oÿt le languaige du roy elle ne monstra pas semblant de entendre son languaige. Mais plus que devant elle contrefist l'enrragee en saillant contre la cheminee. Et des mains elle noircist la face, l'une foys gettoit ung ris gracieulx, l'autre fois ung souspir moult piteulx. Ainsi de ris, de pleurs et de souspirs estoit sa contenance entremeslee pour mieulx et honnestement son entreprinse celer et son honneur garder.

"Par Mahon," dist le roy d'Inde, "de toutes les choses que jamais je veis, voy cy la nonpareille. Or je vous diray comment il nous fault faire. Je veul que la dame soit menee en la mahommerie par devant noz dieux et que pour elle nous façons tous prieres que ilz luy veullent ayder et secourir et sa maladie curer."

Ainsi comme le roy le dit fut la chose bien parfaicte. Et la dame au temple fut menee, mais tant plus la mettoit on aupres de l'ymage de Mahon et son autel, plus faisoit maniere de sa maladie aggraver et acroistre. Dont apres que le roy veit que nul remede ne relache n'y avoit, il la fist remener en sa chambre comme devant ou elle continua son entreprinse sur esperance ferme de Valentin trouver, duquel je vous veul parler.

Iceluy chevalier Valentin, d'ardant desir querant s'amye, la belle et noble dame Esclarmonde, par le pays chevaulcha avec Pacolet que oncques nul jour habandonner ne le voulut. Or chevaulcherent tant qu'ilz arriverent en Esclardie et estoit la terre du roy Trompart, lequel ainsi comme devant j'ay mencion faicte avoit sur le chevalet de bois la belle Esclarmonde emmenee, car il la trompa par ledit cheval de boys de Pacolet. Ilz demanderent en celle cité nouvelles du roy Trompart et on leur a compté la maniere comment il [93verso]avoit esté tué et occis devant Inde la Major, et comment Lucar son filz vouloit sa mort venger, et pour ce parfaire il avoit assemblé quinze roys avec tous compaignons souldoyers qui pour argent vouloent servir et en la guerre aler. Dont parla Pacolet, qui bien sçavoit le langaige du pays, et demanda a son oste plus a plain des nouvelles et de l'estat a iceluy roy Lucar. Et l'oste luy compta comment il avoit fiancé et promis de prendre a femme la fille de Brandiffer, laquelle par avant avoit esté mariee au roy d'Antioche qui par ledit Brandiffer fut desconfit et mis a mort pour ceste cause qu'il avoit laissee la loy et creance de Mahon.

she was shut up in her room, and food and drink were passed to her through a window as if to a beast. From day to day she made it seem that her illness was growing, and she shredded and tore her clothes. She wore her shift over her dress sometimes the right way, sometimes inside out. She rubbed her hands in the chimney and then all over her face so that her lovely pink and rose complexion was soon black and sooty.

While she was in this state, the king came to see her; his heart was stricken by her pitiful state. "Alas, lady," he said, "it is terrible for me to see you like this. For now the time has come when I was to have every solace, pleasure, and happiness from you. Lady, let yourself be helped and be not so depraved by your illness."

When the lady heard the king speak, she pretended not to understand anything he said. Rather, she acted the part of a madwoman more than ever, rubbing up against the chimney. With her hands she blackened her face, sometimes laughing graciously, sometimes sighing most piteously. Thus mixing laughter, tears, and sighs did she reinforce her plan and keep her honor intact.

"By Mohammed," said the king of India, "of all things that I have ever seen, this is the strangest. Now I will tell you what I think we should do. Let us have the lady brought to the temple, to the altar of our gods, and let us pray that they come to her aid and cure her of her malady."

As the king ordered, so it was done. They brought the lady to the temple, but the closer they placed her to the image of Mohammed and his altar, the more it seemed to aggravate and increase her illness. So, once the king realized no remedy or relief was to be found this way, he had her brought back to her room as before, where she continued to follow her plan in firm hope of finding Valentin, of whom I would like to speak now.

This knight Valentin, filled with ardent desire and in quest of his beloved, the fair and noble lady Esclarmonde, rode throughout the country with Pacolet, who had no desire to abandon him for a single day. Now they rode and rode until they came to Esclardy, which was the land of King Trompart, the one who, as I explained before, had borne away the fair Esclarmonde on the wooden horse, for he had duped her with that wooden horse of Pacolet. They asked for tidings of King Trompart in that city, and were told of how he had been killed in India Major, and how his son Lucar wanted to avenge his death, and how, in order to achieve this end, he had assembled fifteen kings with all the mercenary soldiers who were willing to serve and go to war for pay. Then Pacolet spoke up, for he had a thorough knowledge of the local language, and asked his host for more thorough information about the current situation of this King Lucar. And the host recounted how he had become engaged and had promised to take to wife the daughter of King Brandiffer, the one who previously had been married to the king of Antioch, who had been overthrown and executed by Brandiffer for having turned apostate and abandoning the religion of Mohammed.

De telles nouvelles oÿr fut Valentin moult esmerveillé, et sur les fortunes du monde commença fort a penser a par luy, considerant les grans inconveniens, grans debas sont avenus et continuellement aviennent de jour en jour. Et quant il eust ung peu sur la chose avisé, il a dist a son oste, "Sire hoste, dites moy que est devenue une dame moult belle que le roy Trompart menoit avec luy?"

"Par Mahon," ce dist l'oste, "nulles nouvelles n'en avoys oÿ par deça."

"Or me dites," dist Valentin, "ou est pour le present le roy Lucar, car j'ay bien grant couraige d'aler prendre souldoyéz soubz luy pour ce que mon argent me est failly. Et d'aultre part j'ay grant desir et voulenté familiere de la guerre suivyr."

"Seigneur," ce dist l'oste, "le roy Lucar est en Esclardie et la le trouverrez acompaigné de cent mille Sarrasins, car il attent Brandiffer qui en celluy lieu doit amener sa fille pour espouser et prendre a femme."

Quant Valentin entendit toutes ces nouvelles ainsi racompter il eust esperance moult grande de nouvelles avoir de la belle Esclarmonde. Lors partit de celle cité et chevaulcha vers Esclardie faingnant d'avoir desir du roy Lucar servir, mais plus grandement au cueur luy toucha la façon et maniere comment il pourroit s'amye la belle, plaisante et tresnoble dame Esclarmonde recouvrer.

[CHAPITRE 39]

Comment le roy Lucar en la grande et belle cité d'Esclardie espousa et print a femme la belle et gracieuse dame Rozemonde. xxxix. cha[pitre][1]

Ainsi que le roy Lucar, haultement et puissamment acompaigné en grant sumptueulx estat, estoit dedens Esclardie, Brandiffer arriva qui sa fille amenoit. Et quant Lucar sceut les nouvelles il saillit hors de la ville en triumphante et belle compaignie pour luy aler a l'encontre. De veoir Rozemonde fust celuy roy Lucar grandement resjouy, mais de tant qu'il en estoit joyeulx en estoit la dame en son cueur desplaisante, car de tous les aultres a luy elle vouloit mal et de riens ne l'aimoit, mais tousjours regardoit et desiroit Valentin. Au palays royal fut la belle dame menee et convoyee de plusieurs roys, contes, barons et chevaliers, et devant l'ymaige de Mahommet fut a Lucar donnee et espousee. Or ne fault il point demander de l'estat de celle feste, du tresgrant estat qui adonc y fut fait, tant en riches vestemens et joyeulx services et gens de toutes sortes et aussy de viandes que de tous jeux et esbatemens fust parmy la cité d'Esclardie moult grant feste demenee.

Et Valentin si chevaulche sur les champs ardant de parvenir a son intencion. Si avint tout ainsi que il arriva a l'entree d'ung boys qui moult estoit verd et

---

[1] Woodcut of interior scene of king and queen at table with two attendants.

Valentin was amazed to hear such tidings, and began to meditate on the fortunes of this world, considering the great disasters and great conflicts that have happened and continually occur every day. After thinking a bit about these matters, he asked his host, "Sir host, tell me, what became of the lady whom King Trompart was taking away with him?"

"By Mohammed," said the host, "I have heard nothing about her around here."

"Now tell me," said Valentin, "where King Lucar is presently, for I would like to go earn wages under him, because my money has run out. In any case I have a great desire to take part in the war."

"My lord," said the host, "King Lucar is in Esclardy, and there you will find him accompanied by a hundred thousand Saracens, for they await Brandiffer who is supposed to bring his daughter there for him to marry."

When Valentin heard all this information, he had great hopes of having tidings of the fair Esclarmonde. So he left that city and rode toward Esclardy, feigning a desire to serve King Lucar, while what really touched his heart was finding a way to recover the fair, lovely, and most noble lady Esclarmonde.

CHAPTER 39

How King Lucar married the fair and gracious lady Rozemonde in the great and beautiful city of Esclardy.

While King Lucar was waiting in Esclardy, surrounded by all the wealth and power of his sumptuous court, Brandiffer arrived with his daughter. When Lucar heard the news of their arrival, he sallied forth from the city to greet them with a handsome and splendid company. Lucar was quite delighted to see Rozemonde, but as joyous as he was about it, the lady was displeased, for of all the men in the world she wished him most ill, liking him not a jot, but still preferring and wanting Valentin. Numerous kings, counts, barons, and knights conveyed the fair lady to the royal palace, where, before the image of Mohammed, she was wedded to Lucar. No need to ask what the feast was like or in what a grand manner everything was conducted. There were lavish clothes, joyous revelries, all sorts of people and viands, and such games and sports that a grand celebration took place throughout the city of Esclardy.

In the meantime Valentin rode through the fields, burning with the desire to achieve his purpose. It so happened that, as he came to the entrance of a most

plaisant, il oÿt et entendit la voix d'une plaisante dame tresbelle et tresgracieuse laquelle ung Sarrasin par force detenoit soubz ung arbre, et oultre le couraige d'elle en vouloir faire son plaisir et voulenté. Et quant Valentin l'oÿt il dist a Pacolet, "Amy, chevaulchons fort et faisons dilengence. Je ay oÿ une femme en ce boys qui moult fort et haultement crye et maine piteux desconfort; si ferons grant ausmoine de luy porter secours et ayde."

"Sire," dist Pacolet, "laissez la dame et atant ne vous entremettez de son fait, car vous ne sçavez que c'est. Paraventure que elle fait tout par faintise et couverture, et vous en pourroit plus tost venir mal que bien, et vous pourroit on dire que de leur debat vous n'avez que faire."

"Pacolet," dist Valentin, "vous parlez follement, car l'homme n'est pas noble ne vaillant de couraige qui ne maintent les dames, ne confort ne leur donne quant elles sont en necessité; et si vous dy que tous nobles cueurs doivent pour les dames leur corps aventurer et leur honneur garder de toute leur puissance."

Lors toucha des esperons et entra au boys; si aperceult la dame que le Sarrasin tenoit.

"Sire," dist Valentin, "laissez vostre entreprinse, car se la dame voulez a vostre gré avoir, il convient que contre mon corps le vostre vous esprouvez. Vous pouez bien cognoistre que de vostre amour elle n'a cure; si la vous convient laisser ou a moy avoir guerre."

"Par[1] Mahon," dist le payen, "de guerre je le vous ottroye du tout a vostre voulenté. Mais je vous dy haultement et fay assavoir que tresmal vous estes icy venu et arrivé quant pour moy empescher de mon plaisir parfaire estes sur moy [94verso]arrivé sans nulle cause avoir."

A ces motz laissa la dame et monta sur son cheval qui estoit aupres de luy a ung arbre atachié. De l'escu se couvrit et a la lance prinse, puis sont l'ung l'autre eslongnéz. Mais le chevalier Valentin vint de si grant couraige contre le Sarrasin que parmy le corps le passa tout oultre et tant que a la terre l'abatit mort. Et quant il l'eust conquis, il ala vers la pucelle et luy dist, "Damoiselle, vous estes a ceste heure de vostre ennemy vengee. Si vous prie que vous me veullez dire comment et en quelle maniere celuy mauldit homme en ce boys vous a peu amener."

"Helas! sire," ce dist elle, "la verité je vous en diray. Sachez que hersoir au vespre en l'ostel de mon pere il s'en vint logier. Et pour mieulx faire de mon corps a sa voulenté et me emmener a son plaisir, ceste nuyt il est alé en l'ostel de mon pere et l'a faulcement tué et murtry. Puis m'a icy amenee pour mon honneur tollir et oster vituperablement, de laquelle chose par vostre proesse et vaillance m'avez au jour d'uy gardee et deffendue. Si pouez maintenant de mon corps faire et acomplir a vostre bon plaisir et voulenté, car comme chevalier vaillant et hardy champion en danger de vostre vie m'avez gaignee et conquise."

---

[1] Text has *Pa*.

green and pleasant wood, he heard the voice of a gracious, fair, and pleasing lady being held by force under a tree by a Saracen who was trying to have his way with her against her will. When Valentin heard her he said to Pacolet, "Friend, let's hurry and ride quickly. I have heard a woman in great distress crying out in this wood; it would be an act of charity on our part to offer her help and succor."

"Sire," said Pacolet, "forget the lady and do not involve yourself in her fate, for you don't know what is going on. It's possible that she is faking this, and it could likely go badly rather than well for you, and others could say to you that you have no business meddling in their quarrel."

"Pacolet," said Valentin, "you speak foolishly, for no man is noble or of valiant heart who does not defend ladies or come to their aid when they are in need; thus I say to you that all noble hearts must risk themselves for ladies and protect their honor with all their strength."

Then he spurred his horse and rode into the wood; there he caught sight of the lady whom the Saracen was clutching.

Valentin spoke: "Cease your attempt, sir, for if you wish to have your way with that lady, first you must prove yourself against me. You can clearly see that she cares not for your love; either you leave her alone or you face battle with me."

"By Mohammed," said the pagan, "I grant you battle just as you wish. But woe unto you, I say to you, when you come to keep me from my pleasure without having cause."

With these words he let go of the lady and mounted his horse that was attached to a nearby tree. He covered himself with his shield and took up his lance. Then they took up positions at a distance from each other. But the knight Valentin rode with such great courage against the Saracen that his lance passed right through his body, and he threw him down dead to the ground. Having vanquished him, he rode up to the girl and said to her, "Maiden, now you are avenged against your enemy. I beg you to tell me how and in what manner this cursed man was able to carry you into this wood."

"Alas! sir," she said, "I will tell you the truth. Know that he came last night at the hour of vespers to lodge at my father's inn. Then, the better to have his way with me and take me at his pleasure, he came to my father's inn this evening and murdered him despicably. Then he dragged me here shamefully to rob me of my honor, which you, through your prowess and valor, have today prevented from happening to me. Now it is you who may do as you will with me according to your good pleasure and desire, for you have gained and conquered me as a bold and valiant knight through the risking of your life."

"Damoiselle," dist le vaillant chevalier Valentin, "par moy vostre gentil corps n'aura dommaige ne villenie. Retournez en vostre maison et pensez de bien faire et vostre honneur guarder."

Lors Valentin laissa la pucelle et reprint son chemin vers Esclardie. Et les gens du Sarrasin si vindrent devers leur maistre, mais tantost que ilz le trouverent dessus l'erbe gisant mort, sans nul sejour ne dilacion frapperent des esperons pour aler en Esclardie les nouvelles compter. Ilz entrerent en la cité et alerent vers le roy Lucar, desconfortéz et moult dole[n]s, puis luy ont dit, "Hault et redoubté sire, tresmal va de nostre fait, car nostre maistre, le bon mareschal, que vous avez tant aymé et chier tenu, a esté par les larrons en ung boys tué presentement."

Le roy fust moult dolent et a grant quantité de gens saillit hors des portes. Et quant ilz furent dehors ilz veirent venir Valentin et dirent au roy, "Sire, voyez icy celuy qui vostre mareschal a murtry et tué." Valentin fut prins, et tous ceulx de sa compaignie des Sarrasins furent[1] fermement lyéz, et en les batant et frappant par le commandeme[n]t du roy estroitement[2] menéz.

Or estoit Rozemonde en celuy chasteau laquelle cogneut incontinent Valentin, pour laquelle chose elle fust au cueur fort esprinse. Et pour la grant amour de quoy elle l'aimoit elle s'en ala tantost par devers le roy et luy dist, "Helas, sire, gardez vous bien de faire mourir cestuy vaillant chevalier qui pour vostre prisonnier a esté icy amené, car je vous prometz et jure que de tous les vaillans couraiges le plus preux et le plus hardy, il est le souverain [95recto]et en doit l'excellence emporter. Syre, c'est celuy chevalier Valentin du pays de France qui par sa vaillance devant Antioche tua et desconfit le faulx et horrible serpent. Veuillez le garder chierement et en voz gaiges le retenir, car au monde il n'y a si victorieulx homme. Se vous le gardez et sur vous avoit quelque grant bataille, par sa puissance vous auriez victoire et seigneurie."

"Dame," ce dist le roy, "plusieurs foys ay oÿ parler de sa grant renommee et fort ay desiré de le veoir en ma court." Puis appella Valentin et luy dist, "Chevalier, n'ayez de mourir nul doubte, car sachez que dessus tous les aultres je vous veul aimer et chier tenir et tous les vostres souldoyers et a mes gaiges mettre. Mais tant il y a qu'i vous conviendra faire ung messaige pour moy. C'est que vous irez en Inde la Major au roy, et de par moy luy direz que je le deffie, et que je suis pres et appareillé et tout deliberé de ma puissance d'aler venger la mort de mon pere le roy Trompart, lequel cruellement il a fait mourir. Si luy direz que je le somme de venir vers moy par dedens mon palays par devant toute ma baronnye, la corde entour du coul, prest et appareillé de telle mort recepvoir comme par l'assistence de tout mon conseil royal sera jugé et condempné. Et s'i ne veult venir, vous luy direz que dedens bien brief temps je l'iray veoir et viseter en sy grant compaignie que il ne luy demourra chasteau, ville ne forterresse que je ne face du tout exiller et a la terra abatre. Et si ne demourra homme ne femme ne enfans en vie."

---

[1] Text has *et*.
[2] Text has *estoitement*.

"Maiden," said the valiant knight Valentin, "your gentle body will suffer no villainy or harm from me. Go back home and do your best to act rightly and protect your honor."

Then Valentin let the girl go, setting off again on his way to Esclardy. And the Saracen's men came to find their master, but when they discovered him lying dead on the grass, they hurried back to Esclardy without delay to bring tidings. They entered the city and rode straight to King Lucar, where, upset and grieving, they told him, "Most exalted and respected lord, things go very badly for us, for our master, the good marshal, whom you have so loved and held dear, has just been killed by thieves in the woods."

The king was quite upset and immediately went out through the city gates with a great number of men. But as soon as they were outside, they saw Valentin coming and said to the king, "Sire, here is the man who has slain and murdered your marshal." Valentin and his company were seized and tightly bound, and as they were dragged away, they were kicked and beaten by order of the king.

Now Rozemonde, who was in the castle, immediately recognized Valentin, for which reason she was absolutely smitten. Out of the great love she felt for him, she went straight to the king and told him, "Alas, sire, take care not to kill this valiant knight whom you have brought here your prisoner, for I swear to you that of all men with valiant courage, he is the the boldest and hardiest, the greatest of all, and ought to be recognized as superior. Sire, this is that knight Valentin, from the country of France, who by his prowess killed and vanquished the evil and horrible serpent in front of Antioch. You must hold him dear and retain him with wages, for there is no man so victorious in all the world. If you retained him and then some great battle befell you, you would have victory and lordship through his prowess."

"Lady," said the king, "I have often heard of his renown and have greatly desired to see him in my court." Then he called for Valentin and addressed him thus: "Knight, fear not dying, for know that I wish to love and cherish you above all others, and to put you and your men to work for me. But first I have a message I need you to deliver for me. You will go to India Major, to the king, and you will tell him that I challenge him, and that I am ready and waiting and absolutely determined to use my strength to avenge the death of my father King Trompart, whom he cruelly killed. You will also tell him that I order him to come to me, to my palace, before an assembly of all my lords, with a rope around his neck, ready and willing to receive such a death as that to which he will be judged and condemned by my full royal council. And if he is not willing to come, you will tell him that I will come to him quite soon with such a large company that there will not remain to him a single castle, city, or fortress that I do not ravage and utterly destroy. Moreover, there will not remain a single man, woman, or child alive."

"Sire," dist Valentin, "le messaige[1] feray je bien et suffisamment tant que de moy serez bien content. Bien sçay que vous m'envoyerez en lieu dangereulx et de moult fort grant peril plain, mais j'ay fiance en Jesucrist et en la benoitte Vierge Marie qui de plusieurs dangiers moult grans m'a gardé, deffendu et mis hors."

[CHAPITRE 40]

Comment le noble chevalier Valentin partit d'Esclardie pour s'en aler en la grande et puissante cité de Inde la Major porter la deffiance du puissant roy Lucar. xl. chapitre[2]

Quant Rozemonde veit que Valentin estoit pres d'aler en Inde la Major pour le roy deffier, elle entra en sa chambre et par une damoiselle secretement manda [95verso]querir Valentin, lequel moult voulentiers s'y vint par devers elle et en moult grant reverence la salua.

"Chevalier," dist la dame, "bien soyez vous venu, car dessus tous les aultres j'avoye grant desir de vous veoir."

"Dame," ce dist Valentin, "se grant affetion aviez de moy veoir aussi avoy je de vous, ma dame. Depuis que je ne vous veis la chose est bien changee, car j'ay entendu que vostre mary le roy d'Antioche est mort depuis mon departement et que de nouveau estes mariee a ung aultre. Or avez vous peu cognoistre que pour l'amour de vous dedens Antioche je fus grandement chargé de deshonneur et en peril et danger de perdre la vie?"

"Il est vray," dist la dame, "de cela je me tiens coulpable, car la grant amour que je avoye a vous me fist la chose entreprendre, mais sachez que au jour d'uy la faulte que je vous feis vous sera bien recompensee. Et combien que mon pere et ma mere m'aist donnee au roy Lucar, lequel est puissant et riche sur tous les aultres, mais sachez que mon cueur jamais ne le pourroit aymer et non sans cause. Car nonobstant sa richesse et son hault et loyal parentaige, sachez que de tous les aultres il est le plus faulx trahystre deceptif. Et si vous dy que depuis que en son palays vous avez esté arrivé, il est entré en jalousie si grande que durer il ne peult, ne de bon cueur vous regarder. Et pour ceste cause et affin que plus honnestement il soit despeché de vous, il vous envoye en Inde la Major, esperant que jamais vous ne reviendrez par deça, car oncques de messaigier que par luy envoyé y fust, nul n'en retourna que le roy d'Inde ne les aye fait mourir.

---

[1] Text has *mestaige*.

[2] Woodcut depicting messenger down on one knee, holding spear, handing a message to a standing robed and crowned figure, with one attendant partially seen behind him. Repeat of woodcut on 14v and 55r.

"Sire," said Valentin, "I shall deliver your message and do it so well that you will be content with me. I am well aware that you are sending me to a dangerous place full of great peril, but I have faith in Jesus Christ and in the blessed Virgin Mary who have guarded me, defended me, and delivered me safely from many great dangers."

CHAPTER 40

How the noble knight Valentin left Esclardy for the great and powerful city of India Major in order to deliver the challenge of the puissant King Lucar.

When Rozemonde saw that Valentin was about to leave for India Major to deliver the challenge, she went to her chamber and secretly sent a maiden to go get Valentin, who willingly came to see her, greeting her with a deep bow.

"Sir knight," said the lady, "you are most welcome, for I had a great desire to see you more than anyone else."

"Lady," said Valentin, "as pleased as you are to see me, I am just as pleased to see you, my lady. Things have changed since I last saw you, for I have heard that your husband the king of Antioch died after my departure and you have since married another. Were you aware that for love of you I was accused of dishonor and was in mortal peril in Antioch?"

"It is true," said the lady, "I am responsible for that, for my great love for you pushed me to make the attempt, but know that I will make amends today for the harm I caused you then. Even though my father and mother have given me to King Lucar, who is powerful and wealthy above all others, know that my heart will never be able to love him, and not without cause. For, despite his wealth and his lofty and valid lineage, know that he is the most false and deceiving traitor imaginable. Moreover, since you have arrived in his palace, he has worked himself into such a fit of jealousy that he cannot endure it, nor can he consider you in kindly fashion. For this reason, and the more legitimately to be rid of you, he is sending you to India Major, hoping that you will never return, for no messenger ever sent there by him has ever returned — the king of India has killed them all.

"Mais de son intencion par moy sera fraudé et deceu; de cestuy danger vous garderay, et je vous diray comment, franc chevalier. Sachez que il n'y a pas longtemps que celuy roy d'Inde me feist pour femme demander, et qu'i soit vray, trop plus chierement je l'aimoye que le roy Lucar qui est trahystre et de layde facture, desplaisant a veoir et en parler mal gracieulx et peu courtois. Mais du vouloir de mon pere qui fust au mien contraire, je fus au roy d'Inde refusee et a Lucar donnee. Or est il vray que d'iceluy roy d'Inde pour acointance d'amours m'envoya ung aneau moult riche, notabel et beau, lequel j'ay chierement gardé de tout mon cueur pour l'amour de luy. Et sachez que jamais a homme vivant je ne le declairay fors seulement a vous. Mais pour tant que je voy la faulce voulenté et male intencion du roy Lucar lequel en Inde vous envoye pour de vous avoir delivrance, je vous donneray confort et consolacion de ma puissance que de peril vous garderay et seray cause de vostre messaige parfaire et de retourner par deça comme hardy et preux chevalier.

"Et combien que je sçay et cognoy de certain que de mon amour n'avez que faire, si que vous estes a une aultre promis et donné, [96recto]a plus haulte, plus belle et plus excellente dame que je ne suis, si ne veul je point oublier[1] l'amour de quoy pour vous mon cueur fut feru quant je vous veis dedens Antioche, adonc que par vostre victoire le serpent cruel et abhominable fust conquis et vaincu. Et pour les choses dessudictes a vostre honneur acompliez et parfaictes je vous diray que vous ferez. Quant vous serez devant le roy d'Inde arrivé, apres la reverence faicte et le salut donné de par le roy Lucar qui vers luy vous envoye, sans longue demouree, de par moy le saluerez comme mon loyal et secret amy et luy direz que jassoit ce que mon pere m'aist donnee au roy Lucar si n'ay je pas mis en oubly[2] son amour, mais ay ferme propos et bonne voulenté que une foys en ma vie et le plus brief que faire se pourra devers luy me retrairay et de moy pourra faire a sa voulenté et bon plaisir. Et si luy dictes que je trouverray façon et maniere d'aler avec le roy Lucar quant son ost mettera en Inde. Adonc il pourra bien s'il a en luy proesse a sa voulenté m'avoir et emmener. Et affin que le roy d'Inde ne doubte que pour paour ou faintes vous dictes ces parolles vous luy porterez cestuy aneau."

"Dame," dist Valentin, "du bon vouloir que vous avez de moy secourir et donner alegance je vous mercye humblement, et ne vous doubtez du demourant, car vostre messaige feray au plaisir de Dieu au roy d'Inde si bien et si suffisamment que de brief vous en aurez nouvelles bonnes et gracieuses."

A ces motz print congé Valentin de la belle dame Rozemonde et ala vers le roy Lucar qui pour le conduire luy bailla dix mariniers. Lesquelz luy passerent ung grant bras de mer qui est entre Esclardie et Inde, et aussi monterent sur mer et eurent vent aggreable sy bon que a mydy partirent de Esclardie et le lendemain ilz arriverent a ung port lequel est a une lieue pres de la cité d'Inde la Major. Et en ce lieu se descendit Valentin et tira son cheval dehors, puis il monta dessus et dist au mariniers,

---

[1] Text has *omblier*.
[2] Text has *ombly*.

"But his intention will be thwarted by me; I will keep you from this danger, and I will explain to you how, noble knight. Know that this king of India not long ago asked for my hand in marriage, and the truth is that I loved him much more than King Lucar, who is not only treacherous, but ill-made and ugly to behold, ill-spoken and lacking in courtesy. But owing to my father's wishes, which were contrary to my own, I was refused the king of India and given instead to Lucar. Now it so happened that the king of India, as proof of his love, sent me an exceptionally beautiful and costly ring that I have held most dear out of love for him. And know that I never admitted this to any man alive other than you. It is because I see the evil will and false intention of King Lucar, who is sending you to India to get rid of you, that I will give you comfort and consolation as I can, and will protect you from peril, and will make it possible for you to deliver your message and return here like a bold and worthy knight.

"And even though I realize that you have no need of my love, since you are already promised and given to another lady more exalted, more beautiful, and more excellent than I, nevertheless I have no desire to forget the love that pierced my heart when I saw you in Antioch, when you were victorious and had conquered and vanquished the cruel and abominable serpent. For all these reasons mentioned, I will tell you what you must do to do this thing with honor. When you have arrived before the king of India, after having bowed and given him the greeting that King Lucar sent you to him to deliver, you will salute him without delay in my name, addressing him as my faithful and secret beloved, and you will tell him that even though my father has given me to King Lucar, I have nevertheless not forgotten his love, rather I am firmly resolved that, as soon as I may, I will steal away to come to him and then he will have me at his will and good pleasure. Explain to him that I will find a way to go with King Lucar when he takes his army to India. At that time, if he is brave, he will have the opportunity to take possession of me and bear me away. And so that the king of India not suspect that you say these things out of fear or feint, you will bring him this ring."

"Lady," said Valentin, "I thank you most humbly for your generous desire to come to my aid, and have no fear for the rest, for, by the grace of God, I will deliver your message so well and so thoroughly to the king of India that you shall soon have good and pleasing tidings."

With these words, Valentin took leave of the fair lady Rozemonde, and attended upon King Lucar who assigned ten sailors to conduct him. They brought him over a great stretch of sea that lies between Esclardy and India, setting sail with such a brisk wind that, after departing from Esclardy at noon, they arrived the next day in a port a league from the city of India Major. There Valentin disembarked, leading his horse off the ship and mounting it. He said to the sailors,

"Seigneurs, or attendez moy icy tant que mon voyage soit fait et mon messaige acompli. Si plaist a Dieu pas ne feray long sejour que brief je ne retourne."

"Par Mahon," dist ung des mariniers aux aultres tout bas, "jamais ne retournerez se le dyable ne vous ramaine, car de cinquante messaigiers que le roy d'Esclardie y a envoyé, jamais ung seul n'en vint par deça."

Bien l'ouÿt Valentin, que nul semblant n'en fist, mais a part luy dit bassement, "Tel parle des affaires qui ne sçait comment il en va." Ainsi print le chemin et ne demoura pas longuement qu'il arriva en Inde, car pres du port estoit. Et quant il eut ung pont passé il cuida bien estre dedens la ville, mais premier qu'il y entrast luy convint passer cincq portes, dont il fut moult esmerveillé. Et a par soy se print a considerer la fortification d'icelle place, estimant et jugant en son [96verso]entendement icelle ville estre la plus forte place que jamais il eust veue. Et quant il fut en la place du marché il veit une tour moult haulte et belle; sur laquelle tour il y avoit une croix. Si s'esmerveilla Valentin pour cause que bien sçavoit que de la loy paienne n'y avoit point de telles enseignes sans grant cause assise ne souffertte. En celle place trouva Valentin ung Sarrasin auquel il demanda la cause et rayson pourquoy sur celle haulte tour estoit une croix assise.

"Amy," dit le payen, "sachez que celle tour que vous voyez la est nommee la tour Sainct Thomas et est la tour en laquelle il fut lapidé et mis a mort. Or est vray que les crestiens a l'onneur de celuy qu'i dient estre sainct en ce lieu fut fondee une esglise du congé et licence du roy. En laquelle esglise y a ung patriarche et cent crestiens lesquelz en mode et maniere de leur loy tous les jours chantent leurs heures et font messe celebrer. En ce point sont souffers et entretenus a telle chose faire, car ilz paient au roy d'Inde grant tribu par chascun an."

Quant Valentin entendit que a celle tour y avoit monastere et habitacion de crestiens pour l'onneur de Dieu et de monseigneur Sainct Thomais il fust meu en devocion d'aler le lieu viseter. Si se descendit de son cheval et entra dedens[1] l'esglise, puis demanda le maistre d'iceluy lieu. Et on luy fist tantost venir le maistre patriarche qui la place gardoit et les aultres crestiens gouvernoit.

Valentin le salua moult honnourablement, et le patriarche qui saige estoit et homme honneste son salut luy rendit. Puis luy demanda, "Mon amy, de quelle nacion estes vous et quelle creance tenez vous?"

"Jesucrist."

"Helas, sire," dist le bon patriarche, "comment avez vous prins la hardiesse de venir en ceste part? Car se le roy d'Inde a de vous nouvelles jamais n'en partirez que mourir ne vous face."

"Amy," dist Valentin, "de cela n'ayez doubte, car je porte nouvelles et enseignes a luy par lesquelles il n'aura ja couraige ne voulenté de mal contre moy penser. Mais d'une chose vous prie — c'est que me declairez comment ne en quelle maniere vous demourez en ce lieu et comment estes fondéz."

---

[1] Text has *dendens*.

"My lords, wait for me here until my journey is done and my message delivered. May it please God that my stay be brief and that I soon return."

"By Mohammed," said one of the sailors in a low voice to the others, "you'll never return if the devil himself doesn't lead you back, for of fifty messengers that the king of Esclardy has sent there, not a single one has ever returned."

Valentin heard him clearly, but gave no sign of it, saying only to himself, "He speaks of things of which he knows not." Then he set off, and it wasn't long before he arrived in India, for it was near the port. After passing over a bridge, he seemed to be in the city, but before he could actually enter it, he had to pass five gates, which made him marvel. He noticed how well fortified the place was, estimating and judging that this city was the best stronghold he had ever seen. Once in the marketplace, he saw a tall, lovely tower; on this tower there was a cross. Valentin was amazed, since he knew that the pagan religion had no such symbol nor suffered it without good cause. In that place, Valentin found a Saracen to whom he posed the question concerning the reason for which this high tower displayed a cross.

"Friend," said the pagan, "know that this tower you see is called the tower of Saint Thomas, and it is the tower where he was stoned to death. Now it is true that the Christians founded a church here with the permission of the king in order to honor this man whom they call a saint. There is a patriarch and a hundred Christians in the church who chant their hours and celebrate their mass every day according to the mode and manner of their religion. This they are allowed to do, for they pay an enormous tribute every year to the king of India."[1]

When Valentin heard that in this tower there was a monastery, a place for Christians to live and devote themselves to God and to the blessed Saint Thomas, his soul was touched with the desire to see the place. So he got off his horse and entered the church, asking to see the person in charge. Right away they brought him the master patriarch, who kept the place and governed the other Christians.

Valentin greeted him most respectfully, and the patriarch, who was a wise and worthy man, returned his greeting. Then he asked him, "My friend, where are you from and what is your faith?"

"Jesus Christ."

"Alas, sire," said the good patriarch, "how have you had the audacity to come here? For if the king of India has tidings of your presence, you will never depart without being killed by him."

"Friend," said Valentin, "have no such fear, for I bring him tidings and tokens for which he will have no desire or wish to do me harm. But I do beg one thing of you — explain to me how it is that you are in this place and how it all began."

---

[1] This section shows awareness of the St. Thomas Christians of India. See Dickson, *Study*, 230–31.

"Certes," dist le patriarche. "Nous sommes fondéz en l'onneur de Dieu et de monseigneur Sainct Thomas, le martir duquel nous avons le corps en ceste esglise, et ne peult nulz crestiens venir ceans s'i ne sont comme pelerins. Mais telles gens y peuent seurement venir pour cause que les offrandes et oblacions qu'i donnent sont au roy. Et oultre plus nous convient chascun an payer grant tribu."

Et alors Valentin demanda et requist veoir le sainct corps glorieulx et il luy fust monstré en grant reverence et sollennité. Valentin mist les genoulx a terre et moult devotement fist sa priere a Dieu et a monseigneur Sainct Thomas. Apres lesquelles choses ainsy faictes et acomplies il monta a cheval et ala devers le palays auquel le [97recto]roy[1] d'Inde faisoit sa residence acomplir son messaige. En prenant congé du bon patriarche, il luy demanda se nulles nouvelles avoit oÿ dire depuis peu de temps se nulle crestienne fust venue[2] celle part.

"Par ma foy," dist le patriarche, "nous n'en sçavons nulles nouvelles."

Valentin se part et plus n'en enquist, car sans faire bruit secretement vouloit trouver façon d'avoir nouvelles de la belle Esclarmonde. Or ne demoura pas longuement qu'il arriva devant la porte du palays et fist son messaige en la maniere que vous orés.

[CHAPITRE 41]

Comment Valentin fist son messaige au roy d'Inde de par le roy Lucar et de la responce qui donnee luy fust. xli. chap[itre]

Apres que le chevalier Valentin fust arrivé devant le palays du roy d'Inde et que il fut bas du cheval descendu, de cueur hardy et preux, sans doubte ne crainte s'en ala tantost vers le roy lequel estoit en une sale moult richement tendue et paree, acompaignie de troys roys fors et puissans et aussy de plusieurs barons et chevaliers. Et ainsi que Valentin entra en la sale le roy le regarda moult fierement, et moult bien se doubta qu'il estoit au roy Lucar, et luy a dist tout en hault, "Par Mahon, le dyable vous a bien si tost fait venir par deça. N'estes vous pas au roy Lucar servant? Ne le me cele point."

"Sire," dist le noble chevalier Valentin, "ja par moy n'en sera la verité celee. Et sachez que de par luy je vous aporte nouvelles dont vous serez au cueur desplaisant, et d'aultre part je vous aporte certaines enseignes de la belle Rozemonde dont vous serez joyeulx et tout content de moy."

"Messaiger," dist le roy, "je te fay bien assavoir que en despit du roy Lucar qui tant est fier et orgueilleux je estoye deliberé de vous faire mourir, mais pour l'amour

---

[1] *n i* at bottom right corner of 97r.
[2] Text has *vevenue*, probably owing to line break after first *ve*.

"Certainly," said the patriarch. "We were founded in honor of God and the blessed Saint Thomas, the martyr whose body is found in this church, but no Christians may come here unless they are pilgrims. But such people can come safely only because the offerings and oblations they make belong to the king. Moreover, we must pay a large tribute every year."

Then Valentin requested to see the glorious saintly body, and it was shown to him with great reverence and solemnity. Valentin fell to his knees, and said his prayers with great devotion to God and to the blessed Saint Thomas. After having done these things, he remounted his horse and rode to the palace where the king of India resided, in order to deliver his message.

While taking his leave from the good patriarch, he asked him if he had heard any tidings in the recent past of a Christian woman coming to the area.

"By my faith," said the patriarch, "we have had no tidings of such a person."

Valentin left, asking no more questions, for he wished to seek tidings of Esclarmonde without exciting too much attention. It didn't take him long to arrive before the palace gate, and he delivered his message in the manner that you will soon hear.

CHAPTER 41

How Valentin delivered the message from King Lucar to the king of India, and concerning the answer given him.

After arriving at the palace of the king of India, the knight Valentin, with a bold and stalwart heart and absolutely fearless, descended from his horse and strode off to see the king, who, accompanied by three puissant kings as well as many barons and knights, was holding court in a richly decorated hall. As Valentin entered the hall, the king eyed him fiercely, for he suspected he had come from King Lucar, and addressed him aloud, "By Mohammed, the devil has led you here so quickly. Do you not serve King Lucar? Hide nothing from me."

"Sire," said the noble knight Valentin, "never by me will the truth be hidden. Know that I bring you news from him that you will not like, but I also bring you tokens from the fair Rozemonde that will gladden you and make you quite pleased with me."

"Messenger," said the king, "I will have you know that, out of spite to King Lucar, who is so proud and arrogant, I had decided to kill you. But for love of the

de la dame de quoy m'avez parlé n'aurez mal ne villenye non plus que mon corps s'il est ainsi que vrayes enseignes d'elle vous me sachez dire ou monstrer."

"Sire," dist Valentin, "cela feray je bien. Et vous diray mon messaige en telle maniere que d'ung seul mot ne vous en mentiray pour vivre ne mourir. Il est vray et chose certaine ainsi que je vous dy que je suis au roy Lucar lequel devers vous m'envoye, et par moy vous mande que pour vengance et retribucion de la mort de son pere le roy Trompart rendre et satisfaire vous aillez en Esclardie vous rendre en son palays tout nu et la corde au col ainsi comme larron desloyal, trahystre et murtrier publicque. Et en celuy estat veult et vous mande que devant sa royalle majesté en la presence de tous ses barons et chevaliers de sa court comme homme coulpable vous rendez prest et appareillé de telle mort souffrir et recepvoir comme par son conseil sera jugé et deliberé. Et se de telle chose faire et acomplir vous n'estes [97verso]content et me voulez refuser, comme messaiger a ce commis et par luy deputé et envoyé vous deffie et fay assavoir que dedens briefve espace de temps viendra vostre pays courir et ceste cité assieger. Telle est son intention et a voué et juré a son dieu Jupin et Mahon que en toute vostre terre ne demourra cité, ville, ne chasteau ne bourg ne villaige qui ne soient tous mis en feu et par terre ruéz, hommes, femmes et enfans bouttéz et mis a l'espee, si que vous pourrez bien cognoistre que de male heure vous feistes le roy Trompart mourir lequel estoit son propre pere naturel."

"Messaiger," dist le roy d'Inde, "moult bien je t'ay oÿ et entendu, et sachés que peu je tiens de conte des menasses au roy Lucar et de son orgueilleuse deffiance, car on dist communement que tel menasse qui a le plus grant paour. Et pour responce faire sur ceste matiere je feray une lettre faire que vous porterez devers luy et en la lettre sera contenu comment j'ay esté deffié de par luy. Au regard de vous, messagier, acomply et parfait avez vostre messaige. Et si luy manderay la bonne voulenté que j'ay de luy et toute sa puissance recepvoir toutes les fois que il vouldra venir courir sur ma terre. Mais du sourplus de ton entreprinse, c'est assavoir de la belle Rozemonde, declaire moy tout ce que elle me mande, car entre les aultres choses j'ay voulenté et desir tres ardant de en avoir nouvelles."

"Sire," dit le chevalier Valentin, "sur le fait de la dame de par elle je vous salue comme son parfait, secret et loyal amy. Et vous mande que elle est de nouveau mariee et donnee au roy Lucar. Mais tant y a que c'est contre son couraige et oultre sa voulenté, car oncques n'ayma ne ja n'aymera le roy Lucar. Or est la franche dame qui tant a de beaulté au corps est[1] au cueur si frappee et touchee de vostre amour que jamais elle n'aura ne avoir ne veult aultre que vous, s'il est ainsi que vous la veullez recepvoir pour dame. Et pour venir a fin[2] de nostre entreprinse elle m'a dit que elle viendra par deça en la compaignie du roy Lucar son mary quant de Esclardie partira pour s'en venir par deça. Et par ainsi vous pour-

---

[1] Text has *et*.
[2] Text has *fn*.

lady of whom you have spoken, you will suffer no more harm or villainy than if you were I, if indeed you bring me true tokens from her."

"Sire," said Valentin, "that I do indeed. But I will deliver my message word for word as it was given to me, though I die for it. It is true and certain that I serve King Lucar, the one who sends me to you to tell you that, in order to avenge himself and for you to make retribution for the death of his father King Trompart, you are to go to Esclardy, to his palace, in the nude, and with a rope around your neck like any despicable criminal, traitor, or known murderer. He orders you to come in that state before his royal majesty, in the presence of all the barons and knights of his court, and to give yourself up as one guilty and ready to suffer whatever death is judged and decided by his council. And if you are not willing to do this thing, and choose to refuse me, as the messenger commissioned and sent and deputed by him, I challenge you and make known to you that, within a brief space of time, he will come to swarm over your land and lay siege to this city. Such is his intention, and such has he vowed and sworn to his god Jupiter and Mohammed to do, so that in all your land there will not remain a city, town, nor castle, burg, or village that will not be put to the torch and brought down, with men, women, and children all put to the sword, so that you will know for certain that it is woe unto you for having killed King Trompart, who was his own natural father."

"Messenger," said the king of India, "I have indeed heard and understood you, but know that I set little store by the threats of King Lucar and his arrogant challenge, for they say that he who threatens is he who is most afraid.[1] As for a reply, I will have a letter written that you shall carry to him, and in this letter it will be recounted how I was challenged by you on his part. As for you, messenger, you have delivered your message. And to him I express my willingness to receive him and all his forces whenever he deigns to come swarming over my land. But now to the other part of your mission, that is to say, concerning the fair Rozemonde. Tell me everything she told you to tell me, for of all women I desire most to have tidings of her."

"Sire," said the knight Valentin, "as for the lady, in her name, I greet you as her perfect, secret, and faithful friend. She sends you word that she was recently married and given to King Lucar. But this was done against her wishes and her will, for she has never loved nor will ever love King Lucar. Now this noble lady, so beautiful of body, is so smitten to the heart with love of you that she will never have or want anyone other than you, if you are willing to receive her as your lady. And to bring this plan to fruition, she told me she would come here in the company of King Lucar her husband when he leaves Esclardy to come this way. Thus

---

[1] Cf. Hassell, *Proverbs*, 162 (no. M112); Morawski, *Proverbes*, 86 (no. 2363).

rez de legier trouver maniere et façon de la belle dame prendre, lever et emmener a vostre voulenté et bon plaisir."

"Par Mahon," dist le roy d'Inde, "bien me plaisent les nouvelles et moult fort en suis joyeulx. Mais que la chose soit telle comme vous l'avez divisee."

"Sire," dist le chevalier Valentin, "se la chose est vraye ou faulce je n'en sçauroye a parler, mais pour certain signe et enseignes veritables voyez l'aneau qui par vous donné luy fust lequel elle vous envoye. Et nonobstant que femmes soyent de legier couraige et peu arrestees en leur propos, sy me semble bien que celle sur toutes aultres desire vostre amour, et que son entreprinse n'est pas chose faincte."

[98recto]"Amy,"[1] ce dist le roy qui l'aneau bien cogneut, "de ta venue je suis moult fort joyeulx. Or va boire et menger et prendre ton repas et ce pendant je te feray escripre lettres que tu porteras au roy Lucar pour responce de ta deffiance."

Valentin par le commandement du roy fut a celle heure de plusieurs chevaliers haultement festoié et noblement acompaigné. A plusieurs demanda couvertement nouvelles de la belle Esclarmonde en enquerant s'il estoit nouvelles que nulle femme crestienne fust en celle contree, et on luy respondit que non. Si se tint a tant sans plus en parler pour l'eure presente.

Or vint tantost le roy qui les lettres luy bailla, et Valentin les receut qui prent congé de luy qui moult fut joyeulx de partir de ce lieu. Helas! Il ne sçavoit pas que s'amie la belle Esclarmonde fust en celluy palais si pres de luy. Laquelle dame par la cité piteusement pour luy vivoit en priant Dieu devotement que de ce lieu la voulsist delivrer et luy donner de son amy certaines nouvelles et cognoissance prochaine. Or aproche le temps qu'elle le trouva, mais premier soufferra le bon vaillant chevalier Valentin de diverses et piteuses aventures, lesquelles cy apres vous seront declairees et racomptees plus au long.

[CHAPITRE 42]

Comment le bon chevalier Valentin retourna en la cité d'Esclardie; et de la responce que il eut du roy d'Inde la Major. xlii. chapitre

Grant joye et grant liesse eust le franc chevalier Valentin de partir d'Inde la Major et d'estre hors des mains du felon roy qui tant de messaigiers avoit fait mourir. Il monta a cheval et tantost arriva au port ou les mariniers estoient qui moult furent esbahys de sa venue et pensoient a par eulx que son messaige n'avoit pas fait.

"Seigneurs," dist Valentin, "or retournons en Esclardie, car j'ay acomply mon entreprinse dont je doy bien Dieu louer."

---

[1] *n ii* at bottom right corner of 98r.

you will easily find a means to take possession of the fair lady and lead her away according to your desire and good pleasure."

"By Mohammed," said the king of India, "these tidings do indeed please me; I am absolutely delighted. But the situation had better be as you say."

"Sire," said the knight Valentin, "whether the thing be true or false I cannot say, but as a token of its truthfulness, here is the ring you once gave her that she now sends back to you. And notwithstanding the fact that women are fickle-hearted and rarely constant, it seems to me that this lady truly desires your love, and that her intentions are not feigned."

"Friend," said the king, who indeed recognized the ring, "I am truly delighted at your coming. Now go eat and drink and have your meal, while I have letters prepared that you shall take back to King Lucar in response to your challenge."

Valentin was then nobly feted by order of the king, and was kept company in a fine manner by a group of knights. He quietly asked several for tidings of the fair Esclarmonde, inquiring if there was news of any Christian lady in that country, but they answered him in the negative. Then he thought it best to stop talking about the matter for the present.

Now the king came to give him the letters, and Valentin received them and took his leave of him, overjoyed to be gone from that place. Alas! He didn't know that his beloved, the fair Esclarmonde, was so near him in that very palace. For the lady lived in that city in a sorry state, praying God devoutly to deliver her from that place and to give her sure tidings of her beloved sometime soon. Now the time is getting near that she will find him, but first the good valiant knight Valentin will suffer diverse and piteous adventures that you will hear recounted more at length later on.

CHAPTER 42

How the good knight Valentin returned to the city of Esclardy; and concerning the reply of the king of India Major.

The noble knight Valentin was light of heart and full of joy to leave India Major and to be out of the hands of the felonious king who had killed so many messengers. He mounted his horse and soon arrived at the port where the mariners were completely flabbergasted at his arrival, thinking to themselves that he had not actually delivered his message.

"My lords," said Valentin, "now let us return to Esclardy, for I have carried out my mission for which I have good reason to praise God."

"Par ma foy," dist l'ung de ses hommes, "nous sommes esmerveilléz, car oncques jour de nostre vie n'en veismes nul retourner."

"Amy," dist Valentin, "a qui Dieu veult aider nul ne peult nuyre."

A ces motz monta en mer et tant nagerent que en brief temps ilz arriverent en Esclardie. Valentin ne fist nul sejour, mais tantost que bas du cheval fust descendu, il monta au palays. Si trouva le roy Lucar acompaigné du roy Brandiffer et de quatorze puissans et fors admiraulx qui tous estoient venus en Esclardie pour Lucar secourir contre le roy d'Inde. Du retour de Valentin ilz furent tous esmerveillez. Et entre les aultres le trahystre roy Lucar, car jamais ne pensoit que il retournast en vie. Il fist venir Valentin devant tous les barons et luy a dist, "Amy, comptez moy des nouvelles et me dictes se le roy d'Inde viendra par devers moy [98verso]ou point et en l'estat que je luy ay mandé."

"Sire," ce dist Valentin, "a ce n'ayez attente ne fiancé, car il ne prise ne doubte vous ne les vostres vaillant ung petit festu. Il est fier et orgueilleux de couraige et de fait. Pensez que se vous avez grant voulenté de aler par dela, ancores la il plus grant de vous recepvoir. Et affin que vous ne fachez doubte que en mon messaige ait faulte ne deception, je vous presente ceste lettre laquelle il vous envoye; si pourrez clerement cognoistre son couraige et sa voulenté."

Le roy Lucar receut la lettre et devant toute l'assistence haultement la fist lyre; si trouverent que la chose estoit telle que Valentin disoit. Et quant Brandiffer entendit la responce du roy d'Inde et que il cogneut son fier couraige il a juré Mahon et Appolin que jamais en son pays il ne retourneroit tant que mort ou vif le roy d'Inde aient conquis. Lors fit sans nul sejour ne dilation ses gens armer et mettre en point. Sans plus longue attente le lendemain au matin a deux cens mille Sarrasins monta dessus la mer. Et quant la belle Rozemonde entendit que ilz aloyent en Inde la Major tant requist et pria a Lucar qui son mary estoit que avec luy sur la mer la monta. Et devant Inde la mena dont puis apres il se repentit.

Or furent sur la mer maintes barges et galees et de tous vivres garnies assez suffisamment. Le vent fust bon pour eulx si que en peu d'espace arriverent au port. Ilz se sont mis et descendus a terre pour leur ost assoir et fermer lequel ilz ont mis et assis sur une moult belle et plaisante riviere asses pres de la cité d'Inde. Parmy la ville sortit le bruit et sceurent les nouvelles que leurs ennemis estoient arrivéz. Les pons furent a coup levez et les barrieres et portes fermees, et chascun s'en court aux creneaulx pour veoir l'armee. Et le roy monta en une haulte tour pour veoir ses ennemis et du grant peuple que il veit fut moult fort esmerveillé.

"Par Jupin," dist il, "icy aura affaire, mais tant me resconforte que pour deux ans entiers je suis furny de vivres." Il avisa sur la riviere plusieurs tentes et pavillons lesquelz entre les aultres troys en y avoit excellens, richement adornéz et a panonceaulx volans de drap d'or, d'argent et de soye, environnéz d'escussons. Bannieres et estandars arrivoyent de diverses et plusieurs manieres. Le roy d'Inde pour avoir certaine cognoissance a qui telles armes estoient, il appella ung herault

"By my faith," said one of the men, "we are amazed, for never in our life have we seen a messenger return from there."

"Friend," said Valentin, "no one can harm him whom God is willing to help."

With these words he set sail and traveled so quickly that they soon arrived in Esclardy. Valentin did not delay—as soon as he got off his horse, he climbed up to the palace. There he found King Lucar accompanied by King Brandiffer and fourteen mighty emirs who had all come to Esclardy to help Lucar against the king of India. Everyone was amazed at Valentin's return, but the traitor King Lucar more than any of the others, for he never thought that he would return alive. He called for Valentin to appear before his barons and said to him, "Friend, recount to me the news and tell me if the king of India will come to me or not in the manner in which I commanded him to come."

"Sire," said Valentin, "have no expectation of that, for he neither esteems nor fears you and yours a straw's worth. He is fierce and arrogant in heart and deed. Understand that if you are determined to go there, he is even more determined to receive you. And so that you will have no doubt about the truth of my message, I present you with this letter that he sends you; there you will be able to know clearly his intentions and his will."

King Lucar received the letter and had it read aloud in front of his audience; they indeed found that the situation was just as Valentin had described it. When Brandiffer heard the king of India's reply and recognized his arrogance, he swore to Mohammed and Apollo that he would never return to his own land until he had conquered the king of India alive or dead. Thereupon, without delay, he had his men arm and prepare themselves. Waiting only until the next day, he set sail in the morning with two hundred thousand Saracens. And when the fair Rozemonde heard that they were going to India Major, she so begged and implored her husband Lucar that she boarded the ship with him. So he brought her to India, which he regretted much later on.

Now there were many barges and galleys that went with them well stocked with provisions. They had good wind, such that they soon arrived in the port, where they disembarked, setting up the army on a beautiful and pleasant riverbank close to the city of India. News of the arrival of their enemies moved quickly throughout the city. The drawbridges were at once raised, and the barriers and gates closed, and everyone ran to the ramparts to look at the army. The king himself mounted a high tower to gaze upon his enemies, where he was astounded to see such a great multitude.

"By Jupiter," he said, "there will be serious goings-on here, but I comfort myself with the thought that I have provisions for two years." He noticed several tents and pavilions on the riverbank, among which there were three particularly fine, richly adorned with long banners made of gold cloth, silver, and silk, and surrounded by escutcheons. There were banners and standards of various sorts. The king of India called for a herald well versed in armorial bearings in order to

lequel en armes moult bien se cognoissoit, puis luy monstra les tentes et luy demanda a qui ilz estoient.

"Sire," dist le herault, "le premier pavillon que vous voyez la si clerement, luysant et richement fait, c'est celuy de Brandiffer qui moult est roy puissant. Le second que vous voyez apres est a Lucar, vostre ennemy mortel, le filz du roy Trompart que vous feistes mourir. Et le [99recto]tiers[1] pavillon que vous voyez tout au plus bas c'est le tref des dames aux seigneurs que je vous ay monstré et nommé."

Quant le roy d'Inde entendit que en icelluy ost y avoit dames bien se pensa que la belle Rozemonde y estoit. Le cueur luy print a sousrire de la joye et grant liesse; il doubla force et hardiesse en disant a par luy, "Pas n'est temps de dormir qui veult belle amye avoir. Il se doit mettre a l'aventure et corps et biens. Et n'est pas celuy digne de belle dame avoir qui ne veult mettre peine de la conquerir." Pour ceste chose il fist armer tous ses gens et en moult grande puissance saillit hors de la cité desus ses ennemis. Lesquelz a peine eurent espace de eulx mettre en ordonnance et eulx armer, car ilz ne pensoyent pas que le roy d'Inde saillit si tost sur eulx. Mais amours le menoient qui sans grande deliberacion maintes choses font entreprendre et faire.

La fut l'assault moult grant et la bataille moult dure. Et quant le roy d'Inde vit que Brandiffer estoit meslé parmy la bataille pour ses gens conduire et ralier, il laissa la compaignie et en moult grant diligence chevaulcha vers le pavillon des dames, et bien le veit venir Rozemonde et a ses armeures elle le cogneut. Sy saillit hors de la tente seulle sans nulle compaignie et s'en ala courant devers luy. Lors le roy d'Inde qui son ardant desir aperceut frappa des esperons, et de celle part il arriva a la dame et sans faire sejour incontinent sur son cheval la monta. Et fut la dame tantost montee comme celle qui legiere estoit et bonne voulenté avoit de la chose acomplir.

Et apres ce que elle fut montee elle dist au roy d'Inde, "Mon amy parfait et secret, bien puissez vous estre venu, car vous estes celuy que tant je desiroye et que de longtemps j'ay attendu. Et combien que depuis le temps que demander vous me feistes mon pere m'a mariee, et touteffois ce a esté contre ma voulenté et contre mon couraige, car jamais je ne haÿs tant homme que je fay le roy Lucar a qui je suis donnee. Mais or peult il seurement dire que de moy i a eu tout le plaisir que jamais il en aura, car puis que Dieu m'a donné tant de grace que je vous ay trouvé jamais aultre ne quiers avoir et du tout est ma voulenté amoureuse acomplie et parfaicte."

"Dame," ce dit le roy, "de ce ne vous doubtez, car jamais je ne vous feray faulte. Et si vous jure que devant trois jours je vous feray royne de Inde la Major et dame et maitresse de tout mon tenement."

En disant ces parolles le roy d'Inde chevaulcha qui la plaisante dame emporte sur le courant destrier. Et les gardes et les chamberieres du pavillon en grant effroy menant alerent vers le roy Lucar et luy dirent, "Sire, tresmalles nouvelles y a, car au jour d'uy avez fait perte trop grande et villaine, car vostre ennemy le

---

[1] *n iii* at bottom right corner of 99r.

know for certain whose arms these were; then he indicated to him the tents and asked him to whom they belonged.

"Sire," said the herald, "the first pavilion that you see over there so clearly, splendid and richly made, belongs to Brandiffer, a most powerful king. The second one you see next to it belongs to Lucar, your mortal enemy, the son of King Trompart whom you killed. And the third pavilion that you see further down is the tent of the ladies of the lords whom I just showed you and named."

When the king of India heard that ladies had accompanied the army, his mind jumped to the thought that Rozemonde was there. His heart filled with joy and jubilation; he felt himself expand with strength and boldness as he said to himself, "It is no time to sleep for the one who hopes to have a fair friend. He must risk both himself and his possessions. And he who is not willing to take pains to conquer her is not worthy of possessing a beautiful lady." For this reason he had his men arm, and with a great force he sallied forth from the city to descend on his enemies. These latter barely had time to ready themselves and arm, for they hadn't thought the king of India would descend on them so quickly. But love, which makes one undertake many things without much forethought,[1] was driving him.

The assault was violent and the battle hard. But when the king of India saw that Brandiffer was caught up in the midst of the battle to lead and rally his men, he left his own company and rode with all speed over to the ladies' pavilion where he saw Rozemonde, and she recognized him by means of his armorial bearings. So she rushed out of her tent alone and without company to run to him. Then the king of India, who perceived her burning desire, spurred his horse and galloped up to the lady, quickly seizing her and swinging her up on his horse. And the lady was soon mounted, as she was light and willing to accomplish the deed.

After she had mounted, she said to the king of India, "My perfect and secret love, you are heartily welcome, for you are the one whom I most desired and for whom I have waited a long time. Even though my father has married me to another in the time since you asked for my hand, it was done against my will and my heart, for I never hated a man as much as I hate King Lucar to whom I was given. Well, now he can surely say that he has had all the pleasure of me that he will ever have, for since God has had the grace to let me find you, I will never want anyone else, and thus is my amorous desire fulfilled."

"Lady," said the king, "have no fear, for I will never fail you. And so I swear to you that before three days have passed, I will make you the queen of India Major, and lady and mistress of all that I rule."

While saying these words the king of India rode, carrying away the lovely lady on his running steed. But the guards and chambermaids of the pavilion in great dismay rushed to King Lucar and told him, "Sire, we have terrible news, for

---

[1] Cf. Hassell, *Proverbs*, 37 (no. A106).

roy d'Inde a emporté sur [99verso]son cheval la plaisante Rozemonde et tout presentement la desrobee et tolue. Pour ce faictes voz gens apres luy aler pour la dame son honneur garder."

"Or vous taisez," ce dist le roy Lucar, "et plus avant n'en menez parolles. Car qui mauvaise femme tient et il la pert petit en doit estre dolent." Ainsi respond Lucar qui le cueur avoit triste et dolent et non pas sans cause. Et puis vint vers Brandiffer et luy a dit en ceste maniere, "Sire, bien doit avoir vostre fille petit de joye quant elle s'est accordee a suyvyr mon ennemy pour moy laisser et donner ung grant vituperable blasme."[1]

"Beau filz," dit Brandiffer, "ne soyez contre moy malcontent, car au jour d'uy je vous vengeray du trahystre qui ma fille emmaine." Adonc le roy Brandiffer frappa des esperons pour courir apres le roy d'Inde; avec luy grant compaignie de gens pour venger la royne Rozemonde pour l'amour de Lucar.

Mais entre les aultres fut Valentin lequel voulut monstrer au besoing que tous chevaliers doivent leur proesse monstrer. Si frappa des esperons et dist a Pacolet, "Temps est de jouer de ton art et de ta science monstrer." Adonc Pacolet fist ung tel sort qui fut avis au roy d'Inde que devant son cheval estoit tout le champ plain de boys fors et espès et de grosses rivieres. Si eust si tresgrant paour d'estre prins et ataint que il fist la dame bas descendre pour plus legierement fuyr. Et quant la dame fut a terre elle cuida treuver façon de soy apres le roy sauver, mais Valentin fust pres qui luy escria, "Dame, demourez. Il vous convient avec moy venir, car de longtemps m'avez promis que vostre amour je auroye."

"Ha, Valentin, bien peu vous doy aymer et tenir chier; quant d'amours je vous requis par vous je fus escondite, si a esté bien force d'aultre que vous trouver et pourchasser. Mais puis que tant est fortune contraire que j'ay failly a mon entreprinse je me rens a vostre mercy comme vostre propre subjecte et a jamais servante, s'il est ainsi que par vostre moyen je puisse ma paix faire devers le roy Lucar."

"Dame," dist Valentin, "je en feray mon devoir si bien que vous cognoisterrez que bien vous ay servy."

Lors il la mena devers Lucar et luy dist, "Sire, icy voyez la belle et noble dame Rozemonde, vostre femme, laquelle est moult dolentement et piteusement de douleurs atournee pour la force et violence que luy a fait et plus a cuidé faire le desloyal et faulx roy d'Inde."

"Ha, syre," dist la dame, "il vous dist verité, car ainsi comme la bataille commença je le veis devers moy venir. Sy pensay que c'estoit aulcun de voz barons qui pour moi secourir acouroit celle part. Si alay contre luy esperant moy sauver et sans moy de riens enquerir sur son cheval je montay. Mais las! sire, je cogneus tantost sa male voulenté et aperceu bien qu'estoie trahye. Lors la prins par les crins et la face luy a [100recto]esgraffigné[2] tellement de sang fut couvert et que

---

[1] Text has *blsame*.
[2] *n iiii* at bottom right corner of 100r.

today you have suffered too great and painful a loss, for your enemy, the king of India, has carried away on his horse the lovely Rozemonde—just this moment he has kidnapped her and borne her off. Send your men after her so that they may save the lady's honor."

"Be silent," said King Lucar, "speak no more of this. For he who has an evil wife and loses her should mourn little." Thus answered Lucar, who was bitter and aggrieved in his heart, and not without cause. Then he came to Brandiffer and told him thus, "Sire, your daughter must have precious little joy when she has agreed to follow my enemy, leaving me and causing me shameful blame."

"Fair son," said Brandiffer, "do not be angry with me, for today I will avenge you against the traitor who has carried away my daughter." Thereupon King Brandiffer spurred his horse to chase after the king of India; with him rode a great company of men to avenge Queen Rozemonde out of love for Lucar.

But among them was Valentin, who wished to demonstrate his prowess as needed, just as all knights must do. So he spurred his horse and said to Pacolet, "It is time to ply your craft and use your knowledge." Thereupon Pacolet cast such a spell that it seemed to the king of India that there before his horse was a field full of thick and bushy woods and swollen rivers. He was so frightened of capture that he set the lady down, the more easily to flee. Once the lady was on the ground, she began to think how she might find a way to follow the king, but Valentin came up and cried out to her, "Lady, stay. You had best come with me, for you have long promised me your love."

"Ah, Valentin, I have little reason to love you or hold you dear; when I asked for your love, you rejected me, so I had little choice but to seek another. But since fortune is so contrary that I have failed in my attempt, I will yield myself up to your mercy as your own subject and servant forever, if you will thus help me make my peace with King Lucar."

"Lady," said Valentin, "I shall do my duty so well that you will recognize how well I have served you."

Then he led her back to Lucar, saying, "Sire, here is the fair and noble lady Rozemonde, your wife, who is overcome with grief and pain because of the force exercised against her and what might have been attempted by that faithless and false king of India."

"Ah, sire," said the lady, "he tells you the truth, for just as the battle commenced, I saw him come towards me. I thought it was one of your barons come to my aid. Thus I went towards him, hoping to save myself, and, without his saying a word to me, I mounted on his horse. But alas! sire, I realized right away his evil intention and perceived that I had been betrayed. Then I grabbed him by the hair and scratched his face so much that he was covered with blood, and he had

force luy fut de moy laisser a terre descendre. Et ainsi a l'ayde de cestuy chevalier de luy me suis sauvee et eschappee."

"Dame," ce dist Lucar, "vous y avez bien ouvré et n'en convient plus parler pour le present, car nous avons l'assault de par noz ennemys qui trop fort nous donnent a faire." Ainsi laissa la dame sans nulle aultre responce et retourna en la bataille. Et a celle heure retournerent ceulx d'Inde dedens la cité desquelz plusieurs vaillans et bons champions avoient perdus. Mais sur toutes les pertes le roy d'Inde plaingnoit la perte de la dame Rozemonde.

"Helas, dame," dist il, "j'ay bien povrement a mon entreprinse failly. Mais ainsi me ayde mon dieu Mahon, je cognoy clerement que j'ay esté enchanté, car il m'estoit vray semblant que devant moy je trouvoye bois et rivieres fort courans, mais tout aussitost que je vous eux mise bas je ne veis si non beau chemin plain."

Grant honneur eust Valentin et de chascun il fust moult prisé et loué de quoy il avoit la dame Rozemonde delivree et recouvree au roy d'Inde. Et elle aussy luy monstroit beau signe; pour ceste chose fort l'aymoit et de bon cueur. Mais quelque signe d'amour que elle luy monstrast dessus tous le haÿoit et vouloit mal, car bien eust voulu que la chose fust aultrement faicte et acomplye. Mais non pourtant de ceste chose et faulte premiere ne se tint pas atant, mais tant veilla et laboura que son intencion mist a fin et sa voulenté a execucion.

[CHAPITRE 43]

Comment Rozemonde trouva la façon et maniere de soy faire prendre et emmener au roy d'Inde la Major lequel elle aymoit parfaictement. xliii. chapitre[1]

On dist voulentiers et il est vray que se une femme d'elle mesmes ne se chastie, a peine peult nul la chastier, car pluschier ayment a mourir que de faillir a leur entreprinse, comme bien monstra Rozemonde femme du roy Lucar. Car pas ne demoura l'espace de quatre jours que elle saillit de son pavillon et en la plus petite compaignie qu'elle peult monta sur une hacquenee et dist que elle s'en vouloit aler esbatre aux champs pour prendre ung petit de air. Et en ce point s'en ala la dame Rozemonde, chevaulchant vers la ci[100verso]té d'Inde la Major. Or avoit elle secretement fait sçavoir au roy d'Inde que a iceluy jour qu'il fut pres et appareillé pour la venir prendre et emmener. Et il n'y faillit point, car ainsy qu'il l'aperceut il saillit par une faulce porte, monté a l'avantaige, et courust vers la dame. Puis print la hacquenee par le frain et luy a dist, "M'amye, or vous puis je a ceste fois

---

[1] Woodcut of two squires, a queen and her female attendant, all on horseback, exiting the gate of a walled city.

to let me descend to the ground. And thus, with the help of this knight, I have gotten away and escaped him."

"Lady," said Lucar, "you have acted well, but we mustn't speak of this any more for the present, for we are under assault by our enemies and have our hands full." Thus he left the lady without making any other answer, and returned to the battle. At the same time, the forces from India withdrew back into the city, for they had lost many good and valiant champions. But of all his losses, the king of India complained most of the loss of the lady Rozemonde.

"Alas, lady," he said, "I have failed miserably in my plans. But Mohammed help me, I see clearly now that I was enchanted, for it seemed to me that I saw before me woods and rushing rivers, but as soon as I put you down, I saw nothing but a clear road ahead."

Valentin had earned great honor, and he was prized and praised by all for having recovered and delivered the lady Rozemonde from the king of India. She herself acted sincerely grateful, but, whatever sign of love she manifested, she in fact hated him more than anyone and wished him ill, for she had in fact wanted to accomplish what she had set out to do. But despite this first failure, she did not give up, rather she kept watch and worked at it until her plan was brought to fruition and her desire fulfilled.

CHAPTER 43

How Rozemonde found a way to have herself taken and brought to the king of India Major, whom she loved truly.

Everyone says, and quite rightly, that if a woman does not amend her ways herself, no one else will be able to correct her,[1] for women would rather die than fail in their plotting, as was demonstrated by Rozemonde, the wife of King Lucar. For barely four days after the previous events, she mounted on a quiet lady's horse and left her pavilion with the smallest entourage possible, saying that she wished to go amuse herself in the fields and take a bit of air. Then the lady Rozemonde took off, riding straight for the city of India Major. Now she had sent secret word to the king of India that he should be ready that very day to take possession of her and carry her away. And he did not fail when it came to it, for just as he caught sight of her, he came out by a secret gate on an excellent mount and galloped up to the lady. He seized her horse by the bridle, saying to her, "My beloved, now I

---

[1] Cf. Hassell, *Proverbs*, 110 (no. F39).

seurement emmener et vostre voulenté faire." En ce point la mena dedens la cité d'Inde en grant joye et liesse.

Or fut le cry parmy l'ost de Lucar que le roy d'Inde Major emmenoit Rozemonde. Plusieurs monterent a cheval pour la dame secourir, mais leur peine perdirent, car tantost fust entree dedens la cité d'Inde.

"Par Mahon," dist Lucar, "celuy qui la dame me pourra amener je le feray a jamais mon grant seneschal et dessus tous ceulx de ma court maistre et gouverneur."

"Sire," dist Pacolet a Valentin, "se c'est vostre plaisir de la dame avoir, je trouverray tantost enchantement par quoy je la vous feray prendre."

"Amy," dist Valentin a Pacolet, "or la laissez aler. Une foys l'ay rendue a Lucar son mary en espoir qu'elle se chastiast de sa faulte. Et puis que faire ne le veult, aultrement fol serait celuy homme qui remede querir y vouldroit, car femme qui voulenté a de soy mauvaisement gouverner ne peult jamais estre de sy pres tenue que la fin n'en soit mauvaise."

En celluy jour que le roy d'Inde emmena la belle Rozemonde, il la print pour femme et espouse et la nuyt coucha avec elle et engendra ung filz qui Rabaste[1] fut nommé, et lequel en ses jours tint et posseda Hierusalem. Iceluy Rabaste depuis fut conquis par Renyer Montabay qui son frere a nostre foy fut converty avec la fille dudit Rabastre laquelle avoit nom Atibar.

Trop dolent fut le roy Lucar quant sa femme eust ainsi perdue, et Brandiffer le resconforte et luy a dit, "Beau filz, prenez en vous bon couraige, car je jure Mahon et tous mes puissans dieux que devant mon partement je vous en vengerray."[2]

Ainsi jura Brandiffer, mais aultrement ira la chose, car a ce propre jour vers luy vint ung messagier lequel luy a dit, "Sire, entendez mes nouvelles lesquelles seront pour vous desplaisantes. Sachez que le puissant roy Pepin de France, acompaigné du filz a l'empereur de Grece—lequel empereur est en vostre prison enfermé et tenu—sont nouvellement descendus et sont arrivéz sur vostre terre, et ont gasté et destruit plusieurs bonnes villes, chasteaulx et forterresses et grant nombre de voz gens mis a feu et a sang. Et ancores ont fait plus fort, car ilz ont assiegé vostre grande cité d'Angorie en laquelle vostre femme nouvellement est acouchee d'ung tresbeau filz. Or suis je icy venu secours et ayde vous demander, ou aultrement il conviendra vostre belle cité d'Angorie rendre et delivrer a ces mauvais crestiens."

Quant Bran[101recto]differ telles nouvelles oÿt, trop il en fut dolent a son cueur. Lors ala vers Lucar et luy a dist, "Beau filz, voycy ung messager qui de ma terre a mauvaises nouvelles aportees, car Francoys y sont entréz a trop fiere puissance par quoy m'est force de aler celle part pour ma terre garder et mon pays deffendre. Si vous diray que vous ferez—c'est que vous envoyez vers le roy d'Inde

---

[1] The text hesitates between the spellings *Rabaste* and *Rabastre*.
[2] Text has *vengrray*.

can bear you away properly and fulfill your desire." Whereupon he led her into the city of India with great joy and happiness.

Then the cry went up among Lucar's host that the King of India Major was bearing Rozemonde away. Several men mounted their horses to come to the lady's rescue, but their effort was wasted, for she was already within the city of India.

"By Mohammed," said Lucar, "I will reward the one who can bring me back the lady by making him my high seneschal in perpetuity, and he shall be master and governor of my entire court."

"Sire," said Pacolet to Valentin, "if it is your pleasure to recover the lady, I will find an enchantment by which you can capture her."

"Friend," said Valentin to Pacolet, "let her go. I returned her once to Lucar her husband in the hope that she would correct her misconduct. But since she has no wish to do so, it would be foolish to try to remedy the situation again, for if a woman desires to behave badly, she can never be under such close watch that it won't turn out badly anyway."[1]

The very same day that the king of India carried away the fair Rozemonde, he married her and took her to wife, bedding her that night and engendering a son named Rabastre, who, later in life, held Jerusalem in his possession. Later on this Rabastre was conquered by Renaut de Montauban, and his brother was converted to our faith along with the daughter of this Rabastre whose name was Atibar.

King Lucar was grief-stricken that he had thus lost his wife, but Brandiffer consoled him with these words: "Dear son, take some courage, for I swear by Mohammed and by all my powerful gods that, before I leave here, I will avenge you."

So swore Brandiffer, but things went otherwise, for that very day a messenger came to him to announce, "Sire, hear my tidings, which you will find displeasing. Know that the powerful King Pepin of France, accompanied by the son of the emperor of Greece—that emperor whom you hold imprisoned in your dungeon—has just arrived in your lands, where they have already destroyed several good cities, castles, and fortresses, and subjected a great number of your people to fire and blood. And they have done even worse, for they have besieged your great city of Angory[2] where your wife has just recently given birth to a most beautiful boy. Now I have come here to request your help and aid, for otherwise the beautiful city of Angory will be rendered up and delivered to these evil Christians."

When Brandiffer heard these tidings, he was sick at heart. Then he went to see Lucar and told him, "Dear son, a messenger has come bringing such terrible news from my lands that I am forced to go back to guard my land and defend my country. But I will tell you what you must do—send a knight to the king of India

---

[1] Another version of the same proverb referenced in n. 1 above.

[2] Angory is the Old French name of the Turkish city today called Ankara: André Moisan, *Répertoire des noms propres de personnes et de lieux cités dans les chansons de geste françaises et les oeuvres étrangères dérivées* (Geneva: Droz, 1986), 650, 1013. However, the composer knew little of the geography of the region (see page 391, n. 1).

aulcun chevalier et sy luy mandez que il vous renvoye ma fille, la belle Rozemonde, vostre femme, et par tel convenant que vous luy pardonnerez la mort de vostre pere. Si ferez de sa terre lever et partir vostre ost sans nulle guerre luy faire."

"Par mon dieu," dist le roy Lucar, "a cela je pensoye et n'y voy point de meilleur remede ne conseil qui meilleur soit."

A ces motz appella Valentin et luy dist, "Chevalier, de par moy il vous convient devers le roy d'Inde aler et luy direz en ceste maniere, que la belle Rozemonde il m'envoye laquelle il m'a tollue, par tel moyen et convenant que la mort de mon pere je luy pardonneray sans jamais pour ce fait avoir contre luy question. Et si feray mes gens et toute mon armee vuider de dessus sa terre et hors de son pays sans nul oultraige ne dommage luy porter."

"Sire," dit Valentin, "pour vous je vouldroye mon corps aventurer, et plus que pour nul aultre; si feray vostre messaige au mieulx que je pourray, et en petit de temps en aurez nouvelles."

Lors monta a cheval et ala devers Inde et entra dedens la cité ainsi que ung messaiger, et ala tantost au palays auquel il trouva le roy; aupres de luy la belle Rozemonde assise qui moult bien cogneut Valentin, si dist au roy, "Sire, voyez vous cestuy? C'est celuy par qui je vous fus tollue et ostee quant la premiere foys me cuidastes emmener."

"Dame," dit le roy d'Inde, "a ceste heure je m'en vengeray, car jamais en sa vie il ne me eschappera."

"Sy fera," dist la dame, "car de tant je le cognoys que ancores de luy vous pourrez bien estre servy."

Adonc approcha Valentin[1] qui haultement et en grant hardiesse le roy salua et la dame aussi. "Sire," dist Valentin, "je suis messaiger au roy Lucar, lequel vers vous m'envoye et par moy vous mande que luy rendez la plaisante dame Rozemonde laquelle icy est. Et se ainsi faire le voulez il vous pardonnera la mort de son pere, qui mourir fistes, et son armee fera de vostre terre sans nul sejour lever. Mais nonpourtant que je soye chargé de vous faire tel message, mais se croire me voulez jamais ne vous y consentirez, mais garderez la dame que tant a de beauté et que si chier vous aime. Et sachez que jamais jour de ma vie ne seray en lieu ne en place ou je seuffre son blasme et ne deshonneur a vous faire pour l'amour de la dame. Tout le temps de ma vie je luy vouldray honneur porter et a vous faire service."

"Chevalier," dist le roy d'Inde, "vous parlez comme vaillant et moult me plaist [101verso]vostre parole. Mais pour brief vous respondre, dites au roy Lucar s'il a de femmes affaire qu'il pourchasse d'aultres que m'amye Rozemonde, car jamais jour de sa vie a son costé ne couchera ne de son corps n'aura plaisir."

"Chevalier," dist la dame, "saluez moy mon pere et luy dictes que de ce fait la faulte est a luy, car bien luy avoie dist que point ne vouloye estre au roy Lucar

---

[1] Text has *Salentin*.

with the demand that he return my daughter, the fair Rozemonde, your wife, in return for which you will pardon him the death of your father. Then you will release his land and remove your army without waging further war against him."

"By my god," said King Lucar, "I was wondering what I could do, and I see no other possible remedy or better counsel."

With these words he called for Valentin and said to him, "Sir knight, I direct you to go to the king of India and tell him the following: that he send back to me the fair Rozemonde, whom he stole from me, and for that I will forgive him the death of my father and never again hold it against him. Moreover I will withdraw my men and my army from his lands and leave his country without doing any further damage to it."

"Sire," said Valentin, "I would be willing to risk myself in service to you above all others; I will deliver your message to the best of my abilities, and you shall soon have tidings."

Then he mounted his horse and rode towards India, gaining entry to the city as a messenger, and directing his steps directly to the palace where he found the king. Sitting next to him was the fair Rozemonde, who of course recognized Valentin, so she said to the king, "Sire, do you see that man there? He is the one who took me away from you the first time you tried to bear me away."

"Lady," said the king of India, "I will avenge myself right now, for he shall never get away from me with his life."

"Yes, he shall," said the lady, "for from what I know about him, you may still be well served by him."

At that moment Valentin came in, boldly greeting the king and his lady with a flourish. "Sire," said Valentin, "I am the messenger of King Lucar, who sends me to tell you to return to him the fair lady Rozemonde being held here. And if you do so, he will pardon you the death of his father, whom you killed, and he will withdraw his army forthwith from your land. However, despite my charge to deliver this message, believe me when I say you should not consent to his demands; rather you should keep the lady, who is not only beautiful, but loves you dearly. And know that, wherever I go throughout all the days of my life, I will never allow her to be blamed nor you to suffer dishonor for love of the lady. For the rest of my life, I wish only to bring her honor and do you service."

"Sir knight," said the king of India, "you speak like a valiant man and your words please me. But to respond to you briefly, tell King Lucar that if he wants a wife, let him seek someone other than my beloved Rozemonde, for never again in his life will he sleep by her side or have pleasure from her body."

"Sir knight," said the lady, "greet my father for me and tell him that this is all his fault, for I told him I did not wish to be given to King Lucar. Now my father

donnee. Or a mon pere fait a sa voulenté contre la mienne, et j'ay fait a la mienne contre la sienne. Sy dites a Lucar que a moy n'aye plus fiance."

"Dame," ce dist Valentin, "vostre messaige je feray de bon cueur et moult voulentiers." Ainsi a prins congé moult fort joyeulx d'estre hors d'Inde et eschappé du roy. Il est retourné en l'ost et a racompté la responce telle que de Inde a raporté.

"Sire," dist il a Lucar, "pourchassez une aultre dame, car Rozemonde est mariee et espousee au roy d'Inde lequel toutes les nuys couche avec elle et en fait son plaisir."

Et quant le roy Lucar entendit ces parolles ses mains commença a detordre et ses cheveulx a detirer. "Ha! m'amye, pour vous me conviendra il mourir quant j'ay perdu la plus belle, la plus noble et la plus amoureuse qui soit en ce monde. Helas! que vous avoy je fait que sy grant desplaisir m'avez pourchassé? Faulx et desloyal roy d'Inde, jamais mon cueur n'aura cause de toy aymer, car faulcement tu feis mon pere mourir, et puis par ta trahyson ma dite femme m'as tollue!"

Lors parla Brandiffer et dist en ceste maniere, "Mon beau filz, de ceste pitié je suis dolent et fort courroucé, mais pour l'eure presente ne puis confort ne remede donner, car aler me convient en ma terre ou les François sont descendus, ainsi que bien l'avez ouÿ par le messaiger, ou aultrement mon pays sera tout destruit et exillé."

"Sire," ce dist Lucar, "dont nous convient il la cité assaillir devant que partir, car se nous en alons en ce point trop nous seroit reproché villainement."

"Par Mahon," dist Brandiffer, "nul assault n'y vauldroit, car ja aultrement que par famine nous ne les gaignerons. Si demourrez icy et toute vostre puissance en gardant les passaiges que nul vivres n'y puissent entrer, et atant vous suffise que tout aussitost que de mes ennemis seray despeché a forte puissance d'armes et a moult grant compaignie vers vous je retourneray."

[CHAPITRE 44]

Comment le roy Lucar fist tant que le roy Brandiffer sy demoura avec luy devant la cité d'Inde et envoya en Angorie le chevalier Valentin acompaigné de cent mille combatans contre le roy Pepin de France son oncle. xliiii. chapitre

Quant le roy Lucar entendit que le roy Brandiffer le vouloit laisser, moult en fust dolent et moult fort desplaisant et [102recto]luy dist, "Sire, il est vray et bien le sçavez que vous m'avez promis de moy ayder a venger du roy d'Inde qui a vous et a moy si grant injure et villennie a faite."

may have set his will against mine, but I have set my own against his. And also tell Lucar that all obligations are over between us."

"Lady," said Valentin, "I will carry your message willingly and well." Thus he took his leave from them, overjoyed to get away from India and to have escaped the king. He returned to the camp and recounted the answer brought back from the court of India.

"Sire," he said to Lucar, "seek another lady, for Rozemonde is married and joined to the king of India who sleeps with her every night and takes his pleasure with her."

When King Lucar heard these words, he began to twist his hands and pull at his hair. "Ah! my beloved, I should die on account of you, for I have lost the most beautiful, the most noble, and the most lovable woman in the world. Alas! what have I ever done to you that you desire to cause me such distress? False, faithless king of India, I will never have any reason to love you, for you perfidiously killed my father, and then through your treachery you have taken away my own wife!"

Then Brandiffer spoke up in this manner: "Dear son, I am truly sorry and angry over this misfortune, but for the present moment I can give you neither cure nor comfort, for I must go to my land where the French have attacked, as you certainly heard the messenger say, or otherwise my country will be completely destroyed."

"Sire," said Lucar, "we must attack the city before leaving, for if we leave we will be thoroughly shamed."

"By Mohammed," said Brandiffer, "no assault would work, for it is only by famine that we can defeat them. So remain here with your forces and block all the passages and don't allow any provisions to get through, and let it suffice you that I will return to you with a great company of men as soon as I have defeated my enemies."

CHAPTER 44

How King Lucar convinced Brandiffer to remain with him before the city of India and send Valentin to Angory, accompanied by a hundred thousand men, against King Pepin of France, his uncle.

When King Lucar heard that King Brandiffer was planning to desert him, he was very upset, and said to him, "Sire, don't forget that you promised to help me take revenge against the king of India, who has harmed both you and me."

"Il est vray," dist Brandiffer, "et trop suis desplaisant quant ma promesse ne puis acomplir. Mais force me contraint d'aler ma terre secourir."

"Or je vous diray," dist Lucar, "comment bien faire vous pourrez pour le prouffit et honneur de moy, et tant d'une part comme d'aultre. J'ay icy ung chevalier nommé Valentin sur tous aultres vaillant et hardy et couraigeux. Si luy pourrez voz gens bailler, car en toutes choses je l'ay trouvé vray et en ses fais loyal. Et oultre plus vous avez en cestuy ost vostre oncle Murgalent qui de longtemps la guerre a suivye et moult bien s'i cognoist. Si me semble que bon seroit que ces deux feissent le voyaige et vous demourissiez par deça."

A ces parolles se consentit Brandiffer. Si manderent Valentin et Murgalent et leur dirent et declarerent le fait et la maniere de l'entreprinse. "Seigneurs," dist Brandiffer, "vous estes par nous deux esleux pour aler en Angorie lever le siege que le roy Pepin y a mis. Si vous prie et requiers que faces en maniere que ma terre puisse par vous estre deffendue [et] gardee. Et vous, bel oncle Murgalent, ayez le cueur de bien faire et rendu le vous sera, car la ou je auray perte vous n'aurez nul prouffit."

"Beau nepveu," dist Murgalent, "ne vous soussiez plus, car puis que je maine avec moy le vaillant Valentin je n'ay paour, doubte ne crainte que la chose ne se porte bien."

Apres les choses ordonnees et devisees furent bailléz a Valentin et a Murgalent cent mille combatans bien montéz et autant en demoura en l'ost du roy Lucar. Valentin et Murgalent monterent sur la mer et tant bien nagerent et eurent vent aggreable que en peu de temps ilz arriverent au port de Angorie.

Mais premier qu'ilz arrivassent, ung peu de temps premier Valentin avisa une haulte et grosse tour vers les parties d'orient, laquelle estoit couverte de fin leton, lors il demanda aux mariniers quelle place c'estoit. Et ung luy respondit, "Sire, c'est le Chasteau Fort et ainsi est nommé. Et sachez que la place est moult forte et puissante, car si subtillement est l'entré faicte et edifié qu'il n'y peult passer fors seulement que ung homme a une foys. Et si les deux y vouloyent passer ensemble tous cherroient et trebucheroient en la mer qui bat contre les murs. Et en celuy chasteau le roy Brandiffer a moult longuement sa fille Galasie gardee affin que de nul ne luy soit prinse ne robee, car au monde n'est memoire de plus belle que elle, mais tant il y a qu'il ne la veult donner a homme vivant."

Quant le chevalier Valentin oÿt dire ces parolles moult luy print grant desir et voulenté a son cueur de la belle dame veoir, et tout par luy dist que jamais [102verso]il ne sera bien joyeulx tant qu'il l'ait veue.

Or sont ilz arrivéz au plus pres d'Angorie et sur les champs ont leur ost en briefve espace mis et assis. Bien ont regardé et cogneu les tentes et les pavillons de l'ost au roy Pepin qui moult estoient luysantes et plaisantes a regarder. Grant devoir faisoient crestiens de la cité assaillir, mais dedens y avoit ung admiral nommé Bruham lequel tous les jours sans faillir sailloit sur l'ost Pepin et grant proesse faisoit luy et ses gens.

"This is true," said Brandiffer, "and I am not happy that I cannot keep my promise. But I have no choice—I must go help my own lands."

"Then I have a suggestion," said Lucar, "as to how you can save both your honor and mine. There is a knight here named Valentin, more valiant, courageous, and bold than any I have known. You can entrust your men to him, for I have found him true in all matters and loyal in his deeds. Moreover, that army includes your uncle Murgalent, a warrior with long experience. It seems to me a good idea to send those two while you remain here."

Brandiffer consented to his wish. He sent for Valentin and Murgalent, to whom he explained the situation and the undertaking. "My lords," said Brandiffer, "the two of us have chosen you to go to Angory to lift King Pepin's siege. I pray you to do everything necessary to keep and defend my land. And you, dear Uncle Murgalent, have the courage to succeed and you will be properly rewarded, for there is no profit for you where I have loss."

"Dear nephew," said Murgalent, "do not trouble yourself, for since I am taking with me the valiant Valentin, I have no fear or doubt that the matter will not go well."

Once everything was arranged, Valentin and Murgalent were given a hundred thousand well-mounted soldiers, while just as many remained in King Lucar's army. Valentin and Murgalent set sail and had such a good wind that they soon arrived at the port of Angory.[1]

But before their arrival, shortly before reaching that port, off towards the east Valentin spied a tall, massive tower covered with fine brass, so he asked the mariners what place it was. And one of them responded, "Sire, that is Château Fort, and so is it named. Know that it is a most formidable stronghold, for the entrance was built and fashioned so cleverly that no more than one man can pass through it at a time. And if two try to pass together, both stumble and fall into the sea that beats against the walls. And Brandiffer has kept his daughter Galasie in this castle for a long time so that no one may abduct her, for in living memory there has never been any woman in the world as beautiful as she, for which reason he is not yet willing to give her to any man alive."

When the knight Valentin heard these words, he suddenly had a great desire to see the fair lady, and he said to himself that he would not be truly happy until he had seen her.

Soon they arrived close to Angory where they quickly set up their army in the fields. They saw and recognized King Pepin's tents and pavilions that were sparkling and pleasant to behold. The Christians attacked the city with great diligence, but from within there was an emir named Bruhans who sallied forth everyday against Pepin's forces, both he and his men fighting bravely.

---

[1] The real city is actually far inland.

Quant Murgalent avisa l'ost des crestiens qui grant terre tenoit, il appela Valentin et luy dist, "Chevalier, conseillez nous sur cest affaire, car je voy bien et cognoy que les crestiens sont fors et moult grant nombre."

"Murgalent," dit Valentin, "je vous diray mon oppinion. Je conseille que nous envoyons bien tost ung messaigier dedens la cité d'Angorie, et mandons a noz gens que nous sommes icy arrivéz et que demain ilz ne saillent pour riens que ilz ne saillent sur les crestiens et que par devers la ville fierement les assaillent. Et nous de la part de la mer l'assault leur donnerons. Si me semble que par tel moyen ne pourront fuyr ne eschapper que tous ne soyent mors ou prins."

"Par mon dieu," dist Murgalent, "vous avez bien avisé. Or fault trouver messaigier qui ceste chose parfaice et acomplisse."

"Sire," dist Pacolet qui subtil et cautelleux estoit, "ne serchiez aultre que moy, car je sçay parler tous langaiges et feray cestuy messaige si bien que vous cognoisterrez que je y auray esté."

"Amy," dist Murgalent, "tu parles comme vaillant. Or t'en va et Mahon te veulle conduire."

Pacolet se partit qui moult fust joyeulx de faire ce messaige et a par luy dist bassement, "Murgalent, vous m'envoyez faire vostre messaige, mais par le Dieu tout puissant, je le feray en telle maniere et en telle façon que devant qu'i soit demain jour vous cognoisterrez de quel jeu Pacolet sçait jouer."

Ainsi s'en va courant Pacolet tout a pied sans cheval. Et quant il fust eslongné de l'ost de Murgalent il ne tira pas vers la cité d'Angorie mais ala vers l'ost des crestiens, l'une foys tirant comme fol, l'autre foys en soy apuyant d'ung baston. Et quant les crestiens le veirent ainsi venir bien se pensoyent que il estoit espie. Si luy vindrent a l'encontre a moult grant haste et luy demanderent, "Galant, ou alés vous ainsi? Il semble bien a vostre maniere et vostre façon et contenance que vous soyez une espye."

"Seigneurs," dist l'enchanteur Pacolet, "vous avez dit verité. Mais je ne suis pas espye pour aulcun dommaige vous porter. Or me menez bien tost en l'ost du roy Pepin; si me faictes tantost parler a mon seigneur Orson, et je luy diray telle chose dont il sera moult fort grandement esbahy."

Lors les crestiens ont prins le petit Pacolet et puis l'ont mené devers Orson, lequel de le veoir fut moult joyeulx et grant [103recto]chiere luy fist. "Amy," ce dist Orson, "comment se porte mon frere Valentin?" Adonc Pacolet luy compta toutes les aventures qui avenues leur estoient[1] depuis qu'ilz n'avoyent veu l'ung l'autre, et luy parla du serpent que Valentin avoit conquis devant Antioche, et comment il ne peult avoir nouvelles de la belle Esclarmonde. Puis luy dist et declaira comment il estoit arrivé pour combatre a eulx.

"Sire," dist Pacolet, "il est vray que nous sommes au plus pres d'icy arrivéz le nombre de cent mille payens desquelz est conducteur et gouverneur vostre frere

---

[1] Text has *rstoient*.

When Murgalent saw the Christian host holding a large swath of land, he called over Valentin and said, "Knight, advise us concerning this matter, for I can see that the Christians are strong and present in great numbers."

"Murgalent," said Valentin, "I will give you my opinion. I believe we should send a messenger right away into the city of Angory, and let us send word to our people there that we have arrived and that tomorrow they must not fail to sally forth from the city and attack the Christians ferociously. We for our part will conduct our assault from the sea. It seems to me that by such a means not a one will be able to flee or escape with his life."

"By my god," said Murgalent, "you have given good advice. Now I need to find a messenger who can do this thing."

"Sire," said Pacolet, who was subtle and sly, "look no further than me, for I know how to speak many languages, and I will deliver this message so well that you will clearly see that I have been there."

"Friend," said Murgalent, "you speak like a brave man. Now go, and may Mohammed guide you."

Pacolet left, delighted to be delivering this message, and saying to himself, "Murgalent, you send me to deliver your message, but by God almighty, I will do it in such a way that before tomorrow morning you will clearly see what kind of game Pacolet is able to play."

Thereupon Pacolet left swiftly on foot, without any horse. Once he was far enough away from Murgalent's troops, he changed course, wending his way not toward the city of Angory but towards the Christian host, sometimes running madly, other times leaning on a stick. And when the Christians saw him coming thus, they naturally thought he was a spy. Quickly they accosted him, demanding, "Well, my fine fellow, and where do you think you are going? The way you are acting, you must be a spy."

"My lords," said the magician Pacolet, "you have spoken truth. But I am not a spy to bring you any harm. Now take me right away to King Pepin's camp; let me speak at once to my lord Orson, and I will tell him something that will absolutely amaze him."

Then the Christians took hold of little Pacolet and led him to Orson, who was overjoyed to see him and made him most welcome. "My friend," said Orson, "how is my brother Valentin doing?" Then Pacolet recounted all their adventures since last they had seen one another, telling how Valentin had vanquished the serpent before the city of Antioch, and how he had not been able to get any information about the fair Esclarmonde. Then he explained how they had come to do battle against them.

"Sire," said Pacolet, "the truth is that we have arrived nearby with a hundred thousand pagans being led by your brother Valentin along with Murgalent. They

Valentin avec Murgalent. Et sont deça passéz par le commandement du roy Lucar et de Brandiffer, lesquelz nous ont icy transmis et envoyéz pour vous assaillirent et deschasser de ceste terre. Mais se croyre me voulez de cent mille payens qui la mer ont passee n'en retournera ja ung. Ce sont chiens mauldis a nostre loy et a Jesus contraires. Si ne fault pas avoir pitié de leur mort pourchasser en toutes les manieres que on peult et se vous me laissez faire je trouverray la façon et maniere parquoy jamais il[z] ne eschapperont."

"Amy," ce dist Orson, "pour Dieu or y avisez, car se faire le voulez oncques jour de vostre vie vous n'eustes autant d'onneur et si acquerrez merite envers Dieu."

"Sire," dist Pacolet, "or m'escoutez parler ung petit s'il vous plaist."

[CHAPITRE 45]

Comment par le sort et subtil engin de Pacolet fit mettre a mort les payens qui[1] par Brandiffer celle part contre le roy Pepin tenoyent et avoyent esté envoyéz. xlv. chapitre[2]

"Sire," dist Pacolet a Orson, "je suis et seray toute ma vie subject a Valentin vostre frere et a vous. Mais se jamais je vous fis service qui vous deust plaire j'en feray a ceste foys ung. Or escoutez comment il convient tout premierement que vous soyez sur voz gardez et que ceste nuyt vous fachez voz gens armer et mettre en point. Et affin que nul ne puisse dire que Valentin y pense trahyson, je le feray demourer dedens les tentes et pavillons et feray que les payens si iront en moult grant nombre faire le gait. Et quant il sera ainsi fait je getteray mon sort en telle maniere que tous ceulx du gait je feray sy durement dormir que vous pourrez tout seurement passer oultre. Sy viendrez [103verso]tout en leur ost et le feu vous bouterez dedens, en tuant et mettant tout a mort ceulx que vous y trouverrez."

"Par Dieu," ce dist Orson, "vous en parlez moult bien et comme subtil, et monstre[s] que tu as voulenté et devocion de nostre foy soustenir et deffendre."

A ces motz le mena Orson devers le roy Pepin pour compter l'entreprinse. Joyeulx et tres content fut Pepin de telle chose oÿr, et fist Pacolet moult haultement festoier. Pacolet beut et menga, et puis a prins congé et s'en ala en la cité d'Angorie son messaige parfaire, affin que de son fait nul ne se prinst garde et que au roy Murgalent racomptast certaines enseignes. Il entra en la cité et s'en ala au palais ou il trouva l'admiral Bruhans. Haultement le salua et en grant reverence car il le sçavoit bien faire. Puis luy dist son messaige, tel que enchairgé luy estoit par Murgalent donné.

---

[1] Text has *pui*.
[2] Woodcut depicting battle scene of foot soldiers; corpses in foreground.

set forth under the order of King Lucar and Brandiffer, who sent us to assail you and chase you out of this country. But if you are willing to listen to me, not a single one who crossed the sea will return forthwith. They are cursed dogs, opposed to our religion and to Jesus Christ. Thus one need have no compunction about seeking their death however one can, and if you will let me act, I will find a way so that not one shall escape."

"My friend," said Orson, "for God's sake, consider this carefully, for if you are willing to do it, you will acquire more honor than you ever have before, and, moreover, merit in the eyes of God."

"Sire," said Pacolet, "now listen to me for a little, if you please."

CHAPTER 45

How the pagans sent by Brandiffer to fight King Pepin were put to death by means of Pacolet's spell and crafty plot.

"Sire," said Pacolet to Orson, "I am the humble servant of Valentin your brother and you, and will be so all my life. But if ever I did you a service that pleased you, I shall do one this time. Now listen how it goes: first you must be on your guard tonight and see that all your men are armed and ready. And so that no one may suspect Valentin of treason, I will make sure he remains in his tent while a great number of pagans go out on watch. And then, when all is ready, I will cast a spell so that all the men of the night watch fall asleep so deeply that you can pass through. You will penetrate their camp, setting it ablaze and killing everyone you find there."

"By God," said Orson, "you speak well and most cleverly, and show how devoted you are to supporting and defending our faith."

With these words, Orson led him to King Pepin to explain the plan. Pepin was thrilled and happy to hear about it, and feasted Pacolet with great pomp. Pacolet ate and drank, but then he took his leave, for he had to go to the city of Angory to deliver his message so that no one would suspect his true purpose or say anything to King Murgalent. He entered the city and went to the palace, where he found Emir Bruhans. He greeted him with great respect, for he knew how to act. Then he delivered his message, just as Murgalent had charged him to say it.

"Sire," dist Pacolet, "sachez que de la part de Brandiffer nous sommes arrivéz, et pour vous secourir descendus cent mille payens. Sy vous mande le roy Murgalent, lequel de tous les payens a la chairge et gouvernement, que demain au plus matin vous fachez voz gens armer et que vous assaillez les crestiens de la part de la cité d'Angorie, et Murgalent et son ost par derriere les prendront. Si ne pourront fuyr ne eschapper que tous ne soyent mors et desconfis."

Joyeulx fut l'admiral Bruhans de oÿr telles nouvelles, mais il ne sçavoit pas comment il luy en devoit prendre. Lors print congé Pacolet et en moult grant reverence, et s'en retourna vers Murgalent lequel il salua de par l'admiral Bruhans en la façon et maniere comme il le sçavoit bien faire.

"Amy," ce dist Murgalent, "vous estes digne de estre prisé et louenge avoir quant sy bien avez sceu faire vostre messaige."

Puis Pacolet vint vers Valentin et secretement luy a dit, "Vostre frere Orson et vostre oncle le noble roy Pepin vous saluent, ausquelz j'ay fait l'entreprinse sçavoir de vostre venue affin que ilz ne puissent point estre prins en desroy, car grant pitié et dommaige seroit."

"Amy," dist Valentin, "tu as tresbien ouvré." Or ne luy dit pas Pacolet le fait de son entreprinse, car bien le cognoissoit en tant que jamais en jour de sa vie trahyson ne vouloit faire ne consentir.

La nuyt fort aprocha et convint le gait assoir et les gardes de l'ost eslire et establir. Bien vouloit Valentin du gait avoir la chairge mais Pacolet, qui sçavoit bien comment la chose devoit aler, trouva maniere de l'en destourner et le fit aux tentes demourer. Et quant la nuyt fut venue et le gait fust assis, Pacolet entra parmy les payens et son sort getta sur eulx en telle maniere que tous a terre les fist dormir si fort que pour tous ceulx du monde ne se fussent esveilléz.

Or ne dormoit pas le bon vaillant roy Pepin ne toute son armee, car quant vint entour [104recto]la minuyt, acompaigné du duc Millon d'Angler et du vaillant et hardy Orson, a tout soixante mille hommes entrerent sur les paiens. Ilz ont sans faire bruit tout a leur gré le gait passé, puis sont venus dedens l'ost et parmy les trefz, tentes et pavillons ont le feu prins et bouté, et tous les payens mis a mort sans espargner grans ne petis. Tant avant sont entréz en l'ost devant que les payens s'esveillassent qu'i sont venus a la tente du roy Murgalent qui dormoit en son lit. Et tellement fust souspris que au saillir de son lit fut d'ung dart tout oultre le corps passé et a terre cheut mort.

A l'eure de cestuy assault Pacolet vint a Valentin et le print par la main disant, "Monseigneur, pensez de vous sauver, car trop mallement nous va. Sachez certainement que crestiens qui oultre le gait sont passéz et sont dedens nostre ost et ont noz gens de toutes pars environnéz, et mettent tout en feu et en sang. Si pensons de eschapper et sauver nostre vie."

"Helas, Pacolet," dist Valentin, "je cognoy bien que tu as icy ouvré, et que les payens as enchanté et deceu. Si ne sçay comment je doy faire pour mon honneur sauver, car au partir de Brandiffer je luy promis et juray que se vif pouoie

"Sire," said Pacolet, "know that we have been sent by Brandiffer, and that a hundred thousand pagans have come to help you. King Murgalent, who is in charge of this force, bids you to arm your men early in the morning and assail the Christians from the city side, while Murgalent and his host attack them from behind. That way not a one will escape alive or unharmed."

Emir Bruhans was gladdened to hear such news, but little did he know how things would actually turn out for him. Then Pacolet took his leave most respectfully and returned to Murgalent, whom he greeted on the part of Emir Bruhans in his best manner.

"Friend," said Murgalent, "you deserve much praise for succeeding in delivering that message."

Then Pacolet went to see Valentin and said to him quietly, "Your brother Orson and your uncle the noble King Pepin send you greetings. I warned them of your mission here so that they may not be taken unawares, for that would be a great pity."

"Friend," said Valentin, "you have done rightly." Now Pacolet did not explain all of his plan to him, for he knew him well enough to know that he would never in his life consent to or commit treason.

Night approached and it was time to set the watch, to choose who would keep guard. Valentin wished to have charge of the watch, but Pacolet, who knew what was to happen, found a way to deter his purpose and keep him in his tent. Once night had fallen and the night watch was in place, Pacolet stole through the pagan camp, casting his spell in such a way that they all fell to the ground in a deep sleep from which nothing could awaken them.

Now the good and valiant King Pepin was not asleep, nor was his army, for when midnight came, the king, accompanied by Duke Millon d'Angler, the valiant and stalwart Orson, and sixty thousand men descended upon the pagans. They slipped noiselessly past the guard into the heart of the camp, where they set fire to the tents and pavilions, killing all the pagans, sparing no one, great or small. They were so deep into the pagan camp before anyone woke up that they got to the tent of King Murgalent, who was sleeping in his bed. He was taken so much by surprise that he had barely leapt from his bed before he was struck through with a javelin and fell down dead.

With the attack underway, Pacolet went to Valentin and took him by the hand, saying, "My lord, take care to save yourself, for things are going very badly for us. Know that Christians have gotten past the watch and are in the midst of our army, surrounding our men from every side, killing right and left and setting everything ablaze. Let us think how we may escape with our lives."

"Alas, Pacolet," said Valentin, "I recognize your hand in this—you have bewitched and deceived the pagans. And now I don't know what I can do to save my honor, for when I took leave of Brandiffer, I promised him and swore that if

eschapper je retourneroye devers luy. Or suis je seur que s'il a nouvelles de ceste chose, il me fera mourir."

"Sire," dit Pacolet, "de ce ne vous doubtez, car jamais en lieu que je soye vous n'aurez mal ne desplaisir, mais vous delivreray. Et vous eust le roy Brandiffer a mort jugé et au col eussiez la corde et l'eschielle montee, si sçay bien la maniere de vous ramener et de vostre vie sauver."

"Par ma foy," dist Valentin, "tel varlet doit on bien chier aymer et tenir."

Ainsi furent payens par le moyen de Pacolet desconfis et mis a mort. Et quant vint le lendemain au matin l'admiral Abruhans,[1] qui de ceste chose riens ne sçavoit, fist tous ses gens armer pour saillir sur le siege du roy Pepin ainsi que Pacolet leur avoit devisé. Mais bien va aultrement que l'admiral ne pense. Or sont payens yssus hors des murs d'Angorie pour venir sur Pepin, et les crestiens qui de leur entreprinse faicte et de leur conqueste estoient fiers et orgueilleux, et tantost s'en alerent contre eulx. Et en bien peu d'espace furent des deux pars assembléz; lors en ceste place commença la bataille fiere et orgueilleuse. Moult grant fut le bruit des gens et moult fort piteulx a oÿr. La eussiez oÿ maintes tromppettes, busines, clarons et maintz corz d'oliphant sonner. Et la veissiez lances et dars rompre et briser, maintz traitz en l'air voler, et plusieurs vaillans champions a la terre trebucher, de espees et brans d'acier maintz harnoys rompre et membres coupper, maintz chevaulx parmy les champs courir, maintz estandars et maintes bannyeres descouvrir et a la terre abatre.

Et quant l'admiral Abruhans veit que les crestiens faisoyent a ses [104verso] gens si dure guerre, comme hors du sens en la bataille il se frappa. Il a couché la lance et contre ung chevalier qui de Brie estoit est venu, et tellement l'a ataint que tout oultre le corps luy a le fer passé et mort l'a abatu. Puis il tira hors l'espee et courut a ung aultre lequel avoit nom Girad de Paris, et luy bailla si grant coup d'espee que la il mourut. Puis vint a ung vaillant chevalier nommé Robert de Normendie qui moult ses gens grevoit. Sy est alé vers luy et tel coup luy a baillé de son espee qu'i luy a couppee a jambe senestre. Si fort et si vaillamment se combatit l'admiral que devant que il arrestast il fist mourir dix chevaliers crestiens de sa main.

Or l'aperceut le roy Pepin qui vit bien que de crestiens faisoit grant occision. Le roy, qui fust vaillant, a tantost prins une lance, si frappe des esperons, et contre l'admiral est alé de puissance si grande que parmy foye et paulmon la lance passa, et si doulcement l'abatit mort que nul mot ne dit ne nul membre ne remua. Et quant payens veirent que l'admiral estoit mort, pas ne fault demander se furent moult dolens. De tenir le champ ilz n'eurent hardiesse, mais se retirerent dedens Angorie et monterent sur les murs pour la ville deffendre. Crestiens furent diligens et de pres les suivirent, mais ceulx de la cité firent si grant deffence, tant de trait[s] que de pierres, que crestiens trop mallement menerent. Adonc les cappitaines firent faire et amasser fagos et boys de toutes sortes et firent les fosses emplire, et par ce moyen gaignerent les portes et les barrieres. Et a celle heure fut

---

[1] Variant of the emir's name which recurs in the text.

I came out of this alive, I would return to him. Once he knows of this, he will have me killed."

"Sire," said Pacolet, "have no fear of that, for as long as I am here, nothing bad will happen to you—I will deliver you. Even if Brandiffer judged you to death, and you stood on the gallows with the rope around your neck, I would be able to rescue you and save your life."

"By my faith," said Valentin, "such a rascal must be dearly loved and cherished."

Thus were the pagans defeated and destroyed by Pacolet's doing. And when the morning broke, Emir Bruhans, who knew nothing of what had happened, readied his men to assail King Pepin's army just as Pacolet had told him to do. But things went otherwise than expected by the emir. The pagans left the protecting walls of Angory to descend upon Pepin, and the Christians, who had finished their operation and were proud and emboldened by their victory, quickly lined up against them. In no time, the two sides came together and a fierce battle erupted. The uproar of men in combat was overwhelming and most piteous to hear. Had you been there you would have heard countless trumpets, bugles, clarions, and ivory horns sound. And there you would have seen lances and javelins shiver and break, countless arrows fly through the air, multitudes of valiant champions stumble to the ground, many suits of armor pierced and limbs hacked off by swords and brands of steel, numerous horses running through the fields, and many standards and banners torn and trampled on the ground.

And when Emir Bruhans saw the Christians join such fierce battle with his men, he threw himself like a madman into the thick of the press. He couched his lance and rode against a knight from Brie, striking him so hard that the steel passed right through his body and tossed him down dead. Then he drew his sword and descended on another one named Girad de Paris, landing him such a fierce sword blow that he died on the spot. Next he came upon a valiant knight named Robert of Normandy who was wounding a lot of his men. As he came up to him, he swung so hard with his sword that he cut off his left leg. So fiercely and valiantly did the emir fight that before he stopped he had killed ten knights with his own hand.

Now King Pepin perceived him and saw that he was slaughtering Christians. So the king, always a doughty warrior, quickly gripped his lance, spurred his horse, and rode against the emir with such force that he thrust his lance through liver and lung, striking him dead with such deftness that he spoke never a word nor moved a limb. And when the pagans saw that their emir was dead, no need to ask if they were aggrieved. They had no more stomach for the attempt to hold the field; rather, they withdrew into Angory to mount the walls and thus to defend the city. The Christians were hot on their heels, but the city's defenders were so fierce with both arrows and stones that the Christians suffered cruelly. Then the captains had the ditches filled with quickly-gathered wood and sticks, by which means they reached the gates and bars. Then the assault became all the

l'assault moult grant et fort dangereux et y moururent plusieurs bons chevaliers, tant d'une part que d'aultre. Mais non pourtant la deffence que firent les paiens petit leur proffita, car de celuy assault fut la cité prinse et tous les Sarrasins mis a l'espee sans pitié ne mercy. Crestiens entrerent dedens qui maintes richesses y trouverent, et fut par ung vendredy droittement a l'eure que nostre seigneur Jesucrist souffrit mort en la croix pour nous. Le roy Pepin fist apporter et retraire tentes et pavillons dedens la cité pour plus seurement reposer et eulx refreschir.

Sy vous laisseray a parler de Pepin et de son armee, et vous diray de Valentin qui vers Brandiffer retourna.

[CHAPITRE 46]

Comment Valentin apres la bataille retourna devant Inde vers le roy Brandiffer, et en fit porter mort le roy Murgalent. xlvi. chapitre

Apres que la cité d'Angorie fut par les crestiens prinse et que les payens tant dedens que dehors furent mors et deffais, Valentin, qui le corps du roy Murgalent trouva mort sur le champ, appela Pacolet et luy a dist, "Amy, je veul que avec nous cestuy corps emportons. Si pourra le roy Brandiffer plus legierement croyre que nous estions ensemble en [105recto]la[1] bataille."

"Sire," dist Pacolet, "vous ne dites que bien et sy vous pourra estre grant proffit et honneur."

Adonc Valentin fit prendre le corps et moult honnourablement et richement le fist mettre en ung coffre et le couvrir. Puis sont venus au port ou estoient les navirez, et sont montéz sur la mer. Mais de cent mil payens qui la estoient venus n'en retourna pas dix mille que tous ne fussent mors par l'engin de Pacolet.

Or sont ilz sur la mer et tendirent les voilles et tant que ilz vindrent sur le port arriver tout droit ou le roy Brandiffer et Lucar avoient leur ost assis. Ilz prindrent terre et descendirent le corps, puis le chargerent sur deux chevaulx et le porterent faisant chiere piteuse au pavillon de Brandiffer. Lequel pour ceste heure jouoit aux echéz avec le roy Lucar, accompaigné de quinze roys qui le jeu regardoient. Et tout aussitost que Brandiffer a veu Valentin il luy a dist, "Chevalier, bien soyez vous retourné. Or me dictes de la bataille, comment il en va et se vous avez tué tous les crestiens et prins le roy Pepin et Orson son nepveu."

"Helas, sire," dist Valentin, "il en va bien tout au contraire, car perdu avons la journee et y sont tous voz gens demouréz, car le roy Farin, qui la chairge avoit du gait, laissa tous ses gens endormir. Si passerent les crestiens oultre, boutant les

---

[1] *o i* at bottom right corner of 105r. Woodcut of mounted knights entering castle gates.

more brutal and dangerous, and many good knights died on both sides. Nevertheless, the defense mounted by the pagans did them little good, for the city was taken in that assault and all the Saracens were put to the sword without pity or mercy. The Christians entered the city on a Friday, finding incredible riches there, exactly at the hour at which our Lord Jesus Christ suffered death on the cross for us. Then King Pepin had all their tents and pavilions moved into the city, the more securely to rest and refresh themselves.

But now I will cease speaking of Pepin and his army, and will tell you about Valentin, who returned to Brandiffer.

CHAPTER 46

How Valentin returned after the battle to King Brandiffer's encampment before the walls of India, bringing King Murgalent's corpse with him.

After the city of Angory was taken by the Christians and every one of the pagans defeated and killed, Valentin, who had found Murgalent's dead body on the field, called for Pacolet and said to him, "My friend, we must take this body back with us. That way King Brandiffer will more likely believe that we fought together."

"Sire," said Pacolet, "you are perfectly right, and great honor and benefit may come to you that way."

Thus Valentin had the body taken up and placed with great honor in a covered casket. Then they descended to the port, where the boats were waiting, and set sail. But of the one hundred thousand pagans who had come, only ten thousand returned, the others having perished from Pacolet's trick.

Once at sea they sailed so quickly that they soon put in to port near the encampment of King Brandiffer and Lucar's forces. They landed and disembarked the body, loading it on two horses and bearing it with sad faces to Brandiffer's pavilion. At that moment he was playing chess with King Lucar, accompanied by fifteen kings who were watching the game. As soon as Brandiffer saw Valentin, he said to him, "Welcome back, sir knight. Now tell me how the battle went and whether you killed all the Christians and took captive King Pepin and Orson his nephew."

"Alas, sire," said Valentin, "just the opposite, for we lost the day and all your men have remained behind dead, because the man in charge of the night watch, King Farin, allowed all his men to fall asleep. Thus the Christians were able to

feux aux paveillons, tuant et murtrissant a l'espee tous, grans et petis, sans de nul avoir pitié. Et quant je veis que la chose[1] aloit si mal et si mal estoit conduite, je resveillay le plus de gens que je peux pour les mettre a sauveté. Et en ceste bataille est mort vostre oncle Murgalent duquel je ay fait aporter le corps affin qu'il puisse estre mis en sepulture telle qu'il appartient. Et se croire ne me voulez vous pourrez demander aux aultres qui cy sont presens comment il en est alé."

"Sire," dirent les aultres, "il vous dit verité." Lors se leva Brandiffer et comme tout enrragé getta la table auquel il jouoit a terre et tant fust dolent que a peine il ne pouoit mot dire.

"Ha," dist il, "Valentin, je voy bien que tu as fait mes gens mourir."

"Par Dieu," dist Valentin, "c'est mal parlé, car oncques jour de ma vie ne fus tel que vous dictes. Et se nul le vouloit maintenir j'en vouldroye encontre de luy prendre ung champ de bataille."

"Par Mahon," dist Lucar, "de luy il ne s'en fault point doubter. Car se il eust voulu [105verso]faire trahyson il ne fust pas retourné par devers vous."

Adonc se teust atant le roy Brandiffer et moult honnourablement fist enterrer le corps de son oncle. Ceulx de la cité sceurent les nouvelles dont ilz furent moult joyeulx. Adonc le roy d'Inde fist tantost ses gens armer et a quarante mil hommes saillit hors de la cité d'Inde. Et quant Brandiffer oÿt que ilz venoient dessus luy, il fist ses gens armer a toute diligence. Si ne demoura guaires que les batailles s'assemblerent qui moult furent fieres et grandes, tant d'une part que d'aultre. Valentin fut dedens la presse qui de toutes pars fiert et bat tous ceulx qui devant luy se trouvent. Tant fust sa proesse et sa hardiesse crainte et redoubtee qu'il n'y a chevalier si hardy qui de luy ose aprocher. Il entra en la bataille tenant le bran d'acier en sa main si avant qu'i vint au roy d'Inde Major. Et si grant coup luy bailla que de dessus son cheval a terre l'abatit si rudement qu'il n'eust ne force ne puissance de soy relever. Et quant Pacolet veit que il fut bas il ala tantost celle part, luy et plusieurs aultres, si ont prins le roy d'Inde et l'ont rendu a Valentin, lequel le mena au pavillon du roy Brandiffer.

Et quant il sceut les nouvelles que Valentin avoit prins le roy d'Inde, il se escrya moult haultement dessus ses gens. "Or sus!" dist il. "Seigneurs, il n'y a que de bien faire, car au jour d'uy aurons victoire et seigneurie sur noz ennemis. Sy jure mon dieu Mahommet que jamais jour de ma vie au bon chevalier Valentin je ne fauldray ne de corps ne de biens."

Pour ces nouvelles Brandiffer, Lucar et toutes leurs gens prindrent moult grant couraige et se bouterent en la bataille plus fort que devant par telle maniere que plus de trente mille sur les champs demourerent. Et quant le mareschal d'Inde cogneust la perte que ilz avoyent faicte, il fist tantost sonner la retraite pour ses gens recueillir et ralier. Quant Brandiffer[2] et Lucar veirent que ilz se retraioient si les suyvirent de si pres que a l'entree de la cité il y en mourut dix mille. Moult joyeulx estoit Pacolet qui tant de payens veoit mourir, et ne luy chaloit de quelle part la perte deust

---

[1] Text has *hose*.
[2] Text has *bandiffer*.

get past them to set all the tents aflame and put everyone to the sword, both great and small, without pity. And when I saw that matters were going so badly and were so badly conducted, I woke up as many men as I could to get them to safety. And in this battle was killed your uncle Murgalent, whose body I have borne back so that he may be properly buried. And if you do not wish to believe me, you can ask the others present here how they were able to get away."

"Sire," said the others, "he is telling you the truth." Then, like a man enraged, Brandiffer jumped up and knocked over the table on which he had been playing. So bitter was he that he could barely utter a word.

"Ah," he said, "Valentin, I see you have caused the death of my men."

"In God's name," said Valentin, "you speak wrongly, for never a day in my life have I acted as you accuse me. And if anyone were willing to maintain that accusation, I would prove myself on the field of battle against him."

"By Mohammed," said Lucar, "you should not doubt him. For had he wanted to betray you, he never would have returned to you."

Thereupon King Brandiffer fell silent and ordered that his uncle's body be buried with full honors. The people in the besieged city heard the news and were joyful. As a result, the king of India had his men arm themselves, and he set forth from the city of India with forty thousand men. When Brandiffer heard that they were descending upon him, he had his own men arm themselves with great speed. It wasn't long before the battalions were assembled, as large and fierce on one side as on the other. Valentin was within the press, striking and smiting all who stood before him. His prowess and courage were so dreaded and feared that no knight was bold enough to dare approach him. He bore the steel brand in his hand so far forward into the battle that he came upon the king of India Major. He gave him a mighty blow and knocked him off his horse so rudely that the king had neither the force nor the strength to rise again. And when Pacolet saw him down, he and several others rode up, seizing the king of India and rendering him to Valentin, who brought him to King Brandiffer's pavilion.

When he heard the news that Valentin had captured the king of India, he cried out aloud to all his men, "Rally round, my lords!" he said, "we must do well, for today we shall have victory and lordship over our enemies. I swear to my god Mohammed that never a day in my life shall I fail to reward the good knight Valentin, neither in body nor in goods."

Brandiffer, Lucar, and all their men took courage from these tidings, re-entering the battle with greater strength than before and in such numbers that there were more than thirty thousand on the field. And when the marshal of India realized the loss they had suffered, he immediately sounded the retreat to gather and rally his men. When Brandiffer and Lucar saw that they were pulling back, they pursued them so closely that ten thousand died at the entrance to the city. Pacolet was delighted to see so many pagans dying, not caring which side

tourner, mais que luy et Valentin le vaillant chevalier se peussent de leurs mains sauver.

Tant dura la bataille que la nuyt approcha. Brandiffer et Lucar retournerent en leur tentes et pavillons et dirent que on leur menast le roy d'Inde Major, lequel tantost si leur fust presenté. Et quant Lucar le veit il luy a dist tout hault, "Faulx trahystre, or est venu le temps que compte vous me rendrez. Bien pouez estre certain que jamais vous ne me eschapperez, mais je vous feray mourir honteusement."

Bien l'entendit le roy d'Inde que oncques nul mot ne respondit, mais ancores viendra le temps et l'eure que il sera par Pacolet delivré et apres luy livra Bran[106recto]differ[1] en sa subjection, ainsi que apres vous sera declairé.

[CHAPITRE 47]

Comment Valentin oÿt nouvelles de son pere; et comment Pacolet delivra le roy d'Inde par son sort et luy livra Brandiffer a sa voulenté. xlvii. chapitre

A l'eure que le roy Lucar parloit au roy d'Inde, il est arrivé ung messagier lequel apres ce que il l'eust salué il luy a dist, "Treschier sire, je vous aporte nouvelles moult desplaisantes, car sachez que Pepin a prins par force d'armes vostre cité d'Angorie et a mis tout le peuple qui la dedens estoit, hommes et femmes et petis enfans, a feu et a sang sans en avoir pitié."

"Par Mahon," ce dist le roy Brandiffer, "voycy bien mauvaises nouvelles, car ce estoit la plus noble cité qui fust en toute ma terre. Mais puis que ainsi est avenu que j'ay en ma subjection le roy d'Inde, je ay espoir que de brief de mes ennemis je auray vengance." Puis a dist au roy Lucar, "Beau filz, je vous diray que il convient faire—puis que nous avons le roy d'Inde entre noz mains qui tant de dommaige et de villain oultraige nous a fait, je conseille que demain au matin il soit de mort villaine condempné a mourir. Et puis nous irons en Angorie encontre les François qui ma terre degastent et de toutes pars en prendrons vengance, car sachez que dedens Chasteau Fort je tiens en mes prisons l'empereur de Grece et le Verd Chevalier qui nostre loy a delaissé. Si ne me eschapperont jamais que dedens quinze jours je ne les face pendre et estrangler."

Valentin, qui fut la present, entendit bien les nouvelles et moult fust joyeulx de oÿr parler de son pere. Si a fait signe a Pacolet que tantost viendra le temps qu'i luy conviendra jouer de son mestier, puis a part luy dit bassement, "Je prie a Dieu de paradis qu'i vous veulle garder de danger, car jamais jour de ma vie je n'auray en mon cueur liesse tant que je trouve maniere de vous delivrer de prison."

---

[1] *o ii* at bottom right corner of 106r.

they died on, provided that he and Valentin, the valiant knight, could be safe from their hands.

The battle lasted so long that night was falling. Brandiffer and Lucar returned to their tents and pavilions and called for the king of India Major to be brought to them, which was quickly done. And when Lucar saw him he said to him aloud, "False traitor, now the time is come for you to settle accounts with me. You can be certain that you will never escape me before I make you die most ignominiously."

Though the king of India heard him, he made no reply, but the time will come when he will be delivered by Pacolet and Brandiffer given over to him, as will be soon recounted to you.

CHAPTER 47

How Valentin heard news of his father; and how Pacolet freed the king of India with his magic, and delivered Brandiffer up to him to do with as he wished.

Just as King Lucar was speaking to the king of India, a messenger arrived who said to him after a proper greeting, "Gracious sire, I bring you most unpleasant tidings, for you must know that Pepin has taken your city of Angory by force and killed all its inhabitants, men, women, and children, without pity."

"By Mohammed," said King Brandiffer, "here are evil tidings indeed, for it was the noblest city of all my land. But since it has turned out that the king of India is now in my power, I hope soon to be able to take vengeance on my enemies." He turned to King Lucar: "Fair son, I will tell you what you must do—since the king of India, who has caused us so much trouble, is in our hands, I counsel you to condemn him to an ignominious death tomorrow morning. Then we will go to Angory to attack the French who have ravaged my lands, there to take thorough vengeance against them. Know that I hold the emperor of Greece prisoner in Château Fort, as well as the Green Knight who deserted our faith. They will never escape me, for before two weeks are up, I will have them hanged and strangled."

Valentin was there and heard this news, delighted to hear his father mentioned. He motioned to Pacolet that soon he would need to practice his craft, then said softly to himself, "I pray the God of Paradise to keep you from danger, for never a day in my life will my heart find joy until I find a way to free you from prison."

Le roy d'Inde regarda Valentin et dit a part luy, "Mauldite soit l'eure que de mé mains eschapastes, que ne vous feis mourir; pas n'eusse esté en tel dangier comme je suis livré."

Apres ces choses faictes le roy Lucar fist venir cent de ses Sarrasins tous arméz et bien en point et puis leur a dit, "Compaignons, je vous baille cestuy faulx trahystre roy d'Inde. Si pensez de le bien garder autant que vous craingnez de perdre la vie. Puis demain au plus matin quant vous le m'aurez rendu, je le feray mourir et par le col pendre et estrangler."

Les payens et Sarrasins prindrent tantost le roy d'Inde et le mirent en ung pavillon, et la l'ont estaché parmy tout le corps et puis apres luy ont les yeulx bendéz. Il pouoit bien oÿr les jeux, soulas et esbatemens, mais il n'avoit que tristesse[1] et desconfort en son cueur comme celuy qui jamais [106verso]ne pensoit eschapper de mort.

Lors Valentin appella Pacolet et luy a dit, "Amy, je ne cuidoye pas que le roy Brandiffer tenist mon pere en ses prisons, car se je l'eusse sceu, je n'eusse pas mis mon corps en si grandes aventures pour le servir comme je ay fait. Je luy ay esté loyal en toutes ses affaires, mais puis que ainsi va, jamais ne le serviray, mais trouveray voulentiers maniere comment nuire luy pourroye, car je suis petit tenu de servir et faire plaisir a celuy qui sy longuement mon pere tient en sa chartre obscure en moult grant peine et destresse."

"Sire," dist Pacolet, "vous avez bien rayson et cause de luy porter dommaige. Et se vous voulez je vous trouverray bien façon et maniere de delivrer le roy d'Inde la Major[2] et si emmenrra avecques luy le roy Brandiffer. Si croy qu'i le fera mourir honteusement et villainement et a ceste heure la vous en pourrez bien estre vengé. Et par tout pourra seurement vostre oncle, le bon vaillant roy Pepin, tenir la cité d'Angorie et la terre du roy Brandiffer."

"Par ma foy," dist le bon chevalier Valentin, "telle chose vouldroy je bien, et te prie de tout mon cueur et de toute ma puissance que tu faces a ceste heure chose parquoy je puisse le roy Pepin aider et mon pere l'empereur de Grece delivrer."

Quant vint apres soupper les cent Sarrasins, qui le roy de Inde avoient en garde, firent ung grant feu devant leur pavillon auquel il estoit lyé. Et Pacolet qui ne dormoit pas a l'eure pour la nuyt entra dedens leur tente comme celuy qui veult avec eulx veiller et passer le temps. Puis ne demoura pas longuement qu'il getta ung sort par telle maniere que par ung art d'ingromance les fit tous a terre cheoir et les endormit ainsi comme gens mors.

Puis s'en vint au roy de Inde lequel luy deslia les yeulx et le desbenda et luy disoit, "Noble et puissant roy de Inde, prens en moy confort, car je suis ton dieu Mahon qui suis icy du ciel descendu pour toy secourir et delivrer. Tu m'as longuement servy et loyallement honnouré. Si ne te veul pas laysser sans toy donner confort et alegance. Tu t'en iyras en Inde par dedens ton palays sans de nul avoir

---

[1] Text has *tistesse*.
[2] Text has *dinde la ma major*, likely owing to the line break.

For his part, the king of India glared at Valentin and muttered to himself, "Cursed be the hour that I let you get away alive, that I didn't kill you; I wouldn't be caught up in such danger as I am."

After this, King Lucar called for a hundred of his well-armed Saracens, to whom he said, "Friends, I am putting into your keeping this false and treacherous king of India. See that you guard him with a diligence as great as your fear of death. Then tomorrow morning when you bring him to me, I will have him hanged by the neck."

The pagans and Saracens took hold of the king of India, placing him in a tent where they bound his body and blindfolded his eyes. He was able to hear their games and jokes, but his heart was filled with the pain and distress of one who believed himself soon to die.

Then Valentin called for Pacolet and said to him, "Friend, I never imagined that King Brandiffer was holding my father prisoner, for if I had known, I would not have put myself at such risk in his service like this. I have been loyal to him in all his affairs, but as it stands now, I will never serve him. Rather I will find a way to harm him as much as I can, for I am not beholden to serve and please someone who has held my father in a dark prison in great pain and distress for such a long time."

"Sire," said Pacolet, "you have good reason to cause him harm. And if you wish it, I will find a way to deliver the king of India Major, and he will bring back with him King Brandiffer. I believe he will then put him to a shameful and ignominious death, and at that moment you will be well avenged. That way your uncle, the good and valiant King Pepin, will surely be able to keep possession of the city of Angory and the lands of King Brandiffer."

"By my faith," said the good knight Valentin, "I would like that above all things, and I pray you with all my heart to carry out anything that will help King Pepin and deliver my father the emperor of Greece."

After the evening meal, the one hundred Saracens who were guarding the king of India made a great fire in front of their tent where he was being held. And Pacolet, who did not go to sleep that night, entered the tent as if to keep them company and help pass the time. But before long he cast his spell whose magic made them all fall to the ground in a dead sleep.

Then he drew near to the king of India and undid his blindfold, saying to him, "Noble and mighty king of India, take comfort from me, for I am your god Mohammed, come down from the heavens to bring you succor and deliverance. You have served and honored me long and faithfully. Thus I wish to give you comfort and relief, not desert you. You will soon be back in your palace in India without suffering any harm from anyone, for with my mighty powers I have put

dommaige ne encombrier, car par ma haulte puissance j'ay tous ceulx endormy qui te avoient en garde. Et pour mieulx faire ton couraige et ta voulenté tu emmerras le roy Brandiffer qui te tient en prison sans que nulles nouvelles en sache."

"Helas, mon dieu," dit le roy de Inde, "je t'ay bien adouré et de tout mon cueur aymé et chier tenu, quant de ton paradis tu es sy bas descendu pour moy garder et deffendre de mon ennemy mortel. Or cognoy je que tu es vray dieu et tout puissant, quant sur moy tu as voulu monstrer si terribles vertus."

"Roy," ce dist Pacolet, "a moy ayez fiance, car dedens la cité d'Inde la Major seurement et sans danger te retourneray. [107recto]Et[1] si feray pour toy tant que de tes ennemis auras bonne vengeance. Et sur toutes aultres choses croy le conseil de ta femme."

A ces motz le mena Pacolet devers le lit de Brandiffer[2] et tous ceulx de sa garde il fist endormir et cheoir a terre. Puis enchanta Brandiffer tellement que tout incontinent de son lit se leva et en dormant s'est chaussé et vestu en disant au roy de Inde, "Vous soyez le bien arrivé, car avec vous m'en veul aler en vostre palays, et du tout acomplir a faire vostre voulenté."

Adonc le roy de Inde se getta a genoulx en disant, "Souverain dieu, icy pour moy monstré avez vostre grant divinité et souverain miracle dont de tout mon cueur et de toute ma force et puissance je vous rens graces et mercys."

A celle heure amena Pacolet deux moult fort beaulx chevaulx, puis fist monter le roy de Inde et Brandiffer dessus l'ung des chevaulx. Et puis Pacolet dist, "Tenez bien Brandiffer parmy le corps et je monteray sur cestui aultre cheval et je vous emmerray a la cité de Inde."

En ce point chevaulcherent jusques aux portes de la cité et la print Pacolet congié.

"Mahon," dist le roy de Inde, "de tresbon cueur vous rens graces et mercys, et si vous recommande mon ame quant du corps partira."

"Roy," ce dist Pacolet, "je ne vous fauldray pas, car se elle vient en mes mains elle n'aura pas failly a maistre."

Ainsi s'en ala Pacolet et le roy de Inde qui fut aux portes haultement s'escrya ay gayt, "Ouvrez tantost la porte, car je suis vostre[3] roy que Mahon a delivré!" Quant le gayt l'entendit, tantost coururent devers le lieutenant et les nouvelles luy compterent. Puis alerent tantost au palais et firent les barons lever, et a puissance de torches alerent vers la porte. Le roy entra dedens et ala devers son palays.

Et quant Rozemonde l'aperceut elle luy a dist, "Ha! chier sire, bien soyez vous venu. Or me dites comment vous avez ainsy mon pere amené. La paix est elle faicte entre vous et luy?"

"Nennil," ce dist le roy, "la chose va bien aultrement, car ceste nuyt en mon dormant mon dieu Mahon a moy s'est apparu en chair et en sang. Lequel par ses

---

[1] *o iii* at bottom right corner of 107r.
[2] Text has *brandifer*.
[3] Text has *vostrre*.

all those who guarded you to sleep. And to better satisfy your desire, you will abduct King Brandiffer, who now holds you prisoner, without his knowing what is happening."

"Ah, my god," said the king of India, "I must indeed have adored you and loved and cherished you with all my heart, seeing that you would descend from your paradise to watch over and defend me from my mortal enemy. Now I know for sure that you are the true and all-powerful god, since you unveil to me such awe-inspiring virtues."

"King," said Pacolet, "have confidence in me, for I will return you safely and without danger to the city of India Major. And I will arrange things for you so that you will have proper vengeance against your enemies. But above all things, believe your wife's counsel."

With these words Pacolet led him to Brandiffer's bed, and caused his entire watch to fall to the ground asleep. Then he charmed Brandiffer so that he rose immediately from his bed and, still fully asleep, dressed himself, put on his shoes, and said to the king of India, "Welcome, for I will go with you to your palace and do as you will."

Thereupon the king of India threw himself on his knees, saying, "Sovereign god, you have revealed to me both your exalted divinity and a matchless miracle, for which I render you praise and thanks with all my heart and soul."

At that moment Pacolet brought forward two well-made horses, and settled the king of India and Brandiffer on one of them. Then Pacolet said, "Hold fast to Brandiffer by the waist, and I will ride this other horse and lead you to the city of India."

Thus did they ride up to the gates of the city where Pacolet took his leave.

"Mohammed," said the king of India, "again I thank you with all my heart, and commend my soul to you for when it will leave my body."

"King," said Pacolet, "I will not fail you, for if it comes into my hands, it will have a good master."

At that point Pacolet departed, and the king of India cried aloud to the watch at the gates, "Quick, open the gate, for I am your king, whom Mohammed has delivered!" When the watchmen heard him, they ran straightway to the lieutenant and told him the news. Then they rushed to the palace to awaken the barons, who came to the gate with torches. The king entered and proceeded to his palace.

When Rozemonde saw him, she said to him, "Oh, my cherished lord, you are indeed welcome. Now tell me how it came to be that you have brought my father. Has peace been made between you and him?"

"Not at all," said the king, "things went quite differently, for while I was sleeping, Mohammed himself appeared before me in flesh and blood. He not

sainctes vertus et divine puissance m'a delivré des mains de mes ennemis et icy m'a amené et vostre pere baillé."

Et icy faillit le sort et Brandiffer s'esveilla et commença moult effroyement a regarder. Et puis a dist au roy de Inde, "Dont peult estre ceste nouvelle et comment suis je icy venu? Je croy que le[1] dyable d'enfer m'a aporté en ce lieu."

"Non," a dist le roy de Inde, "le dyable n'y a point ouvré, mais a esté le puissant dieu Mahon lequel ceste nuyt a moy s'est apparu, et vous et moy nous a en ceste place aportéz. Sy croy que c'est sa voulenté et son plaisir que vous et moy d'ores en avant faisons bonne paix et soyons bons amis ensemble."

"Par ma loy," dist Brandiffer, "j'aymeroye plus chier [107verso]mourir, car de vostre acointance je ne veul point. Si me laissez aler par devers mon ost ainsi comme j'estoye quant m'avez amené."

"Brandiffer," ce dist le roy de Inde, "ce ne feray je point. Mais puys que Mahon vous a icy aporté je me fie en sa grace de la chose parfaire."

Ainsi est Brandiffer dedens la cité de Inde en dueil et en soussy trop grant de ce que il se voit prins et ne peult a sa voulenté en son ost retourner. Et les cent Sarrasins qui garder le devoyent sont ancores en la tente sur la terre endormis. Or fut le jour venu que le roy Lucar fut levé, si ala tantost en la tente ou il avoit laissé en garde le roy d'Inde. Et quant les payens le veirent qui adonc esveilléz estoient ilz s'escrierent tout hault, "Helas! sire, roy Lucar, nous sommes enchantéz et faulcement trahys, car en ceste nuyt nous avons perdu le roy d'Inde!"

"Ha! faulces gens," dit Lucar, "je cognoy bien comment il en va. Vous estes tous ivres et puis estes tous sur la terre endormis. Je jure a Mahon que le vin que vous avez beu vous sera vendu chier." Adonc les fist tous prendre et a chevaulx atacher et trainer si rudement que de leurs ventres firent saillir les boyaulx et puis les fist tous pendre. De laquelle chose Valentin et Pacolet furent moult joyeulx, car grant plaisir prenoyent a veoir payens destruire et mourir.

Et Valentin appella Pacolet et luy a dit, "Amy, jamais mon cueur n'aura joye tant que je auray trouvé mon pere, l'empereur de Grece, lequel Brandiffer tient en prison dedens Chasteau Fort. Si ne veul plus icy demourer, mais je suis deliberé de laisser ceste gent Sarrasine laquelle j'ay servy assez en espoir de avoir nouvelles de m'amye la belle Esclarmonde. Et croy qu'elle soit morte—Dieu luy face pardon!—pourquoy je m'en veul aler devers le roy Pepin, lequel est en Angorie, pour luy dire et compter les nouvelles comment le roy Brandiffer tient en ses prisons l'empereur mon pere avec le Verd Chevalier."

"C'est bien dit," ce dist Pacolet, "car nous irons apres au Chasteau Fort ou l'empereur est emprisonné. Et je pense jouer de tel art que le chasteau je ouverray et vostre pere metteray hors." Ainsi fut le conseil prins et la chose parfaicte. Valentin et ses gens sans prendre nul congé partirent de l'ost et monterent sur la mer pour leur voyage parfaire et leur entreprinse du tout acomplir.

---

[1] Text has *lo*.

only delivered me from the hands of my enemies through his holy virtues and divine might, but he also placed your father in my power and brought me here."

At that moment the spell broke, and Brandiffer woke up and began looking around fearfully. Then he said to the king of India, "What is going on and how have I come to be here? It must have been a devil from hell who brought me to this place."

"No," said the king of India, "the devil had nothing to do with this, rather it was the almighty god Mohammed who appeared before me this night and brought both of us, you and me, to this place. I believe he wants us to make peace and be true friends and allies from this time forth."

"By my faith," said Brandiffer, "I would rather die, for I have no desire whatsoever for your friendship. Let me return to my camp where I was when you led me away."

"Brandiffer," said the king of India, "that I will not do. However, since Mohammed has brought you here, I will trust in his wisdom to resolve this matter."

Thus Brandiffer was captive in the city of India, feeling mournful and anxious about not being able to return as he wished to his camp. Meanwhile, the hundred Saracens who were supposed to keep watch over the king of India were still in the tent asleep on the ground. Then day broke and King Lucar arose, going straightway to the tent where he had left the king of India under guard. But when the pagans, who were just waking up, saw him, they cried aloud, "Alas! sire, King Lucar, we have been bewitched and falsely betrayed, for the king of India is gone!"

"Ha! false men!" said Lucar, "I can see exactly how things go. All of you got drunk and so every one of you fell asleep. I swear to Mohammed that the wine you have drunk will have been sold to you dearly." Thereupon he ordered them seized, and had them attached to horses and dragged so roughly that their intestines burst out of their bellies, after which they were hanged. Valentin and Pacolet were both glad to see this, for they took great pleasure in seeing pagans destroy and kill one another.

Then Valentin called for Pacolet and said, "Friend, my heart will never be happy until I find my father the emperor of Greece whom Brandiffer holds in his prison in Château Fort. I don't want to remain here any longer, rather I am determined to leave these Saracens whom I have served long enough in the hope of having news of my beloved, the fair Esclarmonde. I believe she must be dead — may God grant her pardon! — for which reason I wish to return to King Pepin in Angory, in order to report to him that King Brandiffer is holding my father the emperor and the Green Knight in his prison."

"A good idea," said Pacolet, "for after that we will go to Château Fort where the emperor is imprisoned. I think I can use my craft to open the castle and rescue your father." Thus did they agree. Without taking leave of anyone, Valentin and his men left the camp and set sail on the sea so as to make their journey and carry out their plan.

[CHAPITRE 48]

Comment Hauffroy et Henry trahyrent leur pere le roy Pepin et les douze pers de France. xlviii. cha[pitre]

Vous avez bien oÿ dire et racompter comment le roy Pepin print la cité d'Angorie. Si vous veul dire et declairer la grant trahyson de ses deux filz faulcement engendréz Hauffroy et Henry. Avint en une nuyt que le roy, estant en ladite cité d'Angorie en son lit couché, songa ung songe merveilleux. Car en dor[108recto]mant[1] luy fut vray avis qu'i veoit clerement les trois clouz dont Nostre Seigneur fut en la croix ataché et la lance de quoy il fust ou costé feru. Puis luy sembloit qu'i veoit ung saint prestre qui au pres du Saint Sepulchre devant luy la messe chantoit. Et luy avint ceste vision par trois fois la nuit continuellement dont moult fust esmerveillé.

Et quant vint vers le matin que le roy pour cestuy songe et pour ceste vision assembla ses barons et tout ainsi que il avoit songé leur declaira, puis leur a dit, "Seigneurs, je ne sçay que il en aviendra, mais puis que telle vision par trois foys m'est avenue, je ne croy point que soit songe abusant. Je suis deliberé devant que retourner en France de aler veoir et viseter le tresdigne et Sainct Sepulchre de nostre redempteur et sauveur Jesus avec les aultres sains lieux qui sont tant hors que dedens la cité de Jherusalem, ausquelz pour chascun jour en l'onneur et reverence de nostre createur et de sa saincte passion sont plusieurs par grans pardons et indulgences donnéz et ottroyéz. Si me veullez respondre se il y a nul de vous qui ait voulenté ou devocion du saint voyaige et pelerinaige en ma compaignie parfaire."

Quant les seigneurs, barons et chevaliers de la court du roy Pepin oÿrent et entendirent le couraige et la devocion du vaillant roy Pepin moult fort furent esmerveilléz; si furent plusieurs deliberéz de aler avec le roy Pepin et l'acompaigner au saint voyaige faire.

Et entre les aultres parla premier Orson et a dit, "Chier sire, je veul se c'est vostre plaisir avec vous aler."

"Et aussi veul je moy," ce dit Millon d'Angler.

Lors pareillement les douze pers de France et disoient en ceste maniere, "Chier et redoubté sire, puis que c'est vostre plaisir de vostre voyage faire et acomplir, nous sommes deliberéz de acompaigner vostre haulte majesté sans de riens vous faulcer, et de prendre chascun l'escharppe et le bourdon."

Le roy tous les mercya qui de leur bonne voulenté fust moult fort resjoÿ. Et alors appella Hauffroy et luy a dist, "Hauffroy, vous sçavez que vous estes mon filz, mais tellement fustes de moy engendré que vous ne vostre frere n'avez en mon royaulme de France vaillant ung pied de terre. Si veul que vous demourez icy pour ceste terre garder et monstrez que vous estes vaillant et loyal, car se bien vous portez

---

[1] *o iiii* at bottom right corner of 108r.

CHAPTER 48

How Hauffroy and Henry betrayed their father King Pepin and the Twelve Peers of France.

You have already heard the tale of how King Pepin took the city of Angory. Now I wish to tell you about the terrible treachery carried out by his two misbegotten sons, Hauffroy and Henry. It happened one night while the king was sleeping in his bed in the city of Angory that he dreamed an extraordinary dream. It seemed to him as he slept that he could see, as clear as day, the three nails with which Our Lord was fastened to the cross and the lance with which he was wounded in his side. Then it seemed to him that he saw a holy priest chanting mass in front of him near the Holy Sepulcher. And this vision came to him three times during that night, for which he was heartily amazed.

Because of this dream vision, the king assembled together all his barons as soon as morning broke in order to retell his dream; then he said to them, "My lords, I have no idea what will come of it, but since the vision came to me three times, I do not believe it to be a false one. I have decided that, before returning to France, I will go visit the most Holy Sepulcher of our redeemer and savior Jesus, as well as the other holy sites both in the city of Jerusalem and nearby, where pardons and indulgences are granted every day in honor of our creator and his holy passion. Tell me whether any of you have the desire and devotion to go on this holy pilgrimage in my company."

When the lords, barons, and knights of King Pepin's court heard the valiant King Pepin's devoted desire, they were all amazed; many of them decided right away to go with King Pepin to accompany him on this holy voyage.

Of them all, Orson was the first to speak, and he said, "Dear sire, if it your pleasure, I wish to go with you."

"And so do I," said Millon d'Angler.

The Twelve Peers of France echoed them, saying in the following manner, "Revered and respected sire, since it is your pleasure to undertake this journey, we are determined, each of us, not to fail you, but to take the pilgrim's purse and staff to accompany your majesty."

Their willingness gladdened the king's heart, and he thanked them for it. Then he called for Hauffroy and said to him, "Hauffroy, you know that you are my son, but you were begotten in such a way that neither you nor your brother possess even a foot of land in the kingdom of France. Thus I want you to stay here to guard this land and to show that you are valiant and loyal, for if you behave

je suis deliberé de vous donner la terre et le royaulme d'Angorie que sy loyallement ay conquis. Et si vous dy bien et fay sçavoir que le roy Brandiffer a une fille sur toutes les aultres belle et gracieuse laquelle je vous feray donner pour femme. Car nostre intencion est de celle conquerir devant que nous retournons en France et de luy faire prendre nostre creance. Et a Henry je luy conquerray ung aultre royaulme qui sera pour luy; si pensez tous deux de bien faire. Et si feray se Dieu plaist en maniere que devant [108verso]ma mort mes enfans seront deuement et suffisamment asignéz et que vous n'aurez cause ne rayson d'avoir debat ensemble."

"Sire," ce dist Hauffroy,[1] "de tant je vous mercye." Puis s'est tiré a part et a dit bassement, "Par Dieu, roy Pepin, j'ay bien vostre cas entendu, car vous n'avez pas intencion ne voulenté que jamais au royaulme de France ay riens. Mais se je devoye renoncer Jesus et sa saincte mere je feray en telle façon et maniere que les choses se porteront a la reverse et au contraire de vostre vouloir." Lors appella Henry et luy a dist, "Beau frere, bien avez oÿ et entendu les parolles du roy Pepin. Il nous veult bailler et assigner noz vies sur royaulmes et terres estranges tout a son appetit et ainsi que ceulx qui ne sont pas dignes de estre appelléz ses enfans. Or cognoy je bien que il a intencion que Charlot[2] soit seul roy de France et que nous n'y ayons riens. Et pour tant se croyre vous me voulez jamais Pepin ne retournera en France que nous ne le façons mourir par les mains des payens. Puis serons roy de France et empereur de romme sans nul contredit, car chose n'y a en celuy monde de quoy j'aye telle voulenté."

"Frere," ce dit Henry, "vous dites saigement. Mais bien il vous fauldroit aviser comment telle chose pourroit estre acomplie et parfaicte."

"Henry," ce dist Hauffroy, "je vous diray comment. Il me fault aler vers le roy Brandiffer et acorder a luy de ceste chose par ainsy que il me donnera sa fille Galasie, et je luy diray les nouvelles comment le roy Pepin et les douze pers vont au Sainct Sepulchre, et comment ilz pourront estre legierement prins, car ilz iront sans armes et peu de compaignie. Et je suis bien certain que les payens seront bien joyeulx de ces nouvelles et se ainsi ne sont prins jamais ne le seront."

"Par Dieu, Hauffroy," ce dist Henry, "vous en dictes la verité. Or vous fault il aler vers Inde la Major et la vous trouverrez le roy Lucar et le roy Brandiffer lesquelz tiennent la cité assiegee. Sy leur pourrez dire et declairer vostre couraige. Et je yray avec le roy en voyaige affin que plus secretement nostre fait si soit couvert et gayt; de trahyson ne se puisse si tost cognoystre."

"C'est bien dit," ce dit Hauffroy, "si me laissez parfaire et acomplir, car jamais je n'auray bon repos tant que icy parfaice ceste besongne." Et ainsy fut la trahyson par les deux freres mauldis et desloyaulx Hauffroy et Henry faicte et composee contre leur propre pere pour sa mort procurer. Helas! ilz monstrerent bien que mal furent engendréz et que de faulce et desloyalle generacion vindrent,

---

[1] Text has *huffroy*.

[2] Text has *charloit*, the only example of such a spelling in the many instances of his name.

well, I have decided to give you the land and kingdom of Angory that I have rightly won. Moreover, I want you to know that King Brandiffer has a daughter, more beautiful and gracious than any other woman, whom I will give you as wife. For our plan is to conquer her before we return to France and to convert her to our faith. As for Henry, I will conquer another kingdom that will be his, so both of you should make an effort to excel. I will do all this, God willing, so that before my death my children will all be properly and sufficiently provided for and there will be no reason for quarrels among you."

"Sire," said Hauffroy, "for all this I thank you." Then he drew back and said softly to himself, "By God, King Pepin, I heard exactly what you said, and it is clear you have no intention that I ever have any part of the kingdom of France. However, even if I have to renounce Jesus and His holy mother, I will do it so that matters come out contrary to your desire." Then he called for Henry and told him, "Fair brother, you have surely heard the words of King Pepin. He wants to give us foreign lands and make us spend our lives in faraway kingdoms just as he likes, treating us as if we are unworthy to be called his children. It is absolutely clear to me that he intends little Charles to be sole ruler in France, and that we will have nothing there. However, if you are willing to accept what I propose, Pepin will never return to France, for we will make sure he dies at the hands of the pagans. Then we will be king of France and emperor of Rome without anyone to contradict us, for there is nothing I want so much in the world."

"Brother," said Henry, "you speak wisely. But you had better explain how such a thing can be accomplished."

"Henry," said Hauffroy, "I will tell you how. I need to go see King Brandiffer to arrange an accord with him by which he will give me his daughter Galasie and I will give him the information about King Pepin and the Twelve Peers going to the Holy Sepulcher and how they may be easily captured, for they will be traveling without weapons and with little company. And I am certain the pagans will be happy to hear this news, for if they cannot manage to capture them this way, they will never do it."

"By God, Hauffroy," said Henry, "what you say is true. You should go to India Major to find King Lucar and King Brandiffer, who are laying siege to the city. There you can explain to them what you want to do. In the meantime I will travel with the king so that he will have no idea we are plotting treason, and thus you can carry out our plan more secretly and securely."

"Well said," said Hauffroy, "let me take care of this, for I will never have rest until I have accomplished this goal." And thus was treason concocted and plotted out by the two cursed and faithless brothers, Hauffroy and Henry, whose purpose was to cause the death of their own father. Alas! they demonstrated that

quant celuy vouloyent faire mourir qui leur pere estoit et qui de toute sa force et puissance prenoit peine, travail et soussy de leur vies assigner et de terres leur conquerir de toute sa force et puissance.

    Or sont le roy Pepin et les douze pers de France, qui [109recto]de nulle trahyson ne se doubtoient, dedens la mer entréz[1] pour faire et acomplir leur pelerinaige. Henry est avec eulx entré pour mieulx couvrir leur trahyson, et Hauffroy son frere s'en ala devers Inde pour trouver le roy Brandiffer qui le siege y avoit mis avec le roy Lucar.

    Or est vray que durant celuy temps entre eulx avoient tresves, car la estoit arrivé le caliphe de Bandas qui ung moys de tresves leur fist l'ung a l'autre donner sur la peine que celuy que premier les romperoit perderoit la moytié de sa terre. Et durant celuy moys le caliphe assembla et fist en ung jour certain venir et assembler Brandiffer, Lucar et le roy de Inde. Et quant ilz furent assembléz l'ung devant l'autre le caliphe de Bandas parla en ceste maniere, "Seigneurs, vous sçavez et cognoissez clerement comment noz mortelz et anciens ennemis les faulx crestiens se sont efforcéz et plus grandement s'efforcent de jour en jour de nous abatre et tout nostre pays destruyre. Et qu'i soit vray, ilz ont ja prins et gaigné toute la terre d'Angorie qui est a nostre grant prejudice et dommaige. Or ne pouez vous aler a l'encontre de eulx durant la guerre de entre vous qui trop grandement nous empesche. Si vous diray quelle chose vous ferez—se mon conseil vous voulez croire, jamais les crestiens ne passeront plus avant ne si ne retourneront plus en leur pays. Je vous conseille que l'ung a l'autre vous pardonnez le maltalent de tout le temps passé. Il est vray que le roy de Inde si fist jadis vostre pere tuer et murtrir honteusement et bien cause en avoit, car a son oncle vostre pere Trompart avoit osté la teste.[2] Or prenez que ce soit mort contre mort, et puis apres le roy de Inde deliverra le roy Brandiffer lequel Mahon luy a baillé. Et au regard de vostre femme la belle et plaisante Rozemonde, elle sera amenee par devers vous et par devers le roy de Inde, et celluy que elle vouldra prendre et eslire sera pour elle, et nul du contraire ne luy pourra dire, mais luy sera tout le temps passé pardonné de toutes ces choses parfaire et de iceluy appointement tenir et acomplir."

    En la forme dessudicte furent tous les seigneurs, roys et barons contens. Lors fut tantost la belle et plaisante Rozemonde amenee devant Lucar et devant le roy de Inde, et luy fut toute la chose declairee comment il avoit esté ordonné. Et quant le caliphe eust parlé a la dame, sans grant avis prendre, elle s'en ala devers le roy de Inde et a luy se rendit, dont Lucar en fut au cueur dolent et courroucé bien amerement. Mais pour l'amour du caliphe aultre chose il n'en fist, car ledit caliphe en ceste paix faisant sa fille luy donna pour femme et espouse. Ainsi fut d'une part et d'aultre le appointement fait et la paix cryee.

---

[1] Text has *entrerent*.
[2] It must be assumed that this is addressed to Lucar.

they were indeed misbegotten, springing forth from falseness and disloyalty, seeing that the one they wished to kill was their father who was taking great pains and making every effort to provide for them and conquer them lands.

Now King Pepin and the Twelve Peers of France, who suspected no treachery whatsoever, left by sea to begin their pilgrimage. Henry set sail with them, the better to cover up their treachery, while Hauffroy his brother set off for India to find King Brandiffer who had besieged that place with King Lucar.

As it turns out, that was the time a truce was called between them, for the caliph of Bandas had arrived and made them agree to a month's truce on pain of losing half one's land for being the first to break the truce. During that month, the caliph fixed a day to assemble together Brandiffer, Lucar, and the king of India. And when they were all together, the caliph of Bandas spoke in the following manner: "My lords, you are most certainly aware how our mortal enemies, the false Christians, have tried and continue to try every day to strike us down and destroy us. And the proof of it is that already we have seen how they have taken and conquered all the country of Angory, to our great harm. Now there is no way you can take up the fight against them while there is this war between you that hurts our effort enormously. Thus I will tell you what you shall do — if you are willing to accept my counsel, the Christians not only will make no further advances, they will never return to their own lands. I advise you to forgive each other's past animosity. It is true that the king of India killed your father shamefully, but he had good cause to do so, for your father Trompart had beheaded his uncle. Accept it as one death for another, and then the king of India will free King Brandiffer whom Mohammed delivered up to him. As for your wife, the fair and pleasing Rozemonde, she shall be brought before you and the king of India, and the one whom she chooses shall be her husband, and no one shall contradict her decision, rather everything done in the past shall be forgiven in order to settle this matter for once and for all."

All the lords, kings, and barons were content to accept this settlement. Then the fair and pleasing Rozemonde was immediately brought forth in the presence of Lucar and the king of India, and everything that had been settled was explained to her. And once the caliph had told the lady everything, without asking for any counsel, she went directly to the king of India, giving herself to him, for which Lucar was sorrowful and deeply bitter in his heart. But out of respect for the caliph, he did nothing, and the caliph, as part of the peace accord, granted him his own daughter as wife. Thus peace was concluded and announced by all sides.

Si vous laisseray a parler de ceste [109verso]matiere et vous parleray de Hauffroy qui descendit de la mer et en celuy propre jour arriva en l'ost du roy Lucar et de Brandiffer.

[CHAPITRE 49]

Comment Hauffroy pour sa trahyson parfaire arriva devant Brandiffer et Lucar, et comment par sa trahison luy propre fut deceu. xlix. cha[pitre]

En[1] celuy propre jour que par le[2] caliphe de Bandas la paix fut ainsi faicte dont icy fait mencion, Hauffroy perseverant en sa malice arriva en l'ost de Lucar et de Brandiffer. Si vint tantost vers le pavillon et demanda aux gardes lequel estoit Lucar et lequel Brandiffer. Et il luy furent tantost monstréz et il les salua haultement. Puis parla Brandiffer disant, "Quelle chose vous demandez et qui deça vous amaine?"

"Sire," dist Hauffroy, "la chose qui devers vous m'amaine n'est pas a dire devant tant de gens." Dont se tirerent a part Brandiffer, Lucar et Hauffroy et avec ceulx le caliphe Bandas.

Lors leur dist Hauffroy, "Seigneurs, escoutez moy parler s'i vous plaist, car pour vostre proffit et grant honneur je suis icy venu. Sachez que je suis filz au roy Pepin de France qui tant est puissant et renommé. Si ay oÿ dire que vous avez une fille laquelle sur toutes les aultres est doulce, belle et plaisante. Si vous fay assavoir que se vous la me voulez donner a femme je vous enseigneray maniere et façon comment vous pourrez prendre et avoir en vostre subjection mon pere le roy Pepin et les douze pers de France qui tant vous ont de dommaige porté. Car sachez que ilz sont partis en habit de pelerin premierement vestus et acompaignéz pour aler en Hierusalem[3] pour le Sainct Sepulchre viseter, et la vous les trouverrez sans grande compaignie."

"Par Mahon," dit Brandiffer, "vous parlez tresnotablement et pour vostre bonne entreprinse je suis content de vous donner ma fille Galasie laquelle a nul homme jamais je ne voulu promettre. Mais une chose y a laquelle je vous diray—c'est que vous renoyrez Jesus."

"Oy," ce dit Hauffroy, "Jesus et sa loy je renonce, car jamais je ne l'aimay trop."

Quant le roy veit et cogneut la faulce trahison de Haufroi, qui son pere vouloit vendre et sa loy renoncer, il s'en ala ung peu a part en conseil, appela Lucar et le caliphe de Bandas, puis leur a dit, "Seigneurs, or pouez vous cognoistre clerement la grande trahyson de celluy mauldit et desloyal homme qui ma fille

---

[1] Woodcut of king and attendants conferring. Repeat of woodcut on 13r and 60v.
[2] Text has *la*.
[3] Text has *hierusalez*.

Now I will leave off speaking of these matters to tell you about Hauffroy, who set sail and that same day arrived in the camp of Lucar and Brandiffer.

CHAPTER 49

How Hauffroy came to Brandiffer and Lucar to carry out his treason; and how by his treachery he was himself deceived.

On the very same day that the caliph of Bandas concluded the peace, as recounted above, Hauffroy, persevering in his evil, arrived at the camp of Lucar and Brandiffer. He came at once to the pavilion and asked the guards which one was Lucar and which one Brandiffer. They were pointed out to him, and he greeted them respectfully. Then Brandiffer spoke up saying, "What are you seeking and what brings you here?"

"Sire," said Hauffroy, "the thing that brings me to you is not something I can speak of in front of so many people." So Brandiffer, Lucar, and Hauffroy drew off to the side a little, along with the caliph of Bandas.

Then Hauffroy said to them, "My lords, please listen to me, for my coming here is to your great profit and honor. Know that I am the son of King Pepin of France, who is powerful and renowned. I have heard it said that you have a daughter more beautiful, sweet, and pleasing than any woman alive. I propose that, if you are willing to give her to me as wife, I will instruct you as to how you may seize and take into your power my father King Pepin and the Twelve Peers of France, who have caused you so much harm. Know that they have left for Jerusalem, already in the dress and manner of traveling pilgrims, in order to visit the Holy Sepulcher, and there you will find them without great company."

"By Mohammed," said Brandiffer, "what you say is very interesting, and for your pains I am happy to give you my daughter Galasie, whom I have never been willing to promise to any man. But there is one condition I set to this deal—you must renounce Jesus."

"I will," said Hauffroy, "I renounce Jesus and His religion, for I never loved Him all that much."

When the king saw Hauffroy's perfidy and realized that he was willing to sell his own father and renounce his faith, he drew off a little to take counsel with Lucar and the caliph of Bandas, saying to them, "My lords, you see how clearly this man who asks for my daughter is a damnable and faithless traitor. I have no reason

demande. Bien peu me deveroye en luy fier quant le propre [110recto]pere qui l'a engendré il veult trahir et mettre en noz mains avec les douze pers de France. Si ameroye plus chier ma fille faire mourir de mort amere et honteuse que de la donner a tel homme qui tant a le cueur faulx, trahystre et desloyal. Nonpourtant convient il trouver maniere de aler en Hierusalem et de maintenir cestuy homme et pourrons de legier avoir a nostre voulenté le roy Pepin de France et les douze pers. Et se nous les avons, bien pourrons seurement dire que de crestienté aurons toute la fleur et de nul n'aurons doubte ne crainte. Et pour mieulx mener ceste besongne a fin, je feray mener a ma fille ce trahystre qui ceans est, et telle lettre je luy envoyeray que tout aussitost qu'il sera par devers elle, elle en sa chartre obscure et parfonde le fera mettre et emprisonner."

A ces motz appella Hauffroy. "Sus, beau sire, moult suis joyeulx de vostre venue. Or entendez que vous ferez—vous irez devers ma fille qui est au Chasteau Fort et vous presenterez de par moy et la vous passerez le temps avec elle jusques a tant que plus a plain sache nouvelles[1] de vostre fait. Puis vous feray ma fille espouser et de ma terre vous donneray a si grant largesse et suffisance que de tout vostre lignaige vous serez le plus heureux."

"Sire," dist Hauffroy, "je vous remercye grandement de vostre bonne voulenté."

Adonc Brandiffer fit tantost habiller cent Sarrasins pour Hauffroy mener a Chasteau Fort. Puis fist escripre une lettre en laquelle estoit contenue la trahyson, et en celle lettre mandoit a sa fille Galasie que elle le feist bouter en la plus obscure prison et chartre qui soit en son chasteau tant qu'i la demandast. Et quant la lettre fut escripte il la clouÿt et la sela de son seel, puis la bailla a Hauffroy et luy a dist, "Chier amy, vous irez devers ma fille ainsi que vous ay dit. Et affin que mieulx elle vous croye vous luy porterez ceste lettre par laquelle je me recommande a elle."

"Sire," dist Hauffroy, "c'est moult bien avisé." Ainsi a prins la lettre et du roy a prins congé. A chemin se sont mis et ou port sont aléz ou sur mer sont montéz. Le vent entra ès voilles et si bien nagerent que dedens brief terme ilz veirent Chasteau Fort ou estoit Galasie qui dessus tous chasteaux estoit beau, fort et plaisant a regarder.

Ilz arriverent au port et prindrent terre assés pres du chasteau. Et quant ilz furent descendus ilz se sont mis a chemin pour aler au chasteau. Et tantost qu'ilz furent devant les portes le portier leur escrya, "Seigneurs, vous ne irez non plus avant car ceans ne peult nul entrer sans certaines enseignes."

"Portier," ce dit Hauffroy, "dites a la dame que nous luy dirons si bonnes enseignes que tost nous cognoisterra."

Le portier monta au chastel et trouva la dame a table assisse et le chastellain qui devant elle servoit. "Dame," dit le portier, "la hors a je ne sçay quelles

---

[1] Text has *nouuvelles*.

to trust him, seeing that he is willing to betray the very father who begot him, and put into our hands the Twelve Peers of France. I would rather have my daughter put to a bitter and shameful death than give her to such a man, one with a false, faithless, and treasonous heart. Nevertheless, it is a good idea to find a way to go to Jerusalem while keeping this man here; it will be easy to seize King Pepin of France and the Twelve Peers and have them in our power. And if we do indeed get hold of them, we will be able to say that we detain the entire flower of Christendom and will need fear no one. And the better to bring this plan to fruition, I will have this traitor brought to my daughter, sending such a letter to her that, as soon as he arrives, she will imprison him in her deepest, darkest dungeon."

After this he called Hauffroy over. "Well, fair sir, I am very happy you have come. Now listen to what you shall do—you will go to my daughter at Château Fort, and you will present yourself in my name, and there you will pass some time with her until I know more about your deeds. Then I will marry my daughter to you and will give you so generously of my land that you will be the happiest of all your lineage."

"Sire," said Hauffroy, "I thank you most heartily for your good will."

Thereupon Brandiffer readied a hundred Saracens to conduct Hauffroy to Château Fort. Next he had a letter written that explained the plot, and this letter directed his daughter Galasie to throw Hauffroy into the darkest dungeon in her castle for as long as he wanted. Once the letter was written, he closed it and sealed it with his own seal, then gave it to Hauffroy, saying, "Dear friend, you will go to my daughter as I explained to you. And so that she will believe what you say, you will bring her this letter in which I commend myself to her."

"Sire," said Hauffroy, "that is a wise move." Thus he took the letter and took his leave of the king. They set out on the road to the port where they embarked and set sail. The wind filled the sails, and they traveled so quickly that before long they saw Château Fort where Galasie lived and which was of all castles the handsomest, strongest, and most pleasing to look at.

They came to the port and landed rather close to the castle. After disembarking, they set out for the castle. As soon as they stood before the gates, the porter cried out to them, "My lords, you will go no further, for no one may enter without proof of having been sent."

"Gatekeeper," said Hauffroy, "tell the lady we will furnish her proper proof by which she will know us."

The gatekeeper mounted up to the castle and found the lady seated at table where the castellan was serving her meal. "Lady," said the porter, "outside there

gens qui ceans veullent entrer. Si me semble qu'i soient[1] [110verso]a vostre pere Brandiffer."

"Chastellain," dist la dame, "alez y tost, car icy grant desir ay d'oÿr de mon pere parler."

Le chastellain descendit, lequel les cogneut et tantost qu'il veit que ilz estoient de par Brandiffer i enchaina les deux lyons qui l'entree gardoient, puis print les clefz et les portes ouvrit. Les Sarrasins entrerent dedens et menoient Hauffroy qui bien pensoit et cuidoit a son honneur et grant proffit estre venu. Mais il luy voulsist mieulx que il eust gardé la terre d'Angorie comme Pepin luy avoit dit et commandé, car de sa trahyson se trouva trahy et en fut dolent et courroucé comme rayson doit estre, car chose mal commencee ne peult a bonne fin venir.

[CHAPITRE 50]

Comment la belle Galasie apres que elle cogneust la faulceté et trahison de Hauffroy elle le fist mettre en ses prisons moult estroitement. l. cha[pitre]

Quant Hauffroy fust entré ou chasteau il se va presenter tantost devant la belle Galasie. Mais quant il veit sa grant beaulté et sa face vermeille en figure coulouree, son gent corps droit et compassé, les yeulx doulx et rians, le nez traictiz et la bouche petit, la forcelle blanche comme nege, ses bras faictiz et ses belles petites mains, d'amours son cueur tant embrasa et si ardamment fust esprins que il perdit le parler et toute contenance. Et tantost apres que il eut prins sa refection, a l'eure il salua la dame en luy disant, "Ma dame souveraine, sur toutes aultres de louenge Mahon, qui fit le firmament, vous doinst force et puissance de voz nobles et gracieulx desirs parfaire et du tout acomplir. Et sachez, dame treshonnouree, que pour la grande renommee que icy je ay a faire de vostre grande et excellente beaulté, j'ay laissé le pays et la contree dont je suis, et pour vostre amour j'ay la mer passee. Or ay je parlé a vostre pere, le puissant roy Brandiffer, auquel j'ay compté nouvelles dont luy et toute payennye en pourra assez mieulx valoir. Et pour verité avoir de ceste chose voycy unes lettres lesquelles par moy vous envoye, et pourrez sçavoir des choses plus a plain."

La dame print les lettres qui moult bien sçavoit lire. Et quant elle eust les lettres aviseez elle regarde Hauffroy d'une chiere hardie. Et puis luy dist haultement devant tous, "Vaussaulx, j'ay vostre lettre regardee laquelle est telle que vous qui estes crestien avez vendu a ceulx de nostre loy les xii. pers de France, et qui plus est vostre pere le roy Pepin qui vous a engendré. Si me mande mon pere que

---

[1] Text has *oients*.

is a group of men I do not know who wish to come in. However, it seems to me they may be from your father Brandiffer."

"Castellan," said the lady, "go see who they are, for I would very much like to hear about my father."

The castellan descended and recognized them, and, as soon as he saw they were Brandiffer's men, he chained up the two lions who guarded the entrance, took the keys, and opened the gates. The Saracens entered, conducting Hauffroy, who thought he had come to his greater honor and profit. However, he would have done better to watch over the land of Angory as Pepin had told him and ordered him to do, for to his sorrow he found himself betrayed by his own treason, as is only right, for a thing badly begun cannot come to a good end.[1]

CHAPTER 50

How, after learning of Hauffroy's great betrayal, the fair Galasie had him thrown into her dungeon under strict guard.

When Hauffroy entered the castle, he went to present himself before the fair Galasie. But when he saw her great beauty—her pink cheeks, her lovely body, straight and well-informed, her sweet laughing eyes, her well-formed nose, her little mouth, her breast white as snow, her pretty arms, and her beautiful little hands—his heart was smitten with such ardent love that he lost both his ability to speak and his self-control. After recovering a bit, he greeted the lady saying, "Most sovereign lady, may Mohammed, who made the firmament, grant you above all others the power and ability to satisfy all your noble and gracious desires and accomplish your will. And know, most honored lady, that for the great renown of your magnificent and excellent beauty, I have left my country of origin behind, and for love of you have crossed the sea. Now I have spoken to your father, the puissant King Brandiffer, to whom I gave information that he and the entire pagan world will know how to use well. And to prove the veracity of these things, here is a message he sends you through me; from it you will understand everything more plainly."

The lady took the message herself, for she knew very well how to read. And once she had considered what was in it, she regarded Hauffroy harshly. Then she said loudly before everyone, "Vassal, I have read your letter and it informs me that you, a Christian, have sold to those of our faith not only the Twelve Peers of France, but also your own father King Pepin, who engendered you. My father

---

[1] Cf. Hassell, *Proverbs*, 115 (no. F90).

de vous je face toute ma voulenté et pour tant que je cognoy que dessus tous les aultres vous estes le plus trahistre et que en vous il n'y a foy ne loyaulté, preudommie ne gentillesse, car quant vous voulez vostre pere trahyr, bien doit par rayson aultruy en vous peu de fiance avoir. Sy vous fay assavoir que par la loy que je tiens que ja de vous je n'en auray ne mercy [111recto][1] pitié, car qui trahyson pourchasse et est en sa trahyson conforté, cil est pire que luy."

Apres ces parolles elle pour son serment sauver l'a fait bouter en prison obscure et parfonde. "Helas," ce dist Hauffroy, "dame, voycy pour moy ung piteulx mariage."

"Sire," ce dist Galasie, "pour femme vous espouserez ma chartre, car jamais vous ne m'aurez."

Or est il vray que en ceste chartre en laquelle fust mis Hauffroy estoit l'empereur de Grece et le Verd Chevalier. Ilz oyent que avec eulx on mettoit ung prisonnier, lors dit l'empereur, "Qui estes vous?"

"Helas," dist Hauffroy, "ne vous chaille qui je soye; je suis Hauffroy, le maleureux bastard de Pepin, roy de France, de tous les douloureux le plus malfortuné."

"Ha," ce dist l'empereur, "moult bien vous cognoissons. Saches que je suis l'empereur de Grece. Si je prie que tu me dies comment se portent mes enfans Valentin et Orson, et comment se porte le roy Pepin de France, Sanson, Gervaz, et le conte de Vuandomme, et le duc Millon d'Angler, et tous les aultres vaillans seigneurs dont je ne sçay leurs noms."

"Seigneur," ce dist Hauffroy, "pour vous faire responce, sachez que ilz sont en ceste terre descendus et si ont ja prins la cité d'Angorie et le païs d'environ. Mais tant y a que je pense que ilz ne sçaivent pas ou vous estes." En ceste maniere deviserent les prisonniers en la chartre dolens et en tristesse de ceste matiere et plusieurs aultres.

Sy vous veul parler de Valentin, de Pacolet qui tant nagerent sur mer que ilz sont arrivéz aupres[2] de Chasteau Fort et sont montéz sur leurs chevaulx et tout secretement sont venus pres des portes a l'ombre d'une muraille.

"Vray Dieu," dist Valentin, "oncques jour de ma vie ne veis place ne forteresse si forte ne si difficille a prendre. Et si croy en ma conscience que il n'est pas possible que il puisse estre prins par force d'armes ne conqueste."

"Sire," dit Pacolet, "je ne sçay que il en aviendra mais nonpourtant je m'y veul essaier." Adonc s'eslongna de Valentin et commença ung art d'ingromance. Mais tout aussitost que le sort eut commencé ung ennemy est a luy venu lequel luy a dit, "Laisse ceste entreprinse, car tu pers ta peine. Ce chasteau jamais ne peult estre prins par nul enchantement ne par assault ne par siege ne peut estre conquis, car il est de telle maniere edifié que jamais homme ne le peult avoir si non par trahison."

A ces motz se partit l'ennemy et puis se leva en l'air et s'esvanuyt, et Pacolet le laissa. Si leva par l'air environ le chasteau si tresgrant bruyne que le bon che-

---

[1] Text has *mercy mercy*, probably owing to the page break.
[2] Text has only *au*, but the *de* seems to indicate that *aupres* was intended.

commands me to do as I will with you, and since I can see that you are the most treasonous of men, possessing neither faith nor loyalty nor honesty nor nobility, for you are willing to betray your own father, there is no reason that anyone should trust you. I will have you know that, according to the authority I hold here, I will show you no mercy or pity, for he who pursues treason and succeeds is the worst of all."

After this speech, in order to keep her word, she had him thrown into a deep, dark dungeon. "Alas, lady," said Hauffroy, "here is a piteous marriage for me."

"Sir," said Galasie, "you shall have my prison to wife, for you will never possess me."

Now remember that the emperor of Greece and the Green Knight were in the same prison in which Hauffroy was thrown. They could hear another prisoner being pushed in, so the emperor called out, "Who are you?"

"Alas," said Hauffroy, "have no care for who I may be; I am Hauffroy, the unhappy bastard son of Pepin, king of France, and I am of all men the most unfortunate."

"Oh," said the emperor, "we know who you are. Know that I am the emperor of Greece. I pray you, tell me how it goes with my children Valentin and Orson, and with King Pepin of France, and Samson, Gervais, and the count of Vendome, and Duke Millon d'Angler, and all the other valiant lords whose names I do not know."

"My lord," said Hauffroy, "I can tell you that they have come to this land and have already taken the city of Angory and the surrounding country. Nevertheless, I am afraid they do not know where you are." In similar fashion the despondent prisoners in the gloomy prison spoke about this matter and many others.

However, now I wish to speak to you of Valentin and Pacolet, who traveled so quickly by sea that they soon arrived near Château Fort. There they mounted their horses and stealthily approached the gates in the shadow of the wall.

"Good God," said Valentin, "never in my life have I seen a fortress of any kind so strong and so difficult to take. I am convinced that it is not possible to capture this place by force of arms or conquest."

"Sire," said Pacolet, "I am not sure what will come of it; nevertheless, I would like to try my hand at it." Thereupon he drew back a little from Valentin and began to weave a spell. However, as soon as the spell was begun, a devil came to him and said, "Forget this attempt, for you are wasting your time. This castle can never be taken by magic or assault or siege, or ever be conquered, for that matter, for it was built in such a way that no man can ever possess it except by treason."

With these words the devil took off, levitating into the air and vanishing, while Pacolet let him go. Then a thick fog surrounded the castle, so impenetrable

valier Valentin ne veoit pas Pacolet, de laquelle chose il fut moult fort esbahy et esmerveillé.[1] Apres que la bruyne fust tout passee Pacolet vint au bon chevalier Valentin et luy dist en ceste maniere, "Sire chevalier Valentin, je veul[2] que nous departons de icy, car trop longuement y sommes. Jamais ce chasteau par nul ne peult estre prins."

Ilz [111verso]ont frappé des esperons et sont retournéz vers la mer et sont en leurs navires entréz et telle diligence ont faicte que en trois jours sont arrivéz en la cité d'Angorie. Et quant ilz furent venus Valentin ala monter au palais et demanda aux gardes des nouvelles de son oncle le roy Pepin et de Orson son frere et des xii. pers de France, et luy fut respondu comment ilz avoient prins habit de pelerin et esoient aléz en Hierusalem viseter le Sainct Sepulchre. Et quant Valentin oÿt les nouvelles il leur a dit que "Dieu les veulle conduire; je les attenderay jusques a leur retour. Et quant il seront venus je les menrray ou mon pere l'empereur de Grece est tenu en prison, car j'ay eu nouvelles certaines qu'il est a Chasteau Fort."

Esmerveilléz furent Françoys quant le lieu oÿrent nommer, car bien ilz avoient oÿ dire que en tout le monde n'avoit point de si forte place. Ainsi demourerent Valentin et ses gens en la cité d'Angorie en attendant le retour du roy Pepin et des douze pers de France. Helas! pour neant il les attendit, car par le faulx trahystre et desloyal Hauffroy sont vendus et piteusement trahys.

[CHAPITRE 51]

Comment le roy Brandiffer et Lucar prindrent dedens la cité de Hierusalem le roy Pepin avec les douze pers de France. li. chapitre

Or sont le roy Pepin et les douze pers de France venus en la cité de Hierusalem[3] pour le Sainct Sepulchre de nostre doulx sauveur et redempteur Jesucrist viseter et adourer, et pour plus devotement faire et acomplyr les sainctz voyaiges qui sont en la terre de promission en laquelle nostre dit sauveur souffrit pour nous mort et passion. Ilz sont arrivéz a ung bon patriarche lequel du Sainct Sepulchre avoit la garde, et il leur a baillé conduitte pour les mener par tout les sains lieux ausquelz sont les indulgences et pardons. Tous les jours ont fait devant eulx par ung prestre moult devotement la messe celebrer, et en grant devocion les sains lieux et esglises viseter et acomplir les sains pelerinaiges.

---

[1] Text has *esmerveil*.
[2] Text has *vous*.
[3] Text has *hierusalez*.

that Valentin could not see Pacolet, which amazed and astounded him. After the fog had dissipated, Pacolet came to Valentin and said, "Sir knight Valentin, I think we should leave here, for we have tarried too long. No one will ever be able to take this castle."

They spurred their horses and returned to the sea, where they embarked on their ships. So quickly did they travel that in three days they arrived in the city of Angory. Once arrived, Valentin mounted up to the palace and asked the guards for news of his uncle King Pepin, Orson his brother, and the Twelve Peers of France, and he was told how they had dressed themselves as pilgrims and gone to Jerusalem to visit the Holy Sepulcher. When Valentin heard the news, he said to them, "May God conduct them safely; I will await their return. And when they return, I will lead them to the place where my father the emperor of Greece is held prisoner, for I have received sure information that he is in Château Fort."

The French were amazed to hear the place named, for they had often heard it mentioned as the most impenetrable fortress in the world. Thus Valentin and his men remained in the city of Angory, awaiting the return of King Pepin and the Twelve Peers of France. Alas! they were waiting in vain, for the false and faithless traitor Hauffroy had sold them and betrayed them most foully.

CHAPTER 51

How King Brandiffer and Lucar captured King Pepin and the Twelve Peers of France in the city of Jerusalem.

Now King Pepin and the Twelve Peers of France came to the city of Jerusalem to visit and worship at the Holy Sepulcher of our sweet savior and redeemer Jesus Christ, and, out of deep devotion, to carry out a holy journey to the promised land where our savior suffered passion and death for our sakes. They arrived at the house of the patriarch who guarded the Holy Sepulcher, and he gave them an escort to conduct them to all the holy places where indulgences and pardons are granted. Every day a priest celebrated mass for them most piously, and, with great devotion, guided them to the sacred places and churches to complete their holy pilgrimage.

Or avint il ainsy comment ilz estoient dedens Hierusalem piteuses choses a racompter, car le roy Brandiffer, le roy d'Inde et le roy Lucar, lesquelz par le trahystre Hauffroy avoient esté de la chose avertis, moult puissamment acompaignéz, arriverent en la cité. Lesquelz estre arrivéz alerent vers la tour David au roy de Surye qui le pays tenoit eulx presenter. Et quant il les veit il fut moult esmerveillé de leur venue, et apres leur salutacion faicte il leur demanda, "Seigneurs, dites moy quelle chose par deca vous amaine, car bien pense et considere que sans grant besoing vous n'estes pas venu icy."

Lors parla Brandiffer et luy a dit, "Sire, sachez que par ung chien crestien nous sommes avertis et suffisamment informéz que dedens ceste cité sont arrivéz les douze pers de France avec [112recto]le roy Pepin. Or sont ilz les drois et principaulx ennemys de nostre loy et ceulx qui de tout le monde nous peuvent le plus grever et dommaiger, et ont desja prins ma cité d'Angorie et grant quantité de ma terre pillee, ma gent mis a l'espee et mon pays destruit. Pour tant sommes icy venus pour les prendre et tenir, car quant nous les aurons de toute France nous pourrons jouyr a nostre apetit et de toute crestienté estre maistres et seigneurs."

"Par Mahon," dist le roy de Surye qui le temple de Salomon tenoit, "vous parlez tressaigement, et de ceste chose suis moult bien content. Or soit fait a vostre apetit, car de telles gens prendre et destruire nous devons estre curieulx. Et pour l'amour de noz dieux nous devons dessus le fait veiller. Sy vous diray que nous ferons pour la chose parfaire et acomplir—je manderay au patriarche se il a nulz pelerins de France, que tost me les amaine et que je veul au pays de France mander par eulx aulcunes lettres."

Ainsi fut la chose faicte. Le messager du roy de Surye ala tantost vers le patriarche et luy dist, "Le roy de Surie par moy vous mande que se vous avez aulcuns pelerins de France, que les luy amenez." Tantost apres il s'en ala au logis ou ilz estoient pres de eulx assoir a table, car ilz avoient leur pelerinage parfait et acomply. Lors leur a dist, "Amis, le roy de Surye par ung messagier vous mande que vous ailez devers luy."

"Helas!" ce dist le roy Pepin, "icy a dures nouvelles, car je sçay de vray se il me cognoist jamais de ses mains je n'eschapperay ne en France ne retourneray. Si vous diray que nous ferons. Je conseille que de Henry qui est mon enfant nous en façons nostre maistre et gouverneur, et je veul apres luy aler comme son serviteur et porteray son chappeau, son bourdon et son escharpe, et par telle maniere nul de moy ne se doubtera."

"Par Dieu, sire," ce dist Henry, qui bien la trahyson sçavoit, "de telles choses ja ne devez parler, car moy qui suis vostre filz et vous doy par droite raison naturelle servir de tout mon pouoir, jamais je ne consentiroye que fussiez a moy subject ne servant. Mais icy est Millon d'Angler lequel est homme preux, tresvaillant et hardy. Si fera bien la chose ainsi que vous la devisez trop mieulx que moy a vostre prouffit et honneur. Et quant faire ne le vouldra, prenez Orson qui tant est vaillant et preux ou Gervaiz ou Sanson, lequel que il vous plaira." Ainsi se excusa le trahystre qui bien la trahyson sçavoit.

Now while they were in Jerusalem, things occurred almost too terrible to recount, for King Brandiffer, the king of India, and King Lucar, all of whom had been averted by the traitor Hauffroy, arrived in the city with a sizeable contingent of troops. Upon arrival they went to the Tower of David to present themselves to the king of Syria, who controlled the country. When he saw them, he wondered at their coming, so that after their greeting, he asked them, "My lords, tell me what brings you here, for I imagine you didn't come without some great need."

Then Brandiffer spoke up and said to him, "Sire, know that we were informed by a Christian dog that King Pepin and the Twelve Peers of France have come to this city. Now they are the most dangerous enemies of our creed, and can cause us the most damage and harm; they have already taken my city of Angory and pillaged a great part of my land, destroying the country and putting my people to the sword. For that reason we have come here to capture them, for once we have them in our power, we shall be able to do as we will with France and be lords and masters of all Christendom."

"By Mohammed," said the king of Syria, holder of the temple of Solomon, "you speak most wisely, and I am quite happy to hear of this matter. Let it be done as you wish, for we must support your effort to seize and destroy such people. And for the love of our gods, we must work diligently to carry out that deed. I will tell you what we shall do to accomplish this: I will order the patriarch to send me any pilgrims arrived from France, explaining that I have some letters I wish them to carry back to France."

Thus was the plan laid. The king of Syria's messenger left right away to go see the patriarch, telling him, "The king of Syria sends me to tell you that, if you have any pilgrims from France, to bring them to him." Right away the patriarch went to the inn where they were about to sit at table, for they had completed their pilgrimage. Then he said to them, "My friends, the king of Syria has sent a messenger asking that you go to see him."

"Alas!" said King Pepin, "this is hard news, for I am sure that if he recognizes me, I will never escape his clutches or return to France. I have an idea what we can do. Henry is my son—I advise that we act as if he is our master and leader, and I will follow him as his servant and will wear his cap and scarf and carry his staff, and no one will suspect who I am."

"For God's sake, sire," said Henry, who excelled at treachery, "you must never speak of such things, for I as your son must by natural right serve you as well as I might—I would never consent that you be my servant. But here is Millon d'Angler, a brave, valiant, and bold man. He can do this better than I, and to your profit and honor. And if he is not willing to do it, take Orson who is so brave and bold, or Gervais, or Samson, whomever you please." Thus the traitor, who excelled in treachery, excused himself.

Le vaillant roy Pepin estoit de estature trespetit et plus que nul aultre prince vivant, "parquoy trop je suis en doubte et en crainte que je ne soye par eulx cogneu par aulcune espie qui me pourroit avoir veu au royaume de France, parquoy je seroye encusé et honteusement mis a mort."

"Sire," dist Millon d'Angler, "tout ce qu'il vous plaira je feray." Lors partirent de leur logis pour aler vers [112verso]le roy payen qui les avoit mandé. Le duc Millon d'Angler fust des aultres fort honnouré comme roy et Pepin va apres mallement vestu et de toutes pars povrement habillé. Meschans souliers portoit et bien sembloit homme de quoy on devoit tenir bien peu de compte. Ainsi ilz s'en alerent vers le roy de Surie. Le bon patriarche les maine qui a nul mal ne pensoit, et tantost qu'il les eut delivré au roy il se partist de la.

"Or ça," dist le roy de Surie, "je suis informé de vostre cas et sçay que vous estes gens françois qui me venez espier, et que en vostre compaignie est le roy de France qui la cité d'Angorie a prinse et grant nombre de noz gens mis a mort. Mais par le dieu Mahon que je tiens chier jamais en France vous ne retournerez."

"Sire," dist ung des douze pers de France, "de ce nous devez pardonner, car en ceste compaignie n'est pas le roy de France."

"Taisez vous," dist le roy de Surie, "je suis de vostre fait tout informé. Et par mon dieu Jupiter, se le roy de France tantost ne se nomme je vous feray tous par les colz pendre et estrangler sans nulle remission."

"Roy," dist tantost Henry le trahystre desloyal, "de moy ne vous doubtez, car ce ne suis je point."[1] Adonc aperceut bien le duc Millon d'Angler que trahyson y avoit, et que par trahyson ilz estoient accuséz. Si a dit tout hault, "Sire roy de Surie, celer ne vous fault riens. Je suis le roy de France puis que vous le demandez. Mais une chose je vous veul dire, s'il vous plaist a l'oÿr. C'est que nous sommes venus le Sainct Sepulchre viseter. Si ne devons en nulle maniere sur vostre terre avoir dommage ne estre prins ne arrestéz, vue et consideré que la loy est telle que tous crestiens peuvent seurement aler et venir au dit pelerinaige par payant le tribu lequel est a vous deu et estably a payer. Or avons nous tout ce payé et toutes les choses acomplies et parfaictes selon les ordonnances et establissemens du pays de par deça, dont me semble avoir injuste et trop grant tort nous faictes si nous voulez pour ceste cause molester ou dommaiger."

"Par Mahon," dit le roy, "seigneurs, vous direz ce que vous vouldrez, mais il n'y a temps ne saison a vous qui guerre nous faictes de venir par deça pour nostre terre espier."

Lors appella Brandiffer et Lucar et leur a dit "Seigneurs, prenez ces faulx crestiens espies et en faictes vostre voulenté car du tout je les metz et delivre en voz mains pour les faire de telle mort mourir que bon vous semblera."

A ces motz furent les pelerins de faulx payens prins et detenus. Si ne fault pas demander se ilz les traiterent durement, car ces vaillans seigneurs non plus

---

[1] Text has *ponit*.

The valiant King Pepin was of very small stature, smaller than that of any prince alive, "for which reason I am afraid that I shall be recognized by them, perhaps by some spy who could have seen me in the kingdom of France, and then I shall be revealed and put to a shameful death."

"Sire," said Millon d'Angler, "I will do whatever you wish." Then they left their inn to go to see the pagan king who had sent for them. Duke Millon d'Angler was treated with honor by the others as if he were the king, and Pepin followed him, dressed in shabby clothes. He wore tattered shoes and looked like a man to whom no one need pay any attention. Thus prepared, they went to see the King of Syria. The good patriarch led the way, never dreaming of any possibility of harm intended, and as soon as he had brought them to the king, he left.

"Well, then," said the king of Syria, "I have full information on you—I know that you are Frenchmen come to spy on me, and that among your company is the king of France who has taken the city of Angory and killed a great number of people there. But by the god Mohammed whom I hold dear, you will never return to France."

"Sire," said one of the Twelve Peers of France, "you must excuse us on that score, for the king of France is not among our company."

"Hold your tongue," said the king of Syria, "I know all about you and your doings. And by my god Jupiter, if the king of France does not make himself known immediately, I will have you all hanged by the neck without delay."

"King," piped up Henry the faithless traitor, "do not suspect me, for I am certainly not he." At that moment, Duke Millon d'Angler realized that there was treachery afoot, and that they had been discovered through treason. Then he said aloud, "Sir king of Syria, we shall hide nothing from you. I am the king of France, since you ask. But there is one thing I would like to say, if it please you to listen. It is that we have come simply to visit the Holy Sepulcher. Thus we should not be harmed or arrested in your land, seeing that the law allows all Christians to come and go safely in the fulfillment of this pilgrimage, once they pay the customary tribute due to you. Now we have paid all this and observed all the customs and laws of the country, for which reason it seems to me you are unjust to wish to hurt us or cause us harm."

"By Mohammed," said the king, "my lords, you may say whatever you like, but you respect no time or season—you make war on us by coming here to spy on our land."

Then he called for Brandiffer and Lucar, and said to them, "My lords, take away these deceitful Christian spies and do with them as you will, for I put them completely in your hands to kill them as you see fit."

With these words the pilgrims were seized and detained by the false pagans. No need to ask if they treated them harshly, for these valiant lords were given

n'eurent de pitié que de chiens enrragéz. Estroitement furent tenus et durement lyéz. Puis parla Brandiffer et dist ainsi, "Seigneurs, je veul que ceste faulce gent soient menéz au Chasteau Fort, et en la plus forte de mes prisons y soient boutéz et devaléz. Puis irons devant Angorie et la cité prendrons [113recto]par[1] grant puissance d'armes. Apres lesquelles choses nous irons en France et tout le pays prendrons et metterons de legier en obeissance, car la nous ne trouverrons roy, seigneur, ne baron qui nous die du contraire. Et pour tant pouez aler chascun en son pays, puis a ung certain jour par entre nous aviserons ensemble a Falezie[2] et les prisonniers entre nous partyrons ainsi comme rayson sera."

"Seigneurs," dist le roy d'Inde, "quant au regard des prisonniers aultre chose je ne vous demande fors que pour ma part me donnez le plus petit. Si en feray mon nayn et avec moy le feray chevaulcher pour tant qu'il est petit, et assés me semble seur. Si luy feray du bien assez mais que la loy de Jesus veulle renoncer." De ceste demande s'acorderent tous les aultres, et au roy d'Inde Major ilz donnerent le roy Pepin qui avec luy le mena. Et depuis moult l'aima nonobstant qu'il souffrit moult de tribulacions ainsi que apres il vous sera declairé.

[CHAPITRE 52]

Comment le roy d'Inde Major pour sa part des prisonniers emmena Pepin mais pas ne sçavoit qu'il fust roy de France. lii. chapitre

Or emmena le roy d'Inde Major le bon roy Pepin mais il ne le cognoissoit pas. Et au departir des douze pers et le roy Pepin y eust entre eulx grant dueil et grant destreste, mais nul ne faisoit semblant fors le plus qu'i pouoyent en leurs cueurs couvertement leur angoisse[3] les vaillans pers piteusement regardoient le roy Pepin, mais nul ne luy osoit dire adieu pour doubte de la cognoisance.

Ainsi s'en va le roy d'Inde et Pepin va apres luy chevaulchant qui n'est pas sans dueil et soussy. "Helas," dist il tout bassement, "vray Dieu de paradis, veullez moy ayder et secourir car se vostre saincte grace ne m'est en ayde je suis de tous povrez qui jamais furent le plus dolent et maleureux. Helas! Millon d'Angler, je vous doy bien aymer quant pour moy en tel danger vostre corps mettez. Henry, Henry! tu m'as bien monstré que tu ne m'aimes pas quant a mon besoing m'as fally. Bien doit mal venir a l'enfant qui au besoing laisse son pere. M'amye Berthe, jamais plus ne vous verray. Helas! Charlot, mon beau filz, Dieu te veulle resconforter, car bien sçay de vray que les trahistres assez te feront de peine souffrir et tu

---

[1] *p i* at bottom right corner of 113r.
[2] Texte has *Faleize*.
[3] Woodcut of mounted army of knights.

no more pity than if they had been mad dogs. They were held closely and bound tightly. Then Brandiffer spoke, saying, "My lords, I want these wicked people to be taken to Château Fort and tossed into the most impenetrable of my dungeons. Then we shall go to Angory and recapture the city with a great force of arms. After that, we shall go to France where we will take the country and easily subject it to our will, for there we will find neither king, lord, nor baron to say us nay. And then each of you can return to his country, but on a fixed day we will gather together in Falezie to decide how to divide up the prisoners among us."

"My lords," said the king of India, "for my part, concerning the prisoners, I ask you for nothing else but that you give me the littlest one. I will make him my dwarf and will have him ride with me, because he is so small and seems safe enough to me. And I will do him good if he will renounce the religion of Jesus." The others all acceded to this request and gave King Pepin to the king of India Major, who led him away with him. Subsequently he loved him very much, notwithstanding the tribulations he suffered, as will be recounted to you.

CHAPTER 52

How the King of India Major took Pepin away as his share of the prisoners without knowing he was king of France.

So the king of India Major took the good King Pepin away with him without knowing who he was. And there was much mourning and great distress as the Twelve Peers and King Pepin were separated, only no one could let anything show, so that, hiding their anguish as much as they could, the valiant Peers watched King Pepin in a pitiful state, not daring to say goodbye for fear of discovery of his true identity.

Thus did Pepin, not without feeling sorrow and worry, ride after the king of India as he left. "Alas," he said to himself softly, "true God of paradise, help me and come to my aid, for if you do not help me with your divine grace, I am of all poor wretches the most unhappy and sorrowful. Alas! Millon d'Angler, I owe you much love, seeing that you have put yourself in such danger for my sake. Henry, Henry! you have demonstrated how little you love me, having failed me in my need. Evil will certainly come to the child who abandons his father in his need. My beloved Bertha, never again shall I see you. Alas! Charlot, my beautiful son, may God comfort you, for I know that the traitors will cause you more than

es jeune et petit et ne pourras contre eulx avoir nul[113verso]le resistance." Ainsi se complaingnoit Pepin et plouroit moult piteusement.

Or a tant fait le roy d'Inde la Major que la dame[1] qui moult la venue desiroit courut tantost au devant et en menant grant joye doulcement l'embraca. Et ainsi monterent au palais en faisant grant feste et grant chiere. La dame regardoit Pepin lequel nonobstant qu'il fust petit il estoit bien furny et fait de tous membres et de face et a regarder tresplaisant. Si demanda la dame au roy d'Inde, "Mon amy, dites moy qui vous a donné cestuy petit homme, car moult semble honneste et gracieux et si peult estre a veoir sa semblance que de bon et hault lieu soit extrait et descendu."

"Dame," ce dist le roy, "il m'a esté donné et si estoit venu avec le roy de France et les douze pers qui estoyent venus en Hierusalem[2] parquoy il a esté prins et s'i veult renoncer sa loy et son dieu Jesus je luy feray moult de biens."

Riens ne respondit Pepin qui bien avoit aultre couraige. Ainsi fut tost l'eure venue que le roy deust souper. Pepin entra dedens la cuisine et le roy luy demanda se riens il sçavoit de la cuisine, et qu'i luy fist la saulce du pain qui rotissoit. Pepin tantost la fist si bien que depuis le roy ne voulut menger ne saulce ne viande que Pepin ne luy appareillast dont tous les aultres maistres de la cuysyne royalle avoient grant despit.

Et sur Pepin eurent envye tellement qu'il avint une foys que le roy luy commanda aprester ung paon, sy ala vers le cuisinier par le commandement du roy et quant il entra dedens la cuisine tous grans et petis le prindrent a mocquer, et l'ung par derriere l'autre le frappe. Il prenoit tout en pacience comme sage et vertueulx, et apres il ala devers le feu pour le paon mettre en la broche. Et le maistre cuisinier qui dessus luy avoit trop grant envye s'approcha pres de luy et ung gros charbon ardant au giron luy getta et trop fort le brusla. Et alors jura Pepin qu'il s'en vengeroie et vint au Sarrasin et tel coup luy donna entre le front et l'oreille qu'il l'abatit a terre. Puis le frappa ung aultre coup si grant qu'i luy a fait la cervelle saillir. Et quant les varlés et soullars de la cuisine veirent que leur maistre estoit mal atourné, ilz assaillirent tous Pepin a bastons et a cousteaulx. Et luy qui fut hardy et preux ne s'est point reculé mais jura Jesucrist qu'il ayme mieulx a mourir que longuement souffrir l'injure de telles gens. Si est alé vers ung garson que d'ung grant pesteil le vouloit assommer et tel coup luy en a donné que a terre l'abatit mort tout roide parmy la cuisine.

La noise et le bruit tant fut grant que le roy en eust les nouvelles. Si demanda tantost que Pepin fust prins et devant luy amené pour en faire justice selon sa faulte, et ainsy fut fait. Et quant il fut devant le roy il luy a dit, "Mauvais garson,

---

[1] This is assumed to be Rozemonde, whose death had been reported as a future event but has not yet occurred, and, in fact, the sixteenth-century English translator added her name to clarify the point.

[2] Text has *hierusalez*.

enough pain, and you are young and little and you will not be able to offer them any resistance." Thus did Pepin complain and weep most piteously.

The king of India Major traveled quickly, and his lady, who greatly desired his coming, ran out right away to greet him, kissing him joyfully and sweetly. And thus did they mount up to the palace together with great happiness and cheer. The lady looked at Pepin who, despite his small stature, was well formed in both face and body and was pleasing to look at. The lady asked the king of India, "My darling, tell me who has given you this little man, for he seems worthy and gentle, and, from the look of him, he could be descended from a high and honorable lineage."

"My lady," said the king, "he was given to me because he had come with the king of France and the Twelve Peers who had come to Jerusalem where they were captured, and if he is willing to renounce his faith and his God Jesus, I will do much good for him."

Pepin, who was opposed to such a step, answered nothing to this. Soon after it was the hour when the king was to dine. Pepin entered the kitchen, and the king asked him if he knew anything of cooking, and that he should prepare the sauce for the peacock that was roasting. Pepin did it right away and so well that from that time on the king would not eat any sauce or dish that Pepin had not prepared for him, which made all the other master cooks of the royal kitchen hate him.[1]

One day the king ordered him to prepare a peacock, and he went to the kitchen as the king had ordered, but they were so jealous of Pepin that, as he entered the kitchen, everyone big and small began to mock him, while one after another they struck him. He suffered this all with patience like a wise and virtuous man, and afterward went to the fire to place the peacock on the spit. But the master cook, who was extremely jealous, came up to him and threw a large blazing coal on his lap, burning him badly. Pepin swore that he would avenge himself, so he turned on the Saracen and smote him with such a blow on the side of his head that he knocked him down. Then he struck him again so hard that his brains burst forth. When the kitchen varlets and scullions saw their master so badly hurt, they all attacked Pepin with clubs and knives. And Pepin, who was hardy and brave, did not retreat, but rather swore by Jesus Christ that he preferred to die than suffer for long the insults of such people. So he came at a boy who was trying to knock him senseless with a huge pestle, and gave him such a blow that he struck him down dead right in the middle of the kitchen.

The noise and the brouhaha were so loud that the king was informed. He demanded that Pepin be seized and brought immediately before him to receive justice according to his crime, and so it was done. And when he was before the

---

[1] Pepin's adventures in the kitchen recall those of Orson in Chapter 14, but also echo the motif of the young Charlemagne as kitchen varlet from *Mainet* (a version of which will appear below in Chapter 64, p. 480). See Dickson, *Study*, 236.

comment as tu esté si hardy de tuer dedens mon palays mon maistre cuisinier? Or me dy tost comment la chose va ou par mon [114recto]dieu¹ Mahon je te feray mourir."

"Sire," dist Pepin, "je vous diray la verité. Il est vray que je estoye en la cuisine pour aprester ung paon pour vostre soupper, ainsi que m'aviez commandé, lors vostre cuisinier, je ne sçay pourquoy ne a quelle cause, il a getté dessus moy ung gros charbon ardant dont moult il m'a dommagé. Et quant je me veis ainsi bruslé je prins ung gros tison et sur la teste luy en ay donné tel coup que je croy bien que n'a mestier de mire."

Le roy fit tost venir les aultres et ilz confesserent le cas tout et en telle maniere que Pepin avoit dit. Et quant le roy d'Inde sceut la verité de la besongne plue que jamais tint chier et aima Pepin. Si commanda que nul de son palays ne fust si hardy de luy faire oultrage. Tant fist Pepin depuis que des petis et grans il fut moult aymé et prisé.

Si laisseray ceste matiere et parleray de la belle et plaisante, doulce et amiable Esclarmonde.

[CHAPITRE 53]

Comment le roy Pepin estant avec le roy d'Inde eust cognoissance de la belle Esclarmonde et de son fait. liii. [chapitre]

Je vous veul parler et faire mencion ung peu de temps de la belle Esclarmonde de laquelle ainsi que devant avez ouÿ tenoit le roy d'Inde, et ja longuement l'avoit gardee. Or avoit ledit roy d'Inde de coustume que des meilleures viandes que il mengoit il envoyoit tousjours a la belle Esclarmonde. Sy avint que a ung soupper il appella Pepin et luy bailla de la viande que devant luy estoit et luy dist, "Alez celle part vers ceste chambre ou il y a une fenestre, et la trouverrez une folle piteusement atournee. Donnez luy cecy et de par moy luy portez."

Pepin print la viande et a la dame il la porta. Mais quant il la veit ainsi povrement aprestee, moult en eut grant pitié et luy dist, "Amye, Jesus qui pour nous souffrit mort et passion vous veulle conforter et donner pacience. Helas! ayez fiance en luy et le servez de bon cueur, et se ainsi vous le faictes sachez certainement que de vostre douleur aurez bonne allegance, mais que en luy fermement vous croyez et prenez le sainct sacrement de baptesme."

---

¹ *p ii* at bottom right corner of 114r.

king, the latter said to him, "Wicked boy, how is it that you dare to kill my master cook in my own palace? Now tell me what happened or, by my god Mohammed, I will have you killed."

"Sire," said Pepin, "I will tell you the truth. What happened is that I was in the kitchen to prepare a peacock for your dinner, as you had commanded me to do, when your cook, for some reason I cannot surmise, threw a blazing coal on me, which hurt me greatly. When I saw myself burned like this, I took hold of a stout partially-burned log and gave him such a blow on the head that I believe he has no need of a doctor."

The king immediately called for the others, and they confessed that the incident took place as Pepin had described it. And when the king of India knew the truth of the matter, he held Pepin dear and loved him more than ever. So he ordered that no one in his palace be so bold as to do him harm. Thus was Pepin loved and prized from that time forward more than anyone, great or small.

Now I will leave off this matter and speak to you of the beautiful and pleasing, sweet, and lovable Esclarmonde.

CHAPTER 53

How King Pepin, while in the custody of the king of India, recognized the fair Esclarmonde and learned her story.

I want to spend some time telling you about the fair Esclarmonde who, as you know, was being held by the king of India, and had been kept there for a long time. Now the king of India had the custom of always sending a part of the best dishes he ate to the fair Esclarmonde. It so happened that at one particular dinner he called for Pepin and, giving him some of the dish that was before him, said to him, "Go over to that chamber where there is a window; there you will find a madwoman in a pitiful state. Give her this; bring it to her as a gift from me."

Pepin took the food and brought it to the lady. But when he saw her in such a miserable plight, he took great pity on her and said to her, "Friend, may Jesus who suffered death and passion for us comfort you and give you patience. Alas! have faith in Him and serve Him with a willing heart, and if you do this, know that for certain you will have a lightening of your sorrow, provided that you believe in Him steadfastly and take the holy sacrament of baptism."

Quant la dame entendit que de Dieu il parloit elle s'approcha pres de la fenestre et luy dist, "Amy, de moy ne vous doubtez. Mais dictes moy si vous estes crestien ou se par faintise dictes telles parolles."

"Dame," ce dist Pepin, "je suis de vray crestien et suis du pays de France venu et nourry."

"Doncques," dit la dame en soubzriant, "vous devez bien cognoistre le bon Pepin et son nepveu Valentin."

"Il est vray," dit Pepin. "Et si cognoy bien son frere Orson et leur pere l'empereur de Grece et Bellissant leur mere et les douze pers de France."

Et quant la dame l'oÿt, tendrement se print a plourer et a dire, "Helas, amy, pourroy je avoir fiance en vous?"

"Oy," ce dit Pepin, "autant que en vostre propre pere ce qu'il vous plaira, car jamais par moy vous ne serez accusee."

"Amy," ce dit [114verso]la dame, "sachez de vray que je contrefay la fole et la malade, mais autant suis saige et saine comme je fus oncques, car je suis crestienne et le beau Valentin avoye pour amy, et a celuy j'estoye donnee pour moy espouser et prendre a femme. Par ung faulx trahystre roy je lui fus longtemps tolue." Lors la dame lui compta tout le fait et la maniere de son estat et comment et en quelle facon elle[1] avoit esté prinse, et la cause pourquoy elle faisoit la malade.

Et quant Pepin eut oÿ la piteuse aventure de la dame escoutee, moult se print piteusement a plourer et souspirer tendrement. Puis en considerant les fortunes et grandes aventures qui de jour en jour viennent sur creature humaine, en gettant grosses larmes, bassement a par luy dit, "Ha,[2] vray Dieu tout puissant,[3] qu'esse des tenebres de ce monde! Or voy je ceste povre dolente pour sa loyaulté tenir estre miserablement atornee et en grande pacience usant ses jours. Helas, Valentin, mon beau nepveu, a ceste foys ne fault il pas demender se pour l'amour de la belle vous estes et avez esté depuis en pacience langoureuse et en soussy moult grant. Or pleust ores a Dieu que de ceste heure vous seussiez comment j'ai trouvé celle qui pour vostre cueur languist."

Et apres ces parolles il regarda la dame en disant, "Amie, je sçai certainement qui vous estes et vous ne sçavez qui je suis. Mais puis que tant en moy avez eu fiance que vostre secret m'avez declaré, je veul dire qui je suis. Sachez que tel que vous me voyez je suis Pepin le roy de France a qui fortune a esté tant contraire qu'elle m'a fait trebuchier en telle servitude et necessité que a present me pouez regarder. Or sçay je bien que mon nepveu Valentin en grant travail de son corps sans sejour ne repos continuellement vous serche. Mais si plaist a Dieu de brief aura de vous nouvelles et en joye et en soulas vous assemblerez ensemble."

---

[1] Text has *el*, probably owing to line break.
[2] Text has *a*.
[3] Text has *puissent*. The typesetter here has a few instances of *en* for what is usually *an*. I have emended only where the sense might be compromised. See *demender* a few sentences below which has not been emended.

When the lady heard him speaking of God, she approached the window and said to him, "Friend, have no fear of me. But tell me if you are Christian, or if you say such things to trick me."

"Lady," said Pepin, "I am a true Christian, and I come from France where I was raised."

"Then," said the lady smiling, "you must know the good Pepin and his nephew Valentin."

"Indeed," said Pepin. "And I also know very well his brother Orson and their father the emperor of Greece and Bellissant their mother and the Twelve Peers of France."

When the lady heard this, she began to sob and said, "Oh, my friend, can I trust in you?"

"Yes," said Pepin, "as much as you would in your own father—say whatever you like, for I will never expose you."

"Friend," said the lady, "know then that I am pretending to be ill and mad, although in truth I am as healthy and right-minded as I ever was, for I am Christian and my beloved is the fair Valentin, to whom I was given that he might marry me and take me as his wife. It was by a false, treacherous king that I was kidnapped a long time ago." Then the lady recounted everything that had happened to her, how she had been captured, and the reason for which she feigned madness.

After Pepin had listened to the lady's sad adventures, he began to weep and sigh in tender sympathy. Then, considering the hazards of fortune and great adventures that befall humankind every day, he said softly to himself through copious tears, "Oh, true almighty God, what shadows there are in this world! I see before me this poor sorrowful girl patiently measuring out her days in this miserable plight in order to keep her troth. Alas, Valentin, my fair nephew, now it is no wonder that you have long and patiently suffered great anxiety out of love for this lady. If it only pleased God that you knew right away how I have found the one for whom your heart yearns."

After these words he looked at the lady, saying, "Friend, I know for certain who you are, while you don't know who I am. But since you have had such trust in me that you have told me your secret, I will tell you who I am. Know that the one you see before you is Pepin, king of France, to whom Fortune has been so contrary that she has made me fall into servitude and want, such as that in which you see me presently. Now I know that my nephew Valentin searches for you constantly in great travail to his body, without pause or rest. And if it please God, he will soon have news of you, and you shall come together again in joy and solace."

A ces motz se pensa la dame et Pepin le[1] laissa pour retourner vers le roy d'Inde lequel a la table estoit. Or vous laisseray ceste matiere a tant et vous parleray du roy Brandiffer et du roy Lucar qui les xii. pers de France et Henry le trahistre prisonnier emmenoient.

[CHAPITRE 54]

Comment Brandiffer emmena a Chastel Fort les xii. pers de France et les fit emprisonner en moult diverses et dures prisons. iiii. cha[pitre]

Vous avez bien oÿ mencion faire du roy Brandiffer qui les douze pers de France avoit prisonniers, et Hauffroy et Henry. Et tant ont fait qu'i sont venus au Chasteau Fort. Brandiffer trouva sa fille Galasie qui tant il avoit et tenoit chiere. Si luy compta le fait et la maniere de l'entreprinse, puis fist sans plus attendre les prisonniers devaler au plus bas d'une tour parfonde ou estoient l'empereur de Grece et le Verd Chevalier. Si avoit esté Hauffroi le trahistre avec eulx bouté. Moult dolent fut Henry quant il n'osa et ne peult au roy Brandiffer declairer son couraige, mais il fut tout le premier devalé es prisons et apres fut getté le duc Millon [115recto] d'Angler[2] qui sur Hauffroy cheut dont Hauffroy moult se complaingnit pour tant que blesé en fut.

"Taisez vous," dist Millon d'Angler, "et vous tirez plus bas, car moult d'aultres il en y a a qui il convient place faire."

Bien entendit Hauffroy le duc Millon d'Angler, si luy demanda dont il venoit et qui l'a amené. "Mais vous!" ce dit Millon, "car je vous avoye laissé dedens Angorie."

"Ha," dit Hauffroy le trahistre, "en ung destour je fus l'autre jour prins et icy amené. Et ainsi furent tous les seigneurs en prison boutéz." Et quant Hauffroy sceut que Pepin n'y estoit point il fist maniere d'en estre bien joyeulx mais eust bien voulu qu'il eust ja esté par le col pendu.

Or sont tous les pers de France en l'orde et obscure prison; la ont cogneu l'empereur de Grece et le Verd Chevalier. Et quant ilz ont tous les ungz les aultres cogneux, il ne fault pas demander les pleurs ne les gemissemens qui adonc furent entre eulx, car nul n'y avoit que la mort plus que la vie n'esperast, fors seulement Orson en les reconfortant leur a dist, "Seigneurs, prenons en pacience. Il plaist a Dieu que ainsi soit et que en ceste façon nous façons nostre penitance. Mais pour tant ne se fault il pas du tout[3] desconforter, mais avoir fiance en Dieu et en noz bons amis. C'est mon frere Valentin et le vaillant Pacolet qui bien sçayt jouer de

---

[1] Another occurrence of *le* for *la* as a feminine direct object pronoun.
[2] *p iii* at bottom right corner of 115r.
[3] Text has *taut*.

With these words the lady grew calmer, and Pepin left her to return to the king of India, who was still at table. Now I will leave off speaking of this matter, and will speak instead of King Brandiffer and King Lucar, who bore off as prisoners the Twelve Peers of France and Henry the traitor.

CHAPTER 54

How King Brandiffer brought the Twelve Peers of France to Château Fort, and locked them up in harsh and horrible dungeons.

You have heard all about King Brandiffer, who had taken the Twelve Peers of France prisoner along with Hauffroy and Henry. They traveled so quickly that they soon came to Château Fort. Brandiffer met up there again with his daughter Galasie, whom he loved dearly. He explained to her all that had happened, and then, without delay, had all the prisoners lowered into the deepest part of the tower dungeon where the emperor of Greece and the Green Knight were already confined. That was also where Hauffroy the traitor had been thrown. Henry was very upset because he could not dare to say anything of his real intention to King Brandiffer, and in fact he was the first to be lowered down into the dungeon. After him they threw in Duke Millon d'Angler, who landed on Hauffroy, hurting him and causing him to cry out in protest.

"Be quiet," said Millon d'Angler, "and back further away, for there are many more of us for whom you had better make room."

Hauffroy heard that it was Duke Millon d'Angler, so he asked where he was coming from and what brought him there. "I could ask you the same thing!" said Millon, "for I had left you in Angory."

"Well," said the traitor Hauffroy, "the other day I was captured in a remote spot and brought here. In a similar way were these other lords thrown into this prison." And when Hauffroy found out that Pepin was not one of the captives, he pretended to be joyful, but in fact he would have preferred to see him already hanged by the neck.

So now all the Twelve Peers of France were trapped in the filthy, dark dungeon; there they recognized the emperor of Greece and the Green Knight. And once everyone had recognized everybody else, no need to ask if there was much sighing and weeping among them, for none of them could truly hope for life more than death, except for Orson, who said to them by way of consolation, "My lords, let us have patience. It pleases God that it be so, and that we do penance in this fashion. But that does not mean we should despair; rather we should trust in God and in our good friends, namely my brother Valentin and the valiant Pacolet, who knows his craft well." Thus did Orson speak, but he did not

son art." Ainsi parla Orson, mais il ne sçavoit pas que le chasteau fust si fort ne de telle vertu que par enchantement il ne sera jamais prins.

Et apres que Brandiffer eut fait emprisonner les seigneurs, il appella sa fille Galasie et luy a dist, "Ma fille, il est vray que je veul aler a la Falezie pour mon ost assembler, et la je doy trouver le roy de Inde et Lucar lesquelz viennent avec moy vers mon pays d'Angorie que les François tiennent. Et pour tant gouvernez vous si bien que de vostre fait je n'aye nul reproche. Et sur tout donnez vous garde des prisonniers qui ceans sont."

"Pere," ce dit la pucelle, "de moy n'ayez doubte ne de eulx aussi, car vous n'en aurez que toutes bonnes nouvelles."

Ainsi partit Brandiffer de Chasteau Fort et s'en ala a Falezie ou il assembla ses gens et son armee. La vint le roy Lucar a moult grant puissance de gens d'armes ainsi que promis luy avoit. Mais le roy de Inde la Major y envoya seulement ses gens et n'y vint point, car adonc estoit sa feme la belle Rozemonde au lit malade en telle maniere que dedens l'espace de neuf jours elle mourut. Donc si grant dueil en print le roy que au lyt malade se coucha, et par l'espace de douze jours fut sans mot dire ne parler; dequoy pas ne despleut au roy Lucar car oncques puis ne l'ayma qu'il luy osta sa femme Rozemonde ainsi comme vous l'avez oÿ devant declarer et plus au long reciter.

[CHAPITRE 55]

Comment le puissant roy Brandiffer apres ce que il eust assemblé tous ses gens a Falezie, il monta des[115verso] sus la mer pour aler en Angorie contre des crestiens. lv. chapitre[1]

Apres que le roy Brandiffer et Lucar eurent leur ost et leur armee assemblee a Falezie, sans nul sejour faire, ilz monterent sur mer et la eurent vent si aggreable que incontinent vindrent arriver au port. Et quant ilz furent arrivéz, ceulx qui les veirent descendre coururent tantost vers la cité d'Angorie et dirent a Valentin les nouvelles qui la cité gardoit en attendant la venue du roy Pepin et des douze pers de France. Helas, il ne sçavoit pas comment la chose aloit. Et quant il vit les tentes et pavillons levéz entour Angorie, moult piteusement print il Pepin a regretter.[2] Puis appella Pacolet et luy a dit, "Amy, trop mal va nostre fait quant je ne puis savoir du roy Pepin nouvelles."

---

[1] Woodcut of sailboat carrying group of figures among whom one is crowned; hilly landscape in background.

[2] Text has *regrettert*.

know that the castle was so strong and so protected by magic that it could never be captured.

After Brandiffer had imprisoned the lords, he called for his daughter Galasie and said to her, "My daughter, my intention now is to go to Falezie to assemble my army, and there I must meet up with the king of India and Lucar, who are coming with me to my territory in Angory held by the French. Therefore, govern yourself well so that I will have no reason to reproach you. And, above all, guard well the captives imprisoned here."

"Father," said the maiden, "have no doubt about me or about them, for you will have nothing but good tidings."

Thus did Brandiffer leave Château Fort and go to Falezie where he assembled his men and his army. There came King Lucar with a great multitude of men at arms as he had promised. But the king of India Major only sent his men and did not come himself, for at that time his wife, the beautiful Rozemonde, was in bed so very ill that she died within nine days. As a result the king mourned so deeply that he took to his own bed in illness, and for twelve days spoke not a word. All of this did not displease King Lucar, for he had never liked him for having taken his wife Rozemonde away from him, as you heard recounted earlier.

CHAPTER 55

How, having assembled his men in Falezie, the mighty King Brandiffer set sail for the city of Angory to fight against the Christians.

After King Brandiffer and Lucar had assembled their army in Falezie, they set sail without delay, and had such good wind that they soon arrived in port. Those who saw them arrive and disembark ran to the city of Angory to give the news to Valentin, who was guarding the city while awaiting the return of King Pepin and the Twelve Peers of France. Alas, he was not aware of what had transpired. And when he saw the tents and pavilions being set up, surrounding the city of Angory, he lamented Pepin's absence bitterly. Then he called for Pacolet and said to him, "My friend, things go badly for us, not knowing what has happened to King Pepin."

"Or me laissez faire," dit Pacolet, "car tantost en aurons nouvelles." Sans aultres choses dire lendemain au matin il partit d'Angorie et s'en ala parmy l'ost des paiens jusques en la tente de Lucar. Et quant Lucar le veit il luy demanda, "Amy, ou est vostre maistre qui aultrefois me servoit?"

"Ha, sire," dist Pacolet, "il est pieça mort et je suis seul demouré. Je vouldroye bien trouver maistre pour loyallement servir."

"Varlet," ce dist Lucar, "bien vous veul retenir; se bien me servez vous serez bien guerdonné."

"Oy," dit Pacolet, "je ne demande aultre chose." Pacolet demoura au service de Lucar, mais mal servy son maistre et mal fust guerdonné, ainsi que vous orrez cy apres, car tantost que la nuyt fut venue il fist ung enchantement entour du roy Lucar et tellement l'endormit que sur ung cheval le monta et sans esveiller le mena en la cité d'Angorie jusques dedens le palays. Moult fut joyeulx Valentin quant il veit Lucar. Or fust il monté en la sale devant ung tresbeau feu et a celle heure luy faillit le sort. Si s'est Lucar esveillé tout effroyé et esbahy de se trouver la. Il regarde de toutes pars le lieu ou il estoit, et Pacolet, qui mal fut avisé, se presenta devant luy et luy a dit, "Beau maistre, je suis vostre varlet; vous plaist il riens commander?"

Lors Lucar qui le cogneut sceut bien que par luy il estoit trahy. Sy print ung cousteau moult pointu qui de telle maniere en ferit Pacolet que a terre cheut mort. Si ne fault pas demander le grant dueil que a ceste heure Valentin mena. Lor dit, "Amy, or estes vous finé. Si puis bien seurement dire que tel a[116recto] my[1] je n'auray jamais. Or suis je de tout point dolent et esperdu, demouré seul en tristesse loing de tous mes amis, pres de mes ennemis. Helas! franc roy Pepin, pourquoy ne venez vous? Car vostre longue demouree vous portera dommaige. Ha, faulx Lucar, tu as celuy occis en qui estoit mon esperance et seul confort. Par le Dieu Jesus tu l'acheteras chier."

"Par Mahon," dit Lucar, "de riens plus ne me chault quant de celuy qui si faulcement m'a trahy je suis vengé." Adonc Valentin ala vers Pacolet et print ses tables qui estoient en son sain esquelles estoient escrips tous les secrez de son art. Et pieça luy avoit dit Pacolet que quant il seroit mort se apres luy demouroit, qu'il print les tables et que la science estoit escripte par laquelle il sçauroit jouer de son art. Et ainsi le fist Valentin et les tables il print qui depuis luy firent bon mestier.

A ceste heure voulut Valentin que Lucar fust a mort jugé. Mais par les seigneurs qui avec luy estoient fut avisé et conseillé que en une tour seroit mis et seurement gardé "affin que s'il avenoit que de nostre partie aulcun noble prisonnier par les payens fust prins que par Lucar peust estre racheté." Le conseil pleut a tous et aussi fut tenu et acordé. Et quant Lucar fust en prison, Valentin fist moult notablement enterrer le corps de Pacolet qui de grans et de petis assez fut plaint et plouré.

---

[1] *p iiii* at bottom right corner of 116r.

"Now just let me see what I can do," said Pacolet, "for I can soon get information." Without saying anything further he left Angory in the morning and infiltrated the pagan encampment all the way to Lucar's tent. And when Lucar saw him he asked him, "Friend, where is your master who used to serve me?"

"Oh, sire," said Pacolet, "he has been dead for some time, and has left me all alone. I would gladly find another master to serve loyally."

"Valet," said Lucar, "I am quite willing to retain you; if you serve me well, you will be well rewarded."

"Very well," said Pacolet, "I ask for nothing better." Pacolet remained in Lucar's service, but he served his master ill and was ill rewarded, as you shall hear, for as soon as night fell, he enveloped Lucar in a spell, and cast him into such a deep sleep that he was able to mount him on a horse and bring him into the city of Angory all the way to the palace without waking him up. Valentin was quite happy to see Lucar. He was brought into the hall before a crackling fire, and at that moment the charm wore off. Thus Lucar woke up, amazed and afraid to see where he was. He looked all around the strange place, and Pacolet foolishly presented himself before him saying, "Fair master, I am your servant; have you anything you wish me to do?"

Then Lucar realized that he had been betrayed by him. He took hold of a sharp knife and stabbed Pacolet, who fell down dead. No need to wonder what grief Valentin felt at that moment. He said, "My friend, now you are killed. I may well say that I shall never have another such friend. Now I am completely wretched and lost, alone with my sorrow, far from all my friends, and near my enemies. Alas! noble King Pepin, why do you not come? Your long absence will cause you losses. Oh, wicked Lucar, you have killed the one who was my hope and my only comfort. By Jesus God, you shall pay for it dearly."

"By Mohammed," said Lucar, "I don't care about anything else, now that I have taken revenge against the one who betrayed me so falsely." Thereupon Valentin went over to Pacolet and withdrew the tablets that he carried in his bosom on which were written all the secrets of his art. In the past Pacolet had told him that when he died, if Valentin survived him, he should take possession of his tablets, for his knowledge, by which Valentin would be able to perform his magic, was written down. And Valentin did so and took the tablets, which afterwards he made good use of.

At that point Valentin wished Lucar to be sentenced to death. But the lords with him advised instead that he be placed in a tower, there to be closely guarded, "in case it happened that there be some noble prisoner captured from among us who could be ransomed by means of Lucar." This advice pleased everyone, and so it was agreed. And once Lucar was imprisoned, Valentin had Pacolet's body buried with all honors, and everyone, great and small, mourned and wept over him.

[CHAPITRE 56]

Comment le roy Brandiffer sceut que Lucar estoit en Angorie; si manda a Valentin pour appointement faire de le racheter. lvi. chapitre

Lendemain au matin fust grant bruit parmy l'ost des payens et grant cry pour le roy Lucar qu'ilz avoient perdu, et dessus tous les aultres grant dueil en menoit Brandiffer. Et ainsi que par tout de luy demandoit, il arriva une espie qui luy dist comment il estoit dedens Angorie et comment il avoit Pacolet tué. Tant fut joyeulx Brandiffer de la mort de Pacolet et au cueur moult dolent de la prinse de Lucar.

Si appella tantost ung messagier qui sçavoit bien parler françois et l'envoya vers Valentin et luy dist, "Tu t'en iras vers la cité d'Angorie par devers Valentin, et luy diras de par moy que s'il me veult rendre Lucar qu'i tient en ses prisons, je luy deliverray le roy Pepin de France, ou l'empereur de Grece, ou Orson son filz, ou l'ung des douze pers de France, ou Hauffroy, ou Henry, ou le Verd Chevalier, lequel de tous mieulx il aimera."

"Sire," dit le messagier, "vostre messaige je feray moult bien et seurement et dedens peu d'espace vous en aurez nouvelles." A ces motz se partit et tira vers Angorie qui assez pres estoit de la. On luy ouvrit les portes sans difficulté faire pour ce que il estoit venu pour messaige faire. Et quant il fut entré dedens il dist qu'il vouloit parler a Valentin et[1] on luy mena tantost. Et quant il fut devant Valentin moult haultement le salua et puis luy fist son messaige tout et en telle maniere [116verso]que du roy Brandiffer luy estoit commandé.

Et qu'il tenoit en ses prisons tant de vaillans hommes moult fut esmerveillé, si dist au messaigier, "Comment se peult il faire que le roy Brandiffer tiengne en ses prisons tant de vaillans seigneurs ne comment les peult il avoir prins?"

"Sire," dist le messagier, "je vous diray comment. Il est vray que le roy Pepin, nagaires acompaigné des douze pers de France, de Orson, et de Henry, alerent en Hierusalem en habit de pelerin pour le Sainct Sepulchre de vostre Dieu viseter. Si vindrent les nouvelles, par je ne sçay quel trahystre, de ceste chose au roy Brandiffer. De laquelle chose il fut joyeulx et en grant diligence et telle puissance assembla que dedens Hierusalem furent tous prins. Et les a Brandiffer a Chasteau Fort menéz qui de toute sa terre est la plus forte place. Si me veullez donner responce briefve de ce que je vous dy, et se change vous voulez faire au change du roy Lucar contre l'ung de voz bons amis."

"Messagier," dist Valentin, "tantost aurez la responce." Et lors entra en une sale et tous les seigneurs fist venir, si leur a dist, "Amis, il est vray que pour rendre le roy Lucar je puis delivrer des prisons de Brandiffer le pere qui me engendra, ou

---

[1] Text has *en*.

CHAPTER 56

How Brandiffer found out that Lucar was in the city of Angory, and so sent a message to Valentin to arrange for ransom.

The next morning a great hue and cry went up among the pagan host for King Lucar, who was missing, Brandiffer grieving more than anyone else. And just as they were searching for him everywhere, a spy arrived who told him how he was within the city of Angory and how he had killed Pacolet. Brandiffer was quite pleased by the death of Pacolet, but terribly sad about Lucar's capture.

Right away he called for a messenger who knew how to speak French well, and he prepared to send him to Valentin, saying, "You will go see Valentin in the city of Angory, and you will tell him from me that, if he will return to me Lucar, whom he is holding captive, I will deliver up to him King Pepin of France, or the emperor of Greece, or Orson his son, or one of the Twelve Peers of France, or Hauffroy, or Henry, or the Green Knight, whichever one he wishes most."

"Sire," said the messenger, "I will deliver your message promptly and well, and you will soon have tidings." With these words he departed and headed towards Angory, which was nearby. They opened the gates to him without any problem, since he had come to deliver a message. Once within, he said that he wished to speak to Valentin, and they took him there right away. Once he was in Valentin's presence, he greeted him respectfully and delivered his message, just as King Brandiffer had directed him to do.

Valentin was amazed that Brandiffer was holding so many valiant men, so he said to the messenger, "How is it that King Brandiffer is holding so many stalwart lords imprisoned; how was he able to capture them?"

"Sire," said the messenger, "I will tell you how. It is true that King Pepin, accompanied by the Twelve Peers of France, Orson, and Henry, journeyed recently to Jerusalem, dressed in a pilgrim's habit, in order to visit the Holy Sepulcher of your God. News of this came to King Brandiffer by way of some traitor (I don't know who). He was delighted, and quickly arranged things so that they were all captured in Jerusalem. Then Brandiffer brought them to Château Fort, which is the mightiest fortress on earth. Please give me an answer soon to the proposal I have brought you, whether you wish to exchange Lucar for one of your good friends."

"Messenger," said Valentin, "you will have your answer presently." Then he called all the lords into a separate room and told them, "Friends, it seems that by returning Lucar I could free from Brandiffer's prison the father who begat me, or

mon frere Orson, ou mon oncle le roy Pepin, qui sont mes trois plus pres et principaulx amis. Si me veullez conseiller lequel je doy demander."

"Sire," respondirent les barons, "icy ne vault riens le songier, car vous sçavez que nul ne peult estre tant tenu comme a pere et a mere, et par droite rayson et naturelle amour devez vostre pere demander par devant tous les aultres."

"Seigneurs," dist Valentin, "vous parlez sagement, mais sauf toutes voz reverences je suis deliberé de faire aultrement. Pour parler de ceste chose justement et selon la vraye equité, vous sçavez tous que ma mere Bellissant par mon pere l'empereur fut a grant tort et a honte villainement de son pays bannye, et en telle necessité que en peril en la forest d'Orleans m'enfanta. Et eusse esté des bestes sauvaiges devouré et mengé, se n'eust esté mon oncle Pepin le roy de France par qui je fus trouvé et lequel m'a fait nourir et eslever sans[1] moy cognoistre en telle maniere que chevalier m'a fait. Et tous les biens que j'ay sont de par luy venus, ne jamais de mon pere je n'eux ung seul confort ne ung povre secours en ma tribulacion. Pour ce veul sur tous les aultres le roy Pepin, qui tant de bien m'a fait sans sçavoir qui je estoye, soit pour Lucar delivré et que mon pere demeure. Et puis si plaist a Dieu tant exploiterons que nous aurons mon pere et tous les aultres aussi."

Quant les barons oÿrent le grant sens et les parolles de Valentin, moult s'esmerveillerent tous de sa grant prudence, et disoient de commun acord que sagement il parloit. Si s'acorderent a sa voulenté pour ce qu'elle estoit raysonnable.

Lors Valentin appella le messagier et luy a dist, "Amy, tu yras vers le roy Brandiffer et luy diras la respon[117recto]ce que je te fay. C'est que je luy rendrai le roy Lucar par tel convenant que il me delivrera le roy Pepin de France, car pour eschange de Lucar aultre que luy je ne veul avoir."

A ces motz partit le messagier et au roy Brandiffer les nouvelles porta et la responce telle que Valentin luy avoit donnee. "Par Mahon," dist Brandiffer, "tousjours les plus puissans sont les premiers honnouréz. Mais puis que celuy il demande celuy je luy renderay comme il me demande."

[CHAPITRE 57]

Comment Millon d'Angler, qui estoit nommé roy de France pour sauver Pepin, fut delivré des prisons de Brandiffer en change de Lucar. lvii. cha[pitre]

Quant le roy Brandiffer sceult que pour eschange de Lucar vouloit avoir le roy de France, tantost manda messagiers a Chasteau Fort vers sa fille Galasie, comment elle baillast et delivrast le roy de France tout seul et sans nul des aultres. Les

---

[1] Text has *sane*.

my brother Orson, or my uncle King Pepin, all three of whom are my dearest and closest friends. You must counsel me on whom I should ask for."

"Sire," answered the barons, "there is no point in wondering, for you know that no one can be more beholden than to a father or a mother, and thus by right and by reason as well as by natural love you must request your father before any of the others."

"My lords," said Valentin, "you speak wisely, but, with all due respect to your opinion, I have decided to do otherwise. For to speak with absolute justice and fairness, you all know that my mother Bellissant was shamefully and wrongfully banished by my father from his land, and sent forth in such penury that she gave birth to me in great peril in the forest of Orleans. And I would have been eaten and devoured by savage beasts if not for my uncle Pepin, king of France, by whom I was found. And without knowing who I was, he raised me and brought me up to become a knight. And everything I have came from him—never from my father did I receive a single thing for my comfort or help in my tribulation. For this reason, I want to exchange Lucar for King Pepin, who did so much for me without knowing who I was, rather than any of the others. Let my father remain for now, and later, may it please God that we succeed in freeing my father and all the others as well."

When the barons heard Valentin's words and recognized his good sense, they marveled at his great prudence and said in common accord that he spoke wisely. Thus they concurred with his wish because it was reasonable.

Then Valentin called for the messenger and said to him, "Friend, you will go to King Brandiffer and will give him this response. I will return King Lucar to him if he agrees to deliver to me King Pepin of France, for I desire no other in exchange for Lucar."

After these words the messenger left and brought his report and the answer to King Brandiffer, just as Valentin had given it to him. "By Mohammed," said Brandiffer, "the most powerful are always the first to be honored. But since this is the one he requests, this is the one I will return to him, just as he asks."

CHAPTER 57

How Millon d'Angler, who was called king of France in order to save Pepin, was delivered from Brandiffer's prison in exchange for Lucar.

Once King Brandiffer knew that Valentin wanted the king of France in exchange for Lucar, he sent messengers right away to Château Fort to his daughter Galasie, explaining that she should send him the king of France alone and none of the

messagiers furent tous pres et entrerent sur mer; si ont tant bien naigé que en bien peu de temps furent a Chasteau Fort arrivéz, et sont aléz vers la belle Galasie, et si luy ont compté tout le fait comment pour eschange de Lucar que les crestiens ont prins ilz sont venus de par le roy Brandiffer querir le roy de France. Et quant la fille l'entendit elle fut tantost preste de faire la vouenté de son pere; si appella le chartrier et l'envoya aux prisons le roy de France demander. Et quant il vint a l'uys de la chartre il se escria tout hault, "Or ça, viengne le roy de France, car delivrer le me convient."

Et quant Millon d'Angler entendit le chartrier il respondit doulcement, "Helas, amy, je suis icy. Pourquoy m'appellez tu? Se mourir me convient premier je prie a Dieu Jesus que de moy veulle avoir pitié, car pour sa saincte foy soustenir veul de bon cueur mon corps a mort offrir."

"Sire," dit le chartrier, "de mourir n'ayez doubte, car delivré vous serez par ung eschange d'ung roy payen que ceulx de vostre loy tiennent."

Et quant Henry entendit les parolles assez se repentit que il avoit escondit le roy son pere et qu'i ne se estoit fait roy de France quant il en fust requis. Mais le faulx et desloyal enfant qui bien sçavoit la trahyson ne pensoit jamais que son pere le roy Pepin en peust eschapper, mais bien cogneut clerement sa faulce et mauldicte et maleureuse voulenté quant il vit que par tel moien le duc Milon estoit delivré. Lequel en grant pitié et en plourant des aultres barons print congé.

"Helas," dit dont l'empereur de Grece, "saluez moy sur tous mon enfant Valentin."

"Voire aussi," dit Orson, "et a luy me recommandez. Et luy declairez la maniere comment nous sommes icy en miserable destresse et en moult grant povreté, et se de par luy n'avons secours de brief, nous conviendra noz jours deffiner."

"Seigneurs," dit Millon, "prenez en vous bon resconfort, car si plaist a [117verso]Dieu de paradis, jamais en France ne retourneray que ne soyez delivré." A ces motz partit de la prison et tous les aultres demourerent plourant moult tendrement et fort piteusement. Lors quant il fut dehors, comme sage et bien aprins il s'en ala par devers la belle et plaisante dame Galasie et de celle print congé en moult grande reverence et honneur. La dame fust doulce et courtoise et a son dieu Mahon doulcement le recommanda.

Ainsi partit le duc Millon et les messagiers qui le estoient venu querir. Le menerent au port, puis monterent sur la mer et en peu de temps ilz arriverent en l'ost de Brandiffer. Lors quant Brandiffer le veit, il luy a dit, "Franc roy, bien puissez estre venu. Assez sçavez la cause pourquoy vous ay mandé. Allez avec mes gens qui vous ont amené jusques a la cité de Angorie et dictes a Valentin que pour eschange de vous me renvoye Lucar comme appointé nous avons."

"Sire," dit Millon d'Angler, "ainsi le veul je faire et telle loyaulté vous tenir que se pour moy Lucar ne vous est delivré je me viendray rendre a vous et pourrez de mon corps faire comme devant."

"Par Mahon," dist Brandiffer, "vous parlez royallement et plus ne vous demande. Or alez a Mahon qui vous veulle conduire."

others. The messengers were ready and set sail; they journeyed so quickly that they soon arrived at Château Fort and went to the fair Galasie, explaining that they had been sent to fetch the king of France in order to exchange him for Lucar, who had been captured by the Christians. When the girl heard this, she was ready to carry out her father's wishes at once; so she called for her warden and sent him to the dungeon to bring out the king of France. And when he came to the dungeon he cried aloud, "Now then, let the king of France step forward, for I am supposed to fetch him."

And when Millon d'Angler heard the warden, he answered softly, "Alas, my friend, I am here. Why do you call for me? If I am to die, let me first pray to God Jesus that He may have pity on me, for I am willing to offer myself up to death in order to sustain His sacred faith."

"Sire," said the warden, "have no fear of dying, for you shall be freed by an exchange for a pagan king, whom those of your religion hold captive."

When Henry heard these words, he repented having refused when asked to help the king his father by pretending to be king of France. But this false and faithless child, who had known all about the plot to betray his father King Pepin, never thought he might have escaped. But it was driven home to him what an unfortunate decision he had made when he saw how Duke Millon was being freed. The latter, weeping and overcome by emotion, took leave of the other barons.

"Well," said then the emperor of Greece, "most of all, greet my child Valentin for me."

"Indeed, for me also," said Orson, "and commend me to him. And explain to him how we are captive here in miserable distress and great penury, and if we do not get help from him soon, we will have to end our days."

"My lords," said Millon, "take some good comfort, for if it please the God of paradise, I will never return to France without first delivering you." With these words he left the prison, and all the others remained behind, sobbing most piteously. Then, once he was outside, he went to take his leave of the fair and lovely lady Galasie with great reverence and honor, like a wise and proper gentleman. The lady was polite and courteous and sweetly commended him to her god Mohammed.

Thus departed Duke Millon and the messengers who had come to get him. They brought him to the port, set sail, and soon arrived in Brandiffer's camp. When Brandiffer saw him, he said to him, "Welcome, noble king. You are sufficiently informed as to why I sent for you. Go to the city of Angory with the men who brought you here, and tell Valentin to send me Lucar in exchange for you, as we arranged between us."

"Sire," said Millon d'Angler, "I wish to act towards you in good faith, such that if Lucar is not delivered in exchange for me, I will return to give myself up to you for you to do with me as before."

"By Mohammed," said Brandiffer, "you speak nobly, and I ask for no more than that. Now go in Mohammed's name and may he guide you."

Ainsi partit Millon d'Angler et ceulx qui le menoient si arriverent en Angorie et entrerent sans nul refus, et apres alerent au palais et la trouverent Valentin qui luy et le duc Millon d'Angler doulcement s'embrasserent. Et parla le duc Millon d'Angler ung petit a secret et a compté l'entreprinse; comment ilz avoient esté prins en Hierusalem et comment le roy d'Inde avoit le roy Pepin emmené sans riens le cognoistre, et ainsi comme il avoit son nom changé a la requeste du roy Pepin. Et puis luy a dit comment les aultres estoient en prison dedens Chastel Fort.

Et quant Valentin entendit il luy a dit doulcement, "Bien avez ouvré, car je cognoy que loyaulté vous avez quise et loyaulté vous est venue, car par le feal service que avez fait au roy Pepin au jour d'uy estes des mains de voz enemis delivré. Bon amy vous monstrastes quant pour le roy Pepin sauver changastes vostre nom, et aussi bien y pouiez vous avoir dommage que proffit, car de propre nature les faulx paiens demandent la mort du roy Pepin pour cause que contre eulx veult la foy de Jesus soustenir et la loy de Mahon destruire."

Quant Valentin eust ainsi parlé, il fist devant luy amener le roy Lucar, puis luy a dit, "Lucar, pour ceste fois estes delivré, mais gardez vous de moy pour le temps a venir, et vous souvienne de mon bon amy Pacolet lequel vous avez tué. Car par le Dieu que je croy se jamais en bataille ou aultre part vous puis rencontrer nous verrons de nous deux qui sera plus vaillant."

A ces motz partit Lucar qui moult fut joyeulx d'eschapper. Et quant il fut dehors des portes Sarrasins a grant puissance luy vindrent au devant en demenant grant feste pour son delivrement; tromppetes, coz et haulx [118recto]clarons firent haultement sonner. Ainsi fut delivré Lucar, et Millon d'Angler rendu a Valentin.

[CHAPITRE 58]

Comment Valentin et le duc Millon d'Angler saillirent de Angorie sur l'ost des payens, et comment les payens si perdirent la bataille. lviii. [chapitre][1]

Tantost que Millon d'Angler fut avec Valentin par dedens Angorie, ilz ne firent pas grant sejour mais ordonnerent leurs batailles et a cincquante mil hommes saillirent de la cité. Bannieres et estandars desployerent et mirent au vent. Et quant Brandiffer en oyt les nouvelles il fist tromppettes et clarons moult haultement sonner et ses batailles ordonna jusques a xxiiii. Et quant elles furent ordonnees, le roy Brandiffer desmarcha acompaigné de xiiii. roys, tous tenans de luy.

---

[1] Woodcut of battle scene with mounted knights and scattered body parts. Repeat of woodcut on 77v.

Thus Millon d'Angler departed, and those who were leading him arrived in Angory and entered without any trouble, and afterward they went to the palace where they found Valentin, and he and Duke Millon d'Angler embraced each other gently. Duke Millon d'Angler took him aside and recounted to him what had happened, how they had been captured in Jerusalem, and how the king of India had taken King Pepin away with him, not having recognized him, and thus how he had changed his name at the request of King Pepin. And then he told him how the others were being held in the dungeon of Château Fort.

And when Valentin had heard all this, he said to him gently, "You have done rightly, for I can see that you sought to act in faithfulness and it has done you good in return, for by the loyal service you rendered King Pepin, today you are delivered from your enemies' hands. A good friend you showed yourself to be by changing your name to save King Pepin, for you were more like to have been harmed by it than helped, for normally the wicked pagans demand the death of King Pepin because he supports the faith of Jesus and wishes to destroy the religion of Mohammed."

When Valentin had finished speaking, he sent for King Lucar, and said to him, "Lucar, this time you are free, but beware me in the future and remember my good friend Pacolet, whom you killed. For by the God in whom I believe, if I ever come across you in battle or elsewhere we shall see who of the two of us is the more valiant."

At these words, Lucar departed, delighted to have escaped. Once he was beyond the gates, a multitude of Saracens came to him, celebrating his release with the sounding of trumpets, horns, and clarions. Thus was Lucar freed and Millon d'Angler returned to Valentin.

CHAPTER 58

How Valentin and Duke Millon d'Angler rode forth from the city of Angory against the army of pagans, and how the pagans lost the battle.

As soon as Millon d'Angler was with Valentin in Angory, they did not delay, but immediately formed their battalions and sallied forth out of the city with fifty thousand men. They unfurled their banners and standards to ripple in the wind. And when Brandiffer had tidings of their movements, he had his trumpets and clarions sounded on high and ordered up his own battalions, to the number of twenty-four. Once they were formed, King Brandiffer set out in the company of fourteen kings, all vassals beholden to him. And the Christians approached to

Et les crestiens approcherent pour frapper dedens mais tant estoyent espes et drus rengéz qu'i n'y peurent entrer.

Lors Valentin frappa dedens et mis en son poing la lance et s'escrya haultement, "Crestiens, prenez couraige! Soyez tous joyaulx!" Et lors commença fiere bataille aupres de l'estandart de Brandiffer, qui aupres de luy avoit Lucar puissament acompaigné. Crestiens assaillirent et Sarrasins se deffendirent, car entour de leur estandart avoit .l. mil. hommes qui devant eulx tenoient targes moult grandes et fortes, parquoy les crestiens peu grever les pouoient.

Adonc ung admiral paien, seigneur de Cassidoine, vit ung François vaillant qui moult de Sarrasins grevoit et plusieurs mors abatoit. Si ala celle part et le crestien d'ung hache frappa ung coup si grant que la teste en deux luy partit. Mais devant son retour il eut de tel pain souppe, car ung moult vaillant escuier du païs de Normendie dessus l'admiral arriva, et devant Millon d'Angler luy a tollue la vie, et pour celle vaillance le fit Millon d'Angler chevalier. A celle heure a dit a ses gens, "Pensés de bien ouvrer, car si povre n'y aura se vaillamment se porte que au jour d'uy je ne face chevalier." Tant en fist a ce jour que chascun prenoit couraige de bien faire pour avoir la colee.

Et en ce point dura la bataille longuement que le soleil commença a obscurer[1] et le jour a delivrer. Mais pour tant que les chrestiens veirent que paiens se vouloient retraire, Valentin ne veult pas se retraire. Trop bien cuidoient Sarrasins en leurs tentes retourner, mais les crestiens furent au devant dont Brandiffer et Lucar moult furent empeschéz. [118v]Toute nuyt dura la bataille forte et tresmortelle. Falloz et grans feuz estoient de toutes pars ardans et flamboyans, et quant le jour fust cler plusfort recommença chascun d'une part et d'aultre. Tant y eut de mors que le sang couroit aval comme les ruisseaux de fontaines.

Si ne fault pas demander de la proesse que fist adonc Valentin, car au plus fort de la bataille malgré Sarrasins se bouta, et le duc Millon frappa des esperons et apres luy ala. Valentin de toutes pars abat gens et chevaulx tant qu'il n'y a payen si plain de hardiesse qui devant luy se trouve. Et tant avant entra en la bataille qu'i vint au plus pres de l'estandart Brandiffer, et lors veit l'admiral d'Inde et devers luy s'en vint si rudement que son cheval tua desoubz luy. Mais Valentin qui fut legier tantost sur piedz se leva et puis print l'espee froubie. De toutes pars tue et abat Sarrasins en criant haultement "Montjoye!" et Dieu reclamant, mais jamais ne fust eschappé se ce n'eust esté le duc Millon qui payens espartit comme le loup fait les brebis, et tous ceulx qui devant luy treuve il abat et gette par terre. Ainsi le secourut et cheval luy bailla. Et quant Valentin fust remonté, il se tira hors la bataille pour prendre ung peu d'air et but une fois de vin que ung de ses gens luy presenta. Et puis retourna en l'estour plus fort que par devant.

---

[1] Text has *obcurer*.

break through their ranks, but they were so thick and numerous that they could not penetrate.

Then Valentin broke through with his lance in his grip and crying out resoundingly, "Christians, take courage! May your hearts be filled with joy!" Then commenced a fierce combat around the standard of Brandiffer, who had Lucar and his cohort near him. Christians attacked and Saracens defended themselves, for around their standard were fifty thousand men holding great shields before them through which the Christians could not harm them.

Then a pagan emir, the lord of Cassidoine, spied a valiant Frenchman who had wounded and killed several Saracens. He dashed over to him and gave the Christian such a stroke with an ax that he cleaved his head in two. But before he could return to his own side he got a taste of his own medicine,[1] for a most valiant squire from the country of Normandy descended upon the emir and took his life right under the eyes of Millon d'Angler, for which valiance the latter made him a knight. Then the duke said to his men, "Do your best to excel, for there is no one so poor that I will not make him a knight today if he shows himself valorous." And he made so many that day, they all took courage to excel in order to be dubbed knight.

The battle lasted so long that the sun began to sink and the daylight darken. And although the Christians saw that the pagans wished to pull back, Valentin did not wish to withdraw. The Saracens were trying to head back to their tents, but the Christians were before them, which blocked Brandiffer and Lucar from doing so. The battle raged on fiercely all night, causing many deaths. Fires burned everywhere, and when the day dawned, both sides redoubled their efforts. There were so many dead that blood flowed like a river.

No need to inquire what marvelous feats of arms Valentin performed, for he threw himself into the thick of the battle despite the Saracens, and Duke Millon spurred his horse and dashed in after him. Valentin smote men and horses all about him, so that there was no pagan so bold as to come near him. But he pressed on into the battle until he drew near Brandiffer's standard, where he saw the marshal of India who rode against him so hard that he killed his horse from beneath him. But Valentin, who was light on his feet, quickly arose and seized his polished sword. He struck down Saracens right and left, crying out "Montjoie!" and invoking God, but he never would have escaped alive had it not been for Duke Millon breaking through the pagans like a wolf through the sheep, smiting to the ground anyone he found before him. Thus did he rush to his aid and give him a horse. And once Valentin was remounted, he withdrew a little from the battle to catch his breath and drink a draft of wine that one of his men thrust at him. Then he returned to battle stronger than before.

---

[1] Cf. Hassell, *Proverbs*, 188 (no. P7); Morawski, *Proverbes*, 32 (no. 869). For the meaning of this proverb, see Le Roux de Lincy, *Le Livre des proverbes français* (Paris: Paulin, 1842; repr. Paris: Hachette, 1996), 643.

Et quant le mareschal de Inde veit que le meilleur n'estoit pas pour eulx, tout le plus secretement que il peut fist ses gens se traire et son estandart en ung petit val pour mieulx se tollir. Bien le vit Valentin; si le dist a Millon d'Angler. Lors appointerent que Valentin et ses gens sans grant bruyt demener iroient sur ledit mareschal et ainsy fut la chose acomplie. Valentin et ses gens tirerent a celle part et frapperent sur les Indois par telle hardiesse que de premiere entree leur bataille rompirent.

Lors Valentin avisa le mareschal qui bien sauver se cuida. Sy frappa des esperons et tel coup de lance luy donna que cheval et homme a terre rua, et crestiens saillirent dessus a maintz glaisves trenchans. Mais il fut si bien armé que de premiere venue ne le peurent pas tuer, mais fut prins tout vif et baillé a Valentin qui le livra en garde a quattre chevaliers. Et furent ainsi a ceste heure les Indois desconfis par le vaillant chevalier Valentin, et fut la premiere bataille qui ce jour fust desconfite. Maintz riches prisonniers ilz furent a ce jour prins, lesquelz Valentin envoya dedens Angorie et commanda seurement les garder.

Or cogneurent tantost Brandiffer et Lucar que le pire estoit pour eulx. "Par Mahon," dit Brandiffer, "je ne puis aviser ne trouver maniere come nous puissons icy contre crestiens resister, et si me doubte fort que ycy mourir ne nous conviengne. Si seroye de oppinion que pour ceste fois nous tenissons atant et retourner en nostre pays. Si pourrons une aultre fois [119recto]a plus grans gens revenir."

"Par Mahon," dist Lucar, "vous dites verité, car nous avons ja perdu des meilleurs de noz gens. Retournons sans plus demourer icy, car il vault mieulx a temps fuir que mourir pour trop demourer."

Ainsy fut par eulx le conseil prins, et firent ploier l'estandart et bannieres et ont dit a leurs gens sauve soy qui pourra. Paiens ont prins la fuitte vers le port de mer et crestiens vont apres, abatant et tuant sans nulle aultre deffence, car gens qui sont en fuytte sont a demy desconfis. Et tant demoura par les champs de payens que avec Brandiffer et Lucar n'en monta que cent a leur retourner. Et apres la desconfiture des payens, crestiens entrerent par les tentes et adonc furent tous riches. Puis alerent en Angorie eulx reposer, car las et travailléz estoient. Lendemain firent les mors ensevelir et pour eulx Dieu prier ainsy qu'ilz estoient tenus.

When the marshal of India saw that matters were not going their way, he pulled his men and banner back into a little valley as surreptitiously as he could. But Valentin noticed him and pointed it out to Millon d'Angler. They decided that Valentin and his men, without drawing attention to themselves, would go attack them, and so was it done. Valentin and his men followed the Indians and attacked them with such courage that they broke their battalion at once.

Then Valentin spied the marshal, who was trying to save himself. He spurred his horse and delivered such a punch with his lance that he brought down horse and rider, and the Christians rallied around with many sharp swords. But the marshal was so well armed that at first they could not kill him, rather they took him alive and delivered him up to Valentin, who put him under the guard of four knights. Thus were the Indians defeated at that time by the valiant knight Valentin, and it was the first battalion vanquished that day. Many rich prisoners were taken that day, whom Valentin sent into Angory with the order that they be carefully guarded.

Now Brandiffer and Lucar soon discovered that they were gettng the worst of it. "By Mohammed," said Brandiffer, "for the life of me I don't see how we will be able to fight off the Christians here, and I fear that we may die here. I think it best that we withdraw this time and return to our country. Then we will be able to come back another time with more men."

"By Mohammed," said Lucar, "you speak the truth, for we have already lost the best of our men. Let us return and stay no longer, for it is better to flee in time than die from having dallied too long."

Thus did they conclude, so they ordered their standard and banners furled and told their men to save themselves as they could. The pagans fled towards the port and the Christians came after them, striking and killing and facing little resistance, for men in flight are half defeated. And so many dead pagans remained on the field of battle that Brandiffer and Lucar set sail with only one hundred for their return trip. And after the defeat of the pagans, the Christians plundered their tents, which were full of riches. Then they returned to the city of Angory to rest, for they were weary and exhausted. The next day, as one should, they buried the dead and prayed God for mercy on their souls.

[CHAPITRE 59]

Comment le roy Pepin fut rendu par le roy de Inde en eschange de son mareschal. lix. chapitre

Apres que les crestiens qui la bataille devant Angorie avoient gaignee et eurent fait les mors enterrer, Valentin monta au palais et commanda que on luy amenast les prisonniers. Lors luy fut tout premier amené le mareschal du roy d'Inde[1] duquel il demanda s'il vouloit croyre en Jesus.

"Par Mahon," dist le mareschal, "j'ayme plus chier a mourir."

Lors luy demanda Millon d'Angler de quel pays il estoit.

"Seigneurs," dit le paien, "je suis mareschal du roy de Inde la Major et moult fort bien son amy."

Quant Millon d'Angler l'entendit il tira a part Valentin et luy a dist, "Bien avons ouvré puis que cestuy payen avons prins; par luy pourrons avoir le roy Pepin que le roy de Inde pour nayn emmena quant nous fusmes prins au Sainct Sepulchre."

"Millon," dit Valentin, "vous dictes verité." Lors appela le payen et luy a demandé se le roy d'Inde Major tenoit point en ses prisons ung crestien de petite estature que pieça avoit prins.

"Par Mahon," dist le mareschal, "en la prison du roy d'Inde n'y a point de crestien. Bien est vray que en sa court il y en a ung petit mais il chevaulche avec luy et n'est point en prison et l'amena de Hierusalem quant les douze pers furent prins."

"Mareschal," dist Valentin, "c'est celuy que nous demandons. Et se tant pouez faire qu'il me soit amené, pour luy vous serez delivré sans nulle ranson payer, car il est mon varlet et longtemps m'a loyallement servy, pour quoy voulentiers ravoir je le vouldroie."

Ce dist le paien, "De ce suis je d'acord," et fut fort joyeulx des nouvelles oÿr. Si escript tost une lettre et au roy d'Inde l'envoye.

Quant le roy d'Inde eut la lettre veue, il fust moult joyeulx de rendre Pepin pour son mareschal, car pas ne cognoissoit quel homme estoit Pepin. Devant luy le fist tost venir et luy a dist, "Bel amy, aler vous convient en vostre [119verso]pays, car par vous je delivre mon mareschal que laisser ne vouldroye pour telz cent comme vous."

"Sire," dist Pepin, "de ce suis joyeulx; et mal vous ay servy et vous plaise a le moy pardonner."

"Amy," ce dit le roy, "a Mahon te commant."

Lors ala Pepin courant a la fenestre d'Esclarmonde et luy dist, "M'amye, prenez en vous bon resconfort, car delivré je suis. En brief vous envoyeray vostre amy Valentin et si sachez de vray que jamais ne cesseray que serez delivree." A ces motz se departit et la dame demoura, qui de grant joye fust paulmee.

---

[1] Text has *din* only, apparently owing to line break.

CHAPTER 59

How King Pepin was returned by the King of India in exchange for his marshal.

After the Christians had won the battle before the walls of Angory and had buried the dead, Valentin went up to the palace and ordered the prisoners to be brought to him. The first one fetched was the king of India's marshal, who was asked if he wished to accept belief in Jesus.

"By Mohammed," said the marshal, "I would rather die."

Then Millon d'Angler asked him from which land he came.

"My lords," said the pagan, "I am the marshal of the king of India Major and his very good friend."

When Millon d'Angler heard this, he drew Valentin aside and said to him, "We have done well capturing this pagan; through him we can regain King Pepin, whom the king of India took away with him to be his dwarf when we were captured at the Holy Sepulcher."

"Millon," said Valentin, "you speak the truth." Then he called over the pagan and asked him if the king of India Major happened to have in his prison a Christian of very small stature who had been captured some time ago.

"By Mohammed," said the marshal, "the king of India has no Christian in his prison. But it is true that in his court there is a little man, but he rides with him and has never been imprisoned, and he did bring him back with him from Jerusalem when the Twelve Peers were captured."

"Marshal," said Valentin, "he is the one we request. And if you can manage to have him returned to me, I will deliver you without your having to pay any ransom, for he was my valet and long served me faithfully, for which reason I would very much like to have him back."

The pagan answered, "I agree to that," and indeed was delighted to hear the proposal. Thus he wrote a letter right away and dispatched it to the king of India.

When the king of India saw the letter, he was more than happy to return Pepin in exchange for his marshal, for he had no idea who Pepin really was. He had him brought to him and told him, "Dear friend, you must now return to your own country, for by exchanging you, I will deliver my marshal, whom I would never desert for a hundred such as you."

"Sire," said Pepin, "I am quite content; and if I have served you badly, may it please you to pardon me."

"Friend," said the king, "I commend you to Mohammed."

Then Pepin ran to Esclarmonde's window and said to her, "My friend, take some comfort, for I have been delivered. Soon I will send to you your beloved Valentin, and know for certain that I will never cease my efforts until you too are delivered." With these words he left, and the lady remained behind, swooning from such joy.

Pepin print le chemin avec le messagier si qu'en petit de temps ilz furent en Angorie. Or ne fault point demander la joye qui adonc fut menee. François alerent a l'encontre sonnant tromppettes et clarons a grant feste demenerent.

"Oncle," dist Valentin, "de bonne heure fust celuy prins par qui vous estes delivré car sur tous les biens du monde vostre corps je desiroye."

"Nepveu," ce[1] dit Pepin, "prenez en vous liesse, car nouvelles vous aporte de la chose du monde que plus chier vous tenez. C'est de la belle Esclarmonde qui tant avez longuement quise. Or l'ay je veue et trouvee et a vous se recommande." Adonc luy compta l'a maniere comment elle avoit esté prinse du roy d'Inde et comment elle s'estoit en toutes ces choses gouvernee et maintenue. Et quant Valentin oÿt ces nouvelles il eust si grant joye que a peine pouoit il parler.

"Ha, dame," dit Valentin, "or vous doit du tout mon cueur aimer et loiallement servir quant pour l'amour de moy tant vous estes gardee. Si prometz a Jesus que jamais ne vous fauldray—ou je y perdray la vie ou je vous delivreray. Ancores ay je les tables du vaillant Pacolet par quoy je pourroie bien de subtil art jouer et de danger me getter."

Apres ces parolles Valentin fist delivrer le mareschal d'Inde. Puis entra en sa chambre secrete et la porte de sa chambre par devers luy ferma, puis print les tables de Pacolet et regarda dedens. Si trouva plusieurs choses merveilleuses a racompter, et entre les aultres choses, il trouva les motz et paroles telles que Pacolet faisoit les gens par son enchantement endormir. Apres a trouvé comment on peult ouvrir la plus forte porte que nul sceust fermer. Et en lisant ces motz la porte de sa chambre soudainement se ouvrit. Puis en la fin trouva come quant il luy plaira, il semblera estre vielle femme et quant il vouldra bel home. Et quant Valentin a toutes ces choses veues, il print encre et papier et, pour doubte des tables perdre, tout en ung brief il les escript et sur luy en ses habillemens les cousit. Si en eut depuis grant mestier pour sa vie sauver, ainsi comme je vous diray.

[CHAPITRE 60]

Comment Pepin partit d'Angorie et retourna en France pour Artus de Bretagne que sa femme vouloit espouser et le royaume tenir. lx. chapitre

En celuy temps que je vous compte que le roy Pepin estoit en Angorie pour payens combatre, et sur ce point luy estoit venu ung messagier de par la royne Ber[120recto]the sa femme, lequel luy a dist apres son salut fait de par ladite dame, "Sire, veullez entendre les nouvelles que je vous aporte de par ma tresredoubtee

---

[1] Text has *se*.

Pepin left with the messenger, and soon they were in Angory. Now there is no need to ask with what great joy he was received. The French poured out to meet him, blowing trumpets and clarions to celebrate the event.

"Uncle," said Valentin, "it was a happy moment when we captured the marshal, for by him you are freed, and of all good things that could happen in this world, I most wanted you returned to us."

"Nephew," said Pepin, "be happy, for I bring you tidings of what you hold most dear in the world. I speak of the fair Esclarmonde whom you have sought for so long. I have found her and seen her, and she sends you her greeting." Thereupon he recounted to him how she had been captured by the king of India and how she had behaved and protected herself. And when Valentin heard this news, he was so overjoyed that he could barely speak.

"Ah, lady," said Valentin, "you deserve to be loved by me heart and soul, seeing how you have kept yourself for me all this time out of love for me. I promise Jesus that I shall never fail you — I will rescue you or lose my life in the attempt. I still have the valiant Pacolet's tablets with which I could perform magic and keep myself from danger."

After these words, Valentin freed the marshal of India. Then he entered his secret chamber where, after closing the door behind him, he took out Pacolet's tablets and looked through them. He found many things marvelous to recount, and, among other things, he found the spells through which Pacolet had made men fall into an enchanted sleep. Then he found a way to open the strongest door so that no one may close it afterwards. And while reading these words, his chamber door opened suddenly. Then finally he found how, when he wanted, he could take on the appearance of an old woman or a handsome man. And when Valentin saw all these things, he took paper and ink and quickly wrote down all these spells, for fear of losing the tablets, and then sewed them into his clothing. And indeed he had great need of them later on to save his life, as I will tell you presently.

CHAPTER 60

How King Pepin left the city of Angory and returned to France because of Arthur of Brittany, who wished to marry his wife Bertha and take over his kingdom.

During this time that I have been telling you about, when King Pepin was in Angory to fight the pagans, a messenger came to him, sent by his wife Queen Bertha, who told him on his wife's behalf, after a proper greeting, "Sire, please listen to the news I bring you on the part of my most respected lady, Bertha,

dame, Berthe la royne de France. Sachez que tous ceulx de par dela pensent et croyent fermement que vous et les douze pers de France soyez mors, pour tant qu'ilz ont oÿ nouvelles que dedens Hierusalem payens vous avoient prins. Si est vray que Artus le roy de Bretaigne, esperant vostre mort et les parolles estre vrayez, en grant puissance d'armes en vostre pays est entré et par force veult de France estre roy, et la royne Berthe oultre son gré espouser. Or suis je venu par deça les nouvelles vous dire. Si pensez sur ce fait, car le cas trop vous touche, et de ceste heure est si grant guerre en France encommencee que Guillaume de Monglive a fait Garin tuer et si a le roy de Bretaigne entreprins de mettre en exil monseigneur Charlot vostre petit filz."

Dolent fut le roy Pepin de telles nouvelles oÿr; si fist les barons de sa court assembler et leurs demanda s'i furent tout d'ung acord que mieulx valloit sa propre terre deffendre que trop soy travailler pour l'autruy acquerir. Tenu fust ce conseil et Pepin l'acorda. Si print congé de tous pour s'en aler en France; le duc Millon d'Angler avec luy ala.

Et Valentin luy dist, "Oncle, demourer me convient pour mettre et peine et force de mon pere l'empereur de Grece et mon frere Orson avec les douze pers delivrer."

"Valentin," dist Pepin, "vous parlez sagement. S'i plaist a Dieu que de mes ennemis puisse avoir victoire, je vous envoyeray aide contre les faulx payens." Apres ces parolles le roy Pepin monta sur mer acompaigné de six mil combatans.

Si vous parleray de Valentin qui pour l'amour de Esclarmonde nuyt et jour ne repose.

[CHAPITRE 61]

Comment Valentin ala en Inde Major et contrefit le medecin pour veoir Esclarmonde. lxi. cha[pitre]

Valentin,[1] qui par le roy Pepin avoit eu nouvelles de la belle Esclarmonde, ne l'a mis pas en oubly,[2] mais partit d'Angorie acompaigné seulement d'ung de ses escuiers, et pour mieulx son fait couvrir, en guise de medecin s'abilla. Et ala vers le port et trouva une nef de marchans qui en Inde vouloient aler. Il entra avec eulx et les marchans le receurent,[3] et tant nagerent sur mer que en brief en Inde arriverent.

Mais premier que Valentin entrast dedens [120verso]la ville il fist faire une robe bien longue et fort honeste. Puis mist sur son espaule ung chapperon fourré, ainsy comme ung grant docteur expert en medecine. En la cité entra; en une

---

[1] Woodcut of seated king and ecclesiastical figure, each with open book. Repeat of woodcut on 7r.

[2] Text has *ombly*.

[3] Text has *recheurent*.

queen of France. Know that everyone there believes most assuredly that you and the Twelve Peers of France are dead, because tidings reached them that the pagans had captured you in Jerusalem. And it is also true that Arthur, the king of Brittany, hoping for your death and the truth of the reports, has entered your territory with a great show of strength, and is trying to become king of France by force and by marrying Queen Bertha against her will. I have come from there to bring you these tidings. Consider what is happening, for it touches you most closely, and at this moment there is so much fighting erupting in France that William of Monglive has killed Garin, and the king of Brittany has undertaken to send my lord Charles, your little son, into exile."

King Pepin was greatly sorrowed to hear these tidings; he assembled the barons of his court and asked whether they were all in agreement that it was better to defend one's own land than to labor to acquire another. Such did they conclude, and Pepin accepted it. So he took his leave from everyone in order to return to France, and Duke Millon d'Angler was to go with him.

Valentin said to him, "Uncle, I must remain here to do my best to free my father the emperor of Greece and my brother Orson along with the Twelve Peers."

"Valentin," said Pepin, "you speak wisely. If it please God that I may have victory over my enemies, I will send you help against the wicked pagans." After this exchange King Pepin set sail, accompanied by six thousand fighters.

Now I will speak to you of Valentin who could rest neither night nor day because of his love for Esclarmonde.

CHAPTER 61

How Valentin went to India, pretending to be a doctor, in order to see Esclarmonde.

Valentin, who had received news of the fair Esclarmonde from King Pepin, did not forget her; rather, he left Angory, taking only one of his squires and disguising himself as a doctor, the better to hide his purpose. Going down to the port, he boarded a merchant ship he found there about to leave for India. He boarded, the merchants welcomed him, and they sailed over the sea so quickly that they soon arrived in India.

Before entering the city, Valentin had a long, proper gown made for himself. Then, just like a successful doctor expert in medicine, he put a furred hood on his

bonne riche hostelerie s'en ala loger. Et tantost que l'oste le veit, il luy demanda de quel mestier il sçavoit user.

"Hoste," dist Valentin, "je suis medecin et si sçay l'art et la science de tous malades guarir."

L'oste plus n'en enquist et moult bien le receust. Bien le servoit son esciuer comme clerc de docteur. En ce point fut Valentin deux jours chieulx son hoste. Puis il luy a dist, "Hoste, ung plaisir me ferez s'il vous plaist. C'est que me demandez ung homme qui voise par la cité crier ma science et que s'il y a nulz maladez je me vante de les guarir. Car sachez que j'ay mestier de gaigner pour vous payer les despens que ceans il me convient faire. Non pourtant se de moy avez doubte, gaige vous bailleray."

"Par Mahon," dist l'oste, "gaige veul je bien avoir," car en estrangiers il se fait mauvais fier.

Dont luy bailla Valentin ung fin manteau fourré. "Tenez," dist Valentin, "et de moy ne vous doubtez point, mais me faictes tantost venir le varlet que je vous ay demandé."

L'oste saillit hors et ung varlet amena qui n'avoit nulz souliers, robe, ne chapperon mais il estoit pres que tout nud. Valentin, pour l'amour de Dieu, le fist habiller, puis luy dist, "Mon amy, sçavez vous que vous ferez. Vous irez par ceste cité et crirez haultement—'Il est venu ung medecin lequel sçait guarir de toutes maladies et aussi de ceulx qui ont perdu le sens, soit homme ou femme. Jamais ne seront tant enrragéz que leur sens ne leur rende.'"

Lors partit le varlet, qui fort joyeulx estoit d'estre bien revestu, et parmy la cité d'Inde toute la journee crya ainsi que Valentin luy avoit dist. Or vindrent les nouvelles au roy d'Inde de la venue de celuy maistre, et pour tant qu'il se vantoit des folz et enrragéz guarir, pour l'amour de Esclarmonde le roy le manda. Nonobstant que desja estoient manches, contrefais, boiteux a tresgrant nombre par devant son logis, mais tous les laissa pour aler vers le roy, car bien sçavoit la fin ou son cueur plus tiroit.

Il salua le roy du grant dieu Jupiter, et le roy luy dist, "Maistre, bien puissez vous venir dedens ma court. Vous disnerez, puis vous diray pourquoy je vous ay mandé." Le roy se mist a table et fist moult richement servir Valentin. Puis apres disner luy a dist devant tous, "Maistre, j'ay en ce palays une dame qui dessus toutes aultres est de beauté guarnye. Si est vray que quant je la prins de l'eure je la vouloye prendre en mariaige et l'espouser. Mais elle me fist entendant qu'elle avoit a Mahon voué que nulle personne n'espouseroit jusques au terme d'ung an. Or luy donnay ce terme tel comme elle me demanda. Mais en la fin de l'an piteuse maladie la print et telle que personne aupres d'elle ne s'ose trouver. Elle brait et crye piteusement; l'une foys rit et [121recto]l'autre[1] pleure. Ne en ses fais n'y a point d'ordonnance dont je suis en mon cueur dolent, car s'elle estoit du fait

---

[1] *q i* at bottom right corner of 121r.

shoulders. Entering the city, he went to lodge in a luxurious inn. As soon as the host saw him he went to inquire of him what craft he practiced.

"Host," said Valentin, "I am a doctor, and I know how to cure all types of illness."

The host asked him no more questions and received him well. His squire pretended to serve him as a doctor's clerk, while Valentin spent two days with his host in this guise. Then Valentin spoke to the host: "Host, will you please do me a favor? It is to find me a man who will roam the city announcing my skills and ability to cure any ill people there might be. For you must know that I need to earn money to pay you the expenses I must accrue here. Nevertheless, if you have any doubts about my ability to pay, I will give you a guarantee."

"By Mohammed," said the host, "I certainly do want a guarantee," for he was suspicious of strangers.

Therefore Valentin handed over to him a fine furred cloak. "Here," said Valentin, "and have no doubts about me, but do send me the boy I asked you for."

The host went out and came back with a boy who had neither shoes, nor tunic, nor hood, and who was in fact almost naked. For the love of God, Valentin clothed him, and said to him, "My friend, let me tell you what to do. You shall go all over the city, shouting out as loud as you can—'A doctor has come who can cure all illness, even madness, in men or women. However deranged they may be, he will restore to them their senses.'"

Then the boy left, delighted to have been clothed, and roamed the city of India all day long, crying his announcement just as Valentin had told him. Now tidings came to the king of India of the arrival of this master, and since he claimed to be able to cure lunatics and madmen, the king sent for him out of love for Esclarmonde. Notwithstanding the great number of the deformed, the crippled, and the lame waiting in front of his lodging, Valentin abandoned them all to go straight to the king, for that of course was where his heart led him.

He greeted the king in the name of the great god Jupiter, and the king replied, "Master, welcome to my court. First dine, and then I will tell you why I have sent for you." The king seated himself at the dinner table and had Valentin lavishly served. Then, after the meal, he announced in the presence of all, "Master, I have in this palace a lady whose beauty exceeds that of all others. It is true that when I first captured her, I wanted right away to marry her and take her to wife. But she explained to me that she had sworn to Mohammed that no one should marry her before a year was up. So I allowed her this term, as she requested it of me. But at the end of that year, a terrible illness took hold of her, such that no one dare approach her. She brays and cries out most piteously; one moment she laughs and the next moment she weeps. There is no sense in her behavior, which breaks my heart, for if she were cured, I would marry her, for my

guarie a femme je la prendroye, car ma femme Rozemonde, fille de Brandiffer, s'est de moy departie. Pour tant se vous sçavez sur ce remede plus en serez payé que demander n'en sçaurez."

"Sire," dit Valentin, "j'en feray toute ma puissance. Mais la maladie est forte a curer. Considerez que de long temps elle est enracinee. Nonpourtant a l'aide de Mahon j'ay fiance de y mettre bon remede. Si me convient toute ceste nuyt estre dedens sa chambre pour sa condicion regarder."

"Maistre," dit le roy, "je vous y feray mener, mais d'elle vous garderez affin qu'elle ne vous morde."

Adonc ung Sarrasin, qui boire et menger luy donnoit, y mena Valentin. Et quant il fut a la fenestre il luy dist, "Regardez la et jouez de vostre science. Le dyable d'enfer la vous fera guarir, mais Mahon, qui plus est puissant, assez aura a faire."

"Va t'en," dist Valentin, "et me laisse tout seul."

Lors s'en ala le Sarrasin et Valentin le[1] regarda moult piteusement. "Helas," dit il, "vray Dieu, tant chier m'avez acheté et chier je vous ay comparé. Mais puis que je vous voy, je suis de tous mes maulx reconforté. Par Dieu, ma doulce amye, jamais en France ne retourneray sans vostre corps mener ou je perdray la vie." Lors la dame le regarde moult effroyement, et encontre luy gette tout ce que trouver elle peult par la chambre, de quoy Valentin fust tresfort esmerveillé.

"Helas, mon Dieu," dist il, "esse[2] faintise ou chose vraye, du mal que je vous voy souffrir? Chiere amie, helas, sans plus faire soyez moderee et m'entendez parler. Je suis vostre amy Valentin pour qui tant de peine avez soufferte. Ne vous souvient il plus de la teste d'arain qui a moy vous donna, et de mon frere Orson a qui le filet fut couppé? Et comment en Acquitaine vous me fustes faulcement par l'enchanteur Adramain desrobee?"

Quant la dame oÿt ces parolles, de grant joye cheut paumee. Et quant elle fut revenue elle a dit a voix moult fort piteuse, "Helas, mon amy Valentin, tant avez eu pour moy de peines, de maulx et de grant doleurs souffertes, et moy pour l'amour de vous. Voyez en quelle povreté je me suis tenue sans avoir a nul homme mon amour accordee."

"Dame," dist Valentin, "on ayme voulentiers chose bien achetee." A ces motz entendit Valentin que les clarons et tromppettes sonnoient pour le roy assoir a souper. Si a dist a la dame, "Je m'en voy au palays, mais apres le souper a vous je retourneray, car au roy j'ay fait entendre que je suis medecin. Si m'a mandé pour vous venir garder et guarir."

La dame a dit, "Dieu vous doinst bien parfaire vostre entreprinse."

Ainsi se partit Valentin et s'en ala au palais, et si tost que le roy le veit il luy demanda, "Maistre, pourrez vous jamais la dame guarir?"

---

[1] Another instance of *le* for the feminine third person singular direct object pronoun.
[2] The phonetic spelling of *est ce*, as recurs below.

own wife Rozemonde, the daughter of Brandiffer, has passed away. Therefore, if you know any remedy for this you shall be paid more than you could even imagine requesting."

"Sire," said Valentin, "I will do my very best. But such an illness is difficult to treat. Consider how long it has held sway over her. Nevertheless, with Mohammed's help, I am confident of finding a cure. I will need to spend tonight in her chamber to observe her condition."

"Master," said the king, "I will have you brought there, but beware of her that she not bite you."

Thereupon a Saracen, who usually brought her food and drink, led Valentin to her chamber. And when he arrived at her window, the Saracen told him, "Observe her and try out your knowledge, but only the devil of hell can help you heal her, for it is too much for Mohammed, the more powerful one, to manage."

"Go away," said Valentin, "and leave me alone with her."

So the Saracen left and Valentin looked at her, filled with pity. "Alas," he said, "my God, how dearly you have paid for my sake, and I for you. But now that I see you, I am comforted for all my woe. By God, my sweet friend, I will never return to France without bringing you back with me or losing my life in the attempt." Then the lady looked at him in fright, and threw at him everything she could find in the room, causing Valentin much astonishment.

"Alas, my God," he said, "is this affliction I see you suffer feigned or true? Dear friend, please try to control yourself and listen to what I have to say. I am your beloved Valentin, for whom you have suffered so much pain. Do you not remember the brass head that gave you to me, and my brother Orson, whose thread was cut? And how you were wickedly kidnapped from me in Aquitaine by the enchanter Adramain?"

When the lady heard these words, she fainted dead away from excess of joy. And when she recovered, she said in a piteous voice, "Alas, my beloved Valentin, you have suffered so much pain, trouble, and sorrow for my sake and I for love of you. See in what sorry state I have kept myself in order not to have to grant my love to any man."

"Lady," said Valentin, "one loves all the more eagerly the thing dearly bought." Just as he said this, Valentin heard the clarions and trumpets sounding to announce the king's sitting to supper. So he said to the lady, "I must return to the palace, but I will come back to you after the meal, for I have told the king I am a doctor. He sent for me to come observe you and heal you."

The lady said, "May God grant you success in your undertaking."

Thus Valentin left to go to the palace, and as soon as the king saw him he asked him, "Master, will you ever be able to cure the lady?"

"Sire," ce dit Valentin, "demenez feste joyeuse, car au vouloir de Mahon demain vous la verrez aussi sagement parler com[121verso]me oncques elle parla, et sera en son sens mieulx que jamais retournee."

Tant fut le roy joyeulx qu'i donna de ceste heure a Valentin ung riche manteau de fin or et de asur, subtillement ouvré, de fines pierres precieuses couvert et broudé. Puis le fit assoir a table et richement comme sa personne servir. Et quant vint apres le soupper Valentin a prins congié du roy et luy a dit, "Chier sire, en la chambre de la paciente me convient toute nuyt bon feu avoir et ung grant cierge alumé, et je seray avec elle. Si deffendez que nul devant elle ne se monstre, car jamais autant ne fut malade qu'elle sera ceste nuyt."

"Maistre," dist le roy d'Inde, "tout ce je vous acorde, et ne faictes que demander et vous serez servy."

Or s'en va Valentin par devers Esclarmonde. Ung gros cierge fit alumer et le mist en la chambre, et bon feu fit faire et demanda tout ce que besoing luy estoit. Puis commanda aux payens que chascun s'en alast et que tout seul luy convient[1] estre, fors que de son varlet qui le devoit servir. Chascun de la se departit et Valentin demoura en la chambre, qui bien ferma l'uys et fenestres.

Puis luy a dit, "M'amye, vous me pouez maintenant embrasser et baiser tout a vostre apetit, car l'eure est venue que trouver vous devoye." Lors Valentin regarda en ung coing de la chambre et veit le chevalet de boys. "M'amye," ce dist il, "n'esse[2] pas la le chevalet de Pacolet?"

"Oy, amy," dist elle, "c'est le cheval par qui Trompart me desroba. Mais mauvais cheval fust pour luy quant il n'en sceut jouer, car dedens ceste cité la teste en eut couppee et je fus du roy d'Inde prinse et retenue."

"Belle," dist Valentin, "or ne vous soussiez, car du cheval de bois je sçauray bien jouer. Et si ay les escrips de Pacolet par quoy bien je m'y doy cognoistre."

Moult joyeuse en fut la dame. "Helas," dist la dame, "partons d'icy quant faire le pouez."

"Par Dieu," dit Valentin, "je l'ay bien en pensee."

Lors ouvrit[3] l'uys de la chambre tout droit a la minuyt et monta sur une fenestre ou la clarté de la lune resplendissoit fort. Puis monta sur le chevalet et mist la dame devant luy et Guerin son escuier derriere. Et quant tous trois furent montéz, Valentin print son brefvet et le conjurement fit ainsi qu'il estoit escript. Puis tourna la chevillette et le chevalet s'en va par dessus mer, roches, villes, et grans chasteaulx tant qu'il fust pres de Angorie. Et n'y eut celuy qui osast dire mot, car ainsi faillit le sort et la se descendirent. Valentin fist ouvrir les portes car il estoit jour cler et le soleil levant.

Or fut en Angorie grant joye demenee pour l'amour de la dame. Valentin la fist richement vestir et de riches draps d'or et de soye, et le lendemain de apres

---

[1] Text has *convent*.
[2] Phonetic spelling of *est ce*, as above.
[3] Text has *ouvrir*.

"Sire," said Valentin, "you may celebrate, for, Mohammed willing, tomorrow you shall see her speak as sanely as she ever did, and she shall have her faculties back better than ever."

The king was so happy that he gave Valentin right away a luxuriant coat of costly gold and azure, finely fashioned and covered and embroidered with exquisite precious stones. Then he seated him at the table and had him served as lavishly as himself. Then, after supper, Valentin took leave of the king, saying to him, "Dear sire, I must have a good fire and a large candle lit all night long in the patient's chamber, for I will stay with her. Moreover, I forbid that anyone show himself in her presence, for she has never been so ill as she will be tonight."

"Master," said the king of India, "I accord you all this; you need only ask and you shall be served."

Now Valentin goes to Esclarmonde. He had a large candle lit in the chamber and a good fire made up, and asked for everything he needed. Then he ordered the pagans all to go away and leave him alone, except for his valet who was to serve him. Everyone departed while Valentin remained in the chamber, closing the door and windows.

Then he said to her, "My love, now you may embrace and kiss me as much as you like, for the hour has come that I was to find you." Then Valentin glanced in the corner of the room and saw the wooden horse. "My love," he said, "is that not Pacolet's wooden horse?"

"Yes, my love," she said, "that is the horse on which Trompart kidnapped me. But it served him ill, for he did not know how to operate it, and when he arrived in this city, his head was cut off, and I was taken and held by the king of India."

"Fair one," said Valentin, "worry no more, for I know well how to operate the wooden horse. Moreover, I have all of Pacolet's writings, which I have studied and from which I have learned what to do."

The lady was delighted to hear it. "Well, then," said the lady, "let us leave here as soon as you can bring it about."

"By God," said Valentin, "that is exactly what I have in mind."

Exactly at midnight he opened the door to the chamber and climbed up on a window where the moonlight shone brightly through. Then he mounted on the wooden horse, putting the lady before him and Guerin, his squire, behind. When all three were seated, Valentin took his notebook and conjured according to what was written. Then he turned the little screw and the wooden horse took off, flying over sea, rocks, towns, and grand castles until they arrived near Angory. And no one dared say a word, for at that moment the spell ended, and they descended on the spot. Valentin opened the gates to the city, for it was clear day and the sun was rising.

There was great joy in Angory for love of the lady. Valentin had her richly dressed with luxurious gold cloth and silk, and the next day, Valentin married

espousa Valentin la dame Esclarmonde. Si ne fault point demander la feste qui adonc fut faicte, car mieulx sembloit estre ung paradis terrestre que nulle joye ou plaisance mondaine. Ainsy [122recto]eust[1] Valentin la douleur perdue et mise en oubly[2] que longtemps pour la dame avoit sufferte et enduree.

Et le roy de Inde Major qui les nouvelles sceut ses dieux en despita disant, "Ha! faulx enchanteur, tu m'as bien trahy et deceu, mais je t'en feray par le col pendre." Assez fit le roy de Inde monter de gens a cheval pour Valentin suivyr, mais nul n'en sceult nouvelles trouver, car il a bon cheval qui tous les aultres passe.

Sy me veul de luy traire et parler du roy Pepin qui en France est alé pour sa femme secourir et sa terre deffendre.

Pour[3] tant que le roy Artus de Bretaigne oÿt dire et racompter que le roy Pepin et les douze pers de France avoient esté prins en Hierusalem, il pensoit de certain que tous fussent mors et dist qu'il seroit roy de France et Berthe il espouseroit. Sy fit une aliance du conte de Monfort, duc de Berry, du conte de Nemours, du conte d'Armignat, et par toute Bretaigne fist cryer que tout homme puissant de porter baston avec luy alast vers les parties de France. Quant la royne Berthe sceut les nouvelles, elle fut moult dolente, mais remedier n'y peult et print son filz Charlot et s'en vint a Lyon pour son ennemy eviter.

En celuy temps y avoit en Anjou ung conte moult loyal et de bonne foy qui, pour la royne secourir et le pays de France garder, fit contre les Bretons tous ses chasteaulx garnir de gens et de vivres, et la ville d'Angiers moult fut fortifié. Lors quant la royne sceut le bon vouloir du conte, elle luy envoya pour secours quatre mille hommes de cheval pour garder les frontieres. Le roy Artus manda au conte de Anjou qu'il luy aprestast passaige pour entrer dedens France, et le conte respondit que il ne le feroit pas. Si ne demoura gaires que sept contes et trois ducz vindrent devant Angiers et la ville assiegerent, et le conte d'Anjou ne saillit point aux champs mais garda la cité et moult fort se deffendit.

Or fist le roy Pepin si bonne diligence que durant celuy siege a Paris arriva. Et les nouvelles en sceurent ceulx de la ville, dont ilz furent moult joyeulx, et notablement des bourgois. Il fut receu et pour l'amour de sa venue menerent feste. Par la ville toutes les reliques des esglises furent portees a l'encontre de luy.

Et quant la royne Berthe qui a Lyon estoit sceut les nouvelles que le roy estoit a Paris, tout au plus tost qu'elle peut ala par devers luy. Et quant elle vint devant luy en plourant luy a requis une vengance mortelle du roy de Bretaigne.

Lequel luy a dit, "Dame, ne vous soussiez, car au plaisir de Dieu vous en serez bien vengee." Adonc fist assembler ses gens et son armee a grant puis-

---

[1] *q ii* at bottom right corner of 122r.

[2] Text has *ombly*.

[3] A line's width of space is left between the end of the last sentence and the beginning of this sentence, and the word *pour* is given a decorative initial, indicating the possibility that a new chapter was to have started here. However, no chapter title or number was ever added and the numbering of the following chapters is correct.

the lady Esclarmonde. It goes without saying that there was a great celebration, for it seemed more like paradise on earth than any usual worldly joy or pleasure. Thus did Valentin put behind him all pain and memory of his long suffering for the lady.

When the king of India found out what had happened, he cursed his gods saying, "Ha! wicked enchanter, you have certainly betrayed and deceived me, but I will see you hanged by the neck." The king sent out many riders in pursuit of Valentin, but none could find any trace of him, for he had a good horse that surpassed all others.

Now I will leave off speaking of him and will speak of King Pepin, who had gone to France to rescue his wife and defend his land.

Since King Arthur of Brittany heard it told that King Pepin and the Twelve Peers of France had been captured in Jerusalem, he was convinced they were all dead, so he declared that he would be king of France and would marry Bertha. He allied himself with the count of Monfort, the duke of Berry, the count of Nemours, and the count of Armagnac, and sent criers throughout Brittany to call all strong men who could wield a weapon to come fight with him in France. When Queen Bertha heard the news she was very upset, but there was nothing she could do except take her son Charles and flee to Lyon to escape her enemy.

At this time there was in Anjou a most loyal count of good faith who, wishing to help the queen and protect the country of France, had all his castles stocked with men and provisions to oppose the Bretons, making sure that the city of Angers itself was well fortified. When the queen heard of this count's good will, she sent him aid in the form of four thousand mounted warriors to guard the frontiers. King Arthur requested safe passage into France from the count of Anjou, but the count replied that he would not grant it. It was not long before seven counts and three dukes came to Angers to besiege the city, but the count of Anjou did not ride out into the field; rather he guarded the city and defended it with all his might.

Now King Pepin made such good speed that, while this siege was going on, he arrived in Paris. The tidings soon spread among the city's inhabitants, making them very happy, especially the town burghers. He was properly welcomed, and they celebrated the joy of his coming. All over the city, church relics were carried out in procession before him.

And when Queen Bertha heard the news in Lyon that the king was in Paris, she returned to him as quickly as she could. And when she came before him weeping, she begged him to take mortal vengeance against the king of Brittany.

He answered her, "Lady, have no fear, for, God willing, you shall be avenged." Thereupon he assembled his men and a large army, sending abroad for men from

sance, et manda querir Picquars, Henaulx, Brabansons et Normans. Grande fut l'assemblee que fit le roy Pepin contre le roy de Bretaigne.

Or eurent les ennemis de sa venue nouvelles, dont moult fu[122verso]rent esbahys, et moult fort se doubterent et non sans cause. Si prindrent tous les aliéz du roy Artus ung conseil ensemble que ledit Artus prendroient qui de ce fait estoit cause, et au roy Pepin le rendroient pour mieulx faire leur paix et leur faulte couvrir; et ainsi le conseillerent et le firent. Car en une nuyt dedens son ost le prindrent et au roy Pepin le menerent, lequel dedens Chastellet a Paris luy fit la teste coupper. Bien pensoient ses aliéz pour tout vray que la guerre leur sourdist, et leur osta le roy Pepin terres et seigneuries, ainsi que plus a plain appert aux croniques sur ce faictes et composees.

[CHAPITRE 62]

Comment Valentin print Chasteau Fort et delivra son pere l'empereur de Grece et tous les aultres prisonniers qui avec luy estoient. lxii. [chapitre]

Valentin, le vaillant chevalier, qui en Angorie demoura, fut en grant pensee nuyt et jour comment son pere pourroit delivrer, car bien sçavoit de longtemps comment le chasteau ne pourroit par puissance d'armes ne par enchantement estre prins, mais bien par trahyson le pourroit on avoir. Si s'avisa d'une chose qui moult bien fut comprinse, et dedens douze navires fist mettre deux mil hommes, et moult richement les fist chargier de vins et de fourment et de couronnes moult riches de perles, saphirs et de toutes aultres fines pierreries, et plusieurs aultres richesses es navires fit mettre. Puis monta sur la mer et ainsi que marchans s'en vont et tant nagerent que ilz arriverent au port du chasteau et la endroit prindrent terre.

Et Valentin se habilla en guise de marchant, puis mist une bien riche couronne sur sa teste, puis dist a ses gens, "Armez vous tous, et prenez voz glaisves, et dedens les bateaulx tout secretement vous tenez que vous ne soyez veux. Et se Sarrasins viennent vers vous, mettez les tous a mort et que nul n'en eschappe."

Et quant il eut ce dit il s'est mis a chemin et est alé vers la porte du chasteau, la couronne sur sa teste. Et quant le portier le veit il luy demanda, "Qu'elle chose vous amaine par deça?"

"Amy," dist Valentin, "je suis marchant qui m'en voy en Espaigne. Si ay dedens mes navires plusieurs riches marchandises. Si ay oÿ dire que nul marchant ne doit passer sans tribu payer sur peine de tout perdre et sa vie en dangier mettre. Si ne veul je pas passer sans payer loyallement."

"Sire," dist le portier, "or m'atendez icy et je voy vers ma dame pour vous donner responce."

Picardy, Hainault, Brabant, and Normandy. It was a great force that King Pepin assembled against the king of Brittany.

Now his enemies had tidings of his return, which astonished and frightened them, and not without cause. All King Arthur's allies took counsel together and decided to take Arthur, the cause of their current situation, into custody, and hand him over to King Pepin, the better to make their peace with him and cover their guilt; and, as they decided, so they did. For they seized him one night from among his host and led him to King Pepin, who had him beheaded in the Châtelet prison in Paris. His allies feared that this war would show them in a bad light, and indeed King Pepin took lands and domains away from them, as is plainly written in the chronicles about these events.

CHAPTER 62

How Valentin conquered Château Fort and delivered his father the emperor of Greece, and all the other prisoners who were with him.

Back in Angory, Valentin, that valiant knight, thought day and night about how he might free his father, for he had long known the castle could never be taken by force of arms or magic, though it might well be had through treason. At last he devised a clever plan. He prepared a dozen ships with two thousand men, had them loaded with a fine array of wines, wheat, crowns richly encrusted with pearls, sapphires, and other precious stones, and other costly merchandise. Then he set sail, and they traveled in the guise of merchant ships, making such good time that they soon arrived and disembarked at the castle's dock.

Valentin dressed himself like a merchant with a rich headdress. Then he said to his men, "Arm yourselves and take up your swords, and hide yourselves in the boats so that you cannot be seen. And if Saracens come upon you, put them all to death so that none escapes."

After saying this, he set out and came to the castle gate, the merchant's headdress on his head. When the porter saw him, he asked him, "What brings you here?"

"Friend," said Valentin, "I am a merchant on his way to Spain. I have a quantity of rich merchandise in my ships. I have heard it said that no merchant may pass this way without paying tribute on pain of losing all his possessions and putting his life in danger. So I do not wish to pass without paying faithfully."

"Sire," said the porter, "now wait here and I will go to my lady to get an answer for you."

Tantost ala vers la belle Galasie et le fait luy compta, et quant elle entendit que tant de beaux joyaulx il a, elle en fut moult joyeuse. Si appella le chastellain et luy dist, "Alez vers le port et le tribu recepvez de ces marchans qui passent, et menez avec vous de mes gens si grant nombre que on ne vous puisse riens tollir."

Et le chastellain fut legier et pensa bien gaigner. Et devers le port les mena a leur male aventure [123recto]car[1] tantost qu'i veirent les riches joyaulx qui aux navires estoient, ilz furent ardans de regarder. Et Valentin leur dist, "Seigneurs, entrez dedens et a vostre droit appetit des joyaulx prenez jusques a la valeur de vostre droit."

Les payens entrerent dedens, qui cuidoyent estre riches, et les crestiens qui estoient mucés saillirent et en plus briefve espace que ne vous sçauroie dire les firent mourir. "Or sus!" dist Valentin, "plus fort faire nous fault pour le chastel avoir." Lors fit il a ses gens les robes des cincquante Sarrasins vestir sur leur harnois pour les faire charger de pierrerie et d'aultres riches draps, et aler devers le chasteau. Et le portier qui les veit venir pensa que ce fussent ses compaignons, adonc il lya les deux lyons qui estoyent en la place, et avala le pont pour cuider avoir aulcun riche joyau, et saillit hors de la barriere. Et Valentin le print et vers la barge le mena. Sy luy a monstré les mors et luy a dist, "Beau maistre, tel que ceulx cy serez sans jamais en eschapper ou vous jurrerez le dieu que vous croyez que dedens le Chasteau Fort a cest jour me ferez entrer et mon corps garderez."

"Sire," dist le portier, "vostre voulenté feray, car mieulx aime vous complaire que de perdre la vie. Si vous jure la foy que je doy au grant dieu que le chasteau vous deliverray tout a vostre bonne voulenté."

"Portier," dist Valentin, "et je te guerdonneray bien. Mais garde toy sur tout de trahyson moy faire."

"Nennil," dist le portier. "Avec moy venez et faictes voz gens qui sont en habit de payen entrer dedens, l'ung apres l'autre, pour le danger du pont, car ilz[2] semblent ceulx qui du chasteau sont partis."

Ainsi que le portier devisa fut la chose acomplie, et Valentin avisa ses gens que il n'en passoit que ung seul, car se deux estoient l'ung cherroit dedens la riviere. En ce point entrerent dedens les cinquante crestiens et Valentin. Et quant ilz furent dedens, le portier leur monstra une faulce poterne. Valentin la fit[3] tantost ouvrir, puis sonna ung cor. Adonc ceulx qui estoient aux bateaulx demouréz celle part acoururent.

Et Valentin pour Galasie entretenir monta au chasteau et ala vers la chambre ou elle s'esbatoit. Et quant elle veit Valentin, qui hault la salua, elle fust toute esmerveillee comment il estoit la venu. "Dame," dist Valentin, "de moy ne vous doubtez, car pour vostre gent corps suis venu celle part." Lors regarda la dame sa doulce contenance et de luy fut au cueur touchee et grant chiere luy fist.

---

[1] *q iii* at bottom right corner of 123r.
[2] Text has *il*.
[3] Text has *fut*.

He went straightway to the fair Galasie to explain the situation to her, and when she heard what lovely cargo he had, she was very pleased. So she called her castellan and said to him, "Go to the port and receive the tribute of these passing merchants, and take such a great number of my men with you that they may take nothing from you."

The castellan was not worried and thought he would easily gain from this. But he led his men to the port to their misfortune, for as soon as they saw the rich cargo in the ships, they were burning to see more. And Valentin said to them, "My lords, go on inside and satisfy yourselves, taking the proper amount owed you from the cargo."

The pagans went in, thinking to enrich themselves, and the Christians hidden inside rushed forth and, in a shorter space of time than in which you could describe it, killed them all. "Let's go!" said Valentin, "for we must strike harder in order to take the castle." Then he had his men cover their armor with the robes of fifty Saracens in order to load them with precious stones and other rich fabrics, and go to the castle. And the gatekeeper who saw them coming thought it was his fellow countrymen, so he tied up the lions who guarded the spot and lowered the bridge, thinking to gain some rich jewel for himself, and crossed over the barrier. But Valentin seized him and led him to the boat. There he showed him the dead men and said to him, "Fair master, you shall be as these are without escape unless you swear on the god you believe in that today you will lead me into Château Fort and keep me safe."

"Sire," said the gatekeeper, "I will do as you will, for I prefer to please you than to lose my life. I swear to you on the faith I owe to the great god that I will deliver you into the castle just as you wish."

"Porter," said Valentin, "for that I will repay you handsomely. But take care to do nothing to betray me."

"No, of course not," said the porter. "Come with me and have your men in pagan dress come in, one by one, past the danger of the bridge, for they look like those who left the castle."

Just as the gatekeeper advised, so the thing was accomplished, and Valentin warned his men to pass one at a time, for if two tried to pass one would fall into the river. In this manner Valentin and the fifty Christians entered within. Once inside, the porter showed them the false postern gate. Valentin had it opened, and then he blew his horn. Thereupon those who had remained on the ships came running.

And Valentin climbed up to the castle to talk to Galasie, going to the chamber where she took her ease. When she saw Valentin, who greeted her respectfully, she was astonished at how he had managed to get in. "Lady," said Valentin, "have no fear of me, for I have come here to honor your noble self." Then the lady saw his sweet countenance, was touched to the heart, and welcomed him.

Or sont les crestiens ou chasteau entréz par la faulce posterne que le portier enseigna. Grant cry et grant bruit menerent tant que la dame saillit aux fenestres; bien veit qu'elle estoit trahye. Elle se tourna vers Valentin et luy a dist en plourant, "Franc chevalier courtois, sauvez mon pucellage, car je me rens a vous. Je voy bien que je suis deceue et trahye."

"Dame," dist le bon Valentin, "n'ayez ne paour ne crainte, car par moy ne par aultre ja n'aurez villennie ne vostre honneur ne sera blessee. Quant est du sourplus ce chasteau sera mien."

Lors commencerent crestiens a serchier de toutes pars; si ne ont laissé en vie la dedens payen ne Sarrasin. Puis est Valentin devallé vers les prisonniers; sy a rompu les portes et a dit haultement, "Entre vous qui dedens estes, parlez se vous estes en vie."

Orson entendit bien son frere Valentin; si luy escria, "Mon frere, bien soyez venu; quelle chose vous amaine?"

"Seigneurs," dist Valentin, "demenez feste, car delivréz serez." Et alors saillirent les prisonniers hors, qui povres estoient et mal colouréz. Si ne fault pas demander la joye qui fut entre eulx. La nuyt se festoient et assez de bon vin beurent qui moult les resconforta. Sept jours furent crestiens dedens Chasteau Fort demenant bonne vie, et en celuy temps s'acointa Orson de l'amour de Galasie, car de Fezonne ne sçavoit s'elle estoit morte ou vive. Nonobstant avint il apres que ledit Orson espousa Galasie apres la mort de Fezonne. Et d'elle eut ung moult beau filz qui eut nom Orsaire, lequel en ses jours tint le noble empire de Constantinoble.

[CHAPITRE 63]

Comment l'empereur de Grece, Orson, et le Verd Chevalier demourerent en garnison a Chasteau Fort; et comment Hauffroy et Henry firent mourir le roy Pepin leur pere. [lxiii. chapitre]

Apres que Chasteau Fort fut prins et que les prisonniers furent ung petit repeux et confortéz, les seigneurs et les barons prindrent conseil ensemble, qu'i seroit bon de laisser aulcun pour le chasteau garder, car icelle place pouoit les payens grever. Si eut aulcuns qui dirent par maniere de couverture que bon seroit que Hauffroy et Henry en ce lieu demourassent.

"Seigneurs," ce dit Hauffroy, "de ce plus ne parlez, car deliberéz sommes de retourner en France nostre pere servir et reconforter en sa necessité."

Just then the Christians entered the castle through the false postern gate that the porter had shown them. They made such a hue and cry that the lady rushed to the windows; she realized then that she had been betrayed. She turned to Valentin and said to him in tears, "Noble and courteous knight, save my maidenhead, for I put myself in your hands. I see now that I have been deceived and betrayed."

"Lady," said the good Valentin, "have no fear or worry, for you will suffer no villainy from me or anyone else, nor will your honor be blemished. As for the rest, though, the castle will be mine."

The Christians began to search everywhere, leaving no Saracen or pagan within alive. Then Valentin went down to find the prisoners; he broke down the gates and called out, "Those of you within, speak up if you be alive."

Orson heard his brother Valentin and cried out, "My brother, you are indeed welcome; what brings you here?"

"My lords," said Valentin, "it is time to celebrate, for you shall be delivered." Then the prisoners came forth, looking ragged and sickly. No need to ask what joy they all felt. That night they celebrated and drank enough good wine that they were quite comforted. For seven days the Christians led a good life at Château Fort, and during that time, Orson was smitten with love for Galasie, for he did not know if Fezonne was alive or dead. Nevertheless it came about later on that Orson did marry Galasie after Fezonne's death. And with her he had a beautiful son named Orsaire, who in his day held the noble empire of Constantinople.

CHAPTER 63

How the emperor of Greece, Orson, and the Green Knight remained to defend Château Fort; and how Hauffroy and Henry had King Pepin, their father, murdered.

After Château Fort was taken and the prisoners were well fed and somewhat recovered, the lords and barons took counsel together, thinking it a good idea to leave someone behind to keep guard over the castle, for that place could be used to cause harm to the pagans. There were some who said disingenuously that it would be good for Hauffroy and Henry to remain there.

"My lords," said Hauffroy, "speak no more of this, for we are determined to return to France to serve and aid our father in his need."

"Par ma foy," dit Orson, "de vostre partement ne devons pas plourer, car onques riens ne vaulsistes, et qui pert malle compaignie il en[1] doit bien Dieu regracier et loer. Et je sçay par esperimance[2] que vous estes gens qui de vostre propre nature ne pourchassez ne demandez que trahyson."

Hauffroy et Henry de ces parolles eurent moult grant despit. Mais force les contraingnit de prendre en pacience, car ilz n'estoient pas gens pour dire du contraire. Il fut en la fin appointié que l'empereur de Grece, qui ja estoit ancien et avoit besoing de repos, avec son filz Orson et le Verd Chevalier demourroient en garnison dedens Chasteau Fort, et Valentin avec tous les aultres retourneroit en Angorie.

Si vous diray des deux trahistres Hauffroy et Henry qui en France s'en vont, lesquelz par leur cruelle malice ont entre eulx pensé et avisé de leur pere avec Charlot leur frere et Berthe leur mere mettre a mort. Or [124recto]ont tant chevaulcé que dedens Paris sont arrivéz. Au palays sont aléz et ont salué le roy Pepin et tous les barons. Le roy Pepin leur fist feste et puis leur demanda des nouvelles de l'empereur de Grece et de Valentin et de Orson et des douze pers de France et des aultres seigneurs.

"Sire," dirent les trahystres, "priez Jesus pour eulx, car ilz sont tous mors en une grande bataille depuis vostre departement et a esté devant Angorie."

Quant le roy entendit ces nouvelles moult fut au cueur dolent et tendrement ploura en regrettant fort les barons et vaillans seigneurs qu'i cuidoit que ilz fussent mors. Mais ce faisoient les trahystres pour le roy courroucer et troubler; lesquelz firent tant en la fin que sa mort pourchasserent, et celle de leur mere Berthe la royne premierement. Et pour tant qu'ilz n'en pouoient pas a leur apetit la bonne dame enpoisonner,[3] ilz s'acointerent d'une damoiselle qui nuyt et jour estoit avec la royne. Et si grant don luy donnerent que la faulce femme consentit et acorda la mort de sa bonne dame Berthe, qui tant luy avoit fait de bien, en telle maniere que au bout de quinze jours par poisons fut morte, dont le roy si desplaisant fut et amerement courroucé que au lit malade se coucha. Et depuis tant firent Hauffroy et Henry que onques puis n'en leva; mais mourut par poisons apres sa bonne dame dont moult plourerent petis et grans, car trop grande perte fut et inestimable dommaige. Semblant monstroyent devant gens d'estre de la mort de Pepin fort desplaisans, mais onques en leur vie ne furent si joyeulx et entre eulx disoient, "Or pourrons nous bien maintenant du royaulme de France faire nostre plaisir, car barons, ducz, contes, ne chevaliers n'y aura qui puisse contre nous resister."

---

[1] Text has *en en*.

[2] Text has *esperance*, which makes no sense in this context. *Esperimance* is a form attested to in Godefroy.

[3] Text has *enprisonner*. However, seeing what follows, it appears to be a mistake of the typesetter.

"By my faith," said Orson, "we need not weep over your departure, for you have never been worth much of anything, and he who loses bad company should thank God and praise Him. I know by experience that you are men who by your very nature pursue only treachery."

Hauffroy and Henry were greatly angered by these words. But they had to keep their patience, for they were not men openly to contradict. In the end it was decided that the emperor of Greece, who was already old and needed rest, would remain in the garrison within Château Fort with his son Orson and the Green Knight, and Valentin would return with all the others to Angory.

Now I will tell you about those two traitors, Hauffroy and Henry, who went back to France and plotted out of cruel malice to kill their father along with Charles, their brother, and their [step]mother Bertha. They rode until they arrived in Paris, where they went to the palace to greet King Pepin and all the barons. King Pepin feted them, and then asked them for news of the emperor of Greece, Valentin, Orson, as well as the Twelve Peers of France and the other lords.

"Sire," said the traitors, "pray to Jesus for them, for they were all killed in a great battle that took place after your departure before the city of Angory."

When the king heard these tidings, he was heartsick and wept bitterly in sorrow over the barons and valiant lords whom he believed dead. But the traitors only did this to upset and trouble the king; they did it because, in the end, they were seeking his death, although, first of all, that of their [step]mother Queen Bertha. Since they could not themselves poison the lady as they would have liked, they became friendly with a maiden who spent day and night with the queen. They gave her such a large bribe that the wicked lady consented to bring about the death of her kind lady Bertha, who had done so much good for her, and in such a manner that within fifteen days she was dead from poisoning. The king was devastated and so terribly upset that he took to his bed in a very ill state. After that, Hauffroy and Henry were able to make sure that he never rose from it again; rather, he too died from poison after his good lady, for which everyone, great and small, mourned bitterly, for it was too great a loss, an immeasurable harm. In public they pretended to be unhappy about Pepin's death, but in fact they had never been so happy in their life, and between themselves they were saying, "Now we can do what we like with the kingdom of France, for there will be no barons, dukes, counts, or knights able to resist us."

[CHAPITRE 64]

Comment apres la mort du roy Pepin, le duc Millon d'Angler voulut faire couronner Charlot son filz. lxiiii. [chapitre][1]

Apres la mort du bon roy Pepin, le duc Millon d'Angler, qui estoit vaillant et saige, assembla le conseil et vouloit faire couronner roy Charlot le petit enfant. Mais Hauffroy et Henry, par dons et par promesses, corrompirent les seigneurs et fut dit que Charlot estoit trop jeune enfant. Et pour tant que le duc Millon soustenoit fort le contraire, Hauffroy et Henry le firent prendre et emprisonner[2] [124verso]dedens le chasteau de Paris, et depuis tenoient Charlot comme varlet de cuysine et de luy se servoient. Dont il avint une foys que Hauffroy commandoit a Charlot une broche a tourner, mais Charlot, qui desplaisant en fut, leva la broche et tel coup luy donna que a terre l'abatit, et Henry saillit avant pour Charlot frapper, mais Charlot, qui bien l'avisa, sur l'oreille le frappa tel coup que le sang courut aval, dont Hauffroy escria a ses gens qu'ilz prinssent Charlot.

Lors vint ung chevalier nommé David d'Elloys qui Charlot print par la main, car aultreffois l'avoit en doctrine. Si le fist tantost monter sur ung cheval et hors de Paris le mena. Et quant les trahistres sceurent que Charlot s'en aloit ilz firent tantost monter a cheval leur gens pour le suivir. Mais ceulx qui apres luy alerent pour tant que le fait cognoissoient n'avoient pas envye de le prendre, mais plus tost cerchoient a revers du chemin; ainsi ne le trouverent point.

Adonc Millon d'Angler[3] manda et escript toute la verité a sa femme qui seur estoit de Charlot. Et quant elle eust veu les lettres, pour l'amour de Charlot moult tendrement ploura, si a juré Jesus que ceulx l'acheteroient chier qui a son frere ont fait villennie et oultraige si grant.

Lors fit escripre unes lettres et par ung messagier les envoya a Valentin et au douze pers de France qui estoient en Angorie. Et quant Valentin vit la lettre il commença fort a plourer et les aultres seigneurs luy demanderent la cause pourquoy il plouroit.

"Helas, amys, se je pleure ce n'est pas sans cause, car le bon roy Pepin est mort et la bonne royne Berthe de ce siecle passee. Si ont Hauffroy et Henry hors du païs chassé le petit Charlot, et vituperablement le duc Millon d'Angler pour tant que l'enfant supportoit ont fait mettre en prison en Chastellet. Si nous mande la dame d'Angler que secours et ayde nous luy façons et je ne sçay comment, car

---

[1] Woodcut of standing robed figure at left who appears to demur as robed figure at right offers him crown, with attendant at far right.

[2] Text has *empisonner*.

[3] Text has *dangle*.

CHAPTER 64

How, after the death of the noble King Pepin, Duke Millon d'Angler wanted to crown his son Charles.

After the death of the good King Pepin, Duke Millon d'Angler, who was valiant and wise, assembled the council and wanted to crown Charles, the young child, king. But Hauffroy and Henry, by means of gifts and promises, corrupted the lords, and it was said that Charles was too young a child. And because Duke Millon tried to convince them otherwise, Hauffroy and Henry had him seized and imprisoned in the Châtelet of Paris, and from that time they kept Charles as a kitchen boy and had him serve them. Then it happened one day that Hauffroy ordered Charles to turn a spit, but Charles, who was not pleased about this, raised the spit and gave him such a blow with it that he knocked him to the ground. Then Henry sprang up to strike Charles, but Charles, who saw it coming, struck him instead so hard on the ear that the blood flowed, for which reason Hauffroy cried out to his men to seize Charles.

Then a knight named David d'Elloys came and took Charles by the hand, for in the past he had been his tutor. Right away he mounted him on a horse and led him away from Paris. When the traitors discovered that Charles had escaped, they had their men mount their horses to pursue him. But those who were sent on the chase had no real desire to catch him, for they knew what was going on, so they looked desultorily, and thus never found him.

Then Millon d'Angler wrote and sent a true account of what had happened to his wife, who was Charles' sister. When she saw his letter, she wept bitterly for love of Charles, then swore to Jesus that those who committed such outrage and villainy against her brother would pay dearly for it.

Then she wrote a letter and sent it by messenger to Valentin and the Twelve Peers of France, who were still in Angory. When Valentin saw the letter, he began to weep, and the other lords inquired of him why he was weeping.

"Alas, my friends, if I weep, it is not without cause, for the good King Pepin is dead and the good Queen Bertha has passed from this world. Moreover, Hauffroy and Henry have chased little Charles out of the country and shamefully thrown Duke Millon d'Angler into the Châtelet prison for having supported the child. The lady of Angler writes to beg us to come to her aid, and I do not know

bien vous sçavez que de jour en aultre nous attendons le fort roy Brandiffer qui nous vient assaillir."

"Par ma foy," dient les barons, "si fault il trouver maniere du bon duc secourir."

"Je vous diray," dit Valentin, "je pense bien tant faire par ung art dont je sçay jouer que devant demain nuyt le duc Millon vous rendray."

De ces motz commencerent a rire tous ceulx de l'assemblee. Et Valentin se part sans plus de delay faire, et de son chevalet a si bien joué que devant la minuyt est alé a Paris et vint en Chastelet, par subtil art a les portes ouvertes, et a tous les prisonniers congé a donné. Puis leur demanda[1] ou le duc Millon estoit, et ilz luy monstrerent la chambre qui bien tost fut ouverte et la porte versee. Le bon duc qui dormoit pour le bruyt se esveilla et demanda, "Qui estes vous qui si rudement entréz?"

"Or sus," dist Valentin, "pensez bien tost de voz habis prendre, car je suis Valentin qui viens d'Angorie pour vous delivrer."

Moult joyeulx fut le bon duc et tan[125recto]tost fut prest. Si le fist Valentin sur le chevalet de bois avec luy monter, et luy a dist, "Gardez de mot dire ne sonner, car nous volerons plus tost que ung oyseau ou fouldre."

"Mais," dist Millon, "puis[2] que si tost alez, pour Dieu, alons par le chasteau d'Angler. Et la verrons et resconforterons ung petit ma femme qui pour moy et pour son frere Charlot est moult au cueur dolente."

Ilz frapperent aux portes et tost le gayt respondit qui cogneut leur seigneur. Si ala vers la dame et luy dist les nouvelles. Et quant elle sceut que son amy estoit venu, elle saillit du lit a tout une petite robe et aux portes acourut. Elle le baise et acolle le bon Millon et des nouvelles luy demande.

"Ma dame," dist Millon, "toutes les sçavez, mais sachez que je m'en voys par devers Angorie ou la bataille des faulx payens attendons. Et au retour, s'i plaist a Dieu, je amenrray les douze pers de France et moult puissante armee pour Hauffroy et Henry confondre et Charlot secourir."

Quant la dame entendit que plus sejourner ne vouloit, vins et viandes fit aporter et la endroit repeurent, car de boire et de menger avoient grant appetit. Puis prindrent congié de la dame et sur le chevalet sont montéz ainsi comme devant, et tellement par l'air s'en sont volléz que tantost par devers les barons les deux chevaliers se trouverent au palais d'Angorie dont tous les seigneurs furent fort esbahys, et moult requeroient Valentin que tel jeu leur voulsist aprendre, et il leur refusa.

Or avint il en ces jours que le roy Brandiffer, qui sur la mer estoit, arriva devant Angorie. Et a une lieue pres de la cité il fist son siege assoir, acompaigné de quinze roys, tous ses subjecz. Ceulx de la cité qui les nouvelles oÿrent de telle venue furent moult esmerveilléz. Si coururent fermer les portes et les pontz et monterent aux creneaulx et regarderent les payens qui tentes, trefz et pavillons a

---

[1] Text has *deman*, probably owing to line break.

[2] Text has *plus*.

how, for you are well aware that we expect from one day to the next that the powerful King Brandiffer will descend upon us."

"By my faith," said the barons, "we must find some way to help the good duke."

"I will tell you," said Valentin, "I think I know a spell I can weave so that before tomorrow night I will render you Duke Millon."

At these words everyone assembled there began to laugh. But Valentin left without delay, and operated his wooden horse so well that before midnight he was in Paris, and came to the Châtelet, where he opened the gates with his subtle art and freed all the prisoners within. Then he asked them where Duke Millon was, and they showed him the room, which was soon opened and the door overthrown. The good duke, who was sleeping, woke up from the noise and asked, "Who are you who have so roughly come in here?"

"Arise now," said Valentin, "take care to dress quickly, for I am Valentin, come from Angory to liberate you."

The good duke, overjoyed, was soon ready. Then Valentin had him get on the wooden horse with him and said, "Be careful to utter not a sound, for we are going to fly faster than a bird or lightning."

"But," said Millon, "since you travel so fast, for God's sake, let us pass by the castle of Angler. There we may see and comfort my wife a little, whose heart aches because of me and her brother Charles."

They knocked at the gates, and the guards, who arrived quickly, recognized their lord. Then he went to his lady and told her the news. When she knew that her beloved had come, she leapt from bed with just her nightclothes on and ran to the gates. She kissed and hugged the good Millon and begged to know how he was.

"My lady," said Millon, "you shall know all, but I must tell you that I am on my way to Angory where we await battle against the false pagans. When I return, if it please God, I will bring back the Twelve Peers of France and a most powerful army to confound Hauffroy and Henry and bring aid to Charles."

When the lady understood that he wished not to tarry, she had wines and meats brought and they dined right there, for they had a great desire to eat and drink. Then they took leave of the lady and remounted on the wooden horse as before, flying so quickly through the air that the two knights soon found themselves among the barons in the palace of Angory, which amazed all the lords. They all begged Valentin to teach them how to do such a trick, but he refused them all.

Now it happened around that time that King Brandiffer, who was traveling by sea, arrived before the city of Angory. Accompanied by fifteen kings, his subjects all, he set up his siege about a league from the city. Those from the city who heard tell of their arrival were astonished. They ran to shut the gates and drawbridges and climbed up to the ramparts to watch the pagans, who were setting up such a great number of tents and pavilions that no one could count them.

si grant nombre disoient que on n'en sçavoit le compte. Valentin et les douze pers de France furent dedens Angorie que murs et portes chascun jour faisoient garder et re[n]forcer. Sy devez sçavoir que les payens furent en leur siege l'espace d'ung mois sans donner assault, et sans que nul des crestiens encontre eulx saillissent.

[CHAPITRE 65]

Comment l'empereur de Grece, Orson, et le Verd Chevalier partirent de Chasteau Fort pour venir devant Angorie les crestiens secourir. lxv. cha[pitre]

L'empereur de Grece qui en Chastel Fort estoit oït parler Brandiffer qu'i Angorie a grant puissance de payens a asiegee. Si fut meu en devocion[1] des crestiens et de nostre foy secourir. Dont ilz eurent entre eulx conseil et avis que ilz laisseroient le Chasteau Fort en garde a ung moult vaillant et hardy chevalier auquel se fioient. Ainsi fut la chose faicte et luy laisserent le Chasteau Fort et luy [125verso]baillerent deux hommes avec luy. Puis partirent pour venir en Angorie l'empereur de Grece, Orson, et le Verd Chevalier, acompaignié de mil combatans.

Si entrerent en la mer et ont levé leur voilles, mais gaires de chemin n'ont fait que tantost aviserent puissance de navires vers eulx approcher. C'estoit ung admiral de payens qui a tout dix mille hommes aloit devant la cité d'Angorie le vaillant roy Brandiffer secourir. Bien cogneurent les crestiens que ilz estoient de leurs ennemis, sy se sont mis en armes et ont prins leurs glaisves. Sur le bort de leurs nefz et en bataille se sont[2] rengéz. Bien veirent les payens que noz gens estoient crestiens; si approcherent fierement et dessus eulx frapperent. Et les crestiens qui Jesus et la Vierge Marie reclamoyent a grande puissance vaillamment se deffendirent. Lors y eut dure et cruelle bataille. L'empereur de Grece, Orson son filz, et le Verd Chevalier a celle heure monstrerent leurs vaillantises et proesses, et en hault s'escrierent, "Jesus, secourez nous!" A ces motz les crestiens prindrent sy grant couraige que tout le plus petit a celle heure avoit force de dix, et pour l'amour de Jesucrist estoient tous pres de mourir, et Sarrasins, qui furent dix contre ung, ont les crestiens encloz. Si ne fault pas demander la proesse de Orson et du Verd Chevalier, car telles proesses faisoient que payens devant eulx ne demouroit en vie.

Et quant l'admiral payen veit leurs proesses si s'approcha d'eulx, et de costé Orson il abatit en la mer ung vaillant chevalier, duquel Orson si fut moult courroucé, car moult fort l'aymoit. Si a prins une hache et a l'admiral payen si grant coup luy a donné que dedens la navire tout mort le reversa. Et quant les payens le

---

[1] Text has *devcion*.
[2] Text has *sons*.

Valentin and the Twelve Peers of France were within the city of Angory, every day guarding and reinforcing the walls and gates. You should know that the pagans maintained the siege for a month's time without carrying out an assault and without any of the Christians sallying forth to confront them.

CHAPTER 65

How the emperor of Greece, Orson, and the Green Knight left Château Fort to come before the walls of the city of Angory to help the Christians.

When the emperor of Greece, who was in Château Fort, heard that Brandiffer had besieged the city of Angory with a huge army of pagans, his sense of piety moved him to come to the aid of the Christians and our faith. Thus they took counsel together and decided to leave Château Fort in the keep of a most bold and valiant knight whom they trusted. Thus it was done, and they left him in charge of Château Fort along with two other men. Then the emperor of Greece, Orson, and the Green Knight left for Angory, accompanied by two thousand warriors.

They had just raised their sails, left the port, and covered a little distance when they saw a fleet of ships approaching them. It was a pagan emir leading at least ten thousand men to the city of Angory to bring aid to King Brandiffer. The Christians recognized them right away as their enemies, so immediately they armed themselves and took hold of their swords, ranging themselves for battle on the sides of their ships. The pagans realized that our men were Christians, so they approached and attacked them fiercely. And the Christians, who loudly called upon Jesus and the Virgin Mary, defended themselves valiantly. There was a hard and cruel battle. The emperor of Greece, Orson his son, and the Green Knight displayed their valor and prowess that day, and they cried aloud, "Jesus, come to our aid!" The Christians took such heart at these words that, at that moment, the least among them had the strength of ten, and for love of Jesus Christ they were all ready to die, while the Saracens, who were ten to one, enclosed the Christians. There is no need to ask about the prowess of Orson and the Green Knight, for they performed such feats that no pagans remained alive before them.

When the pagan emir saw their deeds, he rushed up to them and hurled a valiant knight next to Orson into the sea, for which reason Orson was enraged, for he had loved that knight very much. So Orson seized an ax and gave the emir such a blow that he knocked him dead back into the ship. When the pagans saw

veirent, ilz en furent tous desconfortéz et perdirent toute leur puissance et hardiesse. Si s'en tirerent arriere, puis leurs voilles leverent et mirent au vent et se prindrent a fuyr ceulx qui eschapper peurent. Mais ilz perdirent tant que quinze de leurs navires et quatre mille payens mors y demourerent.

Et apres ces choses l'empereur de Grece parla a ses gens et leur a dit, "Seigneurs, je conseille que de ces Sarrasins et payens nous en prenons les armes et les vestemens et nous en vestons et en mode et en maniere Sarrasine nous apprestons, car trop me doubte que des Sarrasins et paiens sur la mer nous ne soyons rencontréz."

Le conseil pleust a tous affin que parmy Sarrasins et payens ne fussent cogneux. Les robes et les armes et harnois des mors prindrent, et tous les corps getterent en la mer. De male heure d'en avisa l'empereur de Grece, car par les armes qu'i porte il sera desconfit et mis a mort, et par Valentin son propre filz tué et occis comme vous orrez plus a plain declairer cy apres.

Or s'en vont les crestiens sur la mer arméz [126recto]des propres armes des payens et des Sarrasins. Et pour mieulx payens resembler toutes leurs bannieres et estandars ilz ployerent et ceulx des Sarrasins leverent et mirent au vent. Si nagerent si bien et si dilligamment que en bien peu de temps arriverent droitement sur le port de la noble et puissante cité d'Angorie.

[CHAPITRE 66]

Comment les crestiens saillirent de la cité d'Angorie et de l'ordonnance de leurs merveilleuses batailles. lxvi. chapitre[1]

Ung moys apres que le roy Brandiffer et le roy Lucar a toute leur puissance avoyent la cité d'Angorie assiegee, Valentin et les aultres barons avoient ensemble conseil prins de saillir sur leurs ennemis. Si manderent a Brandiffer la deffiance a lendemain, et Brandiffer qui fut fier et orgueilleux voulentiers l'acorda. Lors les crestiens qui dedens la cité d'Angorie estoient leurs batailles ordonnerent en dix eschelles dont Millon d'Angler eust la premiere. La seconde fut Sanson d'Orleans; la tierce fut Gervaiz son filz, le conte de Vuandomme; la quarte le conte de Champaigne; la quinte Quentin de Normendie; la siziesme le duc de Bourgongne; la septiesme le conte de Dampmartin; la huitiesme le conte d'Ausseure; la neufiesme le mareschal de Constantinoble; et Valentin la diziesme, qui a tous donna souvent grant couraige de bien faire. Et les couars qui fuyr vouloient enhardissoit, et avant les faisoit entrer en telle ordonnance que je vous ay devisee.

---

[1] Woodcut of battle scene of mounted knights with lances charging from right and left; one still helmeted but handless corpse prone in foreground.

this, they were discouraged, and lost their strength and boldness. So, raising their sails and setting them into the wind, they retreated, and everyone escaped who could. But they had lost as many as fifteen of their ships, and four thousand pagans were left behind dead.

After these events, the emperor of Greece spoke to his men and said, "My lords, I advise that we take the arms and clothes of these pagan Saracens and put them on to disguise ourselves, for I fear that we may run into other pagan Saracens on the sea."

The advice, which would keep them from being recognized by pagan Saracens, pleased everyone, so they took the tunics, arms, and armor of the dead men and threw all the bodies in the sea. But woe unto the emperor of Greece who thought up this plan, for he will meet his death and be destroyed because of the arms he wears, and moreover it will be by Valentin, his own son, that he will be killed, as you will hear tell a little further along.

Now the Christians are traveling by sea, outfitted in the pagan Saracens' very own armor. Moreover, in order to resemble the pagans all the more, they rolled up their own banners and standards, raising instead those of the Saracens to blow in the wind. They sailed so quickly across the sea that they soon arrived, sailing straight into the port of the noble and powerful city of Angory.

CHAPTER 66

How the Christians sallied forth out of the city of Angory; and concerning the conduct of their amazing battalions.

A month after King Brandiffer and King Lucar began the siege of the city of Angory with the full strength of their forces, Valentin and the other barons took counsel together and decided to sally forth to fight their enemies. They sent a challenge to Brandiffer for the next day, and the fierce and proud Brandiffer accorded it willingly. Then the Christians inside the city of Angory put their battalions in order in ten ranks, the first of which Millon d'Angler was to lead. The second was led by Samson of Orleans; the third by Gervais his son, the count of Vendome; the fourth by the count of Champagne; the fifth by Quentin of Normandy; the sixth by the duke of Burgundy; the seventh by the count of Dammartin; the eighth by the count of Auxerre; the ninth by the marshal of Constantinople; and the tenth by Valentin, who regularly inspired everyone with great courage to do well. He even emboldened the cowards who wished to flee, and put them in the ranks as I just described to you.

Saillirent crestiens hors de la cité d'Angorie pour le roy Brandiffer assaillir, qui de son ost avoit fait quinze fortes et merveilleuses batailles et ne la moindre avoit ung roy. Or ne fault pas demander des pompes, des richesses, des targes, des heaulmes et des harnoys fourbis qui d'une part et d'aultre sur les champs reluysoyent. Busines et tromppettes a celle heure pouoit on oÿr et la grosse bataille commença.[1]

Entour l'estandart des payens estoit le roy Brandiffer, le roy d'Esclardie, le roy d'Inde, le roy de Saleure, l'admiral de Cordes, l'admiral d'Orbie, le roy Damene, le roy Dubias, Josué de Palerne, le conte Braiment, le duc Orchillant, et Croste d'Orcaine. Et quant vint a aprocher des batailles, il y eut ung payen [126verso] de Surie qui jamais n'avoit esté en guerre, lequel pour son corps esprouver passa oultre et vint vers les crestiens, la lance sur l'arrest, moult fier et hardy. Bien le veit Valentin et son cheval frappa des esperons et contre le payen vint si fierement que du coup a la terre l'abatit tout mort. De celle heure commença la bataille moult dure et moult cruelle, et d'une part et d'aultre payens fort assailloient et vaillamment se deffendoyent. Mais toute leur vaillance n'est point a racompter contre la grant proesse que faisoient les crestiens, et entre lesquelz le hardy Valentin, le duc Millon et les douze pers de France.

Le roy d'Inde Major entra en la bataille et crestiens fort greva. Mais quant Valentin le veit il tira devers luy et si grant coup de lance luy donna que a terre l'abatit. A celle heure firent les crestiens reculer les Sarrasins moult loing, et desconfis estoient, quant ung capitaine sarrasin qui en l'arriere garde estoit vint pour les secourir acompaigné de trente mil payens, et la ont commencé la bataille plus forte que devant.

Le roy Lucar trouva le roy de Inde qui moult fort se combatoit et secours luy donna. Tant furent crestiens a celle heure chargéz de payens que par force les contraignit a retraire par devers ung estang qui pres du champ estoit, et trop affaire avoyent se n'eussent esté deux vaillans chevaliers qui celuy jour arriverent en Angorie acompaignéz de vii.cens homes. Les deux chevaliers[2] que je vous dy du Sainct Sepulchre[3] venoient, et moult de affaires et de necessitéz avoient souffert et enduréz, tant de prisons que d'aultres choses, pour faire leur voyage. L'ung de ces deux emmena en France la fille d'ung riche admiral payen, laquelle avoit nom Claradine, et la fist baptiser et prendre nostre loy et nostre creance. Le moindre des deux chevaliers estoit Regnier de Prouvence et l'autre Millon de Dijon, beaux chevaliers et hardis. Les deux eurent nouvelles de la grande bataille qui estoit pres de la, et leurs gens firent armer et a chascun baillerent enseignes et pavillons pour mieulx payens effroyer. Et en ce point vindrent hors de la ville les crestiens secourir.

Si se frapperent en la bataille moult fierement parquoy a l'aprocher furent payens de ceste nouvelle venue fort esmerveilléz, et non pas sans cause, car

---

[1] Text has *commencer*.
[2] Text has *chevalirrs*.
[3] Text has *sepulche*.

The Christians sallied forth out of the city of Angory to attack King Brandiffer, who had arranged his hosts into fifteen mighty and impressive battalions, even the least of which included a king. Now there is no need to inquire about what sumptuous and richly decorated shields, helmets and polished armor shone in the fields on all sides. Just then one could hear horns and trumpets, and then the great battle began.

Surrounding the pagan standard were King Brandiffer, the king of Esclardy, the king of India, the king of Salerno, the emir of Cordova, the emir of Orby, King Damene, King Dubias, Joshua of Palermo, Count Braiment, Duke Orchillant, and Croste of Orcany. When the time came for the battalions to approach each other, a pagan from Syria, who had never gone to war before and wanted to prove himself, pulled ahead of the line and galloped toward the Christians, his lance in its rest, most fierce and bold. Valentin certainly saw him, so he spurred his horse and came against the pagan so fiercely himself that with one blow he struck him down dead to the ground. From that moment on a most harsh and cruel battle was waged, with pagans on all sides attacking and defending themselves valiantly. But all their valor could not stand against the magnificent prowess of the Christians, especially the doughty Valentin, Duke Millon, and the Twelve Peers of France.

The king of India Major entered the battle and caused the Christians great harm. But when Valentin saw him he rode in his direction and struck him so hard with his lance that he knocked him to the ground. Thereupon the Christians forced the Saracens back and were thrashing them soundly when a Saracen captain, who had been in the rear guard, came to their aid with thirty thousand pagans, and then the battle recommenced even more violently than before.

King Lucar found the king of India, who was fighting fiercely, and brought him aid. The Christians at that point were so overcome by the number of pagans that they were forced to retreat towards a pond near the field, and they would have had a bad time of it had it not been for two valiant knights who arrived in Angory that very day accompanied by seven hundred men. The two knights I am talking about came from the Holy Sepulcher, and they had suffered and endured much hardship and privation, imprisonment, and other things in order to carry out their journey. One of them brought the daughter of a wealthy pagan emir to France, whose name was Claradine, and he had her baptized and converted to our religion and beliefs. The smaller of the two knights was Regnier of Provence, and the other was Millon of Dijon, handsome and doughty knights both. The two of them had heard tell of the great battle nearby, so they armed their men and gave each of them standards and banners, the better to frighten the pagans. Thereupon they came out of the city to help the Christians.

They threw themselves fiercely into the thick of the battle, for which reason the pagans were afraid to approach them, and not without reason, for as soon as

Millon de Dijon a son entree tua et abatit mort le roy Lucar et le roy Rubras, dont[1] Brandeffer fut moult esbahy et esperdu. Et apres entra Regnier en la bataille et plusieurs en tua et des plus vaillans.

Moult esmerveillé fut Valentin quant il vit ces deux chevaliers si vaillantes armes faire. Si chevaulcha vers eulx et leur dist, "Seigneurs, bien soyez vous venus. Dites moy, s'i vous plaist, qui deça vous amaine et qui vous estes."

"Amy," ce dit Regnier, "nous sommes pers de France qui du Sainct Sepulcre venons. Si avons oÿ parler de ceste entreprinse et en l'onneur de Jesus sommes venus en ceste part pour vous aider a la sainte [127recto]foy deffendre ainsi que nous sommes tenus. Et se noz noms vous plaist sçavoir je suis appellé Regnyer, seigneur de Prouvence, et mon compaignon est appellé Millon de Dijon, entre les aultres preux et hardy chevalier."

"Seigneurs," dist Valentin, "bien soyez vous venus, car icy est Millon d'Angler et tous les aultres pers de France."

A ces motz entrerent[2] tous en la bataille qui fut dure et mortelle plus que ne pourroye dire. Or se recorde le roy de Inde de Valentin qu'i l'avoit abatu. Si courut contre luy avec trois aultres roys et tellement le presserent que luy et son cheval a la terre abatirent. Mais le preux chevalier tantost se releva et print l'espee froubie, et tout a mieulx qu'il peult de toutes pars se deffent. Mais trop eut a faire quant Millon d'Angler, Sanson et Gervaiz vindrent et secours luy donnerent en telle maniere que ung cheval luy conquirent. Puis coururent vers le roy d'Inde et a terre l'abatirent et son escu luy osterent, si le baillerent a Valentin car le sien avoit perdu.

Or avint sur cestuy affaire nouvelles dont de piteuses choses vindrent, car ung messagier vint dire a Valentin, "Sire, je suis tout maintenant alé vers le port; si ay veu sur la mer grant nombre de Sarrasins qui viennent celle part."

"Seigneurs," dist le bon Valentin, "il y fault aler pour leur garder le passaige." Si se assemblerent Valentin, Millon de Dijon pour aler vers le port. Helas, c'estoit son pere l'empereur de Grece et son armee qui a leur secours venoient. De malle heure vestirent les armes des mauldis et faulx Sarrasins quant il fault que Valentin en mette son pere piteusement a mort.

---

[1] Text has *dung*.
[2] Text has *entreremt*.

he burst in, Millon of Dijon killed and struck down dead King Lucar and King Rubras, which greatly upset Brandiffer. Regnier entered the battle right on his heels and smote many of the most valiant among the enemy.

Valentin was quite amazed at the astoundingly valiant deeds of these two knights. He galloped up towards them and said, "My lords, you are most welcome. Tell me, if you will, who you are and what brings you here."

"My friend," said Regnier, "we are peers of France just come from the Holy Sepulcher. We heard what was going on here, and, for the honor of Jesus, we came this way to help you defend the holy faith as we are bound to do. And if it pleases you to know our names, I am called Regnier, lord of Provence, and my companion is called Millon of Dijon, among others a brave and hardy knight."

"My lords," repeated Valentin, "you are indeed welcome, for here is Millon d'Angler and all the other peers of France."

With these words they all rushed back into the battle, which was more violent and bloody than I could say. Now the king of India remembered Valentin, who had once struck him down, so he galloped towards him with three other kings, and so roughly did they press him that they knocked him and his horse to the ground. But the doughty knight soon arose, and, seizing his polished sword, defended himself on all sides as best he could. But he was nearly overcome when Millon d'Angler, Samson, and Gervais came to his aid with a horse they had seized. Then they descended upon the king of India, knocking him to the ground and taking away his shield, which they handed over to Valentin who had lost his own.

Then there came tidings which caused a great misfortune, for a messenger came to tell Valentin, "Sire, I just went to the port; there I saw a great number of Saracens arriving by sea."

"My lords," said the good Valentin, "we must go meet them to keep them from landing." So Valentin and Millon of Dijon assembled their forces to head to the port. But alas, it was his father the emperor of Greece and his army who were coming to their aid. Woe to them for having dressed themselves in the arms of the cursed and wicked Saracens, when it meant that poor Valentin ended up killing his own father.

[CHAPITRE 67]

Comment Valentin tua son pere l'empereur de Grece piteusement en la bataille. lxvii. chapitre

Aussitost que l'empereur de Grece et ses gens furent a terre descendus, Valentin chevaulcha celle part a force de cheval, la lance couchee. L'empereur de Grece qui grant et hardy couraige avoit, print tantost une lance qui contre son filz vint qui escu de Sarrasin portoit. Si ont rencontré l'ung l'autre par telle force que Valentin passa a la lance oultre le corps de son pere et a terre l'abatit mort sans ung seul mot parler. Puis s'escrya, "Montjoye, vive Grece!"

Et Orson, qui l'entendit bien, cogneut que c'estoit son frere qui son pere avoit tué. Si gette bas lance et escu et leva son heaulme, et puis s'escrie en plourant, "Frere, Valentin, malle vaillance avez faicte et povrement ouvré, car aujourd'uy avez tué le pere qui nous a engendré."

Et quant Valentin l'entendit, du cheval sur la terre se laissa choir, et Orson acourut qui mist les piedz a terre, et son frere acola en menant si grant dueil que de nul homme il ne vous pourroit estre compté. Si vindrent devers eulx Regnyer de Prouvence et Millon de Dijon pour les resconforter. Puis ont [127verso]levé Valentin et luy ont dit, "Chevalier, prenez en pacience, car vostre pere vous ne pouez pour plourer racheter. Ainsi qu'il a pleu a Dieu la chose est avenue."

"Helas," dist Valentin, "que m'est il avenu? Je suis bien dessus tous les aultres le plus mauldit, malleureux, dolent et mal fortuné. Helas! où es tu, Mort, quant tu ne viens a moy? Car je ne suis pas digne que terre me soustienne, ne que nul des elemens me preste nourriture quant j'ay ung fait commis devant Dieu detestable et aux hommes abhominable. Helas! maleureux Valentin, de quelle heure fus tu né, pour commettre sy villain cas et sy desnaturé murtre? J'ay souffert toute ma vie peine, tourment et moult grant soussy, mais dessus toutes choses je seuffre maintenant doleur la non pareille. Faulx roy d'Inde, mauldit soit ton escu et qui le composa, car par luy j'ay esté de mon pere descogneu. Helas! beau frere Orson, quant nostre pere ay mis a mort, prenez mon espee et la vie me ostez, car ce n'est pas rayson que plus je vive sur terre ne que je soye mis ou nombre des chevaliers."

"Frere," ce dist Orson, "prenez en vous meilleur resconfort et vous gardez de desespoir. Souvienne vous que Dieu est assez puissant pour plus grant chose pardonner. Retournez devers luy et pardon demandez, et de vostre peché promettez penitance faire. Certes qui est mort, il est mort—jamais remede vous n'y metterez. Si vault mieulx pour luy prier que sa mort tant plourer. Assez au jour d'uy en avons fait mourir dont ja ne verrez plourer."

Ainsi le conforta Orson qui trop avoit le cueur dolent et marry. Si a tant fait que a l'ayde des aultres barons et chevaliers qui la estoient que Valentin est remonté a cheval. Et ainsi que homme qui la mort ne doubte et sa vie riens ne prise, avec

CHAPTER 67

How Valentin tragically killed his father the emperor of Greece in the battle.

As soon as the emperor of Greece and his men had disembarked, Valentin galloped in their direction with his lance couched and ready. The emperor of Greece, of great and hardy courage, seized a lance himself and rode against his son who was carrying a Saracen shield. They came at each other with such great force that Valentin thrust his lance straight through his father's body and smote him dead to the ground without saying a single word. Then he cried out, "Montjoie! Long live Greece!"

And Orson, who heard him clearly, realized that it was his brother who had just killed his father. He threw down his lance and shield, raised his helmet, and cried out, weeping, "Valentin, my brother, evil is the valor you have shown and calamitous your deed, for today you have killed the father who engendered us."

And when Valentin heard him, he fell from his horse to the ground, and Orson, who had also gotten off his horse, ran up and threw his arms around his brother, wailing with such sorrow that no one could describe it to you. Then Regnier of Provence and Millon of Dijon came to them to try to comfort them. They raised Valentin and said to him, "Sir knight, you must forbear, for you cannot bring your father back through weeping. What has happened is God's will."

"Alas," said Valentin, "what have I done? I am above all others the most cursed, unhappy, sorrowful, and unfortunate. Alas! where are you, Death, why do you not come to me? For I am not worthy to be standing on the earth or to be nourished by any of the elements, seeing that I have committed the most heinous and abominable deed before both God and men. Alas! unhappy Valentin, in what hour were you born, to commit such an evil act and unnatural murder? I have suffered pain, torment, and trouble all my life, but now I suffer a woe incomparably greater than all others. Wicked king of India, cursed be your shield and the one who made it, for because of it, I was not recognized by my father. Alas! dear brother Orson, because I have caused the death of our father, take up my sword and end my life, for there is no reason for me to linger alive on this earth as one of the brotherhood of knights."

"Brother," said Orson, "take some comfort and keep yourself from despair. May you remember that God is powerful enough to forgive even worse deeds. Turn towards Him, ask Him for pardon, and promise to do penance for your sin. It is certain that he who is dead, is dead—you will never find a remedy. It is better to pray for him than to bewail his death so. We have killed enough men today who will never be wept over."

Thus did Orson comfort him whose heart was heavy and burdened with sorrow. Finally he was able, with the help of the other barons and knights there, to remount Valentin on his horse. And like a man who has no fear of death and sets

tous les aultres est entré en la bataille en frappant si grans coups que de tous ceulx qu'i trouva entour de luy, tant fussent ilz vaillans, ung seul il n'en eschappa.

A celle heure retourna le roy Crofle qui sur crestiens frappoit. Si luy donna Valentin ung tel coup que parmi le corps tout oultre le passa. A celle dure bataille furent Millon de Dijon et Regnier de Prouvence qui pour leur vaillance sy avant se bouterent que des Sarrasins furent prins et sans secours tenus. Lors leur benderent les yeulx et dedens leurs navires les firent mener moult piteusement batant. Mais Dieu, qui ses bons amis n'oublie point au besoing, les mettera dehors et dedens France les delivrera. Et menerent Charlot le roy de France a joye, honneur et grant liesse, et au grant dommaige, deshonneur et prejudice des faulx trahistres Hauffroy et Henry.

Ceste bataille dura longuement, car fort ilz se deffendoient et d'une part et d'aultre. Valentin ne regardoit mie a sa vie sauver, mais a frapper et a batre payens prenoit son estudie. Si vint vers Brandiffer, qui fier et puissant estoit, et si grant coup [128recto]l'ung a l'autre donnerent que tous deux a la terre cheurent. Mais Valentin qui fut preux et hardy et sur Brandiffer frappa si durement que a ung seul coup luy a la teste fendue et cheut mort. Et quant le roy Braiment[1] veit que son frere Brandiffer estoit mort, il partit de la bataille avec l'admiral de Courdes et le roy Josué qui retraicte firent sonner, et vers leurs navires alerent pour fuyr et eulx sauver.

Mais les crestiens les suivyrent en reclamant sainct George et sainct Jaques, lesquelz deux sains, ainsi que par aulcuns bons chevaliers depuis fut tesmoigne, pour les crestiens firent et monstrerent ce jour miracle contre payens. Or furent payens de si pres prins et attains que plusieurs dedens la mer faillirent et se noyerent, et aussi en toutes manieres furent payens desconfis. La nuyt fut venue que les crestiens se retrairent dedens Angorie. Puis lendemain au matin s'en yssirent au chemin pour faire les mors enterrer. La furent trouvéz maintz chevaliers mors qui assez furent plains, mais sur tous les aultres, de grans et de petis, fust amerement plouré l'empereur de Grece. Valentin et Orson demenerent sy grant dueil que on ne les pouoit apaiser. Et Millon d'Angler leur a dist, "Enfans, ne plourez plus, mais priez Dieu pour l'ame de luy, car ja pour voz larmes en vie ne reviendra."

Lors ont fait le corps aporter dedens la cité, et l'ont ainsi comme il luy appartenoit fait ensevelir, et plusieurs messes ont fait chanter et assez d'aulmoisnes aux povres departir pour son ame. Mais quiconques face chiere tousjours pleure Valentin qui pour nul confort que on luy donne ne le peult oublier.[2]

---

[1] Text has *vrayement*.
[2] Text has *omblier*.

no price on his own life, he returned to the battle with the others, striking such blows on every side that no one, however valiant, could escape from him alive.

Just then King Crofle returned to the battle and was smiting Christians. Valentin gave him such a blow that it passed right through his body. Millon of Dijon and Regnier of Provence took part in that bloody battle, thrusting themselves so deep into the thick of it that they were captured and held by the Saracens without anyone nearby to help. Then they bound their eyes and loaded them onto their ships, beating them mercilessly the whole time. But God, who does not forget His good friends in their need, will rescue them and will deliver them to France. And they brought Charles back to France with joy, honor, and great happiness, but with great harm, dishonor, and loss to the false traitors Hauffroy and Henry.[1]

This battle lasted a long time, for both sides defended themselves vigorously. Valentin had no regard for his own life, rather he concentrated on striking and smiting pagans. Then he came upon Brandiffer, still as fierce and strong as ever, and each gave the other such a blow that both fell to the ground. But Valentin, the valiant and bold, struck Brandiffer so ferociously that with one blow he split his head open and cast him down dead. And when King Braiment saw that his brother Brandiffer was dead, he left the battle with the emir of Courdes and King Joshua, who sounded the retreat, and they headed towards their boats with the intention to escape and save themselves.

But the Christians pursued them, calling upon St. George and St. James, two saints who performed miracles that day for the Christians against the pagans, as several good knights were able to testify later on. Now the pagans were so closely pressed and attacked that many of them fell and drowned in the sea, and thus in all ways were the pagans destroyed. It was night by the time the Christians withdrew into the city of Angory. Then the next morning they came out again to bury the dead. They found many fallen knights who were to be mourned over, but above all others, everyone great and small bitterly wept over the emperor of Greece. Valentin and Orson bewailed him so much that no one could calm them. And Millon d'Angler said to them, "My children, weep no more, rather pray to God for his soul, for your tears can never bring him back to life."

Then they brought his body back to the city and buried him befittingly, and had many masses chanted and much alms given to the poor for the sake of his soul. But whatever sorrow anyone else expressed, Valentin wept without surcease, unable to forget his sorrow no matter what comfort was offered him.

---

[1] The reference here is to events in another text, *Garin de Monglane*, as pointed out by Dickson in his source study. See *Study*, 249–50.

[CHAPITRE 68]

Comment Millon d'Angler retourna en France, et Valentin et Orson son frere alerent en Grece.
lxviii. cha[pitre]

Apres que payens eurent esté la seconde fois desconfis devant Angorie, le duc Millon d'Angler print congié de Valentin pour retourner en France disant, "Chevalier et amy Valentin, je m'en veul retourner. Si vouldroye bien que aussi legierement m'en partisse que vous me aportastes."

"Amy," dit Valentin en plourant, "ja ne plaise a Dieu que de tel art je joue, car c'est art d'ennemy dampnable. Celuy qui le me aprint en la fin en mourut meschamment, et je croy que pour ce peché je ay mon pere tué." Lors print congé Millon d'Angler et avec tous les barons qui de France estoient se mist a chemin.

Et Valentin et Orson prindrent congé et ensemble conseil de retourner en Constantinoble, mais premier qu'i partissent ilz firent couronner le Verd Chevalier roy d'Angorie et luy firent par les barons et chevaliers du pays faire hommage et feaulté promettre. Puis prindrent de luy congé et monterent sur mer.

Et quant vint au departir Orson appella Galasie. "M'amye, je cognoy que de mon fait estes [128verso]ensainte d'enfant. Mais sachez que pour femme je ne vous puis avoir car j'en ay une aultre espousee. Pourtant s'il vous plaist je vous feray assigner rentes et revenues tant que bien vous pourrez vivre honnestement sans le danger de nul."

"Sire," dit Galasie, "avec vous veul la mer passer, puis me metteray en ung monastere et la deviendray religieuse et pourray Dieu servir pour vous."

"Dame,"[1] dist Orson, "a cela je me acorde."

Lors la mist sur la mer et tant nagerent qu'ilz veirent les tours de Constantinoble. Si descendirent et manderent a la royne leur mere des nouvelles et la mort de l'empereur, mais ne manderent point que Valentin l'eust occis. Dolente et courrucee fut la dame pour la mort de l'empereur, et d'aultre part fut joyeuse de ses deux enfans que en sancté venoient.

Chascun mena grant joye parmy Constantinoble pour la venue de Valentin et de Orson son frere. Chanoynes, clers, prestres et bourgois saillirent de la cité en grande procession, et par toutes les esglises on fist les cloches sonner moult haultement. Ainsi furent receus notablement. Puis monterent au palais qui pour eulx fut paré. Le disner fut pres; a table se sont assis, de plusieurs grans barons acompaignéz.

La dame commença a parler devant tous et a dit, "Valentin mon enfant, or convient sçavoir lequel de vous deux tiendra l'empire de Grece, car ainsi me

---

[1] Text has *dame/ me*, probably owing to line break.

CHAPTER 68

How Millon d'Angler returned to France, while Valentin and Orson his brother went to Greece.

After the pagans had been defeated for the second time before the city of Angory, Duke Millon d'Angler took leave of Valentin in order to return to France, saying, "Sir knight and friend Valentin, I wish to return. But I would very much like to go back as easily as you brought me."

"Friend," said Valentin in tears, "may it never please God that I use such magic again, for it is a damnable devil's craft. The one who taught it to me died from it untowardly, and I believe that it is because of this sin that I have killed my father." So Millon d'Angler took his leave and set out on his way with all the French barons.

And Valentin and Orson also took their leave, deciding together to return to Constantinople, but before leaving they crowned the Green Knight king of Angory, and had the barons and knights of the country pay homage to him and swear fealty. Then they took leave of him and set sail.

When it came time to leave, Orson called for Galasie. "My dear, I realize that you are pregnant by me. But know that I cannot marry you because I have a wife. However, if it please you, I will arrange an income for you so that you will be able to live properly without fear of anyone."

"Sire," said Galasie, "I want to cross the sea with you, but then I will retire to a convent and will become a nun where I will be able to serve God for your sake."

"My lady," said Orson, "to that I agree."

So she joined them on the ship, and they sped so fast over the sea that soon they saw the towers of Constantinople. They disembarked and sent tidings, including the news of the death of the emperor to the queen their mother, but they did not tell her that Valentin had killed him. The lady was full of sorrow for the death of the emperor, but, on the other hand, she was happy for the safe return of her two children.

Everyone in Constantinople celebrated the return of Valentin and Orson his brother. Canons, clerks, priests, and burghers came forth out of the city in a grand procession, and all the church bells rang out on high. Thus were they received with great pomp. They continued on up to the palace, which had been decorated for their sakes. Dinner was ready, so they seated themselves in the company of many important barons.

The lady began an address to them all, saying, "Valentin, my child, now we must know which of you will rule the Greek empire, for as God is my witness, I

veulle Dieu aider que de vous je ne sçay lequel est le plus aisné. Si m'atens bien a vous de y sagement ouvrer."

"Dame," dist Valentin, "je veul que mon frere Orson le soit cestuy premier an."

"Par ma foy," dist Orson, "a moy n'apartient pas de aler par devant vous. Frere, je suis tenu a vous et non pas vous a moy. Si serez empereur, car de ma part je le veul."

Assez debatirent ceste chose. Puis en la fin fut appointié par les seigneurs et barons du pays que tous deux gouverneroient en paix et bonne amour; ainsi fut acordé. Mais le bon Valentin en si hault estat longuement ne demoura pas, comme je vous diray.

[CHAPITRE 69]

Comment Valentin print congé de la belle Esclarmonde pour aler a Romme par devers le pape pour son peché confesser. lxix. chapitre[1]

Valentin, qui pour la mort de son pere nuyt et jour larmoioit, par un matin appella la belle Esclarmonde et lui a dit, "M'amie [129recto]entendez[2] ma rayson. Vous sçavez que devant Angorie j'ay mon pere piteusement tué dont nulle confession je n'ay faicte. Si suis deliberé de m'en aler a Romme mes pechéz confesser et au sainct pere demander penitance. Saluez moy ma mere et mon frere Orson lequel au bout de xv.jours vous l'irez veoir et non plus tost. Et luy baillez cestuy bresvet, et a nulle aultre personne ne le monstrez."

Moult tendrement ploura la dame pour Valentin tant que les larmes luy couroient sur sa face. "Taisez vous," dist le chevalier, "et pour moy ne plourez plus, mais me baillez l'aneau de quoy je vous ay espousee." La dame tantost luy bailla et il en fist deux parties dont il en garda l'une et l'autre l'a baillee a la dame en luy disant, "M'amye, gardez ceste partie de l'aneau et, pour chose que on vous die de moy ne raporte, n'en croyez ung seul mot se vous ne voyez l'autre partye que je porte avec moy. Gouvernez vous sagement et tousjours servez Dieu et de faulces parolles vous gardez, car le monde est au jour d'uy trop faulx et decepvant."

A ces motz embrassa la dame et en plourant piteusement prindrent l'ung de l'autre congié. Ainsi partit Valentin; acompaigné de ung seul escuier il monta a cheval et s'est mis en chemin, et a tant cheminé que en peu de temps est arrivé a Romme. Celle nuyt se loga et puis le lendemain vint a la grant esglise ou le pape chanta la messe. Valentin l'entendit et escoutoit de bon cueur, et puis apres la

---

[1] Woodcut of kneeling male figure at right facing a standing female figure with male attendant at far left. Gestures of leave-taking (?). Cityscape in background.

[2] *r i* at bottom right corner of 129r.

do not know which of the two of you is the elder. Thus I depend on you to make a wise decision."

"Lady," said Valentin, "I want my brother Orson to rule this first year."

"By my faith," said Orson, "it is not fitting for me to rule before you. Brother, I am beholden to you, not you to me. You shall be emperor, for that is what I wish."

They debated the question for some time. Then in the end it was settled by the lords and barons of the country that the two of them would govern together in peace and good love, and thus it was accorded. But the good Valentin did not remain long in such high estate, as I will explain to you.

CHAPTER 69

How Valentin took leave of the fair Esclarmonde to go to Rome to confess his sin to the pope.

One morning, Valentin, who bewailed the death of his father night and day, called for the fair Esclarmonde and said to her, "My dear, listen to what I am thinking. You know that to my woe I killed my father before the walls of Angory, for which I have made no confession. Thus I have decided to go to Rome to confess my sins and request a penance from the holy father. In fifteen days, but no sooner, go to my mother and my brother Orson and greet them. Give Orson this letter, but show it to no one else."

The lady wept such copious tears over Valentin that they ran down her face. "Calm yourself," said the knight, "and weep no more over me, but give me the ring with which I married you." The lady gave him the ring right away and he broke it into two halves, keeping one half for himself and returning the other to her, saying, "My love, keep this half of the ring, and, no matter what anyone ever tells you or brings back as a report concerning me, do not believe a single word of it if you do not see the other half of this ring that I carry with me. Conduct yourself wisely, always serve God, and be on guard against false speech, for the world today is terribly wicked and deceptive."

With these words he kissed the lady, and, weeping piteously, they took leave of one another. Thus did Valentin depart; accompanied by only one squire, he mounted his horse and set off on his road, riding so swiftly that he soon arrived in Rome. That night he took lodgings, and came the next day to the great church where the pope was chanting mass. Valentin heard him and listened with all his heart. Then, after

messe devant le saint pere se agenoulla pour confession demander. Lors le pape, qui bien pensa que de haulte maison fust, luy fist signe que il l'orra. Puis entra le pape en sa chambre et fist venir Valentin qui fort plouroit.

"Beau filz," ce dit le pape, "que peux tu avoir que si tendrement pleures?"

"Helas!" dist Valentin, "de tous aultres pecheurs je suis et me doy nommer le pire." Lors commença sa confession, et entre les aultres faultes en plourant et gettant larmes parfondes commença et confessa comment son pere avoit tué et demanda penitance.

Et quant le pape entendit le cas de Valentin, il regarda la grant et amere repentance que il avoit mort son pere. Au cueur luy print grant pitié; il luy dist, "Mon enfant, ne vous desconfortez pas, car assez est Dieu puissant pour plus grant chose vous pardonner. Alez en vostre logis et demain au matin devers moy retournez; si vous donneray penitance au salut de vostre ame." Ainsi le fit Valentin et en son logis s'en ala sans riens de son fait dire a personne. La nuyt ploura et souspira et gaires ne print de repos.

Et quant le matin fut venu il retourna en l'esglise et le pape trouva qui devant luy faisoit la messe chanter. Apres la messe le pape l'appella et luy dist, "Mon enfant, entend que il te fault faire pour avoir de ton péché pardon. Tout premierement changeras ton habit et povrement iras vestu et ton corps tant tra[129verso] veilleras que de nul ne puisse estre cogneu. Et apres iras en Constantinoble et soubz les degréz de ton palays te logeras, et la endroit seras sept ans sans parler, se Dieu tant de vie te donne, et ne mengeras ne beuveras fors du relief que on donne aux povres. Et se plus tost tu meurs tous tes pechéz te sont pardonnéz. Se ainsi par l'espace de sept ans tu ne fais la penitance jamais pardon tu n'auras."

"Sire," dist Valentin, "tout cela feray je de bon cueur."

Adonc l'apostole de Rome luy donna absolucion. Et ainsi que dit l'istoire que nous tenons pour verité celui jour disna[1] Valentin avec le pape de Rome. Puis apres se partit de la cité et a nul de ses gens ne parla ne congié ne print. Si vous diray comment il partit de sa penitance et de la vie qu'il menoit.

---

[1] Text has *dit a*, which makes no sense.

mass, he knelt before the holy father to request confession. The pope, who realized he was of exalted lineage, indicated that he would hear him. So the pope entered his chamber, inviting Valentin, who was weeping with great emotion, to follow him in.

"Fair son," said the pope, "what is the matter that you weep such copious tears?"

"Alas!" said Valentin, "of all sinners I am and must call myself the worst." So he began his confession, all the while weeping bitter tears, and among the other faults he recounted, he confessed how he had killed his father, and asked for penance.

As the pope listened to Valentin's story, he saw the great and bitter remorse he suffered for having caused his father's death. His heart was filled with pity for him, and he said, "My child, do not torment yourself, for God is powerful enough to pardon you for even a greater crime than this. Go to your lodging and come back to see me tomorrow morning; I will give you a penance for the salvation of your soul." Valentin obeyed his directions and returned to his lodgings without telling anyone anything about what he had done. That night he wept and sighed and slept little.

When morning arose he returned to the church to find the pope having mass chanted before him. After mass the pope called for him and said, "My child, listen to what you must do to have pardon for your sin. First of all, you will change your clothes and go forth poorly dressed, and you will mortify your flesh so much that no one will be able to recognize you. After that you will go to Constantinople and live underneath the stairs of your palace, and there you will stay for seven years without speaking, if God grants you life for that long, and you will not eat or drink except what they give you from the table scraps offered to the poor.[1] And if you die before the time is up, all your sins shall be forgiven you, but if you live seven years and do not do the penance, you shall never have pardon."

"Sire," said Valentin, "all this will I do willingly."

Thereupon the apostle of Rome gave him absolution. And according to the story, which we hold to be true, Valentin dined that day with the pope of Rome. Afterwards he left the city, speaking to none of his men nor taking leave from them. Now I will tell you how he left to carry out his penance and what sort of life he led.

---

[1] Valentin's final years (Chapters 69 to 74) bear many parallels to those of St. Alexis. See Dickson's comparison in *Study*, 251–64. See also *La Vie de Saint Alexis*, ed. Maurizio Perugi (Geneva: Droz, 2000).

[CHAPITRE 70]

Pour racompter comment Valentin en grant doleur de son corps acheva et parfit sa penita[n]ce pour son pere lequel il avoit occys. [lxx. chapitre]

Valentin, qui de Dieu fut inspiré pour sa penitance parfaire, entra dedens ung bois apres que il eust fait resre sa teste, et en celuy boys fust si longuement, mengant pommes et racines et sy traynant parmy les ronces et espines, si que de nul homme vivant n'eust esté cogneu. Apres lesquelles choses il s'en ala en Constantinoble.

Mais premier que il y arrivast pour luy fut grant dueil par la cité demenee, car la belle Esclarmonde, qui son messaige n'oublia pas, ala devers Orson et luy donna la lettre que Valentin luy avoit laissé. Et quant il veit la lettre il s'est mis a plourer moult fort et angoiseusement.

"Frere," dist Esclarmonde, "pourquoy tant larmiez vous?"

"Helas, m'amie," dist il, "ce n'est pas sans grande rayson, car mon frere Valentin s'en va et par ceste letre me fait assavoir que jamais il ne reviendra, mais demoura en exil pour ses pechéz plourer."

Quant la dame entendit que son mary s'en va, a terre elle cheut paumee. Et quant elle fut revenue elle s'escrya bien hault, "Helas! mon amy, pourquoy sans le moy dire estes vous ainsi party? Mal fortunee suis quant je suis demouree et vous en alez sans jamais revenir." Grant dueil menoit la dame et plus grant Orson. Parmy la cité furent tantost les nouvelles de l'alee de Valentin qui en exil s'en estoit alé sans espoir de retourner. Esclarmonde en pleure, Bellissant larmoye, et Orson de cueur souspire. Longuement dura celuy dueil parmy la cité.

Et avint ainsi comme dit l'istoire que en celuy jour on dist a Fezonne que Orson avoit une aultre dame enamouree qui de luy estoit grosse, dont tel couroux print en son cueur que malade en fut et au lit se coucha et en brief temps mourut. Grant dueil en mena Orson mais devant l'an acomply il espousa Galasie dont je vous ay devant mencion faicte.

Or vous diray de Valentin lequel arriva en Constantinoble en si [130recto] povre[1] estat de son corps que de nul de ses amis ne pouoit estre cogneu. Il ala par les rues et parmy les maisons des bourgois l'aumoisne querant pour oÿr des nouvelles. Puis s'en vint au palays a l'eure que son frere Orson et Bellisant sa mere pour soupper vouloyent a la table entrer. Ceulx qui gardoient la table l'ont batu et chassé pour le bouter hors, mais il n'en fait semblant.

"Compaignons," ce dit Orson, qui fort regardoit sa contenance, "laissez ce povre ceans et plus ne le batez, car pour l'amour de mon frere Valentin je veul que tous povres soyent receus affin que Dieu m'en veulle envoyer nouvelles." Lors

---

[1] *r ii* at bottom right corner of 130r.

CHAPTER 70

Recounting how Valentin, with great pain of body, carried out and completed his penance for having killed his father.

Valentin, inspired by God to carry out his penance, shaved his head and entered a wood where he spent such a long time eating apples and roots and dragging himself through the brambles and thorns that no man alive would have recognized him. After that he went to Constantinople.

But the entire city mourned him before he ever arrived there, for the fair Esclarmonde, who had not forgotten his message, went to Orson to give him the letter that Valentin had left for him. When he saw the letter, he began to weep bitterly and with great anguish.

"Brother," said Esclarmonde, "why are you crying so?"

"Alas, my dear," he said, "it is not without good reason, for my brother Valentin has gone away, and by this letter he gives me to understand that he will never return, rather he will remain in exile to bewail his sins."

When the lady understood that her husband had thus left for good, she fell to the floor in a swoon. Regaining consciousness, she cried aloud, "Alas! my love, why have you gone away like this without telling me? How unfortunate I am when I remain here while you go away never to return." The lady grieved deeply, and Orson even more so. The news spread throughout the city that Valentin had exiled himself without any hope of his return. Esclarmonde wept, Bellissant was in tears, and Orson sighed deeply. Such grieving went on for a long time throughout the city.

As the story recounts, it happened that same day that someone told Fezonne that Orson had another lady in love with him who was pregnant by him. She felt such anguish in her heart that she became ill, took to her bed, and soon died. Orson mourned her greatly, but before a year was up, he married Galasie, as I mentioned to you before.

Now I shall tell you about Valentin, who arrived in Constantinople in such a wretched physical state that not one of his friends could recognize him. He walked down the streets and among the houses of the burghers of the town, seeking alms in order to hear news. Then he came to the palace at the hour when his brother Orson and Bellissant his mother came to table to sup. Those who kept the table beat him and pushed him away to throw him out, but he said nothing.

"Fellows," said Orson, who was looking closely at him, "allow this poor man in and do not beat him any more, because, for the sake of my brother Valentin, I want all poor men to be received so that God may one day be willing to send

laisserent Valentin a tant par le commandement de Orson et luy ont aporté bons vins et viandez assez, mais il n'en veult point prendre et regarde une corbeille ou estoit l'aumoisne des povres du relief de la table. Il ala celle part et de celle viande il menga. Ceulx qui le regardoient de sa contenance furent moult fort esbahys. Mais quant vint vers la nuit que les portiers vouloient fermer les portes, sont venus vers Orson et luy ont dist, "Sire, ce malotru qui le fol contrefait, voulez vous que il demoure icy?"

"Je veul que vous souffrez et endurez de luy et que parmy le palays le laissez a sa voulenté faire, car par aventure c'est veu ou promesse que il a Dieu promis. Quant il ne parle point nul ne peult sçavoir qui il est."

Ainsy demoura Valentin soubz les degréz, et fit son lit de la paille et estrain assez il aporta. Lendemain au matin Orson par devant luy passa, qui grant pitié en eut, et l'aumoisne luy donna. Apres passoit pour aler au moustier sa mere et sa femme Esclarmonde qui moult le regarderent et luy donnerent l'aumoisne.

"Helas! povre homme," dit Esclarmonde, "comment pouez vous sans couverture la nuyt icy durer? Sy plaist a Dieu vers la nuyt en aurez."

Valentin s'enclina en les remerciant moult humblement et les dames passerent oultre, mais tout aussitost que elles furent passees Valentin veit deux povres a la porte. Il courut devers eulx et tout leur donna ce que on luy avoit donné.

"Par ma foy," dirent l'ung a l'autre, en soy moquant de luy, "ce quoquin est bien assoté quant il n'a riens vaillant et donne ses aumoisnes que lé autres luy ont donné."

Dist Valentin[1] en son cueur, "Sire Dieu, tout puissant, veullez a tous ceulx pardonner qui de moy font derrision, car ilz ne scevent pas la faulte miserable parquoy ainsi vivre me convient."

Quant vint au disner apres on donnoit a Valentin de toutes viandes, mais il faisoit a sa puissance signe que de riens il ne mengeroit sy non seullement des reliefz. Et quant Orson cogneut sa condicion il commanda que de tout le meilleur de sa table on mist en la corbeille et que le povre homme par devant fust tout le premier party.

"Seigneurs," ce dist Orson, "par le Dieu en qui je croy tousjours me dist le cueur que ce povre [130verso]homme fait quelque penitance que a Dieu a promise et vouee." En ce point fut Valentin moult longuement dedens son palais sans estre cogneu tant que chascun disoit que pieça il estoit mort, parquoy le roy Hugon fist Esclarmonde demander pour femme et depuis grant trahyson entreprint et brassa.

---

[1] Text has *Velentin*.

me tidings of him." So they left Valentin alone by order of Orson, and brought him good wines and plentiful food, but he did not want to take any of it, instead gazing at the basket with the table scraps offered to the poor. That's where he went and ate from its contents. Those watching him were amazed at his behavior. But when night fell and the porters wanted to shut the gates, they came to Orson and said, "Sire, this rascal who pretends to be a fool, do you want him to remain here?"

"I want you to suffer him and allow him to do as he likes within the palace, for perhaps he acts according to a vow or promise made to God. Since he speaks not at all, no one can know who he is."

Thus Valentin stayed under the stairs, making his bed from straw that he brought. The next morning Orson passed by him, and, feeling great pity for him, gave him alms. Afterwards, when his mother and his wife passed by on their way to church, they stared at him and they too gave him alms.

"Alas! poor man," said Esclarmonde, "how can you endure the night without any coverlet? May it please God that you have one before tonight."

Valentin bowed before them, thanking them most humbly, and the ladies passed on, but as soon as they had passed, Valentin saw two poor men at the gate. He ran to them and gave them everything that had been given him.

"By my faith," said one to the other, making fun of him, "this fellow is truly foolish, seeing that he has nothing of value, but he gives away his alms that others have given him."

Then Valentin said in his heart, "Lord God almighty, may you pardon all those who mock me, for they know not for what miserable sin I live in this fashion."

When it was time for dinner, they gave Valentin some from all the food served, but as well as he could, he signaled to them that he would eat nothing but table scraps. When Orson understood his demand, he ordered that the basket be filled with the best from the table and that this poor man be the first to eat from it.

"My lords," said Orson, "by the God in whom I always believe, my heart tells me that this poor man is fulfilling some penance that he vowed and promised to God." In this way did Valentin remain a long time within the palace without being recognized, so that everyone said that he must be dead, for which reason King Hugo asked Esclarmonde to marry him, and afterwards plotted and tried to carry out a treacherous plan.

[CHAPITRE 71]

Comment le roy Hugon fit demander la belle Esclarmonde pour femme; et comment il trahyt Orson et le Verd Chevalier. lxxi. chapitre

En iceluy temps y avoit ung roy en Hongrie que Hugon estoit nommé. Celuy roy oÿt parler de Valentin, qui l'empire de Grece avoit laissé et le pays deguerpy. Si s'en vint en Constantinoble et de Orson fut moult bien receu, tant que par un matin Hugon appella la belle Esclarmonde et luy a dist en beau languaige:

"Dame, sachez que je suis roy d'Ongorie et tiens dessoubz moy plusieurs grans seigneurs. Mais d'une chose je fus mal; c'est que je n'ay point de femme et suis a marier pour laquelle chose je suis venu par devers vous. J'ay entendu que le bon chevalier Valentin jamais plus vous ne le verrez. Je vous requiers que pour mary vous me veullez avoir et recepvoir, et serez royne de Hongrie couronnee et moult grandement honnouree, car sur toutes les aultres vous estes celle que mon cueur plus ardamment desire."

"Sire," ce dist la dame, "du bien et de l'onneur que vous me presentez humblement je vous remercye. Mais pour bien vous respondre, querez une aultre femme, car ancores est en vie mon amy Valentin. Sy suis deliberee de l'attendre sept ans. Et quant il seroit ainsi que mary je vouldroye prendre, a moy il ne fauldroit point parler mais a l'empereur Orson et au Verd Chevalier, mon frere, car sans le conseil de entre eulx jamais je ne m'y consentiroye pour chose que on me sceust dire."

"Dame," ce dist Hugon, "vous parlez treshonnestement et moult me plaist vostre responce."

Lors s'en vint vers Orson et luy demanda se de Valentin avoit eu nulles nouvelles.

"Franc roy," ce dist Orson, qui de luy pas ne se doubtoit aultre chose, "n'en sçay si non par une lettre que a sa femme laissa. Laquelle lettre devise qu'il est alé en exil pour ses pechéz plourer, et dessus luy porte une partie de l'aneau dont sa femme espousa et l'autre luy a laissee. Et sur toutes choses luy a dit que riens de luy ne veulle croire se la part de l'aneau elle ne voit."

"Sire," ce dist Hugon, qui ces parolles bien nota, "Dieu le veulle conduire, car moult est chevalier a louer et a prisier. Or vous diray une chose que j'ay en mon couraige—je suis deliberé en l'onneur de Jesus, lequel souffrit mort et passion en l'arbre de la croix pour nous, de aler en Hierusalem veoir et viseter[1] le Sainct Sepulchre de

---

[1] Text has *viserer*.

CHAPTER 71

How King Hugo asked the fair Esclarmonde to marry him; and how he betrayed Orson and the Green Knight.

At that time there was a king in Hungary named Hugo. This king heard it said that Valentin had left his country and abandoned the empire of Greece. So he came to Constantinople where he was well received by Orson, so much so that one morning Hugo called for the fair Esclarmonde and spoke to her in honeyed language:

"Lady, know that I am the king of Hungary and master over many great lords. However, there is one thing I lack; I have no wife and must marry, for which reason I have come to see you. I have heard that you shall never again see the good knight Valentin. Therefore I ask you to take me as your husband, and you shall be crowned queen of Hungary and greatly honored, for above all others, you are the one my heart desires most ardently."

"Sire," said the lady, "I thank you most humbly for the honor you show me. However, to respond to you properly, I say seek some other woman, for my beloved Valentin is still alive. I am determined to wait seven years for him. Moreover, should the time come for me to take another husband, it is not to me that you would speak, but rather to the emperor Orson and the Green Knight, my brother, for I would never agree to any suit addressed to me without their advice."

"Lady," said Hugo, "you speak most worthily and your answer pleases me well."

Then he went to Orson and asked him if he had received any tidings of Valentin.

"Noble king," said Orson, who suspected nothing concerning him, "everything I know is from a letter he left with his wife. This letter says that he has gone into exile in order to bewail his sins, and he carries with him half of the ring with which he married his wife, the other half of which he left with her. And he said above all else not to believe anything said of him if it were not accompanied by his half of the ring."

"Sire," said Hugo, who took careful note of these words, "may God guide him, for he is a praiseworthy knight. Now I will tell you something that is in my heart—I have decided to go to Jerusalem to visit the Holy Sepulcher of our Redeemer in order to honor Jesus who suffered death and passion on the cross for

Nostre Redempteur. [131r]Si[1] vouldroye bien avoir trouvé compaignie, et se venir il vous plaisoit, a tousjours mais en armes serions compaignons et amis."

"Sire," ce dit Orson, "c'est bien ma voulenté de faire le voyaige et de long temps l'ay de faire promis. Si vous diray que nous ferons—au partir de ceste terre, nous irons en Angorie. Sy sçay bien pour tout vray que le Verd Chevalier qui en Angorie est roy nouvellement couronné voulentiers avecques nous viendra."

"Bien me plaist," dist Hugon. "Alons ou vous plaira."

Lors print congié Orson de la belle Galasie et de sa mere Bellissant. Puis monterent dessus mer et en Angorie tantost sont venus. Et le roy moult honnourablement les receut et de la venue de Orson fut au cueur moult fort joyeulx. Assez se festierent et menerent grant chiere. Puis se apresta le Verd Chevalier pour le sainct voyaige faire. Avec eulx sur la mer monta; si ont tant et si fort exploitié que ilz sont venus en Hierusalem[2] et ont prins logis pour la nuyt reposer. Puis lendemain le matin sont aléz devers le bon patriarche qui devant eulx la messe chanta, puis parmy la cité les fit conduire pour le Sainct Sepulchre et aultres sains lieux viseter. En grant devocion les pardons gaignerent et le voyaige devotement firent, fors le roy Hugon qui devers son cueur portoit la venimeuse trahyson par laquelle il fit les vaillans seigneurs qui en luy se fioyent des faulx payens prendre et moult durement emprisonner. Car ainsi que les bons seigneurs d'entendement les esglises viseterent, le trahystre roy Hugon se partit et embla de leur compaignie; si s'en vint au roy de Surie qui Rabaste avoit nom et iceluy Rabaste estoit frere du roy d'Inde qui devant Angorie mourut.

Hugon de par le dieu Mahon le salua et luy a dist, "Roy, veullez a moy entendre et je diray chose pour vous moult pourfitable. Sachez, sire, que deux chevaliers sont nouvellement venus que dessus tous les aultres doivent estre de vous mal venus et haÿs, car grant partie de vostre terre payenne ont prinse, perdue et exillee, et si ont mis a honteuse mort par leur grande cruaulté le vaillant Brandiffer, Lucar le roy puissant, et vostre frere le roy d'Inde."

Quant Rabaste entendit que son frere estoit mort moult tendrement ploura, puis a dit a Hugon, "Sire, me pourrez vous les deux chevaliers rendre?"

"Oy," ce dist Hugon, "mais que une chose vous me promettez et jurrez, et pour toute ma part vous me donnerez les seaulx d'or que portent les deux chevaliers ou leurs armes sont empraintes."

"Sire," dit le roy de Surie, "trop seroye mal cognoissant se pour tant peu de chose je vous escondissoye. Les seaulx aurez a vostre demande et assez d'aultrez choses se les deux chevaliers me pouez delivrer."

"Oy," ce dit Hugon, "or escoutez comment. En l'ostel du patriarche envoyez voz messagiers et il vous sçaura a dire ou ilz sont."

[131verso]Ainsi le fit le roy de Surye; et huyt cens hommes fit armer, puis alerent vers le bon patriarche qui au commandement du roy leur enseigna le logis. Et

---

[1] *r iii* at bottom right of 131r.
[2] Text has *hierusalez*.

our sakes. I would very much like to find company, and if it pleased you to come, we would forever be friends and companions in arms."

"Sire," said Orson, "it is certainly my desire to make such a voyage, and I have long promised to do it. I will tell you what we shall do: leaving here, we shall go first to Angory. I know for sure that the Green Knight, who has recently been crowned king of Angory, will come with us willingly."

"That pleases me well," said Hugo. "Let us go as you propose."

So Orson took leave of the fair Galasie and his mother Bellissant. Then they set sail and soon arrived in Angory. The king received them most honorably and was delighted to see Orson. They celebrated and feasted together. Then the Green Knight prepared himself for the holy journey. Together they set sail and advanced so quickly that soon they arrived in Jerusalem, where they took lodgings for the night. The next morning they went to see the good patriarch, who chanted mass for them and arranged to have them taken to visit the Holy Sepulcher and other holy sights. With great devotion they earned pardons and consummated their pilgrimage, except for King Hugo, who harbored venomous treason in his heart, and who was planning to have the valiant lords who had trusted him seized and harshly imprisoned by the wicked pagans. Just as these good barons were visiting the churches as planned, the false-hearted King Hugo stole away from their company to go see Rabaste, the king of Syria, who was brother to the King of India who had died in the battle before the city of Angory.

Hugo greeted him in the name of the god Mohammed and said, "King, listen to me and I will tell you something to your great profit. Know, sire, that two knights have recently arrived whom you ought surely to hate and find unwelcome above all others, for they have taken away a sizeable portion of your pagan land, and through their great cruelty caused the shameful deaths of the valiant Brandiffer, the mighty King Lucar, and your brother the king of India."

When Rabaste heard that his brother was dead, he wept with great emotion, then asked Hugo, "Sire, can you hand these two knights over to me?"

"Yes," said Hugo, "but you must promise and swear to me one thing, that in exchange for all I've done, you will give me the golden seals that these two knights carry with them on which their arms are embossed."

"Sire," said the king of Syria, "I would be ungrateful if I refused you so little a thing. You shall have the seals as you request, and much else, if you can deliver the two knights to me."

"Yes," said Hugo, "now listen how it can be done. Send your messengers to the patriarch's lodging place, and he will be able to tell you where they are."

The king of Syria did so; he had eight hundred men arm themselves and go to the good patriarch who, at the king's command, indicated where they were

les chevaliers payens alerent tantost en celle part qui Orson et le Verd Chevalier ont trouvé a disner. Si ont esté prins et liéz et en battant[1] menéz devers le roy.

"Helas," dit Orson, "icy pouons bien veoir trahyson evidente, car tout ainsi que le roy Pepin et les douze pers de France furent en ceste cité aux Sarrasins vendus, ainsy puis je cognoistre que pareillement sommes trahys et vendus."

En ce point furent menéz devant le roy de Surie; et quant il les veit, il leur a dist fierement, "Faulx ennemis de nostre loy, de vous veoir et tenir ay fort grant plaisir. Or me dites voz noms car je les veulx sçavoir et pour cause."

"Sire," dist Orson, "sachez que je suis appellé Orson et ainsi me fays nommer."

Ce dist le roy d'Angorie, "Je suis nommé le Verd Chevalier."

"Par Mahon," dist le roy de Surie, "assez ay oÿ de vous deux parler, et croy que vous estes les deux par qui grant partye de ma terre a esté exillee et mes gens mis a mort. Si avez ung aultre compaignon nommé Valentin lequel se je le tenoye, par mon dieu Mahon, jamais en vie de mes mains ne eschapperoit."[2]

Adonc les fit despouller et leurs seaulx oster, lesquelz depuis a Hugon furent donnéz, roy de Hongrie. Si furent Orson et le Verd Chevalier villainement et honteusement mis en une tour parfonde; en pain et en eaue moult longuement ilz furent. Bien pensoient que le roy Hugon par les payens fust mort. Mais las! ilz ne pensoient pas comment la chose aloit, car il estoit avec le roy de Surye qui les deux seaulx des chevaliers luy bailla, dont il fut si joyeulx que jamais plus ne fut. Si appella Galeran, ung faulx, mauldit et desloyal trahystre qui longuement l'avoit servy, car a tel maistre telle maignie.

"Galeran," dist Hugon, "j'ay trouvé la maniere par quoy je viendray a bout de mon intencion. Et pour tant que vous estes mon nepveu et que long temps m'avez servy, si vous voulez estre secrept, tant de biens vous fray que deverez estre content."

"Oncle," dist Galeran, "de moy ne vous doubtez, car je sçay ou vous pretendez—vous voulez avoir sur tout pour femme la belle Esclarmonde."

"Il est vray," dist Hugon, "ja celer ne le vous convient. Si convient cauteleusement unes lettres faire et dicter ou nom de Orson, car j'ay les propres seaulx de luy dont elle sera seelee, et fault que celle lettre soit ainsi que je vous diray devisee:

"'Orson, par la grace de Dieu empereur de Grece, a vous ma tresredoubtee et souveraine dame et mere, a vous m'amye Galasie, et a vostre seur la belle Esclarmonde, salutacion, toute humble recommandacion premise. Sachez que piteuses nouvelles au pays de par deça nous sont avenues, lesquelles par ces presentes [lettres][3] [132recto]je[4] vous rescrips. Si requiers a Jesus que pacience vous donne et conforter vous veulle. Mes dames, sachez de certain que en la cité de Hierusalem j'ay trouvé mon frere Valentin au lit de la mort malade. Si m'a fait Dieu

---

[1] Text has *bantant*.
[2] Text has *eschapparoit*.
[3] Word is missing in text, probably owing to page break.
[4] *r iiii* at bottom right corner of 132r.

lodging. The pagan knights set out at once, and found Orson and the Green Knight at table for dinner. They were seized and tied and beaten without respite as they were taken to the king.

"Alas," said Orson, "there is certainly treason afoot here, for I realize that just as King Pepin and the Twelve Peers of France were sold to the Saracens in this city, so have we been similarly betrayed and sold."

At that point they were brought before the king of Syria; and when he saw them, he addressed them fiercely: "Wicked enemies of our faith, I take great pleasure in having you in my power. Now, tell me your names, for I have good reason for wishing to know them."

"Sire," said Orson, "know that I am called Orson and so am I named."

The king of Angory said, "I am named the Green Knight."

"By Mohammed," said the king of Syria, "I have heard you say enough, for I believe that you are the two who took possession of a large part of my land and put my people to death. You also have another companion named Valentin, who would never escape my hands, by Mohammed, if ever I had hold of him."

Thereupon he had them despoiled and their seals taken away to be handed over to Hugo, the king of Hungary. Then Orson and the Green Knight were roughly shoved into a deep dungeon, where they survived a long time on bread and water. They thought that King Hugo had been killed by the pagans. But alas! they had no idea how things really were, for he was in the company of the king of Syria who had given him the two knights' seals, for which he was more delighted than he had ever been. Then he called for Galeran, a wicked, cursed, and faithless traitor who had long served him, for such a master always has such a servant.[1]

"Galeran," said Hugo, "I have found the way to achieve what I want. And since you are my nephew and have served me a long time, if you can be discreet, I shall reward you so well that you will be quite content."

"Uncle," said Galeran, "have no doubts about me, for I know what you are thinking—you want to marry the fair Esclarmonde."

"It is true," said Hugo, "no need to hide it from you. What I need to do is quietly write a letter in Orson's name, for I have his personal seals with which to seal it, and the letter must say exactly as I shall dictate to you:

"'From Orson, by the grace of God emperor of Greece, to you, my most respected and sovereign lady mother, to you, my beloved Galasie, and to your sister the fair Esclarmonde, my most humble greetings. Know that sad tidings have come to us here in this country, which I send on to you through this letter. I pray that Jesus may give you forbearance and comfort you. My ladies, know for certain that I found my brother Valentin mortally ill on his deathbed in the city of Jerusalem. God rendered me such grace as to enable me to visit him and speak

---

[1] Hassell, *Proverbs*, 155 (no. M21).

celle grace que devant ses jours finer je l'ay viseté et parlé a luy. Mais tantost apres ma venue il rendit l'esperit, et en la fin de ses jours me charga de vous mander les nouvelles et de saluer de par moy Esclarmonde a laquelle il mande sur toute l'amour de quoy elle l'ayma oncques que tout au plus tost qu'elle pourra qu'elle se marie a aulcun noble prince, et que pour sa mort elle ne prengne desconfort, mais a Dieu prie pour son ame. Et sachez que pas il n'envoye la moitié de l'aneau comme il avoit promis car tantost que malade fut couché il luy fust desrobé.'"

Et quant ces lettres furent ainsi faictes, le trahystre Hugon pour mieulx sa trahyson couvrir en fit faire unes aultres de la part du Chevalier Verd et de Orson ensemble dont la teneur fut telle ou semblable:

"Treschiere et amee seur, assez vous avons fait sçavoir de vostre loyal espoux et nostre bon frere Valentin pour laquelle chose nous deux chevaliers, vostre frere le Verd Chevalier et Orson, considerant la grant beaulté qui en vous est, et que trop est peu de chose de si belle, si plaisante et si tresgracieuse dame sans partie, et aussi pour faire et acomplyr la voulenté du bon trespassé, a qui Dieu pardon face, nous voulons en desirant vostre honneur et prouffit tousjours a mieulx croistre et augmenter, avons deliberé et acordé que le puissant roy Hugon de Hongerie vous ayez pour mary et espoux. Sy veullez a ces choses obaÿr et nostre voulenté parfaire autant que vous doubtez de nous desplaire. Et pour verificacion de ces choses nous avons de noz propres seaulx ces presentes lettres seelees affin de plus grande approbacion de verité. Et sachez que vers vous nous ne pouons aler pour le present, car entre crestiens et Sarrasins est bataille trouvee laquelle nous attendons pour la foy de nostre sauveur et redempteur Jesus soustenir et deffendre, qu'i vous ait en sa garde!"

Quant les lettres de trahison furent par le roy Hugon ainsi dictees il les clouÿt moult bien, et des propres seaulx aux chevaliers et seigneurs redoubtéz les seela. Puis les bailla a son nepveu Galeran et luy a dist que "en Constantinoble vous fault aler par devers la royne Bellissant et la belle, plaisante et gracieuse Esclarmonde ces lettres presenter. Et quant vous y aurez esté, je iray tantost apres comme celuy qui riens n'en sçait pour la belle Esclarmonde requerir. Si ne doubtez pas que elle ne me soit donnee et acordee."

"Oncle," dist Galeran, "le messaige sçauray bien faire, car je cognoy assez vostre cas et vostre intencion."

Lors luy bailla Hugon les lettres, et Ga[132verso]leran se mist a chemin, qui en peu de temps arriva au palays de Constantinoble, a l'eure que on mettoit les tables. Si salua les dames de par l'empereur Orson et le Verd Chevalier, puis leur donna la lettre que sur luy portoit.

"Messagier," dit Bellissant, "que fait mon filz?"

"Dame," dit Galeran, "je l'ay laissé en Hierusalem sain et en bon point. Si pourrez sçavoir par ces lettres de ses affaires tout au plain et au large." Les dames commanderent que le messagier fust fessoyé et bien receu.

Or estoit il de coustume que quant on vouloit boire ou mengier, on faisoit venir Valentin a la table ou en la sale pour mieulx de luy penser, et pour tant que

to him before he ended his days. But soon after my coming he rendered up his spirit, and as he died he charged me to send you the news and to greet Esclarmonde, whom he commands, in the name of all the love she ever bore him, to marry some noble prince as soon as she can, and that she not grieve excessively over his death, but that she rather pray to God for his soul. And know that he is not sending his half of the ring as he had promised, because as soon as he fell ill, it was stolen from him.'"

Once the letter was finished, the false-hearted Hugo, the better to cover his treachery, had another one written from both the Green Knight and Orson, which said something like this:

"Dearest and most beloved sister, we have given you much information about your loyal husband and our good brother Valentin, for which reason we two knights, your brother the Green Knight and Orson, considering how beautiful you are and that it is too much a shame for a lady as beautiful, pleasing, and gracious as you to be without a spouse, and also to accomplish the will of our dearly departed, may God grant him pardon, we have decided and agreed that you should take the mighty King Hugo of Hungary as husband. We pray you obey us in these matters and carry out our will, in as much as you fear to displease us. And for purposes of verification, we have sealed these letters with our own seals so that there will be no doubt of their origin. Also know that we cannot come to you at present, for there is a battle, which we await, soon to be fought between Christians and Saracens in order to sustain and defend the faith of our Savior and Redeemer Jesus, may He have you in His keeping!"

Once the treasonous letters were thus dictated by King Hugo, he had them tightly closed and stamped with the very seals of the two redoubtable knights and lords. Then he handed them over to his nephew Galeran and said to him that "in Constantinople you must go to present these letters to Queen Bellissant and the fair, pleasing, and gracious Esclarmonde. Once you have been there a little while, I will show up as if I know nothing, in order to ask for the hand of the fair Esclarmonde. Have no doubt that she will be accorded to me at once."

"Uncle," said Galeran, "I will deliver your message without any problem, for I know just what you need done."

So Hugo gave him the letters, and Galeran set off, soon arriving in the palace of Constantinople just at the hour when dinner was being served. He greeted the ladies on the part of the emperor Orson and the Green Knight, then gave them the letter he carried.

"Messenger," said Bellissant, "how is my son?"

"Lady," said Galeran, "I left him in Jerusalem hale and hearty. You will be able to learn more details of his affairs from these letters." The ladies ordered that the messenger be feasted and well received.

Now it was the custom that when people ate or drank, they brought Valentin to the table or into the room, the better to care for him, and since they saw from the

on veit au commencement qu'il ne mengoit que reliefz, on luy bailla si bon que plus n'en vouloit user, mais prenoit souvent ce que on gettoit aux chiens, et pour tant donnoit aux chiens largement. Il oÿt bien les nouvelles du messaigier, si se pensa qu'il feroit. Les dames furent tantost levees de table et apres graces rendues Bellissant fist venir ung sien secretaire et les lettres luy bailla pour les lire. Le secreptaire les print et les a leues; de toutes les deux lettres leur dist. Et bien l'oÿt Valentin qui en la sale estoit dont nul semblant n'en fist. Si ne fault pas demander le grant dueil et la destresse, les pleurs, les plains et lamentacions des dames qui furent menéz pour Valentin qu'ilz mandoyent que il estoit mort et deffiné, car ilz cognoissoyent les seaulx des bons chevaliers.

 La belle Esclarmonde ses habis derompit; ses cheveulx tiroit disant, "Povre femme, de toutes les aultres la plus doloureuse! Pourquoy ne vient la mort sans plus me laisser vivre? Las! amy Valentin, pourquoy ne suis je alee avec vous pour vostre corps ayser? Frere, Verd Chevalier, et vous, empereur Orson, trop avez dur couraige que sy tost me voulez marier. Helas! comment doit celle jamais prendre mary qui de tous les vaillans ay perdu l'excelle[n]t, des bons le meilleur, des preux le plus hardy, la rose de honneur, la fleur de chevalerie, des nobles le miroir, des doulx et courtois l'exemplaire, de leaulté le patron, et des sages l'eslite? Faulce mort maleureuse! Que as tu en pensee quant par toy je suis hors de toute humaine joye, ne jamais en ma vie je ne requiers avoir liesse, mais tousjours en languissant celuy plourer que de tous les humains estoit digne de honneur. Ne jamais en ma vie aultre mary n'auray, mais en continuelles doleurs mes jours dolens useray."

 Helas! bien veoit Valentin les grans doleurs que pour luy portoit la belle dame Esclarmonde dont pitié avoit, mais pur la doubte de cognoissance en son cueur portoit sa doleur. Et quant la royne Bellissant veit que Esclarmonde tant se desconfortoit, tout au mieulx qu'elle peult elle la resconforta.

 "Ma fille," dit la dame, "prenez en vous pacience et vous rescon[133recto] fortez. Vous sçavez qu'il estoit mon filz; si en doy assez estre courroucee et au cueur dolente. Mais quant je considere que remedier nul n'y peut, je regarde que mieulx vault prier Dieu pour luy que tant de pleurs getter. Si pensez a ce que vostre frere le Verd Chevalier et l'empereur Orson vous mandent faire."

 "Las!" dist Esclarmonde, "de quoy me parlez vous? Quel mariage peult on faire de celle qui n'a espoir jamais d'avoir joye? Pour Dieu, dame treshonnouree, jamais plus n'en parlez! Car en jour de ma vie je ne veul avoir mary."

 "Fille," dist Bellissant, "vous estes mal avisee, car puis que sy hault homme comme le roy Hugon vous veult avoir a toujours en serez mieulx prisee. Si vous dy bien qu'il pourra ancores tel venir a qui me marieray." A ces parolles entra la belle dame en sa chambre et tendrement ploura. Et Valentin est soubz les degréz qui en son cueur pense dont telle trahyson peult estre venue.

beginning that he would eat nothing but table scraps, they gave him good scraps, such that he would no longer take them, often eating instead what they threw to the dogs, for which reason they gave generously to the dogs. He heard clearly what the messenger said, and thought to himself about what he would do. The ladies soon got up from table, and, after saying grace, Bellissant sent for her secretary, giving him the letters to read aloud. The secretary took them and read them, reciting the whole of both of them. And Valentin heard it all, for he was in the hall, but he gave no sign of reaction. No need to ask if there was great grief and distress, tears, complaints, and lamentations on the part of the ladies over Valentin at the word that he was dead, for they all recognized the seals of the two good knights.

The fair Esclarmonde tore her clothes and pulled her hair saying, "Miserable woman, most sorrowful in the world! Why does death not come and end my life? Alas! my beloved Valentin, why did I not go with you to bring you ease? Brother, Green Knight, and you, Emperor Orson, your hearts are too hard to wish me to marry so soon. Alas! how can I ever take a husband when of all valiant men I have lost the most excellent, of all good men the best, of all courageous men the most bold, the rose of honor, the flower of chivalry, of noblemen the mirror, of gentle and courteous men the exemplar, of loyalty the model, and of wise men the elite? Wicked, unhappy death! What were you thinking, seeing that through you I am cut off from all human joy, nor may I ever in my life think of experiencing happiness, only eternal languishing and weeping for him who of all humans was worthy of honor. Nor will I ever have another husband in my life, for I will use up my sorrowful days in continual mourning."

Alas! Valentin could clearly see the great sorrow the fair lady bore for his sake, which filled him with pity, but, afraid he might be recognized, he had to bear his pain in his heart. And when Queen Bellissant saw how upset Esclarmonde was, she did her best to comfort her.

"My daughter," said the lady, "you must forbear and calm yourself. You know that he was my son; thus I too must needs be much afflicted and have a sorrowful heart. But when I consider that there is no remedy, I find it better to pray to God for him than to weep so prodigiously. So think about what your brother the Green Knight and the emperor Orson command you to do."

"Alas!" said Esclarmonde, "what are you saying to me? What marriage can one make with a woman who has no hope of ever feeling joy? For God's sake, most honored lady, never speak of this again! For as long as I live I shall have no husband."

"Daughter," said Bellissant, "you are not thinking straight, for if so highly placed a man as King Hugo wishes to have you, you will always be the more prized for it. And I tell you that there could very well come along such a one whom I myself would marry." At these words the fair lady entered her chamber and wept bitterly. And Valentin was under the stairs, thinking quietly about how such treachery may have come about.

Si avint que au bout de quatre jours que le trahystre roy Hugon pour son entreprinse parfaire arriva en Constantinoble et la fut en grant honneur receu. Mais la belle Esclarmonde pour riens ne luy portoit semblant de amours.

Lors parla Hugon et dist tout hault, "Madame, bien avez oÿ par les lettres que Galeran vous a baillé comment le vaillant chevalier Valentin vostre filz est mort dont moult suis dolent. Si est la chose ainsi acordee par leur bonne voulenté et gracieuse deliberacion et pour avoir aliance ensemble que je doy avoir Esclarmonde pour femme."

"Sire," ce dit la dame, "je vous prometz la foy que je n'ay nul couraige de vous ne de aultre avoir."[1]

Or estoit Valentin en la sale que toute la trahyson escoute et en son cueur la note. Puis a dit Bellissant, "Ma fille, ne croyez pas du tout vostre courage ne ce que le cueur vous dit, car bien sçaivent le Verd Chevalier et Orson que vous est necessaire pour vostre honneur et proffit et se contre leur voulenté faictes mal en leur grace pourrez estre."

Quant Esclarmonde oÿt ces parolles, fort ala pensant, mais en la fin tant fut la chose demenee que pour complaire au Verd Chevalier son frere et a Orson elle fut d'acord d'avoir le roy Hugon, dont grant joye fut demenee dudit roy Hugon. Mais trop petit luy dura le plaisir qu'il en eut.

[CHAPITRE 72]

Comment Bellissant et Esclarmonde sceurent la trahison et la faulce entreprinse du roy Hugon. lxxii. cha[pitre]

Quant le sainct homme Valentin apperceut que s'amye estoit trahye, moult grant pitié luy en print, si entra en une chappelle de Nostre Dame ou il avoit de coustume de Dieu prier. Si s'agenoulla devant l'ymage de la Vierge Marie disant doulcement, "Marie, des aultres la plus digne, mere, fille, et ancelle du Redempteur de tout le monde, veullez entendre ma priere a moy qui suis povre et miserable pecheur. C'est qu'il te plaise de prier ton chier Filz que je puisse m'amye Esclarmonde deffendre de la trahyson que contre luy est faicte."

Ainsi que Valen[133verso]tin eust son oroison faicte, ung ange vint a luy qui luy a dist, "Valentin, Dieu a oÿ ta priere. Va hors de la ville et tu trouveras ung pelerin. Fay que tu ayez ses habillemens, son bourdon et son escharppe. Et quant ses habis auras vestus, retourne en ton palays et compte devant la compaignie la trahyson telle que tu la cognoys, car ja ne seras cogneu."

---

[1] It is obviously Esclarmonde who makes this response, even though Hugo has addressed his first remark to Bellissant.

So it happened that four days later the treacherous King Hugo arrived in Constantinople to carry out his plot, and he was received with great honor. But for nothing in the world would the fair Esclarmonde show any affection for him.

Then Hugo spoke and said aloud [to Bellissant], "My lady, you have certainly heard from the letters that Galeran put in your hands that the valiant knight Valentin, your son, is dead, for which I am very sorry. Now the matter has been agreed upon through the good will and gracious decision of Orson and the Green Knight that, in order to have an alliance together, I should marry Esclarmonde."

"Sire," said the lady, "I give you my word that I have no intention of having you or any other."

Now Valentin was in the hall, listening to all this treachery and taking quiet note of it. Then Bellissant said, "My daughter, you must not believe what your heart tells you or be headstrong, for the Green Knight and Orson know what is best for your honor and profit, and, if you oppose them, you will not remain in their good graces."

When Esclarmonde heard these words, she thought hard about it, but in the end it turned out that to please the Green Knight her brother and Orson she agreed to have King Hugo, for which King Hugo was delighted. But his pleasure did not last long at all.

CHAPTER 72

How Bellissant and Esclarmonde discovered King Hugo's treachery and wicked plot.

When the holy man Valentin perceived that his beloved had been betrayed, he was filled with pity for her, so he entered a chapel dedicated to Our Lady where he customarily prayed. Kneeling before the image of the Virgin Mary, he said softly, "Mary, most worthy of women, mother, daughter, and servant of the Redeemer of the world, I pray you, hear my prayer, I a poor and miserable sinner. May it please you to pray to your dear Son on my behalf so that I may protect my beloved Esclarmonde from this treachery that has been devised against her."

Just as Valentin had finished his prayer, an angel came to him and said, "Valentin, God has heard your prayer. Go outside of the city and you will find a pilgrim. Contrive to borrow his clothes, his staff, and his scarf. And once you have put on his clothes, return to the palace and recount before the company the treachery as you know it, for you will not be recognized."

"Vray Dieu," dist Valentin, "je te remercie."

Lors se partit et trouva le pelerin et print ses habis; puis retourna au palays ou les dames estoient et le trahystre Hugon que plusieurs faintes parolles disoit a la belle Esclarmonde. Les dames salua et toute l'assemblee. Puis a dit tout hault a la royne Bellissant, "Dame, je vous prie humblement que me monstrez laquelle est la femme de Valentin."

"Pelerin," dist Hugon, que la couleur mua, "Alez en la cuisine et vous aurez l'aumoisne."

"Sire," dist Valentin, "je veul a elle faire ung messaige."

"Pelerin," dit la belle dame, "a moy dont le ferez, car je suis celle que vous demandez."

"Madame, en bonne heure j'ay veu vostre amy Valentin que de par moy vous salue et vous fait assavoir que avant trois jours passéz il sera en ce chasteau."

"Pelerin," ce dist la dame, "avise que c'est que tu dis, car j'ay eu nouvelles certaines que il est mort."

"Dame," dist Valentin, "croyre ne le devez, car je livre mon corps a mourir s'il n'est ancores en vie, et se dedens trois jours icy ne le voyez."

Quant Hugon oÿt ces parolles que Valentin aux dames disoit secretement saillit du palays et sur son cheval monta sans plus retourner. Trop furent esmerveilléz et moult en furent joyeuses les dames et assez vouloient haultement le pelerin festoier. Mais il n'en vouloit riens faire, et leur dit, "Mesdames, vous me pardonnerez, car j'ay mes compaignons en la ville que je voy veoir."

Lors Esclarmonde luy donna grant argent que depuis aux povres departit. Et quant il fut hors on demanda ou estoit le roy Hugon.

"Par ma foy," dit une damoiselle, "je l'ay veu presentement courir sur son cheval." Et sur ces parolles Galeran entra qui son oncle demandoit.

"Par Dieu," dist Bellissant, "de bonne heure estes venu, car jamais n'en eschapperez tant que vous m'aurez la trahyson comptee que vostre oncle a faicte."

Et quant Galeran oÿt les parolles il commença a trambler. "Helas! dames, pour Dieu, prenez de moy mercy et je vous prometz de vous dire tout."

"Oy," dist la dame, "il te sera pardonné."

"Il est bien vray que mon oncle le roy Hugon a ceste trahyson faicte et a vendu et delivré aux payens dedens Hierusalem l'empereur de Grece Orson et le Verd Chevalier." Puis luy compta tout au long comment vous avez oÿ devant. La fut mené ung merveilleux dueil que les dames demenoient; et quant Galeran eut tout dit il se partit, cuidant estre eschappé, mais le prevost le fist prendre et au gibet estrangler.

Et Valentin qui laissa sa robe de pelerin et reprint [134recto]ses habis et s'en vint au palays. "Povre homme," dist Esclarmonde, "ou avez vous esté? Je croy que vous estes desplaisant que marier je me veul."

"True God," said Valentin, "I thank you."

So he left and found the pilgrim and took his clothes; then he returned to the palace where the ladies were to be found with the traitor Hugo, who was speaking lies to the fair Esclarmonde. He greeted the ladies and the whole assembly. Then he said aloud to Queen Bellissant, "Lady, I beg you most humbly to indicate to me which is the wife of Valentin."

"Pilgrim," said Hugo, whose color changed, "Go to the kitchen and you shall receive alms."

"Sire," said Valentin, "I wish to deliver a message to her."

"Pilgrim," said the fair lady, "then deliver it to me, for I am the one whom you seek."

"My lady, in an auspicious hour did I see your husband Valentin, who greets you through me, and informs you that, before three days have passed, he shall be in this castle."

"Pilgrim," said the lady, "be careful what you say, for I have received definite tidings that he is dead."

"Lady," said Valentin, "you must not believe it, for I will give myself up to death if he is not still alive, and if you shall not see him here within three days."

When Hugo heard these words that Valentin was saying to the ladies, he stealthily left the palace and mounted his horse, never to return. Everyone marveled at the pilgrim's words, and the ladies were overjoyed and wanted to treat him to a great feast. But he would have none of it, and told them, "My ladies, you must pardon me, for I have my companions in the city whom I am going to see."

Then Esclarmonde gave him much money, which afterwards he distributed among the poor. And when he was gone, everyone asked where King Hugo was.

"By my faith," said a damsel, "I just saw him running to his horse." And as these words were spoken, Galeran entered, asking for his uncle.

"By God," said Bellissant, "you have come at the right time, for you shall never escape without explaining to me what treachery your uncle has contrived."

And when Galeran heard these words, he began to tremble. "Alas! ladies, for God's sake, have mercy on me, and I promise to tell you everything."

"Yes," said the lady, "you shall be pardoned."

"It is quite true that my uncle King Hugo contrived this treachery to sell and deliver Orson the emperor of Greece and the Green Knight to the pagans in Jerusalem." Then he recounted in its entirety all that you have already heard. Then the ladies began to wail most astonishingly; and once Galeran had told everything, he left, thinking he had escaped, but the bailiff had him seized and hanged from the gallows.

In the meantime Valentin got rid of his pilgrim's robe, took back his usual garments, and returned to the palace. "Poor man," said Esclarmonde, "where have you been? I think you were upset that I thought to marry."

Valentin le[1] laissa et enclina la teste et se print Dieu a prier. La belle Esclarmonde luy avoit fait aporter une coustre mais il couchoit a terre et en ce point parmy les chiens passa long temps ses jours en penitance.

[CHAPITRE 73]

Comment Orson et le Verd Chevalier furent des prisons du roy de Surie delivréz par appointement de la guerre qu'ilz firent puis au roy Hugon. lxxiii. [chapitre]

Le roy de Surie, lequel en ses prisons tenoit le bon empereur Orson et le Verd Chevalier, ung jour les fist devant luy amener, puis leur a dist, "Seigneurs, vous voyez que j'ay puissance dessus vous et que vous ne pouez riens sur moy. Et je sçay que vous estes ceulx du monde que plus avez nostre loy molestee et nostre terre courue et pillee. Si jure mon dieu Mahon que ja ne m'escapperez que mourir ne vous face fors que par ung point que je vous diray: c'est que vous me rendez la cité d'Angorie avec Chasteau Fort et trente aultres fortes places que vous tenez en voz mains."

"Sire," dist Orson, "nous ne le ferons pas se ne nous rendez le roy Hugon que vous tenez."

Ce dit le roy de Surie, "De luy ne me parlez plus, car il s'en est alé et voz seaulx a emporté. Et sachez que par luy avez esté a moy vendus et faulcement trahys."

Quant Orson l'entendit trop fut esmerveillé et a juré que jamais ne cessera tant que du roy Hugon ait prins vengance.

"Par ma foy," ce dist le Verd Chevalier, "je ne vous fauldray pas."

Or ont acordé Orson et le Verd Chevalier au roy de Surye sa demande pour leur vie sauver, et sont retournéz en Constantinoble ou grant dueil fut appaisé. Puis a dit Esclarmonde comment elle a eu nouvelles par le pelerin de Valentin dont joyeulx fut Orson, car sur toutes choses desiroit sa venue. Ceste nuyt coucha Orson avec Galasie et engendra ung filz qui eut nom Morant lequel comme dient les hystoires depuis tint le royaulme de Hongrie.[2]

Ne demoura gaires que Orson mist son armee sus pour aler en Hongrie. Et quant le roy Hugon le sceut, il luy envoya ung messagier disant s'i vouloit acorder qu'i lui laisseroit[3] la cité de Hongrie,[4] pour l'armee recompenser il luy donneroit

---

[1] Another occurrence of *le* for *la*; see Chapter 8, p. 58, n. 1.

[2] Text has *hongre*.

[3] Text has *laissereroit*.

[4] Text has *Angorie*. Due to the closeness in spelling, there is some confusion in the typesetting of this chapter between Angory and Hungary, but the narrative makes it clear that Hugo's kingdom is being spoken of here, since Orson and the Green Knight

Valentin left her, bowed his head and began to pray to God. The fair Esclarmonde had a mattress brought to him, but he slept on the ground instead, and in this fashion spent his days in penitence among the dogs for a long time.

CHAPTER 73

How Orson and the Green Knight were delivered from prison, and of an agreement to wage war afterwards against King Hugo.

The king of Syria, who was holding the good Emperor Orson and the Green Knight prisoners, had them brought before him one day to say to them, "My lords, you see that I have power over you and that you can do nothing against me. And I know that you are those in the world who have most harmed our religion and ravaged and pillaged our land. Thus I swear by my god Mohammed that there is no hope of escaping execution except by one possibility, as I shall explain to you: you must return the city of Angory to me, along with Château Fort and thirty other fortresses of which you have possession."

"Sire," said Orson, "we shall do nothing unless you give back to us King Hugo whom you hold."

The king of Syria replied, "Do not speak of him any more, for he has left, taking your seals with him. And know that it is he who falsely betrayed you and sold you to me."

When Orson heard this, he was amazed and swore that he would never cease until he had taken vengeance against King Hugo.

"By my faith," said the Green Knight, "I shall not fail you in this."

So Orson and the Green Knight agreed to the demands of the king of Syria in order to save their lives, and returned to Constantinople where the great sorrow on their behalf was appeased. Then Esclarmonde explained how she had received news of Valentin from the pilgrim, for which Orson was joyous, for, more than anything, he desired his return. That night Orson slept with Galasie and engendered a son whose name was Morant, who the history books say later held the kingdom of Hungary.

Not long after, Orson raised an army to go into Hungary. And when King Hugo found this out, he sent him a messenger saying that if he were willing to reach an accord with him, he, Hugo, would give him four horses loaded with

quatre fors chevaulx chargéz d'or. S'il y avoit nul que de la trahyson dessus dicte le vouloit accuser il s'en combateroit a tous pourveu que ce ne fust a Orson. Le message fait et le conseil tenu le Verd Chevalier getta son gaige contre le roy Hugon auquel il fist porter et que il se trouvast hors des murs de la cité de Hongrie.[1]

Le roy Hugon vint au champ ordonné a grant triumphe[2] pour combatre, mais le Verd Chevalier y estoit le premier. Et quant ilz furent tous prestz, ilz frapperent chevaulx des esperons [134verso]et de si gra[n]t force sont venus que leurs lances rompirent. Puis mirent les mains aux espees et Dieu sçait quelz coupz ilz se donnoyent, et tant que Dieu aida au bon droit, car le Verd Chevalier bailla si grant coup au roy Hugon sur le heaulme que toute une partie de la teste luy couppa jusques aux espaulles et cheut paulmé. Lors fut honnouré le Verd Chevalier, puis Hugon reprint parolle et devant tous demanda ung confesseur et la compta toute la trahyson et n'arresta gaires que en ceste place mourut.

Orson fit prendre le corps et notablement ensevelir et enterrer en une abaye qui pres de la estoit, et luy fut telle honneur faicte pour tant qu'il estoit roy couronné et en tant monstra Orson la grant noblesse qui en luy estoit. Tous furent informéz de la trahyson du roy Hugon. Par le conseil des sages rendirent a Orson la ville de Hongrie et le pays lequel en print possession et receut les hommaiges des seigneurs. Puis retourna en Constantinoble luy et le Verd Chevalier.

Valentin fut moult joyeulx de ce qu'il les veoit en joye et en prosperité. Moult s'esmerveilloit Esclarmonde de ce que Valentin ne venoit et disoit, "Ha, mauvais pelerin! tu m'as mauvaisement trahye quant tu me dys que mon amy Valentin viendroit au troiziesme jour, et je n'en ay nulles nouvelles en quelque maniere et façon que il soit au monde."

Helas! Elle ne pensoit pas que il fust si pres de elle, car il estoit dessoubz les degréz de son palays ou du vouloir de Dieu tantost fina ses jours. Et adonc le cognoisterra.

---

have just agreed to return the Saracen city Angory to the Saracen king of Syria. The confusion occurs one more time in this chapter.

[1] Second occurrence where text has *Angorie*.
[2] Text has *trumphe*.

gold to pay his army if he, Orson, would leave him the city of Hungary. And if anyone was accusing him of treason, he would fight that accuser himself, as long as it was not against Orson. The message received and counsel taken, the Green Knight threw his gauntlet to King Hugo, to whom it was taken with the message that he meet him outside the walls of the city of Hungary.

King Hugo came out to the prescribed field in fine array, ready to fight, but the Green Knight arrived there first. When both were ready, they spurred their horses and clashed with such great force that they shattered their lances. Then they put their hands to their swords and God only knows what blows they gave one another. And since God helps those in the right, the Green Knight landed a blow on King Hugo's helmet that cut through his head and down to the shoulder so that he crumpled to the ground. Then the Green Knight was honored as the victor, while Hugo recovered speech sufficiently to request a confessor to whom he recounted all his treachery in the presence of all. Hardly had he finished when he died, right then and there.

Orson had the body taken and properly buried in an abbey close by, honoring him in this way because he was a crowned king, and, in doing so, Orson demonstrated how very noble he himself was. Everyone was informed of King Hugo's treachery. The wise men counselled that the city of Hungary and the country around it be rendered to Orson, who took possession of it and received the homage of the lords. Then he and the Green Knight returned to Constantinople.

Valentin was most joyous to see them in joy and prosperity. But Esclarmonde was much amazed that Valentin had not come, and said, "Ah, evil pilgrim! you betrayed me badly, seeing that you told me my beloved Valentin would come on the third day, and I have had absolutely no news whatsoever of him."

Alas! She didn't realize that he was so close to her, for he was under the staircase of his own palace where, according to God's will, he soon ended his days. At that moment she will recognize him.

[CHAPITRE 74]

Comment au bout de sept ans Valentin dedens le palays de Constantinoble fina ses jours; et comment il escript une lettre par laquelle il fut cogneu. lxxiiii. chapitre

Au[1] terme de sept ans que le sainct[2] homme Valentin en peine et en grant tribulacion sa penitance acheva il pleut a Nostre Seigneur de l'oster hors de ce monde et l'appeler en gloire. Et luy print une grant maladie dont moult se sentit affoibly et en mercia Dieu doulcement.

"Helas!" dit le sainct homme, "mon Dieu, mon createur, qui a ta semblance me creas, ayez mercy de moy qui suis povre pecheur, et te plaise de moy vouloir la mort de mon pere pardonner et tous les pechéz que oncques je fis depuis que je suis né. Vray redempteur de tout le monde, ne considere pas le temps de ma folle jeunesse en laquelle trop [135recto]j'ay follement passee en plaisirs mondains, et ne me veulle pas condempner, mais espans et esteng ta saincte misericorde et en tes mains ma povre ame veullez recepvoir et la deffendre du dyable."

Et en disant ces parolles ung ange de paradis a luy apparut qui luy dist, "Valentin, saches de certain que dedens quatre jours de ce monde partiras, car c'est le vouloir de Dieu que devers toy me envoye."

"Helas, mon Dieu!" dist Valentin, "bien te doy gracier, quant par tes sains anges la fin de mes jours me fais assavoir." Adonc le sainct homme fist signe que on luy aportast encre et papier et il fut fait. Lors Valentin escripvit comment luy mesmes avoit en habit de pelerin la trahyson descouverte et tout l'estat de sa vie escript. Puis y bouta son nom et la partie de l'aneau ploya dedens et en sa main le tint. Et apres ces choses fist ung prestre venir auquel devoieme[n]t ses pechéz confessa et les sains sacremens receut, et a celle heure trespassa. En iceluy jour pour luy commencerent a sonner toutes les cloches de la cité dont le peuple moult fort s'en esmerveilla, et l'empereur Orson et tous les barons descendirent et ont trouvé le prestre au plus pres du sainct corps.

"Amy," dist Orson, "pourquoy esse que si fort sonnent par la ville?"

"Syre," dist le prestre, "je croy que ce soit miracle que Dieu veult monstrer pour cestuy sainct homme, car tout ainsi que il a rendu l'esperit les cloches ont commencé de toutes pars a sonner."

Et quant Orson veit que le povre homme estoit en celuy lieu trespassé, moult pensa sur ceste chose et moult en fut esmerveillé.

"Par ma foy," dist il, "je croy que cestuy soit sainct corps et que pour luy Dieu fait miracles." Lors avisa que il tenoit la lettre en sa main et la cuida prendre.

---

[1] Woodcut of interior scene with seated male figure writing at a desk.
[2] Text has *sanict*.

CHAPTER 74

How, at the end of seven years, Valentin ended his days in the palace of Constantinople; and how he wrote a letter by which he made himself known.

At the end of seven years, as the holy man Valentin completed his penance in great suffering and tribulation, it pleased Our Lord to take him out of this world and call him to glory. He fell sick with a terrible illness from which he felt himself much weakened and for which he thanked God sweetly.

"Ah!" said the holy man, "my God, my creator, who created me in your image, have mercy on me, a miserable sinner, and may it please you to pardon me my father's death and all the sins I have committed ever since I was born. True redeemer of the world, do not consider only the time of my thoughtless youth, which I spent too foolishly in worldly pleasures, and please do not condemn me, but extend your holy mercy and receive my poor soul in your hands and defend it from the devil."

While he was saying these words, an angel of paradise appeared to him and said, "Valentin, know for certain that within four days you shall depart from this world, for it is the will of God who sends me to you."

"Ah, my God!" said Valentin, "indeed I must thank you, seeing that you inform me of the end of my days by means of your holy angels." Thereupon the holy man made a sign that someone should bring him paper and ink, and it was done. Then Valentin wrote how he himself had come in the guise of a pilgrim to reveal the treachery, and gave as well a full accounting of his life. Then he signed his own name and wrapped his half of the ring in it and held it in his hand. These things accomplished, he had a priest come to whom he devoutly confessed his sins and from whom he received the holy sacraments, whereupon he died. That very day all the bells of the city began to ring for his sake, for which the people were much amazed, and the emperor Orson and all the barons came down and found the priest next to the holy corpse.

"Friend," said Orson, "why are the bells ringing so loudly throughout the city?"

"Sire," said the priest, "I believe it is a miracle that God wishes to perform for this holy man, for as soon as he rendered up his spirit the bells began to ring everywhere."

And when Orson saw that the poor man had just died in that very place, he thought hard on this and was quite astonished.

"By my faith," he said, "I believe this must be a holy man and that God is performing miracles for his sake." Then he saw the letter in his hand and thought to

Mais avoir ne la peult fors seulement la bonne dame Esclarmonde, car aussy tost que elle le toucha, la main se ouvrit et tout a son plaisir print la lettre. Si fut tantost desploiee, et lors la belle Esclarmonde veit et cogneut la moytié de l'aneau.

"Seigneurs, tantost aura certaines nouvelles de mon amy Valentin."

Si eut ung secretaire qui tantost leust les lettres ou estoient contenus tous les faictz du sainct homme. Si ne demandez pas les grandes douleurs et dures complaintes de Orson, de Bellissant, et de Esclarmonde, car trop avoit dur cueur qu'i adonc ne plouroit. La belle et plaisante dame Esclarmonde ainsi que demie morte se getta sur le corps en faisant telz regretz que bien sembloit que elle deust mourir.

"Helas!" ce disoit la dame, "que doy je jamais devenir quant j'ay perdu ma joye, ma vie et mon confort et ma seule esperance? Helas, mon amy Valentin! que aviez vous en pensee quant sy pres de moy estes venu mourir en povreté et en misere sans moy donner aulcune cognoissance de vous? Helas! je vous ay souvent veu en povreté et froydure [135verso]et travail sans vous donner confort. Or suis je bien sur toutes la plus fortunee quant je n'ai sceu cognoistre ne aviser celuy que tant je devoie servir longuement en amere tribulacion, comme vraye et loyalle espouse!" Puis baisoit sa face et ses mains a merveilleuse destresse.

Et apres le grant dueil le sainct corps fut porté, enterré a la grande esglise de Constantinoble en si grant compaignie que nul par les rues ne pouoit tourner. Et ne demoura pas longuement que le corps fut canonisé et mis en fiertre. Si monstra bien Dieu qu'il estoit bien digne d'estre sainct appelé car le jour de son trespassement furent malades de quelque maladie qu'ilz fussent entachéz qui son corps visiterent tous sains et guairis. Si ne demoura gaires que Esclarmonde apres la mort de Valentin se rendit nonnain et depuis dist l'ystoire qu'elle fut abesse d'une abaye que en l'onneur de monseigneur Valentin fut fondee. Ainsi partit de ce monde le glorieux corps sainct.

Et son frere Orson demoura empereur de Grece, qui sept ans seulement apres la mort de Valentin gouverna l'empire, et en iceluy temps eust ung filz de Galasie nommé Morant. Celuy Morant en son temps posseda et tint le royaulme de Hongrie. Et dedens celuy terme de sept ans mourut Galasie dont l'empereur Orson moult grant dueil demena, et depuis la mort d'elle il ne menga que pain et racines et petis fruis qui parmy les bois trouvoit. Si luy avint une nuyt en vision que il luy sembla qu'il veit toutes les portes de paradis ouvertes, et vit les joyes des sauvéz, les sieges des sains couronnéz en la gloire, et les anges qui melodieusement chantoient devant le sauveur de monde. Puis veit apres entre deux haultes roches au parfont d'une grant vallee obscure et tenebreuse le grant gouffre d'enfer ou estoient les maleureux dampnéz, les ungz en feu ardant, les autres en chaudieres boullans, les

take it. But no one could take it except the good lady Esclarmonde, for as soon as she touched him, the hand opened and she took the letter as she wished. It was soon opened, and then the fair Esclarmonde saw and recognized his half of the ring.

"My lords, soon we shall have definite tidings of my beloved Valentin."

A secretary there read forthwith the letter that contained all the deeds of the holy man. No need to ask whether there was terrible sorrow and anguished complaints from Orson, Bellissant, and Esclarmonde, for anyone who wouldn't weep at that moment has too hard a heart. The fair and pleasing lady Esclarmonde threw herself on his body as if she were half dead, uttering such regrets that it seemed indeed as if she must die.

"Alas!" said the lady, "what can possibly become of me, seeing that I have lost my joy, my life, and my comfort and sole hope? Alas, my beloved Valentin! what were you thinking to come so close to me, but yet die in such poverty and misery without giving me any sign of recognition from you? Alas! I have so often seen you in penury, cold, and travail without giving you any comfort. I am indeed the most unfortunate[1] woman alive, seeing that I was not able to recognize the one whom I should have served for a long time in bitter tribulation, as a true and faithful spouse!" Then she kissed his face and hands in her dire distress.

After this great display of grief, the holy corpse was carried up and buried in the great church of Constantinople, with such a crowd accompanying it that no one could move in the streets. And it was not long before the body was proclaimed saintly and placed in a reliquary. Moreover, God demonstrated clearly that he was indeed worthy of being called a saint, for on the day of his death all sick people, however infected they were, who visited his body came out completely healthy and cured. It was not long after Valentin's death that Esclarmonde became a nun, and the story says that afterwards she was abbess of an abbey founded in honor of my lord Valentin. Thus did the glorious holy man leave this world.

And his brother Orson continued as emperor of Greece, ruling the empire only seven years more after Valentin's death, during which time he and Galasie had a son named Morant. This Morant in his time possessed the kingdom of Hungary. At the end of these seven years Galasie died, for which the emperor Orson mourned greatly, and after her death he ate nothing but bread and roots and berries that he found in the woods. Then one night he had a vision in which it seemed to him that he saw all the gates of paradise open and observed the joys of the saved, the seats of the saints crowned in glory, and the angels who sang melodiously before the savior of the world. Then after that he saw, situated between two massive boulders at the bottom of a great, dark, and shadowy valley, the huge maw of hell[2] where the unhappy damned were to be found, some of

---

[1] The adjective *fortuné* can have both positive and negative meanings. Here it is obvious that Esclarmonde claims to have been mistreated by Fortune.

[2] Cf. Pamela Sheingorn, "'Who can open the doors of his face?': The Iconography of Hell Mouth," in *The Iconography of Hell*, ed. Clifford Davidson and Thomas H. Seiler

ungz pendus par les langues, les aultres assaillis et environnéz de serpens; et generallement veit toutes les peines d'enfer qui sont horribles et trop espoventables[1] a racompter.

Apres laquelle vision il s'esveilla, comme tout effroyé et esmerveillé des choses qu'il avoit veu. Si se recommanda a Dieu et a la Vierge Marie, et en plourant piteusement vint au Verd Chevalier et luy dit, "Amy, je cognoy que le monde est de petit valeur et de petite duree et que tout n'est que vaine gloire des pompes et estas de ce monde desplaisantes a Dieu et au salut trop petit proffitables. Pour laquelle chose je vous prie que de mes deux enfans veullez penser et les confermer en meurs et en condicions en telle maniere qu'ilz puissent l'empire de Grece et les terres qui sont de par eulx gouverner au gré de Dieu et du monde, car la charge vous en laisse comme a celuy qui sur tous les hommes du monde j'ay ma parfaicte fiance. Et sachez que le demourant de mes jours je veul mener vie solitaire et le monde habandonner; et de ceste heure je renonce a toutes honneurs mondaines et prens congé de vous."

Quant le chevalier oÿt [136recto]ces parolles il se print tendrement a plourer[2] et mener grant deuil. Et Orson le resconforte et dit doulcement, "Helas! pour moy ne plourez pas, mais a Dieu priez pour moy, qu'i me doinst force et puissance de mon vouloir acomplir."

Puis se partist Orson en deffendant au Verd Chevalier que son entreprinse ne declairast a personne vivant. Si s'en ala dedens ung grant bois ou tout le demourant de ses jours mena vie saincte tant que apres sa mort il fut sainct canoynisé et plusieurs beaux miracles fist.

Et le Verd Chevalier gouverna les enfans en telle maniere que moult furent saiges, vaillans et bien aprins, et de tous aimés et chiers tenus. Si tindrent paisiblement l'empire de Grece et le royaulme de Hongrie et plusieurs terres payennes qui conquesterent, lesquelles choses plus a plain sont declairees aux livres, hystoires et croniques qui depuis ont esté faictes.

Si me veullez atant pardonner, car de Orson et de Valentin je ne sçauroie plus avant escripre, fors celuy qui pour nous souffrit mort et passion veulle a tous ceulx donner sa gloire qui de bon cueur escouteront cestuy livre. Laquelle gloire nous donne le Pere, le Filz, et le Sainct Esperit. Amen.

Cy finist l'ystoire des deux vaillans chevaliers Valentin et Orson, filz de l'empereur de Grece. Imprimé a Lyon le penultime jour du mois de may par Jaques Maillet, l'an mil quatre cens quatre vingtz et neuf.

---

[1] Text has *espaventables*.
[2] Text has *tendrement a ment a plourer*, probably owing to the line break.

them burning in fire and others in boiling cauldrons, some of them hanged by their tongues and others assailed and surrounded by snakes; and generally he saw all the tortures of hell that are so horrible and too terrifying to recount.

After this vision he woke up, absolutely terrified and amazed by the things he had seen. He commended himself to God and to the Virgin Mary, and, weeping piteously, went to the Green Knight and said to him, "My friend, I recognize now that this world is of little value and short duration, and there is nothing but vainglory in the pomp and estates of this world, displeasing to God and unprofitable to one's salvation. For this reason I beg you to take care of my two children and educate them as to proper manners and behavior so that they may govern the empire of Greece and its territories according to the will of God and the ways of the world. I leave this charge to you as the man in whom, above all men in the world, I place perfect trust. And know that for the rest of my days I mean to live a solitary life and abandon the world; and from this moment on, I renounce all worldly honors and take leave of you."

When the knight heard these words he began to weep with great emotion and grieve deeply. But Orson comforted him and said gently, "Alas! do not weep for my sake, rather pray to God for me, that He give me the strength to accomplish my desire."

Then Orson left, forbidding the Green Knight to say anything about his intentions to anyone alive. He went into a great forest where for the rest of his days he led a holy life, such that after his death he was canonized a saint and performed several beautiful miracles.

And the Green Knight raised his children in such a way that they were very wise, valiant, and well taught, and moreover were loved and cherished by everyone. Peaceably they ruled the empire of Greece, the kingdom of Hungary, and several pagan lands that they conquered, all of which is fully told in the books, histories, and chronicles written afterwards.

Now you must forgive me, for I can write nothing more about Orson and Valentin, but I can write this—may He who suffered death and passion for us give of His glory to all those who willingly will listen to this book. May such glory come to us from the Father, the Son, and the Holy Spirit. Amen.

Here ends the story of the two valiant knights Valentin and Orson, sons of the emperor of Greece. Printed in Lyon the second to last day of the month of May by Jacques Maillet, in the year one thousand four hundred eighty-nine.

(Kalamazoo: Medieval Institute Publications, 1992), 1–19.

Appendix A
Editions

Listed below are known editions of *Valentin et Orson*. Those marked by the letter **E** have been examined by the editor. Those marked by the letter **S** have been attested to by Seelmann, those marked by the letters **Br** have been attested to by Brunet, and those marked by the letters **Bl** have been attested to by Blom. Where Seelmann, Brunet, or Blom mention copies of an edition from a library different from the one where the editor examined a copy, the library has been named. If an edition has been attested to or mentioned without its current location, the listing indicates "location unknown."

1. 1489, Lyon, Jacques Maillet. **E (all three copies), S, Br, Bl**
    a) New York, Pierpont Morgan Library
    b) Paris, Bibliothèque Nationale de France
    c) London, British Library — no initials filled in, only small printed guide letters to indicate what initial was to have been added by hand.
2. 1495, Lyon, Jacques Arnoullet (Chantilly, Musée de Condé). **E, S, Br, Bl**; most of the woodcuts identical to those of the Maillet 1489 edition.
3. 1505, Lyon, Martin Havart (location unknown, perhaps lost). **S, Br**
4. *c.*1515 Paris, Michel Le Noir (location unknown) **S, Br**
5. *c.*1511–1525 Paris, widow of Jehan Trepperel and Jehan Jehannot (Munich, Staatsbibliothek). **S, Bl**
6. 1526 Lyon, Olivier Arnoullet (Wolfenbüttel, Herzog-August-Bibliothek). S, Br, Bl
7. 1539 Lyon, Olivier Arnoullet (Chantilly, Musée de Condé; British Library). **E, S, Br, Bl**
8. *c.*1540 Paris, Alain Lotrian (British Library). **E, S, Bl**
9. n.d., Paris, Alain Lotrian and Denis Janot (The Hague, Royal Library) **S, Bl**
10. n.d. [mid-16th century], Paris, Jean Bonfons (location unknown) **S, Br, Bl**

11. *c.*1569–1572, Paris, widow of Jean Bonfons (Bibliothèque Nationale de France). **E, Bl**

12. n.d. [late 16th century], Paris, Nicolas Bonfons (Mannheim, University Library) **S, Br, Bl**

13. 1579, Lyon, Benoist Rigaud (location unknown). **Bl**

14. 1590, Lyon, Benoist Rigaud (Paris, Arsenal). **E, S, Br, Bl**

15. 1591, Lyon, no named printer (Copenhagen, Royal Library). **S**

16. *c.*1595–1600, Paris, Nicolas and Pierre Bonfons (British Library; Bibliothèque Nationale de France). **E, S, Br, Bl**

17. 1596, Louvain, Jean Bogard (location unknown). **S, Br**

18. 1605, Lyon, Pierre Rigaud (Bibliothèque Nationale de France); probably a reprinting of the 1590 edition by Benoist Rigaud. **E, S, Br, Bl**

19. 1613, Troyes, [Nicolas I Oudot?] (location unknown).[1] **Bl**

20. 1614, Troyes, Nicolas I Oudot (Boston Public Library). **Br, Bl**

21. 1615, Lyon, Jean Huguetan (Bayreuth, University Library; Munich, Bavarian State Library). **Bl**

22. 1621, Lyon, Etienne Tantillon (Wolfenbüttel, Herzog-August-Bibliothek). **Bl**

23. 1631, Rouen, Louis Costé (location unknown). **Bl**

24. *c.*1620, Rouen, widow of Louis Costé (Paris, Arsenal). **E, S, Br, Bl**; Blom places all three of the undated editions brought out by the widow of Louis Costé between 1632 and 1677. The dates in the listing come from the catalogues of the libraries where they are currently located.

25. *c.*1620, Rouen, widow of Louis Costé (Bibliothèque Nationale de France). **E, Bl**; unlike the Arsenal edition, which contains only *Valentin et Orson*, this one contains three additional texts: *Maugis d'Aigremont*, *Les Quatre fils Aimon*, and *La Conqueste de Charlemagne*.

26. *c.*1620–1625, Rouen, widow of Louis Costé (Bibliothèque Nationale de France). **E, Bl**; includes woodcuts not in a similar edition in the Arsenal.

27. 1623, Troyes, [Jean Oudot pour Claude Briden] (location unknown). **Bl**

28. 1629, Troyes, Nicolas I Oudot (La Roche sur Yon, Bibliothèque Municipale). **Bl**

---

[1] The roman numeral in the name is Blom's method for distinguishing between father and son with identical names.

29. n.d., Troyes, Nicolas [II?] Oudot (location unknown). **Bl**

30. 1645, Lyon, (publisher and location unknown). **Bl**; Blom states that this edition is mentioned in two eighteenth-century catalogues of private libraries.

31. 1657, Troyes, Nicolas II? Oudot (location unknown). **Bl**

32. 1665, Troyes, Nicolas II Oudot (British Library). **E, Bl**; contains three texts in addition to *Valentin et Orson*, namely *Maugis d'Aigremont, Galien restauré*, and *Morgant le Geant*.

33. 1670, Troyes, (no editor named, location unknown). **Bl**

34. n.d., Troyes, Yves Girardon (location unknown). **Bl**

35. n.d. [end 16th century], Rouen, Pierre Mulot (Paris, Musée National des Arts et Traditions Populaires). **Bl**

36. 1686, Troyes, Jacques Oudot (location unknown). **Bl**

37. 1694, Troyes, Jacques Oudot (location unknown). **Bl**

38. 1698, Troyes, Jacques Oudot (Bibliothèque Nationale de France). **E, S, Bl**

39. 1700, Troyes, Jacques Oudot (Grenoble, Municipal Library). **Bl**

40. n.d. (probably 17th century), Lille, J. Fourray (Bibliothèque Nationale de France; British Library). **E, S**

41. 1711, Troyes, Jacques Oudot (location unknown). **Bl**

42. 1719, Troyes, widow of Jacques Oudot (Göttingen, Royal Berlin Library). **S, Bl**

43. 1723, Troyes, widow of Jacques Oudot (Bibliothèque Nationale de France; Paris, Arsenal; British Library; Lyon, Bibliothèque municipale). **E, S, Bl**

44. 1723, Troyes, widow of Jacques Oudot (British Library). **E**; contains three texts in addition to *Valentin et Orson*, namely *Le Grand Calendrier et Compost des Bergers* (title page shows Pierre Garnier, Troyes), *Livre second de Huon de Bordeaux, pair de France, et duc de Guienne/ Contenant ses faix et actes heroïques* (Troyes, Pierre Garnier), and *Histoire de Huon de Bordeaux* (Troyes, Pierre Garnier). The volumes are listed and bound in this order with *Valentin et Orson* second.

45. 1726 Troyes, Pierre Garnier (Bibliothèque Nationale de France; Berlin, University Library). **E, S, Bl**

46. *c.*1760, Rouen, Pierre Seyer (British Library). **E**; contains five texts in addition to *Valentin et Orson*, namely *Huon de Bordeaux* (Pierre Garnier, Troyes), *L'Histoire de Melusine* (Jacques Oudot, Troyes), *La Grande Danse Macabre des*

Hommes et des Femmes, Historiée & renouvellée de vieux Gaulois, en langage le plus poli de notre tems (Jean Garnier, Troyes), *L'Histoire des Nobles Prouësses et Vaillances de Gallien Restauré* (J. Oudot, Troyes), and *L'Histoire des Quatre Fils Aymons, Très-Nobles et Très-Vaillans Chevaliers* (P. Garnier, Troyes).

Seelmann describes what may be an identical edition of *Valentin et Orson* published alone, also in the British Library, which he dates as "1727?" and which may be the same edition that Blom mentions as an undated edition by Pierre Seyer from the mid-eighteenth century.

47. n.d. (19th century), Montbéliard, Deckherr (Bibliothèque Nationale de France). E; may be the same as the edition cited by Seelmann from 1820.

48. n.d. (first half 19th century), Rouen, Lecrêne-Labbey (Groningen, University Library). **Bl**

49. 1846, Montbéliard, Deckherr Frères (Bibliothèque Nationale de France; British Library). **E**

50. 1846, Epinal, Pellerin et Cie (Bibliothèque Nationale de France; British Library). **E, S**; Seelmann lists the copy in the British Library as having no date.

Appendix B
Woodcuts

The woodcuts of the Maillet 1489 edition of *Valentin et Orson* are listed and described below. Each is identified by the leaf on which it appears.

- 1v Crowned figure with scepter, strapped-on sword, mounted on horse; both horse and rider have head twisted to the side; small dog in lower foreground; castle on rocky promontory in upper left of frame.
- 5r Wedding scene with four figures, a man and a woman whose hands are joined by a priest standing between them; one attendant at left.
- 7r Two seated figures of which one on left is crowned (king), one on right is ecclesiastical (bishop); both hold books (repeated on 120r).
- 9v Hunting figure of a mounted nobleman with a falcon on his right hand, wearing a feathered cap; walking attendant at left of frame.
- 13r Crowned standing figure flanked by multiple standing attendants, conferring with capped figure; speaking gestures (repeated on 60v and 109v).
- 14v Kneeling figure on left, one hand on spear or lance, handing over or receiving message from a standing crowned figure on right, flanked by attendant (repeated on 55r and 95r).
- 15v Two knights coming together against one another in joust, visors down, rocky terrain in background (repeat on 42r).
- 18r Crowned figure and attendants all mounted on horseback; a few towers just visible on distant promontory in background (repeat on 49r).
- 23v Mounted nobleman with a falcon on his left hand, riding toward trees in left of frame.
- 27r Two standing noblemen, one with sword at his belt, conferring; tree in right background.
- 28v Standing messenger with a spear receiving a scroll from or handing over to a robed and capped standing figure.

30v Two noble horsemen riding through portcullis on left of frame, seen from rear; mounted attendants following from right of frame.

35r King seated on left facing two standing robed figures on right.

42r Repeat of jousting knights from 15v.

49r Repeat of mounted king and noble horsemen of 18r.

51v Two figures seated in boat on a river; left figure holds the oar; crenellated wall on lower bank; walled town with towers on upper bank.

55r Repeat of kneeling messenger with spear, king, and attendant of 14v.

60v Repeat of king and multiple conferring figures of 13r.

64r Woman with wimple on left; two male figures with caps in middle and to the right; middle figure faces woman with his hand on his hip; man on right has a sword on his belt.

69v Two groups of soldiers seen from the rear; one group marching to the left of tents protected by a log barricade; the second group is mounted on horseback and seen riding into far upper distance.

72v Group of mounted soldiers in top right riding toward fortified area of tents on bottom left; walled city on right; marks of previous battle on both barricade surrounding the tents and walls surrounding the city.

77v Battle scene; knights with lances facing each other from left and right of frame; a sword and body parts, including a severed head, strewn across foreground (repeat on 118r).

81r Standing robed and capped figure on left facing a group of standing soldiers on right; leader of group holds a halberd.

84v Mounted knight with lance on left following or attacking from the rear an armed figure on horseback; figures on rising diagonal with rocky terrain on either side.

87r Group of knights crossing a drawbridge and entering through the gate of a walled town on the right, seen from the rear.

91v Execution scene; crowned and robed king on left observing standing executioner with raised sword in the middle about to behead the crowned king kneeling in prayer with his back to the executioner.

93v Interior scene; four figures seated at a table, one female attendant, one queen, one king, and one male attendant; remnants of a meal on the table; two small windows on back wall.

95r Repeat of kneeling messenger with spear, king, and attendant of 14v.

100r Two mounted figures of squires on left riding away from a city; two mounted female figures just emerging through the gate of a city on right.

103r Battle scene; all soldiers on foot with raised swords, one with an axe; body parts strewn across foreground.

105r Mounted knights entering castle gate.

109v Repeat of king and multiple conferring figures of 13r.

113r Group of mounted knights riding and facing to right of frame; most have visors down except for the two near the front.

115v Sailboat at sea carrying group of figures; only heads are visible of which one is crowned; hilly landscape in background.

118r Repeat of battle scene of 77v.

120r Repeat of king and bishop with books of 7r.

124r Standing robed figure on left demurs as figure on right holds out crown; attendant at far right.

126r Battle scene with opposing groups of knights facing each other with lances raised; one fallen knight in foreground.

128v Standing female figure on left with attendant on far left; kneeling male figure on right.

134v Interior scene in which a seated male figure writes at a table.

Bibliography

Primary sources:

L'Abuzé en court. Vienne: Pierre Schenck, 1484. Currently in Bibliothèque Nationale de France.

Baudoin comte de Flandres. Lyon: Jacques Maillet, 1491. (Believed to be privately owned. Known only by reference and photograph in Claudin, *Histoire de l'imprimerie*.)

Dickson, Arthur, ed. *Valentine and Orson: Translated from the French by Henry Watson*. EETS o.s. 204. London: Humphrey Milford/ Oxford University Press, 1937; repr. 2000.

Jason et la belle Medée. Lyon: Jacques Maillet, 1491. Currently in Bibliothèque de l'Arsenal (Paris).

Keller, Hans-Erich, ed. *L'Histoire de Charlemagne (parfois dite Roman de Fierabras)*. Geneva: Droz, 1992.

Kibler, William W., et al., eds. *Lion de Bourges: Poème épique du XIVe siècle*. Geneva: Droz, 1980.

Klemming, Gustaf Edvard, ed. *Namnlös och Valentin: en Medeltids-roman*. Stockholm: Norstedt, 1846.

Langbroek, Erika, et al., eds. *Valentin und Namelos: Mittelniederdeutsch und Neuhochdeutsch*. Amsterdam: Rodopi, 1997.

Miquet, Jean, ed. *Fierabras: Roman en prose de la fin du XIVe siècle*. Ottawa: Editions de l'Université d'Ottawa, 1983.

Paris, Gaston, ed. "*Mainet*: Fragments d'une chanson de geste du XIIe siècle." *Romania* 4 (1875): 303-37.

Perugi, Maurizio, ed. *La Vie de Saint Alexis*. Geneva: Droz, 2000.

Ponthus et la belle Sidoyne. Lyon: Gaspard Ortuin, c.1486. Currently in Bodleian Library, Oxford.

Seelmann, Wilhelm, ed. *Valentin und Namelos*. Leipzig: Soltau, 1884.

Sinclair, K.V., ed. *Tristan de Nanteuil: Chanson de geste inédite*. Assen: Gorcum, 1971.

Valentin et Orson. Lyon: Jacques Maillet, 1489. Currently in Bibliothèque Nationale de France, British Library, J. Pierpont Morgan Library.

Secondary sources:

Aspland, C.W. *A Medieval French Reader*. Oxford: Clarendon Press, 1979.
Bancourt, Paul. *Les Musulmans dans les chansons de geste du cycle du roi*. 2 vols. Aix-en-Provence: Université de Provence, 1982.
Bartra, Roger. *Wild Men in the Looking Glass: The Mythic Origins of European Otherness*. Trans. Carl T. Berrisford. Ann Arbor: University of Michigan Press, 1994.
Bernheimer, Richard. *Wild Men in the Middle Ages: A Study in Art, Sentiment, and Demonology*. Cambridge, MA: Harvard University Press, 1952. Repr. New York: Octagon Books, 1970.
Black, Nancy B. *Medieval Narratives of Accused Queens*. Gainesville: University Press of Florida, 2003.
Blom, Helwi. "*Valentin et Orson* et la *Bibliothèque bleue*." In *L'épopée romane au Moyen Âge et aux temps modernes: Actes du XIVe Congrès International de la Société Rencesvals 1997*, ed. Salvatore Luongo, 611-25. Naples: Fridericiana, 2001.
Blum, André. *Les Origines du livre à gravures en France: les incunables typographiques*. Paris: G. Van Oest, 1928.
Brunet, Jacques-Charles. *Manuel du libraire et de l'amateur des livres*, vol. 5. Paris: Firmin-Didot, 1864.
———. *Supplément*. Vol. 2. Paris: Firmin-Didot, 1880.
Burkert, Nancy Ekholm. *Valentine & Orson*. New York: Farrar, Straus and Giroux, 1989.
Claudin, Anatole. *Histoire de l'imprimerie en France au XVe et au XVIe siècle*. 4 vols. Paris: Imprimerie Nationale, 1900-1914.
Colliot, Régine. "Un prédécesseur de Tartuffe: l'archevêque de Constantinople dans *Valentin et Orson*." In *Mélanges Jean Larmat: Regards sur le Moyen Âge et la Renaissance*, ed. Maurice Accarie, 69-78. Nice: Annales de la Faculté des Lettres et Sciences Humaines de Nice, 1982.
———. "Le Prêtre séducteur dans les fabliaux et dans un remaniement épique du XVe siècle." In *Epopée animale, fable, fabliau: Actes du IVe colloque de la Société Internationale Renardienne*, ed. Gabriel Bianciotto and Michel Salvat, 141-55. Paris: Presses Universitaires de France, 1984.
Cook, Robert F. "'Méchants romans' et Epopée française: pour une philologie profonde." *L'Esprit créateur* 23 (1983): 64-74.
———. "Unity and Aesthetics of the Late *Chansons de geste*." *Olifant* 11 (1986): 103-14.
Cooper, Helen. "The Strange History of *Valentine and Orson*." In *Tradition and Transformation in Medieval Romance*, ed. Rosalind Field, 153-68. Cambridge: Brewer, 1999.
Daniel, Norman. *Heroes and Saracens: An Interpretation of the Chansons de geste*. Edinburgh: Edinburgh University Press, 1984.

Dickson, Arthur. *Valentine and Orson: A Study in Late Medieval Romance.* New York: Columbia University Press, 1929. Repr. New York: AMS Press, 1975.
Doutrepont, Georges. *Les Mises en prose des épopées et des romans chevaleresques du XIVe au XVe siècles.* Brussels: Académie Royale, 1939.
Febvre, Lucien, and Henri-Jean Martin. *The Coming of the Book: The Impact of Printing 1450-1800.* Trans. David Gerard. London: NLB, 1976.
Gardner, Rosalyn, and Marion A. Greene. *A Brief Description of Middle French Syntax.* Chapel Hill: University of North Carolina Press, 1958.
Godefroy, Frédéric. *Dictionnaire de l'ancien français.* 10 vols. Paris: Vieweg, 1880-1902; repr. Geneva: Slatkine, 1982.
Guidot, Bernard. "Formes tardives de l'épopée médiévale: mises en prose, imprimés, livres populaires." In *L'épopée romane au Moyen Âge et aux temps modernes: Actes du XIVe Congrès International de la Société Rencesvals 1997,* ed. Luongo, 579-610.
Harris, J. Rendel. "Valentine and Orson: A Study in Twin-Cult." *Contemporary Review* 126 (1924): 323-31.
Hassell, James Woodrow. *Middle French Proverbs, Sentences, and Proverbial Phrases.* Subsidia Mediaevalia 12. Toronto: Pontifical Institute of Mediaeval Studies, 1982.
Huizinga, Johan. *The Waning of the Middle Ages.* 1949. New York: Doubleday, 1954.
Husband, Timothy. *The Wild Man: Medieval Myth and Symbolism.* New York: Metropolitan Museum of Art, 1980.
Jones, Catherine M. "'Modernizing' the Epic: Philippe de Vigneulles." In *Echoes of the Epic: Studies in Honor of Gerard J. Brault,* ed. David P. Schenck and Mary Jane Schenk, 115-32. Birmingham, AL: Summa Publications, 1998.
Kay, Sarah. *The Chansons de geste in the Age of Romance: Political Fictions.* Oxford: Clarendon Press, 1995.
———. "Contesting 'Romance Influence': The Poetics of the Gift." *Comparative Literature Studies* 32 (1995): 320-41.
Keller, Hans-Erich. "Changes in Old French Epic Poetry and Changes in the Taste of its Audience." *Olifant* 1 (1973-1974): 48-56.
———. "Une *Chanson de Roland* en prose." In *Echoes of the Epic,* ed. Schenck and Schenk, 133-40.
Kibler, William W. "Bibliography of Fourteenth and Fifteenth Century French Epics." *Olifant* 11 (1986): 23-50.
———. "La 'chanson d'aventures'." In *Essor et fortune de la Chanson de geste dans l'Europe et l'Orient latin,* 509-15. Modena: Mucchi, 1984.
———. "From Epic to Romance: The Case of *Lion de Bourges.*" In *The Medieval Opus: Imitation, Rewriting and Transmission in the French Tradition,* ed. Douglas Kelly, 327-55. Amsterdam: Rodopi, 1996.
Krappe, Alexander Haggerty. "*Valentine and Orson.*" *Modern Language Notes* 47 (1932): 493-98.

Le Roux de Lincy. *Le Livre des proverbes français*. Paris: Paulin, 1842. Repr. Paris: Hachette, 1996.

Luongo, Salvatore, ed. *L'épopée romane au Moyen Âge et aux temps modernes: Actes du XIVe Congrès International de la Société Rencesvals 1997*. Naples: Fridericiana, 2001.

Marchello-Nizia, Christiane. *La langue française aux XIVe et XVe siècles*. Paris: Nathan, 1997.

Martin, André. *Le Livre illustré en France au XVe siècle*. Paris: Alcan, 1931.

Moisan, André. *Répertoire des noms propres de personnes et de lieux cités dans les chansons de geste françaises et les oeuvres étrangères dérivées*. Geneva: Droz, 1986.

Morawski, Joseph, ed. *Proverbes français antérieurs au XVe siècle*. Paris: Champion, 1925.

Quéruel, Danielle. "Des mises en prose aux romans de chevalerie dans les collections bourguignonnes." In *Rhétorique et mises en prose au XVe siècle: Actes du VIe colloque international sur la littérature en moyen français*, ed. Sergio Cigada and Anna Slerca, 173-93. Milan: Vita e Pensiero, 1991.

Reinhard, John Revell. *The Survival of Geis in Medieval Romance*. Halle: Max Niemeyer, 1933.

Richard, Jean. "An Account of the Battle of Hattin Referring to the Frankish Mercenaries in Oriental Moslem States." *Speculum* 27 (1952): 168-77.

Rondot, Natalis. *Les Graveurs sur bois et les imprimeurs à Lyon au XVe siècle*. Lyon: Mougin-Rusand, 1896.

Roy, Bruno. "En marge du monde connu: les races de monstres." In *Aspects de la marginalité au Moyen Âge*, ed. Guy H. Allard, 70-81. Montreal: Aurore, 1975.

Schwam-Baird, Shira. "A Husband to Her Liking: The Wily Saracen Queen Rozemonde in the 1489 *Valentin et Orson*." *Olifant* 26.1 (2007): 45-66.

———. "The Romance Epic Hero, the Mercenary, and the Ottoman Turk Seen through the Lens of *Valentin et Orson* (1489)." *Medievalia et Humanistica* 34 (2008) 105-27.

———. "Terror and Laughter in the Images of the Wild Man: The Case of the 1489 *Valentin et Orson*." *Fifteenth-Century Studies* 27 (2002): 238-56.

Sheingorn, Pamela. "'Who can open the doors of his face?': The Iconography of Hell Mouth." In *The Iconography of Hell*, ed. Clifford Davidson and Thomas H. Seiler, 1-19. Kalamazoo: Medieval Institute Publications, 1992.

Stock, Lorraine Kochanske. *The Medieval Wild Man*. New York: Palgrave Macmillan, forthcoming.

Suard, François. "L'épopée française tardive (XIVe-XVe s.)." In *Etudes de philologie romane et d'histoire littéraire offertes à Jules Horrent*, ed. Jean-Marie d'Heur et Nicoletta Cherubini, 449-60. Liège: s.n., 1980.

———. *Guillaume d'Orange : Etude du roman en prose*. Paris: Champion, 1979.

Szkilnik, Michelle. "Pacolet ou les infortunes de la magie." *Le Moyen français* 35-36 (1994-1995): 91-109.

Thompson, Stith. *Motif-Index of Folk-Literature.* 6 vols. Bloomington: Indiana University Press, 1975-1976.
Tinland, Franck. *L'Homme sauvage: Homo ferus et homo sylvestris: de l'animal à l'homme.* Paris: Payot, 1968.
Weever, Jacqueline de. *Sheba's Daughters: Whitening and Demonizing the Saracen Woman in Medieval French Epic.* New York: Garland, 1998.
White, Hayden. "The Forms of Wildness: Archaeology of an Idea." In *The Wild Man Within: An Image in Western Thought from the Renaissance to Romanticism,* ed. Edward Dudley and Maximillian E. Novak, 3-38. Pittsburgh: University of Pittsburgh Press, 1972.